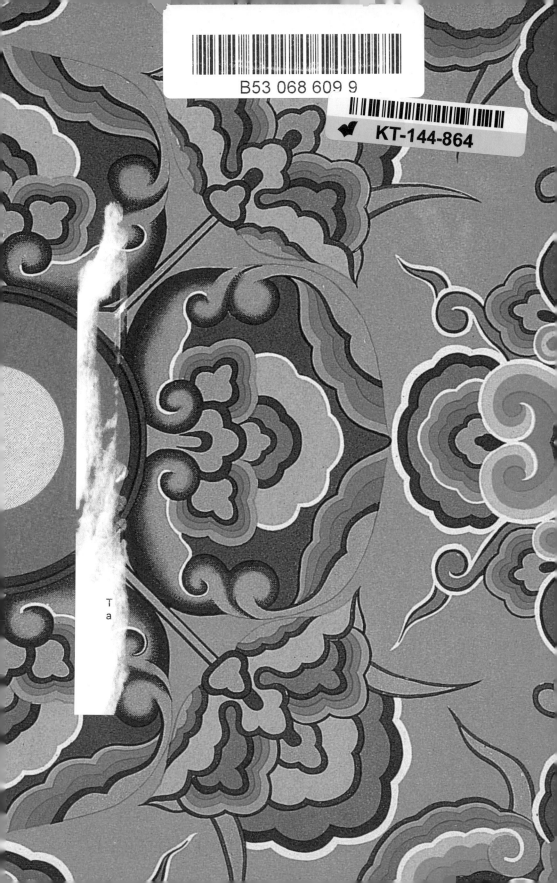

T
a

The Valley of Amazement

ALSO BY AMY TAN

Novels
The Joy Luck Club

The Kitchen God's Wife

The Hundred Secret Senses

The Bonesetter's Daughter

Saving Fish from Drowning

Memoir
The Opposite of Fate

Children's Books
The Moon Lady

Sagwa, The Chinese Siamese Cat

The Valley of Amazement

AMY TAN

FOURTH ESTATE • London

Fourth Estate
An imprint of HarperCollins*Publishers*
77–85 Fulham Palace Road
Hammersmith, London W6 8JB
www.4thestate.co.uk

First published in Great Britain by Fourth Estate 2013
First published in the United States by Ecco 2013

1 3 5 7 9 10 8 6 4 2

HB ISBN 978-0-00-745627-7
TPB ISBN 978-0-00-746887-4

Designed by Suet Yee Chong

Printed in Great Britain by
Clays Ltd, St Ives plc

MIX
Paper from
responsible sources
FSC C007454

FSC™ is a non-profit international organisation established to promote
the responsible management of the world's forests. Products carrying the
FSC label are independently certified to assure consumers that they come
from forests that are managed to meet the social, economic and
ecological needs of present and future generations,
and other controlled sources.

Find out more about HarperCollins and the environment at
www.harpercollins.co.uk/green

FOR

KATHI KAMEN GOLDMARK AND ZHENG CAO

KINDRED SPIRITS

Quicksand years that whirl me I know not whither,
Your schemes, politics, fail, lines give way, substances mock and
*   elude me,*
Only the theme I sing, the great and strong-possess'd soul, eludes
*   not,*
One's-self, must never give way—that is the final substance—
*   that out of all is sure,*
Out of politics, triumphs, battles, life, what at last finally remains?
When shows break up what but One's-Self is sure?

—WALT WHITMAN, "QUICKSAND YEARS"

ACKNOWLEDGMENTS

There are many friends and family who sustained me during the eight years it took to write this book. I will try to repay all of you with sustenance in kind over the years.

For help in keeping this story and me alive: My husband, Lou DeMattei, was so supportive of my need for solitary confinement that he brought breakfast, lunch, and dinner to my desk, where I was shackled to a deadline. My agent Sandy Dijkstra saved me yet again from my own blunders and worries, and thus enabled me to write with peace of mind. Molly Giles, always my first reader, saw the false starts and patiently pushed me forward with astute advice. If only I had followed all of it from the beginning.

For background on courtesan culture and photography in Shanghai, I am deeply grateful to three people for freely sharing through our countless e-mails their research of courtesan culture and photography in Shanghai during the turn of the century: Gail Hershatter *(The Gender of Memory)*, Catherine Yeh *(Shanghai Love)*, and Joan Judge *(The Precious Raft of History)*. I offer apologies for any distortion of their work through my imagination.

For research for the various settings of the story, I thank Nancy Berliner, then-curator of Chinese art at the Peabody Essex Museum,

who arranged for Lou and me to stay in a four-hundred-year-old mansion in the village of Huangcun. My sister Jindo (Tina Eng) got us
to the village by navigating the best route via trains and cars from
Shanghai. Because I had to speak only Chinese to her for four days,
my language skills improved enormously, to the point where I could
understand much of the family gossip necessary for any story. Fellow traveler Lisa See braved the cold, despite predictions of balmy
weather, and she reveled with me over the historic details and unfolding human dramas. She also generously insisted that I use the name
of the village pond in my book, even though Moon Pond would have
been a perfect name for a village in her novel. Cecilia Ding, with the
Yin Yu Tang Service Project, provided extensive knowledge of the history of Huang Cun, the old house, the streets of Old Tunxi in Huang-
shan, and Yellow Mountain.

Museums have always been important in my writing for both
inspiration and research. The Shanghai Exhibition at the Asian Art
Museum in San Francisco opened my eyes to the role of courtesans
in introducing Western culture to Shanghai. Maxwell Hearn, curator
of the Asian department at the Metropolitan Museum of Art in New
York, provided information on the aesthetic and romantic mind of
the scholar as well as on the green-eyed poet who wrote about ghosts
that he purportedly saw. Tony Bannon, then-director of the George
Eastman House in Rochester, New York, opened up the archives of
photographs of women in China at the turn of the century, and he
also showed a rare and restored film of a city girl forced into prostitution. Dodge Thompson, chief of exhibitions at the National Gallery of Art in Washington, D.C., gave me a special tour of paintings
by Hudson River School artists, including those by Albert Bierstadt.
Inspiration for the painting *The Valley of Amazement* came from a hurried visit to the Alte Nationalgalerie in Berlin, after which I recalled
a haunting painting with that title, whose artist, alas, I failed to note,
but who was likely Carl Blechen, a painter of fantastical landscapes,
whose work is prominently displayed in the Alte Nationalgalerie. If

anyone finds the painting, please let me know. I suffer from a sense of failure in not having rediscovered it yet.

For Shanghai research: Steven Roulac introduced me to his mother, Elizabeth, who recounted her days in Shanghai in the 1930s as a foreigner in the International District. Orville Schell, director of the Center on U.S.-China Relations at the Asia Society in New York, gave me insights on several historic periods in China, including the rise of the new Republic and the antiforeigner movement. The late Bill Wu introduced me to the aesthetic world of the scholar—the accoutrements, house, garden, and wall plaques of poetry, all found in his scholar house outside of Suzhou. Duncan Clark found street maps of old Shanghai, enabling us to pinpoint the modern-day location of the old courtesan district. Shelley Lim spent countless hours taking me around Shanghai to old family homes, haunted houses, and the places that provided the best foot massages at midnight. Producer Monica Lam, videographer David Peterson, and my sister Jindo helped me make my first visit to the family mansion on Qongming Island, where my mother grew up and where my grandmother killed herself. Joan Chen laughingly gave me Shanghainese translations for funny expressions, often of the lewd variety, for which she in turn had to ask her friends for assistance.

Many helped me visit places that also influenced the settings in the story: Joanna Lee, Ken Smith, Kit Wai Lee, and the National Geographic Society made it possible to stay in the remote village of Dimen in the mountains of Guizhou Province on three occasions. Kit ("Uncle") spent hours and days and weeks with me, giving me information on customs and village history, and also introduced me to many of the residents, many of whom had lost their homes in a great fire that had destroyed a fifth of the village. Emily Scott Pottruck traveled with me as friend, assistant, organizer, and deflector of trouble. Mike Hawley arranged for us to come to Bhutan and travel to the far reaches of that country, which also served as the setting for certain scenes, including that of the Five Sons of Heaven Mountain.

Among many who assisted with details of the novel: Marc Shuman gave me information on the immortality mushroom *ganoderma lucidum,* which wound up helping me with my health. Michael Tilson Thomas showed me music composed for the left hand, which inspired me to create a character who is a left-handed pianist. Joshua Robison provided lessons on the Lindy Hop and music of the 1920s. Dr. Tom Brady and Dr. Asa DeMatteo gave me insight on the psychiatric profile of children kidnapped at ages fourteen and three. Mark Moffett informed me of what might be learned from the evolution of wasps found in amber. Walter Kirn pushed me to write a long short story for *Byliner,* and that character inched her way into the novel in a major way.

For keeping me from spinning out of control, I thank my assistant Ellen Moore, who kept away many distractions and served as my conscience over deadlines. Libby Edelson of Ecco showed tremendous tact and patience when I was late in sending files or had sent the wrong ones. Copyeditor Shelly Perron worked under tremendous deadlines, and not only kept me from embarrassing myself a thousand times but told me what more she would want to know as a reader. I am so grateful for the help of the many people at Sandy Dijkstra's office and also at Ecco, who have embraced this book—and me as one of their own. You have no idea how much your enthusiasm fills me with guilt that I did not finish this sooner.

I feel so fortunate that this mess of a book fell into the welcoming hands of Daniel Halpern, my editor and publisher at Ecco. He never showed fear after seeing those early pages, only enthusiasm and absolute confidence, which gave *me* confidence. He provided gentle prodding to finish and never exasperation, although the latter was often warranted. His comments, critical analysis, understanding of the story, its whole and its details, were true to my intentions and what I had secretly hoped the book would be. The faults of the book, however, remain mine.

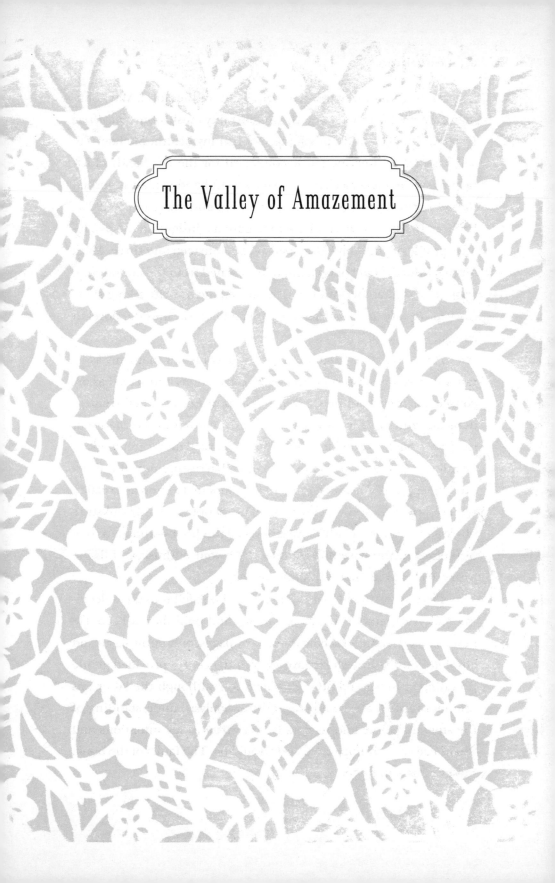

The Valley of Amazement

CHAPTER 1

HIDDEN JADE PATH

Shanghai
1905-1907
Violet

When I was seven, I knew exactly who I was: a thoroughly American girl in race, manners, and speech, whose mother, Lulu Minturn, was the only white woman who owned a first-class courtesan house in Shanghai.

My mother named me Violet after a tiny flower she loved as a girl growing up in San Francisco, a city I have seen only in postcards. I grew to hate my name. The courtesans pronounced it like the Shanghainese word *vyau-la*—what you said when you wanted to get rid of something. "*Vyau-la! Vyau-la!*" greeted me everywhere.

My mother took a Chinese name, Lulu Mimi, which sounded like her American one, and her courtesan house was then known as the House of Lulu Mimi. Her Western clients knew it by the English translation of the characters in her name: Hidden Jade Path. There were no other first-class courtesan houses that catered to both Chinese and Western clients, many of whom were among the wealthiest in foreign trade. And thus, she broke taboo rather extravagantly in both worlds.

That house of flowers was my entire world. I had no peers or little American friends. When I was six, Mother enrolled me in Miss Jewell's Academy for Girls. There were only fourteen pupils, and they were all cruel. Some of their mothers had objected to my presence, and those daughters united all the girls in a plot to expel me. They said I lived in a house of "evil ways," and that no one should touch me, lest my taint rub off on them. They also told the teacher I cursed all the time, when I had done so only once. But the worst insult came from an older girl with silly ringlets. On my third day, I arrived at school and was walking down the hallway when this girl walked briskly up to me and said within hearing distance of my teacher and the younger class girls: "You spoke Chinee to a Chinee beggar and that makes you Chinee." I could not bear one more of her insults. I grabbed her ringlets and hung on. She screamed, and a dozen fists pummeled my back and another bloodied my lip and knocked out a tooth that had already been loose. I spit it out, and we all stared for a second at the glistening tusk, and then I clutched my neck for dramatic effect and shrieked, "I've been killed!" before collapsing to the floor. One girl fainted, and the ringleader and her pack scampered off with stricken faces. I picked up the tooth—a former living part of me—and the teacher quickly put a knotted kerchief to my face to stanch the blood, then sent me home in a rickshaw with no parting words of comfort. Mother decided on the spot that I would be tutored at home.

Confused, I told her what I had said to the old beggar: "*Lao huazi,* let me by." Until she told me that *lao huazi* was the Chinese word for "beggar," I had not known I was speaking a hodgepodge of English, Chinese, and the Shanghainese dialect. Then again, why would I know the word *beggar* in English when I had never seen an American grandpa slumped against a wall, mumbling with a slack mouth so that I might have pity on him? Until I went to school, I had been speaking my peculiar language only in Hidden Jade Path to our four courtesans, their attendants, and the servants. Their syllables of gossip and flirtation, complaints and woe, went into my ear, and came out of my mouth, and in conversations I had with my mother, I had never been told there was anything amiss with my speech. Adding to the mess, Mother also spoke Chinese, and her attendant, Golden Dove, also spoke English.

I remained troubled by the girl's accusation. I asked Mother if she had spoken Chinese as a child, and she told me that Golden Dove had given her rigorous lessons. I then asked Mother if I spoke Chinese as well as the courtesans did. "In many ways, yours is better," she said. "More beautifully spoken." I was alarmed. I asked my new tutor if a Chinese person naturally spoke Chinese better than an American ever could. He said the shapes of the mouth, tongue, and lips of each race were best suited to its particular language, as were the ears that conducted words into the brain. I asked him why he thought I could speak Chinese. He said that I studied well and had exercised my mouth to such a degree that I could move my tongue differently.

I worried for two days, until logic and deduction enabled me to reclaim my race. First of all, I reasoned, Mother was American. Although my father was dead, it was obvious he had been an American, since I had fair skin, brown hair, and green eyes. I wore Western clothing and regular shoes. I had not had my feet crushed and wedged like dumpling dough into a tiny shoe. I was educated, too, and in difficult subjects, such as history and science—"and for no greater purpose than Knowledge Alone," my tutor had said. Most Chinese girls learned only how to behave.

What's more, I did not think like a Chinese person—no kowtowing to statues, no smoky incense, and no ghosts. Mother told me: "Ghosts are superstitions, conjured up by a Chinese person's own fears. The Chinese are a fearful lot and thus they have many superstitions." I was not fearful. And I did not do everything a certain way just because that was how it had been done for a thousand years. I had Yankee ingenuity and an independent mind; Mother told me that. It was my idea, for example, to give the servants modern forks to use instead of ancient chopsticks. Mother, however, ordered the servants to return the silverware. She said that each tine was more valuable than what a servant might earn in a year, and thus, the servants might be tempted to sell the forks. The Chinese did not hold the same opinion about honesty as we Americans. I agreed. Now if I were Chinese, would I have said that about myself?

After I left Miss Jewell's Academy, I forbade the courtesans to call me *Vyau-la*. They also could no longer use Chinese endearments like "little sister." They had to call me Vivi, I told them. The only people who could call me Violet were those who could say my name precisely, and they were my mother, Golden Dove, and my tutor.

After I changed my name, I realized I could do so whenever I pleased to suit my mood or purpose. And soon after, I adopted my first nickname as the result of an accident. I had been racing through the main salon and bumped into a servant carrying a tray of tea and snacks, which clattered to the floor. He exclaimed that I was a *biaozi*, a "little whirlwind." A delightful word. I was the Whirlwind who blew through the famed house of Hidden Jade Path with my nimbus of fluffy dark hair and my cat chasing the ribbon that had once held my hair in place. From then on, the servants had to call me Whirlwind in English, which they pronounced "woo-woo."

I loved my golden fox cat. She belonged to me, and I to her, and that was a feeling I had with no other—not even my mother. When I held my kitty, she kneaded her paws on my bodice, snagging the lace and turning it into fishing nets. Her eyes were green like mine, and she had a beautiful golden sheen over her brown-and-black-splotched body. She glowed under moonlight. Mother gave her to me when I told her I wanted a friend. The cat had once belonged to a pirate, she said, who named her Carlotta after the Portuguese king's daughter he had kidnapped. No one else had a pirate's cat, whereas anyone could have a friend. A cat would always be loyal, unlike a friend. Mother said she knew that for a fact.

Almost everyone in the house feared my pirate cat. She scratched those who chased her off the furniture. She howled like a ghost when she was stuck inside a wardrobe. If she sensed fear in people who approached her, she bristled and let them know they were right to be scared. Golden Dove froze whenever she saw Carlotta prancing toward her. A wildcat had badly wounded her when she was a little girl, and she had nearly died of green pus fever. If anyone picked up my kitty, she bit, fast and hard, and if anyone petted her without my permission, her claws flew out. She murdered a seventeen-year-old boy named Loyalty Fang, who came to Hidden Jade Path with his father. I had been looking for Carlotta and spotted her under the sofa. A boy was in the way and he started jabbering to me in a language I could not understand. Before I could warn him not to touch Carlotta, he reached down and grabbed her tail, and she dug her claws into his arm and peeled off four bloody ribbons of skin and flesh. He turned white, gritted his teeth, and fainted, mortally wounded. His father took him home, and Golden Dove said he would surely die, and later, one of the courtesans said he had and that it was a pity he had never enjoyed any pleasures of the boudoir. Even though it was the boy's fault, I was scared that Carlotta would be taken away and drowned.

With me, Carlotta was different. When I carried her in my arms, she was tender and limp. At night, she purred in my arms, and in the morning, she chirped at me. I kept bits of sausage in my apron pocket for her, as well as a green parrot's feather tied to a string, which I used to lure her out of hiding from under one of the many sofas in the salon. Her paws would poke out of the fringe as she batted at the feather. Together we raced through the maze of furniture, and she vaulted onto tables and chairs, up curtains, and onto the high lips of the wainscoting—to wherever I wanted her to go. That salon was Carlotta's and my playground, and that playground was in a former ghost villa that my mother had turned into Hidden Jade Path.

On several occasions, I heard her tell Western newspaper reporters how she secured the place for almost nothing. "If you want to make money in Shanghai," she said, "take advantage of other people's fear."

Lulu

This villa, gentlemen, was originally built four hundred years ago as the summer mansion of Pan Ku Xiang, a rich scholar and a renowned poet, for what lyrical merits no one knows because his inscribed thoughts went up in smoke. The grounds and its original four buildings once stretched over one-half hectares, twice what it is now. The thick stone wall is the original. But the west and east wings had to be rebuilt after they were consumed by a mysterious fire—the same flames that ate the scholar's poetic thoughts. A legend has been handed down over four hundred years: One of his concubines in the west wing started the fire, and his wife in the east wing died screaming in a circle of flames. Whether it is true, who can say? But any legend is not worth making up if it does not include a murder or two. Don't you agree?

After the poet died, his eldest son hired the best stonemasons to carve a stele that sat on a tortoise and was crowned by a dragon, symbols of honor reserved for a high official—although there was no record in the county that he had ever been one. By the time his great-grandson was the head of the family, the stele had fallen and was nearly obscured by tall prickly weeds. Weather wore down the scholar's name and accolades into unreadable indentations. This was not the eternal reverence the scholar had had in mind. When his descendants sold the place a hundred years ago for a cheap price, the curse began. Within a day of receiving the money, his descendant was seized with a firelike pain and died. A thief killed another son. The children of those sons died of one thing or another, and it was not old age. A succession of buyers also suffered from unusual maladies: reversals of fortune, infertility, insanity, and such. When I saw the mansion, it was an abandoned eyesore, the grounds a jungle of choking vines and overgrown bushes, the perfect haven for wild dogs. I bought the property for the price of a Chinese song. Both Westerners and Chinese said I was foolish to take it at any price. No carpenter, stonemason, or coolie would ever step across that haunted threshold.

So, gentlemen, what would you do? Give up and count your losses? I hired an Italian actor—a disgraced Jesuit with the dark looks of an Asiatic, which became more pronounced when he pulled back his hair at the temples, the way Chinese opera singers do to give the eyes a dramatic slant. He donned the robes of a feng shui master, and we hired some boys to pass out leaflets to announce that a fair would be held on the grounds just outside of the haunted villa. We had stalls of food, acrobats, contortionists, and musicians, rare fruits and a candy machine that pulled saltwater taffy. By the time the feng shui master arrived on a palanquin, along with his Chinese assistant, he had a waiting audience of hundreds—children and amahs, servants and rickshaw men, courtesans and madams, tailors and other purveyors of gossip.

The feng shui master demanded that a pan of fire be brought to him. He pulled out a scroll and threw it into the flames, then chanted a concoction of Tibetan gibberish while sprinkling rice wine over the fire to make the flames leap higher.

"I shall now go into the cursed mansion," the actor told the crowd, "and persuade Pan the Poet Ghost to leave. If I don't return, please remember me as a good man who served his people at the cost of his own life." Forecasts of mortal danger are always useful to make people believe your fabrications. The audience watched him enter where no man dared to go. After five minutes he returned, and the audience murmured excitedly. He announced he had found the Poet Ghost in an inkwell in his painting studio. They had a most enjoyable conversation about his poetry and his past renown. This led to the poet's laments that his descendants had cast him into early obscurity. His monument had become a mossy slab where wild dogs peed. The feng shui master assured the Poet Ghost he would erect a fine stele even better than the last. The Poet Ghost thanked him and immediately left the once-haunted mansion to rejoin his murdered wife.

So that took care of the first obstacle. I then had to overcome skepticism that a social club could ever succeed when it catered to both Western and Chinese men. Who would come? As you know, most Westerners view the Chinese as their inferiors—intellectually, morally, and socially. It seemed unlikely they would ever share cigars and brandy.

The Chinese, by the same token, resent the imperious way foreigners treat Shanghai as their own port city and govern her by their treaties and laws. The foreigners don't trust the Chinese. And they insult them by speaking pidgin, even to a Chinese man whose English is as refined as a British lord's. Why would the Chinese conduct business with men who do not respect them?

The simple answer is money. Foreign trade is their common interest, their common language, and I help them speak it in an atmosphere that loosens any reservations they might still hold.

For our Western guests, I offer a social club with pleasures they are accustomed to: billiards, card games, the finest cigars and brandy. In that corner, you see a piano. At the end of every night, the stragglers crowd around and sing the anthems and sentimental songs of their home countries. We have a few who imagine they are Caruso's cousin. For our Chinese guests, I provide the pleasures of a first-class courtesan house. The customers follow the protocols of courtship. This is not a house of prostitution, which Western men are more accustomed to. We also offer our Chinese guests what are now the expected Western amenities of a first-class courtesan house: billiards, card games, the finest whiskey, cigars in addition to opium, and pretty musicians who sing the old Chinese chestnuts and encourage the men to join in. Our furnishings are superior to those in other houses. The difference is in the details, and as I am an American, that knowledge is in my blood.

And now we've come to where East meets West, the Grand Salon, the common ground for businessmen of two worlds. Imagine the buzz of excitement we hear each night. Many fortunes have been made here, and they all began with my introduction and their exchanging their first handshake. Gentlemen, there is a lesson here for anyone who wants to make a fortune in Shanghai. When people say an idea is impossible, it becomes impossible. In Shanghai, however, nothing is impossible. You have to make the old meet the new, rearrange the furniture, so to speak, and put on a good show. Guile and get. Opportunists welcome. Within these doors, the path to riches is revealed to all who have a minimum of ten thousand dollars to invest or whose influence is worth more than that. We have our standards.

APPROACHING THE GATE of the mansion, you would know at a glance that you were about to enter a fine house with a respected history. The archway still held the carved stone plaque befitting a Ming scholar; a bit of the lichen had been left on the corners as proof of authenticity. The thick gate was regularly refreshed with red lacquer and the brass fittings polished to a gleaming richness. On each of the pillars was a panel with the two names of the house: HIDDEN JADE PATH on the right side, and THE HOUSE OF LULU MIMI in Chinese on the left.

Once you entered through the gate and into the front courtyard, you would think you had stepped back into the days when the Poet Ghost was master of the house. The garden was simple and of classical proportions, from fishponds to gnarly pines. Beyond it stood a rather austere house: the face a plain gray plaster over stone, the lattice windows showing a simple cracked-ice pattern. The gray-tiled roof had eaves that curved upward, not excessively so, but enough to suggest they were the wings of lucky bats. And in the front of the house was the poet's stele, restored to its rightful place, sitting on a tortoise, topped with a dragon, and proclaiming the scholar would be remembered for ten thousand years.

Once you stepped into the vestibule, however, all signs of the Ming vanished. At your feet was a colorful pattern of encaustic Moorish tiles, and facing you was a wall of red velvet curtains. When they were drawn back, you were borne into a "Palace of Heavenly Charms," as my mother called it. This was the Grand Salon, and it was entirely Western. That was the fashion in the better courtesan houses, but my mother's sense of Western fashion was authentic and also daring. Four hundred years of cold echoes had been muffled by colorful tapestries, thick carpets, and an overabundance of low divans, stiff settees, fainting couches, and Turkish ottomans. Flower stands held vases of peonies the size of babies' heads, and round tea tables were set with lamps that gave the salon the honeyed amber glow of a sunset. On the bureaus, a man could pluck cigars out of ivory humidors and cigarettes out of cloisonné filigreed jars. The tufted armchairs were engorged with so much batting they resembled the buttocks of the people who sat in them. Some of the decorations were quite amusing to the Chinese. The blue and white vases imported from France, for example, were painted with depictions of Chinese people whose faces resembled Napoleon and Josephine. Heavy mohair curtains covered the lattice windows, weighted with green, red, and yellow tassels and fringe as thick as fingers, Carlotta's favorite toys. Chandeliers and wall sconces illuminated the paintings of rosy-cheeked Roman goddesses with muscular white bodies, who cavorted next to similarly muscled white horses—grotesque shapes, I heard Chinese men say, which depicted, in their opinion, bestiality.

On the right and left sides of the Grand Salon were doorways that led to smaller, more intimate rooms, and beyond them were covered passageways through courtyards that led to the scholar's former library, painting studio, and family temple, all cleverly transformed into rooms where a businessman could host a dinner party for friends and be entertained by ladylike courtesans who sang with heartbreaking emotion.

At the back of the Grand Salon, my mother had installed a curved carpeted staircase with a red-lacquered wooden banister, which took you up to three curved, velvet-lined balconies modeled after those found in opera houses. They overlooked the Grand Salon, and from them I often viewed the festivities below as Carlotta strolled back and forth on the balustrades.

The parties began after sundown. Carriages and rickshaws arrived throughout the night. Cracked Egg, the gatekeeper, would have already memorized the names of those who were coming, and they were the only ones allowed to enter. From my perch, I saw the men burst through the red curtains and into that palatial room. I could tell if a man was a newcomer. He would gaze at the scene before him, scanning the room, incredulous to see Chinese and Western men greeting each other, speaking with civility. The Westerner would have his first glimpse of courtesans in their habitat. He might have only seen them passing by on the thoroughfare in carriages, dressed in their furs and hats. But here, they were within reach. He could speak to one, smile with admiration, although he learned quite emphatically that he was not allowed to touch. I was delighted to see my mother inspire awe in men of different nationalities. She possessed the power to render men speechless from the moment they walked into the room.

Our courtesans were among the most popular and talented of all the girls working in the first-class houses of Shanghai—elegant, seductively coy, tantalizingly elusive, and skilled in singing or the recitation of poems. They were known as the Cloud Beauties. Each had the word *Cloud* in her name, and that identified the house to which she belonged. When they left the house—whether to marry, join a nunnery, or work in a lower-class house—the cloud evaporated from their name. The ones who lived there when I was seven were Rosy Cloud, Billowy Cloud, Snowy Cloud, and, my favorite, Magic Cloud. All of them were clever. Most had been thirteen or fourteen when they arrived and would be twenty-three or twenty-four when they left.

My mother set the rules over how they would conduct business with the guests and what share of their earnings and expenses they would pay to the house. Golden Dove managed the courtesans' behavior and appearance and ensured they upheld the standards and reputation of a first-class courtesan house. Golden Dove knew how easily a girl's reputation could be lost. She had once been one of the most popular courtesans of her time until her patron knocked out her front teeth and broke half the bones in her face. By the time she mended, with her face slightly askew, other beauties had taken her place, and she could not overcome speculation that she must have greatly wronged her patron to have incited violence in such a peaceable man.

As comely as those courtesans were, every guest, whether Chinese or Western, hoped to see one woman in particular—my mother. From my perch, she was easy to spot by the springy mass of brown curls that graced her shoulders in a careless style. My hair was very much like hers, only darker. Her skin had a dusky tinge. She told people proudly that she had a few drops of Bombay blood in her. No one would have ever honestly described my mother as beautiful, neither Chinese nor foreigner. She had a long angled nose that looked like it had been roughly sculpted with a paring knife. Her forehead was tall and wide—the telltale sign of a cerebral nature, Golden Dove said. Her chin bulged like a pugnacious little fist, and her cheeks had bladed angles. Her irises were unusually large, and her eyes lay in deep, dark sockets, fanned by dark lashes. But she was captivating, everyone agreed, more so than a woman with regular features and great beauty. It was everything about her—the smile, the husky and melodious voice, the provocative and languorous movement of her body. She sparkled. She glowed. If a man received even a glance from her penetrating eyes, he was enthralled. I saw that time and again. She made each man feel he was special to her.

She was without peer in style as well. Her clothes were of her own witty design. My favorite was a lilac-colored gown of near-transparent silk organza that floated above pale pink tussah. It was embroidered with a winding vine of tiny leaves. At her bosom, two pink rosebuds climbed out of the top of the vine. And if you thought the rosebuds were silk as well, you would be only half right, for one was a genuine rose that loosened its petals and released its scent as the night wore on.

From the balcony, I followed her as she crisscrossed the room, the tail of her skirt swishing behind her, the admiration of men in her wake. I saw her bend her face one way to speak to a Chinese man, then at another angle to speak to a Westerner. I could see that each felt privileged that she had selected him for her attention. What all those men wanted from my mother was the same thing. It was her *guanxi*, as the Chinese called it, her influential connections, as the Western-ers put it. It was her familiarity with many of the most powerful and successful Westerners and Chinese in Shanghai, Canton, Macau, and Hong Kong. It extended to her knowledge of their businesses and the opportunities they held, as well as the ones they did not. Her magne-tism was her ability to put men and prospects together for profit.

The envious madams of other courtesan houses said that my mother knew these men and their secrets because she slept with all of them, hundreds of men of every shade of skin. Or, they said, she blackmailed them by learning of the illegal means they had used to gain their money. It could also be that she drugged them nightly. Who knew what it took to get those men to give her what she needed to know?

The real reason for her business success had much to do with Golden Dove. Mother said so many times, but in such a roundabout way that I could gather only bits and pieces, which were as a whole too fantastical to be true. She and Golden Dove supposedly met about ten years ago when they lived in a house on East Floral Alley. At the beginning, Golden Dove ran a teahouse for Chinese sailors. Then Mother started a pub for pirates. So Golden Dove made an even fan-cier teahouse for sea captains, and my mother made a private club for the owners of ships, and they kept outdoing each other until my mother started Hidden Jade Path, and that was that. Throughout that time, Mother taught Golden Dove English and Golden Dove taught her Chinese, and together they practiced a ritual called *momo*, which thieves used to steal secrets. Golden Dove said *momo* was nothing more than being quiet. But I did not believe her.

I would sometimes wander down from my perch with Carlotta and wend my way through a tall labyrinth of dark-suited men. Few paid attention to me. It was as if I were invisible, except to the servants, who, by the time I was seven, no longer feared me as a Whirlwind but now treated me more like a tumbleweed.

I was too short to see past the clusters of men, but I could hear my mother's bright voice, moving closer or farther away, greeting each customer as if he were a long-lost friend. She gently admonished those whom she had not seen in a while, and they were flattered that she had missed them. I watched how she guided those men into agreeing with whatever she said. If two men in the room held opposite opinions, she did not take sides but expressed a view somewhere above, and like a goddess, she moved their opinions into a common one. She did not translate their exact words but altered the tone of intention, interest, and cooperation.

She was also forgiving of gaffes, and they were bound to happen, as is the case between nations. I recall an evening when I was standing next to Mother as she introduced a British mill owner, Mr. Scott, to a banker named Mr. Yang. Mr. Scott immediately launched into a story about his winnings at the racetrack that day. Unfortunately, Mr. Yang spoke perfect English, and thus my mother was unable to alter the conversation when Mr. Scott talked excitedly about his afternoon betting on horses.

"That horse had odds of twelve to one. In the last quarter mile, his legs were slashing the air, gaining steady speed all the way to the end." He shaded his eyes, as if seeing the race once again. "He took the race by five lengths! Mr. Yang, do you enjoy horse races?"

Mr. Yang said with unsmiling diplomacy, "I have not had the pleasure, Mr. Scott, nor has any Chinese I know."

Mr. Scott quickly replied: "We must go together, then. Tomorrow perhaps?"

To which Mr. Yang gravely replied: "By your Western laws in the International Settlement, you would have to take me as your servant."

Mr. Scott's smile vanished. He had forgotten the prohibition. He looked nervously at my mother, and she said in a humorous tone, "Mr. Yang, you must bring Mr. Scott into the Chinese Walled City as your rickshaw puller, and encourage him to make haste like his winning horse to the gate. Tit for tat."

After they shared a good laugh, she said, "All this talk of speed and haste reminds me that we must work quickly together to secure approval for the shipping route through Yokohama. I know of someone who can be helpful in that regard. Shall I send a message tomorrow?" The next week, three gifts of money arrived, one from Mr. Yang, a larger one from Mr. Scott, and the last from the bureaucrat who had greased the way to the approvals and had a stake in the deal.

I saw how she entranced the men. They acted as if they were in love with her. However, they could not make any confessions of ardor, no matter how true. The warning went around that she would not view them as genuine feelings of love, but trickery to gain unfair advantage. She promised that if they tried to gain her affections, she would banish them from Hidden Jade Path. She broke that promise with one man.

BEHIND THE BALCONIES were two hallways, and between them was a common room, where we took our meals. On the other side of a round archway was a larger room we called Family Hall. It contained three tea tables and sets of chairs, as well as Western furnishings. Here my mother met with the tailor or shoemaker, the tax official, the banker, and others who conducted boring business. From time to time, the occasional mock wedding took place between a courtesan and patron who had signed a contract for at least two seasons. When the room was not in use, more often than not, the Cloud Beauties drank tea and ate sweet seeds, while chatting idly about a suitor no one wanted, or a new restaurant with fashionable foreign food, or the downfall of a courtesan at another house. They treated one another like sisters, tied by their circumstances to this house and this moment in their brief careers. They comforted one another, gave encouragement, and also bickered over petty matters, such as their shared expenses for food. They were jealous of one another but also loaned one another pins and bracelets. And they often told the same stories of how they were separated from their families, culminating in all sharing a good long cry of mutual understanding. "No one should have to bear fate this bitter" was the common refrain. "Fuck that lousy dog" was another.

A hallway led to a courtyard flanked by two large wings of the house, laid out as quadrangles around a smaller courtyard. To the left was the southwest wing, where the Cloud Beauties lived. A covered walkway ran along all four sides, which was how each courtesan reached her room. The lowest-ranked courtesan had the room closest to the hallway, which afforded her the least privacy, since all the other courtesans had to walk past her door and window to reach their rooms. The highest-ranked courtesan had the room farthest from the hallway, which gave her the most privacy. Each long room was divided into two parts. On one side of a tall lattice screen, the Cloud Beauty and her guest could have an intimate dinner. Behind the screen was her boudoir. It had a window facing the inner courtyard, and this was ideal for moon watching. The more popular a beauty was, the more well appointed her room, often lavished with gifts from her suitors and patrons. The boudoirs were more Chinese in style than the furnishings in the salon. No patron wanted to puzzle over which divan to recline on for a smoke, where he could relieve himself, or where he might sleep when he had exhausted himself, or was about to do so.

My mother, Golden Dove, and I lived in the northeast wing. Mother had separate rooms on two sides of the building. One was her bedroom and the other her office, where she and Golden Dove met to discuss the evening's guests. I always joined her during her late-midday meal, and also remained with her as she readied herself in her bedroom for the evening. This was the happiest time of my day. During that lean hour, she would ask me about the subjects I was learning, and she often would add interesting facts. She would ask about my reported transgressions: what I had done to cause one of the maids to want to kill herself, whether I had been sassy to Golden Dove, how I had torn yet another dress. I offered my opinion on a new courtesan, or on a new hat Mother was wearing, or on Carlotta's latest antics, and other similar matters that I thought were important to the management of the household.

Mother had another room adjoining her office. These two rooms were separated by French glass doors with thick curtains for privacy. That room was called Boulevard, because its windows faced a view of Nanking Road and it served several purposes. During the day, I took my lessons there with my American tutors. However, if Mother or Golden Dove had guests from out of town, the visitors were given that room as their accommodations. On occasion, a courtesan showed poor planning or excessive popularity by booking two clients for the same night. She would entertain one client in Boulevard and the other in her boudoir. If she was careful, neither client would know of her duplicity.

My room was on the north side of the east wing, and being close to the main corridor, it enabled me to hear the gossip of the four maids who stood just around the corner from my window while awaiting orders to bring tea, fruit, or hot towels and such. As they served the courtesan, they were privy to how well she was succeeding with a new admirer. It always puzzled me why the courtesans assumed the maids were deaf.

"You should have seen her face when the necklace he showed her was worth less than half what she had hoped for. I wasn't surprised."

"Her situation is dire. Within a month, she'll be gone. Ai-ya, *poor girl. She's too good for this kind of fate."*

In the early evening, at least one Cloud Beauty would lead her patron to the larger courtyard below for romantic talk about nature. I stood on the walkway and listened to those rehearsed murmurings so often that I could recite them as wistfully as the courtesans. The moon was a topic they brought up often.

I should be happy seeing the full moon, my love. But I feel sick, because I'm reminded my debts are waxing and your ardor is waning. Why else have you not given me a gift lately? Should my devotion be rewarded with poverty?

It did not matter how generous the patron was. The beauty would press him for more. And often, the long-suffering patron would sigh and tell his courtesan to not cry anymore. He would agree to whatever formula of happiness would quench the girl's complaints.

That was usually how it worked. But one night, I heard with glee as a patron said: "If you had your way, there would be a full moon every day. Don't harangue me with this moon nonsense ever again."

In the late morning, I would hear the girls talking in the courtyard among themselves.

"The cheapskate pretended to be deaf."

"Just like that, he agreed. I should have asked months ago."

"His love is genuine. He told me I'm not like other flower beauties."

By the light of day, they saw different meanings in the sky. How changeable those clouds were, just like fate. They saw ominous signs in wispy streaks high in the sky, noting that they were so far away. They rejoiced when the clouds were as fat as babies' bottoms, and they were fearful when those babies turned over, showing underbellies that were black. So many Cloud Beauties before them had seen their fates change in one day. They had been warned by the older flower sisters that popularity was as lasting as a fashionable hat. But as their reputations grew, most would forget the warning. They believed they would be the exception.

On cold nights, I cracked open the window and listened to the maids. On warm nights, I opened wide the window and stood quietly in the dark behind my lattice screen shutters. Carlotta sat on my shoulder, and together we listened to the maids talk about what was happening in the rooms of the courtesans. Sometimes they said words I had heard the Cloud Beauties use among themselves: Threading the Needle, Entering the Pavilion, Rousing the Warrior, and many other expressions that made them laugh.

How could a child not be curious about the source of that laughter? I satisfied that curiosity the summer I was seven. An opportunity arose when three maids and a courtesan were wretchedly ill from eating rotted food. The remaining maid was called away, to tend to the vomiting courtesan. I saw Rosy Cloud and her suitor walk past my window and toward her boudoir. After a few minutes, I darted to the west wing and crouched under her window. I was not tall enough to see into the room, and most of what I heard was tedious pleasantry.

You're looking well and happy. Business must be good. I imagine your wife singing like a joyful bird.

Just when I was about to give up and return to my room, I heard a sharp gasp of surprise, and then Rosy Cloud's voice quivered as she thanked her suitor for his gift. A short while later, I heard grunts and the same gasp of surprise, repeated many times.

The next night, I was glad to learn that sickness still prevailed. I had come up with the idea of standing on an overturned basin, which made me just tall enough to peek into the room. By lamplight, I saw the dark shapes of Rosy Cloud and her suitor behind the thin silk curtains of the bed. They were busily moving like a shadow puppet play. Two small, silhouetted feet appeared to sprout from the man's head, and all at once, the feet kicked open the curtains. The man was naked and bouncing on her with such violence they fell off the bed. I could not help but give out a shriek of laughter.

Rosy Cloud complained to Golden Dove the next day that I had been spying and that my laughter had nearly caused her suitor to lose interest. Golden Dove told my mother, and Mother in turn said to me very quietly that I should give the beauties their privacy and to not disturb their business. I took this to mean I should be more careful to not be noticed the next time.

When another opportunity arose, I took it. At that age, I did not find what I saw to be titillating in a sexual way. It was more the thrill of doing what I knew would have embarrassed my victims had they known. I had been wicked in other ways: spying on a man as he was pissing into a chamber pot, putting a greasy smear on the costume of a courtesan who had snapped at me, and a few pranks. One time, I substituted metal cans for the silver bells that hung on the marriage bed, and as the man bounced fast and the bed shook, the couple heard clanking instead of clinking. With each transgression, I knew I was doing wrong, but I also felt brave and thus excited while committing my ill deeds. I also knew what the Cloud Beauties really felt about their suitors and patrons. And that knowledge gave me a secret power—one of no particular use, but it was power nonetheless, as valuable as any trinket in my treasure box.

As mischievous as I was, I had no desire to watch my mother and her lovers. It repulsed me to even imagine that she would allow a man to see her without her beautiful clothes. With the flower beauties, I had less hesitation. I watched them writhing on the divan. I saw men stare between their legs. I saw courtesans on their knees, kowtowing to a client's penis. One night I saw a heavyset man come into Billowy Cloud's room. His name was Prosper Yang and he had several factories, some that made sewing machines and others that put women and children to work on those machines. He kissed her tenderly and she trembled and acted shy. He spoke soft words, and her eyes grew wide and tearful as she removed her clothes. He moved his great mass and hovered over her like a dark cloud and she wore a grimace of fear, as if she were about to be crushed to death. He pressed himself against her, and their bodies moved like thrashing fish. She struggled against him and sobbed in a tragic voice. And then their limbs coiled around each other like snakes. He uttered harsh animal sounds. She cried like a little shrieking bird. He leapt astride her backside and rode her as if she were a trotting pony until he fell off. He left her lying motionless on her side. As the moon shone through the window, her body gleamed white, and I thought she was dead. I watched for almost an hour until she finally awoke from near death with a yawn and an outstretched arm.

That morning, in the courtyard, I heard Billowy Cloud tell another flower sister that Prosper Yang had told her that he cherished her and would be her patron, and that one day he might even make her his wife.

What I had been watching suddenly became dangerous and sickening. Mother and Golden Dove had mentioned several times that I might marry one day. I had always viewed marriage as one of my many American privileges, and unlike the courtesans, I could assume it would be mine. I had never considered that my marriage would include a lot of bouncing on me like what I had witnessed with Billowy Cloud and her suitor. Now I could not stop recalling those scenes. They came to me unwanted and gave me an ill feeling. For several nights, I had shocking dreams. In each, I had taken Billowy Cloud's place, and lay on my stomach, waiting. The dark shape of a man appeared against the translucent curtains and a moment later he burst in—Prosper Yang—and he jumped on my back and rode me like a pony, crushing my bones one by one. When he was done, I lay still, cold as marble. I waited to move, as Billowy Cloud had. Instead I grew colder and colder, because I was dead.

I did not spy on the Cloud Beauties after that.

THE FLOWER SISTER I liked most was Magic Cloud. That was the reason I spied on her and her patron only once. She made me laugh by boasting about the rareness of her furnishings in outlandish ways. The wooden marriage bed, she said, was carved out of the trunk of a single hardwood tree as thick as the entire house. I found seams. The gold brocade on the opium bed was a gift from one of the imperial concubines, who she claimed was her half sister. She pretended to be insulted when I said I did not believe her. The batting of her quilt was made of silk clouds and floated up with the smallest sigh. I sighed and sighed to show her that they did not move. She also had a simple Ming table holding scholar treasures, the accoutrements of the literati, which every client appreciated, even if he had never been able to reach the echelons of those who were excessively educated. These pieces, she told me, had belonged to the Poet Ghost. No one else had dared take them. I did not believe in ghosts, and yet I was nervous when she insisted I inspect the objects: an inkstone of purple *duan,* brushes with the softest sheep hair, and inksticks carved with garden scenes of a scholar's house. She held up the scrolls of paper and said they absorbed just the right amount of ink and reflected the exact quality of light. I asked if she could write poetry, and she said, "Of course! Why else would I have all these things?"

I knew that she, like most courtesans, could read and write only poorly. Golden Dove had required the courtesans to have scholar objects in their room. They enhanced the reputation of the house, set it above others. Magic Cloud told me that the Poet Ghost especially appreciated her scholar treasures more than those in the other boudoirs.

"I know what he likes because he was my husband in a past life," Magic Cloud said, "and I was his favorite concubine. When he died, I killed myself so I could be with him. But even in heaven, society separated us. His wife would not allow me to see him, and she arranged for him to be reincarnated before me."

I did not believe in ghosts, yet I grew nervous listening to Magic Cloud's crazy talk.

"He came to me the first night I moved here. I felt cool breath blow over my cheek and I knew the Poet Ghost had arrived. In the past, I would have jumped out of my skin and run off without it. This time, instead of my teeth chattering with fear, I felt a wonderful warmth pour through my veins. I felt love more strongly than I have ever given or received from anyone. That night, I dreamed of our past life and I awoke the happiest I have ever been."

The Poet Ghost visited her at least once a day, she said. She sensed him when she went into the former painting studio, or while sitting in the garden by his stele. No matter how sad or hopeless or angry she had just been, she immediately felt light and happy.

When the Cloud Beauties learned of her phantom lover, they were afraid and angry that she had unleashed the ghost. But they could not criticize her too much, lest her ghost lover, the former owner of the mansion, retaliate against those who had maligned his beloved.

"Can you see him? Can you smell him?" the flower sisters would ask whenever they caught Magic Cloud looking pleased for no apparent reason.

"Today, just before dusk," she answered, "I saw his shadow and felt it sweep gently over me." She drew two fingers up her arm.

And then I, too, saw a shadow and felt a cool sensation sweep across my skin.

"Ah, you feel him, too," Magic Cloud said.

"No I didn't. I don't believe in ghosts."

"Then why are you scared?"

"I'm not scared. Why should I be? Ghosts don't exist." And as if to counter the lie, my fear grew. I recalled Mother telling me that ghosts were manifestations of people's fear. Why else do these supposed ghosts plague only Chinese people? Despite my mother's logic, I believed the Poet Ghost still lived in our house. Sudden fear was a sign that he had arrived. But why would he visit me?

The Poet Ghost was at the mock marriage between Billowy Cloud and Prosper Yang, who had signed a contract for three seasons. I learned that Billowy Cloud was sixteen and he was fifty or so. Golden Dove consoled her, saying he would be quite generous, as old men tended to be. And Billowy Cloud said that Prosper Yang loved her and she felt lucky.

My mother was renowned for holding the best weddings of all

the courtesan houses. They were Western in style, as opposed to the traditional Chinese weddings for virgin brides, a category to which courtesans could never belong. The courtesan brides even wore a Western white wedding gown, and my mother had a variety the Cloud Beauties could use. The style was clearly Yankee—with low bodices and voluminous skirts, wrapped in glossy gathered silk, and trimmed in lace, embroidery, and seed pearls. Those dresses never would have been confused with the Chinese mourning clothes of rough white sackcloth.

A Western wedding had its advantages, as I had already learned from having attended a Chinese version for a courtesan at another house. For one thing, it did not involve honoring ancestors, who certainly would have disavowed a courtesan as his descendant. So there were no boring rituals or kneeling and endless bowing. The ceremony was short. The prayers were omitted. The bride said "I do" and the groom said "I do." Then it was time to eat. The banquet food at a Western wedding was also remarkable because all the dishes looked Western but they tasted Chinese.

For different fees, patrons could choose music from among several styles. Yankee music played by a marching band was the most expensive and suitable only during good weather. A Yankee violinist was a cheaper choice. Then there was a choice of music. It was important to not be fooled by the title of a song. One of the courtesans had asked the violinist to play "O Promise Me," thinking the length of the song would strengthen her patron's fidelity and perhaps increase the length of the contract. But the song went on for so long that guests lost interest and talked about other matters until the song ended. That was the reason the contract was not renewed, the flower sisters later said. Everyone liked "Auld Lang Syne," played with the aching power of a Chinese instrument that looked like a miniature two-stringed cello. Even though the tune was sung on sad occasions, such as funerals and farewells, it was still popular. There were only a few English words to learn, and everyone loved to sing them to prove they could speak English. My mother changed the words to reflect a promise of monogamy. If a courtesan broke that promise, it would lead to the end of the contract, as well as a bad reputation that would be hard to overcome. If, however, the patron was the one who broke the promise, the courtesan would feel humiliated. Why had he dishonored her? There must have been a reason.

Prosper, who fancied he was a Chinese Caruso, sang with gusto.

"Should old lovers be forgot,
And never brought to mind!
Should old lovers be forgot,
For a long, long time.
Clang bowls again, my dear old friends,
Clang bowls one more time.
Should old lovers be forgot,
And never come to mind!"

In the middle of the song, I saw Magic Cloud turn her eyes toward the archway. She touched her arm lightly, looked up again, and smiled. A moment later, I felt the familiar coolness blow over my arm and down my spine. I shivered and went to my mother.

Prosper bellowed out the last note and let the clapping go on for too long, and then he called for the gifts to be brought to Billowy Cloud. First came the traditional gift every courtesan received: a silver bracelet and a bolt of silk—a toast to that! The guests raised their cups, tipped their heads back, and downed the wine in one swallow. Next came a Western settee upholstered in pink sateen— two toasts for that! More gifts came. Finally Prosper handed Billowy Cloud what she wanted most, an envelope of money, the first of her monthly stipend. She saw the amount, gasped, and fell speechless as tears streamed down her face. We would not know until later if her tears were because she received more than she had expected or less. Another toast was raised. Billowy Cloud insisted she could not drink another. Her face wore splotches of red and she said she felt the ceiling lurching one way and the floor the other. But Prosper grabbed her chin and forced down the wine, followed immediately by another as his friends egged him on. All at once, Billowy Cloud gurgled and vomited before she collapsed to the floor. Golden Dove quickly signaled the musician for a final song to hurry the guests out of the room, and Prosper left with them, without a glance toward Billowy Cloud, who lay on the floor, babbling apology. Magic Cloud tried to sit her up, but the senseless girl flopped backward like a dead fish. "Bastards," Golden Dove said. "Put her in a tub and make sure she doesn't drown."

I saw many weddings. The younger beauties had contracts one after another, with hardly a week in between. But as they grew older and their eyes sparkled less, there were no more weddings for them. And then came the day when Golden Dove told a beauty she had to "take the sedan," which was a polite way of saying she was being evicted. I remembered the day that Rosy Cloud was given the bad news. Mother and Golden Dove had her come to the office. I was studying in Boulevard, the room on the other side of the glass French doors. I heard Rosy Cloud's voice growing louder. Golden Dove was citing figures of money, declining bookings. Why was I able to hear this so clearly? I went to the door and saw that it was not completely closed. There was a half-inch opening. I heard Rosy Cloud beg quietly to stay longer, citing that a certain suitor was on the brink of offering to be her patron. But they held firm and were without sympathy. They suggested another house she might join. Rosy Cloud became loud and angry. They were insulting her, she said, as if she were a common whore. She ran out. A few minutes later I heard her howl in the same way Carlotta did when her foot was caught in the doorjamb, as if her voice was coming from both her bowels and her heart. The sound of it sickened me.

I told Magic Cloud what had happened to Rosy Cloud.

"This will happen to all of us. One day fate brings us here," she said. "Another day it takes us away. Maybe her next life will be better. Suffer more now, suffer less later."

"She shouldn't suffer at all," I said.

Within three days, a courtesan named Puffy Cloud was in Rosy Cloud's quarters. She knew nothing of what had gone on in that room—not the bouncing, the sighs, the tears, or the howls.

A few weeks later, I was in Magic Cloud's boudoir in the late afternoon. Mother had been too busy to eat her late-midday meal with me. She had to dash off to some unknown place to meet an unnamed person. Magic Cloud was putting powder on her face, preparing for a long night—three parties, one at Hidden Jade Path, the other two at houses several blocks away.

I was full of questions. "Are those real pearls?" "Who gave them to you?" "Who will you see tonight?" "Will you bring him to your room?"

She told me that the pearls were the teeth of dragons and a duke had given them to her. He was honoring her tonight, and naturally she would bring him to her room for tea and conversation. I laughed, and she pretended to be offended that I did not believe her.

The next morning she was not in her room. I knew something was wrong because her scholar treasures and silk quilt were missing. I peered into her wardrobe closet. It was empty. Mother was still asleep, as were the courtesans and Golden Dove. So I went to Cracked Egg, the gatekeeper, and he said that he saw her leave but did not know where she had gone. I learned the answer when I overheard two maids talking:

"She was at least five or six years older than she said she was. What house would take an old flower with a ghost stuck inside her?"

"I overheard Lulu Mimi telling the patron it was just superstitious non-sense. He said it didn't matter if it was a ghost or a living man, it was infidelity and he wanted the contract money back."

I raced into my mother's office and found her talking to Golden Dove.

"I know what she did and she's sorry. You have to let her come back," I said. Mother said there was nothing more to be done. Everyone knew the rules, and if she made an exception for Magic Cloud, all the beauties might think they could do the same without penalty. She and Golden Dove went back to discussing plans for a large party and how many extra courtesans would be needed.

"Mother, please," I begged. She ignored me. I burst into tears and shouted: "She was my only friend! If you don't bring her back, I will have no one who likes me."

She came to me and drew me close, caressing my head. "Nonsense. You have many friends here. Snowy Cloud—"

"Snowy Cloud doesn't let me come into her room the way Magic Cloud did."

"Mrs. Petty's daughter—"

"She's silly and boring."

"You have Carlotta."

"She's a cat. She doesn't talk to me or answer questions."

She mentioned the names of more girls who were the daughters of her friends, all of whom I now claimed I disliked—and who despised me, which was partially true. I carried on about my friendless state and the danger of my permanent unhappiness. And then I heard her speak in a cold unyielding tone: "Stop this, Violet. I did not remove her for small reasons. She nearly ruined our business. It was a matter of necessity."

"What did she do?"

"By thinking only of herself, she betrayed us."

I did not know what *betrayed* meant. I simply sputtered in frustration: "Who cares if she betrayed us?"

"Your very mother before you cares."

"Then I will always betray you," I cried.

She regarded me with an odd expression, and I believed she was about to give in. So I pushed again with my bravado. "I'll betray you," I warned.

Her face contorted. "Stop this, Violet, please."

But I could not stop, even though I knew that I was unleashing an unknown danger. "I'll always betray you," I said once more and immediately saw a shadow fall over my mother's face.

Her hands were shaking and her face was so stiff she appeared to be a different person. She said nothing. The longer the silence grew, the more frightened I became. I would have backed down if I had known what to say or do. So I waited.

At last she turned, and as she walked away, she said in a bitter voice, "If you ever betray me, I shall have nothing to do with you. I promise you that."

MY MOTHER HAD a certain phrase she used with every guest, Chinese or Western. She would walk hurriedly to a certain man and whisper excitedly, "You're just the one I hoped to see." Then followed the dip of her head toward the man's ear to whisper some secret, which caused the man to nod vigorously. Some kissed her hand. This repeated phrase distressed me. I had noticed that she was often too busy to pay any attention to me. She no longer played the guessing games or sent me on treasure hunts. We no longer lay in her bed cuddled next to each other as she read the newspaper. She was too busy for that. Her gaiety and smiles were now reserved for the men at her parties. They were the ones she had hoped to see.

One night, as I crossed the salon with Carlotta in my arms, I heard Mother call out: "Violet! You're here. You're just the one I hoped to see."

At last! I had been chosen. She gave profuse apologies to the man she had been conversing with, citing that her daughter required her urgent attention. What was so urgent? It did not matter. I was excited to hear the secret she had saved for me. "Let's go over there," Mother said, nudging me toward a dark corner of the room. She took my arm in hers, and we were off at a brisk pace. I was telling her about Carlotta's latest antics, something to amuse her, when she let go of my arm, and said, "Thank you, darling." She walked over to a man in the corner of the room and said, "Fairweather, my dear. I'm sorry I was delayed." Her dark-haired lover stepped out of the shadows and kissed her hand with fake gallantry. She returned a crinkle-eyed smile I had never seen her give to me.

I could not breathe, crushed by my short-lived happiness. She had used me as her pawn! Worse, she had done so for Fairweather, a man who had visited her from time to time, and whom I had always disliked. I had once believed I was the most important person in her life. But in recent months, that was disproved. Our special closeness had become unmoored. She was always too busy to spend time chatting with me during her midday meals. Instead she and Golden Dove used that hour to discuss the evening plans. She seldom asked me about my lessons or what I was reading. She called me "darling," but she said the same to many men. She kissed my cheek in the morning and my forehead at night. But she kissed many men, and some on the mouth. She said she loved me, but I did not see any particular sign of that. I could not feel anything in my heart but the loss of her love. She had changed toward me, and I was certain that it had started the day when I threatened to betray her. Bit by bit, she was having nothing to do with me.

Golden Dove found me crying one day in Boulevard. "Mother does not love me anymore."

"Nonsense. Your mother loves you a great deal. Why else does she let you go unpunished for all the naughty things you do? Just the other day, you broke a clock by moving its hands backward. You ruined a pair of her stockings by using it as a mouse for Carlotta to chase."

"That's not love," I said. "She didn't get mad because she doesn't care about those things. If she truly loved me, she would prove it."

"How?" Golden Dove asked. "What is there to prove?"

I was thrown into mute confusion. I did not know what love was.

All I knew was a gnawing need for her attention and assurances. I wanted to feel without worry that I was more important than anyone else in her life. When I thought about it further, I realized she had given more attention to the beauties than to me. She had spent more time with Golden Dove. She had risen before noon to have lunch with her friends, the bosomy opera singer, the traveling widow, and the French lady spy. She had devoted much more attention to her customers than to anybody else. What love had they received that she had not given me?

That night I overheard a maid in the corridor telling another that she was worried sick because her three-year-old daughter had a high fever. The next night, she announced happily that her daughter had recovered. In the afternoon of the next day, the woman's screams reverberated in the courtyard. A relative had come to say her child had died. She wailed, "How can that be? I held her this morning. I combed her hair." In between her sobs, she described her daughter's big eyes, the way she always turned her head to listen to her, how musical her laughter was. She babbled that she was saving money to buy her a jacket, that she had bought a turnip for a healthy soup. Later she moaned that she wanted to die to be with her daughter. Who else did she have to live for? I cried secretly as I listened to her grief. If I died, would Mother feel the same about me? I cried harder, knowing she would not.

A week after Mother had tricked me, she came into the room where I was studying with my tutor. It was only eleven, an hour before she usually rose from bed. I gave her my sullen face. She asked if I would like to have lunch with her at the new French restaurant on Great Western Road. I was wary. I asked her who else would be there.

"Just the two of us," she replied. "It's your birthday."

I had forgotten. No one celebrated birthdays in the house. It was not a Chinese custom, and Mother had not made it hers. My birthday usually occurred near the Chinese New Year, and that was what we celebrated, with everyone. I tried to not be too excited, but a surge of joy went through me. I went to my room to put on a nice day dress, one that had not been snagged by Carlotta's claws. I selected a blue coat and a hat of a similar color. I put on a grown-up pair of walking shoes of shiny leather that laced up to my ankles. I saw myself in the long oval mirror. I looked different, nervous, and worried. I was now eight, no longer the innocent little girl who trusted her feelings. I had once expected happiness and lately had received only disappointments, one after the other. I now expected disappointment and prayed to be proven wrong.

When I went to Mother's study, I found that Golden Dove and she were laying out the tasks for the day. She was walking back and forth in her wrapper, her hair unbound.

"The old tax collector is coming tonight," Mother was saying. "He promises that some extra attention may make him inattentive to my tax bill. We'll see if the old dog fart is telling the truth this time."

"I'll send a call chit to Crimson," Golden Dove said, "the courtesan at the Hall of Verdant Peace. She'll take any kind of business these days. I'll advise her to wear dark colors, dark blue. Pink is unflattering on someone well past youth. She should know better. I'll also tell the cook to make the fish you like, but not with the American flavors. I know he wants to please you, but it never comes out right, and we all suffer."

"Do you have the list for tonight's guests?" Mother said. "I don't want the importer from Smythe and Dixon to come anymore. None of his information has been reliable. He's been sniffing around to get something for nothing. We'll give his name to Cracked Egg so he does not get past the gate . . ."

By the time she and Golden Dove finished, it was nearly one. She left me in the office and went to her room to change into a dress. I wandered around her office, and Carlotta followed me, rubbing against my legs wherever I stood. A round table was cluttered with knickknacks, the sorts of gifts some of her admirers gave her, not knowing she preferred money. Golden Dove sold the knickknacks she did not want. I picked up each object, and Carlotta jumped up and sniffed. An amber egg with a bug inside—that one would certainly go. An amethyst-and-jade bird—she might keep that. A glass display case of butterflies from different lands—she must hate that one. A painting of a green parrot—I liked it, but the only paintings Mother put on the walls were nude Greek gods and goddesses. I turned the pages of an illustrated book called *The World of the Sea* and saw illustrations of hideous creatures. I used a nearby magnifying glass to enlarge the titles of books in the bookcase: *The Religions of India, Travels to Japan and China, China in Convulsion.* I came across a red-covered book embossed with the black silhouette of a boy in uniform shooting a rifle. *Under the Allied Flags: A Boxer Story.* A note was stuck in the middle of the pages. It was written in the careful script of a schoolboy.

> *My dear Miss Minturn,*
>   *If ever you need an American lad who knows how to obey orders, will you consider using me as volunteer aide? I'd like to make myself as useful as you desire.*
>   *Your faithful servant,*
>   *Ned Peaver*

Had Mother accepted his offer to be her faithful servant? I read the page where the note had been inserted. It was about a soldier named Ned Peaver—aha!—during the Boxer Rebellion. After a quick glance at the page, I concluded Ned was a dull, prissy boy, who always followed orders. I had always disliked anything to do with the Boxer Rebellion. I was two years old in 1900 when the worst of the rebellion took place, and I believed I could have died in the violence. I had read a book about young men who swore themselves into the brotherhood of Boxers when millions of peasants in the middle of China were starving due to a flood one year, and a drought the next. When they heard rumors that foreigners were going to be given their land, they killed about two hundred white missionaries and their children. By one account, a brave little girl sang sweetly as her parents watched her being sent by the whack of a sword to heaven. Whenever I pictured it, I touched my soft throat and swallowed hard.

I looked at the clock. Its newly repaired hands said it was now two o'clock. I had been waiting nearly three hours since she announced we would have lunch. All at once, my head and heart exploded. I ripped up Ned Peaver's letter. I went to the table with my mother's plunder and hurled the case of butterflies onto the floor. Carlotta ran off. I threw down the amethyst bird, the magnifying glass, the amber egg. I tore off the cover of *The World of the Sea*. Golden Dove ran in and looked at the mess, horrified. "Why do you hurt her?" she said mournfully. "Why is your temper so bad?"

"It's two o'clock. She said she was taking me to a restaurant for my birthday. Now she's not coming. She didn't remember. She always forgets I'm even here." My eyes were blurry with tears. "She doesn't love me. She loves all those men."

Golden Dove picked up the amber egg and magnifying glass. "These were your gifts."

"Those are things that men gave her and she doesn't want."

"How can you think that? She chose them just for you."

"Why didn't she come back to take me to lunch?"

"*Ai-ya!* You did this because you're hungry? All you had to do was ask the maid to bring you something to eat."

I did not know how to explain what the outing to the restaurant had meant to me. I blurted a jumble of wounds: "She tells the men that they are the ones she wants to see. She told me the same, but it was a trick. She doesn't worry anymore when I'm sad or lonely . . ."

Golden Dove frowned. "Your mother spoils you, and this is the result. You have no gratitude, only a temper when you do not get your way."

"She didn't keep her promise and she didn't say she was sorry."

"She was upset. She got a letter—"

"She gets many letters." I kicked at the confetti of Ned's note.

"This letter was different." She stared at me in an odd way. "It was about your father. He's dead."

I did not understand what she had said at first. My father. What did that mean? I was five when I first asked Mother where my father was. Everyone had one, I learned, even the courtesans whose fathers had sold them. Mother told me that I had no father. When I pressed her, she said that he had died before I was born. Over the next three years, I pressed Mother from time to time to tell me who my father was.

"What does it matter?" she always said. "He's dead, and it was so very long ago I've even forgotten his name and what he looked like."

How could she have forgotten his name? Would she forget mine if I died? I pestered her for answers. When she grew quiet and frowned, I sensed it was dangerous to continue.

But now the truth was out. He was alive! Or he had been. My confusion gave way to a shaky anger. Mother had been lying all this time when he was alive. He may have loved me, and by not telling me that he was alive, she had stolen him from me. Now he was truly dead and it was too late.

I ran into my mother's office, shrieking, "He was never dead. You kept him from me." I blubbered every accusation that went through my head. She did not tell me the truth about anything that mattered to me. She lied when she told me I was just the one she hoped to see. She lied about lunch . . . Mother was speechless.

Golden Dove rushed in. "I told her that you had received a letter announcing her father had just died."

Mother stared hard at her. Was she angry? Would she dismiss us both, as she did those who displeased her? She put down the terrible letter. She led me to the sofa and sat me next to her. And then she did what she had not done in a long time: She petted my head and whispered soothing words, which made me cry even harder. "Violet, dearest, I truly thought he was dead all these years. I found it too painful to think about him, to say anything about him. And now, to receive this letter . . ." The rims of her eyes were shiny, but the dam of her emotions held.

When I could breathe again, I asked her question after question, and to each she nodded and said yes. Was he nice? Was he rich? Did everyone like him? Was he older than she was? Did he ever love me? Did he ever play with me? Did he say my name? Mother continued to stroke my hair and rub my shoulders. I felt so sad and did not want her to stop comforting me. I continued to ask questions until my mind was exhausted. By then, I was weak from hunger. Golden Dove called for a servant to bring my lunch to Boulevard. "Your mother needs to be by herself now." Mother gave me a kiss and went to her bedroom.

As I ate, Golden Dove told me how hard my mother had to struggle without a husband. "All her work has been for you, Little Violet," she said. "Be grateful, be nice to your mother." Before she left, she suggested I study and become smart to show my mother how much I appreciated her. Instead of studying, however, I lay on the bed in Boulevard to think about my newly deceased father. I began to put together a picture of him: His hair was brown; his eyes were green, just like mine. I soon fell asleep.

I was still drowsy and thickheaded when I heard someone arguing. I realized I was not in my own room but still in Boulevard. I went to the window and looked out onto the hallway to see the cause of the commotion. The sky was dark gray, at that suspended time between night and morning. The hallways were empty. The windows across the courtyard were black. I turned around and saw a warm sliver of light coming through a small opening of the curtains over the glass French doors. The angry voice was my mother's. I looked through the curtain opening and saw the back of her head. She had loosened her hair and was seated on the sofa. She had come back from the party. Was anyone else in the room? I put my ear to the glass. She was cursing in a strange low voice that sounded like Carlotta's deep-throated growl. *"You're spineless . . . a dancing monkey . . . as much character as a filthy thief . . ."* She threw down a folded piece of paper. It landed near the unlit fireplace. Was it the letter she had received? She went to her desk and sat down, seized a sheet of stationery, then slashed at it with her dripping pen. She crumpled the half-written page and threw it onto the floor. "I wish you really were dead!" she shouted.

My father was alive! She had lied again! I was about to rush in and demand to know where my father was. But then she looked up and I nearly cried out in fright. Her eyes had changed. The green irises had turned inside out, and the backs of them were as dull as sand. She had the eyes of dead beggars I had seen lying in gutters. She abruptly stood up, turned down the lamps, and went to her bedroom. I had to see the letter. I opened the French doors carefully. It was dark and I had to move forward blindly, sweeping my hands to avoid bumping into the furniture. I went to my knees. Suddenly I felt someone touch me, and I gasped. It was Carlotta. She pushed her head against me, purring. I could now feel the tiles of the fireplace. I patted the hearth. Nothing. I found the legs of the desk, and raised myself slowly. My eyes had adjusted to the dark, but I saw no sign of anything that resembled a letter. I crept out of the room, bitterly disappointed.

The next day, Mother acted as she always had—brisk and clearheaded as she laid out the tasks. She was charming and talkative in the evening, smiling as always at her guests. While she and Golden Dove were busy during the party, I sneaked into Boulevard, opened the French doors just wide enough to push through the curtains and into my mother's office. I turned on one gas lamp. I opened desk drawers, and one was filled with letters whose envelopes had embossed names of companies. I looked under her pillow, in the little cabinet next to her bed. I lifted the lid of her trunk at the foot of her bed. The smell of turpentine flew out. The source was two rolled-up paintings. I unfurled one and was astonished to see a portrait of Mother as a young girl. I placed it on the floor and smoothed it out. She was staring straight ahead, as if she were looking at me.

Over her chest, she held a maroon cloth. Her pale back glowed like the cold warmth of the moon. Who painted this? Why had she been so scantily dressed?

I was about to look at the other painting when I was startled by the approaching laughter of Puffy Cloud. The door to Boulevard opened. I jumped to the side of the office, where she would not be able to see me. She cooed to a client to make himself comfortable. Of all nights for her to be overly popular! Puffy Cloud pulled the French doors closed. I hurriedly put the paintings back in the trunk and was about to turn down the lamp and leave when Golden Dove came into the room.

We both gasped at the same time. Before she could speak, I asked if she had seen Carlotta. As if she had heard me, Carlotta let out a loud wail behind the doors of Boulevard. Puffy Cloud cursed, "I thought that damn cat was a headless ghost!" I went to the French doors and opened them slightly, and Carlotta darted in.

With Carlotta in my arms, I quickly went downstairs to the party, thinking I might spot my father lurking among the guests. But then I realized my father would not have dared show his face there. My mother would have scratched his eyes out. I looked at the guests and played a game of pretend—imagining one man after another was my father. I picked out the traits I liked—the ones who laughed easily, who wore the best clothes, who received the most respect, who winked at me. And then my eye landed on a man with a pinched and unfriendly expression, and another whose face was so pink he looked like he was about to explode.

In bed, before falling asleep each night, I imagined different versions of my father: handsome or ugly, well respected or loathed by all. I imagined he had loved me very much. I imagined he never had.

A MONTH AFTER my eighth birthday, I entered the common room to have breakfast with the Cloud Beauties and their attendants. I went to sit in my usual spot at the table. But I found that the newest courtesan, Misty Cloud, had placed her bottom on my chair. I glowered, and she returned a glance of indifference. She had miniature features set in a plump, round face, which men found attractive for some reason. To me, she had the ugly face of a baby pasted onto the yellow moon.

"This is my chair," I said.

"*Oyo!* Your chair? Is it carved with your name? Is there an official decree?" She pretended to inspect the arms and legs. "I don't see your name seal. All the chairs are the same."

My temples were beating hard. "It's my chair."

"*Anh?* What makes you think you're the only one who can sit here?"

"Lulu Mimi is my mother," I added, "and I'm an American like her."

"Since when do half-breed American bastards have the same rights?"

I was shocked. Rage was rising from my throat. Two of the beauties put their palms to their mouths. Snowy Cloud, whom I had liked more than the others, told us to calm down. She suggested we take turns sitting in the chair. I had hoped she would have taken my side.

I sputtered to Misty Cloud, "You're a worm in a dead fish ass." The maids burst into laughter.

"*Wah!* The half-breed has such a foul mouth," Misty Cloud said. She looked around the table to the others. "If she's not a half-breed, how is it that she looks Chinese?"

"How dare you say that!" I cried. "I'm American. There's nothing Chinese about me."

"Then why are you speaking Chinese?"

I could not answer at first, because if I did, I would be speaking in Chinese again and give her the upper hand. Misty Cloud picked up a small oily peanut with her thin pointed chopsticks. "Do any of you know who her Chinese father is?" She popped the peanut into her mouth.

My hands were shaking with anger, and I was incensed to see how calmly she was eating. "My mother will punish you for saying that."

She repeated what I said in a mocking tone, then popped a pickled radish in her mouth and crunched it, without bothering to cover her mouth. "If you are pure white, then all of us must be, too. Isn't that right, my sisters?" The other beauties and their attendants tried halfheartedly to silence her.

"You're a dirty hole!" I said.

She frowned. "What's the matter, little brat? Are you so ashamed to be Chinese that you can't recognize your face in a mirror?"

The others looked down. Two made sideways glances to each other. Billowy Cloud put her hand on Misty Cloud's arm and beseeched her to stop. "She's too young for you to speak of this."

Why was Billowy Cloud acting so charitably toward me? Did that mean she believed what Misty Cloud had said? I fell into a cauldron of rage and I pushed Misty Cloud out of the chair. She was too dumbfounded to move for a moment, then grabbed my ankles and pulled me down. I pounded my fists on her shoulders. She grabbed my hair and flung me away from her.

"Half-breed crazy little bastard girl. You're no better than any of us!"

I hurled myself at her and banged the heel of my hand on her nose. Blood gushed from one of her nostrils, and when she wiped at it and she saw her crimson fingers, she threw herself on top of me again and smeared blood across my face. I was screaming epithets and bit her hand. She screamed, and her eyes looked as if they were going to pop out of her sockets. She grabbed me by the neck and was choking me. I struggled to breathe, and in my panic to escape, I punched her in the eye. She jumped up and cried out in horror. I had delivered one of the worst things that could happen to a girl: a black eye. She would not be able to appear at parties for as long as the bruise was visible. Misty Cloud shrieked and lunged at me and slapped my face, vowing she would kill me. The other girls and attendants screamed for us to stop. The menservants rushed in and pulled us apart.

All at once, everyone fell silent, and the only sounds were Misty Cloud's curses. It was my mother and Golden Dove. I thought Mother had come to rescue me. But a moment later, I noticed her eyes had gone as gray as knives.

Misty Cloud cried in a fake way: "She damaged my eye—"

I put my hand to my neck, as if it hurt. "She almost choked me to death!"

"I want money for my eye!" Misty Cloud shouted. "I was making more money for you than the others, and if I can't work until my eye is better, I want the money I would have earned."

My mother stared at her. "If I do not give it to you, then what will you do?"

"I'll leave and tell everyone that this brat is a half-breed."

"Well, we can't have you going around telling lies simply because you're angry. Violet, tell her you're sorry."

Misty Cloud gave me a sneer of victory. "What about my money?" she said to my mother.

Mother turned and left the room without answering her. I followed, puzzled that she had not stood up for me. When we reached her room, I cried, "She called me a half-breed bastard."

Mother cursed under her breath. Usually she laughed at people's insults. But this time, her silence frightened me. I wanted her to quell my fears.

"Is it true? Am I half-Chinese? Do I have a Chinese father?"

She turned around and said in a dangerous voice: "Your father is dead. I told you that. Do not talk about this again, not to anyone."

I was terrified by the deadness in her voice, by the many fears it put in my heart. What was true? Which was worse?

The next day, Misty Cloud was gone. She was kicked out, the

others said. I felt no victory now, only queasiness that I had inflicted greater harm than I had intended. I knew the reason she was gone. She had spilled the truth. Would she now spread it wherever she went?

I asked the gatekeeper if he knew where Misty Cloud had gone.

Cracked Egg was scraping a rusty bolt. "She was too busy spitting insults at your mother to stop on her way out and give me the address of her new house. With that black eye, she might not have anywhere to go for a while."

"Did you hear what she called me?" I was anxious for the answer that would tell me how far the lie had spread.

"*Ai-ya*. Don't listen to her. She's the one who has mixed blood," he said. "She thinks the white part of her makes her as good as you."

White? Misty Cloud had dark eyes and dark hair. No one would mistake her for being anything but pure Chinese.

"Do you think I look half-Chinese?" I asked him quietly.

He looked at me and laughed. "You look nothing like her." He went back to scraping the bolt.

I was relieved.

And then he said, "Certainly not half. Maybe just a few drops."

A cold fear ran from scalp to toes.

"Eh, I was only joking." He said it in a soft tone, one that was too comforting.

"Her mother was half-Swedish," I later heard Cracked Egg tell an attendant, "married to a Shanghainese, who soon died and left her all alone with a baby. Her husband's family refused to recognize her as his widow, and since she had no family of her own, she had no choice but to turn tricks on the streets. And then, when she saw men asking for Misty Cloud when she was only eleven, she sold her to a first-class courtesan house, where she would at least have some chance at a better life than hers. That's what I heard from the gatekeeper at the House of Li where Misty Cloud worked before she came here. If she had not thrown a fit at the madam there, she might have been able to come back."

Later, in my room, I sat on my bed for an hour, holding a looking glass in my lap, unable to bring it to my face. And when I finally did, I saw my green eyes and brown hair and sighed with relief. I put down the mirror. The worry soon returned. I pulled my hair back and tied it with a ribbon so that I could see my face fully. I held my breath and picked up the mirror. Again, I saw nothing Chinese. I smiled, and as soon as I did, my plump cheeks tilted my eyes at the outer corners, and this instant change sent my heart pounding. I recognized too clearly the signs of my unknown father: my slightly rounded nose, the tipped-up nostrils, the fat below my eyebrows, the smooth roundness of my forehead, the plump cheeks and lips. My mother had none of these features.

What was happening to me? I wanted to run and leave behind this new face. My limbs were heavy. I looked in the mirror again and again, hoping my face would change back to what I used to see. So this was why my mother had no special affection for me anymore. The Chinese part of my Chinese father was spreading across my face like a stain. If she hated him enough to wish he did not exist, she must feel the same about me. I unbundled my hair and shook it so it fell like a dark curtain over my face.

A cool breeze swept over my arms. The Poet Ghost had arrived to tell me that he had known all along I was Chinese.

I USED A spyglass to observe every Chinese man who came to Hidden Jade Path. They were the educated, the wealthy, and the powerful men of the city. Were any of them my father? I watched to see if my mother showed greater affection or anger toward any of them. But, as usual, she appeared to be as interested in one as in another. She gave them her special smile, her intimate laugh, her well-acted sincere and special words meant only for each and every one of them.

I was aware of only one Chinese man whom she treated with genuine honesty and respect: Cracked Egg, the gatekeeper. She saw

him every day and even took tea with him downstairs. He knew the
latest gossip about the men on the guest list. The gatekeepers of all
the houses saw and heard everything and shared it among themselves. My mother often remarked to Golden Dove about Cracked
Egg's loyalty and sharp mind.

How Cracked Egg got his name I could not imagine. He was
hardly stupid. Whatever my mother told him about those businesses,
he was able to keep in his head. He could neither read nor write more
than a few words, but he could read people's character. He had sharp
eyes for recognizing which guest should be welcomed, and what their
social standing was. He spotted the faces of their sons who stood awk-
wardly at the gate, and he made them especially welcome, knowing
this visit would be their initiation into the world of male pleasures. He
memorized the names of all the wealthy and the powerful who had
not yet visited the house. From the particular type of eagerness that
a man displayed upon presenting himself at the gate, Cracked Egg
could determine what the man intended to do that night—whether to
court a Cloud Beauty or a business partner—which he then reported
to my mother. He noted the man's appearance—from the grooming
of his hair to the heels of his shoes, the tailored details of his clothes
and his comfort in wearing them. He knew the hallmarks of long-
standing prestige that might separate the man from those who had
more recently acquired it. On his rare days off, Cracked Egg dressed
in a fine suit, a castoff left by a client. From years of observation, he
could imitate the manners of a gentleman, even in his speech. He
always kept himself groomed; his hair was barbered, his fingernails
were clean. After Cracked Egg said I had drops of Chinese blood, I
considered he might be the one who was my father. Even though I
liked him, I would be ashamed if he was. And if he was, perhaps my
mother was too ashamed to tell me. But how could she have taken him
as a lover? He was not cultivated, nor handsome like her other lovers.
His face was long, his nose too fleshy, and his eyes were far apart.
He was older than my mother, perhaps forty. Next to my mother, he

appeared slight of frame. What's more, thankfully, I did not resemble him in any way.

But what if he was my father? His character was good, that's what mattered. He was always kind. To those men on the list who came to the gate and did not meet his standards, he would be apologetic that there was an excessive number of guests who had arrived unexpectedly for a large party. To the young students and foreign sailors, he gave an uncle's advice: "Cross Beaten Dog Bridge and try the opium flower house called Silver Bells. A great old gal named Plume will let you have a go at her once you've bought a few pipefuls."

Cracked Egg had a special fondness for Plume, who had once worked at Hidden Jade Path until she was too old. She's like a daughter, he'd say. He was protective of all the girls, and they often expressed their gratitude by telling stories to others about his efforts to protect them. Cracked Egg feigned he was not listening, and the girls would call out every now and then, "Isn't that what you did?" He would give them his most baffled look.

If my father was indeed Chinese, I would want him to be someone like Cracked Egg. But then I heard Snowy Cloud tell a story a month after the debacle with Misty Cloud. We were having breakfast in the common room.

"Yesterday a drunk came to the gate," she said. "I was sitting in the front garden, just out of view. I could tell by the cheap and shiny clothes that he was one of those overnight successes, no meat to his words, just yellow fat floating in cold broth. He was not an invited guest and would not have been allowed one step over the threshold. But you know how polite Cracked Egg is with everyone.

"This man asked, Hey, are your whores good at acrobatic feats? He patted a fat purse. Cracked Egg put on his sorry face and told him that all the girls in Hidden Jade Path used a technique called 'stiff corpse.' He went on to demonstrate that our limbs were locked in one position by rigor mortis and our mouths were frozen into a grimace. For that, he told the man, they charge three times as much as the loose-limbed girls in the Hall of Singing Swallows on Tranquility Lane. So the man happily toddled off to that low-class brothel, which I heard has just had an outbreak of syphilis."

Everyone laughed uproariously.

"Plume told me he came by last week and smoked a few pipes," she added. "He told her not to cry, that she was still lovely. She wept in his arms. He always shows her his concern and generosity. Every time they have sex, she said, he insists on paying her twice the usual amount."

Every time they have sex. I imagined Cracked Egg crawling over my body, his long face looking at my scared one. He was not my father. He was the gatekeeper.

                                             *

I ASKED MY mother if we could visit an orphanage for abandoned half-breed girls. She did not hesitate in agreeing it was a good idea. My heart beat in alarm. She gathered up some of my old dresses and toys. At the orphanage, I carried them into a large room crowded with girls of all ages. Some looked entirely Chinese, and others purely white—until they smiled and their eyes tilted upward at a slant.

Now, whenever Mother was too busy to see me, I took this as evidence that she had never wanted me. I was her half-American, half-hated child, and I guessed the reason she could not tell me the truth: She would have to admit that she did not love me. I was always on the verge of asking her about my father, but the question remained lodged in my throat. This new knowledge now sharpened my mind. Whenever the courtesans or servants looked at me, I detected sneers. When visitors gave me more than a passing glance, I suspected they were wondering why I looked half-Chinese. The older I became, the more this side of me would show, and I feared that over time, I would no longer be treated like an American, but as no better than other Chinese girls. And thus I sought to rid myself of whatever might suggest I was a half-breed.

I no longer spoke Chinese to the Cloud Beauties or to the servants. I used only pidgin. If they talked to me in Chinese, I pretended I did not understand them. I told them again and again that I was an American. I wanted them to recognize we were not the same. I wanted them to hate me, because this would be proof that I did not belong to their world. And a few of them did come to hate me. Cracked Egg, however, laughed at me and said he had had both Chinese and foreigners treat him worse. He continued to speak to me in Shanghainese and I had to acknowledge that I understood, because he was the one who told me when Mother had returned, or that she wanted to speak to me, or that she had asked that the carriage be brought around to take us to a new restaurant for lunch.

No matter what I did, I feared the stranger-father within my blood. Would his character also emerge and make me even more Chinese? And if that came to pass, where would I belong? What would I be allowed to do? Would anyone love a half-hated girl?

CHAPTER 2

THE NEW REPUBLIC

Shanghai
1912
Violet

At half past noon on my fourteenth birthday, cheers broke out at the front of the house, and firecrackers exploded in the courtyard. Carlotta flattened her ears and flew under my bed.

It was not our custom to lavishly celebrate birthdays, but perhaps I had reached a special age. I ran to find Mother. She was standing in Boulevard, looking out the window at Nanking Road. Every few seconds, I heard rounds of firecrackers popping off in the distance. Then came the whistles of rockets, ripping the air, followed by booms in my chest. Hurrahs rose in crescendo and pitch, then fell, over and over again. So the hullabaloo was not for my birthday after all. I went to Mother's side, and instead of greeting me, she said, "Look at those fools!"

Cracked Egg dashed in without knocking. "It's happened," he announced in a hoarse voice. "The news is all over the streets. The Ching dynasty is over. Yuan Shi-kai will soon step up as president of the new Republic of China." He had a wild look on his face.

It was February 12, 1912, and the Empress Dowager Longyu

had just signed the abdication on behalf of her six-year-old nephew, Emperor Puyi, on the condition that they could remain in the palace and retain their possessions. Manchu rule was over. We had been expecting this day since October, when the New Army staged a mutiny in Wuchang.

"Why would you trust Yuan Shi-kai any more than the emperor's cronies?" Mother said to Cracked Egg. "Why didn't they keep Dr. Sun as president instead?"

"Yuan Shi-kai got the Ching government to step down, so he won the right to step up to the presidency."

"He was commander in chief of the Ching military," she said, "and his imperial roots might still be in him. I've heard some of our customers say that given time, he'll act just like an emperor."

"If Yuan Shi-kai turns out to be corrupt, we won't have to wait two thousand years for the Republicans to let go of our balls."

MONTHS BEFORE THE abdication, the house had been abuzz over the coming overthrow of the Ching dynasty. The guests at Mother's parties did not meet in the middle for several days. The Western men remained on their side of the social club, and the Chinese men remained in the courtesan house. They had talked separately and incessantly about the coming change and whether it would be to their advantage or result in the opposite. Their influential friends might no longer be influential. New associations would be necessary. Plans should be made now, in case new taxes were levied, or if the treaties affecting foreign trade were better for them or no longer in their favor. Mother had had to lure them back to the middle with promises that lucrative opportunities sprout out of the chaos of change.

The servants had also caught the fever of change. They recited a litany of tragedies under imperial rule: Their family land had been seized, and no land had been left to bury their dead. The ancestors' obedience had been punished and the corruption of the Ching had been rewarded. Foreigners had become wealthy on the opium trade. Opium had turned their men into the living dead. "They'd sell their mothers for a gummy wad!" I heard Cracked Egg say.

Some of the maids were afraid of revolution. They wanted peace and no other changes, no new worries. They did not believe their lives would improve under a new military government. From all they had experienced, when there was change, there was suffering. When they married, their lives became worse. When their husbands died, their lives became worse yet again. Change was what happened inside the house, and only they had been there to suffer it.

Last month, on the first of January, we had learned that the Republic had been officially declared and Dr. Sun Yat-sen had been made the provisional president. Mother's smarmy lover Fairweather had come by, unannounced, as usual. Of all the men she had taken to her bed, he was the one who remained in her life, as persistent as a wart. I hated him even more than I had when Mother used me as her pawn to meet him. Fairweather had sat in an armchair in the salon, a glass of whiskey in one hand, a cigar in the other. Between sips and puffs, he had made pronouncements: "The servants in your house have the fervor of heathens newly converted by the missionaries. Saved! Dr. Sun may be a Christian, but do your servants really believe he can perform God's miracle and change the color of their yellow hides?" He had spotted me and grinned. "What do you say, Violet?"

Mother must have told him that my father was Chinese. I couldn't stomach the sight of that worm and had left the room, nearly blind with anger. I had marched down Nanking Road. The sides of British tramcars had been plastered with newspapers that flapped like scales. Civil disobedience had come into fashion over the last year, a daredevil kind of patriotism that delivered symbolic slaps to the imperialists. My Chinese blood had surged, and I'd wanted to punch Fairweather's face. The street had been flowing with students who ran from corner to corner to put up fresh sheets of news on the public walls. The crowds had rushed forward, and the literate ones had read aloud the article about the new president Sun Yat-sen. His words of vision and promise had sent the crowd swooning with optimism. "He's the father of the new Republic," I had heard one man say. I had scanned the wall for a picture of this revolutionary father. Golden Dove had once told me that you could recognize a person's character by examining his face. I had stared at Dr. Sun's photograph and seen he was honest and kind, calm and intelligent. I had heard that he also spoke perfect English from having grown up in Hawaii. If Dr. Sun had been my father, I would have been proud to tell everyone I was half-Chinese. That last thought had caught me by surprise, and I'd quickly tamped it down.

I was never able to talk to Mother about my feelings over having a Chinese father. We could not admit to each other what I knew. And these days, she held back her true feelings on just about everything. China was going through a revolution, and she acted like a spectator at the races—at the ready to bet on the probable winner. She claimed confidence that the new Republic would have no bearing on matters in the International Settlement, where we lived. "The Settlement is its own oasis," she would point out to her clients, "under its own laws and government."

But I could tell that her seeming lack of concern was to mask worry. She, in fact, had given me the skill to discern true feelings by noticing the great efforts used to conceal them. I had often overheard what she and Golden Dove had observed among their customers: bluster that had compensated for fear, a flourish of courtesy that had masked a cheat, indignation that had confirmed wrongdoing.

I, too, had been making great efforts to hide the half-Chinese part of me, and I was always on guard that I had failed to do so. Look how easily I had succumbed to my inborn mind. I had just wished that Dr. Sun had been my father. I had found the students' passion to be admirable. It was increasingly difficult to contort my heart and mind to appear to be a foreigner through and through. I often studied myself in a mirror to learn how to smile without crinkling my eyes into an Oriental angle. I copied my mother's erect posture, the way she walked with a foreigner's assurance of her place in the world. Like her, I greeted new people by looking them straight in the eye, saying, "I am Violet Minturn and I'm most pleased to know you." I used pidgin to compliment the servants on their obedience and quickness. I was more courteous with the beauties than I had been when I was younger, but I did not speak to them in Chinese, unless I forgot, which I did more often than I would have liked. I was not uppity, however, with Golden Dove or Cracked Egg. Nor was I cool-hearted with Snowy Cloud's attendant, Piety, who had a daughter, Little Ocean, whom Carlotta liked.

Ever since my scuffle with Misty Cloud six years ago, no one in the house had mentioned anything that suggested I was of mixed race. Then again, they would not dare to do so after what had happened to Misty Cloud. Yet I was constantly aware of the danger of someone wounding me with the awful truth. Whenever I met strangers, I was shaken by any remarks about my looks.

It had happened not long ago when I met Mother's new friend, a British suffragette, who was fascinated to be in a "Pleasure Palace," as she called Hidden Jade Path. When I was introduced to her, she complimented me on the unusual color of my eyes. "I've never seen that shade of green," she said. "It reminds me of serpentine. The color changes according to the light." Had she also noticed the shape of my eyes? I avoided smiling. My nervousness grew worse a moment later when she told my mother she had volunteered to raise money for an orphanage for mixed-race girls.

"They will never be adopted," she said. "If it weren't for the orphanage and generous women like you, it would have been the streets for them."

Mother opened her purse and handed the woman a donation.

ON THE DAY of the abdication, I welcomed being part of the hated lot of foreigners. Let the Chinese despise me! I ran to the balcony on the east wing of our house. I saw the sparks of firecrackers and shreds of wrappers floating in the air. The paper was imperial yellow and not the usual celebratory red, as if to signal that the Ching dynasty had been blown to pieces.

Throngs were growing by the second, a sea of people with victory banners, their fists punching upward, showing black armbands painted with antiforeign slogans. "End the port treaties!" A chorus of cheers broke out and echoed the words. "No more tra-la-la boom-dee-ay!" The crowd roared with laughter. "Kick out those who love the foreign!" Jeers followed.

Who still loved us? Golden Dove? Did she love us enough to risk being kicked out of China?

The streets were so clogged the rickshaw pullers could no longer move forward. From my perch, I spotted one with a Western man and woman who waved madly to their puller to run over the people blocking their way. The rickshaw puller let go of the handles, and the cab suddenly fell backward and nearly bounced the couple out. He threw his fists up, and the people leapt off. I could not see their faces, but I knew they must have been terrified as they were bumped and pushed about in the mob.

I turned to my mother. "Are we in danger?"

"Of course not," she snapped. She had a knot between her eyebrows. She was lying.

"The greedy ones didn't wait a minute to change colors," Cracked Egg said. "You can hear them everywhere in the market square. *Two bottles of New Republic wine for the price of one!* And then they joke: *Two bottles of Ching wine for the price of three.*" He looked at me. "It's not safe right now for you to go outside. Listen to me, ah?" He handed my mother a packet of letters and the *North China Herald*. "I was able to get them from the post office before the streets closed. But if the riots go on, it may be days before we receive anything else."

"Do what you can to get the newspapers, English and Chinese ones. They'll probably be littering the streets later in the day. I want to see what cartoons and stories appear in the mosquito press. That will give us some idea what we're facing before things settle."

I searched through the house to see if anyone else was worried. Three of the menservants and the cook were smoking in the front courtyard. Confetti from yellow paper littered the ground. They were the ones who had set off the firecrackers, and they were now gloating over the powerlessness of the little Manchu emperor and his haughty eunuchs. No longer would the empress and her Pekingese dogs be more important than starving people!

"My uncle became a Boxer after half our family starved to death," said one servant. "It was the worst flood in a hundred years— maybe even two hundred. It came over us quick as swamp fog. Then came the dry year. Not a drop of rain. One disaster after another." They took turns with a match to light their pipes.

The cook chimed in: "If a man has lost everything, he fights back without fear."

"We've kicked out the Ching," another man said, "and the foreigners are next."

The cook and servants gave me smug looks. This was shocking. The cook had always been friendly, had always asked if I wanted him to make me American lunch or dinner. And the servants had always been polite, or, at least, patient with me when I was making a nuisance of myself. They once scolded me gently when I was a child and had knocked over the platters of food they carried. All children are naughty like that, they had said to my mother. They never openly complained. But I heard them do so in the hallway near my window late at night.

Today they acted as if I were a stranger. The expressions on their faces were ugly, and there was also something odd about their appearance. One of them turned to reach for a flask of wine. They had cut off their queues! Only one man had not, Little Duck, the manservant who opened the door to the house and announced visitors who came in the afternoons. His queue was still wrapped around the back of his head. I once asked him to show me how long it was. As he unwound it, he had said that it was his mother's greatest pride. She said the length of it was a measure of respect to the emperor. "It was just below my waist when she told me that," he said. "She died before it grew this long." It was now nearly to his knees.

The cook snorted at Little Duck. "Are you an imperial loyalist?" The others laughed, baiting him to cut it off. One handed him the knife that they had used to cut off their own queues.

Little Duck stared at the knife and then at the grinning men. His eyes bugged out, as if scared. And then he walked swiftly toward the part of the wall next to an abandoned well. He loosened the coil and stared at his beloved pigtail, then hacked it off. The other men shouted. "Damn!" "Good for him!" "*Wah!* He looks like he just cut off his balls and became a eunuch!"

Little Duck wore such a painful grimace you would have thought he had killed his mother. He lifted the lid from the well and dangled his former glory over it. He was shaking so hard the pigtail wiggled like a live snake. Finally he let go and then immediately looked down the well and watched it drown. For a moment, I thought he would jump into the well after it.

Cracked Egg ran into the courtyard. "What's going on? What's happening with the food? Why is the water not boiled? Lulu Mimi needs her tea."

The men sat there, smoking.

"Eh! When you cut off your queues, did you slice out part of your brains as well? Who do you work for? Where will you go if this house shuts its doors? You'll be no better off than that beggar by the wall with one leg." They grumbled and stood up.

What was happening? What would happen next? I walked throughout the house and saw the abandoned kitchen with water sitting cold in vats, the vegetables half chopped, the washing tubs with clothes half in, half out, as if people had fallen forward and drowned.

I found Golden Dove and the Cloud Beauties seated in the common room. Summer Cloud was shedding rivers of tears for the end of the Ching dynasty, as if her own family had died.

"I heard that the laws of the new Republic will soon shut us down," she said.

"The politicians want to show they have higher morals than the Ching and foreigners."

"New morality. *Pah!*" Golden Dove said. "They're the same ones who visited us and were happy the Westerners let us be."

"What will we do instead?" Summer Cloud said in a tragic voice. She held up her soft white hands and stared at them sadly. "I'll have to wash my own clothes, like a common washerwoman."

"Stop this nonsense," Golden Dove said. "The Republicans have no control over the International Settlement. The Ching did not, and that won't change."

"How do you know?" Summer Cloud shot back. "Were you alive when the Ming dynasty was overturned?"

I heard my mother calling for me. "Violet! Where are you?" She came up to me. "There you are. Come to my office. I want you to stay close to me."

"Are we in trouble?"

"Not at all. I just don't want you to go wandering into the streets. There are too many people running around and you could be hurt." Her office floor was strewn with newspapers.

"Now that the emperor is gone," I said, "will we suffer? Will our house close down?"

"Come here." She took me into her arms. "It's the end of the dynasty. That has little to do with us. But the Chinese are overwrought. They'll settle down soon."

By the third day, the streets were passable, and Mother wanted to pay a visit to some of her clients to encourage them to return.

Cracked Egg said it was dangerous for a foreign woman to be seen out of doors. Drunken patriots roamed the streets with scissors in hand and lopped the queues off any man who still possessed one. They had also bobbed the hair of a few white women just for fun. My mother had never been one to give in to fear. She put on a heavy fur coat, called for a carriage, and equipped Golden Dove and herself with croquet mallets so they could bash the heads of anyone who approached them with shears and a grin.

All of her clients stayed away during the first week after the abdication. She sent the servants out with messages that she had taken down the sign in English that said HIDDEN JADE PATH. But they were still reluctant. The name Hidden Jade Path was too well known, as was the House of Lulu Mimi. The Western clients did not want to show their faces. The Chinese ones did not want anyone to know they had been doing foreign trade with Westerners.

On Sunday the eighteenth, Chinese New Year arrived, reigniting the prior week's furor, and doubling the noise with a cacophony of firecrackers, gongs, drums, and chants. When the rockets shrilled in flight, my mother would stop speaking, clench her jaw, and twitch when the inevitable bang and ka-boom came. She snapped at anyone who spoke to her, even Golden Dove. She was angry over the stupid fear her clients harbored. The clients were slowly returning, five one night, then a dozen, and they were mostly the Chinese suitors whose favorite courtesans had written pining letters to them. No one, however, was in a mood for frivolity. In the salons, the men stood in separate clusters of Westerners and Chinese. They spoke somberly about the antiforeign protests being a bellwether for the future of foreign businesses. One groused, "I heard that many of the student ringleaders were educated in the United States. The Ching government gave them those damn indemnity scholarships, and they returned with knowledge on how to make a revolution."

My mother sailed through the room exuding confidence,

though she had none just an hour before, when she was reading the newspapers. She smiled and dispensed assurances.

"I know for a fact, and from a reliable, highly placed source, that the new Republic is using the antiforeign fuss as a temporary ploy to unify the country. Consider this—the officials who worked under the Ching will still hold their positions under the Republic. That's already been announced. So we'll still have our friends. And besides, why would the new Republic oust foreign businesses? Why would they cut off their own hands and be unable to take from the money pot they're so fond of? This will all blow over soon. It's happened before. Look at the history of past brouhahas of this sort. Western foreign trade came back in even greater numbers and with more profits than ever before. All will settle into place soon enough. But it will require an adjustment at first, fearlessness coupled with foresight."

A few of the men murmured in agreement. But most looked skeptical.

"Calculate how much money foreign businesses bring into China," she continued. "How could the new government be hostile toward us? I predict that after holding back our ships of fortune, they'll welcome us back and make the treaties and tariffs even more favorable. If they're going to stamp out the warlords, they need money to do that. Ours."

More grumbling followed. My mother persisted with her cheerful attitude. "Those who stay will be able to pick up the gold in the streets that the doubting Thomases left behind. And it will be everywhere, yours for the taking. This is a time of opportunity, not of fears or useless scruples. Gentlemen, plan for a richer future. The new path is laid. Long live the new Republic!"

Business, however, remained slow. The gold in the streets lay where no one dared to pick it up.

The next day, my mother ceased all efforts to reinvigorate her business. A letter had arrived just before we were supposed to have a belated birthday lunch at a restaurant. When I reached her door, I heard her talking in an angry way. I looked around and saw no one. She was talking to herself. When I was younger, I had been frightened to hear her babble. But nothing terrible ever came of her moods. Her spells were like someone beating a rug. She purged herself, and then everything quieted inside her again.

"Damn your cursed heart!" she said. "Coward!"

I thought her anger had to do with what had happened to the emperor.

"Mother," I said softly.

She startled and turned to me, clutching a letter to her chest. It was in cursive writing, not Chinese characters.

"Violet, darling, we cannot have lunch right now. Something has come up." She did not mention the letter, but I knew that was the reason. She had done the same thing to me on my eighth birthday. This time, however, I was not angry, only anxious. It was again a letter from my father, I was sure of it. The last one, six years ago, told of his recent death, which was the reason I then knew he had been alive all those years when she had said he did not exist. Whenever I had brought up the subject of my father, she cut me off with the same answer: "I've told you before—he's dead and your asking again won't change that fact." The question had always set her off, but I could not help but ask it, because the answer had changed before.

"Will we have lunch later?" I knew the answer but wanted to see how carefully she answered.

"I have to leave to meet someone," she said.

I would not let her get away that easily. "We were going to have my birthday lunch today," I complained. "You're always too busy to keep your promises to me."

She showed only a small amount of guilt. "I'm so sorry," she said. "I have to do something, and it is urgent and very important. Tomorrow I will take you to an extra special lunch. We'll have champagne."

"I'm important, too," I said. I went to my room and went over what had just happened. A letter. Another birthday lunch put aside. Who was more important?

When I heard her leave, I stole into Boulevard and entered her room through the glass French doors. The letter was not in the drawer, not under her mattress, not in her pillowcase, not in the canisters that held hard candies. Just when I was about to give up, I saw the top of it sticking out of a volume of poetry on the round table in the middle of her room, where she and Golden Dove sat as they went over the business of the day. The envelope was made of stiff white paper and was addressed in Chinese to Madame Lulu Mimi. Below, in English, it said in neat, flowing script: "Lucretia Minturn." *Lucretia.* I had never seen that name used as hers. Was it really her name? The letter was addressed with yet another name I had not heard used for her:

> *My Dear Lucia,*
>
> *I am released from obligation and am at last able to provide what is rightfully yours.*
>
> *I return to Shanghai soon. May I visit you on the 23rd at noon?*
>
> *Yours,*
>
> *Lu Shing*

Who was this Chinese man who wrote in English? He had called her by two different names: Lucretia and Lucia. What was he returning?

Before I could study the letter further, Golden Dove walked in.

"What's going on?" she said.

"I'm looking for a book," I said quickly.

"Give it to me," she said. She took one glance at it and said, "Don't tell your mother you saw this. Don't tell anyone, or you will regret this the rest of your life."

My suspicions were right. This had something to do with my father. On the twenty-third, I feared, my life would change for the worse.

ON THE TWENTY-THIRD, the house was abuzz with news that a certain visitor was expected at noon. I was hiding in the middle balcony, watching the hubbub below. I was supposed to study in my own room, and not in Boulevard, and was under strict orders from my mother not to come out until she said I could. She also told me to put on my green dress, which was one of my best day dresses. I guessed that meant I would meet this man.

Noon came and went, and the minutes ate slowly into the day. I listened for announcements. None came. I crept into Boulevard. If anyone found me here, I would say I was searching for a schoolbook. I placed one under the desk, just in case. As I had hoped, my mother was in her office, just on the other side of the French doors. Golden Dove was with her. Mother was bristling, sounding as ominous as the rumbles that precede lightning. I could hear the threat in her voice. Golden Dove spoke back to her in a soft consoling tone. The exact words were clumps of sound. I had taken a risk in coming into the room. It took an hour before I had the courage to press my ear to the glass.

They were speaking in English. More often than not, their voices were too low for me to make out their words. Soon the pitch of my mother's anger rose sharply. "Bastard!" she cried. "Family duty!"

"He's a coward and a thief, and I don't think you should believe anything he has to say," Golden Dove said. "If you meet him, he'll tear your heart in two again."

"Do we have a pistol in the house? I'll shoot him in the balls. Don't laugh. I mean it."

These snatches of words added to my confusion.

Dusk came, and I heard the voices of servants calling out for hot water. A manservant knocked on my mother's door and announced that a visitor had arrived and was waiting in the vestibule. Mother did not leave her room for ten minutes. As soon as she did, I pushed the French doors open an inch, and moved the bottom of the curtain slightly apart. Then I hurried to my hiding place in the middle balcony overlooking the Grand Salon.

Mother walked down a few more steps, then stopped and nodded to Little Duck, who stood by the velvet curtains.

Little Duck drew back the curtain and called out, "Master Lu Shing has arrived to see Madame Lulu Mimi." It was the same name as the man who had written the letter. I held my breath as he stepped through. In a short while, I would know if this man was who I thought he was.

He gave the immediate appearance of a thoroughly modern gentleman, possessing the carriage of the highborn, erect yet at ease. He wore a well-tailored dark suit and shoes so well polished I could see the gleam from the balcony. His hair was full and neatly cut, smoothed down with pomade. I could not see his face in detail, but I judged him to be older than Mother, not young but not too old. Over one arm, he held a long winter coat and, on top of that, a hat, both of which one of the servants quickly took away.

Mr. Lu glanced casually about the room, but not with the wonderment of most first-time visitors in coming to my mother's house. Western style had become the norm in most first-class houses and even in the respectable homes of the wealthy. But our house had had decorations found nowhere else: shocking paintings, voluptuous sofas with tiger skin upholstery, a lifelike sculpture of a phoenix standing by a giant palm tree the height of the ceiling. The man made a slight smile, as if none of this was a surprise.

Puffy Cloud came over and crouched near me. "Who's that?" she whispered. I told her to go somewhere else. She didn't move. I was about to learn who this man was, and I did not want Puffy Cloud beside me when I did.

My mother resumed walking down the stairs. She had chosen an odd dress for the occasion. I had never seen it before. She must have bought it yesterday. The dress was no doubt the latest fashion— Mother wore nothing less—but the shape was not suited to my mother's habit of flying around the house. It was tightly fitted peacock-blue wool, which accentuated her full bust and hips. The skirt was cinched at the waist, as well as at the knees, preventing her from walking in more than slow, regal steps. The man was patient and looked at her the entire time. When she reached him, she gave no effusive welcome, as she did with other men. I could not hear her exact words, but her tone was flat yet quivering. He made a slight bow that was neither Chinese nor Western, and when he raised himself slowly, he looked at her solemnly, and she abruptly turned away and began walking back toward the staircase at her hobbled pace. He followed. Even from this distance, I could tell her expression was precisely what she despised seeing in the face of any of the beauties. Chin tipped slightly up. Arrogant. Eyes half lidded and looking down over her nose. Disdain. The man acted as if he had no awareness that she was less than amiable. Or perhaps he expected it, was prepared for it.

"*Wah!*" Puffy Cloud said. "Cultivated. And lots of money, too." I flashed an angry look to make her be quiet, and she, being seven years older, showed her usual resentment of my reprimands and returned a sour pout.

I was not able to see his features well, but I felt there was something familiar in his face and was nearly faint with nervousness. Was this man my father?

When they were about to ascend the staircase, I crept away. I hurried to Boulevard and hid under the bed. I would have to remain there another fifteen minutes when dusk turned to dark, and I would not be noticed behind the break in the curtains. The floor tiles were cold, and I regretted that I had not pulled a quilt around me first. I heard the office door open, followed by my mother's and Golden Dove's voices. Golden Dove asked my mother what refreshments she should bring. Usually, depending on the guest, there would be either a selection of fruit or English butter cookies, and tea. Mother said none was needed. I was shocked by her rudeness.

"I apologize for the lateness," the man said. He sounded like an Englishman. "The mobs are tearing down the walls of the Old City and the roads are impassable. I left my carriage and went by foot, knowing you were waiting. It took me nearly three hours just to reach Avenue Paul Brunat."

Mother did not reply with any appreciation that he had made this great effort to come. They moved toward the other end of the room. Even with the French doors ajar, their words were now too faint to understand. His low voice flowed smoothly. Mother's was terse and choppy. Every now and then, she would eject a loud comment: "I doubt that very much." "I did not receive them." "He did not return." All at once, she shouted: "Why do you want to see her now? How long has it been since you cared? You sent not a single word or dollar. You wouldn't have cared if she and I had starved."

I knew she was talking about me. He had never asked about me, had never loved me. Bastard. I immediately hated him.

He murmured fast words I could not understand. They sounded frantic. Then I heard his voice loudly and more clearly. "I was devastated, tormented. But they made it impossible."

"Coward! Despicable coward!" Mother shouted.

"He was with the Office of Foreign Relations—"

"Ah, yes, family duty. Tradition. Obligation. Ancestors and burnt offerings. Admirable." Her voice had come closer to the door.

"After all these years in China," he said, "do you still not understand how powerful a Chinese family is? It's the weight of ten thousand tombstones, and my father wielded it against me."

"I understand it well. I've met many men, and their nature is like yours, predictably so. Desire and duty. Betrayal to both. Those predictable men have made me a very successful woman."

"Lucia," he said in a sad voice.

"Don't call me that!"

"You must listen, please."

I heard the office door open and Golden Dove's voice broke in. "Excuse me," she said in Chinese. "There is an urgent situation."

Lu Shing started to introduce himself in Chinese, and Golden Dove cut him off. "We've met before," she snapped. "I know quite well who you are and what you did." She returned to speaking to my mother in a more even voice. "I need to speak to you. It concerns Violet."

"She's here, then," the man said in an excited voice. "Please let me see her."

"I will let you see her when you're dead," Mother replied.

I was still furious but buoyed that he wanted to see me. If he came to me, I would reject him. It was now dark enough in the room for me to go to the French doors. I wanted to see his expression. I was halfway out from under the bed when I heard Mother and Golden Dove close the office door and walk into the hallway. Suddenly the door to Boulevard opened, and I tucked myself back under the bed close to the wall and held my breath.

"This is too hard for you to bear alone," Golden Dove said quietly in English. "I should be there."

"I prefer to do this on my own."

"If you need me, ring the bell for tea. I'll wait here in Boulevard."

My heart turned over with dread. I would soon turn into a frozen corpse.

"No need," Mother said. "Go have dinner with the others."

"At least let me have the maid bring you tea."

"Yes, that would be good. My throat has gone dry."

They left. I took a big breath.

I heard the maid arrive, followed by the sound of clinking teacups and polite words. I eased my way out from under the bed and was shivering with cold and nervousness. I rubbed my arms and pulled a quilt from the bed and wrapped it around me. When my teeth stopped chattering I went to the glass doors, and peered through the curtain opening.

I knew instantly that this man was my father by my own features: the eyes, the mouth, the shape of my face. I felt a nauseating wave of resignation. I was half-Chinese. I had known it all along, yet I had also clung to the better side of ambiguity. Outside of this house, I would never belong. Another feeling crept over me: a strange victory that I had been right in believing Mother had been lying to me. My father existed. I had exchanged the tormenting question with the awful answer. But why did Mother hate him so much that she had refused to see him all these years? Why had she preferred to tell me he had died? After all, I had asked her once if he loved me, and she had said yes. Now she claimed he had not.

Mr. Lu put his hand on Mother's arm, and she flung it away and shouted, "Where is he? Just tell me and get out!"

Who was *he*?

The man attempted to touch her arm again, and she slapped his face, then beat her fists on his shoulders as she wept. He did not move away but stood oddly still, like a wooden soldier, letting her do this.

She seemed more desperate than angry, and it frightened me, because I had never seen her this way. Whose whereabouts were so important to her?

She finally stopped and said in a cracked voice: "Where is he? What did they do with my baby boy? Is he dead?"

I clamped my hand over my mouth so they could not hear my cries. She had a son and she loved him so much she had cried for him.

"He's alive and healthy." He paused. "And he knows none of this."

"Nothing of me," Mother said flatly. She went to the other end of the room and wept with heaving shoulders. He came toward her, and she motioned him to stay where he was. I had never seen Mother cry so much. She sounded as if she had just suffered a great loss, when, in fact, she had just learned she had not.

"They took him away from me," he said. "My father ordered it. They would not tell me where. They hid him and said they would never allow me to see him if I did anything to harm my father's reputation. How could I go to you? You would have fought. You did before, and they knew you would continue to do so. In their eyes, you respected nothing about our traditions. You would not understand their position, their reputation. I could not say anything to you, because that act alone would have been the end of my ever seeing our son. You are right. I was a coward. I did not fight, as you would have. And what is worse, I betrayed you and justified why I had to do so. I told myself that if I submitted to their will, you would have a chance of soon having him back. Yet I knew that was not true. Instead I was killing what was pure and trusting in your heart. I was tormented by it. Every day, I have woken with that thought of what I did to you. I can show you my journals. Every day, for these last twelve years, I wrote one sentence before all others. *'To save myself, I destroyed another, and in doing so, I destroyed myself.'*"

"One sentence," Mother said in a flat voice. "I wrote many more." She returned to the sofa and sat vacant-eyed, spent. "Why did you finally tell me? Why now and not sooner?"

"My father's dead."

She flinched. "I can't say I'm sorry."

"He collapsed the day of the abdication and lingered another six days. I wrote to you the day after he died. I felt a burden removed. But I warn you, my mother has a strong will equal to my father's. He used his to possess what he wanted. Hers is to protect the family. Our son is not just her grandson, but also the next generation and all it carries forward from the earliest of our family history. You may not respect our family traditions. But you should understand them enough to fear them."

Lu Shing handed Mother an envelope. "I've written down what I'm sure you want to know."

She put her letter opener along the seam, but her hands were shaking so badly she dropped the letter. Lu Shing retrieved it and opened it for her. She pulled out a photograph, and I strained to find an angle that would enable me to see it. "Where am I in his face?" Mother said. "Is it truly Teddy? Are you pulling another trick on me? I'll shoot you with my pistol . . ."

He murmured and pointed to the photograph. Her anguished face turned to smiles. "Such a serious expression . . . Is that really what

I look like? He resembles you more. He looks like a Chinese boy."

"He's twelve now," Lu Shing said. "A happy boy and also more than a bit spoiled. His grandmother treats him like an emperor."

Their voices fell to gentle murmurs. He put his hand on her arm, and this time, she did not push him away. She looked at him with a wounded expression. He stroked her face and she collapsed against him and he embraced her as she wept.

I turned away, slumped to the floor, and stared into the pitch-dark of nothingness, of all possibilities for fear. Everything had changed so quickly. This was their son and she loved him more than she ever had loved me. I went over all that she said. New questions jumped out, each more troubling than the last, sickening me. Her son was of mixed blood as well, yet he looked Chinese. And this man, my father, whose eyes and cheeks I wore, did not bother to take me to his family. He had never loved me.

I heard rustling in Mother's office and turned back to peer through the curtain opening. Mother had already put out the lamps. I could not see anything. The office door closed, and a moment later, I heard her bedroom door open and close. Did Lu Shing and the photo of Teddy go into the room with her? I felt abandoned, alone with my agonizing questions. I wanted to be in my room to mourn for myself. I had lost my place in the world. I was second best in Mother's eyes, a castoff to Lu Shing. But I could not leave the room, now that the servants were rushing through the hallway. If Golden Dove saw me sneak out of the room, she would demand to know why I was there, and I did not want to speak to anyone else about what I was feeling. I lay on the bed and wrapped myself in the quilt. I had to wait until the party began, when everyone would go downstairs to the Grand Salon. And so then and there, I began my bout of self-pity.

Hours later, I was awakened by the sound of a distant door opening. I rushed to the window and looked through the lattice. The sky was a wash of dark gray. The sun would be up soon. I heard the office door open and close and I went to the glass doors. His back was to me and her face was visible just over his shoulder. He was murmuring in a tender tone. She responded in a high girlish voice. I felt heartsick. She held so much feeling for others, such gentleness and happiness. Lu leaned forward and she bowed her head to receive his kiss on her forehead. He tipped her face back up, and said more of those soft words that made her smile. She looked almost shy. I had never known her in so many new ways, so wounded, so desperate, and now bashful.

He embraced her, held her tightly, and when he released her, her eyes were shiny with tears, and she turned away. He quietly left the room. I darted back to the lattice window just in time to see him walking past with a pleased expression, which angered me. Everything had turned out well for him.

I stepped out of the room to return to mine, and immediately Carlotta strode toward me and rubbed my legs. Over the last seven years, she had grown fat and slow. I picked her up and hugged her. She alone had claimed me.

I WAS UNABLE to sleep, or so I thought, until I heard Mother's voice talking to a manservant, instructing him to bring up a trunk. It was not quite ten in the morning. I found her in her bedroom laying out dresses.

"Oh, Violet, I'm glad you're up." She said this in a light and excited voice. "I need you to select four frocks, two for dinner, two for daytime, shoes and coats to match. Bring also the garnet necklace and gold locket, your fountain pens, schoolbooks, and notebooks. And take anything else that is valuable. I can't list everything for you, so you'll have to think for yourself. I've already called for a trunk to be sent to your room."

"Are we running away?"

She cocked her head, which she did when a guest presented her with a novel idea that she actually considered unsound. She smiled.

"We're going to America, to San Francisco," she said. "We're going to visit your grandparents. Your grandfather is ill . . . I had a cable . . . and it is quite serious."

What a stupid lie! If he were truly ill, why was she so happy just a moment ago? She was not going to tell me the true reason, that we were going to see her darling son, and I was determined to force the truth out of her.

"What is my grandfather's name?"

"John Minturn," she said easily. She continued to place dresses on the bed.

"Is my grandmother alive as well?"

"Yes . . . of course. She sent the cable. Harriet Minturn."

"Do we leave soon?"

"Perhaps tomorrow, the next day. Or it could be a week from now. Everything has become topsy-turvy and no one is reliable these days, even when paid top dollar. So we may not be able to arrange immediately for passage on the next steamer. Many Westerners are trying to leave as well. We may wind up settling for a trawler that goes around the North Pole!"

"Who was that man who visited you yesterday?"

"Someone I once had dealings with in business."

I said in a thin voice: "I know he's my father. I saw his face when you were coming up the stairs. I look like him. And I know that we are going to San Francisco because you have a son who's living there. I heard the servants talking about it."

She listened silently, stricken.

"You can't deny it," I said.

"Violet, darling, I'm sorry you are wounded. I kept it a secret only because I didn't want you to know we had been abandoned. He took Teddy right after he was born, and I have not seen him since. I have a chance to claim him back and I must because he is my child.

If you had been stolen from me, I would have fought just as hard to find you."

Fought for me? I doubted that.

But then she came to me and wrapped her arms around me. "You have been more precious to me than you know." A tear formed at the corner of her eye, and that small glistening of her heart was enough for me to believe her. I was soothed.

In my bedroom, however, I realized she had said nothing about Lu Shing's feelings toward me. I hated him. I would never call him "Father."

For the rest of the morning and into the afternoon, as we filled our trunks, she told me about my new home in San Francisco. Before that day, I had not thought much at all about her past. She had lived in San Francisco. That was all. To hear about it now—I felt I was listening to a fairy tale, and gradually my anger turned into excitement. I pictured the Pacific Ocean: its clear blue waters with silvery fish darting through the waves, whales blowing their spouts like fountains. She told me my grandfather was a professor of art history, and I imagined a distinguished gentleman with white hair, standing before an easel. She said her mother was a scientist, who studied insects, like the ones in the amber pieces I tried to smash. I imagined a room with amber drops dangling from the ceiling and a woman with a magnifying glass looking at them. As she talked, now quite easily, I could see San Francisco in my mind: its small hills next to water. I could picture myself climbing and looking out over the Bay and its islands. I was climbing up steep sidewalks flanked by Western houses, like those in the French Concession, busy with all sorts of people of all classes and nations.

"Mother, are there Chinese people in San Francisco?"

"Quite a number of them. Most are servants and common laborers, though, laundrymen, and the like." She went to her wardrobe and considered which of her evening gowns to take. She selected two, then put those back, and selected two others. She chose shoes of white kid leather, then noticed a small scuff on the heel and put them back.

"Are there foreign courtesans or just Chinese ones?"

She laughed. "People there are not called foreigners unless they are the Chinese or the black Italians."

I felt humiliated. Here we were foreigners by our appearance. A cold thought ran through my veins. Would I look like a Chinese foreigner in San Francisco? If people knew Teddy was my brother, they would know I was as Chinese as he was.

"Mother, will people treat me well when they see I am half-Chinese?"

"No one will be thinking you're half-Chinese."

"But if the people there find out, will they shun me?"

"No one will find out."

It bothered me that she could be so confident over what was not certain. I would have to act as confident as she was to maintain the secret that she had a half-Chinese daughter. Only I would feel the constant worry that I would be discovered. She would remain unconcerned.

"We'll live in a handsome house," she went on. She was the happiest I had ever seen her, the most affectionate. She looked younger, almost like a different person. Golden Dove had said that when a werefox possessed a woman, you could tell by her eyes. They sparkled too much. Mother's eyes sparkled. She was not herself, not since seeing Mr. Lu.

"My grandfather built the house just before I was born," she said. "It's not as large as our house here," she continued, "but it's also not as cold or noisy. It's made of wood and so sturdy that even after a very big earthquake shook the city to its knees, the house remained standing without a single brick out of place. The architectural style is quite different from the foreign houses in the French and British Concessions. For one thing, it's more welcoming, without those tall fortress walls and gatekeepers. In San Francisco, we don't need to defend our privacy. We simply have it. A hedge in front and a low iron gate is all we need, although we do have fences on the sides of the house and in back. But that is so we can keep out stray dogs and put up trellises for flowering vines. We have a small lawn, just enough to serve as a grassy carpet on the sides of the walkway. Along one fence, there are rhododendron bushes. And on the other side there are phalanxes of agapanthus, scented roses, daylilies, and, of course, violets. I planted them myself, and not just the ordinary kind, but also the sweet violets, which have a lovely fragrance, the scent of a perfume I once wore that came from France. I had many clothes of that color, and I used to eat candies made of sweet violets and sprinkled with sugar. They are my favorite flower and color, your namesake, Sweet Violet. My mother called them Johnny-jump-up."

"They were her favorite, too?"

"She despised them and complained that I was growing weeds." She laughed and seemed not to notice my dismay. "Once you step inside the house, you're in the vestibule. On one side is a staircase, like the one we have here, but a bit smaller. And on the other side is a thick toffee-colored curtain on a brass rod, not as wide as what we have here. Step through the curtain and you are in the parlor. The furniture is likely old-fashioned, what my grandmother placed there. Through a large doorway, you enter the dining room—"

"Where will I sleep?"

"You'll have a large lovely bedroom on the second floor, with sunny yellow walls. It was my room."

Her room. I was so happy I wanted to shout. Outwardly, I showed little.

"There is a tall bed next to large windows. One window is next to an old oak tree and you can open the window and pretend you're a scrub jay in the branches—those are the noisy birds I remember— they hopped right up to me for a peanut. There are plenty of other birds, herons, hawks, and singing robins. You can look them up in the ornithology books my mother collected. Your grandmother's father was a botanist and a naturalist illustrator. I also have a nice collection of dolls, not the babyish kind you push in a pram. They're prettily painted. And throughout the house are walls of books, top to bottom. You'll have enough to read for the rest of your life, even if you consumed two books a day. You can take your books up to the round turret to read. As a girl, I decorated it with shawls and hassocks and Persian carpets to look like a seraglio. I called it Pasha Palace. Or you can look out the windows through a telescope and see clear to the waterfront and the Bay, to the islands—there are several—and you can count the schooners and fishing boats . . ."

She chattered on, her recollections blossoming. I could see the house in the stereopticon of my mind, a place that took on color and the movement of life. I was dazzled by the thought of room after room with walls of books, of a bedroom with a window next to an oak tree.

My mother was now busy removing her jewelry cases from a locked cupboard. She had at least a dozen each of necklaces, brace-lets, brooches, and pins—gifts she had received over the years. She had sold most of the jewelry, and the ones she kept were her favorites, the most valuable. She placed all the cases in her valise. Were we not coming back?

"Once you find Teddy, will he return to Shanghai with us?"

Again, there was an awkward pause. "I don't know. I cannot pre-dict what will happen. Shanghai has changed."

A terrible thought sprang to mind. "Mother, will Carlotta come with us?"

She immediately busied herself with hatboxes, so I knew already the answer. "I won't leave without her."

"You would stay behind for a cat?"

"I refuse to go if I cannot bring her."

"Come now, Violet. Would you cast away your future for a cat?"

"I would. I am nearly grown up and can choose for myself," I said rashly.

All affection left her face. "All right. Stay if you like."

I had been foiled. "How can you ask me to choose?" I said in a cracked voice. "Carlotta is my baby. She is to me what Teddy is to you. I cannot leave her behind. I cannot betray her. She trusts me."

"I am not asking you to choose, Violet. There is no choice. We must leave, and Carlotta cannot come. We cannot change the rules of the ship. What you must think instead is that we may indeed return. Once we are in San Francisco, I will then know better what to do. But not until then . . ."

She continued her explanation, but grief had already set in. My throat knotted up. I could not explain to Carlotta why I was leaving.

"While we're gone," I heard my mother say through my haze of misery, "Golden Dove can take care of her."

"Golden Dove is scared of her. No one loves Carlotta."

"The daughter of Snowy Cloud's attendant—Little Ocean—she loves her dearly. She will be happy to care for her, especially if we give her a little money to do so while we are gone."

This was true. But my worries remained. What if Carlotta loved the little girl more than she did me? She might forget me and would not care if I ever returned. I fell into a tragic mood.

Although my mother had limited me to four dresses, she was quickly becoming more generous with her own allotment. She decided the two steamer trunks she had were not large enough, and because of their rounded tops they could not be stacked, which would limit what she could bring. Also, they were old, what she had brought from San Francisco. She called for Golden Dove to buy four new steamer trunks, larger ones. "Mr. Malakar told me last month that he had smuggled in a large shipment of Louis Vuitton trunks from France to Bombay. They're the flat-topped ones I want. I also need two steamer bags, the small ones. And tell him he better not think I won't know if he slips me the counterfeit . . ."

She threw her choice of gowns onto the bed. She was bringing so many, I figured she would attend balls as soon as she stepped off the boat. But then she called in Golden Dove and told her to be honest in saying which dresses were more flattering, which brought out the color of her eyes, her complexion, and her mahogany brown hair, and which of these would American women envy, and which would cause them to think she was an immoral woman.

Golden Dove disapproved of all her choices. "You designed those dresses to be shocking and to lure men to your side. And all the American women I've seen staring at you in the park were hardly clapping with admiration."

Instead of having to choose, Mother took most of her evening gowns, as well as her newer dresses, coats, and hats. My four dresses dwindled to the two I would wear during our journey. She promised that many beautiful frocks awaited me, better than those I now owned. My favorite books were not necessary to bring either, nor were my schoolbooks, since those could be easily replaced with better ones in San Francisco, where I would also have better tutors than the ones here in Shanghai. I should simply enjoy a little holiday from study on our voyage.

Into my valise, she placed a maroon box with my jewelry, two other boxes she retrieved from a drawer, two scrolls wrapped in silk, and a few other valuables. On top of this, she placed her fox fur wrap, believing, I suppose, she might need a bit of glamour as we stood on deck and watched Shanghai recede from view.

At last we were done. Mother now needed only to find from among her coterie of influential foreigners someone to buy us passage to America. She gave Cracked Egg a dozen letters to deliver.

A day went by, then a week. The werefox eyes left and her old self returned, the one that was agitated and snappish. She gave Cracked Egg another packet of letters. Two berths, that was all we needed.

What was so difficult about that? Every message came back the same: Her American compatriots were also anxious to leave Shanghai, and they, too, had found that others before them had grabbed every berth on ships for the next month.

During our wait I showed Little Ocean how to make a nest of my silk quilts for Carlotta. Ocean was eight, and as she petted Carlotta, she whispered to her, "I will be your obedient attendant." Carlotta purred and rolled onto her back. My chest ached to see how happy Carlotta already was.

After eleven days of waiting, Fairweather sauntered through Mother's bedroom door, without announcement. He had good news.

I KNOW WHY my mother had once loved Fairweather. He was adept at teasing her out of her bad moods. He was funny, a cure for worry. He made her laugh and feel beautiful. He said he adored her for all her unusual features and manners. He gave her exaggerated looks of befuddled love. He spoke of heartfelt emotions, all of them ones he claimed he had never known with any other woman. And he gave her sympathy for all her indulgent woes. He put her head on his shoulder and told her to cry until her heart was empty of poisonous grief. He shared her indignation when her clients had unfairly used knowledge she had given them in trust.

They had become friends more than nine years ago, and whatever she had needed then, he had given her. They alluded to times in her life when she had suffered a betrayal, a loss of confidence, when she had worried over money. He knew about her early success, about the death of a man who had taken her in when she first came to Shanghai. Remember, remember, remember, he said, to draw out the painful emotions of the past, so he could console her.

I hated that he treated my mother with easy familiarity. He called her "Lu," "Lovely Lulu," "Lullaby," and "Luscious." When she was peeved, he restored her humor by acting like a whipped schoolboy or an errant knight. He recited asinine jokes, and she returned laughter. He purposely embarrassed her in front of others—and in flattering and disgusting ways. At dinner, I watched him obscenely rotate his lips and tongue, claiming there was something stuck on the roof of his mouth. "Wipe that chimpanzee grin off your face," she would say. And he would laugh long and hard, before standing up and bidding her adieu with a comic wink. He would then wait for her in her bedroom. With him, she was weak, no longer herself. She was often silly, drank too much, and laughed too hard. How could she be so stupid?

All the servants at Hidden Jade Path liked Fairweather because he greeted them in Shanghainese and he thanked them for every little thing. They were accustomed to being treated by others as if they were appendages to trays of tea. Everyone made guesses as to where Fairweather might have learned to speak their native tongue. From an amah? A courtesan? A mistress? Clearly a Chinese woman gave him his good Chinese heart. Among Chinese men, he had earned the fond title "Chinese-style foreign dignitary." Although everyone knew his charm, there was little else known about him. Where in the United States did he hail from? Or was he indeed an American? Perhaps an American fugitive? They did not know his true name. He joked he had not used his name for so long, he had forgotten what it was. He simply went by the nickname Fairweather, which his fraternity brothers had given him years ago when he attended a nameless university he had described as "one of those hallowed halls."

"Fair weather followed me wherever I went," he said, "and so my dear friends welcomed me everywhere." In Shanghai, he was invited to parties all over town, and he was the last to leave, unless he spent the night. Yet, oddly enough, no one faulted him for hosting no parties in return.

His popularity, one of the courtesans said, had to do with a skilled man who made counterfeit certificates of every kind. This clever man made visas, birth certificates, wedding certificates, and a valuable supply of documents stamped with the official consular seal, on which he had written in Chinese and English the various "here-with" and "henceforth" proclamations that the person whose name was inscribed had impressed the American consul as having "good character." Fairweather sold them to his "special Chinese friends," as he called them, so special he charged them five times what he paid the translator. They were happy to hand over the money. Any Chinese person, whether a businessman, courtesan, or madam, could wave his or her magic certificate of good character in any court in the International Settlement and have the Stars and Stripes defend his or her honor. No Chinese bureaucrat would have wasted his time chal-lenging an American's opinion, because in those courts, the Chinese would always lose. Since the certificate was good for only one year, Fairweather could assess how special his friends truly were on a regu-lar and profitable basis.

I was the only person who did not fall for his greasy charms. I had suffered much pain seeing how my mother preferred his com-pany to mine. And that pain enabled me to see how false he was. He used rehearsed words of concern, the same ones, the same ges-tures and gentlemanly offers of help. To him, people were prey easily brought down. I knew this because he tried his tricks and charm on me, even though he knew that I saw through his deceit. He sprinkled me with mocking flattery, extolling my messy hair, my bad elocution, the childish book I had chosen to read. I did not smile at him. I was curt if required to speak. My mother scolded me often for being rude to him. He simply laughed. I made it clear through my expression and stiff posture that I found him tiresome. I sighed or rolled my eyes. I did not show him my rage, because that would mean he had won. I left the gifts he brought me on the table in my mother's office. Later, I would return to the table, and sure enough, the gifts would be gone.

Shortly after New Year's Day, Fairweather and my mother had a falling-out. She had learned from Golden Dove that he had been sharing Puffy Cloud's bed before *and* after he had been with her. My mother had made no claim to monogamy. After all, she took other lovers from time to time. But Fairweather was her favorite, and she had assumed that her lovers would not go poking a subordinate in her own house. I listened as Golden Dove told my mother the truth, preceded by this scolding remark: "I told you nine years ago that this man would use you as a fool. Lust leaves you blind long after you've lost your mind in bed." Golden Dove had extracted from her maid the facts and said she would not spare Mother from hearing any of the details so that she would finally banish Fairweather from her bed. "Over the last year, he's been filling her to the brim with so much ecstasy all the maids thought her cries were caused by a sadistic customer. They all heard. They all know—the other courtesans, maids, and menservants. They saw him slithering along the hallways. And guess how Puffy Cloud was able to earn money from him? It was money you had given him for what he had called trifling expenses and a tardy influx of money."

Mother listened to every bit of that sickening truth. I think she felt what had wounded me so often: Someone she loved preferred another. I was glad she felt that pain. I wanted her to know what misery she had given me. I wanted her to give me the supply of love she had given to that cheat.

I had already positioned myself in Boulevard, when Fairweather arrived for his execution. I was ticklish with excitement. Mother had put on a stiff black dress, as if she were in mourning. When he arrived at noon—no doubt from Puffy Cloud's bed—he was surprised to find she was not still asleep, but sitting in her office wearing what he deemed "an unbecoming dress." He offered to help remove it immediately.

"Keep your little trouser friend buttoned up," I heard her say.

I was elated that she finally expressed the same disgust I had always felt for him. She attacked his business acumen. She belittled him for being no more than a paid sycophant. She said he was a parasite who lived on unpaid loans. She could finally see him for who he was, she said, a man whose "cheap charms flowed in spurts from his little fire hose into Puffy Cloud's eager mouth."

He, in turn, blamed his transgressions with Puffy Cloud on an opium addiction. She had seduced him with her pipe, and nothing more than that. His time with her was as memorable as a cup of lukewarm tea. I wished Puffy Cloud could hear what he was saying. Now that he knew how wounded she was, he said, he would take the cure and be rid of both his opium habit and Puffy Cloud. My mother remained silent. I cheered. He shuffled his words, and reminded her that he loved her, and that she knew he had never professed love to any other woman. "We are made of a single heart and thus can never be separated." He beckoned her to look into her heart and find him there. She grumbled strong doubt, but I could hear her weakening.

He kept murmuring, "Darling, darling, my dearest Lu." Was he touching her? I wanted to shout that he was tricking her again. He had given her the poison of his charms. Her tone was wrenching as she told him how pained she was. She had never admitted pain to anyone. He mumbled more endearments. All at once, the pitch of her voice rose.

"Take your hands off my breasts. You embezzled my heart, you bastard, and gave the goods to a courtesan in my own house. You made me a fool, and I won't ever let that happen again."

He confessed more love and said she was wiser than he was. But his sins were not as devious as she made them out to be. It was stupidity, not larceny. He had never wanted to compromise their love with financial favors. But she was the one who offered him so much, and he was overwhelmed with gratitude and also pain of pride that he could neither turn down a gift of love nor repay it. For that reason, he was not going to hold her to the new loan she had promised him a few days ago.

My mother sputtered and cursed. She had never agreed to a loan of even ten cents. He said she had, and recalled his version of a conversation in which he had told her that the glue factory he had invested in needed new machinery. "Don't you remember?" he said. "You asked me how much, and I said two thousand dollars, to which you said, 'Is it really only that much?'"

"How can you imply that conversation to be a promise?" she said. "I would never have agreed to loan money to another of your sticky-fingered schemes—a rubber plantation and now a glue factory."

"The plantation was profitable," he insisted, "until the typhoon destroyed our trees. This glue factory has no such risks. Had I known you never intended to loan me the money, I would not have taken on investors, and some are your clients, I'm afraid to say. We all stand to lose our shirts and I hope they won't mistake you as being part of the reason."

I would have burst through those glass doors if she had agreed to give him the money. Instead I heard her say in a clear voice: "Well, I won't be seeing those clients once I leave Shanghai. And I won't be seeing you, except in my memory of you as a charlatan."

He uttered a string of oaths, among the worst combinations of words I have ever heard. I was overjoyed.

"You weren't even a good fuck," he said at the end. The door banged and he continued swearing as he walked down the hallway.

Golden Dove went to my mother right away. My mother's voice was shaky as she recounted a brief version of what had just happened.

"Do you still love this man?"

"If love is stupid, then yes. How many times did you warn me? Why could I not see who he really was? He must be a hypnotist to have put me under such a spell. The whole house is sniggering at me, and yet, if he came through that door again . . . I don't know. Around him, I'm so weak."

Whispers of gossip drifted through the hallways. I listened from my window at night. The servants were sorry to see Fairweather go. No one blamed Puffy Cloud. Why was Lulu Mimi more deserving of a man? Besides, Fairweather loved Puffy Cloud and had pledged himself to her. She showed everyone the signet ring that bore the seal of his family, one related to the king of Scotland. The menservants gave their verdict: No woman could command a man's fidelity or the natural urges of his manhood. Puffy Cloud left the house before my mother could evict her. She took with her a few farewell gifts— furniture and lamps from her room that did not belong to her.

I thought we were done with the swindler of hearts. But shortly after Mother made her decision to leave Shanghai, Fairweather stood before her in her office. Mother asked me to go to my room to study. I went into Boulevard and pressed my ear against the glass. In a break- ing voice, he expressed sadness she was about to leave Shanghai. He would grieve the loss of her, she who was a rare being no woman could ever replace, a woman he would have adored through poverty and old age. He wanted nothing, except to give true words she could take with her and remember during troubled times in the future. He wept to good effect, and then left, no doubt overcome by his own bad acting.

My mother told Golden Dove what had happened. Her voice was shaky.

"Did he tempt you?" Golden Dove asked.

"He never touched me, if that's what you mean?"

"But were you tempted?"

Silence followed.

"The next time he comes," Golden Dove said, "I am going to be right here in the room."

They did not have to wait long. He came soon with dark circles under his eyes and disheveled hair and clothes. "I haven't been able to sleep since I last saw you. I'm in agony, Lu. Your words inflicted pain on me, and deservedly so, because what I feel is the pain of truth. You have never been cruel, not intentionally, at least. But your hatred toward me is unbearable. I feel it here, and here, and here. I feel it day and night, and it's like coals and knives. I, of all people, knew you had been betrayed by Lu Shing and deserved better. You deserved the better part of me, and that's what I gave you. I was unfaithful with my body, yes, but my heart and spirit remained yours, completely, constantly. Lu darling, I ask nothing of you except for you to understand and acknowledge that I do genuinely love you. Please tell me you believe me. I won't think life is worth living if you don't."

Mother actually laughed at what he said. He ran out of her room. She later told Golden Dove what had happened and was pleased to say she had rebuffed him without her help.

He showed up the next day, freshly groomed and wearing smart clothes. "I'm leaving Shanghai and going to South America. There's nothing here for me now that you're leaving." His voice was sad but calm. "I simply came by to tell you I won't bother you anymore. Can I kiss your hand good-bye?"

He went to his knees. She sighed and held out her hand. He kissed it quickly, then pressed her palm to his cheek. "This will have to last me a lifetime. You know I could not possibly have meant what I said about your lack of skills as a lover. You alone were able to take me to spasmodic heights of pleasure I did not know existed. We had such good times, didn't we? I hope that one day you can forget all this ugliness and recall those times when we were too exhausted from pleasure to utter a single word more. Are you remembering? Oh, dear God, Lu, how can you remove such sweetness from me? Can you leave me with just one more memory? It won't hurt, will it? I would like nothing more than to give you one more bout of pleasure."

He looked at her from bended knee, and she said nothing. He touched her knee, and she still said nothing. He lifted her skirt and kissed her knee. I knew what would happen next. I saw it in her eyes. She had grown stupid. I left the room.

Golden Dove scolded her the next morning: "I can tell he leeched onto your body and heart again. It's in those bright eyes and the tiny turned-up corners of your mouth. You're still remembering what he did last night, aren't you? That man must possess the magic of a thousand men to put enough lust between your legs to remove your brain at the same time."

"Last night meant nothing to me," my mother said. "I gave in to an old itch. We had our lewd fun between the sheets and now I'm finished with him."

Three weeks later, Fairweather sauntered into the common room with his chimpanzee smile and went to Mother with arms wide open. "You better give me a kiss, Missy Minturn, because I've just reserved two cabins on a ship that leaves two days from now. Is that not proof of love?"

Her eyes went wide, but she did not move. He told her in a rush that he had heard the call for help through the Shanghai business grapevine, and although she was angry with him, and he with her, he felt he could redeem her trust in him and win her back by providing what she so desperately needed.

They left the common room and went to her study. I finished my breakfast quickly and then went to Boulevard, arranged my books and writing sheets sloppily on the table into a picture of studiousness, and then put my ear to the cold glass. I heard his sickening love talk of heartaches and a life without purpose, how purpose was renewed when he found a way to help her. He provided a copious number of endearments, along with the usual declarations of pain everlasting. And then he switched tack. "Lu darling, we had such fun the other night, didn't we? My God! I've never seen you with that much sexual fire. I feel the flames in my loins just thinking about it, don't you?" There was a long silence, which I hoped was not a kiss—or more.

"Get off me," she said roughly. "I want to hear more about this latest peace offering first."

He laughed. "All right. But don't forget about my reward. And when you hear what I found you, perhaps you'll consider doubling the award. Are you ready? Two cabin reservations on a steamer— only three stops—Hong Kong, Haiphong, and Honolulu. Twenty-four days to San Francisco. The cabins are not first class. I'm not God enough to pull that miracle. But the cabins are decent, port-side. All I need are your passports. Don't worry. I have the reservations, but I am required to show the passports by tomorrow to secure the booking."

"I'll give you mine. But a child traveling with her mother does not require one."

"The steamship's purchasing agent told me the passport is required of all passengers, man, woman, and child. If Violet does not have one, it's a simple matter of presenting her birth certificate at the American Consulate to have one issued. She does have a birth certificate, doesn't she?"

"Of course. I have it right here."

I heard the scrape of chair legs, the click of a key, the squeak of a drawer pulled out. "Where is it?" she exclaimed.

"When did you last look?"

"There was never a reason to look. All my important documents are here, under lock and key." She cursed, opened more drawers and slammed them.

"Calm yourself," he said. "Another one can be issued by the consulate easily enough."

It was hard to hear what my mother was saying. She was mumbling to herself . . . something about an orderly office . . . never misplacing anything.

"You're losing your mind, Lulu," Fairweather said. "Come here. We can fix this easily enough."

She mumbled again and all I could hear was the word *stolen*.

"Come now, Lu darling, be rational. Why would anyone want to steal Violet's birth certificate? It doesn't make sense. Put it out of your mind. I can get both her birth certificate and passport from the consulate tomorrow. What name did you put on the birth certificate? That's all I need to know."

I heard her say the name "Tanner," and "husband" and "American."

"Married?" Fairweather said. "I knew you loved him and the two of you lived together. But you certainly went to extremes for Violet's sake. Well, that's all good to hear. It means she is an American and of legitimate birth, a citizen. Just think how difficult it would have been if you had used the name of her real father, the Chinese one."

I felt punched by his words. Why did this despicable man know so much about me?

In the evening, Fairweather returned with a downcast face. He and my mother went to her office. I took my usual position in Boulevard. I had already taken care earlier in the day to put the doors ajar and part the curtains. "They have no record of birth for Violet," he said.

"That's impossible. Are you sure you used the right name?" She wrote furiously on a sheet of paper and showed it to him.

"I used the very name and spelled it correctly, as you've written it. There is no record for Violet, no child at all for Lulu Minturn. I was thorough and checked that as well."

"How stupid of me," Mother said. "We used my given name, Lucretia, on both the marriage certificate and her birth certificate. Here, I'll write it down."

"Lucretia! I must confess, the name doesn't suit you. What else have you kept from me? Another husband? Any more names I can use to investigate further?"

"This is absurd. I'll go down immediately and get the damn certificate myself."

"Lulu darling, there is no point in doing so. They likely lost a box of records, and no amount of strong-arming is going to unearth it in time for your departure from Shanghai."

"If we cannot get her a passport," Mother said, "we are not leaving. We'll simply have to wait."

She would wait for me. She loved me. This was proof I had never had before.

"I figured you would say that, so I've come up with my own timely solution. I've found someone highly placed, a genuine pooh-bah who has agreed to help. I cannot reveal his identity—that's how important he is. But I did him a favor once, which I have kept secret for many years—an indiscretion involving the son of a man whose name you would recognize, a Chinese celestial to many. So the pooh-bah and I are excellent friends. He assures me we can obtain the necessary paperwork that will allow Violet to enter the United States. I simply have to declare that I am her father."

I nearly shouted in disgust. My mother laughed. "How fortunate that is not the truth."

"Why do you insult your daughter's savior? I've been going to a great deal of trouble to help."

"And I am waiting for you to tell me how you would accomplish that and what you want in exchange for your trumped-up fatherhood. I won't deceive myself into thinking our catapulting passion the other night is compensation enough."

"Another round of that will be. I take nothing as profit. The money needed is for necessary expenses only."

"By the way, since honesty is at issue here, what is your real name, the one you propose to give Violet?"

"Believe it or not, it really is Fairweather, Arthur Fairweather. I turned it into a joke before others could make it one."

The fake father laid out his plans. Mother would have to give him the money now to purchase the two cabins on the ship and to compensate the pooh-bah. He would deliver the tickets in the morning and whisk me to the consulate. At noon, she should send the trunks on to the ship and board early to safeguard the cabins from squatters. Fairweather sounded too lighthearted, too practiced to be telling the truth. He wanted her money.

"Do you doubt that I can accomplish this?"

"Why would I not go to the consulate as her mother?"

"Forgive me for being frank, Lulu dear, but the American government is not inclined to show the new Chinese government that it provides special favors to those whose establishments cater to happiness of the flesh. Everyone has suddenly developed shining morals. You are too famous, too notorious. I do not think my pooh-bah friend would push the limits of his position. Violet will be registered under my name and I can say that her mother is my late wife, Camille—and yes, I had a wife, but I will not talk about her now. Once we have both her birth certificate and passport, Violet and I shall board the ship as father and sweet child and then happily rejoin you. Why are you frowning? Of course I am coming with you, darling. Why am I going to all this trouble? Do you still not believe that I truly love you and want to be by your side forever?"

There was a long silence, and I imagined they were kissing. Why did she believe him without question? Did a few kisses once again empty her brain that quickly? Was she going to introduce this crook to her son as "your sister's dear devoted father"?

"Violet and I will share a cabin," my mother said at last, "and you will have the other to yourself—in consideration of the late Mrs. Fairweather and my notoriety, as you put it."

"You want me to woo you all the way to San Francisco, is that it?"

Silence followed. They were kissing again, I was sure of it.

"Let's get to the business end of this," she said. "What do I owe you for this show of affection?"

"It's fairly straightforward. The cost of the cabins, the monetary gratitude to the pooh-bah, and his inflated price of whatever bribe he had to pay someone else. Influence of this sort does not come cheaply or honestly. When you see the sum, you may think the berths are dipped in gold. It's a painful amount, and it has to be paid in the old standard of Mexican silver dollars. No one knows how long the new currency will hold."

More silence followed. My mother cursed. Fairweather went over the details again. She pointedly asked how much of that amount was profit to him, to which he rumbled with anger at her ingratitude for all he was doing. Not only was he calling in all his favors, he stated, but he was also leaving Shanghai a pauper. He was due to be paid a large sum in two weeks. But for her, he was leaving that behind, as well as unpaid bills, which meant he had little chance of ever showing his face in Shanghai again. That was proof of how much he loved her.

Silence followed. I was nervous she would give in to his lies. "Once we're on the boat," she said at last, "I'll show my gratitude. And if you have duped me, you will know that my revenge has no limits."

The next morning, I argued with her over the wretched plan. Mother was already dressed in her chosen travel costume: a cornflower-blue skirt and long jacket. Her hat, shoes, and gloves were cream-colored kid leather. She looked as if she were going to the races. I was supposed to wear a ridiculous sailor blouse and skirt, which Fairweather had sent over. He said it would make me look like a patriotic American girl, a guise that was necessary to douse all doubt that I was anything less than snowy white. I was certain he wanted me to wear the cheap dress to humiliate me.

"I don't trust him," I said, as Golden Dove helped me into the dress. I laid out my argument. Did anyone go to the consulate to verify that what he had said was true? Maybe there was a birth certificate. And who was this influential man he claims to know? The only reason he was doing this was for money. How could she be sure he would not abscond with the money?

"Do you really think I haven't asked all those questions and five times again more?" She acted annoyed. But I saw her eyes dart about, looking for danger in dark corners. She was frightened. She had doubts. "I've gone over it," she continued, speaking quickly, "looking for every possible rat hole he can jump into." She rambled about her suspicions. Cracked Egg had sent people out to learn if the tickets were genuine. They were indeed reserved, paid by someone expecting to get reimbursed at twice the cost, not thrice, as Fairweather had said. That was his usual greed, and she could overlook that as long as she received the tickets. She confirmed that the passports were indeed required. And Golden Dove had already gone to the consulate to see if it was true that my birth certificate could not be found. Unfortunately, they would not give such information to anyone but the child's American parents.

"Why would Fairweather go to the trouble of doing all this?" my mother said, and a moment later, she answered herself: "Pulling strings is his favorite game, as is looping them, one through the other. What do you think, Golden Dove? Should I trust him?"

"Never with love," she said. "But if he comes here with the tickets, that's a sign he's capable of performing what he says. If he does not bring the tickets, Cracked Egg will bring back the money and a slice of his nose."

"Why do we have to leave right away?" I cried. "If we wait, we won't need his help. All this is for Teddy. For Teddy, I have to pretend Fairweather is my father. For Teddy, I have to give up Carlotta and suffer heartbreak."

"Violet, don't become hysterical. This is for all of us." She was fiddling with her gloves. She was nervous, too. "If we cannot get your documents, the answer is absolute: We will not go until we obtain them." A button popped off one of her gloves. She removed the gloves and tossed them onto her desk.

"But why do we have to hurry now? Teddy will still be in San Francisco."

She had her back to me. "Shanghai is changing. There may not be a place for us here anymore. In San Francisco, we will start afresh."

I prayed Fairweather would not come. Let him abscond with the money and prove his stripes. But he showed up promptly at nine, when Golden Dove and I were in Mother's office. He sat down and handed my mother an envelope.

She frowned. "This is a ticket for only one cabin and one berth."

"Lulu darling, how can you still not trust me? If you had both tickets, how would my daughter, Violet, and I board later?" He pulled the other tickets from his breast pocket and held them up. "You need only knock on my cabin door to verify your daughter and humble servant are there." He stood and put on his hat. "Violet and I better make haste to the consulate or this whole effort will be for naught."

Everything was happening too quickly. I stared hard at my mother. *No, don't let him take me,* I wanted to beg. She gave me a look of resignation. My heart beat so fast I was dizzy. I scooped up Carlotta, who had been sleeping under the writing table, and I began to sob, rubbing tears into her coat. A manservant whisked away my valise.

"No tears for me?" Golden Dove said. I had never even considered she was not coming with us. Of course she was not. She and my mother were like sisters. She was like an aunt to me. I went to her and threw my arms around her, thanking her for her care. I could not comprehend I would not see her after today, not for a while, and maybe forever.

"Will you come to San Francisco soon?" I asked tearfully.

"I have no desire to go there. So you'll have to return to Shanghai to see me."

Golden Dove and my mother walked down the stairs with me. I clutched Carlotta so hard she squirmed. At the gate, I saw that the courtesans and their attendants had already gathered for my farewell. I thanked Cracked Egg for keeping me safe. He smiled, but his eyes were sad. Little Ocean, who loved Carlotta, stood by. I pressed my face into Carlotta's fur: "I'm sorry! I'm sorry!" I promised I would always love her and that I would return for her. But I knew I would probably never see her again. Little Ocean held out her arms, and Carlotta rolled into them. She showed no distress in my leaving and this hurt my heart. But as my mother and I walked through the gate, I heard Carlotta cry out. I turned around and she was twisting her body, trying to reach me. My mother put her arm around my waist and firmly led me forward. The gate opened and a chorus of beauties shouted, "Come back!" "Don't forget us!" "Don't get too fat!" "Bring me back a lucky star!"

"It won't take long," my mother assured me. I saw a small knot of worry in her forehead. She stroked my face. "I've asked Cracked

Egg to wait at the consulate and to send a message to me once you have your passport. I won't board until I have that message. You and Fairweather will go directly to the boat, and we'll look for each other at the back of the boat and stand together as the ship gets under way."

"Mother . . . ," I protested.

"I won't leave until you are beside me," she said firmly. "I promise." She kissed my forehead. "Don't worry."

Fairweather led me to the carriage. I turned back and saw my mother waving. I saw the knot on her brow.

"Five o'clock, at the back of the boat!" she called out. Above her fading words, I heard Carlotta howl.

CHAPTER 3

THE HALL OF TRANQUILITY

Shanghai
1912
Violet—Vivi—Zizi

When I stepped down from the carriage, I saw the gate of a large house and a plaque with Chinese characters spelling "Hall of Tranquility." I looked up and down the street for a building with the American flag.

"This is not the right place," I said to Fairweather.

He returned a look of surprise and asked the driver if it was indeed the correct address, and the driver affirmed that it was. Fairweather called for assistance from those by the gate. Two smiling women came forward. One of them said to me, "It's too cold for you to stand outside, little sister. Come in quickly and you'll soon be warm." Before I could think, they grasped me at the elbows, and pushed me forward. I balked and explained we were going to the consulate instead, but they did not let go. When I turned to tell Fairweather to take me away from there, I saw only shimmering dust floating through the sun's glare. The carriage was moving at a brisk pace down the road. Bastard! I had been right all along. It was a trick. Before I could think what to do, the two women locked their arms in mine and moved me forward more forcefully. I struggled and shouted, and to everyone I saw—the people on the road, the gate-keeper, the menservants, the maids—I warned that if they did not obey me, my mother would later have them jailed for kidnapping. They gave me blank-faced stares. Why didn't they obey? How dare they treat a foreigner this way!

In the main hall, I saw red banners hung on the walls. "Welcome Little Sister Mimi." The characters for *mimi* were the same ones used in my mother's name for "hidden." I ran to one of the banners and pulled it down. My heart was racing and panic choked my throat. "I'm a foreigner," I squawked in Chinese. "You are not allowed to do this to me . . ." The courtesans and little maids stared back.

"How peculiar that she speaks Chinese," a maid whispered.

"Damn you all!" I shouted in English. My mind was racing and all in a jumble, but my limbs were sluggish. What was happening? I must tell Mother where I am. I needed a carriage. I should notify the police as soon as possible. I said to a manservant, "I will give five dollars if you carry me to Hidden Jade Path." A moment later, I realized I had no money. I became more confused by my helplessness. I guessed they would keep me here until five o'clock, when the boat would have sailed away.

A maid whispered to another that she thought a virgin courte-san from a first-class house would have worn nicer clothes than a dirty Yankee costume.

"I'm not a virgin courtesan!" I said.

A squat woman of around fifty waddled toward me, and by the watchful expressions on everyone's faces, I knew she was the madam. She had a broad face and an unhealthy pallor. Her eyes were as black as a crow's, and the hair at her temples had been twisted into tight strands that pulled back her skin and elongated her eyes into catlike ovals. From her lipless mouth, she said, "Welcome to the Hall of Tran-quility!" I sneered at how proudly she said the name. *Tranquility!* My mother said that only second-class houses used good-sounding names like that to convey false expectations. Where was the tranquility? Everyone looked scared. The Western furniture was shiny and cheap. The curtains were too short. All the decorations were imitations of what they could never be. There was no mistaking it: The Hall of Tranquility was nothing more than a brothel with a sinking reputation.

"My mother is a very important American," I said to the madam. "If you do not let me go this instant, she will have you convicted in an American court of law and your house will be closed forever."

"Yes, we know all about your mother. Lulu Mimi. Such an important woman."

The madam beckoned the six courtesans to come meet me. They were dressed in bright pink and green colors, as if it were still Spring Festival. Four of them looked to be seventeen or eighteen, and the other two were much older, at least twenty-five. A maid, no more than ten, brought steaming towels and a bowl of rose water. I knocked them away and the porcelain smashed onto the tile with the bright sound of a thousand tiny bells. While picking up the slivers, the frightened maid apologized to the madam, and the old woman said nothing that would assure her that the damage was not her fault. An older maid gave me a bowl of osmanthus tea. Although I was thirsty, I took the bowl and threw it at the banners with my name. Black tears ran down from the smeared characters.

The madam gave me an indulgent smile. "*Ayo!* Such a temper."

She motioned to the courtesans, and, one by one, they and their attendants politely thanked me for coming and adding prestige to the house. They did not appear genuinely welcoming. When the madam took my elbow to guide me toward a table, I yanked back my arm. "Don't touch me."

"*Shh-shh,*" the madam soothed. "Soon you will be more at ease here. Call me Mother and I'll treat you just like a daughter."

"Cheap whore!"

Her smile disappeared and she turned her attention to ten plates with special delicacies that had been set on a tea table. "We'll nourish you for years to come," she said, and blathered on with other insincere words.

I saw little meat buns and decided I would spare the food from being destroyed. A maid poured wine into a little cup and set it on the table. I picked up the chopsticks and reached for a bun. The madam tapped her chopsticks on top of mine and shook her head. "You must drink the wine before eating. It is custom."

I quickly swallowed the foul liquid, then reached again for a bun. With two claps and a wave of her hand, she wordlessly signaled that the food be taken away. I thought she intended that I eat in another room.

She turned to me and said, still smiling, "I've made a hefty investment in you. Will you work hard to be worth the burden of feeding you?"

I scowled, and before I could call her foul names, she delivered a fisted blow to the side of my head next to my ear. The force of it nearly snapped my head off my neck. My eyes watered and my ears rang. I had never been struck before.

The woman's face was contorted and her shouts were faint, distant. She had deafened one ear. She slapped my face and more stinging tears rose. "Do you understand?" she said in her faraway voice. I could not gather my senses long enough to answer before more slaps followed. I threw myself at her and would have pummeled her face if the arms of the menservants had not pulled me away.

The woman slapped me again and again, cursing. She grabbed my hair and yanked back my head.

"You brat, I'll beat that temper out of you even after you're dead."

She then let go and shoved me so hard I lost my balance, fell to the floor, and into a deep dark place.

I AWOKE IN a strange bed with a quilt on top of me. A woman hurried toward me. Fearing it was the madam, I wrapped my arms around my head.

"Awake at last," she said. "Vivi, don't you remember your old friend?" How did she know my name? I unlocked my arms and opened my eyes. She had a round face, large eyes, and the questioning look of one raised eyebrow.

"Magic Cloud!" I cried. She was the Cloud Beauty who had tolerated my antics when I was a child. She had come back to help me.

"My name is now Magic Gourd," she said. "I'm a courtesan here." Her face looked tired, her skin was dull. She had aged a great deal in those seven years.

"You have to help me," I said in a rush. "My mother is waiting for me at the harbor. The boat is leaving at five o'clock, and if I'm not there, it will sail away without us."

She frowned. "No words of happiness for our reunion? You're still a spoiled child, only now your arms and legs are longer."

Why was she criticizing my manners at a time like this? "I need to go to the harbor right away or—"

"The boat has left," she said. "Mother Ma put a sleeping potion in your wine. You have been asleep most of the day."

I was stunned. I pictured my mother with her new trunks stacked on the dock. The tickets had gone to waste. She would be furious when she learned how cleverly Fairweather had tricked her with his greasy words of love. It served her right for being in such a rush to see her son in San Francisco.

"You must go to the harbor," I said to Magic Gourd, "and tell my mother where I am."

"*Oyo!* I am not your servant. Anyway, she is not there. She is on the boat and it is already sailing to San Francisco. It cannot turn back."

"That's not true! She would never leave me. She promised."

"A messenger told her you had already boarded and that Fairweather was looking for you."

"What messenger? Cracked Egg? He did not see me go in or out of the consulate." To everything Magic Gourd said, I countered senselessly, "She promised. She would not lie." The more I said this, the less sure I was.

"Will you take me back to Hidden Jade Path?"

"Little Vivi, what has happened is worse than you think. Mother Ma paid too many Mexican dollars to the Green Gang to leave even the smallest crack for you to slip through. And the Green Gang made threats to everyone at Hidden Jade Path. If the Cloud Beauties help you, they would be disfigured. They threatened to cut all of Cracked Egg's leg muscles and leave him in the streets to be run over by horses. They told Golden Dove the house would be bombed and that you would suffer the loss of your eyes and ears."

"Green Gang? They had nothing to do with this."

"Fairweather made a deal with them in exchange for settling his gambling debt. He got your mother to leave so they could take over her house without interference from the American Consulate."

"Take me to the police."

"How naive you are. The chief of the Shanghai Police is a Green Gang member. They know about your situation. They would kill me in the most painful way possible if I took you away from here."

"I don't care," I cried. "You have to help me."

Magic Gourd stared at me openmouthed. "You don't care if I'm tortured and killed? What kind of girl did you grow up to be? So selfish!" She left the room.

I was ashamed. She had once been my only friend. I could not explain to her that I was scared. I had never shown fear or weakness to anyone. I was used to having any predicament solved immediately by my mother. I wanted to pour out to Magic Gourd all that I felt—that my mother had not worried enough for me, and instead she became stupid and believed that liar. She always did, because she loved him more than she loved me. Was she with him on that ship? Would she return? She had promised.

I looked around at my prison. The room was small. All the furniture was of poor quality and worn beyond repair. What kind of men

were the customers of this house? I tallied all the faults of the room
so I could tell my mother how much I had suffered. The mat was
thin and lumpy. The curtains that enclosed the frame were faded and
stained. The tea table had a crooked leg and its top had water stains
and burn marks, making it suitable only for firewood. The crackle-
glazed vase had a real crack. The ceiling had missing plaster and the
lamps on the walls were crooked. The rug was orange and dark blue
wool woven with the usual symbols of the scholar, and half of them
were worn bare or eaten by moths. The Western armchairs were rick-
ety and the cloth was frayed at the edge of the seats. A lump grew in
my throat. Was she really on the boat? Was she worried sick?

I was still wearing the hated blue-and-white sailor blouse and
skirt, "evidence of my American patriotism," Fairweather had said.
That evil man was making me suffer because I hated him.

At the back of the wardrobe, I spied a tiny pair of embroidered
shoes, so worn there was more grimy lining than pink and blue silk.
The backs of the shoes were crushed flat. They had been made for
small feet. The girl who wore them must have wedged her toes in
and walked on tiptoe to give the effect of bound feet. Did she rest
her heels on the backs of the shoes when no one was looking? Why
had the girl left the shoes behind instead of throwing them away?
They were beyond repair. I pictured her, a sad-faced girl with large
feet, thin hair, and a gray complexion, worn down like those shoes,
a girl who was about to be thrown away because she was no longer of
any use. I felt sick to my stomach. The shoes had been placed there
as an omen. I would become that girl. The madam would never let
me leave. I opened the window and threw them out into the alley.
I heard a shriek and looked down. A ragamuffin rubbed her head,
then grabbed and clutched them to her chest. She stared at me, as if
guilty, then ran off like a thief.

I tried to recall if Mother had worn a guilty expression as I was
leaving her side. If so, that would be proof she had agreed to Fairweather's plan. When I had threatened to stay in Shanghai with Car-

lotta, she might have used that as an excuse to leave. She might have said to herself that I preferred to stay. I tried to remember other fragments of conversations, other threats I had made, promises she had given, and protests I shouted when she disappointed me. In those pieces was the reason I was here.

I spied my valise next to the wardrobe. The contents would reveal her intentions. If they were clothes for my new life, I would know she had abandoned me. If the clothes were hers, I would know she had been tricked. I slipped over my neck the silvery chain with the key to the valise. I held my breath. I expelled it with gratitude when I saw a bottle of Mother's precious Himalayan rose oil perfume. I petted her fox stole. Underneath that was her favorite dress, a lilac-colored one she had worn on a visit to the Shanghai Club, where she had boldly strolled in and seated herself at the table of a man who was too rich and important to be told that women were not allowed. I hung this impertinent dress on the wardrobe door and placed a pair of her high-heeled shoes below. It gave the eerie appearance that she was a headless ghost. Below that was a mother-of-pearl box with my jewelry: two charm bracelets, a gold locket, and an amethyst necklace and ring. I opened another small box, which contained lumps of amber, the gift I had rejected on my eighth birthday. I lifted out two scrolls, one short, the other long. I unwound the cloth wrapper. They were not scrolls after all, but oil paintings on canvas. I put the larger one on the floor.

It was the portrait of Mother when she was young, the painting I had found just after my eighth birthday, when I rifled her room for a letter she had just received that had upset her so. I had had only enough time for a glimpse before putting it back. Now, while examining it closely, I felt a peculiar discomfort, as if I were staring at a terrible secret about her that was dangerous for me to know—or perhaps it was a secret about me. Mother's head was tilted back, revealing her nostrils. Her mouth was closed, unsmiling. It was as if someone had given her a dare and she had taken it without hesitation. Although, perhaps she was also frightened that she had done so and was trying to hide it. Her eyes were wide open and her pupils were so large they turned her green eyes black. It was the stare of a fearful cat. This was who she was before she had learned to disguise her feelings with a show of confidence. Who was the painter enjoying her state of fright?

The painting was similar in style to that of European portraits commissioned as novelties by rich Shanghainese, who had to have the latest luxury that the foreigners enjoyed, even if they were renderings of other people's ancestors in powdered wigs and their beribboned children with spaniels and hares. They were popular decorations in the salons of hotels and first-class flower houses. Mother had mocked those paintings as poorly executed pretensions. "A portrait," she had said, "should be that of a person who was breathing at the time it was painted. It should capture one of those breaths."

She had held her breath when this portrait was done. The longer I looked at her face, the more I saw, and the more I saw, the more contradictory she became. I saw bravery, then fear. I recognized in it something vague about her nature, and I could see she had already possessed it when she was a girl. And then I knew what that was: her haughtiness in thinking she was better than others and smarter than them as well. She believed she was never wrong. The more others disapproved of her, the more she showed her disapproval of them. We ran into all sorts of disapproving people while walking in the park. They recognized her, "The White Madam." Mother would give them a slow appraisal head to toe, then a sniff in disgust, which always sent me into near fits of giggles as the recipient of her stares and rebukes came undone and retreated speechless.

Usually she gave no further thought to people who had insulted her. But the day she received the latest letter from Lu Shing, she had a festering anger. "Do you know what morals are, Violet? They're other people's rules. Do you know what a conscience is? Freedom to use your own intelligence to determine what is right or wrong. You possess that freedom and no one can remove it from you. Whenever others disapprove of you, you must disregard them and be the only one to judge your own decisions and actions . . ." On and on she went, as if an old wound still festered and she had to cleanse it with venom.

I looked hard at the painting. What conscience did she have? Her right and wrong were guided by selfishness, doing what was best for her. "Poor Violet," I imagined her saying. "She would be taunted in San Francisco as a child of questionable race. Much better that she stay in Shanghai where she can live happily with Carlotta." I became incensed. She had always found a way to defend her decisions, no matter how wrong. When a courtesan was forced to leave Hidden Jade Path, she said it was a matter of necessity. When she could not have supper with me, she would tell me it was a matter of necessity. Her time with Fairweather had always been a matter of necessity.

A matter of necessity. That was what she said to suit her own purposes. It was an excuse to be selfish. I recalled a time when I had felt sickened by her lack of conscience. It happened three years ago, on a day that was memorable because it was strange in so many ways. We were with Fairweather at the Shanghai Race Club to watch a Frenchman fly his plane over the track. The seats were filled. No one had ever seen an airplane in flight, let alone right above their heads, and when it soared up, the crowd murmured in unison. I believed it was magic. How else could you explain it? I watched the plane glide and dip, then tilt from side to side. One wing fell off, then another. I thought this was meant to happen, until the plane flew into the center of the racetrack and cracked into pieces. Dark smoke rose, people screamed, and when the mangled aviator was dragged from the wreckage, a few men and women fainted. I nearly vomited. The words *dead, dead, dead* echoed through the stands. The debris was hauled away, and fresh dirt was poured over the blood. A short while later, the horses entered the track and the races began. I could hear the departing people angrily say that it was immoral to continue the races and shameful that anyone would enjoy them. I thought we would also be leaving. Who could stay, having just seen a man killed? I was shocked that my mother and Fairweather had remained in their seats. As the horses pounded the track, my mother and Fairweather cheered, and I stared at the moist dirt that had been poured to hide the blood. Mother saw no wrong in our watching the race. I had no choice but to be there, and yet I felt guilty, thinking I should have told them what I thought.

Later that afternoon, as we walked back to the house, a little Chinese girl, who might have been around my age, ran out of a dark doorway, and claimed to Fairweather with her smattering of English words that she was a virgin and had three holes for a dollar. The slave girls were a pitiful lot. They had to take at least twenty men a day or risk being beaten to death. What more could we give them besides pity? And even that was difficult to do because there were so many of them. They darted about like nervous chickens, tugging on coats, beseeching men, to the point of being a nuisance. We had to walk briskly past them without giving them a glance. That day, my mother reacted differently. Once we were past the girl, she muttered, "The bastard who sold her should have his little cock cut off with the guillotine for a cigar."

Fairweather laughed. "You, my dear, have bought girls from those who sold them."

"There's a difference between selling a girl and buying her," she said.

"It's the same result," Fairweather said. "The girl becomes a prostitute. It is a collusion of seller and buyer."

"It's far better that I buy a girl and take her to my house than for her to wind up as a slave like this one, dead at fifteen."

"To judge by the flowers in your house, only the pretty ones are worth saving."

She stopped walking. The remark had clearly riled her. "That is not a reflection of my conscience. It is pragmatism. I am a business-

woman, not a missionary running an orphanage. What I do is a matter of necessity based on the circumstances at hand. And only I know
what those are."

There were those words again: *a matter of necessity.* Right after
she said them, she abruptly turned around and went to the doorway where the girl's owner sat. She gave the woman some money,
then took the girl's hand and rejoined us. The girl was petrified. She
glanced back at her former owner. "At least her eyes don't have the
deadened gaze that most slave girls have."

"So you've just bought yourself a little courtesan," Fairweather
said. "One more saved from the streets. Good on you."

My mother snapped, "This girl won't be a courtesan. I have no
need of one, and even if I did, she'd never be suitable. She's already
ruined, deflowered a thousand times. She would simply lie on her
back with a beaten look of submission. I'm taking her as a maid.
One of the maids is marrying and going to her husband's village." I
learned later that no maid was leaving. I thought for a moment that
she had taken the girl because she had a good heart. But then I realized it was her arrogance in showing up anyone who had disapproved
of her. She had stayed at the race club for that reason. She bought the
girl because Fairweather had made fun of her conscience.

I scrutinized again the oil painting, noting every brushstroke
that had created her young face. Had she possessed more sympathy
for people when she was my age? Had she felt any for the dead pilot
or the little slave girl? She was contradictory, and her so-called matters of necessity made no sense. She could be loyal or disloyal, a good
mother, then a bad one. She might have loved me at times, but her
love was not constant. When did she last prove that she loved me? I
thought it was when she promised not to leave me.

On the back of the painting were these words: "For Miss Lucretia Minturn, on the occasion of her 17th birthday." I did not know
my mother's birthday or her age. We had never celebrated them
and there was never any reason to know. I was fourteen, and if she

had given birth to me when she was seventeen, that would make her thirty-one now.

Lucretia. That was the name on the envelope of Lu Shing's letter. The words below the dedication had been lashed to oblivion by the dark lead of a pencil. I turned the painting faceup and found the initials "L.S." at the bottom right corner. Lu Shing was the painter. I was certain of that.

I unrolled the smaller painting. The initials "L.S." appeared on the bottom of that one as well. It was a landscape of a valley, viewed from the edge of a cliff, facing the scene below. The mountain ridges on each side were ragged, and their shadow silhouettes lay on the valley floor. The pendulous clouds were the shade of an old bruise. The upper halves were pink, and the clouds receding in the background were haloed in gold, and at the far end of the valley, an opening between two mountains glowed like the entrance to paradise. It looked like dawn. Or was it dusk? I could not tell whether the rain was coming, or the sky was clearing, whether it was about arriving there with joy or leaving it with relief. Was the painting meant to depict a feeling of hope or was it hopelessness? Were you supposed to be standing on the cliff charged with bravery or trembling in dread of what awaited you? Or maybe the painting was about the fool who had chased after a dream and was looking at the devil's pot of gold that lay in that glimmering place just beyond reach. The painting reminded me of those illusions that changed as you turned them upside down or sideways, transforming a bearded man into a tree. You could not see the painting both ways at the same time. You had to choose which one it was originally meant to be. How would you know which was right unless you were the one who had painted it?

The painting gave me a queasy feeling. It was an omen, like the worn slippers. I was meant to find it. What happened next was salvation or doom. I felt certain now that the painting meant you were walking into the valley, not leaving it. The rain was coming. It was dusk, turning dark, and you would no longer be able to find your way back.

With shaky hands, I turned the painting over. *The Valley of Amazement* it said, and below that were initials: "For L.M. from L.S." The date was smeared. I could make out that it was either "1897" or "1899." I had been born in 1898. Had Mother received this one along with her portrait? What was she doing before I was born? What was she doing the year after? If Lu Shing had painted this in 1899, he would have still been with my mother when I was a year old.

I threw both paintings across the room. A second later, I was overcome with fright that some part of me would be thrown away and destroyed, and I would never know what it was. She hated Lu Shing for leaving her, so there must have been a very strong reason she had kept the paintings. I ran to claim back the paintings. I cried as I rolled them up, then shoved them into the bottom of the valise.

Magic Gourd walked in. She threw two cotton pajama suits on a chair—loose jackets and pantalets, green with pink piping—the clothes worn by small children. "Mother Ma figured these clothes would keep you from trying to escape. She said you are too vain to be seen in public dressed like a Chinese maid. If you keep your haughty Western ways, she'll beat you worse than what you already received. If you follow her rules, you'll suffer less. It's up to you how much pain you want to endure."

"My mother is coming for me," I declared. "I won't have to stay here much longer."

"If she does, it won't be soon. It takes a month to go from Shanghai to San Francisco and another month to come back. If you're stubborn, you'll be dead before two months pass. Just go along with whatever the madam says. Pretend to learn whatever she teaches you. You won't die from doing that. She bought you as a virgin courtesan and your defloration won't happen for at least another year. You can plot your escape in between times."

"I'm not a virgin courtesan."

"Don't let pride make you stupid," she said. "You're lucky she isn't making you work right away." She went to my valise and dipped her hands inside and pulled out the fox stole with its dangling paws.

"Don't touch my belongings."

"We need to work quickly, Violet. The madam is going to take what she wants. When she paid for you, she paid for everything that belongs to you. Whatever she does not want she will sell—including you, if you don't behave. Hurry now. Take only the most precious. If you take too many things, she'll know what you've done."

I refused to budge. Look what Mother's selfishness had done. I was a virgin courtesan. Why would I want to cling to her belongings?

"Well, if you don't want anything," Magic Gourd said, "I'll take a few things for myself." She plucked the lilac dress hanging in the wardrobe. I stifled a shout. She folded it and tucked it under her jacket. She opened the box with the pieces of amber. "These aren't good quality, misshapen in a dozen ways. And they are dirty inside— *aiya!*—insects. Why did she want to keep these? Americans are so strange."

She pulled out another package, wrapped in paper. It was a little sailor suit, a white and blue shirt and pantalets, as well as a hat, like those worn by American sailors. She must have bought those for Teddy when he was a baby and was planning to show them to him as proof of her enduring love. Magic Gourd put the sailor suit back into the valise. Madam had a grandson, she said. She picked up the fox wrap with its dangling baby paws. She gave it a wistful look and dropped it back in. From the jewelry box, she removed only a necklace with a gold locket. I took it from her, opened it, and peeled out the tiny photographs on each side, one of Mother, one of me.

And then she fished in deeper and pulled out the two paintings. She unrolled the one of my mother and laughed. "So naughty!" She laid out the one with the gloomy landscape. "So realistic. I have never seen a sunset this beautiful." She put the paintings in her pile.

As I dressed, she recited the names of the courtesans. Spring Bud, Spring Leaf, Petal, Camellia, and Kumquat. "You don't have to remember their names for now. Just call them your flower sisters.

You'll know them soon enough by their natures." She chattered on. "Spring Leaf and Spring Bud are sisters. One is smart and one is foolish. Both are kind in their hearts, but one is sad and does not like men. I will leave it to you to guess which is which. Petal pretends to be nice, but she is sneaky and does anything to be Madam's favorite. Camellia is very smart. She can read and write. She spends a little money every month to buy a novel or more paper for writing her poems. She has audacity in her ink brush. I like her because she's very honest. Kumquat is a classical beauty with a peach-shaped face. She is also like a child who reaches for what she wants without thinking. Five years ago, when she was with a first-class house, she took a lover and her earnings dwindled to nothing. It's the usual story among us."

"That was the reason you had to leave, wasn't it?" I said. "You had a lover."

She huffed. "You heard that?" She fell silent, and her eyes grew dreamy. "I had many lovers over the years—sometimes when I had patrons, sometimes when I did not. I gave too much money to one. But my last lover did not cheat me out of money. He loved me with a true heart." She looked at me. "You know him. Pan the Poet."

I felt a cool breeze over my skin and shivered.

"Gossip reached my patron that I had sad sex with a ghost and that he was stuck in my body. My patron no longer wanted to touch me and asked for his contract money back. Puffy Cloud spread that rumor. That girl has something wrong with her heart. In every house, there is one like her."

"Did you really have the Poet Ghost in your body?"

"What a stupid thing to ask! We did not have sex. How could we? He was a ghost. We shared only our spirit, and it was more than enough. Many girls in this business never experience true love. They take lovers and patrons, hoping they will become concubines so they can be called Second Wife, Third Wife, even Tenth Wife, if they are desperate. But that is not love. It is searching for a change of luck. With Pan the Poet, I felt only love, and he felt the same for me. We had nothing to gain from each other. That was how we knew it was true. When I left Hidden Jade Path, he had to remain because he was part of the house. Without him, I felt no life in me. I wanted to kill myself to be with him . . . You think I'm crazy. I can see it in your face. *Hnh*. Little Miss Educated American. You don't know anything. Get dressed now. If you're late, Madam will poke another nostril into your face." She held up the pajamas. "Madam wants all the girls to call her Mother. Mother Ma. They are just sounds without true meaning. Say it over and over again until you can swallow them without choking. Mother Ma, Mother Ma. Behind her back, we call her the old bustard." Magic Gourd imitated a big squawking bird flapping its wings and swooping around to guard her flock. And then she announced: "Mother Ma did not like your name *Vivi*. She said it made no sense. To her, it was just two sounds. I suggested she use the Chinese word for the violet flower."

She pronounced the word for "violet" as *zizi,* like the sound of a mosquito. *Zzzzz! Zzzzz!*

"It's just a word," she said. "It's better that they call you that. You are not that person. You can have a secret name that belongs to you—your American nickname, Vivi, or the flower name your mother called you. My courtesan name is Magic Gourd, but in my heart I am Golden Treasure. I gave that name to myself."

At breakfast, I did as Magic Gourd had advised. "Good morning, Mother Ma. Good morning, flower sisters."

The old bustard was pleased to see me in my new clothes. "You see, fate changes when you change your clothes." She used her fingers like tongs to turn my face right and then left. It sickened me to be touched by her. Her fingers were cold and gray, like those of a corpse. "I knew a girl from Harbin who had your coloring," she said. "Same eyes. She had Manchu blood. In the old days, those Manchus were like dogs who raped any girl—Russian, Japanese, Korean, green-eyed, blue-eyed, brown-eyed, yellow or red hair, big or tiny—whatever was in grabbing distance as they raced by on their ponies. I wouldn't be surprised if there's a pack of ponies that are half-Manchu." She grasped my face again. "Whoever your father was, he had the Manchu bloodlines in him, that's for certain. I can see it in your jaw and the longer Mongolian taper of the eyes, and also their green color. I heard that one of the concubines to Emperor Qianlong had green eyes. We'll say you're a descendant of hers."

The table was set with savory, sweet, and spicy dishes—bamboo shoots and honeyed lotus root, pickled radishes, and smoked fish—so many tasty things. I was hungry but ate sparingly and with the delicate manners I had seen courtesans use at Hidden Jade Path. I wanted to show her she had nothing to teach me. I picked up a tiny peanut with my ivory chopsticks, put it to my lips and set it on my tongue, as if it were a pearl being placed on a brocade pillow.

"Your upbringing shows," the old bustard said. "A year from now, when you make your debut, you can charm men to near insanity. What do you say to that?"

"Thank you, Mother Ma."

"You see," she said to the others with a pleased smile. "Now she obeys." When Mother Ma picked up her chopsticks, I had a closer look at her fingers. They resembled rotting bananas. I watched her peck at the remaining bits of food on her plate. The sneaky courtesan Petal stood up and quickly served the madam more bamboo shoots and fish, but did not touch the last of the honeyed lotus root. She waited until Spring Bud helped herself to the last big piece, then said in a chiding tone, "Give that to Mother. You know how much she loves sweets." She made a show of shoving her own lotus root pieces onto Madam Ma's plate. The madam praised Petal for treating her like a true mother. Spring Bud showed no expression and looked at no one. Magic Gourd looked sideways at me and whispered, "She's furious."

When Mother Ma rose from her chair, she wobbled, and Petal ran to steady her. The madam crossly swatted her away with her fan. "I'm not a feeble old woman. It's just my feet. These shoes are too tight. Ask the shoemaker to come." She lifted her skirt. Her ankles were gray and swollen. I guessed her feet under her bindings were even worse.

As soon as the madam left the table, Camellia said to Magic Gourd in an overly polite tone, "My Peer, I cannot help saying that the peach color of your new jacket flatters your coloring. A new client would think you're at least ten years younger."

Magic Gourd cursed her. Camellia smirked and walked away.

"We tease each other all the time like that," Magic Gourd said. "I flatter her thin hair. She flatters my complexion. We laugh rather than cry about our age. The years go by." I was tempted to tell Magic Gourd that the peach color did not flatter her at all. An older woman wearing a younger woman's colors only looks as old as she is pretending not to be.

I followed Magic Gourd's advice. I did what the madam expected. I performed the toady greetings, answered politely when she talked to me. I showed the rituals of respect to the flower sisters. How easy it was to be insincere. Early on, I received a few slaps whenever I had facial expressions that Mother Ma judged to be American. I did not know what they were until I felt the blows and she threatened to grind down any part of me that reminded her of foreigners. When I stared at her as she scolded me, she slapped me for that as well. I learned that the expression she wanted was cowering respect.

One morning, after I had been at the Hall of Tranquility for nearly a month, Magic Gourd told me that I would be moving into a new room in a few days. The old one was meant to humble me. It was a place to store old furniture. "You'll have my boudoir," she said. "It's almost as nice as the one I had at Hidden Jade Path. I'm moving somewhere else."

I knew what this meant. She was leaving for someplace worse. I would have no ally if she did. "We'll share the room," I said.

"How can I do my wooing when you're in the room playing with dolls? Oh, don't worry about me. I have a friend in the Japanese Concession. We're renting a two-story *shikumen* and will run an opium flower house, the two of us, with no madam to take the profits and charge us for every little plate of food . . ."

She was going to lower herself to an ordinary prostitute. They would simply smoke a few pipes and then she would lie down and prop open her legs to men like Cracked Egg.

Magic Gourd frowned, knowing what I was thinking. "Don't you dare pity me. I'm not ashamed. Why should I be?"

"It's the Japanese Concession," I said.

"What's wrong with that?"

"They hate Chinese people there."

"Who told you that?"

"My mother. That's why she didn't let Japanese customers into her house."

"She didn't allow them because she knew they'd take away the best business opportunities. If people hate them, it's because they envy their success. But what does any of that matter to me? My friend told me they're no worse than other foreigners, and they're scared to death of the syphilitic pox. They inspect everyone, even at first-class houses. Can you imagine?"

Three days later, Magic Gourd was gone—but for only three hours. She returned and dropped a gift at my feet, which landed with a familiar soft thump. It was Carlotta. I instantly burst into tears and grabbed her, nearly crushing her in my hug.

"What? No thanks to me?" Magic Gourd said. I apologized and declared her a true friend, a kind heart, a secret immortal. "Enough, enough."

"I'll have to find some way to hide her," I said.

"Ha! When Madam finds out I brought her here, I wouldn't be surprised if she hangs red banners over the door and sets off a hundred rounds of firecrackers to welcome this goddess of war. Two nights ago, I let some rats loose in the old bustard's room. Did you hear her shouts? One of the servants thought her room was on fire and ran to get the brigade. I pretended to be shocked when I heard the reason for her screams. I told her: 'Too bad we don't have a cat. Violet used to have one, a fierce little hunter, but the woman who's now the madam at Hidden Jade Path won't give her up.' The old bustard sent me off immediately to tell Golden Dove that she paid for you and everything you own, including the cat."

Golden Dove had been glad to relinquish the beast, Magic Gourd reported, and Little Ocean cried copious tears, proof she had treated Carlotta well. But Magic Gourd brought back more than Carlotta. She had news about Fairweather and my mother.

"He had a gambling habit, a fondness for opium, and a mountain of debt. That was not surprising. He took money that people had invested in his companies and used it to gamble, thinking he could then make up for his previous business losses. As his debts piled up, he reported to his investors that the factory had suffered from a typhoon or fire, or that a warlord had taken over the factories. He always had an answer like that, and he sometimes used the same excuse for different companies. He did not know that the investor of one of his companies was a member of the Green Gang, and the investor of another was also with the Green Gang. They learned how many typhoons had happened in the last year. It is one thing to swindle a gangster and another to make fools of them. They were going to hang him upside down and dip his head in coals. But he told them he had a way to pay them back—by chasing away the American madam of Hidden Jade Path.

"*Ai-ya*. How can a woman so smart become so foolish? It is a weakness in many people—even the richest, the most powerful, and the most respected. They risk everything for the body's desire and the belief they are the most special of all people on earth because a liar tells them so.

"Once your mother was gone, the Green Gang printed up a fake deed that said your mother had sold Hidden Jade Path to a man who was also a gang member. They recorded the deed with an authority in the International Settlement, one who was also part of the gang. What could Golden Dove do? She could not go to the American Consulate for him. She had no deed with her name on it because your mother was going to mail it after she reached San Francisco. One of the courtesans told Golden Dove that Puffy Cloud had bragged that she and Fairweather were now rich. Fairweather had exchanged the steamer tickets to San Francisco for two first-class steamer tickets to Hong Kong. They were going to present themselves as Shanghai socialites, who had come to Hong Kong to invest in new companies on behalf of Western movie stars!

"Golden Dove was so angry when she told me this. *Oyo!* I thought her eyes would explode—and they did, with tears. She said that a new gang with the Triad did not care about the standards of a first-class house. They own a syndicate with a dozen houses that provide high profits at low costs. There is no longer any leisurely wooing for our beauties, and no baubles, only money. The Cloud Beauties would have left, but the gangsters gave them extra sweet money to stay, and now they are caught in a trap of debt. The gangsters made Cracked Egg a common manservant, and now the customers who come are swaggering petty officials and the newly rich of insignificant businesses. These men are privy to the attentions of the same girls once courted only by those far more important. There is no quicker way to throw away the reputation of a house than to allow the underlings to share the same vaginas as their bosses. Water flows to the lowest ditch."

"They have no right," I said over and over again.

"Only Americans think they have rights," Magic Gourd said. "What laws of heaven give you more rights and allow you to keep them? They are words on paper written by men who make them up and claim them. One day they can blow away, just like that."

She took my hands. "Violet, I must tell you about pieces of paper that blew back and forth between here and San Francisco. Someone sent a letter to your mother claiming it was from the American Consulate. It said you had died in an accident—run over in the road or something. They included a death certificate stamped with seals. It had your real name on there, not the one Fairweather was going to give you. Your mother sent a cable to Golden Dove to ask if this was true. And Golden Dove had to decide whether to tell your mother the death certificate was fake, or to keep the beauties, you, and herself from being tortured, maimed, or even killed. There was really no choice."

Magic Gourd removed a letter from her sleeve and I read it without breathing. It was from Mother. The letter rambled on about her feelings in getting the letter, her disbelief, her agony in waiting to hear from Golden Dove.

> *I'm tormented by the thought that Violet might have believed before she died that I had left her behind deliberately. To think those unhappy thoughts might have been her last!*

I seethed. She chose to believe I was on board because she was eager to sail away to her new life with Teddy and Lu Shing. I asked Magic Gourd for paper so I could write a letter in return. I would tell Mother I wasn't fooled by her lies and false grief. Magic Gourd told me no letter from me would ever leave Shanghai. No cable could be sent. The gangsters would make sure of that. That's why the letter Golden Dove wrote to my mother had been the lies they told her to write.

I BECAME A different girl, a lost girl without a mother. I was neither American nor Chinese. I was not Violet nor Vivi nor Zizi. I now lived in an invisible place made of my own dwindling breath, and because no one else could see it, they could not yank me out of it.

How long did my mother stand at the back of the boat? Was it cold on deck? Did she miss the fox wrap she put in my valise? Did she wait until her skin prickled before she went inside? How long did she take to choose a dress for the first dinner at sea? Was it the tulle and lace? How long did she wait in the cabin before she knew no knock would come to her door? How long did she lie awake staring into the pitch-dark? Did she see my face there? Did she see the worst? Did she wait to watch the sun come up or did she stay in bed past noon? How many days did she despair, realizing each wave was one more wave farther from me? How long did it take for the ship to reach San Francisco, to her home? How long by the fastest route? How long by the slowest route? How long did she wait before Teddy was in her arms? How many nights did she dream of me as she slept in her bedroom with the sunny yellow walls? Was the bed still next to a window that was next to a tree with many limbs? How many birds did she count, knowing that was how many I was supposed to see?

How long would it have taken a boat to return? How long by the fastest route, by the slowest route?

How slowly those days went by as I waited to know which route she took. How long it has been since the slowest boats have all come and have all gone.

THE NEXT DAY, I moved into Magic Gourd's boudoir. I had kept from crying as she packed up her belongings. She held up my mother's dress and the two rolled-up paintings and asked if she could take them. I nodded. And then she was gone. The only part of my past that remained was Carlotta.

An hour later, Magic Gourd burst in the room. "I am not leaving, after all," she announced, "thanks to the old bustard's black fingers." She had been concocting a plan for two days and proudly unveiled how it unfolded. Just before she left, she met with Mother Ma in the common room to settle her debts. When Mother Ma started doing calculations on the abacus, Magic Gourd raised the alarm.

"'*Ai-ya!* Your fingers!' I said to her. 'They've grown worse, I see. This is terrible. You don't deserve this misfortune of health.' The old bustard held up her hands and said the color was due to the liver pills she took. I told her I was relieved to hear this, because I thought it was due to something else and I was going to tell her to try the mercury treatment. Of course, she knew as well as anyone that mercury is used for syphilis. So she said to me: 'I've never had the pox and don't you be starting rumors that I do.'

"'Calm down,' I said to her. 'My words jumped out of my mouth too soon and only because of a story I just heard about Persimmon. She once worked in the Hall of Tranquility. That was before my time, about twenty years, but you were already here. One of the customers gave her the pox, and she got rid of the sores, but then they came back, and her fingers turned black, just like yours.'

"Mother Ma said she did not know of any courtesan named Persimmon who had worked in the Hall of Tranquility. Of course, she didn't. I had made her up. I went on to say she was a maid, not a courtesan, so it was no wonder she would not know her by name. I described her as having a persimmon-shaped face, small eyes, broad nose, small mouth. The old bustard insisted her memory was better than mine. But then the clouds of memory lifted. 'Was she dark-skinned, a plump girl who spoke with a Fujian accent?'

"'That's the one!' I said and went on to tell her that a customer used to go through the back door to use her services for cheap. She needed the money because her husband was an opium sot and her children were starving. Mother Ma and I grumbled a bit about conniving maids. And then I said Persimmon's customer was a conniver, too. He called himself Commissioner Li and was the secret lover of one of the courtesans. That got the old bustard to sit up straight. It was an open secret among the old courtesans that the old bustard had taken the commissioner as a lover.

"'Ah, you remember him?' I said. She tried to show she was not bothered.

"'He was an important man,' she said. 'Everyone knew him.'

"I poked a bit more. 'He called himself Commissioner,' I said. 'But where did he work?'

"And she said, 'It had something to do with the foreign banks and he was paid a lot of money to advise them.'

"So I said, 'That's strange. He told you and no one else that.'

"Then she said, 'No, no. He didn't tell me.' I heard it from someone else.'

"I made my face look a little doubtful before going on: 'I wonder who said that. As the rumors go, everyone thought he was too important to question. One of the old courtesans told me that if he had said he was ten meters tall, everyone would have been too afraid to correct him. He sat at the table with his legs wide apart, like this, and wore a scowl on his face, as if he were the duke of sky and mountains.' That was the way all important men sit, so of course, she could picture him in her mind.

"The old bustard said, 'Why would I remember that?'

"I sprang my trap. 'It turns out he was a fake, not a commissioner at all.'

" '*Wah!*' She jumped out of her chair, and then immediately pretended the news meant nothing to her. 'An insect just bit my leg,' she said. 'That's why I leapt up.' To improve the lie, she scratched herself.

"I gave her more to scratch: 'He never came with friends to host his own parties. Remember that? People were expected to invite him to their parties once he arrived. Such an honor! Everyone wanted to please him. In fact, one of the courtesans was so impressed with his title, she gave her goods away, hoping he would make her Mrs. Commissioner. She took him into her boudoir and she never knew he had already stuck himself into Persimmon just before visiting her.'

"The old bustard's eyes grew really big when I said that. I was beginning to feel a little sorry for her, but I had to go on. 'And it is even worse than that,' I said. I told her what I had heard about Commissioner Li, facts she would clearly remember. 'Whenever he shared this courtesan's bed, he told her to go ahead and put a full three-dollar charge on his bill—a charge for a party call, even though he had not held a party. He said he did not want her to lose money from spending so much time with him instead of with other suitors. Anyone would think he was generous beyond belief. By the New Year, he owed nearly two hundred dollars. As you know, it's customary for all clients of the house to settle their accounts that day. He never did. He was the only one. He never showed his face again. Two hundred dollars' worth of fucks.'

"I saw the old bustard's mouth was locked into an expression of bitterness. I think she was trying to keep from cursing him. I said what I knew she was thinking: 'Men like that should have their cocks shrivel up and fall off.' She nodded vigorously. I went on. 'People say that the only gift he gave her was syphilitic sores. They assumed he did, since the maid had it—a sore on her mouth, then her cheek, and who knows how many more in places we couldn't see.'

"The blood drained from the old bustard's face. She said, 'Maybe it was the maid's husband who gave her syphilis.'

"I was not expecting her to come up with this, so I had to think fast. 'Everyone knew that the old sot could barely lean over the side of his bed to piss. He was a bag of bones. But what difference did it make whether she had it first or he did? In the end, they both had the pox, and everyone figured he must have given it to the courtesan, and she probably did not even know. Persimmon drank *mahuang* tea all day long, to no avail. When her nipples dripped pus, she covered them in mercury and got very sick. The sores dried up, and she thought she was cured. Six months ago, her hands turned black, and then she died.'

"The old bustard looked as if a pot had fallen on her head. Really, I felt sorry for her, but I had to be ruthless. I had to save myself. Anyway, I didn't go on, even though I had thought to say that someone learned that the Commissioner of Lies had died of the same black hand disease. I told her that was the reason I had feared for her when I saw her hands. She mumbled that it was not a disease but the cursed liver pills. I gave her a sympathetic look and said we should ask the doctor to check her chi to get rid of this ailment, since those pills were doing no good. Then I went on: 'I hope no one believes you have the pox. Lies spread faster than you can catch them. And if people see you touching the beauties with your black fingers, they might say the whole house is contaminated. Then the public health bureaucrats will come, everyone will have to be tested, and the house closed down until they verify we are clean. Who wants that? I don't want someone examining me and getting a peek for free. And even if you're clean, those bastards are so corrupt, you'll have to give them money so they don't hold up the report.'

"I let this news settle in before I said what I had wanted all along. 'Mother Ma, it just occurred to me that I might help you keep this rumor from starting. Until you correct the balance in the liver, let me serve as Violet's teacher and attendant. I'll teach her all the things I know. As you recall, I was one of the top Ten Beauties in my day.'

"The old bustard fell for it. She nodded weakly. For good measure, I said: 'You can be sure that if the brat needs a beating, I'll be quick to do it. Whenever you hear her screaming for mercy, you'll know that I'm making good progress.'

"What do you think of that, Violet? Clever, eh? All you have to do is stand by the door once or twice a day and shout for forgiveness."

THERE WAS NO single moment when I accepted that I had become a courtesan. I simply fought less against it. I was like someone in prison who was about to be executed. I no longer threw the clothes given to me on the floor. I wore them without protest. When I received summer jackets and pantalets made of a light silk, I was glad for the cool comfort of them. But I took no pleasure in their color or style. The world was dull. I did not know what was happening outside these walls, whether there were still protestors in the streets, whether all the foreigners had been driven away. I was a kidnapped American girl caught in an adventure story in which the latter chapters had been ripped out.

One day, when it was raining hard, Magic Gourd said to me, "Violet, when you were growing up you pretended to be a courtesan. You flirted with customers, lured your favorites. And now you are saying you never imagined you would be one?"

"I'm an American. American girls do not become courtesans."

"Your mother was the madam of a first-class courtesan house."

"She was not a courtesan."

"How do you know that? All the Chinese madams began as courtesans. How else would they learn the business?"

I was nauseated by the thought. She might have been a courtesan—or worse, an ordinary prostitute on one of the boats in the harbor. She was hardly chaste. She took lovers. "She chose her life," I said at last. "No one told her what to do."

"How do you know that she chose to enter this life?"

"Mother never would have allowed anyone to force her to do anything," I said, then thought: *Look what she forced on me.*

"Do you look down on those who cannot choose what they do in life?"

"I pity them," I said. I refused to see myself as part of that pitiful lot. I would escape.

"Do you pity me? Can you respect someone you pity?"

"You protect me and I'm grateful."

"That's not respect. Do you think we are equals?"

"You and I are different . . . by race and the country we belong to. We cannot expect the same in life. So we are not equal."

"You mean I must hope for less than you do."

"That is not my doing."

Suddenly, she turned red in the face. "I am no longer less than you! I am more. I can expect more. You will expect less. Do you know how people will see you from now on? Look at my face and think of it as yours. You and I are no better than actors, opera singers, and acrobats. This is now your life. Fate once made you American. Fate took it away. You are the bastard half who was your father—Han, Manchu,

Cantonese, whoever he was. You are a flower that will be plucked over and over again. You are now at the bottom of society."

"I am an American and no one can change that, even if I am held against my will."

"*Oyo!* How terrible for poor Violet. She is the only one whose circumstances changed against her will." She sat down and continued to make chuffing noises as she threw me disgusted looks. "Against her will . . . You can't make me! *Oyo!* Such suffering she's had. You're the same as everyone here, because now you have the same worries. Maybe I should do what I promised Mother Ma and beat you until you learn your place." She fell silent, and I was grateful that her tirade had ended.

But then she spoke again, now in a soft and sad voice, as if she were a child. She looked away and remembered when her circumstances changed, again and again.

Magic Gourd

I was only five, just a tiny girl, when my uncle took me away from my family and sold me to a merchant's wife as her slave. My uncle told me he was doing only what my father and mother had ordered him to do. To this day, I don't believe that was true. If I did, my heart would turn completely bitter and cold. Maybe my father wanted to be rid of me. But my mother must have been grief-stricken when she discovered I was gone. I am sure she was. I have a memory that she was. Although how could I know that when I did not see her after I was stolen? I have thought about this for many years. If my mother did not want me, why did the bastard take me away in the middle of the night? Why did he sneak me away?

I cried all the way to the rich man's house. He bargained and sold me as if I were a piglet who would grow fat and tasty. The merchant had a wife by an arranged marriage, as well as three concubines. The middle concubine was called Third Wife, but she was first in his heart. She was the wife who took me as her maid.

The merchant, I soon discovered, found excuses to go to her room more often than to the others. Looking back, it seems strange that she had such power over him. She was the oldest of the wives. Her breasts and lips were larger than what was considered ideal. Her face was not delicate. But she did have a certain way about her that mesmerized her husband. She spoke with a slight tilt of the head and in a soft melodious voice. She knew the right thing to say to soothe his mind, to restore him. I overheard the other concubines say she came from the brothel life in Soochow and she had wrapped her legs around a thousand men and sucked out their brains and good sense. They were jealous of my mistress, so who knows if their gossip was true.

Like my mistress, I was not born with great beauty. My big eyes were my best feature; my big feet were my worst. They had been bound, and they burst from their bindings after I arrived in the merchant's house, and because I walked on tiptoe, no one knew any better and I did not wrap them up again. Unlike the other maids, I was not just obedient but eager to do anything to please my mistress. I felt proud that I was the maid to the merchant's favorite, the most highly valued of his wives. I brought her plum flower blooms to put in her hair. I always made sure her tea was scalding hot. I brought her boiled peanuts and other snacks throughout the day.

Because I was so attentive, my mistress decided I would one day be a suitable concubine to one of her younger sons—not as the second wife, but perhaps the third. Imagine me being called Third Wife! From then on, she treated me more kindly and gave me better food to eat. I wore prettier clothes and better-made longer jackets and pantaloons. To help me become a suitable concubine, she criticized my manners and the way I spoke. And that is who I would have become if the master, that ugly dog's ass, had not ordered me one day to take off my clothes so he could be the first to break me open. I was nine. I could not refuse. That was my life, to obey the master because my mistress obeyed him. When it was over, I was bleeding and could barely stand from the near-fainting pain. He told me to get hot towels for him. He made me clean him, to wipe away all trace of me.

Whenever he visited my mistress, I would be standing outside the room, waiting. I could hear her teasing high voice, his low murmuring, "This is good, this is good. Your moist folds are like a white lotus." He was always talking about his sex organs and hers. He would grunt, and she uttered little cries that sounded like fear and girlish delight. Then they would fall silent, and I would run and get the hot towels, so that by the time she called for them, I could bring them in immediately.

I would pretend I could not see the master behind the gauzy bed curtain. I saw the shadows of my mistress as she washed him. She would throw the dirty towels on the floor, and I rushed forward to take them away, nauseated by the smell of the two of them. I then had to return and wait. When my mistress left, I went in, and he lay me on my back or stomach, and he did what he wanted, and sometimes I fainted from the pain. So that became part of my circumstances, to open my legs, to bring him hot towels, to remove my scent from him, to return to my room, and to rub his scent off me.

When I was eleven, I became pregnant, and that was how my mistress discovered her husband had been rutting me. She did not blame me, and she did not blame her husband. Many husbands did this to maids. She simply said I was no longer suitable to be her son's concubine. Another maid brought me a broth and she put this in a long glass tube and stuck this inside me. I had no idea what she was doing until I felt it pierce me and I screamed and screamed as other servants held me down. Later, I had terrible cramps for two days and then a bloody ball fell out and I fainted. When I woke I was feverish and in terrible agony. My insides were turned outside and were so swollen, I thought the baby had not fallen out but was growing. I found out later the maid had sewn me up with the hair from a horse's tail so that I could break open again like a virgin. But now pus was growing where a baby would have been.

During my fever days, I could not rise out of bed. I sometimes heard people say that my color was green and that I would soon die. I had seen a green corpse once and imagined myself looking the same. I would be afraid of myself. "Green ghost, green ghost," I kept saying. The master came to see me, and I saw him through the slits of my eyes and gave a scream of fear. I thought he was going to rape me again. He looked nervous and said soothing words, telling me he had always tried to take good care of me and that I should remember that he never beat me. He thought I was so stupid I would be grateful and not come back to haunt him as a ghost. I had already told myself I would. A doctor came, and my arms and legs were tied down before he inserted sacs of medicine, which felt like burning rocks. I begged them to let me die instead. The fever stopped after a week, and my mistress let me stay another month until my insides were no longer outside, and the horsetail stitches no longer showed. And then she sold me to a brothel. Luckily, it was the first-class house where she had worked before the merchant took her as his concubine. The madam inspected me, top to bottom, and poked around the opening of my vagina. She was satisfied that I was unbroken.

They named me Dewdrop. Everyone said I was very clever because I quickly learned to sing and recite poetry. The men admired me but did not touch. They said I was precious, a little flower—all sorts of things that made me truly happy for the first time in my life. I had been so starved for affection I could not eat enough of it. When I was thirteen, my defloration was sold to a rich scholar. I was fearful that he would discover the truth about my virginity. What if he could tell I had been sewn up? He would be angry and beat me to death, and the madam would be furious, and she, too, would beat me to death. But what could I do?

When the scholar took my hips, I clamped my legs together out of fear that he would soon discover the truth. But when the scholar finally broke through the horsetail thread, it was just as painful as the first time and I screamed and cried genuine tears. Blood poured out. Later, when the scholar inspected the damage he had caused, he pulled out the loose hair of a horse's tail. "Ah, we meet again," he said. So this was not the first time the ruse had been played on him. I shivered and cried, telling him the master of my old house ordered me to fetch hot towels when I was nine, and that my mistress sewed me up after the baby fell out. I babbled about my fever and how I nearly became a green ghost.

He stood and got dressed. The maid brought in hot towels, and he said he would clean himself. He seemed sad. After he left, I waited for the madam to come into the room and beat me. I imagined I would be driven out of the house. Instead, she came to me and inspected the blood on the bed. "So much!" she exclaimed in a pleased voice. She gave me a dollar and said the scholar had given this extra gift for me. He was a very kind man, and I was sorry to hear that he died a few years later of a high fever.

So that is what it is like to be kidnapped and later taken to the underworld of the living. You are not the only one. And one day, whether your defloration happens here or in the arms of a lover or a husband, you probably won't need a horse's tail to be part of your marriage bed.

A MONTH AFTER Magic Gourd told Mother Ma the pox story, the old lady turned for the worst, and everyone agreed she might not last to Spring Festival. Not only did her fingers remain black, but her legs also took on the same hue. Because of the story Magic Gourd had made up, she truly feared she had the pox. We did not know what she really had. Maybe it was the liver pills. Perhaps it really was the pox.

But then the old bustard's maid came to us in the common room when we were having our breakfast. While carrying out her mistress's chamber pot, she said, she stumbled and some of the piss hit her face and went into her mouth. It tasted sweet. Another maid had told her that a former mistress had sweet-tasting urine and that her hands and feet had turned black as well. So then we knew she had the sugar blood disease.

A doctor came, and over Mother Ma's protests, he cut off her bindings. Her feet were black and green, oozing with pus. She refused to go to the hospital. So the doctor cut off her feet right there. She did not scream. She lost her mind.

Three days later, she called me to sit with her in the garden where she was airing her footless legs. I had heard that she was making amends to all. She believed her disease was caused by her karma and that it might not be too late to reverse its direction.

"Violet, ah," she said sweetly, "I hear you have learned good manners. Don't eat too many greasy foods. It will ruin your complexion." She patted my face gently. "You are so sad. To keep false hopes is to prolong misery. You will grow to hate everything and everyone, and insanity is certain. I was once like you. I was the daughter of a scholar family and I was kidnapped when I was twelve and taken to a first-class house. I resisted and cried and threatened to kill myself by drinking rat poison. But then I had very nice customers, kind patrons. I was the favorite of many. I had many freedoms. When I was fifteen, my family found me. They took me away, and because I was damaged goods, they married me off as a concubine to a nice man with a vicious mother. It was worse than being a slave! I ran away and went back to the courtesan house. I was so happy, so grateful to return to the good life. Even my husband was happy for me. He became one of my best customers. This is the beautiful tale you can one day tell a young courtesan about your own life."

How could any girl think that was a lucky life? And yet, if I were Chinese and compared this life with all the possibilities, I, too, might believe over time that I was lucky to be here. But I was only half-Chinese, and I still held tight to the American half that believed I had other choices.

The doctor came a few days later. He cut off one of Mother Ma's legs, and the next day, he cut off the other leg. She could no longer move around and had to be carried on a little palanquin. A week later, she lost the black fingers, then her hands, one piece after another until there was nothing left, except the trunk and head. She told everyone she was not going to die. She said she wanted to stay alive so she could treat us better, like daughters. She promised to spoil us. As she weakened, she became kinder and kinder. She praised everyone. She told Magic Gourd that she had musical talent.

The next day, Mother Ma did not remember who I was. She did not remember anything. Everything disappeared, like words in breath. She talked in dreams and called out that the ghosts of Persimmon and Commissioner Li had come to take her to the underworld. "They said I am nearly as black as they are, and we three would live together and comfort one another. So I'm ready to go."

Magic Gourd felt very bad that Mother Ma believed in her lie, even to the end. "*Shh- shh*," she said. "I'll bring you a soup to turn your skin white again." But by morning, the old lady was dead.

"Hardship can harden even the best person," Magic Gourd said. "Remember that, Violet. If I become this way, remember the good things I did for you and forget the wounds."

As she washed Madam Ma's body to prepare her for the underworld, she said, "Mother, I will always remember that you said I played the zither especially well."

GOLDEN DOVE CAME to the house a week after Mother Ma died. It had been five months since I had seen her and yet she seemed to have aged a great deal. I felt a flash of anger at first. She had had the opportunity to tell my mother I was still alive. She took away my chance to be saved. I was about to demand she write my mother again, then realized I was acting like a selfish child. There had never been an opportunity for her to save me. We all would have suffered. I had heard many stories since coming to the Hall of Tranquility about people who had been killed when they went against the wishes of the Green

Gang. I fell into Golden Dove's arms and did not have to say anything. She knew the life I had had with my mother. She knew all the ways in which I was spoiled. She knew how much I had suffered as a child, believing that my mother did not love me anymore.

Over tea, she told us that the house had lost its luster. The corners were filled with dirt, the chandeliers had grown chains of dust. And after only a few months, the furniture had become shabby, and all that was unusual and daring in my mother's house simply looked odd. I imagined my room, my bed, my treasure box of feathers and pens, my rows of books. I saw in my mind the lesson room, where I looked through a crack in the curtains of the French glass doors and saw my mother and Lu Shing talking quietly, deciding what to do.

"I'm leaving Shanghai," Golden Dove said. "I'm going to Soochow, where life is kinder to those who are growing old. I have a little money. Maybe I'll open a shop of some kind. Or maybe I'll do nothing except drink tea with friends and play mahjong like the old matriarchs."

One thing was certain in her mind: She would not become the madam of another house. "These days, a madam has to be ruthless and mean. She has to make people afraid of what she might do. If she is not harsh, she might as well open the doors and let the rats and ruffians come in and take what they want."

She gave me news of Fairweather. He was a favorite topic among patrons and courtesans at parties. After he duped my mother, they recounted how cunning and handsome he was. No one thought he had done anything terribly wrong. He was an American who had swindled another American. I was wounded to hear how unsympathetic people were toward my mother. I had never known how much they disliked her.

In Hong Kong, he and Puffy Cloud lived in a villa halfway up the peak. Within a month, due to his gambling habit and Puffy Cloud's love of opium, they ran out of money. Puffy Cloud returned to brothel life, and Fairweather tried one more time to swindle a businessman, a taipan who was a member of another Triad. "Fairweather wasn't able to steal the taipan's money. Instead he stole the heart and virginity of his daughter. All the rumors were the same: Fairweather was stuffed headfirst into a large sack of rice, and with his feet paddling in the air, he was thrown into the harbor, where he promptly sank. To picture it made me feel a little sick, but I was also not sorry to hear he had a frightful death."

When Magic Gourd left to order tea and snacks, Golden Dove spoke to me in English to avoid feeding gossip to the eavesdroppers. "I've known you since the day you were born. You are like your mother in so many ways. You often see too much, too clearly, and sometimes you see more than what is there. But sometimes you see far less. You are never satisfied with the amount or kind of love you have. You want more and you suffer from never being able to have enough. And even though more may be in front of you, you don't see it. You are suffering greatly now because you are unable to escape from this prison. You will find a way out of this place one day. This is a temporary place of suffering. But I hope you don't suffer forever from keeping love from your heart because of what has happened. That could have happened to your mother, but you saved her after she was betrayed. All the love she has been able to feel is because you were born and you opened her closed heart. One day, when you leave this place, come visit me in Soochow. I will be waiting."

"TAKE OFF YOUR shoes," Magic Gourd ordered. "Stockings, too." She frowned. "Point the toes." She sighed and shook her head and continued to stare at them, as if she could make them disappear by thought alone.

The new madam of the house was coming in two days, and Magic Gourd was anxious that I be allowed to stay, so that she could remain, too, as my attendant. She had the shoemaker make a pair of stiff slippers that forced me to stand on just the balls of my feet.

He added cuffs to mask the heels of my feet and wrapped red ribbons around my ankles. The slippers gave the illusion of a tiny hobbled foot.

"Walk around the room," she ordered.

I pranced like a ballerina. After five minutes, I limped stiffly like a duck without feet. I fell into a chair and refused to try any longer. Magic Gourd pinched my arm hard to make me stand. As soon as I took one step, I toppled and knocked down a flower stand and its vase.

"Your pain is nothing compared with what I had to endure. No one let me sit. No one let me take those shoes off. I fell over and bumped my head and banged my arm. And it was all for nothing." She lifted one of her misshapen feet. It was nearly as large as my natural ones. The instep was a hump. "When I was sold to the merchant's family, no one bothered to keep my feet wrapped, and I was glad at the time. Later, I realized my feet were unlucky two ways—ugly and still big. When I first started in this business, lily feet mattered. If my feet had been smaller I could have been voted the number one beauty of Shanghai. Instead, I wore shoes like the ones on your pampered feet, and I only became number six." She was quiet for a moment. "Of course, number six is not so bad."

In the afternoon, she dyed my hair black, oiled it, and pulled it tight so it would lie flat. In between, she talked.

"No one is here to please you. Don't expect that from me. You are here to please others. You should never displease anyone—not the men who visit you, not the madam, not your flower sisters. Ah, perhaps you do not need to please the menservants and maids. But do not turn them against you. Pleasing others will make your life easier. And the opposite leads to the opposite. You must show the new madam that you understand that. You must be that girl she wants to keep. I promise you—if you are sent to another house, life will be worse. You would not move up in popularity and comfort, only down, down, down. Up and down—that's our life. You mount the stage and do everything to make men love you. Later they will remember those moments with you. But they are not memories of you, but the feeling they were immortal because you made them gods. Remember this, Violet, when you step on the stage, you are not loved for who you are. When you step off, you may not be loved at all." She daubed powder on my face, and clouds of white dust rose. She read my face. "I know you don't believe me now." She ran a brush of kohl over my eyebrows and painted my lips. "I will have to tell you these things many times."

She was wrong. I believed her. I knew life could be cruel. I had seen the downfall of many courtesans. I believed something cruel had happened to my mother. That was why she was loveless and could not truly love anyone, not even me. She could only be selfish. No matter what happened to me in the future, I would not become like her.

Magic Gourd brought out a headband. "I wore this when I was your age. These are just tiny seed pearls, but in time, you will have your own, and maybe the pearls will be real." She placed the headband around the back of my head and pushed it over my face, tucking in the loose strands.

"It's too tight," I complained. "It's pulling at the corners of my eyes."

She lightly slapped the top of my head. "*Oyo!* Are you unable to endure even *this* small amount of pain?" She stood back and looked sternly at the result, then smiled. "Good. Phoenix eyes, the most attractive shape. Look in the mirror. Eyes shaped like an almond and tipped up at the corners. No matter how much I pull back the sides of my hair, I cannot make a phoenix eye. Those eyes came from your father's side of the family."

I could not stop staring at myself in the mirror, turning my head, opening and closing my mouth. My face, where was my face? I touched my cheeks. Why did they look larger? The headband formed a V at my forehead and framed my face into a long oval. My eyebrows tipped upward at the ends as well. The center of my lips was painted into a red pucker, and my face was pale with white powder. With just these few touches, the Western half of me had disappeared. I had become the race I once considered inferior to mine. I smacked my lips and raised my eyebrows. I had the face of a courtesan. Not beautiful, not ugly, but a stranger. At night I scrubbed off the new face, and when I looked in the mirror, I saw how black my hair was. My true face was still there, what had always been there: the phoenix eyes.

The next day, Magic Gourd taught me to put on powder and rouge. The same Chinese mask appeared. I was taken aback but not shocked this time. I realized that all the courtesans looked different after they had prepared their faces for the evening. They wore masks, and throughout the day, I picked up the mirror and looked at mine. I added more powder and tightened the headband so that my eyes were pulled higher. No one, not even my mother, would have recognized me.

THE NEW MADAM was named Li, and she brought with her a courtesan whom she had bought when the girl was four. Under Madam Li's tutelage, Vermillion had grown to become a well-known first-class courtesan, now nineteen years old. She had earned the affection of the madam, who called her "Daughter." They had come from Soochow, where Madam Li owned a first-class courtesan house. It was widely thought that the courtesans from Soochow were the best. That was the opinion of everyone, and not just those in our world. The Soochow girls had a gentle manner, a leisurely way of moving, and their voices were sweet and soft. Many Shanghainese flowers advertised that they were from Soochow. But in the presence of one who truly was, the lie was apparent. Madam Li believed that she could have even greater success in Shanghai, where money flowed from across the sea, and after she bought the Hall of Tranquility, in keeping with the custom of naming first-class houses after the madam or the star, she renamed it in honor of her daughter: the House of Vermillion. It was good advertising as well. All the courtesans were sent away. I was not yet a courtesan, so I had no second-class reputation to overcome. There was a lot of crying and cursing among the departing flower sisters as their trunks were inspected to make sure they were not taking along furs and dresses that belonged to the house. The courtesan Petal threw me a hateful look. "Why is she keeping you? A half-breed belongs on the streets, not in a first-class house."

"What about the courtesan Breeze?" I countered. Magic Gourd had told me recently about Breeze to give me encouragement. She was one part Chinese and another part American.

"The quantity of blood from each is not known," Magic Gourd said. "And there were other rumors—that she had been not only a courtesan, but, early on, a common prostitute. Whoever she was, she worked step-by-step to raise herself to a better status every few months. According to plan, she attracted the affection of a wealthy Western man who took her for his wife. Now she is too powerful for anyone to speak openly about her past. That is what you should do. Step-by-step, higher and higher."

Madam Li invited three courtesans from top-ranked houses, who had been lured by an agreement that they could keep any money earned in the first three months without sharing it with the house.

"Very smart of Madam Li," Magic Gourd told me. "Those girls will work hard to take advantage of the deal, and the House of Vermillion will get off to a fast start."

The cheap furniture and decorations in the salon were replaced that first day with the latest styles. And the courtesans' boudoirs were sumptuously refurbished with silk and velvet, painted glass lamps, carved high-back chairs with tassels, and lace-curtained screens that hid the toilet and bathing tub from view.

My room remained the same. "You won't be entertaining any guests in your room for at least a year," Magic Gourd said, "and we still have to pay rent. Why run up our debt?" I noticed that she had said "our debt," making it clear that she also meant "our money." "What I have in this room," she continued, "is much nicer than what the other girls had. It is still in style and it's all paid for." The furniture was dowdy and worn.

On the second day, we were seated at a table with Madam Li and Vermillion. Magic Gourd had already warned me to remain silent or she would pinch a hole in my thigh.

"Do you know why I am keeping her?" the madam asked Magic Gourd.

"You have goodness for this unfortunate waif and recognize her promise. We are most grateful."

"Goodness? *Pah!* I'm keeping her as a favor to my old flower sister Golden Dove, only that. I have always been indebted to her for something that happened many years ago, and she extracted that debt from me when she moved to Soochow."

Now the debt to Golden Dove had changed hands to me. Madam Li stared hard at me. "You better behave. I did not promise you could stay forever."

Magic Gourd thanked her with excessive words. She said she would be a worthy tutor and attendant. She blathered on about her experience as a first-class courtesan, her ranking as one of the top Ten Beauties of Shanghai.

The madam cut in. "I don't need to hear more of this boasting. It's not going to change the fact that she is mixed race. And I don't want Violet bragging to guests that she's Lulu Mimi's daughter. Everyone's laughing about the American madam who fell into the trap of an American lover who was nothing more than a convict who had escaped from prison before coming to Shanghai."

Fairweather was a convict? "How do you know—" I started to say until Magic Gourd pinched my leg and said to the madam: "As you can already see, she looks nothing like a Westerner now. No one will recognize her. We have given her the name Violet."

Madam Li scowled. "And can you dye her green eyes? How do we explain that?"

Magic Gourd had already prepared an answer. "It can be a literary advantage," she said in an overly elegant voice. "The great poet-painter Luo Ping reputedly had green eyes, and he saw the deepest qualities of the spirit."

Madam Li snorted. "He also saw ghosts from the underworld." She paused. "I don't want paintings of ghouls hanging in her room. That would scare the pants off any man."

Vermillion broke in. "Mother, I suggest we simply say her father was a Manchu, whose family originated from the north. Many on the border have foreign blood and light-colored eyes. And we can add that her father was a high-level official with the Ministry of Foreign Relations who died. It's close enough to the truth anyway."

Madam Li stared at me, as if to see how well the lies fit my face. "I don't remember Golden Dove telling us those things," Madam Li said.

"Actually, she said her father's mother was part Manchu, and it was her grandfather who was the official. Her father was just a big disappointment to the family. Complete truth is not an advantage."

Manchu blood! A disappointment to his family! I was stunned that Golden Dove had told them about my father. She had never told me these details.

"Don't say he worked in the Ministry of Foreign Relations," Madam Li added. "People might joke this girl was the result of his relations with a foreigner. Did she ever tell you his name?"

"I couldn't pry that out of her," Vermillion said. "However, this is already enough explanation to turn your debt to Golden Dove into an opportunity. Some of our customers are still loyalists to the Ching. And since the Ching emperors and empresses were Manchu, the bit about her Manchu blood might be useful. And since Manchu women don't bind their feet, that can easily explain why her feet aren't small."

"We still need a story about her mother," Madam Li said, "in case anyone hasn't already heard the truth."

"Might as well make her part Manchu as well," Vermillion said.

"We can say she killed herself after her husband died," Magic Gourd said. "An honorable widow, an orphaned innocent girl."

Vermillion ignored her. "The usual reason will do. After the death of the father, his younger brother gambled away the family fortune and left the widow and her daughter destined to a life in the gutter."

Madam Li patted her arm. "I know you're still bitter about that. But I'm glad your mother sold you to me." Madam Li turned to me. "Did you hear what we said about your father and mother? Is it straight in your head?"

Magic Gourd spoke quickly. "I can test her and make sure she knows every detail by heart, no mistakes."

"She has to be ready in a month's time to attend her first party. It won't be an official announcement that she is our virgin courtesan, just an appearance to spread the word."

I felt as if she had said I would soon die.

"Don't worry," Magic Gourd said. "She's a good girl, and I'll beat out any bad temper that remains."

Madam Li looked hard at each of us and then she relaxed. "You may call me Mother Li."

When she left, Magic Gourd pinched my arm. "There is nothing more important than a good beginning. Do you want a good life? Do you want to be first class? Tomorrow I'll start your lessons, and one day, when you are popular and shimmering with jewels, you'll say to me, 'Magic Gourd, you were right, thank you for giving me a happy life.'"

CHAPTER 4

ETIQUETTE FOR BEAUTIES OF THE BOUDOIR

Wherein Magic Gourd advises young Violet on how to become a popular courtesan while avoiding cheapskates, false love, and suicide

Shanghai
1912
Magic Gourd

Do you want to wear out your insides by the time you are sixteen? Of course not. Then learn these lessons well.

While you are still a virgin courtesan, you must learn all the arts of enticement and master the balance of anticipation and reticence. Your defloration won't happen until the New Year, when you turn fifteen, and I expect you to have many ardent suitors by the time Madam is ready to sell your bud.

You might be thinking, *What does my attendant, old Magic Gourd, know about romance?* When I was nineteen, I was one of the top Ten Beauties of Shanghai. And not too many courtesans last until they are thirty-two. So you see, I know more than most.

REPUTATION

Always remember, little Violet, you are creating a world of romance and illusion. When you play the zither, it should be the aching or joyous companion to your song-poem. Sing to your suitor as if no one else is in the room, as if it were fate that brought you two together at this moment, in this place. You cannot simply pluck the silk strings or let memorized words fall from your mouth. You might as well not play at all and just take the sedan directly to a brothel where no one bothers with illusions or preludes.

Most beauties learn only ten song-poems throughout their career. You will not be like most. You will be unusual. Over the next year, you will learn three melodies about mountain retreats, three rustic ballads about maidens and young boys who meet in the mountains, three classic song-poems about returning from war and slaying tigers, one sing-speak tune to make guests laugh, one lively favorite for happy celebrations, and one farewell hymn about companions who will soon depart, which adds warmth at the end of a party and extends an invitation to get drunk together again.

You are an educated girl, so I know you are capable of learning quickly if you are disciplined. If you want to become one of the top Ten Beauties of Shanghai, your repertoire must be large enough to choose a different song for each suitor who hosts a dinner in your honor. When you sing it to him, he will forget all other women. When it comes time for the customers of all first-class houses to nominate the top Ten Beauties, guess which beauty will get the most votes? Each month, you will learn another song, and with each you must sound natural and honest, as if this song is flowing from your heart. I will accompany you on the zither until your warbled notes don't sound like two cats screeching over the same dead mouse.

We'll choose your song-poems carefully. Forget winter mountain poems, because they are always cold and bare in mood. But those having to do with spring thaw are fine, because they speak of renewal and abundance, the opposite of death and loneliness. Songs of summer yielding to autumn are acceptable, especially if they include the tasting of fruits your suitor enjoys. Make sure the fruit is not overly ripe, however, because that suggests worms will follow. The sounds of nesting swallows carry promise, but avoid any songs that have to do with the arrival of magpies or the departure of phoenixes, since they herald bad news and the retreat of life.

Later, when you are closer to your defloration, you will learn a few song-poems about the death of a beautiful girl. I know it seems strange to choose sad songs, but tragedy opens the aching heart and increases longing, passion, and desperation. A man will do anything to remove regret and feel his loved one back in his arms. Even if he has never lost anyone he truly loved, he will want to pretend he has and lie next to you, to unite with your departed spirit, to revel once again at the peak of passion. The tips to attendants and maids are especially good when the songs are tragic, to say nothing of the gifts that will be placed at your goddess feet.

In time, we will add to your repertoire those song-poems that match each man's idea of his self-importance. Is he a scholar, a businessman, or a politician? These are songs you would perform for the host in front of his friends, and the more songs you know, the better you can sing praises not just to a scholar but also to the president of a university, not just to a businessman but also to the chief officer of Renji. There are many captains of industry; you need to know the nature of those industries. Occasionally you might entertain the abbot of a temple. That one is easy: He loves songs for the gods. When sung with whispered intimacy, words sound true, and his chest will swell, knowing that others are there to hear these honest praises. The effect is the same for every man: He will feel more powerful, more virile, and in a conquering, generous mood, the more so if he has drunk plenty of wine. You must be attentive to filling the half-empty cup.

Madam said you will attend your first dinner party in a month. It is not your formal debut. Madam wants you there so that gossip will reach the mosquito press. The buzzing of men who were at the party will make others eager to host debut parties night after night. But don't do anything that leads to stinging gossip. Why do you think it's called the mosquito press? Each party will breed more stories in *Social Shanghai*. How you behave next month can set the course of your career. I don't want you to act like a little girl, nor a seductress. And don't show off your fancy Western education or your smart opinions. If you laugh, cover your mouth. You never remember to do that. No man at this party will want to see what's ugly inside of your mouth. If the older men are becoming impertinent, call them Grandpa. Some of those old men will try to pull you onto their laps. Bastards. If that happens, I will come quickly to you to say, "Mr. Wu on East Prosperity Road is waiting for us." I will always say this whenever I want to remove you from an undesirable situation. Don't be stupid and ask me who Mr. Wu is.

The first party is for an important man named Loyalty Fang. *Important* means he is very rich. He is hosting a big banquet and wants two courtesans for each of the eight guests. So that also tells you how important he is. It's good for you to start out at a rich man's party. You'll see just how fierce the competition will be. All four beauties of our house will be there and also twelve from other houses. He asked if our house had a virgin courtesan, and Madam was happy to say she had a new one, fresh and naive. He was pleased and said he liked a variety of ages for interest. Maybe he has a special eye for virgins. Even so, don't try to charm him—Madam has her eye on him for Vermillion's husband. If you make slight mistakes of etiquette the first time, everyone will be forgiving. They may consider it proof that you are pure and innocent. If you are terribly clumsy, stupid, or haughty, there goes any chance of a comfortable life. You'll be lucky if Madam lets you stay on as a maid to pay your debt.

You may not be asked to do anything special, but don't think that means you don't have to do anything at all. First, you must observe and learn my cues. Greet the guests, ask the customer you are standing behind whether he desires more tea or a particular dish, and then let me know. I will bring what he ordered. I doubt the host will ask you to provide entertainment, since there will be several accomplished beauties who are popular in the storytelling halls, but I've been taken by surprise before, and it was unfortunate. Just in case, I have come up with a story you can learn over the next week. You will tell it while I accompany you on the zither.

The story is about eternal youth. If it is told in the right way, any man who hears it will wish to have your youth rub off on him. The actual rubbing, of course, will not happen until your defloration. With this story, you are creating a promise for the future. Immortality. The tale has been promising immortality for over a thousand years. It is called "Peach Blossom Spring," and even a child can recite some version of it.

Because it is an oft-told tale, you must use special talent in performing it. Lots of expression—sadness, wonder, surprise, genuine regret, and so forth. You pause here, look there, and move your eyes sideways to increase anticipation. In my younger years, many men said they had never felt closer to immortality than they did while listening to me. Even the other courtesans said so, and they are not ones to flatter another beauty, except insincerely.

My version went more or less like this: A poor fisherman falls asleep on his boat, which floats into a secret grotto. He emerges on the other side in a haven where people dress and speak in the style of a bygone era. The people are free of war and worry, hate and envy, sickness and old age. There is only one season, spring. The maidens are always virgins, the wine is always sweet, the peonies are always blooming. Standing on every hillside are trees whose branches are heavy with voluptuous peaches.

"What is this place?" the fisherman asks a young maiden, and she replies, "Peach Blossom Spring," and then pleasures him in ways he never imagined possible. ("With wine and song," you should say with innocence. Everyone will get a big laugh out of that.) Time does not pass in this heaven on earth. It renews itself, as does his insatiability. Eventually he regains his senses, realizing that everyone back home must be worried sick about his absence. He sails for home laden with delicious meats and fruits for his mother, father, and wife. He will tell his friends to come with him to this utopia. The boat is a leaky wreck by the time he reaches his hometown. Half the village has burned down, the pagoda has collapsed, and the people are frightened by his long, matted beard and hair. He learns that two hundred years have passed, three civil wars have been lost, and his family and friends are long dead. Sadly, he returns to his boat and sails back toward the grotto. Many years pass, and he is still sailing, unable to find Peach Blossom Spring.

That is the story everyone knows, but I like to add a happy ending. It goes like this: The fisherman is about to drown himself when he spots the same pretty maiden on the riverbank, eating a peach so enormous she has to use both hands to bring it to her cherry lips. She waves to him, and together they sail through the grotto to Peach Blossom Spring. Nothing has changed. The maidens. The peach trees. The weather. The contentedness. The fisherman is again young and handsome—and, of course, looks remarkably like the host of the party. The maiden looks like you.

When I recited this ending, I mentioned the erotic pleasures the lucky man would enjoy. Everyone knows them. Swimming with Goldfish, Tasting the Watermelon, Climbing Higher on the Peach Tree. Often they were the ones I already knew that the host loved. But, of course, you should not include these details while you are still a virgin courtesan. Maybe next year. As I accompany you on the zither, my playing will help you know what you say next: a bit of glissando to signal the surprise arrival, tremolo for mounting passion, a sweep over all twenty-one silk strings for the return to the past. During the next few weeks, I will train you to deliver every word with precise gestures of your face and body while still looking natural and spontaneous, as if the story is unfolding before you, as if all your emotions are genuine and unexpected. You will learn to use an innocent girl's melodious voice, with its sweet trills up and down, its hesitant pace, or a mounting rush of pleasurable release.

There is another quality to a superior performance. Some girls perform with mere skill but without emotion. They may be masters of technique, but they wear a frown of concentration. I call that style "Looking at the Arrow and Not the Target." So boring. After three minutes, the men are hoping the story will soon end so they can return to a more boisterous evening.

Another style is called "Plucking Your Own Heartstrings." That kind of beauty closes her eyes and appears to be caught in another world. Her face beams with pleasure, and she might raise her eyebrows a little or smile to herself to show she is pleased with the way she is playing the music. So conceited.

I call the third style "Floating Together in Ravishment." This is the one you'll learn. Think of the story as I tell you what to do. You'll start with your eyes partly open, your lids still weighted by dreams, and as your eyes drift side to side to take in the surroundings, they meet your host's. Try that now. No, no, *slowly* move the eyes. If you move them fast like that, you look suspicious. Next, you will look at him fully with a longing gaze. Then let your eyelids fall halfway closed again—too much, that looks like you are asleep. Look as if you have entered paradise together. Let your mouth relax, your lips part—not that far. Now keep your eyes on him as your face flushes with uncontrolled pleasure. Suddenly, you gasp—*softly* with pleasure not fright—and you show uncertainty—no, no, not a frown—a questioning look that changes to acceptance of fate. With this dream of him in your eyes, you are being swept away. You're an innocent girl, a little frightened because you don't know where you are going. Close your eyes, breathe quickly, warble uncontrollably to match the zither's tremolo. Then close your eyes and say "Ah!" with ecstasy that devastates your senses. That means you should wear a slightly painful expression, as if you have died, but it's a small pain, a temporary death, so don't move for a few seconds. Don't grit your teeth. The pain is what you feel in your heart. Finally, let your face relax, and when your dreamy eyes meet his, he won't be able to loosen his purse strings fast enough in hopes he'll win your defloration.

Understand that the story of Peach Blossom Spring is not simply about the desire for immortality. It is also about the secret place in a man's past that now eludes him, the place where he felt the most alive. When he thinks of it, he realizes his life has been barren and lonely. He is sentimental, regretful, and keenly aware of elapsed years.

His nostalgia may be for a lurid episode from the days of his youth. That is typical. What romance did a married cousin initiate? Or was it an older girl who seduced him? What did he see when he wet his finger and made a hole in his young aunt's paper window? Was she with his uncle, his father, or a boy his age? What did she do when she caught him? Did she punish him? Did he enjoy his punishment? What erotic memory does he now rely on to reach the heights?

Remember also that a grown man may have nostalgia for his ideal self. He was supposed to leave a legacy of high morals so his descendants would worship him for the lofty reputation he built. Few men are capable of preserving their ideal self. If he is a scholar, what philosophical principles were sacrificed to ambition? If he is a banker, what oath of honesty was dirtied by favors? If he is a politician, what civic-minded policies were destroyed by bribes? You must cultivate his sentimentality for moral glory and help him treasure his myth of who he was. And when you do, he will not be able to let you go for at least a season or two.

You are too young to know yet what nostalgia truly means. It takes time to become sentimental. But for the sake of your success, you must quickly learn. When you touch a man's nostalgia, he is yours.

PATRONS AND CHEAPSKATES

As a courtesan, you must work toward the Four Necessities: jewelry, furniture, a seasonal contract with a stipend, and a comfortable retirement. Forget about love. You will receive that many times, but none of it is lasting. You can't eat it, even if it leads to marriage. And unless you become famous, you would become another of many concubines—and not Second Wife, but maybe Fourth Wife, Fifth, Sixth, or worse. You would have to eat whatever the man's first wife chooses. When you think of retirement, consider what will still provide a small bit of the freedom you now enjoy. You could do no better than to be the madam of a house like your mother's. You may hate her now, but that has nothing to do with your freedom and comfort in later years.

To gain the Four Necessities, you must be popular, desired by many suitors who give you costly gifts. You must be as clearheaded, firm, shrewd, and quick-thinking as a businessman. You offer no bargains, and you never accept anything less than what you are worth. I will let you know what that is after the first year of your defloration. If you do not follow my advice, you will lower your value, and even my efforts may not be enough to lift it up again.

My duty is to increase the competition among suitors before Madam decides who will enjoy the privilege of deflowering you. I will attend all your parties, all your calls to other houses. I will hint to your suitors that you have others vying for your favor, and I may mention the gift you are wearing—a hairpin of diamonds, a ring of imperial green jade. Each week you will wear jewelry that is a bit more valuable. These are things I may have to loan you. I might say that your favorite color is green, and thus jade and emeralds are your favored jewels. Do not contradict me and say you love pink. That kind of truthfulness is stupidity and will lead to gifts of flowers. Some suitors must be drawn in gradually, no matter how wealthy. Even the wealthiest man may have had frugal beginnings. Habits remain. When he has provided enough gifts to prove his sincerity, I will prepare the boudoir and let him know he is welcome to have tea with you after the party. Only serious suitors will be invited—and for tea only, perhaps a song. They'll see a hint of the inner chambers where they might lose their minds.

We will develop a language between us, using our eyes and eyebrows, the small movements of our fingers on fans and collars. You will know when to be subtle so I can be clear. When I mention Mr. Wu's party, I am taking you away. When I mention Mr. Lu on Pebble Road, you will know that the man who is eyeing you is Vermillion's suitor. I will single out men of generosity. When a man's desire for you increases, so will his gifts. When gifts increase, so does your worth, and when your worth increases, so will the favors Madam bestows. Bring in a rich patron, and she will call you Daughter. When you have no patron, no suitors, and no callers of any kind, she will declare you a parasite and threaten to kick you out.

I tell you these things so you can avoid the pain of truth later. Our world is full of temporary promises and guile. It is necessarily so. We are not evil people; this is just how we survive. There are only a few steps that separate success from failure. Understand this and you will not suffer from disillusionment as often as I did.

You will have favorites among the suitors for your bud: the charming ones, the handsome ones. I will try to nurture those. But the madam will choose whoever she feels is the best for your defloration, the one who offers the most. If it is a man whom you find distasteful, I will ask Madam to let you have a little fun with the next. That way, if a man is odious, you'll remember that better is yet to come.

Just remember, the first week is the most profitable. After that, you're no longer a virgin. Interest in you falls, the gifts are less. That always happens to young beauties. Once they've sold their inexperience, no one wants the rest of their inexperience. But you will surprise everyone. That's what I'm teaching you: to use your brain as cleverly as you use your hips and mouth.

In the House of Vermillion, all the hosts for parties and dinners will be rich, just as they were at Hidden Jade Path. The guests of hosts—maybe they are, maybe not. That's where my skills come in. I can quickly find out. Since we're part of a new flower house, we must depend at first on Vermillion's fame and following to establish our reputation as first class. So never steal her patrons or I'll hand you the silken cord by which you can hang yourself. News of the House of Vermillion has already been reported in the mosquito press, and the madam will ensure that there is more to come. The tabloids love exciting gossip—and scandal even more. There's always some story about a bumpkin who claims he was fleeced by a dishonest courtesan. I think most of these accusers are simply cheapskates who thought they could throw down a dollar and get their stem caressed just as they did by a cheap whore at an opium flower house. Or they think that love in a courtesan house is truly love, and they claim later they were betrayed. But some courtesans are genuine connivers. And if they are caught, that spells the end of their careers in Shanghai. They would have to move to another province to attract unsuspecting clients. I despise their kind. They make men think all flowers are pickpockets of the heart. You won't find any courtesans like that in this house, so don't you become one.

I will get you off to a quick start by spreading good rumors in the tabloids. The editor of the most popular mosquito daily is a former lover of mine, and because I did not charge him for many of our trysts, I can ask him to put in a favorable word. We may have to make something up in the beginning. "A well-known shipping magnate said that the virgin courtesan at the House of Vermillion is worth an early look-see before she makes her official debut." That will add intrigue as well as make it clear that you are with a first-class house, not the kind that charges one dollar for this, two dollars for that. That's what the old bustard did, and it lowered us to a second-class house and encouraged customers to bargain for sex. Here, we don't go back and forth on the price. It is three dollars for a party, and it does not include riding on the stem. No argument.

The extras at the House of Vermillion will cost slightly more than most places. Your mother did the same, and it is a good strategy. If the prices are higher and the beauties are higher class, a man feels all the more privileged. Vermillion has stocked French wine and special virility mushrooms. A good host would never deny his guests the fine wine just recommended by his courtesan. But she should never make the cost of saving face so high that a man must go elsewhere to show how generous he is. One man reviled a greedy house to the press, and as a result the house lost most of its business and had to close so it could start a new life under a different name. The man's factory later burned down, and, fortunately for the reincarnated house, no one could prove the disaster was related to a grudge.

At the party next month, there will be two beauties to stand behind each guest. The host of the party or Madam will make those arrangements. Whichever man you are assigned to, keep in mind that he has no special rights to you. If he tries to sneak a hand onto your leg, move back, and apologize for being too close. Even so, you should be attentive to his needs—more wine, more tea. They expect to be pampered, and other men will notice if you are too lazy to do so. If he is playing the Finger Guessing game with the other men and he loses, he may give the penalty cup of wine to a beauty to drink.

I know that often happened in your mother's house. But do you know why? Why does the man not enjoy the wine himself? To stay clearheaded while gambling? No, he enjoys having a woman take the punishment for him. After all, a little cup of wine is not like a beating. But it weakens her a little, makes her drunk so she loses her calculating ways, especially in the boudoir. That's what they think, anyway. They don't know how cunning we are. When the beauty accepts the cup, the beauty next to her exchanges it for an empty one, then empties the wine into a vase. Have you ever wondered why there are so many vases and spittoons about the place? Do you now see why it is unwise to make enemies with the other beauties of the house? You should practice this sleight of hand many times. I don't want you drunk and sick. That would make a lasting impression.

To entice a guest with your eyes, wait until the man stares at you. Look past his gaze before returning your eyes for only a moment. As the night progresses, let your eyes linger, longer each time, and let your smile grow, so his confidence does as well. Forget that demure technique of casting the eyes downward and pretending to be flustered. That may have worked ten years ago. These days, fake coyness just makes a man confused. You don't have to be brazen, but your meaning should be clear. Some of my clients reached the heights through eyes alone. You think that's victory? Ha. Once the stem shrinks to normal, the man is no longer urgent. He's content to go home.

Watch out for cheapskates. They may come as guests of the host. A country cousin, an old schoolmate, the kind who's used to second-class houses or worse. You can tell who they are because they don't know the rules. They woo courtesans who already have patrons. They think they can bed a beauty the first night. They don't bother to tip attendants or maids. That's the worst. I'll be quick to excuse you from such parties, announcing that you have a call chit for a party hosted by the ever-useful Mr. Wu on East Prosperity Road. But some of the cheapskates may be newly rich and don't know our customs. For those I have a pamphlet, which many beauties use: Li Shangyin's "Advice to Men Visiting Flower Houses." Tried-and-true for hundreds of years. *A man should not brag about the size of his stem. He should not make false promises. He should not piss in front of the courtesan.* And so on. I added that a man should give generous tips to maids and attendants. Why not? It saves everyone time and embarrassment.

The guests to really watch out for are tagalongs who are disreputable. Some of them have manners of the highborn, but they've gambled away their family's wealth. Or they burned it up into opium smoke. They come bearing jewelry they've stolen from their mothers or sisters or wives. (Nothing would follow after they've disbursed those.) Worse are thieves who took jewelry from the boudoirs of beauties they lured with their lies. They carry stolen bracelets and rings from one house to the next. A friend of mine lost her entire retirement savings to just such a thief. We all thought he should have had his stem cut off and fed to the dogs, and the madam of the house thought so, too. She hired gangsters to track him down, and let's just say that they fed that dog much more than his stem. I will always be on the lookout for scoundrels and thieves. If I steer you away from a man, that may be the reason. Never question what I do or you'll be on your knees for thugs and their friends as repayment for the help you didn't want.

There are tempting young men—rich, handsome, but spoiled and heartless, too. They show off to their friends. They toss out gifts—jeweled hairpins to this flower, bracelets to that one. They woo so passionately that the beauties vie among themselves to have them stay the night. Those beauties dream of making them their patrons. They give them everything in one night, but the next day those young men are courting another. They want only to trample as many flowers as they can. They compete and brag about how little time it took. They describe the pudenda, as proof they entered her gates. This is why I require a courtship of no less than a month. You may have only three or four intimate suitors during this period, and only those who might become patrons. These three or four will keep you busy enough.

There is another kind of suitor I will help you avoid. They are like stallions and never seem to exhaust themselves. As soon as they're done, they're ready to mount you again. With them, you will have no strength to rise in time to take tea with the first-time guests, the new opportunities. You will not look your best when you take carriage rides. And you know what the mosquito press will say. Is the flower Violet wilting and about to fall?

A man's manners may be impeccable until he is in your bed. There is a type who thinks he can order up any kind of sex, like dishes on a menu. He brings his pillow book to ask for the outlandish positions he's illustrated in the back. It's one thing to lash a beauty's arms to the high corner of the bed and quite another to hang her upside down like a monkey from the chandelier. They don't care if the chandelier crashes down or an arm is twisted loose from its socket. I know of one girl who fell on her head, and afterward she put her clothes on backward and never said two words that made any sense. The house couldn't keep her, and I don't know where she went.

The most dangerous is the Lover of Bloodcurdling Screams. He would just as soon poke a pig and your mother. Most of those men go to streetwalkers. But the wealthy ones can afford to torture even a famous beauty. He loves to give a woman pain—and it does not come from a few slaps on the buttocks. The conceited girls are his favorite. They refuse him at first and are lured by his money. The innocent ones are entranced from the start. He can only be satisfied when he sees a beauty's eyes bulge when she has no breath to cry out for help. A few years ago, that happened to a courtesan in the House of Vitality. She was young and naive, like you, only seventeen. She knew everything—no one could tell her what to do. The demon encouraged her haughtiness. He asked to be her humble servant. He came laden with gifts and threw a banquet in her honor. The attendant invited him into the beauty's boudoir. In the morning, the attendant found her dead and went insane. I won't describe what the monster did. I can already see you're sufficiently scared.

The suitors I'll find for you will treat you like a lily made of white jade. A few will even be so overly polite you'll be bored to tears when they seek your permission for every peek and touch. Rich old men can be among the best suitors and patrons. They're experienced, generous, and they know how to tip. They enjoy adulation, but don't need praise all night long. You'll know who they are by how warmly I receive them. "Come sit here," I'll say, "your favorite spot by the window. Eat this, it's your favorite snack. Drink this wine, it makes you hearty. Violet will sing your favorite song." In the boudoir, they'll treat you like the Goddess of Mercy in a holy temple. They'll place offerings on your belly so that you might grant their stem a longer life. You may have to apply some herbs to get their stem to stand up, and the potions I have almost always work. Often he will simply fall asleep and dream of what he couldn't do. Tell him your dream of what he did. There is another good trait of old men: They are loyal. They won't chase after flowers, one after the next. They don't want to educate a new girl about their inabilities. The only problem with old men is that they die, sometimes suddenly. You may have one as your patron who gives you a handsome stipend. It's a sad day when you learn his sons are burning incense for him at the family temple. You can be sure that his wife won't be toddling over with your stipend in hand.

With all these things in mind, I will choose the very best suitors and patrons, who will go crazy to have you. My plan is to pay off our debt to Madam in three years or less. She paid a lot of money for you, Violet. On top of that, some of your furniture and clothes are provided by this house and that adds up to one hundred fifty dollars—that's Mexican silver dollars, not the new Republican money. And don't forget, you also have to pay your monthly rent, not to mention your share of the food and use of the sedan. So you can see why we must be very careful about money. Some girls spend, spend, spend, and their debt goes up, up, up. By the time they have to leave, they have nothing but tears. Once you're free of debt, you can do as you please, as long as you pay your rent and give Madam a portion of your earnings. When your savings have mounted, we can rent our own house and start a business of our own. I already have one in mind, and it is not an opium flower house.

For your defloration, I would like you to earn a full set of jewelry. Most beauties are happy with the usual two gold bangles and bolt of silk. If I have my way, you will receive much more than that. An expensive ring or necklace might be enough, but once he's in your room, I'll suggest that he celebrate by giving you the rest of the set. After your defloration, we'll need to work hard to accumulate more sets. We may have to rent jewelry from older courtesans who are hanging on and in need of cash. All those necklaces and bracelets will show future patrons how popular you already are. Once a man is your patron, always wear your most expensive set. Praise it lavishly, but add a small criticism. Tell him dark rubies do not flatter your complexion. Mention that the style is a little old-fashioned for a girl as young as you. Say that you saw a beauty who wore a more modern set, and that it showed what good taste her patron had. Now he has the opportunity to offer you jewelry more to your liking. If he says nothing, then that will be the last evening he comes to your boudoir until he offers a suitable form of admiration.

If he offers to take you to a jewelry store, let him know that Eight Virtues, on Felicity Lane, has the best selection and that they are also very honest and never claim that gold over silver is pure gold, unlike Eight Precious Garden, on Fourth Avenue. I know the owner of Eight Virtues, Mr. Gao, and I would ask him ahead of time to set aside two sets, one quite expensive, the other not as expensive but also very nice. When we arrive, Mr. Gao will ask your suitor what he has in mind. If he does not ask for a specific piece of jewelry, Mr. Gao will bring out the expensive set—bracelet, necklace, ring, and hair ornament. You should murmur that if you had a set like that, you would no longer wear the jewelry you have now. If the suitor tells you to try it on, remove the jewelry you have on, throw it on the counter, and tell Mr. Gao to give it to the memorial fund for chaste widows. Don't worry, Mr. Gao will later come to the house and return the set. Now that you've discarded the other jewelry, what can your suitor do? He should buy the set you love so much to show he values you more than anyone, and since you value this set more than any other, the feeling is mutual. At the very least, he should buy a set worth a little more than the one you gave to the faithful widows. You cannot accept anything less.

Yet you also cannot appear greedy and wheedle your future patron. I, on the other hand, can bargain with Mr. Gao on behalf of your suitor. I'll tell you to take off the necklace so I can examine it. I will call attention to a flaw in one of the jewels, a little blur. Mr. Gao will look at it and acknowledge this with dismay and immediately offer a lower price. You can admit you still like the set but are not sure if it's the right thing to get. You should then ask your suitor what he thinks. Is it still worth it? Notice how the question is phrased. You are not asking him to buy it; you are asking if it is worth the money. If he does not answer immediately, Mr. Gao will lower the price again, saying he does not want anybody claiming his merchandise is flawed. He adds that he is willing to sell the set for such a small sum because you said you liked it more than anything you've ever had. And when others see it, you might tell them the same. They will also think you paid full price. So this is beneficial to all. At this point, your suitor will likely buy it. After all, he's struck a bargain without even trying.

On the other hand, he could decline to buy the set, and now he has a reason to do so without losing face. The set is imperfect. You said so yourself. Ask Mr. Gao if there is anything similar in style that is without flaws. Mr. Gao will bring out the second set I selected. It will be less expensive than the first set but more than the discounted price. You can exclaim over this unbelievable price. If the suitor does not immediately say he will buy it, what does that mean? Whatever it means, so you do not lose face, look at the set again and find something else that is not to your liking that you had not noticed before. I will ask Mr. Gao if he will have new sets next week. He will say yes, and I will suggest we return. Then we can see what happens. You might be surprised.

One beauty told me that she was once confronted with a similar humiliating situation. She walked toward the door and tried for one last gift, stopping to admire a headband. It was decorated with small pearls and was expensive for a headband, but not extraordinarily so. The suitor said that it did not become her. She was disheartened and prepared to walk away empty-handed when the man called out to Mr. Gao to bring out the headband he had seen the other day. When she saw it, she wept. It was encrusted with pearls and diamonds and was more expensive than the entire first set of jewelry. Mr. Gao had been in on this ruse. The suitor knew how courtesans played the game, but he truly loved this beauty, and he showed her it was not her tricks that had won his heart. When he became her patron, he gave her enough money to pay off her debts and open a house of her own. She was so devoted to him that when he died suddenly, she killed herself to be with him. None of his wives did that.

As you can see, the strategies for winning a pledge from a patron must be carefully played. You don't want to return home empty-handed too many times. That's why I should accompany you on any visits to the jewelry store. And until you get a top-quality headband, study the one Vermillion has. It is almost as nice as the one I told you about, studded with pearls and diamonds and shaped to enhance the roundness of her forehead and the angle of her phoenix eyes. You should openly admire the headband. Say aloud how precious it is. Praise the patron who bought it. She will appreciate your flattery, because it will show in front of other men how valuable she is and that the gifts from her future suitors should be equal in quality to her headband. Her patron will also be encouraged to give her another nice gift. One day, Vermillion will do the same for you. Her flattery will also give your suitors an idea of the sort of gift that could win your heart. As you grow in popularity, you should eventually receive a headband worth ten times more than the one I gave you.

My own fault lay in accepting something less. You are lucky you can benefit from my mistakes.

THE ILLUSIONS

The illusion of romance depends on a man's willingness to believe, and his willingness comes from thwarted desires. All of your illusions should lead to one thing: to make him fall in love with you. If he does, time will stand still when he is with you. He will fancy himself immortal and be willing to give up his worldly goods for you.

A few men may wish for special illusions. I call one the Illusion of Tragic Love. Remember the songs I said you should learn? The one about maidens who died young? You might take on the role of a girl he grieves for, someone to whom he secretly pledged his love. You will become that girl and either allow him to fulfill the pledge or be released from it. He may even ask you to perform the role of the cousin who dies in the novel *A Dream of Red Mansions* or that of the lover of the scholar in the opera *The Legend of White Snake.* A real weeper. This will require flowing robes for a costume, more white powder on the face for a ghostly effect. You should memorize scenes from the novel and master expressions of betrayal and forgiveness. It's harder than you think. You don't want to look murderous or like a fool. But if you master the look of tragedy, you can make a fortune. If you have truly lost someone, as I have, you will not need to pretend. You simply remember. Someday I will tell you all about him. I can't ever speak of him without having tears from my heart flood out from my eyes.

The most common request from suitors is the Illusion of the Noble Maiden. The man wants you to put on the same airs of a noble-man's daughter, whom he can woo into bawdy adventure, and without the meddling of a gabby mother-in-law. To achieve the Noble Maiden role, you wear clothes that are rich and dramatic, refined yet also a little daring. Perhaps the undergarments are skimpy and in a happy red color.

Some courtesans are asked to play what we call the Illusion of the Night Scholar. A little kohl to darken the eyebrows, the Ming hat of a philosopher, long robes. If he wants a warrior, the hair is oiled, parted on two sides, combed over the forehead, and knotted tightly at the back. The Night Scholar illusion has become quite popular these days, even in a few first-class houses. I don't know if the courtesans here do that. But it used to be done only in the second-class houses. That's what the old bustard allowed in the Hall of Tranquility. The customer asked her for the Night Scholar, and she called the courte-san who was known for performing the role with some enthusiasm. A lot of that enthusiasm came from being older and having a last chance to make some good money. The customers piled on the gifts for a few days, and the gates to heaven opened. When I reached thirty, I became the Night Scholar most often requested, even though I look nothing like a man. There's no shame when you do it in your own boudoir. I didn't boast in the storytelling halls.

The old bustard also came up with another specialty to draw more business: Two Scholars. I played one of them, and whoever was not so busy played the other. The customers did the usual wooing, but with two beauties. One of us would complain, "Hey, I do all the work. Why should she get the same amount?" Then the other of us made the same complaint. That's how we both cooperated to get more money. But we made it worth it to the man. He would enter the boudoir, quaking and close to bursting when he saw two stern Confucian scholars. I held the ropes while the other wore a girdle with an ivory stem. I threw him silky undergarments to put on and called him a wife-whore. While he dressed, we sat at the tea table with legs crossed, smoking Western cigars. We commanded that he put on a headband, that he powder his face and rouge his lips. *Oyo!* What an ugly courtesan he made. Still, we flattered his prettiness, his youth, and called him "Little Pink Lotus." He had to call us "Lord Scholars," and I would bind him seated in the chair with his legs dangling over the arms, the usual position, nothing that special. He cried and begged, but alas, it was no use, and the other beauty crossed the threshold with the ivory stem. Where? you ask. How can you be so stupid? Where else would a stem go into a man? In his little pink lotus!

For the very generous ones, we let him rest a bit and then brought out another stem, and he now had to call us "Master Teachers." I would wear the ivory stem this time. For the extremely generous ones, there was a third stem, usually called "Uncle" or "Brother." That was the request. Family was always last, the most exciting.

Some men just liked a little variety. Others were homosexuals who pretended they were not, to hide their true nature from other businessmen. They didn't realize that some of those businessmen had the same secret. We were very discreet. We knew who was dabbling in the dew with the pretty opera singers, because some of those singers were our lovers. The singers didn't enjoy their work, but the money was good. When I was still a courtesan at the Hall of Tranquility, I had one old man who liked to use the ivory stem both ways. That's the kind of customer a madam in a second-class house will take. I had to wear the Night Scholar clothes and apply Heavenly Showers ointment to get the man's ancient warrior to stand up. And because he quickly burst, he wanted to draw things out by using the ivory stem on me. He gave me an extra gift, but I still didn't like it. Those fake stems never grow soft. It was too much work.

The only reason I am telling you this is so you will be prepared if a man asks for these things. If you know what they want, you won't be tempted by offers of extra money once they are inside your boudoir. I don't want you to play the role of a man. You are first class. Your reputation is still that of a young beauty. Maybe Puffy Cloud did that. Ha. She was probably crazy for it. But if a man hints that he wishes to wear your robes or he brings out an ivory stem on a girdle, you should go behind the screen and ring the chimes for me. Those customers know they are supposed to make those requests to the attendants ahead of time. I will politely tell him the Night Scholar is not available but that his teacher can take care of whatever lessons he needs. If he's urgent, he'll accept my offer. I won't mind doing this from time to time. A lot of the attendants who were once courtesans do the specialties no one else wants to do. I still have a girdle and different-size stems in my trunk. The bigger the tip, the bigger the stem—that's how it usually goes. Too bad I never had a big talent for playing the Scholar. I was not genuinely enthusiastic.

On occasion, we have clients who wish to receive instruction. Most are inexperienced. Formerly devout monks, young boys whose fathers are clients of ours, or customers who wish to learn the skills of an expert lover to woo another man's wife. If you come across these men, let me know. In fact, the initiation of young boys was a specialty of mine, and that's because the fathers who brought their sons remembered how encouraging I was when they were young. I am always moved to tears when these same young boys come back as grown men and say to me, "Because of you, my wife and concubines are content." Often they ask for a lesson, just for old times' sake. You should let me take care of any client like this. They are not as choosy about how old the courtesan is. What matters to them is gaining knowledge that will last a lifetime.

Whatever any man requests, you should never degrade him for his desires, nor should you accept being degraded. If he's drunk and pisses on you, ring the chimes and I will come and remove him from your room. Don't accept extra money to let him do these things. You know what happens to a woman who lets herself be degraded? She winds up with a pimp and lies on the floor of a chophouse, where rickshaw pullers and laborers rub her raw, one after another, a hundred a day. She never has a chance to close her legs or her mouth until she's pounded into raw meat and dies. I've always wondered why those women don't kill themselves. Maybe they think it's their fate and if they endure it they will have a better life in the next. I would rather kill myself and return as a fly.

FASHION

Don't let yourself become too thin. No man likes bony limbs poking him. And it's bad business if a suitor accidentally snaps a girl's ribs. Just before you came to the Hall of Tranquility, that happened to one beauty. She screamed so loud that the madam, the attendant, and two menservants ran into the room, thinking the man was killing her. The servants flung the naked man onto the streets. The old bustard learned he was an official who determined the fees for business licenses. This did not end favorably for anyone.

A fat courtesan holds no appeal, either. It limits what positions she can do without breaking the man's stem in two. Right now, you have a good shape. I think your breasts might grow to be a little larger than ideal. Large breasts were not considered attractive when I started my career, and those who had them would bind them up. But these days, younger men find large breasts lurid and exciting. It's the influence of pornographic Western postcards. I still think that large flopping breasts belong on a wet nurse. Don't do anything to grow them on purpose.

When it comes to clothes, everything about you should convey that you are a high-ranking courtesan. The best clothes should be worn in public—on carriage rides, in restaurants, at the theater. Your jacket will be so tight, everyone can see your shapeliness. The skirt will be well-fitted so that no imagination is needed to see the curves of your rump. There will be shocking Western details: buttons instead of clasps, frills, and pleats. Or it could be men's trousers, or a Western skirt. This is where you must use your imagination. As you ride around in a carriage with your suitor, think of yourself as being onstage, like an actress. All eyes are on you. Your suitors and patrons are proud to show you off. It gives them face. They enjoy seeing envy in other men.

You'll have to share the carriage at times with another courtesan, and I'll do my best to avoid pairing you with a beauty who might draw more attention. You are not the loveliest of the flowers, not yet, and who knows if you ever will be. And with carriage rides, loveliness and fashionable clothes are what the public will see, rather than intimate skills of enchantment. So other means are needed to attract attention when you are in public.

I have several ideas we will use over the coming months. And we'll have to keep them a secret lest the other beauties steal them. First, I am having the tailor make a costume in the colors of the imperial family. We've used golden yellow in the past, but only with underwear, and for many men, this alone sent them into paroxysms of clouds and rain. Now that the emperor is gone, what laws forbid us to wear any color, and anywhere that pleases us? Imagine what an imperial-yellow jacket and kingfisher-blue pantalets will do to a suitor and to every loyalist who sees you in public. We'll have costumes made in imperial violet, the exact shade. I am hoping we are the first to flaunt these colors. What a story that will make for the mosquito press: the courtesan Violet wearing violet clothes!

I've also been mulling over getting you a European hat. I saw one that was quite outlandish. It was the size of a seat cushion and had a fan of baby ostrich feathers on top, dyed violet. You'd be visible from blocks away, and with the color being the same as your name, you would be the talk of the tabloids every time you wore it. It's an expensive hat, so I may see if I can have it copied. Then again, if we wait, we run the risk that another courtesan will buy the hat and wear it first, and you can't be seen imitating another courtesan. That would be reported in the tabloids, too.

The clothes at dinner parties will depend on the host and the other courtesans there. As I said, you cannot outdazzle Vermillion. But for a party in your honor, you must wear your best evening costumes. The weave of the cloth has become the fashion. It is always a pattern that only the most skilled of craftsmen can make. We'll have to wait a bit before we can afford the one I have in mind. It looks like layers of petals. Clothes made out of fabrics like that will cost you a month's worth of earnings at least. Never eat anything at the party. A grease stain will ruin an outfit, and that would be a costly bit of greed. Some beauties have embroidered a flowery pattern to cover a stain, but everyone knows why a branch of plum blossoms suddenly sprouts over the breasts.

In winter, the silk must be thick and as lustrous as a pearl. The collar looks best when lined with Russian shaved white fox or chinchilla. But rabbit will do the first year. In the summer, the top layer of silk weave will be delicate, tissue thin, and of a perfectly even weft, light but also crisp. You don't want to look wilted. Every detail must be perfect, from the clasp at the throat to the frills at the hem.

Women on the streets will envy and admire your clothes for their clever details. You'll enjoy seeing that. For many young girls, a glimpse of you will provide the greatest excitement of their lives. They'll be talking about you until they go to their graves. Rich young girls will take note as we pass by in carriages and run to the tailors we use and ask for a costume just like that worn by the famous courtesan Violet. It is annoying that rich girls imitate us, but it is also flattery. If many girls from rich families copy your fashions, this will raise your status. Men are not the only ones who make us popular. Look at those who are the top Ten Beauties each year. Are they the most beautiful? No. They are the ones who understand human nature, that of men and women both. They know how to attract attention and envy and bend it to their advantage.

Don't be surprised if a few wives pay you handsomely to visit your boudoir—to see your wardrobe, your makeup, and even to learn the unusual positions their husbands enjoy. Show them. They think it is only about coupling, rather than prolonged courtship and the engorged pleasure of two lovers in conspiracy. They can no longer be courted. Their husbands make demands, and they comply. So you need not worry that you are giving away your secrets and your patrons will become so satisfied with their wives that they never pay you a visit. But be sure you charge those wives a lot, at least five dollars.

Remember that envy is one of mankind's greatest flaws. It leads to recklessness in the one who envies and possessiveness in the one who has you by his side. You can use one suitor to increase the ardor of another. Beware not to do this between brothers or with friends who are like brothers, though. If they have a falling-out, people will say that you were so strong a plow cow you pulled two brothers apart.

After you've been to a few parties here and at other houses, you will understand more about envy among courtesans. You may have seen it at your mother's house. You will feel it bite you. Envy is a poisonous snake around your ankle. You may hate your competitor or your suitor. You may want to destroy her, him, and yourself. Take note of these feelings. Another courtesan may feel this way about you and will do everything to cause your downfall. But if you inspire envy in everyone, a strange thing happens. That envy eventually turns into respect, an acknowledgment of your superiority. Do not flaunt your victories, however. Your rivals may envy you one day and cheer your demise the next.

That reminds me: We must have a souvenir photograph made and decide on a nickname to set you apart from others.

If we don't choose one ourselves, people will give you one without asking. I already heard one of the other courtesans call you "the White Daylily." A lot of virgins are called by that sweet name. But you don't want to be stuck with it forever or you'll be the butt of jokes—"no longer so white," that sort of thing. The nickname must be unique. I know of beauties who compared themselves to birds. "The Voice of a Sparrow." One girl chose that, even though she had a harsh voice. Besides, sparrows are so common and noisy with their chitter-chitter-chirp-chirp in the morning. Another girl I knew chose the description "As Classic As a Weeping Willow." I think she chose it because the painted backdrop in the photo studio showed a willow and a lake. What's so special about that? "Weeping Willow"—someone who is wooden and weeps until her eyes are red and as big as eggs? These are not traits that men cherish. I'm thinking yours might be "A Waterfall Dream." It sounds good. A man can picture it: falling in love, swept away, torrential love. Something like that. We can come up with the exact meaning later when I decide who you really are.

You are young and inexperienced, Violet. No one will envy anything about you today. The beauties are much lovelier and trickier than you. So don't try to compete. Just observe. Few girls receive the kind of advice I am giving you. They learn it later, as I did, through agonizing mistakes. They thought beauty, poetry, and a sweet voice would last forever. They depended on it. They did not realize that what matters the most is a mix of strategy, cunning, honesty, patience, and the readiness to grab every opportunity. Above all, a girl must always be willing to do what is necessary.

ACCIDENTS

Clothes are like a theater curtain. Some courtesans always keep the curtain closed until they open the curtains of the bed. They go by the old rules. No touching of hands. Everything very proper, as if they are a proper bride. How boring. The man may as well be with his wife. That kind of modesty may have been the custom years ago, but these are modern times. If you provide a glimpse of the future, it won't cheapen you. You're still holding back. In fact, the more you let them peek, the more they will want what you are holding back. Just remember there is a difference between giving a man a glimpse and letting him examine the goods in detail.

Some of the best glimpses occur during garden strolling accidents. These must seem perfectly innocent. It might go like this: You are wearing a tight jacket and trousers whose seam fits into the crease of your pudenda. You walk by the rockeries and pond, engaged in lively conversation. Suddenly you cry out and pretend you have stepped on the sharp stone I secretly placed there earlier. Quickly sit on a garden stool and cross your legs so you can examine your imaginary wound. The pain has caused you to forget the lewdness of this position. When you catch the man staring at your pudenda, act embarrassed at first, then coy. He will play the role of the gallant gentleman who insists on examining the wound to ensure you are not crippled for life. This ploy was once successful only with girls whose bound feet were three-inch stubs. But nowadays, even the daughters of scholar families no longer have their feet bound. So there is no shame that your feet are unbound. Of course, some men will be disappointed, especially the older ones. If you notice ahead of time that the man is aroused by tiny "golden lilies," it's best not to bother with the injured-foot ploy.

Another trick is to ask your suitor to pluck a flower for your hair. Turn away from him as you attempt to slip it along the side, by your ear. Then let it fall. In your hurry to retrieve the flower, you bend over, and the jacket that had barely covered your hips now lifts like fog from the moon. Be sure he has a view of your rump for at least three seconds. When you stand and see his face, cover your mouth with the flower and laugh. Give the sly happy look of mutual conspiracy. When he is standing beside you, push your finger into the center of the flower and note for him the darker, more flushed color, the deeper fragrance. He will nearly be insane at this point, unless the flower that fell has lost its petals and is a weedy little thing.

There are some simple garden positions you can use. Stand next to a tree, and as you admire its age and strength, straddle it ever so slightly. Columns are also good for this purpose.

After your defloration, I will lend you some of my special skirts. Here is one in your color, a rich imperial violet. The whiteness of the skin is best against a darker-colored skirt. The middle panel conceals a split, like the part between two curtains. You can close the split with frog clasps. Or you can unfasten them to show the knees, or the thighs, or the pudenda. This skirt is only for very special suitors or patrons who enjoy showing you off in public. Never cheapen yourself by revealing what is beneath the skirt if your suitor requests a look. Everything with this skirt must be an accident you control. The more generous the suitor, the more accidents you should have. You might catch your skirt on the arm of a horseshoe chair. The flap opens, the whiteness of your skin flashes, and with your coy look of surprise you've given your patron two seconds of titillation. A variation is to loosely sew the clasps on so that they easily rip away.

You can have accidents of the skirt at the theater. Patrons are especially fond of this if you are seated in a curtained box. Once he discovers the opening, you can allow him to stroke you throughout the performance, but only if he's given you a gift that night. Climbing into, and descending from, the carriage are also good opportunities for suitors who need only a nudge to become a patron. Blustery days are also advantageous. Let your fingers help the gusts raise your skirt. If the man is already your patron, you can allow him other privileges. When you are at a banquet in your honor, let his hand under the table slip between your legs to explore the forbidden in front of his guests. Converse brightly but hesitate every so often, and provide the half-lidded look you learned for your songs. The others will know exactly what is happening. Nothing is openly said, but all will know. Always maintain the appearance of propriety. In this way, you can enhance the agony of desire in your patron and in his envious guests. I guarantee the party will end earlier than usual.

PREPARING THE BOUDOIR

I have furnished your room with every comfort to set the stage for lovemaking. You saw that I already had your bed placed closer to the middle of the room so I could move the screen that hides the toilet and bathing tub. It was so cramped and uncomfortable before. And how can you feel clean if the bathing tub resembles an old threshing box? The chamber pot was so low that old men on rusted legs had a hard time seating themselves and standing back up. I don't know why I did not think of that when this was my boudoir. Now your suitor and you can refresh yourselves in more spacious surroundings. The new chamber pot is set under a carved seat with armrests. And the pot is porcelain, a nice oxblood red, easy to clean. I've ordered a new bathing tub, one of the Western ones, copper, with lions' feet. Very fashionable. It has already arrived, but I cannot have it put in your room until next week. Vermillion saw the same one, and she must be the first to have it. There will be a Western coatrack for your dressing robes, a tufted bench, and a table with ointments, perfumes, and snuff bottles containing invigorating powder. To call the servants to tidy up, you simply strike the four bars of the new chimes I bought. It is the same instrument used on the finest railways to announce that dinner will be served.

I have thought of even more decorations and luxuries. They are all the things I should have thought to use with my own suitors. I decorated my room one way and then never changed it. As I grew older, my room appeared increasingly old-fashioned. I recognize that now. The furniture is still high quality, though, and I'm sure I can sell it for a good price. But to buy the new furniture we need, we will require money gifts. So you see how important it is that you do well at the parties right from the start. We cannot borrow money endlessly from the madam, or we'll be slaves to her for the rest of our lives. At the very least I will reupholster the chairs and sofa, and I am having new curtains made for the bed. Silk batiste in golden emperor yellow with blue embroidered characters that mean longevity. I bought yellow and blue ribbons and dozens of little bells. They'll be tied to the corners of the bed and above and will sound merrily with the slightest jiggle of your hips, letting the man know he's headed toward heavenly ecstasy. It's a clever touch. I might even take a customer every now and then just so I can hear the sound of those bells.

FOUR WAYS TO DAMAGE YOUR CAREER

There are four ways you might find you are out of business for a short time, a long time, or forever.

The first is your monthly flow. You do not want to rise from a fancy chair at a party, only to discover you have left a red map of Chongming Island on the brocade of the chair and a matching one on the back of your skirt. I will give you a set of special sea sponges, which you can put inside you. If your flow is heavy, you can also add a little silk sac of moss at the front of the gates of your pudenda. Never allow intimate relations with a suitor during this time. Be flirtatious but coy at parties. Meet with new suitors for afternoon tea. A patron, however, is another matter. A few of them may enjoy a make-believe defloration with the spillage of blood. In those cases, we will ask for a small defloration gift to make the fantasy more realistic. You will have to act reluctant as your patron strips away your clothes, and then just do what you did during your real defloration, only not as loud.

If the patron is not interested in a fake defloration, he may ask you to pleasure him with your mouth, or watch you do something to yourself, or many other things we don't need to talk about now.

It will only scare you. If a patron wants something unusual, I can advise you then what to do, what not to do, and what requires more negotiation.

The second way to lose business is to have a baby. You can avoid this if you are diligent in following my instructions every time you have intimate relations. I will bring you a warm soup of musk and *dong quai* to drink before you bring a man to your boudoir. I will remind you to place a small silk pouch containing my secret ingredients of herbs. There is nothing that will cause your pudenda to pucker or the man's stem to shrivel or burn. I've heard that the concoctions at other houses have had this effect, immediately or over time. And never listen to another courtesan who tells you to use slices of persimmon. That is an old joke some courtesans play on one another. It will dry out the pudenda and make it impossible for a man to come in. When your suitor has satisfied himself, quickly go behind the screen and wash your pudenda with saffron water. If you forget to use the pouch with my secret ingredients, I will give you a strong *dong quai* broth that will give you cramps and end anything that got started. If you have gone for two months without your monthly flow, I will call in a woman who will take care of the problem. She is quite good, although a few girls over the years got pus fever, and not all of them were as lucky as I was in avoiding death.

The third way to lose business is to get pus fever and die. So do not get pregnant. There are many other sicknesses. Don't assume that a man who is deathly ill would stay at home. Some men who know they are not long for this world want one last squeeze of pleasure. That's how strong the instinct is. If a customer is coughing and spitting and unable to catch his breath, do not drink from the same bowl of wine, no matter how much he insists. He may have tuberculosis. If a customer has red eyes and is vomiting, it may not be drunkenness but typhoid fever. You must be especially careful about sex diseases, like syphilis. You should inspect every man in your bed quickly to make sure he has no sores. Admire his stem, praise it, while giving it a thorough inspection. Even a little sore is dangerous. If you see one, pretend you are overcome suddenly with dizziness or the need to vomit, and then summon me. This is an ugly disease. Over time, sores as big as red peonies will bloom. Then the poison flowers will eat away your flesh and rot your brain. You've seen beggars in the street who have what I'm talking about. If you get the pox, don't listen to anyone who says to take mercury or rat poison. Many girls have taken the wrong amount and that's the end of them after screaming for hours in agony. I know of a better remedy that sometimes works. I'm not telling you what it is because I don't want you to think you can be careless and that old Magic Gourd can easily get rid of your sores. One last thing: Never touch a foreigner. They brought the pox to China, and I'm sure many of them have it.

The fourth way to lose business is to lose your mind. Do not become addicted to opium. You will not be able to take care of your customer if you are asleep all the time. Do not get drunk. This might cause you to laugh at a man's shortcomings. Do not cry all the time in front of others. We all have reasons we are sad. If you weep constantly, it's like you are saying your sadness is sadder than the sadness of others. How do you know? If you weep in front of suitors, they will see that trouble lies in the future if they successfully win your affections. A few tears in front of your patron is another matter. He can be moved to be kinder and more generous. But you must cry sparingly to be effective. Crying can come from genuine feelings as well, and the one your patron will love best is happiness.

PREPARING THE PUDENDA

Tomorrow, Vermillion's maid will come with her threads and remove all the hair from your pudenda, armpits, and upper lip. A virgin must be pure white. And right now you are as hairy as a man. Curly hair on the pudenda is unattractive, like seaweed, not at all silky. We'll simply have to call in Vermillion's maid once a week to keep your little mound a white tigress. Don't be tempted by ointments and poultices recommended by other courtesans as having the power to remove hair forever. Those have been known to shrivel up a woman's pudenda so that it looks like an old woman's crack. One so-called remedy ate away the girl's skin, and it was the color of raw meat after that. The courtesans who recommend them may swear they were not aware it would cause this damage, but everyone knows it was done as revenge. So if anyone comes to you with potions of any kind—to remove hair, to increase your desire or that of your suitor—come to me immediately and tell me what she said and show me what she gave you. I'll threaten to pour it on her until she admits it was an evil ruse.

For the next year, you will learn a dozen positions each month. Never do just one position. They must be used in combinations that surprise him, one rotation after another. You should provide the unexpected even on the night of your defloration. Innocence and bafflement quickly become tiresome. You cannot be lazy and helpless, expecting that your first lover will serve you, unless it is clear that this is what he desires. When a man buys your defloration, he wants your innocence, some hesitation, and cries of pain as proof that he is the first. At the same time, he does not want the awkwardness of a girl's inexperience and screaming all night long. What man wants to pry apart a girl's crossed arms and legs every few minutes without gaining headway? Men are romantic. What they hold as the ideal is not what comes naturally to women. Over the next year, we will go through lovemaking possibilities that will convince your first suitor you are worth the price. There's a famous joke told in brothels: Two men ask a man who has just deflowered a virgin, "How was the battle opening the pavilion gate? Was it as intoxicating as ten cups of wine?" The other man answers, "I got through the gate easily enough, but inside there was only half a cup." Half a cup. That's what some men say when they have paid dearly for disappointment.

I know you are not ignorant of what a man looks like in a fully florid state. When I worked at Hidden Jade Path, I used to see you peeking through my lattice window. You were like a little moth, and I couldn't yell at you without spoiling the man's arousal. I'm sure your snoopiness continued over the years, and now you yourself will practice what used to interest you so much. I have hired a young man from the opera troupe. He's a talented actor and capable of doing whatever I tell him, all the positions, the dramas, and illusions—all without piercing your bud. And there's no chance he will try. He is a homosexual and finds no pleasure in a woman's body, only in the actor's art. You will call the actor by the names that fit the lesson: Lord Yang, the Hermit, the Sage, the Marquis, and others I conjure up. He will call you Miss Delight, Madam Li, Widow Li, Lady Li, Fairy Maiden, Slave Girl, and such.

Don't worry: You will both be clothed in loose pajamas, although at times I will have him wear only bandages to cover his stem and pouches, and he'll wear the girdle and fake stem so that you can pay attention to where things fit. He won't touch you, of course, only aim in the right direction. He won't be aroused by the sight of you, so I'll ask him to caress himself so you can also see the changes in his coloring, his breathing, his pupils, and the tension and relaxation of his limbs. The bandages will be wrapped tight, so there is no danger anything will pop out.

To begin, you will learn the Four Basics: embracing, opening, piercing, and rolling. They may seem obvious, but there is an art to each of these, a rhythm and a gracefulness. The same skills of patience and gracefulness apply to all of the positions. We will practice the art of all your movements—how quickly to move your limbs, when to arch your back. Every courtesan has a hundred methods at her disposal. Upward, backward, seated, standing, feet pressed on his stomach, legs in the air, the Bucking Horse, the Swaying Bamboo Shoots, Tigress Meets the Dragon, Oysters in the Turtle Shell— all the ways that five thousand years of lovemaking, excitement, and boredom have devised. Learning takes a lifetime. To enhance your reputation, we'll invent a few ourselves.

The actor will give you lessons on convincing expressions so that you can display the Nine Urges—moaning, groaning, pleading, and so forth, but not all of them on the first night. But by the second night, you will need to show up to the eighth to prove he has awakened the maiden in the grotto. The actor will also mimic for you the Two Responses of the male: groaning with desire and then grunting with satisfaction. Gratitude should be the third, and a nice gift the fourth.

I'm going to make finger-shaped sacks—some thin, some thicker—with uncooked rice inside. He can use them to show you how to pleasure men who have difficulties getting their stem to stand up. Sometimes it falls asleep. To give him confidence, you must always refer to his stem as the Warrior or the Dragon Head. Men are very easily pleased by these words. You might be with a man who seems quite virile at the party but is ashamed later that his warrior is more of a foot soldier. For both these cases, the actor will show you how to use rings and clips, so you can see how the rice bulges upward and makes the stem straight and thick. Many customers have also favored our gold and kingfisher-blue ribbons. They become quite commanding when they wear the emperor's colors. Of course, now that the emperor has abdicated, that color may not have the same effect. I will also place in your room lust-arousing potions. Use only those, never any given to you by another courtesan. Those could be anything from vinegar to chili oil. Happiness in the Pavilion is a good brand, and it won't set the stem on fire and send your suitor leaping about in agony. It has happened with other brands. Men may think the more potions they drink, the larger they will become. That will only make them vomit or will loosen their bowels all night long. So pay attention to the amount.

Each night, I want you to lie in your bed and try to arouse yourself. I will give you a pearl polisher and a lotion called Gates Wide Open. When you can't stop yourself, you'll know what I'm talking about. If these things do not bring you to the heights, I will ask the actor to help you practice the expressions you should make. He's very professional. When a man sees a woman with urgency in her face, that's like love to him. You might as well get used to the pearl polisher. Many suitors will bring their own bag of toys, and pearl polishers are a favorite among those who like seeing a beauty writhe and gasp like a fish out of water. You will know later what I am talking about. I have received quite a few of these pearl polishers as gifts over the years. Frankly, I would have preferred a bolt of silk.

You may discover you feel little in the way of pleasure at the beginning. Many new beauties dislike sex. It may be that the first suitor is rough or the patron is old or has no lovemaking skills. Or he may be spoiled and have many ridiculous requirements, and you feel more like a nursemaid to a demanding child. Be patient. Not all of them are terrible. I am telling you about the bad ones so that if these situations happen, you will not be surprised. If you don't have romantic ideas in your head about this work, you won't be crushed.

Who knows—after your first patron, you might be surprised that your second treats you with such tenderness you will think this career is not work but play. That is seldom true with the first, however. They have purchased your defloration, and tenderness won't be what gets them through the gates. If you cry, they won't stop and soothe you. They won't apologize.

But later there will be suitors who act like true lovers, and perhaps they will genuinely want to give you pleasure. A man like this loves to watch a woman reach the immortal heights. It gives him power when he has seduced a courtesan using the same ruses she used with him. You'll be tempted to believe you are no longer a courtesan with this man. You will give yourself freely, without expectation of money, and you will believe with all your heart that this happiness will last forever. The scent of this man will cause you to abandon everything I have taught you. This will happen to you many times, with many men.

And I will be there to restore your common sense.

CHAPTER 5

THE MEMORY OF DESIRE

Shanghai
August 1912
Violet

At Loyalty Fang's dinner party, Magic Gourd and I stood by the wall near the far end of a long table crowded with revelers. Madam Li told me I would be no one special at the party, "just a little ornament," and that I should simply look pleasant and smile. "Nothing more," she warned and flashed her eyes as a threat to obey. She was nervous because the party was larger than expected, the room was too small, and a few of the extra courtesans who arrived did not meet her first-class standards of dress and manners. She was irritated that their attendants had accompanied them, and she informed them this was not the place for them to be casting for new business, so they would have to remain outside the room.

It had been nearly six months since I had been kidnapped, and over those six months, my hopes had calcified into bland acceptance in everything but the failure of my mother to return. I blamed her gullibility and carelessness for delivering me to a life in hell. During those earlier months, I had vowed to remain steadfast to who I was— the independent thinker, the student of Knowledge, the American girl who used ingenuity to solve any problem. How quickly that former self had retreated. Magic Gourd was right: My strong will had been nothing more than haughtiness, and when my freedoms were taken away from me, I was not even equal to a courtesan. Tonight, I was glad to be the little ornament. There would be no expectations and no criticism. I would simply pass the night, as if I were at the theater—once again the seven-year-old girl peering from the balcony at the guests of Hidden Jade Path.

Before the party, Madam Li had reviewed with the courtesans the names of the guests, what businesses they had, whether they were married and had concubines, and what flattery they might like to hear. Loyalty Fang, the host, was the best of the prospects. Madam Li did not have to say anything about him to the others. He was a celebrated habitué of courtesan houses. I asked Magic Gourd why there was such a clamor when it was announced that he would host a party.

"Besides being wealthy," she began, "he is well educated and from a literati family with modern business sense. He is twenty-four and still has no wives or children, which is a great worry of his mother's. Every courtesan, of course, would like to ease his mother's mind and provide her with the next generation."

"What does he look like?"

"He is not handsome in a typical way. But when he walks in the room, you see his aura of being from an elite family. He presents a cultured demeanor but is not a snob. He is at ease in whatever situation he finds himself. He immediately stands apart from those newly polished overnight successes. His eyes and mouth are sensuous—not the shape of them but how they move and express his delight and his sexual imagination. That's what everyone says. I have not verified that what he seems to express is what he also expresses in bed. But many have said that when he looks at them, they instantly picture themselves beneath him. You'll see what effect he has on the women tonight."

Like an army general, Madam Li laid out our positions. Two courtesans would stand behind each of the eight men seated at the table. Madam Li placed her daughter Vermillion across the table from Loyalty Fang's seat. He would be able to see her attributes and gracefulness, from smiling face to graceful swaying hips. And she would have opportunities to capture his attention and speak in the soft, caressing Soochow-style voice she had perfected. Madam Li would put a courtesan from another house next to Vermillion, one with far less appeal. Our three other courtesans, Little Phoenix, Green Plum, and Spring Grass, would stand opposite the next best prospects, Eminent Tang, Unison Pan, and Perceptive Lu.

From my vantage point, I could freely observe the entire scene. I had watched many handsome men at Hidden Jade Path, Westerners and Chinese, young and old, those who acted important and those who actually were. Loyalty Fang entered the room, and it felt as if the temperature and brightness of the room had warmed. I scrutinized his face to see why he was so famously handsome. In dress, he looked Western and modern. But that was typical of many guests. His hair was groomed and pomaded in the style seen in fashion magazines. Nothing unusual about that. His face was long and, to my mind, his features were ordinary. But a few minutes later, they were not. I could not put my finger on what the exact difference was, because from moment to moment, his features changed: His eyebrows rose in attention while listening to his friends. When he smiled, his eyes crinkled. His eyes grew large and dark when the talk was serious. After studying him even longer, I decided he looked like a nobleman I had seen in a painting. I saw how his eyes fell on women and captured them. With each woman, his eyebrows rose just a bit, as if it were the first time he had beheld her beauty, and the smile that followed was mischievous, mysterious, and promising. He would gaze at her, giving her his full attention, which never lasted more than a few seconds. But in those seconds, it was clear that those courtesans were engulfed with desire. Even the courtesan who had no sexual desire for men at all seemed flattered that he had noticed her. And then I saw he gave the long stare to attendants, as well, and many had been courtesans in their younger years and had not enjoyed lingering stares for a long time. He revitalized them.

He had a charismatic way with men as well, which had more to do with his easygoing manner and the sense he seemed to give each man who he had chosen as his most trusted confidant. He drew his peers into conversation; no one was left out. He posed questions, listened well, brushed off their modesty, and cited their accomplishments, without apparent glibness. I was mesmerized and believed he was genuine in who he presented himself to be.

I saw which woman had drawn his attention and on whose face he had lingered the longest, and who had received a smile more secretive than the others. Thus far, that woman was Vermillion, as expected. "Of the hundreds of parties I have attended," Vermillion said, "the food has never been more splendid. Our gratitude goes to our host for his generosity."

Loyalty, in turn, thanked Madam Li for arranging the banquet. I wondered if he knew Vermillion's flattery was insincere. She had not eaten a bite. We were not allowed to eat. If I was lucky, I would be able to taste what remained when the night was over.

A drunken guest called to me. "Eh, little flower! Eat! Enjoy!" He picked up a glistening scallop with his chopsticks, brought it over to me, and aimed for my mouth. How could I deny this man a chance to fulfill his generosity? The moment the scallop touched my parted lips, it slipped out of the man's chopsticks and slid down the front of my new jacket, from breast to lap. The man mumbled apology, and as Madam Li led him back to his seat, she assured him that this was not his fault, but that of the clumsy girl. Magic Gourd's mouth was agape. The oily stain had slithered down like the trail of a slug. "A month of earnings," she grumbled. I refused to look chastised. This was not my doing.

A moment later, I heard a ruckus. Two courtesans—the ones

Madam Li had not been pleased to see—were squabbling. A wind of whispers flew around the table and I learned that they were rivals for the same portly man they stood behind, and he had been going back and forth between them over the last two years. Madam Li quickly escorted the angry women out of the room. The portly man turned around as they left and faked confusion, as if he were the last to know what had happened. When Madam Li returned, she went to Magic Gourd. "Hurry. Take their places, both of you." Magic Gourd nudged me forward. I stood on the portly man's right side, and Magic Gourd was on his left. I had joined the theater and now had to be careful not to make mistakes, and the best way to do that was to do nothing.

I put on my simpleton smile, and was quite pleased with my acting, until Magic Gourd pinched me. She handed me a bottle of rice wine. "Hurry. Fill his bowl." Then came another pinch. "Hurry. Offer to put more of the fish on his plate." She pinched me again. "Remove the bones." She pinched me again and again to hurry do this and hurry do that. She pinched me for scowling back at her, and that's when I finally pinched her back, hard. She yelped. I heard great roars from the men and amused murmurs among the courtesans. Magic Gourd explained that I had stepped on her foot. Vermillion and Madam Li wore tight-lipped expressions, as if to keep from bursting with anger. My face was burning, and when I saw Magic Gourd staring at me, I refused to look ashamed. I looked away. And that's when I saw that Loyalty Fang was beaming at me.

"She has such spirit," he said, his eyes fixed on mine. Was he being sarcastic?

Madam Li hastened to apologize: "Our virgin courtesan has much to learn. As you can see, Violet is still very young."

"Has she been learning to recite stories or poems?" he asked.

"She is learning everything."

"Let her do a little something, then. A story, a song, a poem. She can choose."

Madam Li demurred. She had seen me rehearse the other day and had criticized Magic Gourd for my poor training. "She is not accomplished yet," Madam Li said, "not ready for your ears. Wait a few more months. One of our other beauties can play the zither for you tonight." She turned to Vermillion with bright eyes and gave a slight nod to signal this was her big chance.

But Loyalty Fang acted as if he had not heard her and beckoned me to go to where Vermillion's zither lay waiting. "Take as much time as you need to prepare," he called out. He then led the men into singing a ballad about youth and tigers. Magic Gourd arrived and seated herself by the zither. She looked as if we were about to be executed. "We will do 'Peach Blossom Spring.'" I protested that I could not. I could not remember most of it. "Pay attention to what I play on the zither," she said. "Tremble with the tremolo, sway with the glissando, and sweep your eyes upward as the music rises. Don't forget to act natural. And don't shame me," she said, "or you will be the reason we sleep on the streets tonight. Tonight, you have an opportunity to build your reputation—and whether it is good or bad will depend on what you do."

The room quieted. All eyes were on me. Loyalty Fang smiled broadly, as if he were already proud that he had discovered a talented singer in their midst. Magic Gourd swept across the zither and plucked the first few notes. I closed my eyes and opened my mouth to speak the first sentence. Nothing came out of my throat. The words were stuck. I tried for several minutes, and Magic Gourd continued to sweep across the zither, adding a few plucks that signaled the beginning of the story. I finally pushed out a strangled sound, and then trembling ones followed: "Has anyone heard the story of Peach Blossom Spring?" Of course, everyone had. A three-year-old child knew it. "I will tell it as it has never been told before," I said. Loyalty Fang grinned, and when his guests looked at him, they complimented his choice of entertainer. "This is quite special." "Excellent choice."

I began in spurts of jumbled words, and when I related how the fisherman's boat drifted lazily down the stream to paradise, I did so in a torrent of words that would have capsized the boat. Magic Gourd motioned for me to slow down and follow the zither's music. I did so, stiffly, coming in either too late or too early, and being unsure whether my expressions matched the story. When I recounted the fisherman's arrival in Peach Blossom Spring, I struggled to recall which facial expression I was supposed to show—the half-closed eyelids, or the parted lips, or the swooning tilt of my head. I did all three in sequence, and when I saw Magic Gourd, her eyes were wide with panic and she repeated a tremolo. At that point, I was so confused the jumbled contents of my memory congealed and turned me into a blockhead. I blundered into paradise like a terrified refugee. "The fisherman finds his wife still alive two hundred years later . . . even though everyone else is dead . . . and also the village is burnt to the ground. They get in the boat and return to paradise together, where virgin maidens greet him and provide him with immediate pleasure . . ."

The men burst into roars. "Immediate pleasure? *Wah!*" "This is a paradise where I want to go!" "No need to do any courting." In a wobbly voice, I added that the pleasures were delicious peaches and wine—and that the fisherman shared those with his wife, too. That elicited more laughs. Magic Gourd blinked and her mouth was open, as if she were silently screaming. Vermillion and the madam were stony-faced statues. The courtesans from other houses were barely able to contain their delight, knowing I would not be future competition of any concern.

I returned to the far end of the table to resume my place as the "little ornament." Magic Gourd stood by me and mumbled to herself, "She shamed me. She made me a fool. What will happen to me?"

I was incensed. Her shame? Were they laughing at her?

A servant brought me a bowl of wine. What's this? None of the other women had received one. Loyalty Fang stood and held up his bowl. "A single bloom, a swarm of bees, a single pierce, ten thousand slain." It was mockery made to sound like a classical witticism from a thousand years ago. "Tonight, little Violet," he continued, "with one song, you have stung all our hearts, and we would kill each other in our battle to win you." The men thundered in agreement and everyone tipped back their bowls. Magic Gourd nudged me to do the same. How cruel to make me toast my fiasco. Amid cheers, I drained my cup of humiliation in one continuous swallow. Done! I smiled. I didn't care what they thought.

"And now, little bloom," Loyalty said, "sit here beside me."

What did this mean? I looked toward Madam Li. She frowned and hurried a servant to place a chair next to the host. Vermillion was busy talking to the man whom she stood behind. She was such a good actress she knew to act as if she were unaware of what was happening. I looked to the far end of the table where Magic Gourd still stood. She gave me a weak smile. She was puzzled, too. I was helped into the chair. I saw two beauties across the table whisper to each other, blatantly eyeing me. Loyalty called for a courtesan to sing a lively ballad, and Madam Li selected one of the newer girls of the house who was known to be a songster. Everyone pretended to listen, but I knew that much of the attention was on me. I knew what they were thinking: How strange that he had singled out such a silly girl to sit next to him. The room grew noisier. With each refrain of the ballad, the men raised their cups for a toast. Loyalty Fang encouraged me to take a few sips but did not require I finish the bowl. A plate laden with food was set before me. Loyalty Fang beckoned me to eat. I looked at Madam Li, and she nodded. I tasted one dish and then another. The fish was succulent, the prawns were sweet.

I felt Loyalty Fang lean in close to me. "Seven years ago, I went to Hidden Jade Path. I was seventeen, and I thought I had entered a dreamworld. Beautiful women. Western surroundings. An American madam. I had never met a foreigner. Then I heard a naughty girl shouting as a cat darted by me. The cat flew under the sofa. Do you remember?"

I looked at his face, and after a few seconds, I saw within his grown features traces of the awkward boy who had stared at me. "It's you!" I said. "But I heard you died!"

"This is terrible news. Why am I the last to know?" The awkward boy had grown into this sensual and self-assured man.

Now I remembered the rest of the incident. Carlotta bit his hand and then slid down his arm, leaving long bleeding furrows. He had tried to pretend the ghastly wound did not hurt, but seconds later, his face went white, his teeth clenched, and then his eyes rolled back and he sank to his knees and fell forward. A crowd gathered around, and someone shouted for his father to come right away. A short while later, his limp body was carried away by two men. The next day, one of the courtesans said he had died. I feared Carlotta would be branded a murderer and I her accomplice!

"Do you remember what I asked you that night just before I died?" he said. "No? I asked in my poor English if you were a foreigner. And what was your answer? Do you recall?"

I did not recall the conversation, but the only answer I would have given was yes.

He continued: "You said in Chinese that you did not understand what I was saying. And then you bent down to search for your cat. I saw the tail flicking from underneath the sofa and grabbed it to pull the cat out. Here is the souvenir of that mistake."

Loyalty Fang pushed up one sleeve. "Violet Minturn," he said in his unsteady English. "Look what your cat done me." I shivered to see those pale white scars. He spoke again, this time in his beautiful Chinese. "I have waited a long time for your apology, Violet. And now I have been more than compensated for my pain."

So he had indeed meant to humiliate me. "I apologize to you for the bad cat and the bad story I recited tonight," I said tersely.

"I did not mean it that way. I cherished your telling of the tale. I know it was your first performance. And it was for me. You were truly charming."

I did not believe him.

He took on a serious expression. "When I was seventeen, my father took me to Hidden Jade Path for my initiation into the world of flowers. I felt as if I were in a dreamland of fairies and gods. He said that when I became a success, I would be able to visit however often I wanted. Just being there caused excruciating yearning for romance, and I was angry my father had shown me the delights and then denied them to me. I was determined to be richer than he one day and to woo all the beautiful flowers I wanted in this dreamland. I had remained single-minded about this goal. Within a few years, I became successful in business and had all the pretty flowers I could possibly want. But I had forgotten the dreamland that had motivated me. I forgot to return and fulfill that seventeen-year-old boy's yearning. I grew complacent, although not content. But I was too busy to notice anything was missing.

"Over the last two years, I have been feeling both a little bored and vaguely dissatisfied. I still enjoyed my life, but I felt I was not moving forward. There was nothing to move forward to. I decided I needed to stir myself up, and come alive—stretch my tendons, my mind, my spirit. But how? Until I knew, I felt this unease would stay with me like a bothersome toothache.

"A few months ago, I was at a party with one of my old school-mates, Eminent Tang—he's seated at the end of this table. He was telling me about all the businesses that had been taken over by either the Japanese or the Green Gang. Hidden Jade Path was one. As soon as he said that name, I recalled the dream and my promise to return. I hurried over to the place with seven years of anticipation coiled in my body. But the dreamland was gone. The house was no longer the same.

"I told Eminent about my disappointment and asked what had happened to the American madam. He gave me the story. I'm truly sorry about what happened, Violet. I admired your mother very much and the world she created. But I must be honest that when I heard you were now living at the House of Vermillion, I felt as if a string of firecrackers had gone off in my head, heralding the return of the dream. I know that you did not come here willingly, and I assure you I was not thinking about you in a lustful way. After all, in my mind, you were still a seven-year-old brat. What I realized about the dreamland, however, was the power it once held simply by being withheld from me. It created yearning—and also purpose. It demanded the best of me to meet my purpose: diligence, intelligence, and an understanding of myself and of others. I had to weigh opportunity and morality, ambition and fairness. My early resolve to be successful and independent came from that hunger of desire, which had yet to be sated.

"As I had hoped, when I saw you here, the memory of desire returned, the power of yearning, excitement rippled through me, and I knew it would lead me forward again—to where, I don't yet know. I feel with you the deep aching of a new desire. The desire is the elusive dream that will infuse me with new purpose. Without purpose, I can't see my future. I'm stuck in the present, counting off the days, with mortality staring me in the face."

My heart was racing with pride and excitement, but I was also confused. I did not want to make any mistakes in fulfilling—or rather, not fulfilling—his dream. "You want to think of me as someone who is not real? Is that it?"

"Oh, you are very real. But you are from the dream that was my touchstone, and still can be. You are my memory of desire. Do you mind if I think of you this way? Someone I will forever yearn for, based on what I remembered in my youth?"

"I'm sure I can help you keep the dream strong. What should I do to withhold myself from you? Should I ignore you?"

"Not at all! You should be as charming as you are. In fact, you should do what you can to increase my desire. I will use my willpower and do all the withholding. Give it your best efforts. The stronger my desire, the stronger my willpower, and the stronger my purpose in life. That's what I need to rid me of this nagging complacency."

He wanted an unconsummated romance. I was a little disappointed. I imagined what would be denied him—our bodies pressed together, limbs encircled, our cries of endearment, the little nap afterward. At that moment, I longed for him—and a second thought followed. I longed for a Chinese man, and until this very second I had not considered him to be one race or the other. How strange! I had practiced the arts of seduction, believing I would never have to use them here. In refusing to believe I would not, I had never imagined I might desire one of the customers of the house. I wanted romance, knowledge of him and our bodies together. I felt freed, relieved, and joyful to be unbound. I had fought all these years against the Chinese half becoming mine. I resented it was there. But now I was no longer wavering between the two halves. I had stepped across a threshold that had divided my American and Chinese halves only to discover I had imagined there was any such line. I was still myself, no different, and I did not have to deny who I was. He yearned for all of me and not half. I yearned for all of him. Such tragedy for the two of us! We were monk and nun to each other. By suffering desire, we helped each other become—what was it he said?—invigorated with purpose? I would have to find one. But at least Loyalty Fang was mine for the night, and everyone could see that.

I sat confidently beside him as he conversed with his friends. I admired his leisurely manner of speech, typical of literati families, perfectly articulated without a hint of a regional burr, and embellished with a few archaic phrases. This was the man who longed for me. He casually mentioned heroes and maidens from novels to emphasize a humorous point. He talked about his work with a consortium concerning the new government and the United States. He asked his guests for their opinions on the new president and rephrased each person's answer to make it seem that they were better informed than they actually were. This man, who discussed so knowledgeably the reasons why the rubber factories went bankrupt, had never-ending yearning for me. He addressed his friends but glanced often at me and smiled. I was his dream.

"Little Violet," he suddenly said, "tell us what you think. Should I invest in Japanese companies with new equipment, as the bankers say I should? Or should I buy the failing Chinese companies and equip them with new machinery and management? Which way would make enough money to pay for this very expensive banquet?"

Magic Gourd had told me I should answer any questions asking for my opinion by deferring to a man's better knowledge of the situation. Agree with him. Anything else would signal I was brainless to think I knew more than he did and that I would also be annoyingly chatty in bed. But I was flush with tipsy bravado, bolstered by his recent confession, along with two bowls of wine. I had listened to countless heated discussions between my mother and her clients on the subject of foreign investments. I had always thought the conversations were tedious. The guests asked the same questions. Mother gave the same answers, chock-full of facts and figures, predictions and projections. She used to practice them in front of Golden Dove, and Golden Dove would suggest that she move her hands a certain way. I would listen through the door in Boulevard and then deliver those lines to Carlotta, who purred, quite happy to listen.

And so I mimicked my mother once again. I rose from my chair and stood with erect posture and delivered the memorized phrases, along with the hand gestures—and with far more ease than I had earlier with my sad rendition of "Peach Blossom Spring." I imagined I was she, confident and with erect posture, as I spoke in her theatrical authoritative voice of optimism: "I recommend a farsighted approach to the answer. Who benefits if your company contributes to Japanese expansion of their businesses, buildings, and profitability? Is it to the detriment of our fledgling Republic? Of course, a businessman cannot make decisions based solely on nationalism. But I believe the new Republic presents an unprecedented opportunity.

Buy up the failing Chinese cotton mills to start, select new partner-
ships with American investment companies, using the new policies
to come under the Republic. You can then rebuild the cotton mills
with modern equipment, infuse them with better management, and
receive a larger share of the profits than what you would have had by
investing in a Japanese company. The growth of Japanese businesses
is the growth of Japanese power, and we should all look to the future
and be wary. You, then, can be a model for commerce in the new
Republic: one that is progressive, Chinese controlled, and supportive
of foreign trade policies that benefit the Republic." I sat down.

Loyalty Fang nodded solemnly. The men at the table were quiet,
stunned. No one agreed or disagreed. The courtesans were baffled,
and I knew what they were thinking: Was this flaunting of opinion
good or would it prove damaging?

Loyalty smiled. "What you said is precisely what I intend to do.
I am dazzled by your knowledge and, more so, your spirit, how vivacious you are, so full of surprise."

At the end of the night, Loyalty Fang gave Magic Gourd a large
tip. He apologized for the behavior of his drunken younger brother,
the man who had dropped the scallop on my jacket. He added a sum
of money that was enough to buy three new jackets to replace the
ruined one. "Lake green," he said. "That color would complement
her eyes." And then he told Madam Li that he wished to be the first to
host a party in honor of the virgin courtesan Violet.

"I hope you won't spend too lavishly," I teased, "since you can
never have me."

"Why can't I have you?"

"You said you want to yearn for me forever, to have the dream
withheld."

"Ah! That is exactly right. In the dream it's this way. But we are
awake and can control our lives. I can yearn for you, I can woo you,
and I can eventually, with your permission, fulfill my desire in your
bed—unless you still have that cat."

Back in our room, Magic Gourd bubbled over our success. "The story of Peach Blossom Spring needs more polishing, of course. But now we do not need to hide your half-Western origins. Everyone is talking about your Eurasian blood as an advantage."

This was the first time I had heard her use the word *Eurasian*.

"I heard Loyalty and another man describe you that way. They did not say it as an insult. It was rather like elevating your value. That was why the men thought you were captivating when you told the story. You are Eurasian, they said, yet you speak Chinese so well. And now he is hosting your debut party! It must mean he will buy your defloration." I did not tell her what Loyalty had said. She would ruin it with her interpretation of what it meant.

I picked up Carlotta. As she purred, I reminded her of the boy she nearly killed. She was as happy as I was that he had returned.

The gossip from the first party was reported in all the tabloids. "She is Eurasian and accomplished in both languages." "Her storytelling was charming and natural in an unrehearsed way." "She was at ease entertaining men of importance, conversant on all topics, even those concerning foreign control." All the tabloids dropped names of the famous and powerful: Eminent Tang, who had formed a partnership with several banks to finance the construction of new buildings that were rising along the Bund. Perceptive Lu, whose father had met with the United States consul general to discuss foreign loans. One man was dating a famous actress. Another had an enviable collection of rare scroll paintings.

Most of the gossip concerned Loyalty Fang, the host. The gossip columns in the mosquito press mentioned the shipping companies he owned, the favorable trade routes he had managed to negotiate. They listed his porcelain factories in Hong Kong and Macau. They touted that his family was among the most distinguished of the literati in Shanghai who had been important in building the new Republic. And every one of the tabloids reported that the virgin courtesan Violet had a Chinese face and Western green eyes, which she inherited from her mother, the famed American madam, Lulu Mimi. "How lucky that the House of Vermillion was able to capture this unusual flower. What gifts will he next bring her? Will it be teacups and saucers or large tureens with foreign family crests? Whose family crest would appear on hers? That of her American mother?"

Eurasian looks had become my advantage and not my flaw. Besides Loyalty, eleven men hosted debut parties for me. Madam Li boasted about the number by saying it was excessive to call them debuts after two. None was more lavish than my first debut, which was the one hosted by Loyalty. I sat at the table beside him. The courtesans sat behind the men who were Loyalty's guests. The banquet had foods more rare than the last—tastes no one had ever had, food for the gods. He hired musicians, and, in my honor, they included an American who played the banjo, an instrument I had never heard and which sounded to me like a zither whose musician had gone mad.

I expected Loyalty would come daily and ply me with gifts to increase his yearnings in anticipation of my defloration. Instead, he came once every five or six days and would then be absent for one or two weeks, with not even a card to tide over the period in between. Magic Gourd sent messages to his house, using all kinds of pretexts: "Violet will perform a new song tonight." "Violet will wear a new jacket, made possible by your generosity." The answer was always the same: "He is away from Shanghai."

Without notice, he would appear in the late afternoon when the house was quiet. He always brought an unusual gift. One was a goldfish in a large bowl with seven goldfish painted on the interior. "This little fish is the lucky eighth. With so many painted fish, he will not be lonely."

"You must leave me with seven replicas of you so that I am not lonely as well." After that, I did not hear from him for ten days. When he showed up—unexpectedly, as usual—I had to keep my growing annoyance hidden. I could not presume I could make demands. Our romance was clouded by commerce. He spent money on me, gave

Magic Gourd tips and me gifts. Meanwhile, Madam Li and Magic Gourd were tallying the amounts, calculating how much more he might be willing to spend. "We can't expect the amount will be as big as what Vermillion received," Madam Li said. Back in my room, Magic Gourd said, "You will fetch more than Vermillion. And then we'll show Madam Li to never underestimate us."

Two and a half months before my scheduled defloration, Loyalty arrived and stayed only an hour. He told Magic Gourd and me that he was leaving for the United States on a business matter. He said it nonchalantly. I knew it would take a month to simply reach San Francisco! If he did go, he might not return in time for the bidding of my defloration. Maybe he would never return, like my mother.

I had assumed too much. He wanted an unconsummated romance. I was naive. I did not understand him, or Chinese men, or the purchase of sexual favors.

"You will be gone so long," I said, "you will likely miss my fifteenth birthday on February twelfth."

He frowned. "When I return, I will make amends with a lovely birthday gift."

"Madam Li expects my defloration will take place at the same time."

He frowned again. "I did not realize . . . This is unfortunate timing. I know it's disappointing." He took my hand but did not say he would cancel his trip. I fell mute with disappointment.

Magic Gourd tried to dissuade Loyalty from making the voyage. She cited the recent sinking of *Titanic*. A Japanese ship also went down not that long ago. Ice and typhoons were very bad this year.

A month later, Madam Li told me that eleven men who had hosted parties for me were eager to buy my defloration. Loyalty Fang was not among them. She patted my arm. "I called. I asked the secretary to send a cable urging him to consider. The secretary said it was hard to reach him, even by cable. But she said she would try."

Madam Li went on to review the men who wished to bid. For the first time, I had to confront the fact that one of those eleven men would win the privilege of breaking me open for business. I could not recall a single one who did not repulse me in that regard. Would it be the blowhard, or the man old enough to be my grandfather, or the one covered in oily perspiration even on the coldest days? What about the dimwit with ridiculous opinions? There was one who frightened me: a thin man with small eyes and a piercing stare. He never smiled. I thought he was a gangster. There were a few who would not have been objectionable to other courtesans. They did not mind if they were dull, as long as they had money. Those same men did not ask for my opinions. They did not expect me to understand their conversations with their friends. They did not compliment me on my high spirit. They were not interested in me, only in the prize that lay between my legs. At their dinner parties, they asked only that I tell the story "Peach Blossom Spring." They had read in the tabloids that I did this quite well.

A date was announced for my defloration: February 12, 1913, the day of my fifteenth birthday, the one-year anniversary of the emperor's abdication. A doubly auspicious day to be celebrated. I did a quick calculation. It was five weeks away. Was Loyalty on his way home?

More parties were thrown in my honor. But Madam Li said I was so listless she had to tell each man that I was suffering from a headache.

The contenders were allowed into my boudoir for tea. Magic Gourd was always present to make sure no man pried from me an early sample. I could no longer ignore the inevitable. I imagined each man touching my pristine body. They were all revolting trespassers.

The days went by with relentless speed. I was always cognizant that Madam Li would soon make her final decision based on the offers received. I begged her to consider my feelings and wait for Loyalty Fang to return. I would not be able to hide my disgust with any of the current prospects, I explained, and they would feel cheated. If the man proved brutal, I might never overcome the horror of the first time. It would ruin me for any future courtships. For once, she seemed a little sympathetic.

"I felt the same with my defloration," Madam Li said. "I hoped for one suitor and won a different one, a man old enough to be my grandfather. I thought of killing myself. When the time came, I kept my eyes shut tight and pretended the man was someone else. I pretended I was someone else. I was somewhere else. When he broke through my gates, there was so much pain I genuinely forgot who I was. I realized the pain would have been the same, regardless of who might have broken me open. The man told me afterward that just as he was making headway, I shouted for him to take back his money. And then I fainted. The man was pleased about that. He said it was proof that I had been a virgin. You can pretend to faint. It may also happen without pretending." Madam Li's words were not consoling.

One afternoon, with less than two weeks before my scheduled defloration, Madam Li ran on and on about a suitor who owned seven factories that manufactured parts of things: headlamps for automobiles, pull chains for porcelain toilets, and the like. Every year, his wealth tripled. He was not from the most prestigious family, but in today's Shanghai, prestige could be bought and people did not care as much about your origins. The offer he made was so large compared with the others that it would be foolish to refuse. Until then, she would not tell me whose offer was the highest. That was a matter I should not be concerned with. But now the highest bidder was growing impatient. He would wait another three days and then his offer would evaporate. If that happened and news of it went around, the others would rescind their offers as well. And the bidding would begin again with lower offers because the men would then know that time was too short to recover from the rejection. She told me with an apologetic face that the one who would likely buy my defloration was the thin man who never smiled.

"This is not a tragedy. If you delight him, you can change his expression into smiles," she said. "Then he will look less unappealing."

For two days I could not sleep or eat. I pitied myself. On the second day, I loathed myself. On the morning of the third, I recalled what Madam Li said about closing my eyes and pretending I was someone else. I did not want to be a girl who had no mind of her own. That would be a brainless living death. I wasn't going to stand around like an ornament or wear a simpleton's smile all night long. I did not want my happiest emotion to be relief.

I recalled that hated phrase my mother used: "a matter of necessity." I once thought she applied that like a tarp over selfish desires. It occurred to me that she also used that view to accept a bad situation, to let go of how she thought of herself. She did what was a matter of necessity. "Every difficult situation has its particular circumstances," she had said, "and only you know what those are. Only you can decide what is necessary to achieve the best possible outcome." I thought about my circumstances. I did not know what the best possible outcome might be. I did not know what I would decide was necessary to achieve it. But I resolved I would not kill myself nor lose myself. And with that, I no longer pitied or loathed myself. I was no longer helpless in spirit. But it did not remove my disgust for the bony man.

That afternoon, just before Madam Li was supposed to give her answer to the bony man, a cable came from Loyalty notifying Madam Li that a letter would arrive that day. "It concerns the privilege of Violet's defloration. Please forgive the tardiness of my offering. I will explain in person why it was delayed."

For two hours, I paced, wondering if the offer would be large enough. When the letter arrived, Madam Li took it into another room. A minute later, she emerged, and quickly nodded her head with a big smile. "All that you wish," she said.

I should have been jubilant. But fear prickled me. We began with the romance that we would always yearn for each other and never be fulfilled. All that I wished might not be all that I received. I was afraid to trust happiness. Why did I hear nothing from him for so long? I lay on my bed, away from everyone, to think about what I wished. I had a sobering thought: I was entering into the life of a courtesan—willingly. Before, I had no choice but to become one. Now I chose to be with Loyalty. Within this life was all that I wished. But I also knew what lay ahead: all the changing futures of being a courtesan. Even if I could leave the courtesan world one day, I would not be able to completely shed that I had once been a courtesan, not in my mind and not in the mind of others.

Two days before the defloration, Loyalty returned. He begged forgiveness for the torment I had been through. He had prepared his offer long ago, he said, and his secretary was supposed to deliver it. She never did. It was found on her desk below another letter she had written to him. He showed it to me:

> *I am a virtuous woman and a faithful employee. For three years, I have done all that you asked without complaint, without mistake. It is my own misfortune and fault that I harbored love for you, and it was increasingly unbearable that you never noticed. I could have continued in obscurity. But I could not see you give yourself to a creature with no morals, who wants none of your goodness and only your money. I apologize that I did not do as you asked. It is the only time I have disobeyed you.*

"She hanged herself in my office after everyone had left for the day," he said. "That was how I learned that my letter to you had never been sent."

I was horrified. I imagined her pain. I, too, harbored love for Loyalty. I would not have been able to hide it for three years. But I would not have killed myself.

FOR MY DEFLORATION ceremony, Madam Li, with Magic Gourd's encouragement, chose to hold a mock Western wedding. Loyalty's offer had included a contract to be my patron for one year. I allowed myself to believe I would not be simply a bride but a wife. I had already started yearning to be a real one.

The day before the wedding, a dress arrived, a gift from Loyalty. It was an American wedding dress, made in New York, ivory silk with seed pearls, which flowed in one piece from bosom to ankles, wrapping around the shape of my body. He included satin shoes with heels, and, by his written instructions, I should let my hair hang loose, unbound, with only the pearl beaded veil of organza over my face. When I looked in the mirror, I did not recognize myself. I was not a young naive girl. I looked sophisticated and modern, elegant and elongated. I turned my hips one way and then the other. The veil wafted upward, and I gasped to see a different face. And then it was gone. I turned sideways and again I saw the other face. This time I recognized my mother's features in me. I had never seen them so clearly. This was the sort of dress she would have worn. This was how she would have turned her hips. This was the look on her face, knowing a Chinese man—my father—would soon bed her.

Loyalty was pleased to see me in the wedding clothes. He wore a tailored English suit. I leaned against him and whispered that I would be his fairy maiden tonight, the one he had wished to court in Hidden Jade Path. After twelve banquet dishes, Loyalty's wedding gifts were toted out, which would enable me to refurnish my boudoir: a dining table and chairs in the latest Western style, an armchair, sofa, and chaise longue, three flower stands, a desk, a bookcase, novels in English, a bureau, two wardrobe closets, a Western canopy bed, a Persian carpet, three Tiffany lamps, and a tabletop Victrola. At the very end of the ceremony, he placed on my finger a jade-and-diamond ring. He discreetly left on one of the flower stands a red silk envelope of money, which I saw Madam Li take away.

We thanked the wedding guests and made our way to the boudoir. As I passed Magic Gourd, she gave me a nod of encouragement but her face bunched into worry. Or was it sympathy in knowing what awaited me?

The doorway was hung with dozens of red banners, and pots of flowers crowded the entrance. Inside, two lamps glowed and the room was scented with roses and jasmine. The marriage bed was enclosed within golden curtains of silk batiste.

Magic Gourd entered bearing hot towels and tea. She held the matches we would use for the Lighting of the Big Candles.

"We don't need to perform those old-fashioned customs," Loyalty said. I was disappointed. I liked the mock-wedding rituals I had watched as a child. He gave Magic Gourd a tip, an indication that she should leave. The door closed, and we were alone for the first time.

"My little captive," he said, and stared at me fully, head to toe. He kissed me. Magic Gourd had not allowed the actor to do that. He ran his hands over my back, my sides, and kissed my neck, and my eyes blurred with the sensation. He returned to my mouth. This was the feeling of love. He unbuttoned my dress. Everything was happening so quickly I could not remember what I was supposed to do. I was glad he had not asked me to sing a song. The dress fell to my ankles. He lifted off the slip, and as he removed the rest of my clothes, he kissed each newly revealed part of me. He freely inspected me, touched my breasts. This was love.

He motioned for me to go to the bed. I slipped behind the curtains and lay as gracefully as I could on my side. Through the golden scrim, I watched his shadow as he lazily removed his clothes. I saw he was already aroused when he parted the curtain. I had expected this would not occur until later. Suddenly I became frightened. I knew what would come, the cracking of the watermelon, the burning rocks, Peach Blossom Spring gushing blood. He lay next to me and inspected my face and stroked the slopes of my cheek, chin, nose, and forehead. When he touched my trembling mouth, my lips naturally parted.

"Keep your lips sealed. Do not open them, no matter what I do. Do not make a sound." He again traced the curves of my face and I closed my eyes. Suddenly I felt his hand cup my pudenda. I gave out a gasp of alarm, then murmured I was sorry.

He laughed. "Ah, good, this was not rehearsed. It is truly you." He reminded me to close my mouth. He squeezed my pudenda softly, as if determining the ripeness of a peach. I pressed my eyes closed as he parted the lips of my pudenda. "There it is, the pearl, the center of you," he said. "Such a lovely pale pink. I chose the color of your pearl necklace correctly." He showed me the necklace and then tucked the beads along my cleft. "There," he said, "pearls joining the pearl." He suddenly drew the necklace upward, and I caught my breath with a spasm of surprise.

"Keep your mouth closed," he ordered firmly. I was disappointing him. I clamped my lips tightly, and over and over, they opened, despite my efforts. He tucked pillows under my hips so that my pudenda was lifted high. My panic was growing. Was this Climbing the Mountain? He bent my legs and pressed them wide open. Double-Winged Bird? Seagull Wings on the Edge of the Cliff? He knelt between my knees. I felt his stem nudge my opening and he slowly pushed in the tip, and I prepared myself for pain. But now we were rocking from side to side. Pair of Swooping Eagles. I smiled at him, thinking he had already entered me. He lifted his hips away from me. I assumed he was one of those men who finished quickly. No matter. The defloration was a success. I would tell Magic Gourd she was wrong. There was no pain.

Then, all at once, his stem thrust hard into me, farther this time, through my center, gutting me inside out. Against everything Magic Gourd had warned me not to do, I screamed and tried to push him off. He pinned my arms down and stared at my mouth. "Now you can keep your mouth open. The other mouth is open, too."

Nothing had prepared me for this. Magic Gourd's instructions, her warnings, his nostalgia, my urges, the actor's lessons, our yearning, unfulfilled and filled—all vanished as I pleaded for him to stop.

But why should he stop? This was not romance or yearning. He had paid for my pain. This was business.

YEARNING RETURNED, UNFULFILLED.

All that I wished became an illusion the moment he deflowered me and I saw victory in his face. He had instantly satisfied his own dream as a seventeen-year-old boy—to have any of the flowers he desired at Hidden Jade Path. I thought our romance was love, but it was the commerce of romance that had brought us together and would also lie between us for the duration of his contract as my patron.

As I lay clutched with pain, he murmured, "You were expensive, Violet, nearly twice what I gave to another popular courtesan." He must have expected I would be pleased to hear this kind of flattery. Instead, I felt I had instantly become a whore. He had wooed me, as any suitor would his favorite courtesan. He wanted the chase and capture, the self-denial and mock agony in between. My agony was real.

Magic Gourd brought me a soup with special herbs that she said would ease my suffering and allow me to sleep. Only then did Loyalty ask in surprise if I was in pain. He had not considered that his ecstasy might not be mine. He helped me up and carried me to the divan. Each of his steps jostled my wounded body. Magic Gourd removed the bloody sheets and quilt. Loyalty studied it with solemn interest. "I did not realize there would be so much blood."

The next morning, when I awoke, I thought I was swaying in a boat. Magic Gourd was nearby. "I gave you too much soup." The scorching pain had been replaced with a dull ache. Loyalty had left for a business meeting, and she arranged for dinner to be brought to my room when he returned in the evening. Persian pajamas and a robe lay on the bed.

"Rest," she said. "I'm sorry you suffered so much. Some girls have brief pain and then it is over. Others are like you and me. You had your gate locked with two bolts. The harder it is to break in, the more pain. You will feel better by tomorrow."

I did not believe her. "Will I have to endure this again tonight?"

"I will speak to him. You have a year together. I will suggest he explore your mouth instead. He may be kind and simply let you rest."

That evening, he was kind. He asked many questions about the pain. Was it stabbing or searing or pounding . . . He almost seemed proud that he had injured me. He lay on the bed, facing me. There was no longer any need to be flirtatious or mysterious. That had been our intimacy, and I did not yet know what would replace it. I was no longer the virgin and I did not know whom I should mimic. His face looked larger and his features had changed slightly, as if he were the brother of the man who had once ached for me.

"Was it my free spirit that made you think I was more valuable than the other courtesan?" I asked.

He laughed. "Your spirit always invigorates me—suddenly."

His penis was standing straight up like a soldier. "What part of my spirit did you like best?" I said tersely. "Was it my business advice? If you made money because of my advice, would you have paid more?"

He was quiet, then turned my face toward him. "Violet, I misjudged you. You weren't ready for this life, and now you find it demeaning to be here. But don't demean me as if I were an inconsiderate customer."

"You paid for my bud, not for my spirit."

"My words have always been true. You are my living dream. I met you when I was the awkward boy who became a successful man and is beside you now. You took me to my past and back again, and when I am with you, I feel you know me—or did, until I became your patron and made you regret this change."

"Please take me away from here."

"How can I do that? Where would you go?"

"Your house."

"Now you're asking the impossible."

He was saying I did not belong in his society. He would never take me as his wife, and since he had no wife, he could not take me even as a concubine. I would have refused to be one, in any case.

"We have a year together, Violet. We've pledged fidelity. Here we are lovers, together in a world like Peach Blossom Spring. We can freely enjoy romance and pleasures. You have freedom from worry for a year. Let's be happy."

"Freedom from worry is happiness? What happens at the end of the year?"

"When a contract is over," he said carefully, "my affection for you will remain. The expectations will be different. But I will still visit you, if you let me."

"Will you have affection for another and visit her as well?"

"This talk has become absurd! You lived in a courtesan house nearly all your life. You saw the nature of that world. Yet now you cannot understand how it possibly pertains to you. Yankee privilege. I will not give that back to you. And I don't want to speak about this again."

"I cannot speak? Have you bought my mind and words as well?"

He dressed, and when he stood in the doorway, he said with surprising gentleness: "You are overwrought and my presence makes it worse. So I'll leave you to reflect on what I've said over the months since we first met. Ask yourself whether I have ever been dishonest. Did I delude you? Why am I here? I won your heart because you won mine."

I was afraid he was leaving for good and that he would ask Madam to cancel the contract.

But then he said, "By tomorrow, you'll be better rested and your mind will be clearer. I have a little gift for you, but I prefer to wait until tomorrow."

The following night, I pretended to be calm. I apologized. I said it was true that I found it hard to accept my new station in life. He gave me a bracelet of twisted gold braid. There was only a little pain when he entered me this time, and he murmured endearments, which eased my heart and mind: "You are my timeless dream;" "Our spirits are together;" he thanked me tenderly for bearing the pain and his ignorance that I had suffered. He said that I would always be his timeless dream.

Over the next year, we had many arguments. When he paid his generous stipend each month, instead of being grateful, I was reminded that I had been purchased. He did not visit every day. Sometimes I did not see him for a week. "Business in Soochow," he said. Soochow—the city of the most desired courtesans, who had soft voices. Shanghai courtesans lied and said they were from Soochow. And he went there for business! I wanted him to take me along. Madam Li had allowed me to go on carriage rides with him into the countryside, believing I had no desire to run away from the house. But I did want to run away—to his house, if only he would take me. I held out hope that he would change his mind. I was faithful, of course, but I did not believe he was. At parties, I saw him give his seductive gaze to many women—to even the attendants. He protested to me that he had no such "mesmerizing eyes," as I had accused him of having. "I have two eyes like everyone else."

The thought of his future delight with other women tormented me. Another woman would feel this same pleasure with him. She would have his seductive gaze, intimate words, his mouth, tongue, and cock, his understanding of her, his love. She would convince him he could not live without her, a woman who was purely Chinese and did not bear the stigma in elite society of careless breeding. With each wave of joy came another one of fear. Perhaps his love was only temporary as well, a season's worth.

"This is the jealousy I warned you against," Magic Gourd said. "It is an illness. It will destroy everything. You'll see soon, if you cannot stop it." She repeated her warnings every day, and they stayed in my head like the noise of mosquitoes in my ears.

The noise in my head disappeared in the summer. As if it were a sign of our future together, Carlotta rubbed against him and allowed him to pick her up. We had a season of calm, a lull in worries. He visited me at night nearly daily. At the parties, he gave his gaze to me alone. We laughed and did not argue. I made an effort to show him the endless joy we would have during a lifetime of Peach Blossom Spring. He was more attentive to me and I was inattentive to what I imagined were his faults.

On hot afternoons, we lay naked atop the sheets and took turns fanning each other. We poured cool water over our necks as we lay together in the tub. On some evenings, I teased and seduced him, and on other nights, he seduced me and I succumbed. We talked about the past, about our childhoods. We often retold how we met in Hidden Jade Path. The next day, we would lavish the story with more details. He imagined the delights he would have enjoyed if Carlotta had not wounded him. Whatever he imagined, I fulfilled. I, in turn, told him about my loneliness, my abandonment by both my mother and father. Just in telling it, my loneliness vanished. He laughed as I recounted the naughty things I had done to the courtesans when I was growing up. He asked about the American details of my life—what was the famous Lulu Mimi like? "She was driven by success," I said. "Like you."

He lit incense coils to keep the mosquitoes away, and I took those small gestures as love. He often said the words I wanted to hear: "I am consumed by you." "I ache for you." "I adore you." "I love you." "You are the greatest treasure of my life." I had never before felt the wideness of love.

And then the fears began when I saw him speak to his former favorite courtesan at a party. She flirted, and he seemed delighted. We argued that night, and I continued to press him on his feelings for me compared with others, questions he refused to answer because, he said, it was like feeding stones into a deep well. He knew how angry

I could become, and that was also knowledge of me he would take when he left, along with the secrets I had confessed about my childhood and loneliness and pranks. He possessed an understanding of my needs, and yet he would no doubt roll and twist his body in bed with another woman after I had become a former favorite in his lifetime of conquests and stipends.

"It pains me, Violet," he said, "that I am the source of your greatest unhappiness when I had once been the opposite."

Two months before the end of the contract, when we were having the usual late-night tea, snacks, and arguments, he said he did not want to be drawn into any more of my endless misery. "I was enchanted with your free spirit, and jealousy has killed that in you. You live in a prison of fear and suspicion. The truth is, I've indulged you in ways no patron ever would have. You say my words were never genuine. A patron is not required to be genuine and yet I have been. I know you will never stop with this harangue unless I ask you to marry me, and that I will never do. Even if society let me, I would not consign myself to a wife who berates me, imagining that I have withheld part of me that does not exist. Since we are both unhappy, I think it's best that I not visit you anymore. You should use these two months to prepare yourself to be a real courtesan. You will learn the difference, and in time, I hope you look back and appreciate my feelings for you." He gathered his coat and hat. "Accept love when it's offered, Violet. Return love and not suspicion. Then you'll receive more."

He continued to pay the monthly stipend. I waited for his anger to subside, as it always had, and for him to return to me. I waited for two months. He was considerate enough to wait until the contract had officially ended before he pursued a popular courtesan. When I heard this news, I refused to be brokenhearted. Every day I refused.

THREE MONTHS AFTER the end of the contract, I was invited to attend a party hosted by Loyalty's friend Eminent Tang. He said he had been interested in me when he saw me at Loyalty's party, but he could not say anything once he saw Loyalty was besotted.

Magic Gourd was quick to tell me Eminent Tang was a good prospect. She reminded me that he was the one who had made a fortune in the construction of new buildings along the Bund. He was bound to grow even richer as Shanghai grew. As she had hoped, Eminent became my most ardent suitor. He was also my first customer and not someone I loved or yearned for. When I imagined him touching me, I felt neither dread nor excitement. "Are you losing your eyesight?" Magic Gourd said. "That man is pleasing enough to look at all day without blinking. After you've been on your knees as long as I have, you'll kowtow to the gods to finally have a client who won't cause you to pretend he is someone else."

He was thirty-two, and every time I saw him, I noticed he wore shoes of another kind of leather—lamb, calf, young snake, baby alligator, baby ostrich . . . How many times would I see him before he ran out of a variety of baby animal skins? His shoes made me think he was eccentric. I hoped he was not a member of the Green Gang. If he was, I would not be able to bear touching him. I had accepted my life in the world of flowers, but I would never accept what the gangsters had done to bring me here.

"If you refused every man who has dealings with the Green Gang," Magic Gourd said, "you would be without half of your customers. They are part of government and business. Even some of the police in top positions are members. They are not all terrible people. In any large society, you have good people and bad." She pointed out Eminent Tang's good qualities: He was the favorite customer of many courtesan houses in Shanghai and had had his share of great beauties. If I secured his patronage it would increase my status. This, to my mind, did not sound like a recommendation of fine qualities.

"He's dull," I said.

"*Oyo!* He is not there to entertain you. Just make sure you are not dull. You are the one who has to provide excitement, and in the ways they want but don't yet know it. This is not like being with Loyalty Fang. He was different. You were lovers. That does not often happen."

She allowed Eminent to visit me in my room for tea. The boudoir was behind a twelve-panel screen, and Magic Gourd had positioned the screen so that part of the bed could be seen. It was glowing by lamplight. She found an excuse to leave, letting us know she would return in ten minutes. This would discourage him from starting his patronage without a contract. Eminent rushed to tell me how much I occupied his mind. He never forgot the business advice I had provided at Loyalty's party last year. In fact, he said, whenever he recalled it, his admiration for me rose. They were the same words Loyalty had used to joke that he had an erection. Eminent Tang, however, said them with such seriousness, I knew he meant it was admiration alone and that I should not laugh.

He requested me at parties hosted by his friends at other houses. He had a businesslike demeanor with everyone, except me. When his eyes found mine, he grinned and became boyish. Magic Gourd had pointed out to me that every suitor who was infatuated with a courtesan transformed into his youthful self-being at that stage of his life when his sexual urgings were new. When suitors became boyish they were reckless and vulnerable to being generous.

Eminent Tang had given me extravagant gifts over the past month, including a ring with rare imperial green jade and diamonds. I allowed him to visit my boudoir twice more—tea and snacks only. He professed that he was besotted to near insanity and wanted nothing more than to please me—and I understood his meaning: He wanted to please me in my bed. Tedious politeness. Magic Gourd advised that I invite him to spend the night when we met at the next party he hosted. "Do so with the same subtlety he uses with you. While admiring the banquet food, say you would enjoy learning about his mother's Shanghai cooking, what his favorite dishes are. This subject is always very special to a man. They all have a warm feeling with this sort of talk. When he asks when he can see you, simply say, 'Tonight, if you are not too tired of talking.'" As Magic Gourd had predicted, his mother's cooking put him in an erotic mood. The party ended early that night.

Magic Gourd had already prepared my room by placing gifts from other men in places where he would see them. Mosquito coils were lit, so that we could be naked without slapping and scratching. "We will allow him intimate favors this first night and then he will need to wait another three. Then he can have a second. If necessary, we may need to let him have a third. But if you do, don't provide him with everything he wants. Put him off without being obvious. Promise to provide more the next time, but then let him know that you will also be seeing another suitor the next night. In all likelihood, he will offer to be your patron so that no one else can have your attentions."

"Perhaps he will lose his admiration for me after one night and not care if I withhold anything after that," I said. I was certain I could not feign the same intimate feeling or excitement I had with Loyalty. He would be merely a customer.

In the early evening, just an hour before the party, Magic Gourd told me that Loyalty would attend as well. "He is, after all, a friend of Eminent Tang's."

"He must know I'll be there. Everyone knows Eminent Tang is wooing me." She said quietly that he was bringing his favorite courtesan. "What do I care which giggling girl he brings?" I was angry that Magic Gourd told me this and then tried to console me. He was a past client. That was all. I was inexperienced at the time and allowed myself to expect too much.

"Madam Li was wrong to let you take a contract with Loyalty for a year. You had the glimmer-eyed look of a girl who thinks she will marry. Loyalty led you to think this by being too good to you. Of course, you confused that with love. If Eminent Tang becomes your patron, act like a true courtesan and make him feel carefree and so happy that he reports nothing but praise to those who gossip."

Eminent Tang greeted me with his besotted, boyish face. He invited me to sit next to him rather than have me stand. He encouraged me to eat special dishes he had ordered. I was about to invite him to spend the night when I saw Loyalty enter with his favorite. He came toward me. But it was only to politely greet Eminent Tang, the host. He then greeted me warmly yet with the distance of politeness. He complimented my jacket, one of the three I had made with the money he gave me to replace the one ruined by his brother. I regretted wearing it, but I thanked him for the compliment.

"The color suits you," he said.

I did not need to think of what I should say. A courtesan with plump cheeks and big eyes came to his side and reported merrily that after Eminent's party, there would be a drinking game at her house. He could play until exhausted and then spend the night. She made it clear that he was likely to become her patron. He was going to a drinking party. I was going to have a conversation about Eminent's mother's cooking. Loyalty said a few more customary polite words, ones that he could have said to anyone, and then his favorite pulled him away. How did other courtesans accept the kind of humiliation of seeing a lover with another courtesan? A few minutes later, I invited Eminent Tang to my room to play an American game of cards. He accepted immediately.

True to his word, he wanted nothing more than to please me. He was polite and asked if he could touch me: my face, my arm, my leg, my breast, my pudenda. It was tedious, but I was also glad I could anticipate what he would do. When I removed my clothes, he was grateful rather than charged with the mutual lust that Loyalty and I had shared. I kept my eyes on Eminent's face to remove Loyalty from my mind. He was kind, gentle, and polite. He could not possibly be a gangster. I closed my eyes, and each time I opened them, I studied more of his face. He was attractive, yet I felt no desire. I pretended to be the slowly awakening virgin. My eyes enlarged with mock uncertainty as he pressed against me. I closed my eyes and let him move inside me. And with his predictable rhythmic strokes, I was comforted and began to cry.

Before he awoke in the morning, I had already bathed and donned a loose robe. He looked like a sleeping boy. Even his body was slim and youthful. I was about to call for breakfast, but he pulled me toward him, and we began again. I was careful to provide the right balance: no longer the awakening virgin, but one who has been newly awakened. I remembered those courtesans at Hidden Jade Path who knew what suited their clients. I had imitated saying the words they said with every suitor. I did not find it beneath me to say them now. I was proud of my skill, and with Eminent Tang, I already knew he wanted to feel he had conquered my reticence, and I seduced him into thinking he had.

That afternoon, Eminent Tang met with Madam Li and offered a contract for two seasons. I was taken aback that I had been reduced in value to just the summer and fall. Magic Gourd assured me that this was a good offer and a better arrangement than more seasons. If a patron proves unbearable you would not be stuck for too long. "You may think he is easy to please now. Once he has a contract, he will want much more. Do what you can to keep him besotted for as much of those two seasons as you can. That way you won't have to work so hard. In two seasons, he won't be besotted with you. Then he will seek another so he can become besotted once again."

"Have you ever known a man whose love was genuine and lasted more than a few seasons?"

"Every flower wishes she could find a man like that," she said. "Eventually, we learn not to wish. But hope came true for me twice. Once it was with the Poet Ghost. You know about him. The other was a living man. He was not as rich as most. He owned a small paper factory. And he already had a wife and two concubines. But he declared he loved me. He said this many times and he told me all the reasons. It was not my talents or my skill at flattery or my knowledge of all the different pleasures. He loved my strong character, my genuine heart, my simple good-hearted nature. I spent a lot of my savings to buy him a gold watch. He told me that he drew it out of his pocket every half hour to determine if his workers were keeping pace. One day, two factory workers killed him. Before they were executed, they said they killed him for both the watch and for his mistreatment of them. My lover's widow kept the watch. I did not want it anyway. I thought it had killed him. However, that was true love. It can happen."

1915

Over the next few years, I discovered that men are alike in many ways. They enjoy flattery of their character and their expression of that in bed. Their leadership. Their hard work. Their generosity. Their persistence and diligence. Their superiority. Most needed a continual stream of flattery from many women. I understood that. I also knew from the start how long a patron's interest would last by the length of the contract. This ceased to surprise me, and thus, it did not bother me—although in a few instances I was pleased that the contract had been extended for another season. And with some I was also less than grateful that it had been.

Each man had his particular erotic fantasies, which on the surface seemed similar. It might be a caress on his back—and it might be with a finger, a toe, a breast, a tongue, a feather duster, a flyswatter, or a whip. The more skilled I was at recognizing these subtle differences of need, the more I could find what else he might like and use that knowledge to good advantage. I could provide it once more, then withhold it, then provide it again without warning, or after he had given me another gift. One man liked to wash my pudenda. Another liked to peer into the back of my mouth. Another wanted me to sing a mountain maiden song as I undressed with my back to him. Another wanted me to titillate myself using the pearl polisher he gave me while he hid behind the screen. I told Magic Gourd what each man liked, thinking there would be one she had never seen. "I've encountered the same," she always said.

I was proud when I could finally tell her about a fetish she had never experienced, nor would she ever. It was to wear prim Western clothes and say in English that I did not understand the man's repeated sexual demands, which he gave in Chinese. He would then push me down—I preferred the bed and not the floor—and bounce and buck until I said in Chinese that I could now understand him perfectly because his bold knight coming through my gates had united our minds as well.

NEARLY THREE YEARS after my defloration, Loyalty Fang sent a note, asking to meet me. I thought about whether to accept.

I was no longer haughty and naive, spirited and stupid. I did not let my feelings run wild and imagine paid romance was love. I was a popular courtesan and took pride that I could create the most convincing romance possible for each man and that I provided this within the limits of time, be it one season or two. I never accepted a contract that was longer. It was not wise to be out of circulation. I built a reputation as a courtesan who was not dishonest with her clients. And if a suitor made promises, I did not believe him, but I was not cynical about his infatuation. I reminded myself of all this as I considered Loyalty's request to see me. But still my heart raced.

I had seen Loyalty at parties from time to time—with courtesans and without. He was always polite, and I became more at ease each time, and eventually I discovered I could greet him with the faint affection of former friendship. Finally I was ready to meet him without bitterness or humiliation. As Loyalty once predicted, I would one day see him as a patron who treated me far better than most.

I told Magic Gourd about the request. She made a round mouth and twitched her eyebrows to be humorous. "Could it be he wishes to court you?"

I allowed him into my room. I resolved there would be no favors for old times' sake.

"I've watched you for almost three years," he said, "and not without a wish we could still enjoy each other. I feared, however, the old pain would return."

"I was young and naive," I said.

"You've learned so quickly and know more than most, I suspect. I see you have your spirit back, your independence. I wondered if you had truly forgiven me. If only we had met now, for the first time. You would have been able to see me as a patron and we could have enjoyed our time together without the burden of expecting more."

"You don't require forgiveness. You did nothing to wrong me. I should ask you to forgive me. I was unbearable, wasn't I? I look back and wonder why you stayed as long as you did."

"You were fifteen." He then gave me the familiar gaze. "Violet, I would like to be your patron for a season. Could you bear to do that, given your past resentment of me?"

I said nothing. I usually had a ready answer to any request a man might make. But this one concerned my once-damaged heart. I had carefully repaired it. I was a different person. My desire for him was so strong I could easily lose myself. The next moment I thought: Why not enjoy a season without having to pretend I was in ecstasy, as I had to do with other men? I would have a holiday from work. Whatever happened, whether heartache came later, I wanted to feel the old addiction of love.

"Before you answer, I need to tell you something else," he said. "I have a wife."

The old pain instantly returned.

"We didn't marry for love," he said. "Our families have known each other for three generations, and she and I grew up side by side, like brother and sister. From the age of five, we were destined to marry. She delayed the marriage as long as possible, and you'll be pleased to know the reason. She has no sexual desire for men. Both families believe she is the reincarnated spirit of a nun and they had hoped I would be able to change her religious tendencies. But the real truth is, she loves a woman, my cousin, whom she's known since childhood. After my wife gave birth to a son, everyone was happy, and those two reincarnated nuns went off to live together in another part of the house. Nonetheless, she is still my wife. I tell you this, Violet, so that you don't think another courtesan is luring her way into becoming my wife. I have a wife and I don't want the chaos of concubines."

As pledged, he was my patron for a season. For that time, I did not have to play a role. I simply gave in to love and pleasure, and put aside the knowledge that I would be wretched later.

When the season was over, Loyalty made a different pledge to me.

"I will always be your loyal friend. If you are ever in trouble, you can come to me."

"Even when I am old and wrinkled?"

"Even then."

He had just pledged friendship for a lifetime. He was giving me his loyalty, the meaning of his name. He would always help me. Wasn't that the same as love? Wasn't that worth all the seasons over a lifetime? Every few weeks, he would visit me for a night or two. I hoped for another contract each time I saw him. I delayed pressing suitors to become patrons so that I would still be available to him. Finally, I chided him gently. "Instead of having a night with me here and there when I am not busy, why not do a contract and have me at your beck and call whenever you wish."

"Violet, my love, I've told you many times you know me better than anyone else. I have no mirror, but you truly see me. When I'm with you, I feel the old yearning, the vital force, and if I did not resist, I would fill the emptiness, and I would not strive harder. And then I would feel the passage of time, along with the terror that something important had eluded me, my better purpose in life, which I would never find before I died. I would sense the days going by, the edge of life coming closer. I don't have to say more. You know me better than I do myself."

"I know that what you just said is stink from a dog fart. If I knew you that well, I'd make you do what I want." He laughed.

With each question I asked, he gave me a better answer than I had expected, but it was contained within a worse one, a riddle of hope. He had pledged himself to me for life, yet he did not want to ever be fulfilled by me, and so we had to remain apart. What did he think I would fulfill? Why couldn't I simply fail to fulfill it? What about my yearnings? I felt as if I were running in a labyrinth, chasing after something I could not see yet knew was important. I sensed it was just ahead, and then it would go around a corner, and I would be lost. I would have to decide what to do next, where to go, and what I needed to get out of that confusing place. If I stopped running and stood still, I would be accepting that what I had was all I would ever have. And then I would no longer be lost, because there would be nowhere else to go.

As time went by, I discovered the stranger I had been running after—my happier self, which all my worries and discontent had chased away. I left behind my yearnings, and I continued on with a sharper mind and clearer eyes, ready to take what was in front of me.

CHAPTER 6

A SINGING SPARROW

Shanghai
March 1918
Violet

Spring Festival came and went, and Magic Gourd lamented that I had again failed to become one of the top Ten Beauties of Shanghai. I had not garnered any good gossip worth mentioning in the mosquito press, she said. I had worn the wrong colors. I had failed to cultivate more influential clients. "Do you think those girls who win are prettier or more talented? Not at all! But they don't lie around cracking watermelon seeds, thinking popularity always goes up and never down."

The popularity contest was a sham, but she refused to believe it. The courtesans who won worked for houses run by the Green Gang, and the tally of votes by their members outnumbered the competition tenfold. "Even if the contest were not crooked," I said, "I'm twenty, a picked peach, no longer new and intriguing. And being a Eurasian flower is not an advantage anymore."

She gave a dismissive sniff. "If you already think like that, you better look now for some way to attract more attention, or you'll wind up as an attendant to a girl as ungrateful as you."

The world of flowers was full of Eurasian weeds—half-American, half-English, half-German, half-French—50 percent of a hundred varieties. And there were more in the second-class houses, even more in the opium flower houses. All of us in the first-class houses resented the newcomers, both the sojourners and those who would plant roots and reach out for opportunity. They were changing Shanghai to fill a bottomless greed. The Japanese had taken over more Chinese businesses, buildings, and houses. They owned little shops and big stores. Their geishas had higher status than our first-class courtesans while offering only music that sounded like raindrops, no sex. Why was that popular? If that were all that our flowers offered, they would have been tapping out tunes on a brass begging bowl.

Last week we were surprised to hear that three of the best first-class houses now welcomed foreigners as customers. At Hidden Jade Path, foreigners had come every night, but they had not been allowed in the courtesan house, except as a guest of a Chinese customer. And even then, they could only look and not touch. We heard rumors that the Western customers who visited first-class houses did not follow the customs and protocols. They did not have the patience to woo a beauty for a month. They did not compete with other men. They flirted and played games, drank, ate, and listened to the beauty sing. The more forceful and generous ones were invited into the boudoir the same night. In our opinion, those first-class houses had fallen beneath the standards of second-class houses. On the other hand, the Westerners left handsome gifts, usually in silver dollars. The houses had been less profitable in recent years. No wonder they were letting exceptions creep in. The jewelry that their Chinese suitors gave them might have been worth more than those dollars, but when the courtesans traded them in at the jeweler or pawnshop, they received less than their value and the money was in Chinese yuan. Many worried that the currency would fall in value with the least little problem among the warlords and the Republicans, but it would be unpatriotic to say so aloud.

What would happen to our house? If we did not take in the foreigners, what else could we offer? There were over fifteen hundred first-class houses, and many had newer and more fashionable furnishings, more card games, radios, and phonographs in each room, as well as modern toilets that carried away the dirtied water with a pull on the chain. Madam Li said she could not afford to change the furniture and decorations whenever a fresh breeze went by.

In the lesser houses and on the streets, there were choices, beyond imagination, for salacious sex. Nothing was sacred or too precious to defile. Some prostitutes were widows of noblemen—so they said—who allowed men to rub off their gilt. The wives who called themselves "half-open" welcomed visitors from morning until late afternoon, when their husbands were away. One aging woman claimed she was a famous singer. She had decorated her room with posters from the days when she was at the height of her fame. We did not think she could possibly be the famous singer we had once admired—but we discovered she was when we went to visit her. For the foreigners, there were Eurasian girls, who claimed they were the daughters of diplomats, pale white girls, who advertised themselves to be the daughters of missionaries, many pairs of virgin twins, and pretty courtesans who were, in reality, pretty men. But the lies still drew the foreigners, who were too ignorant to know they were being tricked or too embarrassed to say so later. Those foreigners, we imagined, would be the same ones who might walk through our doors.

Vermillion was almost twenty-five, past her bloom and luster. She refused to recognize it. Her reputation had carried her far, and she still attracted old-fashioned suitors who threw parties and requested her to play the zither and sing. But now the suitors did not have to wait several weeks before she was available. And not all the suitors were the ones with great power and wealth, although, luckily, some of our longtime customers remained steadfast.

I saw her eyes widen with horror the day when Madam Li broached to her the idea of welcoming foreigners—respected, wealthy ones, she assured her, not sailors or clerks. "It has become not only acceptable, but fashionable," her mother said. "We will still be selective about our clientele. A foreign guest would have to be introduced by a longtime customer of the house who can vouch for the foreigner's good standing."

Vermillion looked as if fire would shoot out of her eyes. "They are crude in manners," she said, "and they carry gonorrhea, syphilis, and bugs that leave you covered head to toe with red itchy bumps. Do you want me, your beloved daughter, to become a diseased whore overnight?"

Madam Li's eyes narrowed. "If you want to inherit this house," she said, "you better take gangsters as your patrons from here on out."

THE FOLLOWING WEEK, Loyalty Fang told Madam Li he was happy to make an introduction. Our foreign guest would be the American son of a distinguished family whose shipping company had done business in China for over fifty years. Loyalty said he was more than satisfied with their services in transporting his porcelain to Europe and America. This commendation attested to the father's good character and, apparently, the son's.

"He's been in China for nearly a year," he told me over tea. "Very earnest, but very Western in his thinking. He told me he's been teaching himself Chinese, although I must say, whatever Chinese he is trying to speak is so atrocious it's impossible to understand. I have resorted to using my English to converse with the man, and since I'm a little rusty, our conversations have been limited to the weather, the country where his family lives, their state of health, when his grandfather died, the food he has eaten in Shanghai, and whether there was any particular dish that he thought was strange but delicious. It's laborious making small talk. Every few minutes, I have to use that damn Chinese-English dictionary you gave me. I know how to say in English *vegetable, meat,* and *fruit.* But how do you say *cabbage, pork,* and *kumquat?* Anyway, from those few conversations, I can assure you he is polite, humble, and bashful—ha!—truly unusual in an American, don't you think? The last time we spoke, he said he wanted to meet a Chinese woman who spoke English well enough that he could enjoy interesting conversations. Of course, I thought of you."

"So I am no longer your little Eurasian beauty," I said. "For your friend, I've become Chinese?"

"Eh, are you ashamed to be Chinese? No? Then why are you so quick to criticize me? When we met, you were Lulu Mimi's Eurasian princess. That was how everyone saw you. Since then, I have not thought of you as one race or two. You are simply who you are—a hotheaded vixen who will not forgive me—and for what, you won't tell me."

"I don't know why I bother to talk to you at all," I said.

"Violet, please, let's not argue now. I have an appointment soon, in thirty minutes. Anyway, this man said he wanted interesting conversation. And I hope this one we're having is not the kind you will provide."

Now that I was no longer infatuated with Loyalty, I could clearly see his faults, his insults and arrogance, the worst being his careless attitude about my past feelings for him. He greeted me at parties with an intimate look but did not request my attendance at his next party. At a previous party, we enjoyed flirting as he reminisced about my defloration. I took this as a sign that he wished to spend the night. When I boldly invited him to relive the past, he begged off, saying he was exhausted from having just returned from Soochow. I was humiliated. "Ah, Soochow, Land of Beautiful Courtesans," I had replied. "No wonder you are depleted." He retorted that I did not appreciate that he had made the effort to visit me. I said he had made the effort to attend a party where I happened to be. The last time he showed interest in spending the night, I said I was too tired to take visitors, and he became angry. He knew why I had answered him that way. We had been bickering for nearly two years and yet we could not be rid of each other—until now. I suspected he had so little feeling for me he did not hesitate in referring an American to me, knowing the man would want to fuck me as soon as he learned a few useful phrases in Chinese.

In the late afternoon, a manservant announced that the foreigner had arrived. He was expected, and he was also an hour late, which already made us feel we were not going to be treated with respect. I was in a sour mood when I walked into the salon. The man stood up. I looked at the clock on the credenza and said in English with mock surprise: "Oh my, is it already four o'clock? I hope I did not keep you waiting. We thought you were coming at three." I gave a slight smile, expecting he would apologize for his tardiness. "No need to apologize. Loyalty Fang said I should come at four." Damn Loyalty and his shitty English. The American stared at me, no doubt disappointed that I was not the exotic flower he had hoped for. "I am half-Chinese," I said bluntly.

Madam Li and Magic Gourd were already seated. Vermillion was absent, as she had said she would be. Shining and Serene soon entered. They were new to the house—sisters, who had been at another first-class house, until its madam died and the house quickly went downhill. Madam thought they should see how Westerners behave. I had been tempted to dress like a Westerner, but decided I should not let my irritations toward Loyalty guide what I do. My hair was pulled back into a chignon and my dress was Chinese but modern, long and slim with a high neck. He was seated in an armchair and I took a seat across from him. I could tell by the stiff-lipped expressions on the other courtesans' faces that they found it disturbing to see their first foreigner in the house. His presence changed the status of our house. He did not have the air of sophisticated Americans or the demeanor of the wealthy businessmen my mother had entertained.

His name was Bosson Edward Ivory III. Loyalty told me he was perhaps twenty-five, but he appeared to be older. He was slight in frame, and he had the typical bony-faced features of an Anglo-Saxon. His head was shaped like a turnip—a large crown and forehead, which tapered to a long chin. His eyes were hazel, and his sandy hair was wavy and unkempt, as was his mustache, a feature on men that reminded me of a dust broom for collecting half-eaten debris. His clothes were well tailored, crisp with starch, but also rumpled. A disheveled appearance was always a sign of disrespect, unless you were a starving beggar.

"Please call me Edward," he said, and kissed each courtesan's hand in a laughable courtly manner.

"Edward is difficult for the Chinese to pronounce," I said. "Bosson is much easier."

"Bosson is the name of my dead forebears and carries the onus of success and hard work, neither of which I have." I knew he meant this humorously, but I translated what he said, as if it were not. "He is too honest," Magic Gourd said.

"Of course, if it's easier for them," the foreigner said, "I would be pleased if they call me Bosson."

I told them in Chinese: "bo-sen"—the *bo* that means "radish" and the *sen* that means "huge." Giant radish! They appreciated my joke.

Tea arrived with a little pitcher of milk and a plate of butter cookies and jam. Madam Li said she had had to go to the foreign marketplace to find milk for spoiling the tea.

He and I made small talk about his time in China and what he had seen. Every so often, I gave brief translations. He claimed he had arrived a year ago but had not seen as much as he would have liked, but he planned to stay for a while, years even. He leaned back against the sofa and sat with his legs far apart, as if he were in a saloon. He did not seem bashful, as Loyalty had described him. In fact, he was too much at ease.

"I like to visit places people don't ordinarily see," he said. "Most Americans aren't adventuresome about delving into the foreign world."

"In China, you are the foreigner."

"Ha! After a year here, you'd think I would remember which way it goes. Perhaps over the next five years, I'll get the hang of it."

"Five years is a long time for a visitor. Or do you intend to live here?"

"I came here with an entirely open mind. All I know is that I will not be leaving soon."

"Are you comfortable where you're staying? That is always important with a long visit. Otherwise, you'll have nothing but bad things to say about Shanghai, and that would be a pity when it is so easy to discover what is heavenly."

"I'm completely pampered. I'm at a guesthouse not far from here on Bubbling Well Road. It belongs to an old friend of my father's, a Chinese fellow, Mr. Shing. While studying abroad, he lived with our family in upstate New York. I was too young to remember much about him, but he made an impression of being Old World and mysterious, even though he was quite young at the time, as well as friendly. I think he's the reason I've long been curious about China."

As he continued to talk, I translated for the beauties, abbreviating more and more as the conversation went on. His family owned a shipping company, which his great-grandfather started eighty years ago.

"I'm sorry to say the Ivory family made its fortunes on opium. These days we transport manufactured goods, like Loyalty Fang's teacups and saucers."

The family sent him to Shanghai to become acquainted with the business, since he would one day inherit it. I translated this to the beauties and they took more interest. "That was the story he gave," I added, "and Americans are known to make up all kinds of things when they're away from others who know better."

"The truth is, I haven't learned anything about the business," he said. "I ran away from responsibility and I would be better described as a vagabond, without plans. I would like to discover China in a spontaneous way, and not by schedules to see shrines and pagodas. I don't want to read a guidebook and be told what I will find and that I will feel *transported to the ancient days of the first emperors.*" He pulled a leather notebook from his coat pocket. "I am writing a travelogue— putting down a pastiche of scenes, which I've illustrated with pencil sketches."

"Will you publish them?" I asked politely.

"I will, if my father buys a publishing company."

The man did not have a serious thought in his brain.

"I write for myself," he said. "I would not foist my rough little stories on others. That would be cruel."

"Do you have titles for books you write only for yourself?"

"*To the Farthest of the Far East.* I came up with it last week. You're the first to know. Of course, I've had a dozen titles before this one, and another may strike me later. That's the problem when you have neither goal nor destination nor readers."

"How far east have you gone so far?"

"Not east at all. Only to the southwest boundaries of Shanghai. However, what I mean by *farthest* is not as much distance as it is a state of mind. Do you know Walt Whitman's *Leaves of Grass*?"

"We have many things in Shanghai from around the world, but, alas, not all the English books that have ever been published."

"Mr. Whitman is admired by all. His poems serve as my travel guide, so to speak, like this one:

> "Not I, nor anyone else can travel that road for you.
> You must travel it by yourself.
> It is not far. It is within reach.
> Perhaps you have been on it since you were born, and
>   did not know.
> Perhaps it is everywhere—on water and land."

I had never read the poem, yet I had lived the heartache of those words—the loneliness, being on a road to an unknown place,

set there with no understandable reason. It was like the painting of
the valley between the mountains, with clouds that were both dark
and rosy pink, and a bright place ahead that was a glowing paradise
or a burning lake.

"By the look on your face, I assume the poem is not to your liking," Edward Ivory said.

"Quite the opposite. I would like to read more one day."

Magic Gourd broke in: "Ask him if he is planning to sell a story
about his visit to this courtesan house."

He gave his answer to her directly, as if she understood English:
"If I write about you, I will likely sell more copies on the basis of that
alone."

I translated and Magic Gourd snapped: "Tell the liar to make
me young and beautiful."

Edward Ivory laughed. Shining and Serene smiled, although
they did not know what was being said.

"Lovely girls," he said. "The one on the left looks barely older
than a child. So young to have fallen into this life."

A stone fell down my throat. Who was he to pity us?

"I don't see myself as a fallen woman," I said.

He choked on his biscuit. "Poor choice of words. And I was not
referring to you, of course. You are not one of them."

"I am indeed one of *them,* as you put it. But you don't need to pity
us. We live quite well, as you can see. We have our freedom, unlike
American women who cannot go anywhere without their husbands
or old maid aunts."

His face became serious for once. "I apologize. I have an unintentional habit of offending people."

I decided to put a close to this unsuccessful encounter. "I think
we have had enough conversation for the day, don't you?" I stood up,
which forced him to stand, and I waited for him to give his thanks
and farewell.

He gave me a look of surprise, then reached into his waistcoat pocket and drew out an envelope and handed it to me. It contained twenty American silver dollars.

Damn Loyalty! "Mr. Ivory, it seems that Mr. Fang neglected to explain to you that this is a courtesan house, not a brothel with whores you can bed as soon as you walk through the door with a few coins jingling in your pocket." I poured the silver dollars onto the table and some of them spilled onto the carpet.

Madam Li and Magic Gourd cursed. The beauties cried that Vermillion had been right about foreigners and their diseased minds and bodies. They left at once.

Edward was baffled. "Is it not enough?"

"Twenty dollars is the amount charged by your Yankee whores on the painted boats in the harbor. I thank you for thinking we're worth an equal amount. However, we are closed for business today."

THAT EVENING LOYALTY came to the house and Magic Gourd took him to my room to avoid having others listen to my tirade. I did not wait for the door to close before shouting, "Your foreign devil friend treated me like a saltwater whore! Are you spreading rumors that we're a come-and-go brothel?"

His face showed anguish. "It's my fault, Violet, and I know that's not hard for you to believe. But it is also not what you think. The man and I were speaking in English about his wish to meet a companion who spoke English. I told him I knew a woman who was highly unusual and I described you in ways that are completely true—that you speak perfect English and are beautiful, cultured, intelligent, educated—"

"Enough flattery," I said.

"I then told him you were a courtesan and I asked him if he knew what a first-class courtesan house was. That's what I thought I had said. He said yes. I asked if he knew the customs. It turns out that instead of saying the English term for *first-class courtesan house,* I used the English dictionary you gave me and it translated those words into 'number one whorehouse.' Edward later went to the American Bar and asked a man who had lived in Shanghai many years what a Shanghai whorehouse was like. And that man said that Edward's wildest dreams would come true after a little chitchat and an offering of a dollar or two for a regular visit and up to ten for one with specialties. When Edward later told the same man about the fiasco, the man laughed and told him what a courtesan house was and why he would never be allowed to set foot in one again. Edward immediately called and told me everything. Violet, when you said you were done with the conversation, he thought you were ready for his wildest dreams. You can't blame either Edward or me entirely. Some of it was due to that damn Chinese-English dictionary you gave me. And this is not the first time it's caused me to make embarrassing mistakes. I can show you, if you don't believe me, which these days, it seems, are too often the case. Can't we call a truce?"

Loyalty placed two elegantly wrapped boxes on the tea table. "Edward asked me to bring these gifts to ask for your forgiveness. He worried he had made you angry at me as well. I told him, 'Don't worry about that. She's been mad at me for years.' Eh, Violet, can't you simply laugh for once."

The larger box contained a book with green leather covers and a gold-embossed title: *Leaves of Grass.* Sprouting from the title were vines and tendrils that wound around the letters and ran freely to the edges. I found a thick sheaf of deckle paper inscribed with the passage that had felt so familiar.

The smaller box contained a gold bracelet with rubies and diamonds, an extravagant gift from someone who might not ever see the recipient again. I read the note.

Dear Miss Minturn, I am deeply ashamed of my unintentional crude behavior. I cannot expect forgiveness, but I hope you believe the sincerity of my apology. Yours, B. Edward Ivory III

Magic Gourd went with Madam Li to Mr. Gao's jewelry store, where they learned that Edward had paid two thousand yuan. Mr. Gao said it would have been half that price if the foreigner had known to bargain him down. Nonetheless, we should still consider that Edward Ivory had paid us that higher amount of respect.

"The bracelet is worth forgiveness," Magic Gourd said, "especially since it was Loyalty's fault to begin with. Madam Li and I agreed." She added: "The foreigner should not expect anything to go further than that—unless you want it to, of course, in which case, this bracelet is a nice start."

Loyalty rang two days later and asked if he might host a small dinner and bring Edward as one of his guests. "I must be honest, Violet, he asked if I would do this. He received your note of forgiveness, but he is still in a terrible state. He has not slept or eaten. He spouted nonsense about wounding everyone he meets. I told him it was my fault, not his. That did nothing to put his mind at ease. Maybe all Americans who suffer from melancholy act as if they have gone mad. But I truly thought he might throw himself in the river, and I don't want his ghost visiting to keep telling me he's sorry."

His reasoning was always exasperating. "So instead, you're making me responsible for whether a crazy man kills himself, is that it? Why did you tell me this? Host your party. I'll be there to accept his apologies in person. If he drowns himself afterward, I can't be blamed. As for you, you should have taken English lessons from me when you had the chance."

Loyalty brought Edward and four other guests, enough people for a noisy party of drinking and games. Edward was quiet and did not speak to me at first, except to say "please," "thank you," and "you're very kind." He stayed his distance, as if I were a scorpion. But I felt him watching me. He was solicitous toward Madam, Vermillion, and Magic Gourd, and was excessively polite to the other beauties. They smiled as if they had understood all his English words. At the end of the evening, he gave Magic Gourd and the maids generous tips and then placed another gift before me, wrapped in green silk. He bowed gravely and left. I opened the gift in private, without Magic Gourd's prying eyes. This time, it was an emerald-and-diamond bracelet. The card said:

> *Dear Miss Minturn, I am grateful to be allowed in your company again. Yours, B. Edward Ivory III*

I had not received such an extravagant gift in nearly two years. The next night I wore the bracelets to three party calls. When I went on my afternoon carriage ride with Shining and Serene, I pointed out beautiful birds and clouds so that those on the sidewalks could see the brilliant conquest I wore on my wrist.

THE NEXT MORNING, Madam said I had a phone call from the American. Edward apologized for the intrusion, as well as for presuming I might talk to him. His host, Mr. Shing, had said invitations should be written by letter a week in advance. But he hoped I would understand his haste. The manager of the shipping company had reserved two seats in his box at the Shanghai Race Club, and because he had fallen ill with influenza, he could not go. He had offered them to Edward. As it happened, Sir Francis May, the governor of Hong Kong, would also be present and seated two boxes away. "I thought I might press my luck to see if I could persuade you . . ."

A chance to meet the governor! I immediately regretted my meanness to Edward from the day before. "I would be also pleased to see you again," I said, "so I can personally thank you for your lovely gifts."

Since Chinese people were not allowed at the race club, Magic Gourd said we had to ensure there was no doubt about my right to be there. She brought out the lilac dress my mother had worn at the Shanghai Club. The dress still looked new and fashionable. I pictured

my mother the last time she wore it. The old heartsickness remained
and it could fan quickly into anger. I told Magic Gourd the weather
was too cold. I found another that I had worn with success to a Western restaurant, an excursion costume in cerulean-blue velvet. It
had a capelet and narrow skirt with a provocative cascade of folds
at the back. I tried on a brimmed hat with a few modest feathers.
But when I thought of sitting among foreigners vying for the attention of the governor, I exchanged modesty for plumage that would
give me confidence. I wore my hair loosely bound and I fastened a
strand of pearls Loyalty had given me the night of my defloration. An
hour later, Edward arrived driving a long-nosed automobile—a sharp
contrast to the boxy black cars that sputtered and wheezed. He said,
almost apologetically, that his father had sent the Pierce-Arrow town
car on one of his ships as a gift for his twenty-fourth birthday. He was
twenty-four, four years older than I was. As we drove to the race club,
I realized I did not need to do anything to attract envy and attention.
The car brought people on the streets to a standstill as they watched
us go by.

When the governor of Hong Kong arrived, a hubbub arose, and
people followed him like an unloosened hive of bees. We watched
from our seats, and when the governor turned in my direction, he
nodded and smiled. "How nice to see you, Miss Minturn." This led
to a buzz of questions. "Who is she?" "Is she his secret lover?" I was
baffled that he knew my name and was immediately light-headed
with happiness in attracting temporary fame among the foreigners.
Edward was impressed as well and poured me glass after glass of delicious cold wine, enough for me to become giddy, and I soon found
special beauty in everything around us: the muscles of the horses,
the brilliant blue sky, the sea of hats, of which mine was the loveliest.
In my state of tipsy exhilaration, I could have smelled manure and
thought it was perfume. After the third race, the governor stood, and
again glanced my way, smiled, and tipped his hat. "Good afternoon,
Miss Minturn." This time I knew who he was. He had been one of my

mother's favorite clients, a kind man who greeted me warmly whenever I wandered through the parties. He had a daughter, my mother later told me, who died when she was my age. I had not been pleased to hear that. But the unpleasantness of his remark then was worth his acknowledgment of me at the race club. I had been elevated to a person of importance. Edward slyly passed along a rumor to a few people nearby that he had heard that the governor was a friend of the family. "She won't confirm it. But I believe her father was the governor before Sir May."

Edward asked that day if he and I could be friends. He said he would be pleased to serve as my companion, an escort to the places an American girl might want to see and could not unless accompanied by a maiden aunt. I assumed he was asking to be my suitor. If he was, he would be my first foreigner.

I SOON DISCOVERED that Edward's offer to be my companion meant exactly that and nothing more. During the first week, we walked through the Public Park, dined at a restaurant, and visited American bookshops. I knew he was fond of me, but he did not hint that he would like to become more than a friend. I guessed he was afraid to press further, given our disastrous beginning. Or perhaps he knew I had other suitors and thought it was unseemly to compete. Maybe he thought one of them was Loyalty.

During the second week, he took me to see a temple, but as soon as we arrived, he developed a crushing headache and had to quickly return home. He told me he had suffered from migraines since childhood. But I worried that he had caught the new Spanish influenza. The Ivory Shipping Company had been secretive in reporting the arrival of three sick men from the United States. Almost immediately, the manager in the Shanghai office also fell ill. They recovered, and no one knew for certain if it had been the deadly influenza, but during the scare, the Ivory Shipping Company had put all its employees under quarantine—all but Edward, who was not, strictly speaking, an employee. If Edward was indeed infected, he might infect me, and then everyone in the House of Vermillion would be imperiled and the doors would be closed. Each day we read terrible stories of the number of people in other countries who had died. Even the Spanish king had nearly died of it. We expected the wave of death to arrive in Shanghai any day. Thus far, except for families in poor sections of the city, few people we knew had taken ill with it. At our house, we drank bowls of bitter herbs, and we noted whether any guests were flushed or dizzy, a symptom that was easily confused with drunkenness. If a man coughed, Madam Li was quick to rise with a kerchief over her nose and ask the guest to return another time. Those asked did not take offense. The streetcars were washed down each night with limewater, and Madam Li followed that precaution and had the servants wash the courtyard leading to the house with a strong dose each morning.

Edward recovered from his migraine headache, only to fall victim to another a few days later. He said it felt as if poison had entered his brain. It began like a pin poking into his eye. It then went into his skull and the poison spread like fire. His mood was always dark just before an attack, and that was how I could predict when one was about to occur. I would not hear from him for days, and then he would return in a bright mood. He told me that he was forced to stay in a darkened room. He could do almost nothing, not even think. But he knew he was getting better when he could sit up. He took that time to write in his travelogue and it helped alleviate his malaise, as if the written words had purged the last of the poison in his brain.

When he suggested we take a long excursion in the car, I asked if it was wise. If he suffered from an attack, how would we return? That was when he decided to teach me to drive.

During my first lesson, I drove slowly, and he told me how happy he was to have the opportunity to admire the passing landscape. To me, it looked monotonous. There was not a spot of flat land that had not been tilled and planted. He had me practice making turns at every intersection. He tossed a coin, and if it showed heads, I turned right, and if it showed tails, I turned left. Edward took the wheel when we had to go in reverse where the road was blocked by buffalo cows or a pile of rocks set there for whatever odd reason farmers set rocks on roads. Wherever we went, we attracted the attention of peasants bent over in the fields. Edward honked and waved. They stopped work, stood up, and stared solemnly at us, never waving back. Here and there, we saw walls of houses whitewashed with lime. We passed villages where men were hewing logs into coffins. We watched a line of people dressed in white treading over the narrow paths between rice fields, headed up to a cemetery on the hillock. As I became a more competent chauffeur, I drove faster. The pages of his book flapped open, and a letter fluttered out and was gone before he could catch it. I asked if we should turn the car around, and he said we did not need to retrieve the letter. He knew the contents well enough. It was from his wife, telling him that his father's health was poor.

I was disappointed to learn he was married. But I was not much surprised. Most of my suitors had wives, at least one, and whenever a man mentioned the fact, I was reminded of my standing as a momentary diversion, a pastime for now and not necessarily the future. To many men, I was a woman who existed only in a particular place, like a singing sparrow in a cage.

"Is your father's condition serious?" I asked.

"Minerva always makes it seem so. She uses my father's health to lure me home, and I don't appreciate being baited. I know that sounds unfeeling. But I know the lengths to which Minerva will go. Our marriage has never been a happy one. It was a mistake and I'll tell you why."

He spoke frankly. Many men did, assuming that courtesans would not be shocked, given what they had done. But I also felt he confided in me as a friend, someone he hoped would understand.

When he was eighteen, he said, he was walking alongside a fence outside of a horse pasture. A blond-haired girl in the pasture waved and ran up to him. She was plain-looking and stared with open infatuation. She knew his name and who his family was, which was odd. "That was Minerva," he said, "and her father was the horse doctor who treated our horses. She had accompanied him twice to our house." Edward told her to hop over the fence and he took her into the nearby woods, not sure what they would do. She lifted her skirts and said she knew how. Without a word more between them, they had sex. He stopped before he finished so she would not get pregnant, and she told him to go ahead because she would later wash herself out. Her uncle had taught her how to do this. She said that so breezily, as if it were normal. For two years, they met in the woods. She always brought along a spout and a jar of quinine solution, what her father used to treat horses with staggers. As soon as they finished, she poured this into her vagina while lying down, then stood and jumped up and down for half a minute to wash away his semen. She didn't think it was embarrassing, but he usually turned away. They hardly ever spoke except to say when they would next meet.

One day, the horse doctor, his wife, and Minerva were seated in the Ivory family's parlor, demanding that Edward marry their pregnant daughter. Edward was stunned because Minerva had always used the quinine. Mr. Ivory declared his son could not possibly be the father. He tried to bully Minerva into admitting she had been promiscuous with others. Out of defiance of his father—and not in defense of Minerva—Edward said it was indeed his child. His father then offered the family a large sum of money to be rid of them, and that moved Edward to say he would marry Minerva. The girl cried in disbelief, as did Edward's mother, and Edward was proud that he had stood up to his father—until the wedding night a week later. He was appalled to find this idolizing girl lying on her back in his bed and not in the woods, with no jar of quinine necessary. Soon after the wedding, Minerva told her mother she had never been pregnant and feared what Edward would do when no baby came. Her mother said to wait another month and tell him she had a miscarriage. So she did, with tears and sobs, and he was compassionate and managed to get himself to say "love" to assuage her grief. She mistook it for actual love that had finally blossomed in him. She then confessed she had never been pregnant, thinking he would now be grateful for the subterfuge. He asked her if anyone else knew and she said that only her mother did.

"I thought I was being morally good by marrying her," he said, "and goodness had punished me. I told Minerva I would never love her. And she said in turn that if I tried to divorce her, she would kill herself, and to prove her threat was real, she ran out into the frigid night wearing only a nightgown. Later, after she thawed, I said I was leaving, and she should divorce me on grounds of abandonment, and if she did not, she would live out her days like an untouched childless widow. I left the house and came home only occasionally—whenever I received her letters claiming my father or mother was gravely ill. We never shared the marriage bed ever again. That was six years ago. My mother has actually become fond of her. She encourages me to return from wherever my latest adventures have taken me so that I can resume fathering a child. It's a sad arrangement, and all of us have played a role to make it so."

"Including her uncle," I said.

When it was time to return, I had no idea how to take the same hopscotch route back to Shanghai. Edward, I learned, had an indelible geographic memory. He was like a living compass and map. He remembered all the turns, the detours, the potholes, and the smallest landmarks—a notched tree, a large boulder, and the number of whitened walls in each village. He claimed his indelible memory did not extend to memorizing what he had read. He had to work hard to learn the poems from *Leaves of Grass,* he said. But once he learned them, he could retrieve any passage that perfectly suited the view or our mood.

I had grown fond of him. He depended on my companionship, and I was delighted to provide it because he treated me as his friend. Yet I also worried that he might one day wish to become my suitor, and then we would no longer be friends, but a courtesan and her customer, who met with different expectations. Intimacy of that kind would not strengthen friendship.

We often talked about the war. We walked up Bubbling Well Road two or three times a day to a café or bar to hear the latest reports. He admired the leaders of the Republic of China, Sun Yat-sen and Wellington Koo. He admired Woodrow Wilson even more. In his opinion, those three had what it took to finally return the German Concession and Shandong Province to China. He hoped to enlist in the service. If he could not find a navy recruiting station in Shanghai, he might hitch a ride aboard one of the ships taking Chinese workers to France.

"Why didn't you enlist while you were in New York?" I asked.

"I tried. But my father and mother did not want me to be drafted and risk having their only son killed. My father sent off a letter to a bigwig general. It said I had a serious heart murmur and it was signed by a well-known doctor. I was not allowed to join."

"Do you really have a heart murmur?"

"I highly doubt it."

"Why would you not know for sure?"

"My father turns lies into the official truth. Even if I had nothing whatsoever wrong with my heart, the doctor wouldn't tell me if I asked."

One afternoon, when he returned me to the house, he asked if I had any free evenings available. I had seen the signs in his eyes. The time had come and I was sad that we were going to exchange friendship for business. He knew that my evenings were booked with parties and that I had suitors whom I invited to my boudoir. He had certainly given me enough gifts to be treated with favor. "I can set aside any evening you would prefer," I said.

"Wonderful!" he said. "I want to take you to a play that the American Club is putting on."

I felt oddly disappointed.

ON THE FIRST warm spring day, two months after we met, we drove to Heavenly Horse Mountain in the southwest corner of Shanghai. The mountain was not high, but it spread itself wide over the land with a graceful skirt of green trees, shrubs, and wildflowers. Edward said we could hike to a spot where a tunnel-like cave would lead us to a different world on the other side. He had gone once by himself. As we set out on our hike, I thought of the poem he had recited when we first met.

> Not I, nor anyone else can travel that road for you.
> You must travel it by yourself.
> It is not far. It is within reach.
> Perhaps you have been on it since you were born, and
>   did not know.
> Perhaps it is everywhere—on water and land.

This time, I felt no haunting loneliness. I was with a friend who calmed me. We walked side by side through a forest of bamboo, white oak, and Chinese parasol trees. The forest was thick with shrubs and fragrant wild jasmine. When the path narrowed, I walked behind him. He wore a knapsack, and his brown leather journal peeked out of the top. I watched him take long strides as he leaned forward into the mountain. The path grew rocky and steeper. Our walk had become more strenuous than what I had in mind. I removed my short jacket. My blouse was already damp with perspiration. My skirt felt heavy and cumbersome. When we finally reached the cave, I proposed an early lunch, and we sat on boulders. While eating our sandwiches, I saw his travelogue lying to the side of his knapsack and reached for it.

"May I?"

He looked hesitant at first, then nodded. I turned to the page where his pencil had been inserted. He had lovely smooth handwriting that demonstrated an assured rhythm, as if he had never hesitated in writing his words.

When the rice fields flooded and turned the roads into slow rivers of mud, our beasts of burden—both men and mule— sank and became stuck. The carters were cursing. I was still on the cart, and saw that a plank of wood on the side of the cart had been dislodged when the cart sank. It was about five feet long. I instantly devised a plan. I placed the plank over the mud. I would walk to one end, swing it out like a clock dial, and then walk to the other end and swing it out again. Once I reached the mule, I would place the plank in front of the beast and encourage it to take the first step, and with one foot extricated, it would have the momentum to haul itself out.

As I stepped onto the board, one of the carters held up his hands and gestured for me to stop. I ignored him. They watched me with skepticism etched across their faces. They mumbled to one another and grinned. I did not need to speak Chinese to know they were belittling me for trying.

I took my second step, then a third. My plan was clearly a good one. What a clever lad I was! Yankee ingenuity. Reader, I am sure you are smarter than I in knowing what was about to happen. When I crouched to spin the board around, I heard a loud sucking noise as the board pulled away from the mud. The teeter-totter tipped me face forward into the mud and I received a good whack at the back of my head to teach me not to ignore Chinese advice again.

I had laughed throughout, and I saw how pleased he was that I liked it. "Stupidity must be rendered with subtlety," he said.

I turned back the pages to read more, but he snatched it from my hands.

"I would like to read it aloud to you later when we visit those places that inspired the words."

I was glad that he spoke of future adventures. There were many pages yet to read. We finished our lunch quickly. He took my hand as we went into the dark cave. The coolness of the cave sank into my damp clothes. Halfway in, I could no longer see Edward in front of me. He must have sensed my trepidation. He squeezed my hand. He moved steadily, and I was glad I could depend on him. This was the safety and trust I had grieved for in my heart. I wanted to stop in this dark place and simply stand there with Edward holding my hand. But we continued to move ahead, and in a short while I saw the soft light of an opening around the curve. We emerged into a beautiful bamboo forest with green and yellow light. This was the other world, a peaceful place, more lovely than the sex-wracked Peach Blossom Spring. We moved forward along a slippery path. He laced his fingers more firmly through mine. His hand was warm. My damp blouse, which had felt unbearably hot, now chilled me. "Careful," he said every now and then, and squeezed my hand. The forest was thick with vegetation covering the ground. There was no path that I could make out. I was confident that Edward would know how to return us safely. At that moment, I was filled with longing for him. It was not sexual. I wanted the physical comfort of being held. I wanted to feel protected and safe. Giving my body was the only way I could express what I needed. And yet, in the past, once I had done so, the brief comfort and safety the man had provided became tawdry, merely sexual urges satisfied, which left me feeling foolish and lonelier than ever. Golden Dove had warned me not to close off my heart because of bitterness. Loyalty had told me that I should take love and kindness when they are offered. Had love ever been offered? He claimed it had. Was a contract love? Was inconstancy love? Maybe the kind of love that would comfort me did not exist. Perhaps I expected too much of love and no one existed who could ever meet my unceasing and bottomless need for it. I certainly would not find it with a vagabond who took no responsibility for anyone. Yet I still wanted his arms around me.

"It's cool in the shade," I said, and shivered. This was not a lie.

"Are you cold?" he said.

"Could you wrap your arms around me to keep me warm?"

Without hesitation his arms enclosed me. I lay my face on his chest. We stood in the green light, still and quiet. I could hear his fast heartbeat. I felt his warm breath over my neck. His rigid penis pressed against me.

"Violet," he said. "I think you know how happy you make me."

"I know. I'm happy, too."

"I always want to be your friend." He stopped and was quiet. I could feel his heart beating faster. "Violet, I've held back saying something because I don't want you to think that my feelings for you as your friend are not true. But now that you've allowed me to hold you, I must tell you that I desire you, too."

I was light-headed, anticipating what would soon follow. I remained still. He tipped up my face, and I must not have shown what he had hoped to see.

"I'm sorry. I shouldn't have presumed."

I shook my head and stepped back. I watched his face change from confusion to gratitude as I unbuttoned my blouse and camisole to reveal my breasts. He kissed each breast, then my lips and eyelids. He embraced me once again. "You make me so happy," he said. We moved deeper into the forest, and when we saw an old tree with a thick trunk that listed to one side, we hurried toward it. He gently leaned me against it and lifted my skirts.

Our lovemaking was simple and necessarily brief, owing to the discomfort of an upright arboreal bed shared with ants. I did not lose my head to wild sexual desire, as I had experienced with Loyalty. I was elated that our friendship, which was so dear to both of us, had safely crossed the threshold into intimacy. We had shared the same neediness. We were glad to let go of loneliness. We were happy to make each other happy.

All the way home, we talked exuberantly about places we wished to visit, and the emotions we had at dawn and dusk—the expectations of the new day, the reverie at dusk—often tripping over each other's words. But when we returned to the house, our mood turned awkward. Evening was coming, and I would have to prepare for the parties. Once again, I would become a courtesan with suitors waiting to gain my attention and my favors in bed. I decided immediately that tonight there would be no suitors.

"Can you come to my room?" I asked. "I must attend the parties, but I will return alone."

That night he memorized the geography of me: the changing circumference of my limbs, the distance between two beloved points, the hollows, dimples, and curves, the depth of our hearts pressed together. We conjoined and separated, conjoined and separated, so that we could have the joy of looking into each other's eyes, before falling into each other again. I slept tucked into him and he wrapped his arms around me, and for the first time in my life, I felt I was truly loved.

In the middle of the night, I felt a shudder followed by three smaller ones. I turned around. He was weeping.

"I'm terrified of losing you," he said.

"Why would you fear that now?" I stroked his brow and kissed it.

"I want us to love each other so deeply we ache with the fullness of it."

He had expressed the kind of love that I had nearly convinced myself did not exist, except in the spiritual twin of my own self-being.

He fell quiet, then took a deep breath and slipped out of bed and began to dress.

"Are you leaving?"

"I am preparing for you to ask me to leave." He sat down on a hard chair and buried his face in his hands. And then he looked at me and said in hollow voice: "I'm damaged, Violet. My soul is damaged, and if we were to join our souls, I would damage you. There is something about me you should know. I've never told anyone about it, but if I kept it from you, I would feel vile that I had accepted your love. Once you learned what I had been hiding, it would poison your soul. How could I let that happen to you? I love you too much."

I immediately put up the old ramparts that had shielded my heart and waited. I still wanted to believe that nothing he would say could be as dire as he felt it was.

He looked me in the face. "I've told you my family is rich. I was privileged, spoiled. My parents and grandparents gave me whatever I wanted. I didn't have to take responsibility for anything. They acted as if I could never do wrong. I'm not blaming them for what I did later. By age twelve I had my own conscience. I could have chosen to do right or wrong.

"What I did happened on a beautiful summer day. My parents and I had gone for a walk in the mountains, to a place called Inspiration Point, where we would have a clear view of Haines Falls. My father had a painting of that waterfall. In fact, he had many paintings of waterfalls, and the one of Haines Falls was not even particularly special. When we arrived, we saw that a family had beaten us to the spot and set up a picnic. I heard my father say 'dammit' under his breath. They were exactly where my father had wanted to stand to see the falls. It was an outcropping of flat rock, set back a safe distance from the cliff, about twenty feet. The man and woman greeted us. They had a son about my age, and a girl who was perhaps six or seven. The girl had a large porcelain doll seated next to her, and it looked like her—the same blue dress, curly blond hair.

"I had always been a prankster and liked to scare people. I enjoyed their misery. That day, I grabbed the girl's doll and swung it up in the air. The girl shrieked, as I expected she would, and then I caught it in time. No harm done. She was relieved, and came toward me to retrieve her doll. I threw it up in the air again. Again she shrieked and begged me: 'Don't let her fall! She'll break!' She started to cry and I was about to stop, but then the boy got up and shouted at me: 'Let go of her doll right this instant!' No one ever ordered me around. I said to him, 'What will you do if I don't?' And he answered: 'I'll give you a black eye and a bloody nose.' The girl was screaming, 'Give her back!' Their father said something in a warning voice. All this excitement of emotion made me determined to keep up what I was doing. Their mother and father rose and were coming toward me. I shouted: 'If any of you comes one step closer, I'll let the doll fall right onto this rock.' They didn't move. I remember the feeling of power seeing them so distressed and helpless. I kept swinging that beautiful doll up in the air. Meanwhile, my father had moved to the spot the family had vacated, where he was looking at the falls through his binoculars. The boy took a step toward me and I swung the doll up by one arm to make it go higher. But then the arm tore off, which surprised me. I stared at that odd little arm and wasn't paying any attention to the doll in the air until I saw the boy rush by me, his face turned up, holding out his arms so he could catch the doll.

"I can still see every bit of what happened next: the doll was falling headfirst. The girl's mouth was open, horrified. The boy wore a fierce heroic face. 'I'll get it!' he called to her, still looking up. All at once, I saw the doll was not coming down where I had caught it before. It must have been that the torn arm had pitched it to the right, toward the cliff. I saw the doll plummet past the cliff. The boy managed to stop at the edge and his arms were bent and flapping like chicken wings. I willed him to tilt backward to safety. But instead he tipped forward and he groaned—it was an awful sound that came from his gut—and then he was gone and there was nothing but clear blue sky. All the air in my lungs emptied. It couldn't be true, I told myself.

"I heard the boy's father call sharply: 'Tom!' as if to order the boy to come back. His mother called, 'Tom?'—as if to ask if he was hurt. The little girl was screaming, 'Tommy! Tommy! Tommy!' I heard his name so many times. His mother and father went to the edge. I don't know if he was still falling and they could see this. They kept saying his name, louder and higher. I was shaking. I was hoping there might be another ledge right below, and that he was still alive. I slowly walked toward the cliff. But my father grabbed my arm, and led me away, and my mother immediately joined us. The man saw us and yelled, 'Stop! You stop! You're not getting away with this!' My father did not look back. He shouted: 'He did nothing wrong.' He pushed me forward to make me go more quickly. My mother said to me: 'It was an accident.' My father added: 'What kind of boy would run toward a cliff without looking?' And then I heard the woman wail: 'My boy, my boy! He's gone! He's dead!' So then I knew. My father did not need to push me anymore. I was running as fast as I could.

"At home, they said nothing more about what had happened. Everything went on as usual. But I could tell they were still thinking about it. I went to my room and vomited. I was terrified because I could not stop seeing the boy pitching forward. I kept hearing the girl calling him—Tommy! Tommy!—making him alive and gone at the same time. He was gone and I was alive, but evil. Two days later, I saw my father tear a page out of the newspaper, crumple it up, and throw it in the fireplace. He lit it on fire and did not bother to watch it burn. He walked away, just as we had walked away from that family and what I had done. It occurred to me then that he had been standing at a vantage where he would have seen the boy falling. How could he remain so unaffected by what he had seen? Yet he said nothing and I said nothing. I hated myself for not being able to speak. He had saved me from blame, and I was a coward for letting him. I never confessed what I did to anyone.

"I've lived with this for thirteen years, and no matter where I run to, the memory of what happened is still with me. It's as if that boy were my constant companion. The way I imagine him, he's looking at me, quiet, waiting for me to admit I killed him. In my mind, I do tell him it was my fault, that I was cruel. He doesn't forgive me. He wants me to tell everybody, and I need to but can't. Every day, all around me, I see reminders—the clear blue sky, a little girl, the newspaper on the table, those paintings of waterfalls—and I think, It was not an accident. I meant to be cruel. I caused it to happen, and I never admitted it to anyone."

His eyes looked emptied of life. I was standing on the other side of the room by the time he finished.

I could not stop picturing the boy. I had become the little girl watching her doll and brother disappear from view. I was sickened by his confession. I had allowed myself to trust him and that trust had turned into a poison in my brain.

"Condemn me," he said.

"Don't give me that burden," I said. I was shivering, suddenly cold. "That girl is your judge. Go find her."

"I've tried. I've looked for the newspaper story. I asked those who lived in the area."

Edward put on his coat and gathered his belongings. I would no longer see him. He was leaving me with his confession. He had entrusted his secret to me, and I wished he never had. He meant only to be cruel to that girl, but the death of that boy was still his fault. What he had intended was evil enough—his selfish need, his disregard of others. My mother intended to go to San Francisco to see her son. She may not have intended to leave me behind. Or perhaps she did. The result was the same and she should bear the guilt for all of it, and no matter what excuse she had, whatever trickery it was, she wasn't any less to blame. Look at my life. I could not go back to being that girl I once was any more than that girl with the doll could. I would always feel betrayed. Edward would always carry guilt, and that was how it should be. We understood that, as victim, as culprit. We both suffered from a hollow in our souls, and only two damaged people could understand what that meant and suffer in that hollow together.

He asked if he should leave. I shook my head. "Oh, Edward," I said. "What now?" I allowed him to embrace me. I could feel his chest heaving and shaking. He had wanted love so great we would ache with the fullness of it. I ached, knowing it would be less.

OVER THE NEXT few days, Edward and I talked about our wounds. "I have had storms of rage," I told him, "and when I was caught in them I could think of nothing else and my whole body was filled with poison. Why does love end so quickly and hatred last without end?"

"Could you ever hate without hurting so much?" he said. "Is there no relief? Would constant love from me fill your mind with thoughts of another kind so that there was no room for rage?"

Edward asked if I could trust him enough to leave the courtesan world and live with him. He had asked the very thing I desired for so long. Yet I was not prepared to exchange one uncertain life for another. He had once been reckless with other people's hearts and lives. Instead of believing he would keep me safe, my need for him made me fragile. I needed honesty, and I was afraid to hear what his next confession might be. I needed complete trust in him, but I could not rid myself of doubts. Instead of loving him freely, I restrained myself, unable to let go.

Over the weeks, I slowly gave in to my longing to entrust myself to love. He poured out every transgression he could recall to prove he would not keep anything from me. He kept to himself after his despicable act and had storms in his mind, as I had, but his were of such ferocious guilt that he thought he would go mad. He had released them to no one. When his parents hired the tutors to write his essays, he now confessed, he let them. When he met Minerva, he had sex with her in a field and had little feeling for her. He had seen prostitutes after he left his wife. He had gone through drunken spells. He masturbated. I laughed at that one. I confided in him my loneliness as a child and the terrible fear I had had that I might be half-Chinese.

I told him the story of my father enflaming my mother with emotions I had never seen in her, about my shock to discover she had a son, who was more important to her than I had ever been. I spoke of her heartlessness in putting me in the hands of her lover, a man even she did not trust, and who turned out to be an animal who would eat his own mother. I spoke briefly of those days when I believed my mother would return, how I alternated between hope and hatred, until I gave up, and all that remained was hate.

He comforted me. He wanted to understand my sadness and anger. But how can anyone truly understand another's suffering unless he has felt the wound being made and the moment trust died? He could not go back in time and inhabit my mind as a child, an innocent heart, and my spasms of uncertainty day after long day, night after long night. How could he ever truly understand what it was like to see love fleeting like migrating birds, leaving you with the horror that you were never loved and never would be? He felt only my sadness, just the aftermath. And it would have been enough had I not heard his confession. Now there would always be doubts and not complete trust. Our love would never increase with more gifts of ourselves. Our love would be solace, companionship, and the careful mending of wounds.

I CONTINUED TO attend parties and charm men who might become suitors. I was a good actress caught between love and necessity. Loyalty came back on occasion and tried to renew the better days, as he called them. "Should I be sorry I introduced you to the American?"

The hot moist weather of June descended and made me feel heavy and listless. I brought out my lightweight dresses. One was too worn to wear at parties but was good for idle afternoons. I slipped into the dress. How strange: I could not close the fasteners on the bodice. Had I gained that much weight? Or perhaps it was all those salty pickles I had been eating. I looked at my breasts. The nipples were larger than before. Another thought came hard on the heels of the last. I cast back to when I last had my monthly flow: seven weeks ago, just before a big party. Or was it eight? I had recently complained to the cook that he had served food that was spoiled and had made me ill.

I was pregnant. Magic Gourd always talked about pregnancy as if it were a sex disease you could catch from men. This was Edward's baby, my baby, and I would give this baby love, trust, and complete devotion. The moment I thought that, I knew the baby was a girl. I could see her, opening her eyes for the first time. They were green, a shade between my green eyes and Edward's hazel ones. I imagined her at age four, walking next to me in the park, pointing to birds and flowers, and asking me to name them. And then she was six and reading aloud from a book as I listened. She was twelve, learning history and elocution, and not the tricks of seducing a man. I imagined her at age twenty, my age, with men who tried to win her favor—not to deflower her or bed her in her boudoir—but to ask her to marry. Or maybe she would not marry at twenty or ever. She would run the Ivory family business. She would be Edward's only heir. This baby girl would have too many choices to count. She would be who I was supposed to have been.

When I told Magic Gourd I was pregnant, she wailed and ran over to stare at my belly.

"*Ai-ya!* Didn't you stick the little herb pillows inside you? Did you drink the soup? Or did you do this on purpose? Do you know what trouble you've given us? How many weeks? Tell me the truth. If it's less than six, I can still pack the herbs inside you—"

"I want this baby."

"What? You want to look like you're growing a watermelon in your belly and two winter melons for breasts? You'll soon be big out to here and even a man with the cock of a horse wouldn't be able to reach your precious portal. *Baby!* What man wants to ride a nurse-maid with soppy tits squirting all over the place? You'll lose your suit-

ors, your money, your position in this house, be kicked out, and soon
you'll be a whore—"

"—lying in a filthy shack with my legs wide open for dogs and
rickshaw pullers. You don't have to tell me anymore."

"Good. Now you've come to your senses. I'll call a woman who's
taken care of this same problem for a lot of careless girls. And don't
you listen to those maids from the countryside who tell you to drink
tadpole soup. That's a recipe for twins."

"This is Edward's baby. I want to keep it."

"*Wah!* Edward's? What difference does that make? You've
known him for only four months and now you're willing to ruin
your figure and throw away your life for a spoiled American who
deserted his wife.

"How many times have you learned that a man's loyalty never
lasts more than a few seasons? Look at Loyalty. He told you he
couldn't live without you. He said you knew him better than he knew
himself. He was your patron for four seasons, then he came by one
night here, two nights there, he took another season with you, then
it was again one night here, one night there, and now it's *how are you*
and *see you later*. You loved him, Violet. It has taken you so long to
overcome the wounds. And now you love Edward, who was disloyal
to his wife."

I regretted telling her that part of Edward's confession. I only
did to let her know he was not a prospect for marriage.

"How loyal will Edward be in another year—or another five
when you have no looks or suitors? And how do you know this is his
baby? What if your baby pops out with black hair, crying *wah-wah* in
Chinese? Is your Edward so stupid to think he's the only one to shoot
seeds into you?"

"No other man could possibly be the father," I said.

"Nonsense. You were still seeing Auspicious Liang last month.
You were probably too lazy to use the herbal pillows with him, too.
Or did you just recite poetry together and look at the moon?"

"We did other things. There is no possibility that he is the father."

"And who will take care of your yowling Yankee bastard? Don't expect me to be amah to your whim."

"I'll hire an amah. I'll live with Edward. He asked me long before this happened."

"You've already told him?"

"I will tonight."

Magic Gourd walked slowly around the room talking to herself: "*Ai-ya!* Little Violet, why must I do all the worrying? Of course he wants you to live with him. Why pay when he can have you for free? You cannot trust a man to be steadfast. If you depend on one man you can also depend on disaster. Edward's life is like drifting seaweed. He has no plan. He could drift back to America soon. If you leave this house, Violet, you may not be able to come back once you realize your mistake. You are twenty. At this age, each year goes by more quickly than the last. And the men who would want you when you are older are often the cruel and cheap ones."

The maid announced my bathwater was ready. I went behind the screen and quickly immersed myself. I would decide what to do with my life, not Magic Gourd. And I had already decided I was going to have the baby. But as soon as I said that to myself, I was doused with fright. Magic Gourd's worries appeared before me. Edward said he loved me. But she was right. We had known each other for only four months. He had once been a cruel and careless boy. He might have been born that way and this might come out later. He might have other secrets he had not yet told me. And there was much he did not know about me—the number of men who had visited my bed, and all that I had done with them. We might be in bed one night, and he would sit up and say, "Hey, where did you learn to do that? Who enjoyed these talents you have? What else do you know?" If I told him the truth, he would be shocked and disgusted. He might be so shaken his cruel nature would return. Or maybe he would turn to religion.

Many Americans did so when faced with heartache and hardship. Or maybe the prodigal son would return to his family when he was broke. They would lure him with money, and he would make amends with his wife, and this time, she would give him a real baby. He would be with his own people, a mature man in his own society. His happiness would be greater than what it was with me now.

I pushed those terrible thoughts away. A different future appeared before me. A ship. It would take me across the sea to where I should have gone six years ago. Edward could get me a visa. Fairweather had lied. My birth certificate had probably been at the consulate all along. If we worked fast enough, the baby might even be born in America, and in America, no one would know what I had done in the past—except my mother. She would have no way of knowing I had come. Let her continue to think I died in Shanghai. And where would I live in America? His family would not welcome me.

Magic Gourd's smug face sprang to mind. "You see. You do not fit in his world. You never will." She would not either. What if she spoke without thinking and bragged about how well she had taught me the tricks of a courtesan? I would suffer a permanent fall in society. Edward would defend me at first, but what kind of fortitude did he have? It would be dangerous to bring Magic Gourd with me. In any case, no amount of bribery money could buy the paperwork for her to come to America. And even if I got her a visa, she would never leave Shanghai to live among foreigners. She complained whenever Edward spoke to me in English. It was settled then. She would stay in Shanghai, and I would give her money to help her start a business. Perhaps she could rent a few rooms in a small house and train an appreciative virgin courtesan. I would make sure she was comfortable. Edward would contribute to make that possible, I was sure of it. With guilt dispelled, I could freely imagine life without Magic Gourd's ceaseless meddlesome ways: her criticism, unwanted advice, and more criticism for not following what she said. I would not have to see her victorious face when the dangers she had warned of came to pass. As terrible as it was to say, it would be a relief to be free of her.

As if she had heard me, Magic Gourd said: "I know you never like hearing what I have to say." Her voice sounded tired and sad. "You think that baby growing inside you will fill the emptiness your mother left behind. But listen to me, Violet. You would give that baby your bad fate, and then the two of you would share the same emptiness. I know you do not want to hear that. But I am only being honest, and who else would tell you the truth?"

I did not answer.

"If you decide to have the baby and live with Edward, I will say nothing more. I will not be happy for you, but I will always be here to help you when you realize you're in trouble, unless I have already perished on the streets."

THE NEXT MORNING, I told Edward in a straightforward manner that I was pregnant. "This isn't your burden," I said, "and there is nothing you must decide, because I have already decided."

"What did you decide?"

"I am keeping the baby and will raise it myself."

I watched his face change from shock to jubilance. "Violet, you have no idea how happy you've made me. If I could jump to the moon to show you, I would." He enclosed me in his arms and rocked me. "A beautiful innocent baby we created out of love. She's part of us, the best part—which means she is more you than I. But I'll claim what I can, a thumb, a toe, a smile . . ."

He said *she*. "How do you know it's a girl?"

He paused, clearly surprised by his slip of the tongue. "I instantly saw her in my mind as you . . . It must be because I was wishing today that we could start our lives from the beginning. I was wishing that I had known you all your life and all of mine."

Who would Edward have become if he had not been cruel when he was a boy? He would not have met me in China. He would have remained at his family home, married a woman he loved, had a baby with his wife, and would never have left them. He would have had no need for additional companionship. He would not have come to the House of Vermillion and plunked down twenty silver dollars on the table. I never would have met him. But we did. It was our fate and our natures, flawed and wounded, that brought us together.

Edward took my hands and kissed them. "Violet, I know you didn't intend to become pregnant. I'm deeply grateful that you've decided to keep the baby. We'll start afresh, without the old sadness. She'll be our future. And we'll love our baby completely and perhaps we'll be able to love each other just as fully. Can we live together, the three of us? Can you bear it? I know there is nothing I can do to prove without a doubt that you can trust me. But if you give me a chance, I would prove it to you every day."

The next afternoon, Edward returned with good news. He had told his host, Mr. Shing, he would be departing soon. "I said we were getting married. It's not a lie. I feel that there is more truth to our unity than there ever was with my legal wife. No one in Shanghai would ever know I had been married before. And I do plan to press more strongly for a divorce. In the meantime, you are my Mrs. Ivory and we will have a wonderful place for raising our child. Mr. Shing has kindly offered his own house—not the guesthouse but the mansion. I had wanted only his advice on where to look for a suitable house to rent. He nearly wrestled me to the ground, insisting I move into his house. He said he was leaving for Hong Kong soon and would be gone for at least two years. If we want to continue to live in his house when he returns, he will take the guesthouse, which he prefers anyway. The main house, he says, is too big for a man who spends only a few weeks a year in Shanghai."

I felt uneasy. A favor this generous was not to be trusted. Mr. Shing might be a gangster who would extract a debt from Edward.

"Does Mr. Shing know who you're marrying? Is he aware that I'm a courtesan."

"I told him about you early on, right after our meeting that went awry. I had told him at the time that you were Eurasian but could pass as an Italian countess. Mr. Shing found it interesting that I had fallen in love with a courtesan. He said it was not hard to believe, since courtesans tend to be far more interesting than most women who have led sheltered lives and have done only what good society has told them to do. He asked all sorts of questions about you—all of them proper. Your name, your age, the usual facts. And it turns out he has heard of your mother. He acknowledged she was well known but he said he had not been aware of what had happened to her daughter."

Edward went on bended knee. "Now that we have a threshold over which I can carry you, I would like you to make me an honorable man." He took from his pocket a ring. It was a large oval diamond surrounded by smaller ones. "Violet," he began, then broke down and wept.

I was ashamed I had ever doubted Edward. I was not accustomed to the magnitude of such love. I had been influenced by Magic Gourd to disbelieve anything a man might say that moved my heart.

Just then Magic Gourd walked into the room. "What's going on here?"

"Edward has asked me to live with him," I said. "And he's given me a ring." I held it up. The size of the diamond spoke to its significance.

Her face turned rigid. "I'm so happy you showed me I am wrong." She left the room.

A half hour later, she returned, her eyes red and her jaw stiff. It was the most emotion I had ever seen her express, and I knew that had she been able to hold it back, she would have. She laid out on the bed the jewelry she had put in safekeeping for me. Next, she tossed onto the divan the gifts I had given her over the years: the jacket, the hat, the shoes, the necklace, the bracelet, the mirror, the valise with my mother's dress, and the two paintings. "Look them over and tell me if everything is there. I don't want you to later accuse me of stealing from you."

"Stop talking nonsense," I said.

"Soon you won't have to hear my nonsense."

"What is going on?" Edward asked. "Why is she angry? I thought she'd be pleased."

I answered in English. "She's accused me of abandoning her."

"Well, that is easy to remedy. The house is certainly big enough. She can have a whole wing to herself, if she wants."

I was stunned. I had no time to tell Edward what I had planned to do for Magic Gourd. She was standing in front of us. She would detect what I was saying and Edward's puzzlement that I would turn down his offer. On the other hand, I should translate what Edward said. She had once said she would refuse to live with a foreigner.

"He has empty rooms?" Magic Gourd said. "You have an empty heart. He offered to have me live with you. I could see your sneaky face, trying to think how you could be rid of me. Well, don't worry. I wouldn't live with two foreigners, even if they begged me."

If I did not beg, that would have settled it. And it would be her decision, and I would not feel guilty about it. Edward had offered. I had translated. But an awful feeling washed over me. If I did not ask, it would be like killing her. I owed her a debt of gratitude. More than gratitude, much more.

I could finally see what had always been there. She had been more than an attendant, more than a friend, more than a sister. She had been a mother to me. She had worried, sought to protect me from danger, guided me toward the best. She had looked out for my future, assessed the worthiness of everyone to be in my life. And in that way, she had taken me as her purpose in life, the one who gave her meaning. I had had constant love all along. And in recognizing that, I felt moved to tears.

"How could you step out of my life?" I told her. "If you don't join me, I will be lost. No one would worry about me as much as you. No one knows me better, knows my past and what this new life means. I should have told you a long time ago." I became teary-eyed. She kept her lips sealed, but her jaw was trembling. "You are the only loyal person in my life, the only one I can trust."

Tears fell from her eyes. "Now you know. I was always the only one."

"We love each other," I said with a light laugh. "In spite of all the trouble I've given you, you stayed with me. So it must be that you loved me like a mother."

"*Wah!* Mother? I'm not old enough to be your mother." She was crying and laughing. I could tell by her strong protests that this was exactly what she had wanted me to realize and what she had wanted to hear. "I'm only twelve years older. How could I be your mother? Maybe you could say I was like an older sister."

She had made herself even younger than the last time she lied about her age. "You have been like a mother to me," I repeated.

"That can't be. No, no, I'm too young."

I had to repeat it a third and final time, so that she would finally accept this and not doubt I was being genuine. "No one could have loved me more, except a mother."

"Not even Edward?"

"No one. Only a mother, only you."

MAGIC GOURD AND I had to quickly decide which of our belongings to take and which to part with. We sold the furniture, including the pieces Loyalty gave me for my defloration. Magic Gourd kept a few knickknacks. The costumes we loved most could never be worn anywhere other than a courtesan house. I had to sort them into ones that were more or less valuable than others. At first it was simple to decide. I set aside the costumes with stains and rips. I gave those to the maids to sew and clean as best they could. Magic Gourd took those to the pawnshop, but we were offered a ridiculously low amount. We had no time to go back and forth over the week to bargain. So we gave them to the maids who had repaired them. I would have thought they would be grateful beyond tears, but they accepted the clothes with a look of disappointment. I assured them that they would also receive the customary tip, after which they admired the clothes and praised me for being more generous than other courtesans who also left to live as concubines of rich husbands.

I gave a very nice winter costume to Shining. It was well made, of good silk, and had an exaggerated sleeve shape that resembled a lily. I gave another to Serene. It was an excursion costume for carriage rides, a showy one, with a high-neck fur collar, and it was beautiful, all but the color, an odd shade of mauve that did not suit my complexion. It was supposed to be the color of oxblood, but which I had come to feel was closer to the tinge of a bleeding pig. Whenever I wore it, I had bad luck with suitors who did not pay or with slights by Loyalty. But the color enhanced Serene's pale skin, and thus it would likely bring her better luck. She was overcome with emotion when I gave her the costume. She told me I was a good person—and with genuine feeling, I believed.

I gave Madam a fur wrap and Vermillion a long opera coat. I had already settled my debt with Madam, which included the original fee she had paid for me, interest, and other expenses, which I did not know she had charged, including a percentage of the "protection services" provided by the Green Gang and special taxes levied by the International Settlement administration. My retirement savings dwindled down to a quarter of what I thought I had. I sold back a few costumes to the tailor, who felt they were in fine enough condition to present as new. We agreed to share fifty-fifty whatever these clothes fetched. I knew he would cheat me out of at least a quarter of my half, so I also made him agree that he would give me a good price when I returned to have new clothes made in a Western style. When I did, I would point out how little money I received for the clothes he sold for me and he would lower the price even further.

There was one dress I could not part with, a lucky one, which had brought me many suitors and two patrons, including my second contract with Loyalty. It was a green watered silk, the upper half Chinese with pearls for frog clasps and silk thread dipped in gold that had been sewn along the plackets of the collar and edges of the sleeves. The upright Chinese collar was slightly flared to show a hint of Western lace lining. It was tightly fitted around the bodice. Below the waist, it tapered wide to accommodate a full Western skirt with large pleated folds. A false hem ended at the knees, and below that were three layers of scalloped silk of a dark emerald shade. The dress looked like the folds of a theater curtain as it was being raised.

This was my greatest achievement in fashion, one I had created without Magic Gourd's interference, and its success created a ripple through the courtesan houses, so that by the end of the next week after I had first worn the dress, some courtesans had already copied a few of its features—the lace, the false hem, the scallops, and the collar's flared shape. But, as I had planned, they were unable to imitate the expensive pearl clasps or the delicate gold threading that had required weeks of careful sewing. As a result, the ones worn by other courtesans looked like the cheap replicas that they were.

In the costume, I'd had not only luck but also a sense of confidence and calm, which I took to be my true self. I was afraid to leave the dress behind. Yet, to keep it might pull me back to my old life, whether I wished it or not. Tucked inside me was a fear that I would have to return for any number of reasons I had imagined a hundred times. In the end, I kept the dress. I might be able to make a few adjustments, so that it was more suitable to a life without suitors.

I fretted over which dress I should wear for my arrival at the house. It should be Western. Other Chinese people treated Westerners with respect—or at least with fear. But the dress should not be too fancy, lest it appear that I had made too much of an effort to compensate for my station in life. I finally chose a dark blue walking suit.

Magic Gourd appeared at my door, and I had to keep myself

from laughing. She wore a dull brown Western dress with a blouson that hid her breasts and waist. She said the dress was ugly, but it suited her new life. Although Magic Gourd had retired as a courtesan six years ago, she had remained attentive to her best features, her perfect skin and a graceful undulating walk that acted like a switch in throwing her hips from side to side. When she was training me as the virgin courtesan, she demonstrated the walk, emphasizing its subtlety and lewdness, which I could never achieve. I saw men stare at her as she seduced them with the provocative movement of a retired courtesan whom they otherwise would not have noticed.

"I'm too old now to wear beautiful clothes. I'm already thirty-five."

Now she had made herself older. And she was—close to forty-five, by my guess. As the years went by, she had aged more quickly. I now appreciated how well she had done in prolonging her career.

She set a valise on the sofa. Inside were pouches of jewelry, hers and mine. She put aside the pieces she thought I should sell: the gaudy and less expensive ones. She picked up a ring that Loyalty Fang had once given me. She eyed me. She and I knew this would reveal what I still felt for him. If I kept it, I would feel unfaithful to Edward. "Sell it," I said.

There were more valuables she felt were too precious to put in the trunks: a small jade carving, a pair of porcelain dogs, and a small mantel clock. I saw she had also included two scrolls wrapped in cloth. But then I realized they were not scrolls but those damn paintings that had belonged to my mother and that had been painted by Lu Shing.

"I thought I threw these away," I said.

"I told you that day that I was keeping them for myself. I like the painting style and I don't care who painted them."

"Just make sure they're hanging in a place where I can't see them."

Magic Gourd frowned. "You have a good heart and you have a

hard one. Now that you have Edward and a new life, you can soften your heart a little, put it at ease. You don't have to be like me."

THE CAR ARRIVED to take us to our new home. Edward had gone ahead to make sure everything was in order. My heart beat fast, making me feel like I should run to keep pace with its rhythm. I was leaving my courtesan life at last, yet I saw omens everywhere that this was a mistake: a laughing bird, a tear at the bottom of my skirt, a sudden breeze. Whenever I had tried hard to avoid bad luck, it came anyway. And whenever I had ignored the signs, the result was the same.

WE DROVE THROUGH the gates and into the courtyard. The house was tall, like Hidden Jade Path, but the stone walls made it look like a fortress.

Edward ran to the car and swept open the door. He helped Magic Gourd first. "Do you think you can be happy here?" He wore a boyish grin.

I looked at the large house and the small guesthouse opposite it. To the left, the grounds extended to gardens and several smaller buildings in a similar style. It looked as if the former stone wings of the house had broken off and floated away. Small rosebushes had been planted on both sides of the pathway to the house. Beneath them were violets with purple-and-yellow faces. I did not often see those flowers and decided I would take that as a good omen and stop thinking that everything unusual was a sign of bad luck to come.

"Is Mr. Shing here? We should thank him right away."

"He's already left," Edward said. "We can send him a letter. Once you go inside, you'll see how much there is to thank him for."

We walked between double doors twice our height and into a chilly vestibule. A servant quietly entered and whisked away our long coats. Magic Gourd would not let him take her small valise with her valuables. The cold sank through my skin into my bones and I was about to call for the servant to return the coat when Edward led me through another doorway and into a large, comfortably heated square hall. Across the room was a fireplace and above that an enormous mirror, like those found in the lobbies of hotels. I walked toward it and saw my face. Was that really how I looked—timid and lost? I mustered the assuredness I had always had as a popular beauty. But I could not shake the feeling that I did not belong here and never would. The house was sparely furnished, but each chair, sofa, and table was clearly expensive and tasteful. There were no spittoons or velvet curtains that cascaded onto the floor. The air smelled sharp, and felt thinner. Magic Gourd walked around the room tentatively, as if her footsteps might break the tile floor.

I ran my hand across the fireplace mantel. Its rounded marble corners and sides had the look of wax that had melted into soft ripples. The flames were tall and bright, and as I grew warmer, I gradually felt more at ease.

"Look at that servant staring at me," Magic Gourd hissed, "as if to tell me I am lower than he is." She looked at herself in the mirror. "This dress is even uglier than I thought. It looks cheap."

Edward signaled a servant to push open a row of painted fanfold screens to reveal a dining room whose furniture was made of a golden wood. The legs were carved with the same swirled wax patterns of the fireplace. At one end of the room was a Chinese pond with miniature rockeries. As Magic Gourd and I approached the pond, a mass of openmouthed goldfish swam toward us with the eagerness of begging dogs. "They want to eat us alive!" Magic Gourd exclaimed. She went to a chair and sat down heavily. "All this excitement has worn me out. I need to take off these clothes. Where's my room?"

Edward signaled a maid, who shouted, "Mousie!" A girl, around ten years of age, ran out and offered to take Magic Gourd's valise, and when Magic Gourd refused to let go, the woman rebuked the girl for not helping Auntie. "That woman called me Auntie," Magic Gourd said, "as if she is younger than I am. I am going to tell her I am Mrs. Wang and that I am the respectable widow of a rich and educated man . . . and very handsome, too. Why should I have an imaginary husband who is old and ugly?"

Edward took me up a wide stairway and into a library lined with walls of books. At one end was a billiard table with a rounded belly and green-and-red fringe, and at the other an arrangement of two brown velvet sofas facing each other, along with armchairs, square tables stacked with books, and reading lamps.

We made our way to the other end of the hall and to a closed door. Edward said it was our bedroom. He opened it and revealed a small room with only a small table. I was puzzled until he led me farther in, to another door. Edward opened it slowly. Before me was a large room, darkened by green curtains. It was stately, without excess, and conveyed the power of the man who owned the house. An enormous bed with a carved headboard and footboard faced the door. This was bad feng shui and could draw disharmony and expel our luck . . . I stopped myself. I should no longer think this way. I quickly took in the rest: walls covered in green silk, a thick Persian carpet, a rose marble fireplace, small tables, tulip-shaped sconces. I caught Edward watching me.

"Are you pleased?"

"Yes, of course. But I feel like an intruder. It will take time to feel I belong here."

He took me through a doorway and into a large dressing room with a rose-covered divan and two walls of cabinetry. Beyond that was a bathroom with white marble floors and walls and shiny silver faucets that resembled a collection of pistols. The pedestal sink looked like a bird fountain, and, in fact, a marble dove sat in each corner. On one side of the bathroom was yet another door. I opened it and stepped into another bedroom, decorated in shades of rose.

"Is this for the baby?"

"The baby's room is down the hallway. This is your private bedroom."

"Why would I have a private bedroom separate from yours?"

"It's a ridiculous American custom of the very rich. The more money you have, the more privacy you require. You would not sleep here, of course. But you can use this room to place your personal belongings, your dresses, and such. I have similar rooms on the other side of the bedroom."

"Look at that enormous chandelier and that bureau. Everything looks so proper and also as if no living, breathing person ever slept here." My eyes passed over a painting on a wall next to the bed. It looked familiar: the shadowed land, the sharp-toothed mountains, a false glow of life that would soon be extinguished. I walked up to read the name of the artist: Lu Shing. My heart beat fast. In the other corner it said *The Valley of Amazement*. Someone had taken it from Magic Gourd's valise. But how had they put it into a frame so quickly? It did not make sense. Someone was mocking me, giving me bad omens.

Edward came over and stood behind me. "Mr. Shing's artistry is not as dreadful as he made it out to be."

I nearly jumped out of my skin. "Mr. Shing? Lu Shing is the owner of this house?"

"The very one. I was also struck by the painting. We had a similar one in our house, only much larger. He painted it when he was our guest. It's the southwest view of the valley we saw from our house. He must have painted this smaller one as a study for the larger one."

I was breathing fast, unable to take in enough air. Like many Westerners, Edward had mistaken Lu Shing's first name as the given name and the second as the family name. "Mr. Shing" should have been "Mr. Lu."

Why was Edward living in his house? Was this a secret plan?

Just then Magic Gourd crossed the room. "The bed is so soft it's like a pile of autumn leaves. The fireplace is not even lit, but it's as hot as an oven. She stared at me. "*Ai-ya!* What's wrong? Are you sick? Is it the same nausea or do you have a fever?" She took my arm and guided me to the bed, and then she, too, saw the painting. "*Eh!* How did this get here? Did someone steal it from my bag?"

"This house belongs to Lu Shing," I said. "He is Edward's host, the one he called Mr. Shing."

Her eyes grew round. "How can this be? Are you sure it's the same person?" She studied the painting from corner to corner, and put her finger on the name.

Edward did not understand what we were saying. "She likes it as well, I see."

I asked Magic Gourd to give me some privacy. She quickly left, giving a parting glare at Edward.

"I don't know what Lu Shing's plan is or his reason for letting us stay here, but I cannot live in this house."

"What's wrong? Violet, you're trembling. Are you ill?" He sat me on the bed.

"Your generous host, Mr. Shing, as you call him, is actually Mr. Lu, the father who abandoned my mother and me when I was a baby, and who then entranced my mother into leaving Shanghai for America to find her long-lost son. He is the reason I wound up in the courtesan house."

Edward fell silent, staring at the painting with vacant eyes. He started to speak several times, then stopped.

"Did he have anything to do with our meeting?" I said. "Was this a plan you and he concocted?"

"No, no. Violet, how could you think that? If Lu Shing had a plan, I did not know it. It sickens me that he knew who you were and tricked me into bringing you here. Did he think we wouldn't find out?" Edward stood up. "Of course we must leave. I'll call for the servants to remove our things immediately."

And we would have done exactly that had Magic Gourd not fallen sick with Spanish influenza.

CHAPTER 7

A BLUE DISEASE

Shanghai
June 1918
Violet

I had never seen Magic Gourd rendered so helpless. She moaned that she wanted to return home rather than die in a stranger's house. When she could not breathe easily, she stared at me with bulging eyes, shiny with tears.

Edward called for a doctor from the American Hospital, and an officious portly man with a beard, an Englishman, arrived wearing a white mask. He had the unfortunate name of Dr. Albee, which sounded like the Chinese words for "eternal suffering." Magic Gourd said to him, "King of Hell, I am Chinese. Don't take me to the fire pit where foreigners burn forever." Later, she lied that she was a Christian and deserved to go to heaven. She listed the good deeds she had done, which consisted primarily of having to deal with my haughty attitude, teaching me well, and being patient when I did not follow her advice. I was full of remorse that she would leave this world thinking of me as an ungrateful charge. She further cut into my heart by saying I was her beloved little sister and she worried about what would happen to me after she was gone. That led to her plea that he allow her to stay until I became one of the Ten Beauties of Shanghai.

Dr. Albee said there was nothing to do but encourage her to drink water and make her as comfortable as possible. He advised that everyone in the house wear a mask and, in parting, informed us that we were all under a two-week quarantine. No one was allowed to leave. Only then did I remember that I wanted to leave this house the moment I learned it belonged to Lu Shing. None of that mattered now. As the fever progressed, she confused me with her mother. Her face glowed and she explained why she had not returned to the village to see her sooner. I told her I was happy she had come back to me. I cried as she recounted in terrible detail her mistreatment by the husband of her mistress.

When the Chinese doctor arrived, I asked that he introduce himself to Magic Gourd by a Chinese name that sounded like "good health." He gave her bitter soup and a plaster of camphor to place over her chest. She soon breathed more easily. I went to her side and said, "Mother is here. Now you have to get well and stay longer on earth so you can take care of me in my old age." Her eyes rolled toward me and she frowned. "Have you lost your mind? You're not my mother. Look in a mirror. You're Violet. And why should I take of you? You should take care of me for all the trouble you caused me." That was when I knew she would recover.

The Chinese doctor told the servants to wash the floors thoroughly with limewater each day so that the rest of us would not become ill. But that evening, I suddenly became feverish and cold at the same time. My bones felt as if they would break. The room floated, Edward shrank to the size of a doll. I awoke and saw a girl sitting next to the bed dozing. I did not recognize the room at first and thought Fairweather had kidnapped me again and dropped me off at another courtesan house. At least it was first class this time. And then I saw the Lu Shing painting and remembered where I was, and in an instant I was seized with fright. "Where's Edward?" The slumbering girl sat bolt upright then ran out. Moments later, Edward arrived and petted my forehead, murmuring endearments as his tears fell onto my face. I told him not to touch me lest I infect him, and he assured me that I was no longer contagious. No one else had become ill. They had been drinking the bitter soup day and night. "I know how vile it is because Magic Gourd made me drink the same daily potion. I've concluded that if you don't die from the awful taste, you won't die of influenza."

When I was well enough to sit, Edward carried me to the garden where a chaise longue had been placed in the shade of a tree.

"I already sent Lu Shing a letter excoriating him for his abandonment of you and his deceit in not telling me who he really was. I let him know that as soon as you had recovered completely from illness, we would leave. He sent back a reply." I asked Edward to read it aloud, and I lay back, steeling myself.

"My dear Violet," Edward began. "I claim no excuses that override immorality. I expect no forgiveness. I can never adequately make amends. I can only try to add to your comfort . . ." He said that I could stay in the house as long as I wished. He would provide for the expenses and the servants there. He wanted me to inherit the house, but it would require acknowledging that he was my father. If I were willing to do so, he would have the documents drawn up for his will. He closed by saying I should let him know if I ever wanted to meet him, even if it was only to vent my anger. But unless I said so, he would not return to the house and cause me further upset. The envelope showed the letter had been posted from Hong Kong. It was signed: "Yours, Lu Shing."

"I will do whatever you wish," Edward said.

"Bastard. He said nothing about my mother. He did not say whether she or he knew I had been alive all these years." I was quickly overcome with exhaustion and Edward took me inside so I could sleep. The next morning, Edward told me he had written a letter to Lu Shing demanding he tell me the answer to those questions. He often found ways to show me he loved me and would protect me, just as he had promised he would. I put my arms around him and clung to him like a child.

"I don't really want to know the answers," I said. "I've already gone through every possible reason and circumstance why my mother did not return to save me, and none would be adequate to explain why, unless he said my mother had died before she ever set foot on American soil. And even if he told me that, I could not be certain if he was telling the truth. All that pain consumed me for so long. I don't want its hold on me again. If I change my mind later, I will ask you to read me what the coward says." In keeping with my wishes, when Lu Shing's second letter arrived, Edward put it away.

I waged a small war with myself over what to do with the house. My immediate impulse was to leave and also to refuse the inheritance. I tried not to think of the comfort we had settled into. Of course, one of the first things I did was to remove the loathsome painting from the bedroom. By necessity, we stayed on, so I could recover fully from illness. And then it was because I had daily morning sickness and the upheaval of moving might be harmful to the baby. I was already worried that my illness might have affected her health. I finally made peace with living there for reasons of fear: If Edward's parents ever tried to cut off his funds, as they once had, we would be cast into poverty, without a roof over our heads. I told Edward we would stay.

He later admitted that he was relieved because of worries he had for our future child. If anything happened—if he became ill and he was not around—where would the baby and I live? We went to the lawyer for the Ivory Shipping Company to ask for general advice. He was an odd-looking man with a bushy head of hair, and an equally bushy beard and eyebrows that were as thick as squirrels' tails. Edward introduced me as his wife, "Mrs. Ivory," and explained that I had an eccentric American uncle in Soochow who had sent me a letter saying that he wished to leave his house to me.

"We don't want to appear avaricious and ask that the bequest be placed in his will," Edward said. "Would his letter be sufficient when the inevitable comes to pass?"

The lawyer believed a will was best, but he said that the letter might be sufficient if it was dated, in his handwriting, and there were no descendants, like some ne'er-do-well son. When we returned home, we found that Lu Shing's two letters were indeed dated, and Edward put them in a safe place where no one but he could find them.

We lived in our little world, in the cozy intimacy of married life. When the weather turned cold, we lay quietly in each other's arms in front of the fireplace, knowing what the other was thinking, about happiness now and in the future and the luck that we had found each other. We read to each other in the library—from the newspaper, a novel, or Edward's favorite book of poems. On rainy days, we played the Victrola and danced while Magic Gourd watched. Edward would always gesture to her to take a few whirls with him. She, in turn, would always refuse the first request, and only after Edward had pointed to me and gestured that my stomach was too large to dance to such a fast song, would she happily relent. It was amusing to watch them communicate in a guessing game of gestures and facial expressions, which often led to hilarious misunderstandings. Edward once pantomimed licking and biting into ice cream on a stick and our walking to the new shop down the road that sold the confection. Magic Gourd thought a stray dog had been eating food on his plate and ran off with it when he saw Edward coming. I wound up having to translate. We found boxes with various games and amusements, including table tennis. Magic Gourd proved to be quick and agile, and Edward was surprisingly clumsy and slow. He did not mind that we often broke into laughter. I learned later that he was actually quite skilled, but he had loved seeing us so happy. We took walks twice a day to reach the cafés where customers discussed the latest news about the war. Victory was drawing near and we all felt impatient for war to be over. We talked in bed about our childhoods, recalling everything we could, so that we would feel we had known each other all our lives and more deeply than other people had. We debated whether it was Chinese Fate or American Destiny that had brought us together. Our meeting each other could not possibly be as random as two leaves from two trees being blown together.

The only blemish in our perfect life was Lu Shing. My rage toward my mother and him used to consume me. They could never sufficiently compensate me. How could they return the life I should have had? But now I had the life I always would have wanted. I would never forgive Lu Shing. But while living so blissfully in his house, I no longer dwelled on his despicable actions that had changed my life.

THE EPIDEMIC WAS over by the summer of 1918. And when the war ended in November, we had a second reason to celebrate. Although the International Settlement had claimed its neutrality during the war, now the flags of different nationalities flapped their colors to signal the world was at peace. Westerners broke out the French champagne they had been saving, and people on the streets exchanged kisses with strangers. They also exchanged germs, and those kisses were later blamed when a new wave of influenza broke out—and it was worse in strength than the last. Shanghai was not as affected as other places in the world. That was the report we read in the newspaper, which also noted that, similar to the last time, the greatest toll was on young men and women. Oddly enough, those who were the most physically fit were the most likely to be struck down.

Magic Gourd and I had already suffered influenza and were no longer at risk of infection. But Edward had escaped the first round. I was more than seven months pregnant, and out of fear for our coming baby, we had everyone in the house practice strict hygiene. If Edward and I went outside of the house, he wore a mask and we avoided crowded cafés and restaurants. Despite those precautions, Edward fell ill, and I flew into action, having already read up on all that was needed to treat the patient. We boiled water sprinkled with camphor and eucalyptus. We made him drink hot tea and a broth of bitter Chinese herbs. We had at the ready wet towels to cool the fever, most of which was rejected by Edward, who said his symptoms were so mild they suggested he had been too much a weakling to qualify for the endangered category of the physically fit. He was in bed for only a day and bragged that influenza was no worse than the common cold. He recovered quickly, easing our worries. Now that he, too, was protected from ever getting the flu again, we would not have to worry about passing it on to our baby.

On a frigid bright day in January, our baby girl was born. The Paris Peace Conference started the same day, and we took this as a sign she would be a calm baby. That proved to be true. She was fair-colored and resembled Edward more than me. Her eyes were hazel and she had tufts of light brown hair. I claimed the whorl on the back of her head was mine, as well as the faint blue birthmark on her rump, which many Chinese babies had. The curves and lobes of her delicate leaflike ears matched Edward's. I claimed her rounded chin. Edward said that when she frowned in her sleep, she looked like me when I was worried. I said that when her nostrils flared, she looked like him when food arrived on the table. Edward pronounced her "the most perfect replica of the most perfect woman in all eternity." And upon receiving that love-soaked endearment, I asked him to choose our baby's name. He thought for two days. The name would be part of our new family legacy, he said. Bosson would not be her inheritance.

"Her name shall be Flora," he said at last. "Violet and Little Flora." He cradled her and brought his face close to her sleeping one. "My little Flora."

I was secretly stricken. In courtesan houses, we were known as "flowers." I had had mixed feelings all my life about my name. Violets were the flower my mother loved, a meager-faced one, easily trampled, that grew with little care. I had changed my name over the years, from Violet to Vivi and Zizi, and many nicknames in between. Now it had returned to me as Violet. It was like fate. I could not permanently change it. In the library the other day, I had been listening to an opera aria, the loveliest of them all. I read the accompanying pamphlet tucked into the sleeve of the record. It was sung by the character Violetta, a courtesan, it said, and then added "and at this stage of her life, a fallen flower."

Edward was singing sweetly in his tenor voice—"Flora! O Sweet Little Flora! Dewdrop in the morning. Rosebud in the afternoon . . . Look at her eyes!" he said. "See how alert they've become when I say her name. She recognizes it already. Little Flora, Little Flora." How could I ask him to choose another name?

We could not bear to have Little Flora away from our sight and decided she would remain with us rather than in the nursery with the amah. In the middle of the night, I woke to her soft complaints and grunts, and lifted her from the bassinet by my side of the bed, and put her to my breast. I sang softly to her: "Flora, O Sweet Little Flora, dewdrop in the morning, rosebud in the afternoon." She quieted and her eyes drifted until she found mine and there she remained. In that small moment of recognition, I found my greatest joy.

March 1919

In March, the Spanish Influenza returned yet again. "The war is over, and this should be over as well," Magic Gourd said. Everyone was saying this one was more powerful than the last. Fewer were infected, but those who did fall prey suffered more and died faster.

Edward, Magic Gourd, and I had already overcome influenza, so we were grateful we were not in danger. But Little Flora, who was only two months old, had never been ill with any malady, and we were exceedingly cautious. We required everyone in our household to wear gauze masks whenever they left the house. Before coming into the house, they had to drop their used masks into a pot by the door, so they could later be boiled clean and dipped into camphorated water, and made ready for use again. When we took Little Flora for fresh air walks, we placed a covering of camphorated gauze over the baby carriage. We avoided crowded places. Large warning signs appeared everywhere: big fines would be levied against those caught spitting, coughing, or sneezing in public rooms or on tramway cars. Two of the boys' academies and one of the girls' closed due to outbreaks in the dormitories. Along Bubbling Well Road, we passed stores and stalls offering remedies to prevent influenza or to cure it. The best way to avoid sickness, we learned, was to drink Dr. Chu's elixir eight times a day, or to gargle with Mrs. Parker's Potion, or to bathe in hot onion water. Those who took ill should rest and drink alcohol, the best whiskey being the most effective.

Two weeks later, we learned that only a hundred or so foreigners in the International Settlement had died, and at least half of them were Japanese. The schools reopened. There were no piles of bodies along the sidewalks, only piles of unsold masks. We lost our concern and our caution.

When several days later Edward developed the sniffles, he was the first to say he should not go near Little Flora. In any case, he had no appetite and would not join us for supper.

Since I was vulnerable to getting a cold, Edward and I each slept in our private bedrooms that night. His manservant Little Ram set a glass of whiskey on his bedside table. The next morning, when I went to Edward, I was alarmed to see that his eyes were rimmed red and his face was pale and sweaty. He claimed he was warm because the evening was humid. The weather was, in fact, chilly. He coughed as if choking and explained that Nanking Road was flying with dust from buildings that were being torn down. He had a headache from the pounding effort of coughing.

"It's Chinese disease," he joked. The Americans and British called all sorts of maladies "Chinese disease," from stomach ailments to anything puzzling, especially if it led to death.

In the afternoon, I went to Edward's side and was shocked to see he had become more feverish. He was coughing so violently he could barely find his breath or balance to stand. "I already told you. It's Shanghai swamp fever," he managed to joke. "Please don't worry. I'm going to lie in a cool tub." An hour later, he asked me to summon a doctor at the American Hospital, but only so he could get medication for his cough. He required the help of two servants to rise out of the tub and return to his bed.

Dr. Albee arrived. Magic Gourd recognized him. "King of Hell," she called him. She told me she would also send for the same Chinese doctor who had treated us when we were ill. He would likely have better remedies than this one, who has said there was not much that could be done, except tap your toes and twiddle your fingers.

I assured him that Edward had overcome influenza during the second outbreak, so this was another kind of illness. Typhoid? He peered into Edward's mouth, did a few more inspections of his nose and ears, felt around his neck, thumped and listened to his back, then said with great authority: "The patient has an infection of the adenoids." He measured laudanum from a larger bottle into a smaller one. He gave Edward a capful to ease the cough and an aspirin for the fever. He also prescribed fresh sheets, since this would contribute to a sense of ease rather than dis-ease and thus hasten a return to health. To enable Edward to breath more comfortably, he used a syringe to draw out some of the mucus. As he prepared his instruments, he said to Edward that he should have the troublesome adenoids removed once he recovered from the infection.

"It promotes good health and a clear mind," he said cheerily. "Removal can also cure conditions such as bed-wetting, poor appetite, and mental retardation. Everyone should be rid of them. If you and your wife decide to have them removed, there is no one better than I to do the operation. I've removed them from hundreds of patients."

He inserted a bulb syringe into one of Edward's nostrils. When the doctor looked at what he had withdrawn, his expression changed to dark puzzlement. It was thick and tinged with blood. He reassured me that it was not serious. Edward coughed up sputum. It, too, had streaks of red.

The doctor babbled on as Edward coughed violently and tried to catch his breath. "This sort of bloody discharge is typical," Dr. Albee said in a quick professional tone. "The tissue becomes irritated and bleeds." He said we should feed him plenty of tea, no milk. I was glad to see the very cheerful doctor leave.

I sat by Edward's bed and read aloud from the newspaper. An hour later, bloody foam bubbled out of Edward's nostrils. "Damn the adenoids!" I cried. "Damn that doctor!"

Magic Gourd flew in and saw Edward. "What's the matter with him?"

I was shaking and breathing so hard I could barely speak between breaths. "Edward told us last fall that he had a touch of influenza. He said it was no worse than a common cold. I think that's what it was, not influenza. He was never protected from it."

I wanted Magic Gourd to tell me he was already better and would be well by evening. Instead, her eyes widened with fright.

The Chinese doctor took one look at Edward and said, "It's Spanish influenza and it is the fierce one." He added, "We've had many more cases than your American doctors have seen—fifteen hundred so far. Of those I have seen hundreds. There is no doubt, it is influenza."

He told a manservant to remove Edward's pajamas, which were damp from the fever. He ordered a maid to bring clean cloths, large cloths, twenty of them. The doctor turned to me and said, "We can try."

Try? What did he mean by this frail word *try*?

"If he is better by tomorrow morning, he has a chance." He doled out medicine in packets, which we were supposed to boil for an hour.

The doctor twisted hair-size acupuncture needles into Edward's body. Soon Edward's rigid grimace softened into mindless surrender. He breathed in a regular fashion, more slowly and deeply. He opened his eyes, smiled, and whispered hoarsely, "Much better. Thank you, my love."

I wept with relief. The day was new, the world was different. I took his hand and kissed his damp forehead. We had turned the corner on this crisis. "You scared me," I gently complained.

Edward rubbed his throat, "It's trapped in here," he whispered.

I stroked his hand. "What is?"

"A piece of meat."

"My darling, you had no dinner. There is nothing in your throat."

The doctor said in Chinese. "A sensation of something lodged in the throat—many complain of that."

"What can be done to remove what's in his throat?"

"It is a symptom." He looked grave, then shook his head.

"It's in here," Edward said, now gasping as he pointed to his neck. He looked at the doctor and said in English, "Doctor, if you would be so kind. Please give me some medicine I can swallow." The doctor answered in Chinese. "You will not suffer too much longer. Be patient." Before the doctor left, he said that if a blue color spread throughout his body, it was a very bad sign.

His hair was so damp from the fever it looked as if a pail of water had been poured over his head. He was no longer burning; he felt cool. His eyelids were slack, one lid lower than the other. "Edward," I whispered. "Don't leave me." He turned his head slightly but could not find my face. I set my hand in his palm. His fingers moved. He mumbled without moving his lips. I thought he said, "My dearest love." We laid poultices over his body, drew the poisonous air out of his lungs with hot cups. He took one hundred tiny pills and they rolled down his tongue. He immediately coughed them out with bloody sputum. He took small breaths, fast and shallow, and when he exhaled, it sounded like fluttering paper in his chest. We sat him up, and tapped his back, then slapped and pounded with our fists to remove the sputum of demon influenza. I tended to him without feeling in my body, seeing and hearing nothing but Edward, willing him to stay alive. I buoyed him to take in the air, another gulp and another. I must not be inattentive, not for a moment. He depends on me. I remained steadfast and sure, sitting near him, praising him as his chest rose. He would wake from senselessness, open his eyes every now and then, and look at me, surprised to see me. I heard him mumble, "What a fearless girl you are," and then, "I love, I love . . ." But he drifted off again.

By late afternoon, Edward's face took on the faint bluish splotches we had dreaded. His lips were cold, his eyes were dry. Magic Gourd pulled back the sheet to replace it with a clean one. His legs were mottled gray. The darker tide was flowing up his legs. I called to him and said he would be cured by morning. "Do you believe me?" I held my breath when he sucked noisily for air. I could barely breathe. I was suffocating. But I refused to cry; that would mean defeat. I recounted for him all the wonderful moments that had bound us. I talked without pause to sustain the thread between us. "Do you remember the day we emerged from the cave and into that green heaven? I loved you then. Did you know that? Edward, do you remember?"

And then I realized I had been shouting. The room was quiet and I could hear with terrifying clarity the gurgle and hissing, the small bubbling, popping sound of bloody froth flowing from his nostrils, his mouth, and his ears. In the evening, just after sunset, when his face was as gray as the shadows, he gurgled once more and drowned.

I stayed with him all night. At first I could not release his hand. The life force might still be in his veins and I might be able to squeeze it back. But without air, he deflated, and he had hollows in his cheeks. His eyes sank, then all of him. His hand had turned cold. I could not press my warmth into his. "How can you be gone? How can you be gone?" I murmured. And then I wailed. "How can you be gone?" Agony still showed in his face and I was angry. Where was the peaceful departure that people claimed comes with death? I cried angrily then in despair and grief. I covered his face, and cried, imagining him, as he had been in life, not still, not quiet.

The door opened and light poured in. Magic Gourd looked stricken. I jumped up. How could I have forgotten about Little Flora! "Is she ill?" I cried. "Did she leave me, too?"

"She is with the amah in the other wing and not at all sick. But you cannot see her until you wash yourself completely. We need to burn your clothes and Edward's, too—and the bedding, the towels, everything, including your shoes."

I nodded. "Be careful that the servants don't save the clothes for themselves."

"Most of the servants are gone." She said this so plainly I did not understand her at first. "They ran away after Edward died. Only three stayed: the amah, the menservants Bright and Little Ram, the chauffeur Ready. They had influenza the first time it came around, so they have no fear. I will have the men wash the body."

Body. How unfeeling that word was.

"Use warm water," I said, then left to draw my own solitary bath. Tears fell into the bathwater. When I arose from the bathtub, I became dizzy, and sat on the bed. I kept myself from crying with one thought: I had to appear calm when I went to Little Flora. I closed my eyes to gather my thoughts. She must always know she is safe and protected.

I awoke six hours later, in the afternoon. Edward was no longer in the bedroom. The sound of his voice was now silence. I wandered downstairs.

Magic Gourd came out from the dining room, where Edward now lay. She took me into the parlor. "You must say your farewell quickly. Bright said that in the Chinese Old City, they are stacking bodies and putting them into one large grave. Families cannot send their dead family member to their ancestral villages. You can imagine the wailing that broke out when they heard that. We don't know what the foreigners are doing with the bodies, but we must take no chances that they will decide for us."

It was too soon for Edward to leave. I would have delayed as long as I could, had Magic Gourd not taken charge. She had loved Edward and I knew she would be caring and wise. I was grateful I did not have to think about what to do. Bright and Little Ram had devised a coffin, using a large cabinet. They would use candle wax to seal the top and all the sides. They had already dug out the pond to make a grave. It was the spot where Edward and I sat on warm days, read to each other under the elm tree, kicked our feet in the pond to splash water on each other.

"The King of Hell came by to see how Edward was," Magic Gourd said. "Here is the death certificate. I can't read what the farting dog wrote."

Pneumonia, secondary to influenza. He had admitted his mistake. He must have reported Edward's death to the American Consulate and authorities of the International Settlement. The amah brought Little Flora to me. I examined her face and felt her forehead. Her eyes were clear and sought mine. I looked at her face once again, at her ears, brow, hair, and eyes that were Edward's legacy.

Magic Gourd led me into the dining room, "ready to catch the baby," she said, "if I fainted." The large table was gone and the coffin stood in its place. Edward's skin still had a gray pallor. He wore a suit that he had worn when we went for walks. I stroked his face. "You're cold," I said. "I'm sorry." I apologized to him for every doubt I had ever had about his goodness, honesty, and love. I said that I once believed I was incapable of giving him love because I did not know what that was, only that I needed it. He showed me how natural it was to take it, and how natural it was to give. And now my heartache was unendurable, and that was proof that we loved each other completely. I turned Flora around so that she faced him. "Our daughter, our greatest joy, showed me I could love ever more deeply. I'll tell her that you held her every day and sang to her." The blue-faced man said nothing. That was not Edward. I did not want the torturous moments of the past two days to become what I remembered most strongly about him. I handed Magic Gourd the baby, and I went upstairs to the library.

I sat on the sofa across from its twin and recalled our conversations—his wit, his seriousness, his sense of fun, and even the dark moods he sometimes fell into when we talked about what he had called his soul and moral self. What was redemption? Where did he go when he left us? I spied the new journal he had started using just last week and held it against my chest. This was who he was. But it also was not. It was sad and beautiful knowledge that a person cannot be found elsewhere but in his own spirit. No one could possess it.

Before I reached the top of the stairs, I heard deep voices and a shrieking child. I hurried downstairs. Two Chinese policemen stood in the hallway. They each held on to an arm of my personal maid's daughter, Mousie. The frightened girl was around ten years old, and had flinched at any sudden sound or movement. Magic Gourd and I had long suspected that her mother regularly beat her. The policemen shook her. The whites of her eyes showed. "My mother made me take it to the store," she said with chattering teeth. "She said she would beat me to death if I did not."

One of the officers said that the little girl had taken a valuable necklace to a jewelry store run by a man named Mr. Gao. The jeweler claimed he was immediately suspicious when he saw the necklace. He knew whom it belonged to. He took it to the police station so he would not be accused of stealing it. Although he appeared to be telling the truth, he was being held at the police station until his claims could be verified.

"Please," Mousie cried. "Don't let them kill me!"

"Someone here must describe the missing necklace," the sterner policeman said.

Magic Gourd went to my room and took out the jewelry to see which piece was missing.

She came back. "The necklace is studded with small emeralds. Two curlicues join a third in the middle . . ."

The policeman brought out the necklace. Magic Gourd examined it for damage. She then scolded the little crying girl.

"She was born with a small brain," I quickly explained to the policemen. "She thinks like a little child without any good sense. We have the necklace back, so no harm has been done. We'll watch the girl and the jewelry more carefully. And I can assure you that Mr. Gao is someone we have known for many years and is very trustworthy."

"The girl told us a foreigner died of a blue disease," one of the men said gravely. "We do not handle matters concerning foreigners. But if it was influenza, an American doctor must examine the body and verify the cause, then report it to the American Consulate."

"We already have a death certificate, signed by Dr. Albee with the American Hospital. He treated Mr. Ivory."

The men asked to see Edward to verify it was a foreigner who had died and not a Chinese citizen. They stopped before reaching Edward. "*Ai!* The blue face," one murmured.

An hour later, a detective from the British police station came, followed by a consular officer from the American Consulate. They offered brief condolences and apologies for the intrusion.

"Who is the deceased?" the American said.

"Bosson Edward Ivory III." The words resounded like a death knell. I handed them the death certificate. They examined Edward and asked for his passport. I went to Edward's desk, and before I gave it to him, I looked at his photo. So somber, so young. And then I saw below his name the word *married*. Under the words *wife's name*, it said: "Minerva Lamp Ivory." At that moment, I leapt into a new life.

The men scanned the passport.

"I am his wife, Minerva Lamp Ivory."

They jotted this down. "May we have your passport?" the American said.

I hesitated.

"It is only a formality."

I excused myself and went to my bedroom, supposedly to retrieve the nonexistent passport. I went through the motions of opening empty drawers, searching in my mind for plausible excuses.

I returned to them in distress. "My passport is missing. I've looked in the usual places, and it's gone. One of the servants must have stolen it."

"Please don't concern yourself. As I said, it's just a formality. If it is missing, we can help you get it replaced. Would you like us to notify the family?"

I thought fast. "It would be better that I do it. It will be such a shock to his father and mother. I need to use the exact words to soften the blow and let them know he did not suffer—and I wish that were true. I know they will also ask that Edward's body be returned to their home in New York."

"I'm sorry to inform you but that is not possible," the consular officer said. "The bodies of those who have died of influenza cannot be transported outside of the city."

"We had already heard, which is why I have made private arrangements. I need to tell his parents with great delicacy that we will bury him here at home. His body will stay within these garden walls."

"You're fortunate you have land for burial. Fifteen hundred Chinese have perished so far and are being buried in a mass grave. Some of the Chinese are throwing the bodies into the river. We're concerned that the drinking water has been contaminated with influenza. Boil your water well. I also recommend you not eat fish."

Little Flora began to fidget and whimper. I felt her forehead. I worried constantly that she might fall ill.

The British detective gave her a clown smile and rolled his eyes to make her laugh. She cried instead. "A pity to lose her father so young," he said.

An hour after they left, we buried Edward in the garden under the large tree. At Edward's gravesite, Little Ram and Bright spoke words of gratitude. Magic Gourd provided a bowl of fruit and lit a handful of incense sticks. The two men filled in the grave with dark moist earth. After they left, I dug up the violets that lined the pathway to the house, and I replanted them so that they covered his grave.

I turned to the familiar page in *Leaves of Grass*, and I read aloud in a steady voice.

"Not I, not anyone else can travel that road for you.
You must travel if by yourself.
It is not far. It is within reach.
Perhaps you have been on it since you were born, and
    did not know.
Perhaps it is everywhere—on water and land."

CHAPTER 8

THE TWO MRS. IVORYS

Shanghai
March 1919
Violet

After Edward died, I sat each day on the stone bench and sand to read to Little Flora, and talk to her about her father's love for her, and she stared at me with a look of concentration, as if she understood what I was saying. On the fourth day, I heard pounding on the gate. I put down my book and opened the gate to find a solemn man who looked like an undertaker.

He removed his hat and introduced himself as Mr. Douglas of the legal offices of Massey & Massey, which represented the Ivory Shipping Company. "My deepest sympathies," he said. "I am sad to meet again under these tragic circumstances."

I searched my memory. I had gone to see the lawyer with Edward to determine whether Lu Shing's letter, in which he offered me this house, was legally sufficient for us to later make a claim. But the man we saw then looked different from this man.

"I should have come sooner," the man said. "It took time to draw up the documents. As you know, Mr. Ivory made financial arrangements for your daughter and you."

I learned that Edward had written a letter to his lawyers and Little Ram had taken it to them. The date revealed it was six days ago, the day when he first felt ill, when he said he had no appetite. He had known already he would die.

The lawyer put the documents before me. Edward had stipulated that, in the event of his death, the entirety of his Shanghai bank funds was to be immediately transferred to a new account for his daughter, Flora Ivory. His wife, the mother of his child, would be given full authority as the signatory. This would be in addition to any sum provided later by inheritance.

Mr. Douglas leaned toward Little Flora. "What a beautiful child. I see the resemblance to both you and the late Mr. Ivory." He handed me a sheet of paper covered with dark type and handwritten names and the sum of $53,765. "You need only sign here to accept."

It was an astonishing sum of money, enough to last a lifetime. How wise that Edward had put the money in Flora's name. She was his heir and the money could never be taken from her. I stared at the name at the bottom: Minerva Lamp Ivory. "I assume your name is spelled correctly," the lawyer said. "That is the information the company lawyers have in their records. We only need to verify it with your passport."

Edward would never have called Minerva the mother of his child. It would have angered him, as much as it did me. I wanted to declare the truth, but I knew that doing so would be dangerous.

"The name is correct, Mr. Douglas. But I lack the passport to verify it. A former servant stole it. I mentioned to an officer with the consulate that I would come soon to replace it . . . but it has been difficult." Genuine tears fell. I could not speak.

"May we assist you and secure it for you?" Mr. Douglas said. "A new widow would hardly be expected to leave her house. The consulate can easily find the record of your passport and visa. A photograph is all that is needed."

"You are too kind. However, I regret to say that I never registered my passport with the consulate. When I stepped off the ship, I was eager to see my husband and disheartened to see a very long line at customs. I spoke to a guard with urgent pleas to locate a WC due to nausea. It was wrong of me. But I saw no harm at the time whether I declared myself now or later. Edward and I were going to remedy that and have Little Flora registered as an American citizen as well. That's when I discovered the passport was not in my drawer. I suspect the thief was a maid who had left a month before."

"It is not the first time we've encountered this problem. American passports fetch a large sum of money. We can obtain a new one with the help of an officer I know at the consulate. He knows my word is trustworthy. I will personally vouch that you are indeed Minerva Lamp Ivory. I was witness to hearing Mr. Ivory introduce you to me as Mrs. Ivory, his wife. By the way, have you done anything further about your uncle and the house he wishes to leave you?"

It was only then when I realized that Mr. Douglas and I had indeed met. Since our last meeting, he had cropped his wild hair and shaved off his beard.

"We will record a birth certificate at the same time," the beardless Mr. Douglas said. "What is the child's full name?"

"Flora Violet Ivory," I said without hesitation. "My husband chose the name."

"A very good name. Sweet and delicate. I need only your photograph. Do you happen to have one?"

I went to my bedroom and found a souvenir card for suitors and patrons. I was adorned in a slim sheath and was leaning provocatively against a pedestal in a studio. I carefully cut out the head and came back with a less racy photo showing the much-improved Minerva Lamp Ivory.

After the man left, I sat on the stone bench, dizzy from the effort of my ruse. I was an accomplished actress in the wiles within the courtesan house, but not in matters involving grief and the future of my child. Little Ram brought me tea. I asked him if he had seen Edward write the letter.

He nodded. "He told me not to tell you. He said it would upset you. I did not know what the letter said."

"Was he very sick when he wrote it?"

"He had a fever and a headache. He asked me to bring him aspirin. But his mind was still clear."

That night I saw a beatific vision of Edward writing his letter. He was glowing at first, and as he reached the end of the page, he began to fade until he joined the shadows. Suddenly he appeared again and was radiant. This time, when the image faded, I was left with a sense of peace I knew I could call upon. I allowed the possibility that I had fallen asleep and dreamed the whole scene. It did not matter. What I felt was true.

If only he could help me write a letter to the Ivory family informing them of his death. They had idolized him, their only son. What guise could I take? What tone should I use? A doctor, the ineffectual Dr. Albee? An official who set rules and regulations for handling the bodies?

Magic Gourd brought me a letter. "It's from Lu Shing. If you want, I can throw it away."

"I do not need to be protected from anything Lu Shing might have to say. The worst has happened. Everything will seem like bad weather in comparison."

> *Dear Mrs. Ivory,*
>
> *I am deeply saddened by the passing of your husband and the son of friends I have known for over twenty years. I hope you will continue to reside in the house. All arrangements have been made for your continued comfort. If you are in need of any assistance in matters big or small, please do not hesitate to let me know directly.*
>
> *Yours,*
>
> *Lu Shing*

He called me Mrs. Ivory. He acknowledged both the distance between us and my new status as Edward's wife. I sent a reply asking him to write the letter to the Ivory family—his good friends for over twenty years—informing them of Edward's death: Their beloved son, Edward, had succumbed to influenza, quickly and without suffering. I told Lu Shing he should not mention Little Flora or me.

I had once reviled him for not acknowledging that I existed. I was now asking him to continue to do so.

My passport arrived the next day, along with a birth certificate for Little Flora. It sickened me to see the bottom half of it.

Flora Violet Ivory, born January 18, 1919, in Shanghai, China
Father: Bosson Edward Ivory III, businessman
Age 26. Race: White. Birthplace: Croton-on-Hudson, New York
Mother: Minerva Lamp Ivory, housewife
Age 23. Race: White. Birthplace: Albany, New York

I DEVOTED MYSELF to Little Flora's future. She would never be aware of my past, never aware of the circumstances of her birth. I remade myself into Edward's legal wife and widow, Minerva Lamp Ivory. To impersonate her and not raise suspicion, the new Mrs. Ivory spoke no Chinese in public. She wore a hairstyle different from mine, parted on the opposite side of my natural one. She had her hair bobbed and waved. Her clothes were tailored, conservative, and not fashionable by my standards. And she joined the American Club, where she attended tedious luncheons for wives, listened to lectures on buying porcelain, volunteered to assist with a charity ball to raise money for Russian refugees, and explained repeatedly with genuine pain that her husband had died of influenza and that she was living alone in a house on Bubbling Well Road with their only child. The street name let them know Mrs. Ivory was well off.

During the day, Little Flora and I visited the park, went to the movie theater for foreigners, and rode in the car along the Bund, passing the building of the Ivory Shipping Company. In my role as Mrs. Minerva Ivory, I was at first easily unnerved. I would see the face of a woman emerge from the blurred crowd to stare at me. Each disapproving face was different, but all were foreign, and they seemed to be saying that they knew I was not who I said I was. I recalled that my mother had said that I should disregard anyone who disapproved of me. I had the freedom to think for myself. But that was not true now. I had to think about Little Flora.

I had no true friends, other than Magic Gourd. Ever since Edward died, she had softened in manner and showed more concern than criticism. She had once refused to be Little Flora's amah. But she now believed that the amah was going deaf. She called her several times the other day when the amah was facing the other way, and she did not respond. What if Little Flora fell and cried for help? She insisted on accompanying Little Flora on our outings.

"If you can pretend to be a woman you do not want to be," she said, "then I can pretend to be an amah."

At the shops, she bought good tea for us and bright yarn for the amah. The amah now knit dresses, shoes, hats, coats, blankets, and mittens for Little Flora, day and night, it seemed. When Little Flora outgrew them, another set was ready. We gave the old clothes to the American Club, which donated them to a rotating list of charities for the poor. I learned one of them was the orphanage for mixed-caste girls, and I was glad.

"Could any of the girls ever pass for white?" I asked the woman in charge of charity donations.

"I've seen some who at first glance seem as white as you or me," she said. "But on second glance, you see the eyes are slightly slanted or the lips are thick and the skin has a yellowish cast."

By her answer, I knew she believed the girls' Chinese blood was inferior. I used to worry incessantly over being exposed as Chinese for that reason. I had suffered as a child, feeling ashamed, or suspicious that I was being insulted. I did not belong to the good society of either the American or Chinese worlds. Little Flora would never suffer from doubts over where she belonged.

One afternoon, I returned home and heard Flora's squeals of laughter in the library. She and Magic Gourd were kneeling before a low table with a photo of Edward, incense bowls, plates of fresh fruit and candies. Magic Gourd held incense sticks with curling smoke. "If only your Edward were alive to hear my thanks," she said to me. "At least I can send him my admiration, wherever he is."

Edward would have thought it a charming tribute. I wondered whether Little Flora would one day believe incantations for Chinese ghosts were backward superstitions.

September 1922

Three and a half years had passed since Edward's death.

Edward's vividness receded from me. When it was a month after his passing, I felt he had been gone a very long time and that it was also a moment ago. I marked the passing months by the new clothes that the amah knit for Little Flora: green and yellow in April, yellow and blue in July, lavender and rose in September. I noted the week that different flowers bloomed and when the trees lost their leaves and when bright green buds appeared on twigs. I counted the number of times Flora asked to be lifted, or turned her head to smile at me, or came running on her little legs calling my name, a number that became as innumerable as the number of days since Edward had been gone.

I found the journal Edward had started just before he died. How sad that he did not have enough time to fill a hundred more. I used this one to record Little Flora's new words, funny sentences, and precocious ideas. Soon I could not keep up. I would have had to spend the entire day writing down all that made her special. I loved in turn the succession of toys she loved: the rag doll, the balls that fit into holes on a wooden board, and, when she was three, the sketch pad and crayons, on which she drew a sleet of colors and bent lines.

I kept Edward's habit of reading the newspapers. Little Ram brought me two newspapers each day, a Chinese one and a Western one. I had no one except Magic Gourd to discuss the events of the day. At first, she took no interest. But then a story arose—the murder of a Western child and the uproar that arose among all foreigners in the International Settlement. She protested that a thousand little Chinese girls could be murdered and they mattered to no one. I agreed that was true, but I also worried that the murderer, who had not been found, might snatch Little Flora next. After that, when I read the news to Magic Gourd, she had an opinion on everything.

Outside our haven, Shanghai was becoming a different place. There was more of everything—and they were more modern, more fashionable, more luxurious, more bizarre, more exciting. The villas were larger, the cars more numerous, a sign of how rich you were. And there were movie stars. Whatever they did became instantly popular. The three movies Magic Gourd and I saw concerned young innocent girls who had been lured to the big city and forced into prostitution. Magic Gourd cried throughout the first movie, whispering, "That's my story," but at the end, she complained: "That kind of happy ending never happens." At the end of another, she said, "Many girls kill themselves for the same reason."

I watched what was happening in Shanghai through the eyes of a mother. To protect Little Flora, I needed to know where the dangers were. Shanghai was being pulled and stretched, tense with foreigners and Chinese living side by side, disregarding each other as best they could. There were days when we thought the air between them might snap and explode again. The university students found more reasons to protest the rights of foreigners and the ill-treatment given to Chinese workers. An anti-Christian campaign was the latest, and we watched to see if there were signs that it would spread and become more serious, as had happened during the Boxer Rebellion. I was frightened that violence would break out and put Little Flora in peril. My life had changed when the emperor abdicated. During revolution, there were heroes and enemies, but there were also hoodlums who grabbed whatever they could when everyone else was busy fighting. For now, the protests had led to strikes but not violence. And the longest one started just after the Paris Peace Treaty was signed.

"If I were educated," Magic Gourd said, "I probably would be a revolutionary right this minute."

I wondered what Edward would have thought of Woodrow Wilson now. Instead of returning Shandong Province to China, the Allies had decided it was best to let the Japanese continue to occupy and control it. In the United States and Europe, they celebrated the Peace Treaty. In Shanghai, the students called for strikes and the universities, workers, and merchants all joined in and everything shut down. When the strikes stretched on for months, Magic Gourd joked she should go on strike, too. We couldn't buy anything or go to the movies. There was no gasoline for the car. I was disturbed by what I heard at luncheons with the ladies at the American Club. They saw no harm in Japan retaining Shandong Province. After all, Japan had joined the war against Germany earlier than China had and they were also very good managers. They were puzzled why the Chinese government would have believed the transfer of the province back to them was practically guaranteed.

I was most puzzled by my own reaction. No matter how American I was—or wanted to be—China was, in my heart, my homeland. In my opinion, what the Allies had done to China was wrong. That meant I was not a patriotic American. I resented what Woodrow Wilson had done.

What would Edward have thought of that? I could no longer guess. We had once been able to guess what the other was thinking. Now that he had been dead longer than we had known each other, I felt I had hardly known him. I knew less and less of him, because what I wished I had known grew vast. He would always remain deeply loved, the romantic who saved my life, the one who knew me best and laid to rest all doubts that he truly loved me.

Through Little Flora, he returned to me. I thought of him when little moments caught me by surprise, and I thought of them as his moments. This morning, it was a fly that had landed on Little Flora's toast. She asked why I said the fly was dirty when he was washing his hands. She transformed what might be ordinary and annoying into his humor and new wonder. Edward would have laughed so many times. I could imagine that clearly.

In appearance and manner, Little Flora was Edward's child. Her lank hair was his shade of ripe wheat with its variations in shadow and sun. It swung as she ran on her sturdy legs. Her hazel eyes were set deep. She had his thin ears, which were a nearly transparent pink. He had teased me that she had my expressions: the frown of worry, a different frown for displeasure, the reluctant smile, the stiff stubborn chin, the openmouthed surprise.

One day I watched her pluck a hydrangea ball in the garden and examine its hundreds of petals. She pressed it with her palms, peered inside, and then held it up, as if she had discovered the secret of life. Edward had shown me that same look when he examined my face.

I wanted to give her my best qualities—my honesty, persistence, and curious mind. I did not want her to have my worst, the contradictions that also existed in me: my dishonesty, hopelessness, and skeptical mind. I did not want her to waver, as I had, between what she believed to be true of herself and who others thought she should be. She would not be a captive figure in a painting, like my mother had been.

Before she was born, I believed she would be the girl I was supposed to have been. But she was not. She was her own self-being. How lucky I was.

WE HAD THREE unexpected visitors, who came on the most ordinary of days.

It was September 16, in the hot mid-afternoon. We were in the garden, under the shade of the elm tree. Little Ram had planted a lawn that ringed the tree. The violets I had planted over Edward's grave three and a half years ago had gone wild and ran under the stone bench, around the lawn, and up the path to the house. We had brought out a sofa and two wicker chairs, small tables, and a quilt. Our picnic was over and I was on the sofa reading a story in a magazine. Little Flora was napping with her head in my lap. She wore two periwinkle ribbons in her hair. Magic Gourd was furiously fanning herself. The amah had fallen asleep, still holding her knitting needles and the beginning of Little Flora's new dress. Above the whirring sounds of summer insects, we heard the crunch of wheels over gravel, a door slam, and voices. Little Ram gave a shout, and a moment later, he was running toward us. He had only enough time to say that three people had pushed their way through the gate and demanded to see me immediately.

There they stood, three Westerners in clothes unsuited for a hot day: a tall man with spectacles and a mustache, a woman with a mannish jaw and high-rounded brow, and a younger woman with blond hair and a bland face. Her eyes darted nervously at Flora and me. I did not invite them into the shade. I lifted Flora and put her against me. She awoke and made small protests as she was dragged away from dreams.

"Are you Minerva Lamp Ivory?" the man said. And when I affirmed that I was, the square-jawed woman said, "That is a lie. This is Minerva Lamp Ivory." She pointed to the younger woman. "And Bosson Edward Ivory III was her husband."

Edward was right in how he had described Minerva. There was nothing about her that would have bound him to her. Her eyes showed no spark or intelligence, hardly any expression other than puzzlement and discomfort. Her lips were pressed tightly in the manner of a child who had been told to be quiet. She appeared to be thirty-five, although I knew she was younger, and she was dressed like a schoolgirl in a white blouse and gray pleated skirt. A damp fringe of pale blond hair lay flattened against her forehead.

The man introduced himself as an American lawyer in Shanghai, Mr. Tillman. He handed me a document with blocks of tiny black words, and pronounced in an unemotional voice the charges against me:

IMPERSONATION OF BOSSON EDWARD IVORY'S WIFE, MINERVA LAMP IVORY, EMBEZZLEMENT, FRAUD, AND THEFT, AND THE UNLAWFUL POSSESSION OF FLORA VIOLET IVORY, DAUGHTER OF BOSSON EDWARD IVORY III AND MINERVA LAMP IVORY.

I had to use all my wits to not appear shaken. I had expected this day, had imagined many versions of it. "You are here uninvited and must leave," I said. "If you wish to discuss anything, we can arrange to do so at your lawyer's offices." I gestured toward the direction of the gate and then let Magic Gourd know in a few words what was happening and that we should hurry to the house and have Little Ram and Bright lock the doors. I started to leave, and Tillman blocked my way and commanded in English that I could not take the child. Magic Gourd gathered herself up, as if she could stretch and become his height. "Fuck your mother and your dog," she said in Chinese. Little Flora told Magic Gourd in Chinese that she had spoken bad words. Magic Gourd pointed to the three people and said, "They are bad people and you should tell them to leave."

Flora twisted around to look at them and repeated Magic Gourd's Chinese words. The two women were startled. Flora turned back and wrapped her arms around my neck and made a few snuffling complaints about the sun. I whispered that as soon as the people went away, we could go to the ice cream shop.

Flora looked up at them and said in English, "Go away." Again, the women were stunned. Little Flora had the powers of a goblin. The older woman nudged the younger one.

"Flora," Minerva said weakly, and took a step toward us. Little Flora eyed her with suspicion.

"Don't you dare come near my child," I said. "You frighten her."

"We have proof that you are not the mother of this child," the lawyer said in his laconic voice. He drew out two pieces of paper. "This is the birth certificate of Minerva Lamp Ivory." He handed it to me and I let it fall to the ground. "And this is Minerva Lamp Ivory." He gestured toward blank-eyed Minerva and then retrieved the paper.

The older woman broke in: "You will find my name recorded there as Minerva's mother. Mildred Racine Lamp." She smiled. "There is no question that I am not your mother."

"I am glad to hear it, Mrs. Lamp." I received the reaction I intended.

Mr. Tillman pulled out another piece of paper. "This is the birth certificate for Flora Violet Ivory." I refused to look at it. "The father is Bosson Edward Ivory III. The recorded name of the mother is Minerva Lamp Ivory. I think you have seen this document before. We received it from the American Consulate."

I spoke directly to Minerva. She was the weak one. "Do you claim you gave birth to my daughter while you were in New York? Did she spill from your womb? By what religious miracle?"

Minerva started to speak and her mother said that the lawyer should speak for her. "We are referring to the legal record, not biology," Tillman said. "Do you dispute that the names on the documents were not the recorded ones. If so, that will be the assertion you will have to defend in the American Court in Shanghai."

"What you assert to do is to steal my child." I saw that Mrs. Lamp was wearing a necklace with a small silver cross. "That is evil condemned by God."

"Who are you to accuse us of evil?" Mrs. Lamp said. "You stole Minerva's name to steal Edward's money. Minerva Ivory—it's on Edward's passport, the birth certificate, and the bank account. Minerva Ivory, wife of Bosson Edward Ivory III. We have the marriage certificate. You were his half-Chinese mistress—a woman who lured him to become his concubine. That's the word you use here, isn't it?"

"An informal relationship," Tillman said, "does not confer legal rights to money. All rights belong to the person of record."

I met him with an uneven voice: "Edward wrote a letter. It is in his handwriting and states that it is his dying wish that money be provided for his daughter, Flora Ivory, and he asked that the mother of his child be the signatory. I am the mother of this child. You cannot use legal hocus pocus to change that." I was back on confident ground.

"We examined the letter at the offices of Massey and Massey. Mr. Douglas provided it when this became a case of fraud, which had unknowingly involved him. The letter does not give any name, except Flora's."

"You've lived quite lavishly on Edward and Minerva's money," Mrs. Lamp said. "A grand house." She swept her hand across in an arc. "And with servants and an expensive car that belonged to Edward Ivory, the property of his widow, Minerva Ivory—the true one."

"This house belongs to my father, Lu Shing."

"We've never heard of any Lu Shing."

"You know him as Shing Lu. You had his name backward."

Tillman gave a slight nod to Mrs. Lamp and Minerva. "It's the Chinese custom with names that the family name comes first." They were chagrined to learn I was right.

At last, I had gained some ground. "He gave me use of the house for as long as I desire," I continued. "And I will also inherit the house. I have it in writing." The letter, where was it? Edward said he put Lu Shing's two letters where no one would find it. Where?

"Chinese daughters of concubines are not in the line of succession of property in China," Tillman said. "Inheritance by males is preemptor."

"We have both a legal right and moral obligation," Mrs. Lamp said. "Flora deserves to be raised to have dignity, respect, legitimacy, and an education—and not one provided by a prostitute. If you love her, how can you selfishly let her remain with you?"

Tillman cut her off. "We must finish with other matters first." He had shown part of his hand—that there were other matters. He was following a sequence of legal traps.

"If a letter executed by Mr. Lu Shing exists, produce it. Does he acknowledge you are his daughter, legal or illegitimate? We found no record of your birth with either the American Consulate or various Chinese offices of records. It is difficult for you to make legal claims when you have no proof that you exist." Mrs. Lamp laughed.

I was furious. I did have a birth certificate, the one my mother said had been stolen from her desk. She had recorded it under the name of someone she had married when I was born, a name that sounded like "Tanner." It had been hard to make out when I listened from Boulevard. And Lu Shing's letter—I struggled to remember what the letter had said exactly. My proof lay in shreds of memory.

"Another point the court will consider: It was Edward Ivory who had a strong prior relationship with Mr. Lu Shing. He has known the Ivory family for over twenty years. He lived with them for a number of years as their protégé. They exchanged letters of friendship. Mr. Lu Shing offered Mr. Ivory's son, Edward, a place to live in Shanghai on that basis. There are letters attesting to that as well."

"You can ask Mr. Lu Shing directly," I said. "Speak to him. I have the telephone number of his company office." I was counting on Lu Shing's remorse to save the day.

"We did contact Mr. Lu's company offices," Tillman said. "Mr. Lu Shing no longer owns the company. It was taken over by a Japanese enterprise two months ago. Mr. Lu Shing was bankrupt and left the country. His last communication to his former manager was from the United States."

"Tell her that we know what she did for a living," Mrs. Lamp said.

"We learned that you were engaged in the profession of courtesan. That is not illegal in the International Settlement, as you know.

We have no legal charges. However, we would call into question your moral suitability, as well as the environment Flora would be forced to live in, if you were to make an argument to keep her."

Magic Gourd was shouting that I should call the police and kick the hooligans out on their foreign asses.

"Be reasonable, Miss Minturn," Tillman said. He even knew my name. "The Ivory family has made a generous offer. They will drop all charges and require no repayment of money you took from the bank account if you relinquish Flora today. You will soon have no home or money. You have no legal argument to fight these charges. You would lose and go to prison for theft. The Ivory family would then be given Flora. If you tried to run away with her, you would be charged with the kidnapping of a child who legally belongs to the Ivory family. Police officers are already outside the gate. However, if you relinquish her today, you will be doing the best by her. She will have a life of privilege in the United States. She will have legitimacy, a chance at a proper life with an upstanding family."

Magic Gourd babbled on about kicking the intruders out. She did not know yet the devastation that awaited Little Flora and me. "I might be reconciled in my heart that what you say is the best. But I ask myself, how can I let my child go to the very people Edward despised? He came here, to China, to escape you and your soulless-ness. You, Minerva, tricked Edward into marrying you by claiming you were pregnant—all this to gain the money and prestige of the Ivory family. Your mother told you to feign a miscarriage. You both plotted and manipulated and lied and you led Edward into doing what was right for you and the coming child. He wanted to be honor-able and good, and when you told him you had made up the whole thing, you made a mockery of his goodness. You repulsed him in all ways. Yet you schemed to have him return to you. He never would have touched you."

Mr. Tillman glanced at the two women. Minerva was shocked. Mrs. Lamp said in the hurried tone of someone trying to stamp out the truth: "These are lies and we won't hear any more of it. Minerva, don't listen. Take Flora so we can leave." Minerva was frozen, and her lower lip was trembling.

"You know that what I'm saying is true. He left you and his mother and father because he felt gutted by your selfishness, your manipulations. You want to steal Flora away from me, and it proves that you are all that he hated. You have your documents and certificates with your names and hateful facts. But those are words and the rest is false. Edward would never have wanted his daughter to live with the very people whom he loathed and left. He and I made this child out of love for each other. You want to cover her with your web, and spin your lies around her until you suffocate her soul. I won't give her to you. You can arrest me and throw me in prison. But I will never willingly give her to you."

I could not bear to look at them, knowing that they would have Little Flora soon. I hugged Flora closer to me, feeling the full weight of her. She buried her face into my shoulder. And then I ran. Magic Gourd took off with me. I heard Mrs. Lamp shout. Tillman said, "Let them. The policemen will get her."

Little Flora whimpered, "I'm scared." I said in a cracked voice, "Don't be afraid. Don't be afraid." I ran toward the back gate and heard shouts to send the men to that side. I knew that escape was hopeless. Where would I go? Where could I hide? But I would fight for her as long as I could.

And then I reached the gate and ran through. Two Sikh policemen grabbed my shoulders and Little Flora shrieked as her hands slipped away from my neck, as her body rose up and out of my arms. Her eyes were fastened on mine.

The policeman who took her walked away briskly and another man held me. I could no longer see her face. But I heard her sob: "No! Let me go! Mama! Mama!" I called back: "Little Flora! Little Flora!"—crying out her name long after she was gone.

I don't know how long I stood there before I allowed Magic

Gourd to lead me away. I was confused and I could only think that I should wait. She took me back to the house and I went to Little Flora's room. I had the crazy hope that Little Ram would rescue her and put her safely in my arms. The room was silent and airless without her. Magic Gourd came in, breathing hard. Little Ram said he saw Mrs. Lamp and Minerva get into a black car and drive up Nanking Road. A police officer was guarding Edward's car. So they ran after the black car until they could no longer see it. Magic Gourd bit her lips and cried as she walked around Little Flora's room. She found a silver bracelet she had given Little Flora when she was born. It was supposed to lock her to the earth. "I should have made her wear it."

Only a short while ago, Little Flora had lain with her head in my lap and I had been stroking her hair. Mrs. Lamp and Minerva had never looked at Little Flora with motherly eyes. To them, Little Flora was nothing more than a legal document. I had been so naive to not have realized the danger. She was Edward's daughter, his only child. And Edward had been the Ivorys' only child, their beloved son who could do no wrong. Little Flora was now the legitimate daughter of Edward and Minerva, and the heiress of the Ivory family estate, which Minerva would help her spend. On the Ivory family tree, Little Flora would claim her place and so would the false mother.

I went to Edward's room and closed the door. I railed against the American laws, the deaf god, blind fate, and the cruelty of humans. I asked Edward to tell me those monsters would not damage Little Flora's heart. I walked around the room beseeching him, as if he were God and knew all things and could make promises and decrees. Don't let Little Flora lose her curiosity. Don't let Minerva dull her mind. Strike down dead Mrs. Lamp. Bring Little Flora back to me now. Let me find her. Tell me how.

I ran my hand over the soft bristles of a shaving brush that had once swirled around Edward's jaw each day. I used to watch him. How could he be gone, while his shaving brush remained? I picked up Edward's gold pocket watch on its heavy chain. I found cuff links that he had tucked into a pocket of a waistcoat. He had been fastidious and negligent at the same time.

I wondered which of my habits Little Flora would have had, if she had remained with me. Through what kaleidoscope of wonder would she have viewed the world? Had she inherited Edward's conscience, his humility and humor, his expressions of deeper, wider love? I had a gnawing need to know who she would be ten years from now. Let her be curious, let her be strong-willed. If I could give her anything she could keep, let it be the knowledge that she is loved, so that she would have the ability to love as well.

I placed her photograph next to Edward's and stared at her face. And then I saw in her photograph that she was wearing the heart-shaped locket Edward and I had bought soon after she was born. Inside were tiny photographs of Edward and me. I had had the locket sealed so that when Little Flora wore it, our three hearts would always be together, never broken. Little Flora loved that locket and would scream if anyone tried to take it off. I hoped she would scream and lash out at her false mother.

I kissed Edward's face in the photograph and thanked him for his love and for Little Flora. I kissed Little Flora's face in the photograph and thanked her for showing me how deeply and freely I could love. I recited to her the words of Whitman that Edward quoted, the pledge that had enabled him to leave his family and find himself: "Resist much, obey little."

WE RECEIVED A letter of eviction a few days later, no doubt hastened by the Ivory family's thorough plan to dig me up like a weed and be rid of me. A representative from the Ivory Shipping Company confiscated the car. Someone from the Japanese company made a list of all the belongings of the house. When they tried to claim the paintings by Lu Shing that Magic Gourd wanted to keep, she pointed to the dedication on the back of each that showed it had been given to my mother.

I found positions for the amah, Little Ram, and Bright through the help of a kind woman at the American Club, who had recommended them as servants to recent arrivals from San Francisco. Magic Gourd and I brought out everything of value we owned: my jewelry, the dresses, the carvings, whatever we could sell, and we made a list of the order in which we would part with them. I would not let go of Little Flora's and Edward's belongings. I would never have the heart to sell them, but I could not leave them behind for someone else to sell or throw away. "When the time comes," Magic Gourd said, "I will find a use for them and you will never know."

The one possession of Edward's I most wanted was his leather diary, his words and thoughts, his view of the world and himself. I had been searching for it ever since he died. I had to find it now. Magic Gourd and I went through his dressers, looked under the bed, the one we shared and the one he died in. We looked behind the furniture and even moved the heavy wardrobe. We looked at every book in the library and ran our hands behind the books. The brown leather covers made it nearly indistinguishable from a thousand other books. It sickened me that we might not find it. I had already set aside his fountain pens, pencils, blotter, the beautiful green leather volume of *Leaves of Grass* he had given me as an apology soon after we met, and on top of that the beaten copy he had purchased for himself to replace it. I picked it up. He had held this book. I opened it and I cried to see what was inside. The pages had been cut out to make a secret vault for his journal. Here he was before me: his words, his thoughts and emotions. I opened it, turning the pages, no longer sad but joyful in remembering the moments he had read the pages to me. Here was the story of his heroics that ended with his face in the mud. He had been so pleased when I laughed. I saw another entry, toward the back. I did not recognize it, and I was frightened that there was a reason he had withheld it from me, that it might contain a confession that he felt differently about me.

> Violet was driving slowly. This was her first time behind the wheel and she kept her eyes fastened on the road while I enjoyed the scenery. We glided past villages and I saw the somber faces of farmers who had never seen anything go this fast. We exuded vitality and joy. But then I noticed the lime-whitened walls of the houses, where the colors of life had been blanched by death. I observed a cortege of mourners in white, trudging up a hill. Illness was spreading like a dark pestilence in the field. I urged Violet to drive faster to feel the wind of life that comes with speed. I wanted to pass sorrow on a day when I was with the one I loved.

He had loved me then. He had been so careful to keep his feelings from me. I turned the pages and saw only the blur of my tears. At the back, I found two letters stuck between pages. They were Lu Shing's. Edward had promised to put them where no one would find them until I told him I was ready to read them. I opened one. It was addressed simply to "Violet." This was the one that had offered me the house. He had also said that it required amending his will and that, in turn, this required that I allow him to acknowledge that he was my father. He asked my permission to do so. I had never responded. The second letter was the one I had refused to read:

> *My dear Violet,*
>
> *I have wanted to say these words for many years. I am ashamed it has taken this long for them to reach you. I give you the answers as a confession, not as an explanation, with no excuses for my dereliction of your happiness and safety.*
>
> *From the day you were born, I loved you, but inadequately. I loved your mother, but inadequately. Because of my lack of character*

and courage, I did not stand up to my family. I yielded to their demands to carry out my duties as the eldest son. When your mother gave birth to our son, my family took him from her. He was the firstborn son of the next generation. She did not know where to find him and I could not tell her because of threats by my family that I would never see him if I did.

When my father died in 1912, I was at last able to tell your mother that her son was in San Francisco. She knew nothing of the evil that awaited you. Through trickery, she boarded the boat. Through trickery later, she believed you were dead.

I now confess to you the great evil I did to you. Five years ago, I was at the party hosted by my friend Loyalty Fang when you performed your first story. That was when I learned you were alive. I was horrified that my actions had led you to this life. But then I saw how enamored you were of Loyalty, and I heard several men remark they had never seen Loyalty so infatuated and that it would not be surprising if Loyalty became your patron or even your husband. How could I pull you away from this chance? This was the inner world you knew, and if I took you to the outer world and said you were my daughter, you would have been shunned. I truly believed you would find happiness with Loyalty.

I used this as my shameful reason to avoid my responsibility to you once again. I never told anyone that I was your father before I left Shanghai.

A number of years passed before I returned. As you know, the Ivory family asked that I take care of their son, Edward, who knew no one and could not speak Chinese. I introduced him to Loyalty, who knew a bit of English. Loyalty introduced you to Edward. You know the rest. I am grateful beyond words that you have found the happiness you have always deserved. However, I also know that your happiness does not absolve me of my moral shortcomings.

I have not seen or spoken to your mother since our meeting in

Shanghai. She did not meet me in San Francisco as planned. After I
had written her numerous letters, she finally sent back just one. She
said she had no desire to see either me or her son. She said she had
only one child and she grieved for her every day. That was you. If
you would like me to contact her, I will do my best. In the meantime,
I will say nothing, in case you do not wish to open doors you may
have already permanently closed. I hope this letter has provided you
with the answers you needed. I fear that it may have also stirred up
more turmoil.

Please let me know your wishes. I am ready to serve as your father
and your debtor.

Yours,

Lu Shing

His letter was a pallid summary of his own spiritual agony.
Beyond his claims that he did not deserve forgiveness, he left off
with the happy ending. How would he serve as my debtor without any
means to reach him? The one surprise was his mention that Mother
had not met her son. To think she left me for naught. Lu Shing had
provided the answers to the questions that had tormented me over
the years. But beyond those inadequate facts, I knew now the nature
of two people whom I had reviled for so many years. They were simply
weak, selfish, and careless of others. I wished to push them out of my
mind. My grief left no room for them. And now I had to determine
quickly what to do next. For the first time since I was fourteen, I could
choose. I would look at my abilities and match them to opportunities.
I was more intelligent than most. I had persistence.

But, as I soon learned, those qualities could not make the world
turn in a different direction. I sought a job as an English teacher at a
school for Chinese translators. The students were men and they could
not hire a woman. I offered myself as a governess. Word had gone
around the American Club that I had been a courtesan who imper-
sonated a widow. They were horrified at the thought that a prostitute

would teach their children. I inquired about teaching positions at schools run by Canadians and Australians, thinking they might not have heard reports of my past. If they had, they masked it by saying they could not hire someone who had no experience.

My only opportunity was to return to the courtesan world. But now I felt as I had when I was fourteen. I would defile myself by offering myself to men. I felt I would be betraying Edward. Even if I returned, I might be able to survive for only a few more years. And then what? It sickened me to realize that I truly had no choices. I had to accept defeat.

Magic Gourd thought we should start a small courtesan house. We would call it a private teahouse, which would set us apart from the opium flower houses. It suggested a place that was more refined, which might require men with manners and at least some amount of courting—perhaps not as much as in a first-class house. In any case, we had heard that even in first-class houses, the courting time required had been much reduced. We could take four rooms, one for her as madam, one for me as entertainer and courtesan. The two other rooms would be for two courtesans we would recruit. I listened dully to her plan and told her it was too early to think about this. She told me to rest. And she went to look for a suitable place to rent. She wrote down expenses that needed to be paid to the Green Gang for protection, and taxes that would be assessed in the International Settlement. We tallied up the cost of furnishing a refined teahouse. We obtained prices from Mr. Gao for the value of our jewelry. And we realized in the end we could afford one teacup.

Magic Gourd came up with another idea: "Loyalty Fang made a promise to you—if you ever needed help when you were in trouble, you could ask him."

"That was seven years ago," I said. "He probably doesn't remember what he said and to which girl."

"He gave you a big ring as a pledge that his promise was true."

"He gave many flowers a ring for something or other that was true for that moment. You told me yourself: As time passes, the ring is no longer a promise but a souvenir."

"Do you remember when I asked if we should keep the ring or sell it with the other unwanted jewelry? I saw the look in your eye. You hesitated a little too long before you told me to sell it. So I didn't."

"Then you should sell it now."

"It's pride that keeps you from asking him. You don't have to ask for money. Ask him to help us get a position in a first-class house. Two feet in the door, yours and mine, that's all. It would take him two minutes, a phone call, a little flattery to the madam."

I had never thanked Loyalty for introducing me to Edward. There was nothing to thank in the beginning. He was the one who had apologized to me for Edward's crude behavior. It had occurred to me later that I should have been friendly to Loyalty and his wife, that I should have perhaps invited them to dinner. But then I held off because he would remind me of my past. I told Edward, and he had understood. Now, to Loyalty again, I would be reminded not only of my past but also of the times I was devastated by him. He had known me intimately—sexually and emotionally. He knew my weaknesses both ways and how to make me succumb. I had never loved him deeply, as I had Edward. But if I saw him, he might make one small expression that once made me believe he loved me, or had made me livid, or might remind me of certain erotic nights. He knew me too well. Magic Gourd was right. I was too proud. I would be stupid not to see him, simply because I did not want to be reminded of my past with him. The worst he could do was to fail to remember his promise. I would be humiliated, and so be it. I could not afford pride.

When I finally picked up the telephone to call Loyalty, I apologized quickly that the years had gone by without thanking him. I was honest and said I had wanted to leave my former life behind. I told him briefly about Edward's death.

"When I heard, I felt great sadness for you. Truly, I did. I imagined you in your grief." I then told him about Little Flora's abduction. He groaned. "I had not heard, and I have no adequate words to tell you how sorry I am. I can only say that if that had happened to my son, I would find those who did it and tear off their limbs. I'm glad you still have Magic Gourd to keep you company. She has been a good friend to you for so many years."

"Like a mother," I said.

"By the way, do you still have that cat who tried to eat my arm?"

"You asked me that seven years ago. Carlotta died." A small knot of old sorrow rose in my throat.

"Has it really been that long?"

"So much time has gone by you may have forgotten something you said seven years ago. If you did, I will not remind you—"

He broke in. "I've already guessed the reason you are reaching out to me," he said.

I thought he meant this as criticism.

"I know you had to put away pride and old wounds to call me."

"You are not obligated to help. It was many years ago."

"Ah, Violet, you are still resisting kindness. I would like to help, if I can. Speak freely."

"I need to return to my old job. I don't know if the House of Vermillion would take me back. I am almost twenty-five years old, and you can't make me young again, no matter how much praise you give on my behalf. Grief and worry have worsened what age has not. But with your word, they would at least consider me. I am realistic. I would appreciate whatever you can do, without your having to lie, at least not too much."

He was quiet for a few seconds, and I was sure he was composing a tactful answer to explain why he was unable to help.

"Let me think more about what I can do. Can you come to my office tomorrow?"

I guessed that he wanted to see how aged I had become to know which house might take me. He sent his chauffeur the next day to bring me to his office. I was surprised at how simple and messy the room was: a desk, two hard chairs, a small sofa, armchair, and low tables.

He kissed my hand quickly. "Violet, I am always happy to see you." He gave me his famous long gaze. "You look as lovely as ever."

"Thank you. You flatter as well as ever." I gave him a pleasant smile, friendly but not flirtatious. I saw he was already assessing my appearance more critically.

He sat back, crossed his legs, and lit a cigarette. It was a superior businesslike pose. "I have given much thought as to what I can do. And here is what I propose. I will go to Vermillion—she now owns the house. I'll mention that you've decided to return and will choose a house soon. I will then say that I am eager to be one of your suitors, and since the House of Vermillion is my favorite, I hope that she will do what she can to convince you to rejoin them."

"This is very generous." I was trying to decipher what he really wanted.

"In any business negotiation, it is better to make the other party think they are benefiting more than you. Don't denigrate yourself, Violet. You are lovely and able to understand men and you are kind to their failings. I know you hesitate, given your feelings for Edward. My actual proposal is that you give me English lessons in your room. I am serious. I should have improved my English years ago. My business requires it. I am relying on translators and don't know if they are saying what I intend. I propose that I visit you two or three times a week in your room. I need you to be a strict teacher and make me practice. No excuses. I'll pay for the lessons, and it will be equal to what a suitor might give you. If I fail to practice hard enough, you can fine me. Naturally, since I am not an actual suitor, I will continue to court other women—at other houses, of course. That leaves you free to receive suitors when you are accustomed to life in the house again. We must have a clear understanding that this is the arrangement. I have no hidden meaning. I want only to help you as an old friend. And I want to learn enough English that I don't have to use a dictionary that tells me a courtesan house is where you find whores for ten dollars."

LOYALTY WAS A bad student and paid me many fines. After two weeks we were back to our old ways and became reacquainted in my bed. I had missed the comfort of being with someone, and he was familiar. After another four weeks, we were arguing every night over the same misunderstandings of what was said and what was meant. He made excuses why he could not see me on a few occasions. I learned he was seeing another courtesan.

"If you had known sooner," he said in exasperation, "you would have been mad at me sooner. By doing it my way, you were happy with me for two weeks more."

"I don't care whether you see someone else. Just don't insult me with dishonesty."

"I am not obligated to tell you everything."

In the old days of my infatuation, he could cause havoc with my emotions. Now his antics simply made me angry. I was not in love with him anymore, and his selfishness was tiresome. My heart was full of yearning for Edward and Flora. I wanted them back. The yearning I had for Loyalty had been that of a fifteen-year-old virgin who grew older but continued to believe she would marry the man who had deflowered her. I was glad to be free of the delusion.

"We'll never understand each other," I said. I was neither angry nor sad. I said it as if I were reciting a lesson, one I had just learned. "We should admit that you won't ever change, and neither will I. We make each other unhappy. It's time we stop."

"I agree. Maybe in a month we can both be more reasonable . . ."

"We will never be reasonable. We are who we are. I want to stop. I won't change my mind."

"You are too important to me, Violet. You are the one who knows me. I know I don't always make you happy. But in between our fights, you are happy. You've told me you are. Let's try to have more happiness and fewer fights—"

"I cannot continue this way. My heart has become frayed."

"You never want to see me?"

"I will see you as my student and you can see me as your English teacher."

A calm fell over me. I felt no acrimony toward Loyalty. For many years, I had waited for proof of love from him. No amount of patience would bring it, because I did not know what love was beyond the discontent that I did not have it. Now I did know, and I realized I would never find lasting love with Loyalty. His abiding love lasted as long as I was by his side. I wanted a deeper love, in which we felt we could never know enough of each other—our hearts, our minds, and how we saw the world. To finally understand that was a victory over my own self.

CHAPTER 9

QUICKSAND YEARS

Shanghai
March 1925
Violet

Loyalty was throwing a big party at the House of Lin to celebrate the fifteen-year-old virgin courtesan Ruby Sky and her upcoming defloration, which he had bought for a price greater than what he had paid for mine. As with the party where I first met him, he had invited seven friends and there was a shortage of courtesans. As usual, he requested my presence, and as usual, I appreciated the business.

Over the last few years, I had worked hard to improve my skills as a zither player, as well as a singer of Western tunes. Loyalty cited to his guests my unusual musical talents as reason for others to request my services at their parties. In truth, my skills were only passable. Despite his recommendation, my desk was not burdened with stacks of requests. Who among the younger clients wanted to hear plucky zither music when they could spin out a fast song on the phonograph? They preferred whatever was modern, and Shanghai was all about modernity. I had added one musical advantage by singing a few songs in the melodic Western style with the zither providing only the harmony. One guest who had visited the United States said it sounded like I was playing the American banjo, and thereafter I advertised myself as a banjo singer, "widely sought for parties with a buoyant atmosphere."

The madam of the House of Lin was the former Billowy Cloud at Hidden Jade Path. She greeted me with much enthusiasm. "I'm so grateful you had no engagements tonight," she exclaimed before the others arrived. "I should call upon you more often. Our girls are busy every night." At one time, I would have been insulted by her insinuation that I had no regular suitors. Now Magic Gourd was telling Billowy Cloud that she should always think of me to give a party a lively touch. I entered the banquet room and saw Loyalty with his wiggly new favorite. He was gazing at her with the same tender expression he had given me when I was his virgin and he had claimed no other girl had stirred such new and surprising emotion in him.

Loyalty came over to us and greeted Magic Gourd and me in the courtly British manner—a kiss on my hand and a slight bow. I complimented him on the lovely new flower he was honoring. She threw me a suspicious eye. Magic Gourd had complained of stomach problems but still insisted on attending because she had a feeling I would make a new conquest.

Halfway through the party, Loyalty begged that I entertain everyone. I began the party with two sentimental Chinese songs, followed by the banjo-style tunes "Always," "Tea for Two," and "Swanee River," the last being my best, because of my joke that *suh-wan-nee* meant in Chinese "thinking about grabbing you," and that *fa fa e wei* meant, the first time it was sung, "to show you the beautiful rising clouds," and, in the second, "to show you my hunger for your raging fire." "Swanee" always ended the party in a high mood, generous tips for me, and, on occasion, a new suitor.

Loyalty jumped to his feet. "Thank you, Maestro!" He used the traditional term reserved for the famed singers at Storytelling Hall. "You make us swoon, you raise our spirits. We must show our appreciation." He gave a toast and then slipped me an envelope with money, so that others knew they should do the same. Then Loyalty gave another toast. More obligatory clapping and roars of admiration followed.

One man toward the end of the table opposite Loyalty was overly effusive. "I have never heard such a combination of delicate and forceful notes rise from the zither as those your fingers plucked tonight. And from a foreigner no less!"

That tiresome comparison to foreigners, yet again. "Only half," I said in apologetic tones. "But I still try to be impressive."

"I did not mean to suggest your talent had to do with the short-comings of race. I meant it was an added benefit that you can sing also in English. Truly, I've never heard such a dazzling banjo performance by anyone."

It was the usual banal compliment. I doubted he had ever heard another courtesan play banjo music, but I responded with ritual modesty. "I lack great skill but I'm glad you enjoyed it nonetheless."

"My admiration is genuine. I'm not trying to gain favor to be invited into your boudoir. I speak from my respect and knowledge of the arts." He looked to be thirty, but he wore the earnest face of a young boy filled with awe visiting a courtesan house for the first time. Young boys wanted to have knowledge of the arts in bed. This man's bullshit was a ploy I had heard many times before. He introduced himself as Perpetual of the Sheng family of An-hwei Province, second cousin to Mansion, who was one of Loyalty's friends.

Although he was from An-hwei, he spoke Han without the province's accent, so it was clear that he was educated. As for looks, compared to Loyalty, he was not unattractive, but he was not the first man on whom your eyes would fall when scanning a room of prospects. As he continued to heap praise, I elevated his attractiveness to pleasing but in an ordinary way, which is to say, he did not have any of the features I disliked. He was not narrow-shouldered and bony nor did he have the broad Mongolian look. The eyes were not squinty like those of a cheapskate. The nostrils were not large like those of a blowhard. The lips were not thick with crude intent. He did have the missing teeth of a man whose neglected hygiene likely extended to less visible parts of his body. He did not have the coarse features of someone with questionable morals. He had no patchy eyebrows like that of a syphilitic. His hair was abundant, but not so wildly thick as to suggest he had tribal blood. His hairstyle was not chopped like a bumpkin but precisely cut and smoothed back with silky pomade. By all that he was not and a little of what he was, I found him somewhat attractive.

It was difficult to tell whether he was well-to-do. He had come as Mansion's guest. His clothes were clean but somewhat creased, though that had always been a problem with Western linen suits in warm weather. His fingernails were trimmed and lacked the long nail on the little finger, which opium sots used as an entrenching tool to dig out the sticky residue of a pipe and the waxy crevices of their ears. He spoke again in a serious voice: "Your delicate fingers pranced like fairies and made the music all the more entrancing."

This was too much. "Do you belong to one of the literati societies in Shanghai?"

"Trying to find out if I'm worthy of your company?" Now he smiled, but only with his mouth, not his eyes. I maintained my aplomb and waited patiently for his answer. "I don't seek the society of like-minded intellectuals," he said. "I'm a painter-poet who prefers solitude. I have moods, you see, best not seen in public. The moods give my paintings a moody style, which is not popular with most collectors."

"Most collectors think popularity is a style," I said.

"Anyone can have original style," he countered. "And yet no one truly does. We're influenced by those who came before us, beginning with the painters thousands of years ago who imitated nature."

What a pretentious boor. "Why do scholars always apologize for ignorance?" I asked.

"You persist in wanting to know if I'm from a scholar family . . . Ah, now I've annoyed you, I can tell."

"Not at all," I said pleasantly. "We courtesans enjoy playful banter. That's what you like and I'm happy to accommodate." I turned to Magic Gourd, who was standing to the side, slightly behind me. "It's warm. I need my fan." If I later put my fan in my lap, that was the signal for Magic Gourd to call me aside to let me know someone had sent me an urgent message. She always kept a note in her pocket for that reason. I was sure now that he was a poor prospect. If he had any money at all, he'd make me turn upside down for it. I had already been at the party for well over two hours and it was unlikely that further monetary appreciation would come my way from the other guests.

I turned back to Perpetual. "Are you ready to confess? Do you have a ship of gold? Are you the bureaucrat we must bribe?"

"I confess I am indeed from a scholar family—and a wastrel."

"Have you spent the entire fortune? Isn't there still some for me?"

"It wasn't money I wasted. It was my education. I passed the third-level examinations five years ago, when I was twenty-six and I have nothing to show for it."

"Twenty-six! I don't know of any man younger than thirty who passed at that level, and that includes the cheaters."

"From the moment I sprang from the womb, I started studying to pass the examinations at the national level. While still at my mother's breast, my father laid out the plan for my life, the typical one of the old Ching dynasty days: take a high civil post in a small district, adhere strictly to form and custom, and at the end of the two-year appointment, move to successive posts in more and more important counties and provinces. That's what my father did."

"And what happened after all that breast milk?"

"I excelled in the six arts. Revenue and taxation were my undoing. I couldn't apply my mind to a system that robbed the poor and enriched the rich."

"Those are not lively topics, I agree." I placed the fan in my lap. Soon I could leave this tiresome man.

"The Ching system was unjust. The new system? It's just different hands taking the money now."

What an idiot he was. The men in the room might occupy the positions he maligned.

Mansion shouted out, "Eh, cousin, are you tormenting her with your usual revolutionary talk? Let's forget about all the injustices tonight. You can fix them tomorrow."

Perpetual kept his eyes on me. "My criticism of the old system left me unemployed. Like many without a job, I call myself a painter-poet. And now you have your answer. I am too poor to be your suitor. I wouldn't have been able to afford to be here if my cousin had not invited me."

"I'm not as mercenary as you make me out to be," I said, one of my oft-used lines. "Recite me a poem to compensate me for my time."

"Listen to the street vendor calling outside the window right now—his praises about the virtues of fermented rice soup. That's one of my poems."

"Your humility is bottomless. I will not give you any peace until you recite a poem for me. Just choose one that has nothing to do with bureaucrats or fermented rice soup."

He paused, then said, "Here is one suited to you." He looked steadily into my eyes.

> "It was an endless time before we met, but longer still
>   since she left.
> A wind starts up from the east, blowing a hundred
>   flowers into flight,
> And the spring silk-worms begin to weave, weave on till
>   they perish.
> In her morning mirror, she sees her halo of hair
>   changing color,
> And yet she taunts the chill of moonlight with her
>   evening song.
> And by late evening the candles weep under their wicks.
> It's not far, not so far to her Enchanted Mountain.
> Blue birds, listen with care to what she says, bring her
>   words to me."

I was stunned almost to tears. It touched the sadness I had over my separation from Little Flora. We were parted, time went on, and she was alive somewhere else. The man had awakened me from the lassitude of a meaningless routine.

"It's magnificent," I exclaimed. "Truly. I'm not being polite. It's vivid but not overly so, and so natural that it seems written without effort. There is no forced sense of style or effect. It rises out of true emotions. I feel the wind, see the candle. The poem reminds me of those by Li Shangyin. In fact, it is just as good."

Magic Gourd came at that moment to tell me about my pre-planned urgent message. We walked out of earshot. "I'll stay. He's interesting, and the poem he just recited is surprisingly moving. I want to recite it tonight. It may increase interest in me."

"Is he a prospect?"

"He has the thin pocket of a last-century scholar. But he may keep me amused."

"My stomach is still churning, so it's home for me."

I returned to Perpetual's side, and his eyebrows rose. "What's this? You're not using polite excuses to desert me?"

"I want to hear more of your poems."

"I don't dare. Your ear is too good. You liked the first, but you might tell me the next sounds like the slop of minstrel troupes. I would suffer from your bad opinion of me."

"Criticism, the death from a thousand cuts."

"I've had only a few people who have listened to my poems. Most are relatives who opine on with the same complaints they have for boils and bad weather. 'Ai! It's too painful to bear. When will it end?' My wife was my best critic. She had strong opinions and saw the good and the bad in what I wrote. We could talk freely about everything because we were like-minded. Her name was Azure, like the blue skies where she dwells." He was quiet and turned his head away from me. "She died of typhus five years ago." He remained silent, and I did not feel right interrupting him. "I apologize," he said at last. "I should not burden you with my sadness. You don't even know me."

"Not many understand the loss of profound love," I said. "My husband died six years ago, and my daughter was stolen from me three years ago. Edward and Flora."

"They were foreigners?"

"Edward was an American. Flora was born in Shanghai."

"I noticed something different about you—an absence of a part of your spirit. Your eyes see but have stopped looking. The grief."

Such understanding was unusual in a man.

"In my case," he went on, "grief did not lessen over time. It renewed itself each morning when I awoke and discovered my wife was not beside me. It was as if I were learning for the first time that she was dead. I would climb the hill to her gravesite every day to remind myself she was gone forever. I recited my poems to her headstone, remembering I had read them to her when she breathed beside me in bed."

"I talk to my husband, too. I gain comfort when I think of him, but when he doesn't answer, I am devastated once again."

"I have thought many times of killing myself so I can join my wife. Only my little son keeps me bound to earth. My cousin forced me to come here. 'Come see beautiful women, not graves,' he said. And so now you know, I have no heart to pursue pleasures of any kind, even if I could afford to. But this evening, you revived a deadened part of me—my spirit. You speak so openly about all things. That was her nature as well."

"Your grief is the depth of this poem. It stirs me. Will you let me recite it tonight to our guests?"

"You're kind to ask. But I think the others don't want the intrusion."

"There's a lull in the party now, and it's my role to add some luster with entertainment. Will I be the first courtesan to recite this poem in public?"

"My wife in her grave is the only one who has heard it."

I went to Loyalty and asked if he would like me to recite Perpetual's poem as part of the entertainment. As I read it, I felt profound longing for Edward and Little Flora. I imagined Little Flora waiting for me. Perpetual was astonished at how well I captured his intent.

That night I received more accolades and money gifts than I had in several years. I was immediately invited to numerous parties that would be held in the next week, and as the requests piled up, I had to tell my hosts I could come only for a brief amount of time, due to my numerous engagements. I had returned to the days when men pursued me and increased their gifts to compete for my favor. Three men pursued me with special interest, vying for my favor.

By the end of the second week, one suitor went elsewhere. After another week, the passion I had momentarily stirred had spent itself, by which time a dozen courtesans had recited Perpetual's poem. I lived in terror once again that I would have no visitors, not even occasional ones. And to those who did come, I allowed the wooing to be brief, a few days and not weeks. A man these days had too many choices and would not wait to see if a flower chose him above others. He could date modern college students for free who did not care about scandal and shame. They even kept sponges to prevent pregnancy pinned to their panties so they could slip them into their vaginas the moment opportunity arose. When I accepted one man on the first night, Magic Gourd berated me, saying I was behaving no better than a girl at an opium flower house. Two men came to visit the next night, mentioning they were friends of the man who had visited the night before.

"You see!" Magic Gourd said. "You're attracting cheapskates like flies to rotten fruit. There is no quicker way to ruin a reputation."

At least I continued to receive requests to perform at parties, most recently from Perpetual's cousin Mansion. He was honoring two important men who had the ear of the president of the Republic. I was told they especially liked the American songs.

"Will your cousin Perpetual return to us?" I asked. "I want to thank him again for his poem. It led to quite a stir." I also hoped he would let me recite another of his poems.

"I'll invite him the next time I see him. He comes and goes. I think he has some sort of business outside of Shanghai. Or maybe he's taken up with a courtesan at another house. Hah! He's quite secretive."

A business. So he was not as poor as he made himself out to be. And I knew there was no truth to his being at a courtesan house. Poor man.

A FEW NIGHTS later, Perpetual returned as Mansion's guest at a small party of drinks and games with close friends. Magic Gourd hurried over to me and told me to extract another poem from him.

"Do you think I'm so stupid I would not have thought of that already?"

I welcomed Perpetual with genuine gladness. After my performance, I seated myself beside him. "I'm glad Mansion forced you to come back."

"I certainly didn't need much persuasion. Your music lifted my spirits, and I deeply appreciated our conversation."

Mansion and his friends started the Finger Guessing game. Perpetual declined to play. He said he disliked gambling. We watched a few rounds with amusement. But then I saw his face become somber. He turned and looked at me with haunted eyes.

"It's been difficult since the last time I saw you. I was grateful I could speak openly about my wife, but it also created an upwelling of nearly unbearable sorrow. I was so desperate to alleviate the pain that I wandered the streets for hours until I found myself in an opium flower house. It was dark inside and the shadow of a woman led me to a divan. I heard the voices of other men and women. I took two puffs on the pipe and soon the pain eased and I entered the blue smoke heavens. All the joy I had ever experienced in my entire life poured back into me at once. I did not think I could feel any greater bliss—until I felt a hand on my arm. Azure was sitting beside me. I swear, it was as vivid as seeing you here. I kissed her and caressed her face to make sure she was real. She assured me she was. She lay down on the divan, her clothes disappeared, and her beautiful pale body undulated in eagerness for me. Once again we were conjoined in mind, heart, body, and spirit. She made the same cries of joy, accompanied by the peals of tiny bells tied to her ankles. We swirled weightless in silk and air. We rose to the heights, higher than we had ever gone, and after each peak, we began again. Every time I entered her—" He stopped. "Forgive me. What's dear to me must sound obscene."

"Nothing shocks me," I said. I secretly considered I, too, might smoke opium to bring back Edward as a vivid illusion.

"The joy does not last long enough," he said. "The blue smoke eventually disappears and the reality emerges and is much harsher than before. One moment I was lying with my wife, sighing with contentment, and the next I was staring into the eyes of a vamp. This girl was no more than twenty, around the age of my wife when she left me. Other men would have thought she was pretty. But I was revolted that my wife had been exchanged for this empty-headed girl who talked like a whimpering baby. I looked for my clothes so I could leave as soon as possible. But then I felt her firm hand on my privates. I was disgusted and about to order her to stop, and then I was even more disgusted with myself because my penis had hardened in her hand. I am a normal man and it had been five years since I had touched a woman, other than that illusion of my wife. The girl lay back on the divan, pulled up her dress, and spread her legs. I could not repel the urge. I thrust myself into her—and then, what I did . . ." His chest heaved, as if to keep from sobbing. He looked down. "I did something revolting, and it makes me sick to even think about it now." He shook his head.

I waited for him to continue. But he stood up.

"I can't talk about this anymore." He looked around. "If anyone else heard me they would think I was a lunatic. I think I've subjected you to enough accounts of my miserable life. You're extraordinarily kind for listening."

"There's no need to apologize. Truly. It's necessary to purge the worst that grief brings. Perhaps you could do so by writing more poems."

"I have. Much of it is sentimental blather. The next time my cousin invites me I will bring you some. Then you can have a good laugh. No more of these gloomy self-indulgent recollections."

"You don't need to wait until he invites you," I said, thinking quickly. "Come tomorrow in the late afternoon. I can listen to your poems in the privacy of my sitting room and have tea."

As soon as he left, Magic Gourd rushed over. "Did he give you a poem?"

"Tomorrow afternoon. He'll come for tea."

"If he gives you a poem, will you let him into your bed?"

"What? And make him think I'm a prostitute?"

HE ARRIVED THE next day wearing Chinese clothes. I was a bit surprised. Some of our clients still did, but they tended to be older. Then again, he did hail from An-hwei. As if he knew what I was thinking, he said, "Western clothes can't compare to the Chinese long gown in terms of comfort. Look at me. Don't I look more like a poet?" He did, and I also thought he was more handsome, perhaps because he seemed relaxed.

I invited him to sit in the armchair. I took the sofa then waited for an opportune time to ask him for a poem. I waited as he told me about the new problems facing Shanghai. I waited as he recounted the injustices to workers and peasants. I tried to be an interesting conversational partner, but I was also impatient. I asked Magic Gourd to bring wine instead of tea. Finally the conversation returned to his misery and torment. His speech became slurred.

"I hesitated to tell you yesterday what happened at the opium flower house because I was scared thinking I had gone mad. I know I can speak frankly to you, but if I tell you what happened, can you be honest with me and tell me if you think I've lost my mind or have become evil?"

I gave him my most sympathetic look and honest assurances.

"I already told you about my wife and the girl. As I was saying, the girl was lying on her back and I was on top of her, grinding her by instinctual need alone. She was smiling. All of a sudden I could not bear to see her face. I asked her to turn away and close her eyes. And then I could not stand to feel her body latched onto mine moving as if we were one. So I told her to stop moving, to lie still. I told her to make no sound. I closed my eyes and I imagined this still body was the corpse of my wife. I was crying out of joy and shame because I had joined with my beloved again, only now she was dead. I pounded into her harder and harder, as if I could fill her with life. But she remained a corpse, and it filled me with fresh anguish, so I stopped. I asked the girl for the pipe. Soon I was in blue smoke heaven with the illusion of my wife fully alive. What joy I felt as I slipped between those familiar soft folds and into her secret chamber. I made love with this illusory living body. Hours later, I returned again to my senses, and saw the prostitute, and again I made her assume the role of my wife's corpse. I was there for three days. I could not stop because the bliss increased the torment and the torment increased the need for relief . . . Are you repulsed yet?"

"Not at all," I lied. His fantasies were revolting. Yet it was admirable that a man could grieve for his wife so much he would resort to such gruesome measures to be with her. A dead wife would be flattered.

He clasped my hands in gratitude. "I knew you would understand. You've told me already that you imagine your husband when another man is penetrating you."

I had not said that—and what a crude way to put it—"penetrating you." When I imagined Edward, it was when I was alone, when I was missing our quiet times, and I was remembering what he had said.

Perpetual looked around the room and complimented me on the tasteful decor. "When you imagine your husband," he said, "is it just his face?"

"What I remember most is the sound of his voice," I said, "certain conversations we had. And I also can see his different smiles, a contented smile, a smile of relief, one of surprise, or the way he looked at our baby when she was born."

"Expressions. That's interesting. How about scent, the odor of his body and breath?"

"That's not what returns to me unconsciously. With effort just now, I can remember it somewhat."

"I remember everything, especially the sex scent, the two of us together. It's my poet nature to remember and imagine the forbidden. Misery is the source of my poems."

Here was my chance, at last. "Did you know your last poem caused a flurry of requests for me to perform it again in other houses?"

"Mansion told me. I'm glad. I looked through the hundreds I've written, trying to decide what else you might like."

Hundreds. My career was saved.

"I chose one of my newer poems, part of a collection I call City of Two Million Lives. You should be completely frank in your opinion of it. I am always working to improve my poems." He cleared his throat.

> "The rich surge in power like a flooded river,
> and wash downstream the honor of men.
> On ocean waves, the foreigners land
> and erode our homeland shore.

Their anthems become our funeral songs
for our forebears who drowned in their rising tide.
They make our heroes lie in their beds
then proclaim, 'Shanghai is our bastard slave!' "

I was struck dumb. It was nothing like the beautiful poem he had read before. This was like a speech given by students with black armbands on Nanking Road. Down with imperialism! Abolish port treaties! Take back the concessions!

"It's quite powerful," I managed to say, "inspiring . . . excellent commentary on the problems our Shanghai faces."

"You may use it anytime," he said proudly. "Tonight even. My cousin has invited me to come. I already told him I have a new poem."

I had to tell him the truth: "This would not be the best poem for our guests to hear. Our customers are the people your poem denounces."

"Where's my brain? I'll try to find others that might be better suited. What's your desire?"

"Perhaps one about wistful love," I said, "like the last, the aching suspension of having what you desire. Youthfulness is also good. Our guests enjoy remembering their first love."

The following week, Perpetual gave me a new poem, which he said was about wistful love.

Through the window of my studio,
I see the peonies, still unfurled.
I see the path, the bridge uncrossed.
How I long to hear her footsteps
And hold her tiny feet once more!
How I long to embrace her
and watch her robe unfurl!

But alas, my breath steams the window
and clouds all memory but of that day
she crossed the bridge to the underworld.

At least it had nothing to do with a depraved society. Magic Gourd suggested I take out the words *to the underworld*, so that it would sound like the lady in the poem might be late, rather than dead. Against my better judgment, I performed the poem that night as it was written, and a pall fell over the room. Only one man was enthusiastic. He had just lost his favorite concubine to suicide.

Perpetual was encouraged by my false report that it was well received. He brought me another, even more wistful than the last.

The leaves once fluttered, as did my heart.
The nude branches are now burdened with snow.
And the silkworm weavers are gone,
But her silk robe remains beside her empty bath.
Under cold moonlight, no longer golden,
But white as her corpse on her new slab bed.

I was aghast. The corpse of his wife had returned. I summoned up effusive praise, noting how beautifully the still branches contrasted with fluttering leaves, how wrenchingly he had placed the white image of silkworms next to the cold one of snow and the final one of a corpse.

Magic Gourd and I debated whether I should perform the poem. We finally agreed it was so bad it would inspire only laughter and damage my career. I would lie once again and say it was a great success.

Magic Gourd was disappointed, but not discouraged. "If he has hundreds, as he says he has, perhaps he can give them all to you so you can choose the best. Poets are blind to what is good or bad in their poems. You've already known him for over a month. You should have been able to pull out a few good poems by now. Yearning love, wistful love, love fulfilled, anything but tragic love. I think the best way to do that is to take him to bed. Give him some fresh inspiration to replace the tiresome one of his wife."

"I FEAR MY mind is withering," I said to Perpetual a few days later when he returned to Shanghai from what I assumed was a business trip. "Would you be willing to give me lessons in calligraphy? Perhaps I could practice by copying all your poems. That would provide both discipline and inspiration."

As I had expected, he was flattered and instantly agreed to help. I had already bought the brushes, ink, and a thick stack of rice paper. He took his role as teacher quite seriously. He told me I had to prepare my mind, prepare the ink, and prepare to create each character by seeing the flow of the brushstrokes required. I prepared to seduce him.

"You can't write the character as if it were broken pieces glued together," he said after my first effort. "It's done with a rhythm and a stillness. No shaky hand, no stiffness either." He showed me how to hold the brush perpendicular to the paper, and I deliberately held it at a slant. He put his warm hand around mine and guided me through the strokes. I deliberately made my arm stiff and jerky so that he had to stand behind me to guide my movements. I swished my hips in rhythm to his guidance and brushed against his thigh. Most men would have stiffened and immediately taken the subtle invitation to finish the lesson in bed. Perpetual, the faithful widower, moved away.

The poem I copied was the turgid diatribe from the collection he called City of Two Million Lives. Shanghai is our bastard slave! Perpetual had said true love came from sharing higher ideas, and this poem contained a heavy assortment of them. I had to show an interest in them if I were to compete with a dead wife who had already inspired five years of chastity. "People should want to live by higher ideas—altruism, self-sacrifice, honor, and integrity. They shouldn't give in and simply say, 'Oh well, that's impossible, so I'll just go along and be greedy like everyone else.' "

"But men must be pragmatic. Ideas do not feed mouths or create progress."

This fueled him to explain what he meant. I stopped listening after ten minutes and he went on for an hour. My plans to seduce him were a failure. He was excited, but not in the manner I had planned. I suggested we stop and resume our lessons again the next day.

"This has been fortifying to me. It's good to talk aloud about these ideas. My wife and I used to do this all the time."

I later told Magic Gourd that any inspiration I might have over his poems could not compete with the combined forces of his high ideas and his dead wife. It was useless—and costly, given how much he enjoyed snacks with tea. When Perpetual next called on me, I told him a new suitor wished to visit me in the afternoon. I would let him know when we could resume our calligraphy lessons again. He could not hide his disappointment.

"You've been much too kind to have spent so much time with me," he said in a formal manner.

The afternoons went by without visitors. I read a novel, then another. I sent a manservant out to buy newspapers, one in Chinese, one in English. While I had often tired of Perpetual's political talk, I now found myself reading the news from his point of view, the one that despised progress: more ships, more buildings, more ribbon cutting, more handshakes between two tycoons about to make themselves even richer. I thought of my mother telling each customer: "You're just the one I hoped to see," which served as a prelude to fostering the merger of power. As I read the news I asked myself whose view was better—Mother's or Perpetual's? Which was self-serving? Which one destructive to those left behind?

When Perpetual returned two weeks later, I was genuinely pleased to see him. I had been lonely. He hurriedly said he knew that I was busy and only wanted to tell me that I had inspired him to write new poems, more like the first one he had shown me the night we met.

"Poems rise from the force of emotions," he said. "Mine arose from our separation. I found that I missed your company, and then I yearned for it, and after a while, I ached for it, and that's when poems of wistfulness poured out, unstoppable. For that reason, I'm grateful that I have been away from you. But I must also confess something that may shock you. I have been dishonest. I told you that grief for my wife blocked all desire for other women. Shortly after I met you, I no longer imagined that the corpse of my wife was the illusion before me. It was you. So it was both my longing for you and shameful dishonesty that created the most powerful poems I have written in many years. They are still quite poor, I'm sure, but, if you like, I offer them as gratitude for poetic inspiration and for stirring feelings of love I thought I would never again experience. Be assured, I don't expect anything from you in return. I will remain your admirer, since I'm too poor to transform myself into anyone else. The pain of unreciprocated love will lead to even more powerful poems over the years."

Of all the bashful men I have had, he certainly had the oddest way of telling me he wanted to bed me. Imagine it: I was more desired than the corpse of his wife! Nonetheless, I was eager to see the poems I had inspired. "If I gave you what you yearn for," I said, "would you lose your inspiration?"

His face contorted into the agony of sexual desire. "The poems would be different, yet no less powerful. They might be even stronger, given the strength of my love."

I was quiet as I thought about this prospect: If I allowed him into my bed, I would have conversation that would fill otherwise lonely afternoons. I would receive a flood of poems to choose from. Those were reasons enough, yet there was another. I would also fulfill my own longing for love—and it was not for him. I wanted to feel that I was loved once again, and by someone who ached to have me.

"I'd like to see the wistful poems you wrote," I said, "as well as the ones that will be different."

I lay on the bed and let the new poems begin.

His POEMS ABOUT his yearning for me were not bad, but they were still not good enough to perform. At least they were not about politics. He visited me in the afternoons three or four times a week. After a month had gone by and no worthwhile poems had come as a result, Magic Gourd said Perpetual might be more of a one-rocket pop-and-fizzle kind of poet. She regretted telling me I should seduce him. "Look at all the time you've wasted—and he did not even pay for all the tea and snacks, let alone those afternoons he happily wallowed in your bed."

Naturally, I was disappointed with my inability to inspire better poems from him. It was a matter of pride. But I did not feel those intimate afternoons had been a waste of time. For one thing, my calligraphy was much improved. I had what he called "a lightning blur literary style." I had also enjoyed being treated as an equal during our debates over subjects I knew little about: antifeudalism, social realism, the rural worker class, and the like. The boring subjects had become more lively now that I actively argued. I also felt a sense of accomplishment in having conquered his five years of chastity and laid to rest his wife's corpse. As every courtesan knows, marriage as the First Wife would be the best ending for a career. Marriage to Perpetual, however, would mean living somewhere in An-hwei Province, and I could not draw from him any information that would indicate whether his family home was fifty miles away from Shanghai or a hundred and fifty. He still remained secretive about his finances. He claimed to be poor, but Mansion said he had businesses elsewhere. Obviously, it did not involve foreign trade, but at least he had means for making money. And it goes without saying that any family with ten generations of successful scholars would have accumulated some degree of wealth over the years.

If I had deeply and wildly loved him, any distance from Shanghai would not have mattered. But I did not love him. Instead, I had a feeling for him that was like love. These lovelike feelings were far from the light-headed, cross-eyed, stormy-hearted ones I'd had for Loyalty. They were not at all like what Edward and I had shared. This kind of love was more one of growing contentment that would come from being adored for the rest of my life. It would not matter that sex with Perpetual was not that exciting. He was inexperienced, I reasoned, having made love to only one woman. I could teach him without him even knowing it. Then again, I would not mind having nights of less demanding sex. After years of work, retirement had its pleasures, too, as did the aphrodisiac words *Ten Generations of Successful Scholars,* which conjured in my mind the thrusting power of ten generations of important and respected men.

PERPETUAL AND I were engaged in another of our debates of higher ideas when I heard our gatekeeper shout: "The bastards shot him!" We ran to the front courtyard where almost everyone had gathered.

"Is he dead?" Vermillion asked.

"No one knows for sure," a manservant said.

A distant rumble of voices grew louder. Magic Gourd told us that people were angry to the point of crazy because the British police at Louza Station had fired into a crowd of student demonstrators who had surrounded the station, demanding the release of their leader who had organized the antiforeign protest. None of us knew how many were wounded or dead, only that our manservant Little Ox had gone out on an errand and had not returned well beyond the time when he said he would. Five minutes before, a manservant from the house across the street told Old Pine that Little Ox was lying in the road. He did not know if he was dead. Old Pine was Little Ox's uncle who had raised him since infancy. The old man was moaning between words: "He must have detoured to Nanking Road to see how big the demonstration had become. Why else would he have gone? The bastards!"

We opened the gate and looked out. A stream of chanting people was rushing by. The noise was getting louder by the second.

"We have to find him!" Old Pine said, and he slipped into the running masses.

"I'll go with him," Perpetual said. He looked at me, and I knew he was asking me to join him. This was a moment that represented all that we had talked about: justice, fairness, unity in making change. I paused for perhaps three seconds, and then I took his hand.

"Don't go!" Magic Gourd shouted. "Stupid girl. You want to be lying next to Little Ox?"

Perpetual and I reached an area where it was so crowded no one was moving. We were caught in a squeeze box of anger from both sides. Perpetual yelled, "Let us through! My brother was shot!" We pushed in.

I was the first to see Little Ox lying facedown on the road. I recognized him by the crescent scar on the back of his head. We saw Old Pine coming toward him and he fell to his knees and turned his nephew's head to see his face, then wailed. Epithets and a unified groan of sorrow rose. Just then the ground shook with an explosion, and in an instant, I was swept into a stampede of rioters. I felt a hand on my back. Magic Gourd shouted, "Don't fall! Don't fall!" I could not turn around for fear that I would do exactly what she warned me not to do, and then I would be trampled. So I let myself be carried in that millipede of legs. Around me were students with armbands, bare-chested laborers, servants in white jackets, rickshaw men and streetwalkers. I might die with these strangers and felt the numbness of acceptance and an odd dismay that I would be found dead wearing a dress I had never liked. It occurred to me only then that Perpetual was nowhere to be seen.

Along the sidewalks, protestors were hurling rocks at shop windows with Japanese characters and stepping inside to help themselves to the loot. "Out with the Japanese." "Down with the British." "Kick out the Yankees."

As I approached the House of Vermillion, I was relieved to see Old Pine standing near our gate. He was looking upward at a burning effigy with a sign that said it was the police commissioner.

"They've taught that bastard the last lesson he'll ever learn."

His eyesight had been worsening over the years. From three meters' distance, he wouldn't have been able to tell the difference between a white-turbaned Sikh and a white-haired missionary. He was crestfallen when I told him that the commissioner was not burnt to a crisp and would live to learn a few more lessons. We pounded on the gate, and Vermillion's frightened voice asked who we were before sliding the bolt. We rushed into the large reception hall. My flower sisters were clustered in a corner. I was about to tell them the sad news about Little Ox when a rock sailed through a window and everyone ran to the back of the house. We heard jeering. Old Pine said that people thought our house was where the British diplomat lived. They were going to break down the gate. Two days ago, the diplomat had thrashed a pancake seller with his cane for refusing to make way, and an outraged crowd had descended on him in reprisal and broken his legs. When word went out that the pancake seller had died, the furor had mounted to the pitch of madness. And now this!—a rumor that the damned diplomat lived in our house.

The girls ran to their rooms to gather their jewelry from hiding places, in case they had to flee. Where would they go? What would happen if they were caught with those hard-earned baubles? I was glad that mine were in a shallow false bottom I had made under the bed. Only Magic Gourd knew where the cases were and which panels had to slide open first. It was only then that I realized I had not seen Magic Gourd. I had assumed she had returned to the house.

"Where's Magic Gourd?" I cried aloud as I ran through the room. "Did she return?" I went to Old Pine. "Did you see her?"

He shook his head. Of course he had not seen her. He was nearly blind! "Open the gate! I have to find her." He refused. It was too dangerous, he said.

"Get away from here!" I heard Magic Gourd say on the other side of the gate. "Are you so blind and stupid that you cannot see this sign? Read it. House of Vermillion. Are you all from the countryside and can't read? You, over there, you look like a student. Do you know what this place is, or are you still drinking mother's milk? This is a first-class courtesan house. Where does it say House of British Diplomat? Show me!" We heard pounding on the gate. "Old Pine, you can let me in now." When it swung open, only a few sheepish young men were standing outside. They craned their necks to see inside.

Perpetual's anguished face suddenly appeared. He grabbed me and hugged me so strongly I thought he was going to crack my ribs. "You're safe! I was about to kill myself, certain you had died." He released me. His face became puzzled. "Weren't you worried for me?" he asked.

"Of course," I said. "Scared out of my mind." I secretly wondered why I had not worried where he was. I fingered his torn sleeve and kept my faced turned down. I could feel his eyes on me. When I looked up, he was staring hard, disappointed, almost angry. We both knew I should have burst into tears of relief when I saw that he was safe.

DURING THE WEEK of riots, Perpetual did not come back. I reasoned it was dangerous to walk in the streets when small riots erupted without warning. The word was out that the police commissioner had left an underling in charge of the Louza Station and went off to enjoy an afternoon at the Shanghai Club and horse races. The underling had panicked when the students entered the doors. He ordered his men to fire, and twelve were killed and many injured. It would take a while for things to quiet down in our neighborhood.

The parties were canceled. Vermillion rang our best patrons, one at a time, and claimed that everything had calmed down and that she was hosting a grand banquet to celebrate the new peace. My flower sisters and I rang our suitors and former patrons. Everyone said it was inconvenient to come. Nothing was going our way. Just this morning the corpse of an old man was placed on our steps. Vermillion did not want his ghost to enjoy his afterlife in our flower house. "Let him do his business in the Hall of Pleasure Gates down the street," she said. Everyone laughed except Old Pine, who had been told to remove the body.

He had already refused. "I'm not letting this man's ghost take over my body so he can fuck the girls with my cock."

I saw a beggar across the lane. "Hey, old grandpa! Ten cents to you if you take this body away."

"Fuck your mother," the man said in a thick, drunken voice. "I was mayor of this city. Give me a dollar." After some haggling, we paid the dollar.

As the days wore on, we heard rumors that some of our patrons had become paupers. Bank loans were taken back. Factories burned down. Warlords seized their unattended businesses in other provinces. There were stories abounding that the Japanese were turning this chaos to their advantage, and soon there would be a Japanese landlord behind every door, as if there were not already too many. What was happening? The world had gone mad.

Vermillion did an account of the house finances, listing the parties that had been booked and canceled, the courtesans whose patrons provided regular income. She calculated what that represented in terms of money to each girl and money to her pocket. I listened with a sick heart as she named my suitors as among the least successful and reliable. Since no one was giving parties, I received no requests to provide banjo-style zither music and songs. Perpetual had stayed away. He was probably angry at me. But I could not worry about him now. He would not be of any help with my finances. He had contributed only one good poem.

When at last the riots ceased and we had visitors again, they were not the same powerful men who had come before. These men had money, but they did not lavish it on us. They wanted less courting and more proof in the boudoir that we were better than the courtesans of other houses. And even without much business, Vermillion expected us to pay our full rent and expenses, but she quickly saw that if she kicked out everyone who lacked enough money each month, she would have no courtesans left. I portioned out my savings to keep my room.

I felt great relief when Vermillion came to me with a new client. Mansion had said he wanted to hold a private party at his house in honor of his guest, a middle-aged business partner named Endeavor Yan. The guest had expressed specific interest in a courtesan skilled at storytelling. Vermillion said no one was as seasoned as I was in the literary arts. I was flattered and thanked her for choosing me.

I wondered, of course, if Perpetual was staying at Mansion's house. If he attended the party, this would be a good chance to secretly show my affections and have him forgive me for my failure to worry sufficiently during the worst of the riots. That night I dressed in Westernized Chinese clothes, a blend of new and old. I also brought my zither. I was happy to see that Perpetual was indeed present at the dinner party, and I cast fond looks his way while still being attentive to the guest of honor. When it came time for the storytelling, my suggestions were brushed away. Endeavor Yan asked that I read a scene from *The Plum in the Golden Vase*. I was taken aback. This was a pornographic novel. It was popular in the courtesan houses, but only after a suitor had been invited to the boudoir. I had never been asked to perform this before a group of men during a dinner party. Perpetual looked away. More wine was poured for all. Mansion came around and said softly that he had persuaded Endeavor Yan to agree that I read a selection in his room instead.

"He is here for only three nights," Mansion said, "and I suggested that he provide the equivalent of a month's worth of gifts, fifty dollars for the favor. He may ask for another performance the next night. I know this may be much to ask, Violet. Forgive me if you find it insulting."

Before I could answer, Perpetual came up to Mansion to bid him good night. He said to me that he was pleased to see me, then left. I took his departure to mean he disapproved of what I was doing. For all these months, this pompous man had let me pleasure him and had paid nothing for the privilege. I told Mansion I would be more than pleased to entertain his business partner. Fortunately, Magic Gourd was not here to see what I had agreed to do without even one night of courtship. I had enacted scenes from the book before—but only for patrons. Tonight's decision signaled the rapid descent of my career.

Endeavor was solicitous of my comfort. Was it too cold? Would you like tea? We talked for a few minutes about nothing in particular and then he brought me the book. He wanted me to read from the passage in which the character Golden Lotus cuckolds her master by lascivious encounters with the young gardener. He said he would play the role of both the young gardener and the master of the house. He brought out a hairbrush with a long tapered handle, which I used to punish the naughty but compliant gardener. After a few smacks, he thanked me, then brought out a whip. He was now the master of the house and I was Golden Lotus. He angrily accused me of infidelity and I pretended to weep as I declared that nothing had happened between the gardener and me except lessons in horticulture. But, as the story went, my pleas were for naught, and Endeavor wielded the whip and I provided the requisite shrieks, begging that he forgive me before he killed me. The whip was constructed so that it was not that painful, but what stung was my humiliation when Endeavor asked me to squirm a bit more and to scream with more realism and volume. At the end of my performance, he was again solicitous and asked if I was cold. He then requested to see me the next evening.

The following evening I performed the purchased shrieking with even more realism. Mansion gave me an extra gift and was voluminous in his gratitude for my being so accommodating. Vermillion was pleased that all went well, and I suspected she knew from the start what had been in store for me. I waited until I had finished both nights before I told Magic Gourd what had happened. She was mad only that I had not told her. She was my attendant and was supposed to watch over me. I had taken away her purpose in life. So that was how I knew that she accepted the need to do whatever was necessary.

Two days later, Perpetual stopped by in the afternoon. He said nothing of that evening at Mansion's party. We talked animatedly about the usual subjects. I was his equal and I was grateful he had renewed my self-respect. I did not have to shriek and humiliate myself. I welcomed him into my bed, and while lying in his arms, he gave me a new poem and asked me to read it aloud so that he could see the words form and spill from my beautiful lips.

> "Untouched paper is the colorless sky.
> When washed by brushes, carapaces emerge,
> vast mountains rise wet against dry clouds.
> With a single hair and meager ink,
> I am a daub of hermit in an ancient crag,
> Who asks the gods where immortality hides.
> But mountain shadows and streaks of cliff
> now block the heavenly sky from view."

I cried. It was a masterly poem. His talent had come back. I had begun to have doubts, but no longer. I told Magic Gourd the news. I told her to sit while I performed it.

"It's pretentious," she said when I finished. "What did you see in it? Is your mind that hazy after sex? It's all about how important he thinks he is—as great as the mountain and the sky, which he believes he created with his brush. How can he be a real scholar? I'm beginning to think the first poem he gave you was not one he wrote."

I resented her belittling him. What did she know about a good poem or a bad one? She was uneducated. And her suspicions about his character were ridiculous. I had never met a man more forthcoming. His confessions about his wife were heartrendingly honest.

"Don't answer right away if he asks you to marry him," she said. "You know next to nothing about him except for his talk-talk-talk about ideas that are useless and that he has written only one good poem. Why does he stay with Mansion? Where is his family home? He said he is from An-hwei, but where? And where does he get his money from?"

"He has a business," I said.

"Mansion *guessed* that he had a business. Now you are saying it's certain? Where is the proof?"

"He can't be poor. He's from a scholar family of ten—"

"Ten, ten, ten. That is what you love, this number of generations. I have had a growing uneasiness about him. I feel in my stomach what you feel in your heart. He claims to be a man of high ideas. Ideas are like air. What does he do with his ideas? He gives opinions and feels important, and you are his audience, who gives him applause in your bed. He criticizes his own poems. Yet he gives you bad ones and thinks they are suitable to be performed. And the grief he had for his wife until he met you—no sex for five years?—that claim alone tells you something is wrong with his head—although more likely that's another one of his lies. And think about this: He has never given you anything, no money for all the tea and snacks he's had. Vermillion told me that she was hoping he would make up for the cost with a few good poems. She told me she's charging us, since nothing came of her temporary generosity. You must think, Violet. Don't be tempted to marry this man. He is not the easy answer to your future."

Until Magic Gourd put up her resistance to him, I had had doubts about my feelings for him. But each suspicion she put up, I knocked down, and love grew stronger out of stubbornness. I reasoned that my conversations with Perpetual about high ideas were far better than listening to a man talk about port treaties and taxes. He admired my mind, which I would always possess, whereas most men wanted charming words that told them how virile they were. When my looks withered, those men would have no interest in applying their virility on me. Perpetual would love me, whether I slept beside him in bed or in a grave. Magic Gourd wanted me to wait until a repulsive rich man collected me as one of his concubines. She would rather I perform degrading scenes from pornographic novels than perform a poem.

The next day I received a letter from Perpetual and another poem. The poem was another masterpiece.

> Vaporous clouds hide the mountain,
> clear pond reflects his majesty.

He said he was the mountain whom no one understood, and I was the pond, whose depth of feeling could show him his best qualities. Those two lines were Perpetual's declaration of love and his wish that I be his wife. I waited three days before telling Magic Gourd that I had decided to marry him. I did not want her to ruin my newfound happiness with her warnings of doom. They came soon enough.

"Are you telling me his gauzy lies have so thoroughly swaddled your judgment?" Magic Gourd said. "Vapors, majesty? What kind of poem is this? He's placed you in the pond and thinks he's majestic for doing so. If you think this poem is a masterpiece, that's proof that you have poetic clouds in your head and can no longer think."

The following day a letter arrived:

Dearest Reflection of My Soul,

In Moon Pond Village, you will no longer be bothered by the decay of Shanghai. You won't have to tolerate the daily boatloads of arrogant foreigners with their coarse habits, slabs of meat, demands, and insults. You won't have to entertain men with rootless morals. There are no conniving madams, no cutthroat competitors.

In my home village, it is peaceful. You will be with like-minded

people. Every evening, you will be able to see the sunset at the
moment of its blazing glory against a pink sky that is not obscured
by columned buildings built by foreigners.

Imagine it, my darling, together we will have all the riches we
need, the beauty of mountains, pond water, and sky that inspired
the poems I wrote for you. You will have the respect of being Wife
in a scholar household, with five generations of family under one
harmonious roof.

Ours will be a simple life, to be sure. You are used to one that is
more exciting. But I feel there is more to all that I have said so far.
It is what I would give you, far more than the equal of what you
have given me when you moved me beyond grief and into joy. I will
shower you with poems in praise of you, which I will read just before
you fall sleep and upon waking, when we will share each new day
as the beginning of love.

Magic Gourd raised one eyebrow. "He certainly has the wooing words. So effortless. And the quiet village life he brags about—*oyo!*—I never knew there were so many advantages to boredom in the backwaters! Of course, those five generations will keep you on your toes. So many people to please, so many arguments, just like a courtesan house. And you'll be busy lighting incense and bowing all day long to revere ten generations of continuous scholars. Their altar table must be ten meters long. Don't give him an answer."

"I already did. I have agreed."

"Then you'll have to go back to him and say you now disagree."

"Why do you think you can decide my life?"

"Because I talked to Mansion today. I asked about Perpetual's business. He said he didn't know if he had a business, since he never talked about one. I asked what he knew about his family. He said he didn't know them at all, only that Perpetual was his second cousin by way of his mother's brother whose wife was the sister of one of Perpetual's aunt. Mansion said his mother might have known more about the family, but she had died long before meeting Perpetual. I asked if he knew anything about Perpetual's dead wife. He was surprised to hear that Perpetual even had a wife. He had never mentioned her. Mansion then said that men don't think to ask these kinds of questions of their relatives. It would be like accusing them of hiding something. And that's exactly what I think Perpetual is doing."

She could not change my mind. Who would I become if I did not take this chance? What would remain of my self-esteem? Waiting for something better was a luxury of young girls. I had a chance to keep my self-respect and to also have respect from others. I could pass the days without worry over where I would live the next month or the next year or when I was old. I would have the leisure to sit in a garden and reflect on my life, my character, and my memories of Edward and Flora. I could form opinions and share them as a peer with my husband. No man was perfect. I was not perfect. We two would come together with our faults, and together we would learn to forgive ourselves and accept inadequacies. We would come with our pain and console each other. We would bring our individual hopes, some impossible, some sentimental, and we would find those we could share and fulfill, perhaps even with a child. If he did not have great wealth, we would still have like-mindedness, which cannot be purchased. And we would have love, not infatuation, not what I had with Edward, but one that would be our own. That love would endure and enable us to hold each other through whatever troubles might come.

I appreciated all that Magic Gourd had done for me over the years. She had been like a mother to me. But I didn't need her approval. She had already threatened she would not accompany me to my husband's home. Her threats over the years had usually proved false. But this time, she might actually make good on it when she learned, as I recently did, that Perpetual's family home was in a little village called Moon Pond, and it was three hundred miles away.

CHAPTER 10

MOON POND VILLAGE

From Shanghai to Moon Pond Village
1925
Violet

Summer heat poured into my body and rose from my face like a damp fever, turning the dust on my face into tears of mud. Then rain came once again and diluted the tears, softened the roads and deepened the ruts, until, once again, we were stuck.

We had started on our journey to Moon Pond three weeks ago. Perpetual had said he would accompany us to make sure we were safe and comfortable. But just days before we were going to leave, he had been called away from Shanghai. He had business somewhere in the south, important matters, he said. He would take a different route to get to Moon Pond, and with luck he might arrive even before we did. We would be perfectly safe traveling alone, he had assured us. The way there was easy and he had never heard of problems with bandits or anything like that. "The worst that can happen," he had said, "is that you'll be bored."

He was right. I was already weary of travel and wondered how I could endure more. We had been moving ever west and inland along a zigzag route no devil would want to follow—past cities, then county seats, and later, smaller and smaller market towns, until there were no trains or trucks, no steamers or tenders, nor barges or poled fishing boats that could take us from one fork to the next. At the last river town, Magic Gourd found a cartman waiting for fools at the dock. He had an honest face and called himself Old Jump, a name that promised he had much industrious experience. He claimed he had the best carriage in five counties, one that had belonged to a warlord. She bargained for the prized carriage, sight unseen, which came with two donkeys, an extra cart, the man's services, and the shoulders of two strong men, who happened to be his addle-minded sons. And now we were jiggling and bouncing over ruts and potholes on the spring-coiled banquette of a rich man's carriage—a broken-down seat that had been yanked out of its high social standing and roped onto a mule cart with a tattered canopy of oilcloth and moth-eaten silk. The cartman still insisted that the contraption was indeed the best, and that Magic Gourd should walk through all five counties if she thought he was lying.

Each morning she cursed Old Jump and his two sons anew for faults besides his dishonesty—such as smiling when there was no reason to do so other than to mock her. "They're the kind of idiots who live in a place named after a pond," she said to me. "You have no idea what village life is like, Little Violet. You might change your mind, but that's all you'll be able to change. Women kill themselves in places like that, because there's no other way to escape."

Today the wind was blowing, and to keep out the dust, she wore a scarf around her neck and face. With just two squinted eyes showing, she looked like one of the mummy-wrapped walking dead. The wind grew stronger and whipped away the scarf. Only moments before, the sky had been filled with cauliflower-headed clouds. Now there was a sea of churning black mushrooms. I had thought we were leaving trouble behind, but maybe we were catching up to it. There were already many signs that we should turn back. The day before yesterday, a cartwheel had come loose, and it took two hours to repair.

Another delay. Yesterday it appeared that a donkey had gone lame. It refused to move for several hours. The wind blew my hair loose and across my face, and raindrops the size of leaves fell on our heads. Before we could jump down to take shelter under the cart, lightning cracked the yellow-green fields of rice. The thick grass swayed in one direction and then the other, as if the field were a living creature, heaving deep breaths as it changed yellow to green. With another bright crack, rain poured all at once, and washed my dirty face and soaked my clothes. In minutes, the downpour softened the ruts and deepened them, so that when we tried to move, we sank and were stuck. Edward had written about a similar predicament in his travelogue. He used boards and swung them like a clock dial, then fell face forward into the mud. I laughed out loud at the memory, which made Old Jump think I was belittling his efforts to extricate us.

Magic Gourd pulled her foot out of her shoe, then her shoe out of the mud. "This may be your fate, but why is mine tied to it? What wrong did I commit to you in a past life? Tell me, so I can make amends and then be on my way. I don't want to come back as your donkey in my next life and have you staring at my ass telling me to go faster."

When we were finally on our way, she said, "Why should we hurry to get there? To meet a bunch of country bumpkins with literati pretensions?"

BEFORE WE LEFT Shanghai, Magic Gourd threw up all sorts of worries to make me reconsider.

"They'll be Confucian down to the tips of their fingers," she said, "the same ones that will yank out your hair when you're slow to obey. You'll have to revere each member of the family in proper order and with the right amount of obeisance from old to young. And your position will be at the bottom with the chickens. You think Mother Ma was cruel? Wait until you work like a slave for a mother-in-law! You can't even imagine it. I lived through it, just barely. My sweet-talking rascal said I'd be free of worries through old age and into heaven. He did not say I would make a detour first to hell in his ancestral village. I couldn't endure it even one month. I said to myself, Why should I die for this idiot's mother? I'd rather be a streetwalker than a concubine."

"I'll be the wife, not a concubine."

"*Oyo!* You think they'd treat you any better, a fancy woman from Shanghai with your American face? Look down at those big flapping feet of yours. People from the countryside will be shocked to see them. And those lizard-green eyes. They'll think you're a fox-maiden. They'll pounce on every mistake you make. You'll have to swallow being unjustly accused, speak sparingly and never complain, endure gossip about you without showing anger, and agree heartily that the old ways are best." And then she said in a false simpering voice: "Yes, Mother-in-law, you are wise to slap me so I can learn." Her hands imitated mincing steps going backward in retreat. "You better practice now."

Surely there were some mothers-in-law who were either kind or stupid. And even if Perpetual's mother turned out to be cruel, I could gradually change whatever I did not like. I was clever. It would simply take time. Besides, a mother-in-law could not live forever. My biggest worry was boredom.

For my role as Perpetual's wife, I went to the tailor and asked him to make me the proper attire of a scholar's wife and capable daughter-in-law.

"A wife! *Oyo!*" he crowed. "You must have put the jealous worm in every courtesan's stomach. I've made clothes for very few who graduated to a position like yours."

"I'll be living in their countryside estate in An-hwei—the ancestral home of a scholar family. Ten generations. Did you know that many famous scholars come from An-hwei? It may not be as glamorous as Shanghai, but it will be civilized, more like a scholar's retreat. The clothes should not be too fancy or modern. No Western touches like last season's clothes. I am guessing they are a bit traditional out there. Of course, that does not mean my clothes have to be hideously old-fashioned."

"I will make them look more historic in style—like the clothes of heroines in romantic novels."

"Don't use the style of the tragic characters," I said. "I don't want to wear a memorial to their bad fate."

The tailor made four fancy jackets, one for each season. The work was as fine as usual, the silk was the best, smooth and not slippery, glossy but not shiny. But they lacked, in my opinion, any hint of the historic. They were dowdy, like the clothes that faithful widows wore so as to not incite lust, so voluminous that two more of me could have fit inside them. The tailor assured me I looked the epitome of a lady of noble birth. He also made three simple costumes for daily wear, without embroidery. The winter jackets had a silk padding, instead of thick cotton. The summer clothes had a cotton lining as fine as baby hair, and the halter underneath was of the same light cloth. The placket was plain. The shape of the jacket was similar to what I had had made years ago in a style Magic Gourd had called "breezy." It fit more tightly at the top and widened toward the bottom. And the slits on the sides ran past my waist and were loosely held together with small frog clasps. The clothes were still sedate in appearance and would be suitable for a life of repose and garden reverie. At the last minute, I packed a few of my *chi-paos*, choosing ones without too high a collar or too long a side slit. It might turn out that Moon Pond Village was less of a backwater than I thought.

Perpetual had chosen my new name the night before he left on his business trip: Xi Yu, "Fine Rain," taken from the famous lines of the Tang poet Li Shangyin, whom we both admired. The choice suggested that I was from a family of literati, which, in some respects, was true. My Western mother had been educated in America, and she and tutors had schooled me to be literate in both Chinese and English. We would not, however, explain that to his family. I later cursed when I remembered that Li Shangyin was famed for romanticizing illicit love. If his family was scholarly, they might recognize the origins of the name. It was too late to tell Perpetual we had to choose another.

Beyond the unsuitable name, I worried about his family's reaction to my slightly Western appearance. Perpetual had told me he would think of a way to make it acceptable. If they had objections, I would surely be able to win them over. I had supplied him with the made-up lineage of the Manchu family distantly related to royalty and from a northern part of China, where a thousand years ago invaders of all races galloped back and forth. To bolster the story, Magic Gourd dyed my hair black.

Just when I had solved one problem, Magic Gourd threw up another: "His mother will wonder why you are so old and never married. For me, it is easy. I'll say I'm a widow to an honorable bureaucrat who never took bribes, and hence, as a woman of modest means, I have led a traditional, quiet, and mournful life. As virtue requires, I have never given in to men tempting me to remarry."

"You'll have a hard time convincing them that's true if you can't control your temper and foul mouth."

"And you better not say you're a widow. You'll also have to explain your relationship to me."

"Mother and daughter?" I said, and waited for her to cite one of her fluctuating ages.

"*Chh!* How could I be old enough to be your mother? We are only twelve years apart. I'll be your older sister instead." She quickly corrected herself. "That is, *if* I decide to go with you. I don't recall whether you actually asked."

This had been an ongoing accusation because of my having stupidly said to her: "Where else would you go?"

She accused me of handing her pity for a beggar. I said I had already told Perpetual I could not possibly go alone to his village without her as my companion—companion, not beggar. She said a companion could be anyone—a cat, even. I might find many companions in my new home.

"You are going there to be Perpetual's wife. You have a purpose. If I serve no purpose, I shouldn't come. I don't want to go all the way there and discover that. I can make my own way in life. You don't have to pity me." A few minutes later, she said, "But if there is a reason and I decide to go, I'll need a name as well." She said aloud the possibilities. Some were coquettish, others were too literary for her level of education. She finally chose Wan Xia, "Dusk Glow," which, in my opinion, was ridiculous. There was nothing about her that gradually faded. "Lightning" or "Thunderstorm" would have suited her better.

Magic Gourd had waited until the day before we were due to leave to come up with her face-saving reason for accompanying me: "Little Violet, I just heard something terrible from one of the maids. She worked for a Chinese scholar family about twenty-five years ago. An American girl became the eldest Chinese son's concubine. He brought her home and his mother treated the girl like a slave. No matter what the American girl did, she could not please anyone in the family, including her husband. Soon after joining the household, her mother-in-law beat her to death, and no one did a thing about it. The American side said they could not interfere in Chinese family matters, and it was the reason they discouraged Americans from marrying Chinese. The Chinese side said she deserved it because she was insolent. It's the truth! She died because of American insolence in her blood and there was no one there to protect her."

She waited for my reaction. I had told her that story years ago. I overheard my mother and Golden Dove talking about it. But I knew what I was supposed to say. "*Ai-ya!* I'm so glad you're coming with me! You must protect me against anything like that happening. You're willing to do that for me, aren't you?"

ON OUR JOURNEY, Magic Gourd often gave me sisterly wisdom that would be useful in adjusting to my new life.

"Soon you won't need that book you're reading. You'll be busy embroidering handkerchiefs until your eyes dry up and go blind. And forget about eating what you want and when you want. There's no restaurant in those backwaters, no runners to get what your tongue desires. You can't send the soup back to the kitchen just because it's a little oily. What you'll get is yesterday's food that nobody touched because it was already rotten. And here's the worst. You'll have to rise at dawn every day. The only times you've seen the sunrise is when you haven't yet gone to bed. That's life in the countryside. I remember."

She was interrupted by the guffaws of the two sons who had been telling jokes. ". . . That idiot from Dog Tail Village believed the conniver, paid two cents for flying feathers, and jumped off a cliff. The idiot said he doubted the feathers would work, but he didn't want to waste two cents."

The old cartman rushed over and beat his sons with a crop. "I'll crack your heads open and take out whatever shit and piss are in your brains that makes you too stupid to understand what it means to work."

"You see!" Magic Gourd said. "That's the kind of vulgar talk you'll hear from now on."

Magic Gourd had gone mad. It was as if she had an unreachable itch, she could not stop digging up warnings and stories of suicidal escape, and soon I would lose my mind as well.

"We had so much freedom in Shanghai," I heard Magic Gourd say in a wistful voice. She started up with the same arguments she had made when we were in Shanghai, the identical words: "You should have taken my advice and used your savings to start your own house. We could have gone to another city where the rent was cheaper, and with little competition. But instead, you wanted to become a respectable wife. Did you give him all your money? What about your jewels? And for what? To be respectable in a place where hermits go to die! With our two brains, we could have thought of something—"

"Two brains? These ideas are brainless, as foolish as my dream of marriage. What would have happened if we had followed your plan? If we failed, what would become of you and me? We're too old to start off on our own. You're already close to fifty."

"*Wah!* Fifty? Now you're adding years to insult me?"

"If I had stayed in Shanghai, I would have soon been headed for a cheap brothel in the Japanese Concession, where I would have had to spread my legs as soon as a customer called my name. That's where you were headed before I let you be my attendant."

Magic Gourd leaned back. "*Oyo!* You let me be your attendant?" She huffed and lowered herself out of the carriage. "No gratitude! If you don't want to listen to me, fine. I'll never speak about this again. I'll never say anything to you for the rest of my life. You're a ghost as far as I'm concerned. As soon as we reach the next town, I'll be on my way back and out of your life. I promise you that. Forever. Do you hear me? Then we'll both be happy!"

She had often rewarded me over the years with days of silence. Unfortunately, this time, after only two hours, she broke her promise and resumed her harangue.

"One day, you'll weep over my grave and say, 'Magic Gourd, you were right, I was stupid. If I had listened, I would not be lying in a cheap shack in Moon Pond letting peasants have a go at me for two cents a poke. I would still be a human being with a name and a mind that remembered who I could have been . . .' "

I stopped listening. I had already tormented myself with everything she had said—and with even more than that. I had changed my life so many times, had stepped onto the stage so often to create an illusion of love, that I no longer remember what love really was. I looked at the ring Perpetual had given me: one thin band that was so easily crushed. I was traveling three hundred miles to pretend to be someone I was not, to live with a man I had had to convince myself to love. I was chasing after happiness, that false salvation, all the way to a desolate place. I might not find it. And if I did, it might simply be the illusion I had created in my mind, and if I held on to it as real, I would exist only as part of that illusion.

I had once feared this might happen to Little Flora. I used to look at her and Edward's photographs each night until Perpetual said it bothered him that I might be thinking of Edward while he was making love to me—at any moment—comparing him to Edward, wishing I was with Flora. So I put away the photographs. But I still recited to Little Flora the words that would keep her strong until I found her: "Resist much, obey little."

As THE DAYS plodded on, I regretted not having clothes made for suffering in hot sun and pouring rain. From among my simple summer jackets, I had chosen the one I liked best, a green gauze silk. It pained me when the first blotches of dirt appeared on the sleeves. The jacket's panels looked like funeral banners as the wind whipped them sideways.

Magic Gourd was now in a sentimental mood and was tallying all the comforts and pleasures we were leaving behind: the storytelling halls, the music, the singing, our freedom to laugh, and also our shocking clothes, which had left a wake of envy among women who called themselves respectable. And what about the bets we had made for our patrons at the gambling table and the money we received when the bets were lucky?

"Remember the carriage rides we took with our clients," she said, "how much fun we had as we rode through the city, waving to pious women making offerings at temples? Remember how we laughed when foreign women scowled and their husbands leered at us. Think of the many men who admired you, swooned over you, and bestowed you with gifts. Those were the days and now they're done . . ."

I closed my eyes and pretended to doze.

The cart stopped, and when I opened my eyes, I realized I had indeed been dozing. On the right side of the road was the steep slope of a mountain. On the left was a cliff. About a hundred feet in front, the road was covered by a mudslide that had swept away another cart—only ten minutes before, a boy told us. An entire family of six people went over when their cart became a boat carrying them to death in a waterfall of mud. "You can't see any of them," he said, "except for one arm and the top of a head. The arm stopped waving a while ago." He gestured for us to come look. Everyone did, even Magic Gourd, but I stayed by the cart. Why did I need to see some-one else's bad luck? To feel glad it was not mine? To scare myself into thinking it still might be?

The road was impassable, Old Jump announced. We had to turn back, but he knew of a shortcut that would save us time. We soon learned the shortcut was not even a road, just a path through a rape-seed field and barely wide enough for the wheels of the cart. As we plunged forward, Old Jump praised himself. "You see? What books would tell you where to go?" A few hours later, Old Jump cursed and the donkeys stopped. The path was cut with a zigzag of trenches so that a cartwheel or donkey leg could not avoid slipping in one. We turned around and cut through another field, and hours later, we came upon a blockade of huge boulders that would take ten men to move. We took another route. That farmer had dug a maze of holes with broken clay shards awaiting those who fell in. "Hatred makes men clever," Jump muttered. We were now three days behind where we should have been, rolling backward because we could not turn the cart around. At this rate, Perpetual would likely arrive at his home before we did. I would prefer it.

"Good news," Old Jump announced a few days later. "We will soon reach Magnificent Canal. From there, we cross the river by ferry, and then we are only two days from Moon Pond Village." The town, he said, was a bustling port and county seat. The river was choked with boats and sampans bringing in food of all kinds. We would have our choice of a dozen inns. "Clean enough to please even you," he said, looking at Magic Gourd. "I haven't been there since I was a young man, but I still remember it sharp as yesterday. The outdoor theater and acrobats, little boys stacked hands on hands, then feet on feet, then hands on hands. The girls were prettier than ones I'd seen anywhere else. Nice and shy, too. Oh, and those spicy snacks—I've been savoring them in my memory ever since . . ."

Whatever he had savored would remain a memory. Magnificent Canal had no canal, no river, not even a trickle. It was a flat plain of silt. Old Jump ran back and forth, cursing. "I must have taken the wrong road." A man standing in a dark doorway said, "It's the same place."

We learned that twenty years before, the river that had fed the canal flooded and changed course, drowning many villages in both its old and new path. When the floodwaters receded, it left behind a colorless ghost town. The only inhabitants were old folks who wanted to be buried in their ancestral home beside those family members who had drowned.

"What fate brought me here to see this?" Magic Gourd said. "Why this?"

Old Jump snapped, "Don't blame me! You think I know every disaster that's happened over the last twenty years?"

One lane of the town remained, and its buildings were covered with the soot of cooking fires, which gave the town the appearance of having nearly burned down. A badly listing teahouse was propped up by a splintered beam of wood. Why bother? If you stepped inside for tea, the place would become your casket. The stage of the acrobat theater had caved in and the cavity contained whatever the floodwaters had brought—broken buckets, sickles, and stools. I shuddered to think that the owners of those everyday things might be underneath the heap.

The innkeeper was overjoyed to see us, his first customers in over twenty years. As he led us to our quarters, he boasted about a duke who had nearly passed through Magnificent Canal. "We built a grand archway painted red and gold, carved with dragons at the corners. We also widened the road, planted trees, spruced up the temple, washed the gods, and patched them up . . . But then the flood came."

When he opened the door to our room, swirls of dust rose, as if a ghost tenant had awakened. A skeletal wooden bed held a nest of dead mice, and the quilt was nothing more than feathery shreds. This was not the worst we had seen along our journey. In some places, the mice were still alive. Magic Gourd and I removed the mess and washed down the floor. We set our mats down on the bed's bare wooden platform. I slept fitfully. Magic Gourd shrieked often, waking me, one time claiming she had opened her eyes to see a rat twitching his whiskers, as if he were deciding which of her ears to eat first. Then I screamed because I saw it above us, crossing along a crossbeam. The next morning, we saw Old Jump talking to one of the local farmers, a man with handsome features so leathered by the sun he could have been any age between thirty and fifty. He eyed me, and I heard Old Jump explaining that I looked foreign but was actually Chinese.

"Good news, miss," Old Jump said, full of smiles. "This man knows exactly how to go from here to there. There's a hard clay road up ahead. The flood washed away the rocks and filled the potholes, and the drought baked the clay good and hard. Hardly anyone uses it, so there aren't any ruts."

"If it's so good, why doesn't anyone use it?" I said.

"Everyone calls it the Ghost Road," the man replied, "because a whole village higher up got swept down the mountain—houses, people, cows—and they were all ground up and washed down to the next landing of the road where this tragic sludge became a smooth white road. That's what people say, anyway."

Old Jump was no longer smiling. "You've been on this road?"

The man paused. "I have no reason to go in that direction," he said. "You can take another road going east, but it's a day out of your way. The road is not as smooth, and in the last few years, brigands have attacked people. I heard they killed only a couple of people this year. It was much worse in the past because of famine. You can hardly blame them. They had to eat. If you decide to go that way, you shouldn't worry too much. They've been using some old muskets left by foreign trappers who died, and they don't fire half the time. Anyway, it's your choice."

Old Jump nodded uneasily. "We'll take the shortest route."

"The Ghost Road it is. Listen carefully then. You take this road toward the west, and at the next village, where the road divides, go west again. That's about two days from here. Then you'll get to that white stretch with the bones I told you about. That'll take another two days. When you reach a place where you can keep going west on Ghost Road or turn north and take a rough road, go north, and head upward for another two days. Where the road splits, take the left toward the Undulating Hills. You can't miss them. They look like buttocks and breasts. You'll enjoy a couple of days winding in and out of those." He looked at Magic Gourd and me. "Pardon me." He grinned at Old Jump. "Go through a narrow opening between two hills. Once you come out of those hills, you'll be looking down on a long narrow valley between low mountains and a river wiggling down the middle. At the end of the valley are five mountains. Moon Pond lies at the foot of those mountains. You'll know you've arrived because the road ends there. They're tall mountains, so don't be fooled into thinking you're almost there. You'll need a full day just to wind down the Undulating Hills. And you better have plenty of rope fastened to the sides of your carts. The road down is steeper than it looks. Grab on to keep your load from pushing those donkeys over the ledge. There's a village at the bottom. You can stay there or go another seven or eight hours to reach Moon Pond."

Two days later, when we reached the Ghost Road, Magic Gourd, Old Jump, and his sons fell quiet. They stared at the white ground. The road looked to me like ordinary clay.

"It's whiter," Magic Gourd said, "like bones dug up by grave robbers. I've seen bones this color in the village where I lived with the mean mother-in-law."

We rolled ahead. One of the wheels creaked like a wounded animal. Every time we heard sounds in the woods, Magic Gourd gasped and grabbed onto my arm. I felt a chill run through me before I told her to stop being ridiculous. Old Jump let the donkeys rest only briefly, and they protested when water was taken away too soon.

"How can you believe this ghost nonsense?" I said to Magic Gourd.

"What's nonsense in Shanghai is not nonsense in the countryside. Those who don't heed the warnings don't live to admit they were stupid not to do so." At nightfall, Old Jump and his son argued whether it was better to keep going, or to stop for the night and place one man on guard. The donkeys balked and made the decision for us. If they died of exhaustion, we'd be stuck there for good. Whenever we heard rustles in the bushes, the sons shouted and jabbed the air with their long knives—as if they could kill a ghost that was already dead.

We started again just before dawn, and by mid-morning, the wheels crunched noisily over pits and rocks. We had left the Ghost Road and were on the rough one headed north. We moved through the Undulating Hills. Just before dusk the next day, we reached the opening squeezed by two hills. We saw the valley below and a twisting river running its length. It was bounded by low hills that had been carved with terraced rice paddies, which were just now turning the gold-tinged green of harvest. At the far end were the dark shadow heads of four mountains, each one rising above the other. Between the second and third was a dark thundercloud with a pink udder. Sunlight shot through it and the land beneath it glowed. Moon Pond lay in that light.

It was beautiful, yet it gave me an ominous feeling. All at once, I knew why. I had seen a valley like this many times, the one in the paintings Lu Shing had given to my mother and to Edward. I was looking at the Valley of Amazement. Had I always been destined to come here? I had secretly examined that painting a dozen times.

Edward believed the valley was illuminated at dawn, at the waking hour. And I had said it was dusk, when life closes down. He thought the dark clouds were leaving and that the storm was over. I thought it was about to begin. And so we were both right and wrong. It was dusk, and the storm was leaving.

"Only four mountains, not five," Magic Gourd said. "That farmer can't count."

Four mountains. The painting had five, two on one side of the golden opening, three on the other. The sky shifted and the thundercloud moved slightly, and we saw the fifth, an enormous dark mountain that lay just beyond the other four. The painting had been an omen. I looked for ways it was different and I found them. Here the valley was longer, and the hills were terraced with rice paddies. The mountains in the other were more jagged along the ridge. In fact, other than the five mountains, a river valley, and stormy clouds, it hardly looked the same. In the painting, there was something at the back that glowed. Here there were just the mountains.

The valley gradually took on its own shape and coloring. It was not gloomy, I told myself. Dusk would bring a close to my past and leave it behind as a secret. Tomorrow would be a bright beginning. I would be a Wife. Perpetual would be there to welcome me, and we would live the serene life of scholars in repose. We would walk in the mountains, and we would both be inspired to write poems. Who knows, we might even have a child together. All at once, sadness rolled over me as I thought about Little Flora. By living so far from the sea, I would never be able to find her. I would have to insist to Perpetual that I return to Shanghai to see if there had been any word.

We stepped out of the cart and Old Jump led the donkeys down the path. The sun fell and we saw the smoky glow of cooking fires. We passed through a lane of houses along the river and reached a small market square with a temple at one end. A man called out from the dark mouth of a wine shop that we should stop to quench our thirst. Old Jump was happy to accept his invitation. We stood in the cool shadow of a stone wall. Men, women, children, and even dogs were staring at us. I saw the wine seller giving directions to Old Jump. He pointed to some unknown place ahead, angled his head one way and bent his hand in the same direction, then twisted his body sharply, and rose up on his toes as he looked down at some imaginary danger we might fall into. As he continued to look downward, he again rose on his toes, gritted his teeth, and then he sank to his knees and bounced up. His hands moved downward, wiggling like the tail of a thrashing fish. Suddenly, he went still. His arms shot straight forward, and he cocked one eye, as if staring through a telescope. Then his arms fell to his sides and he gave Old Jump a satisfied look to indicate we had safely arrived in Moon Pond. Old Jump repeated the gestures, and the man nodded and corrected him twice. Satisfied, Old Jump bought the man a small bottle of wine, and the man again pointed in the direction we should go and shot his hand forward, as if we would now travel even faster. Two other young men came out of the shop's doorway and leered at me. They made no effort to lower their voices as they discussed my foreigner looks and wondered what I tasted like in bed.

"Fuck your mother," Magic Gourd said.

They laughed.

Old Jump returned after paying. "Good news—" he started to say.

Magic Gourd cut him off. "Stop saying good news *this,* good news *that.* It's like a curse."

"All right, I'll tell the bride," and he faced me. "There's a widow who went mad after her husband died. She can't stop washing the walls and floors, except when she welcomes boarders."

That evening, I took a cool bath. As I twisted mud out of my hair, the madwoman dragged in another small wooden tub with clean water, and had me climb in, then removed the other. She did this twice more until I insisted I had nothing more to wash off but my own skin.

We woke early the next morning. I slipped into my clothes. The madwoman had shaken the dust off them. It was the leaf-green jacket and trousers. Magic Gourd put on a deep blue jacket. We had never worn such dowdy clothes, but when the widow saw us, her eyes and mouth rounded, and for the first time, I heard her speak. "I can die in peace," she said in a rustic accent, "knowing the wives of the gods took a bath in my house." I was pleased we had given that impression. These were the clothes I would wear to meet my new mother-in-law and the rest of the clan. And I would see Perpetual. Counting all our delays, we were over a week behind schedule.

As we mounted the carts, the heat sank into my body. The cart-wheels once again turned, milling dust onto our faces and clothes. Every now and again, we slapped at each other's clothes and raised small choking clouds. The wind gusted and the fine grit clung to us again. As we drew nearer, the sky was blocked by the wall of Heaven Mountain and its four sons. We rode now in their shade.

"The closer we come, the less we see," I murmured.

"We'll be blind by the time we arrive," Magic Gourd replied.

We were quiet the rest of the way. I grew more and more nervous, imagining Perpetual's family, scholarly yet old-fashioned, friendly in a fussy way, lamenting the many difficulties we'd had in reaching them. I imagined a grand courtyard house, the beautiful pond with the mountain in its mirror. The road wound next to the river, and on both sides farmers were harvesting the rice, splaying the grain where they slashed. They stopped work to stare at us, blank-faced.

We reached a narrow and dilapidated bridge, clearly what we had been warned was the perilous part of the journey. The water ran fast, streamed over large boulders and churned at the bottom of them with such force we had to shout to be heard. Across the river, we reached the main road leading into the village, which quickly nar-rowed into a path that tunneled between the outer walls of houses. A few minutes later, the path opened onto a market square next to a pillared temple with peeling red lacquer. It was an hour before dusk and most of the food vendors had already left, but there were still a few stalls that displayed baskets, funeral necessities, wine, salt, tea, and plain cloth. My life was changing for the worse second by second. Past the square, we entered another tunnel. We emerged, and straight ahead was a large round pond. It was not clear blue but green with algae. And it was not ringed with trees and grassy banks, as I had imagined. On both sides stood a mishmash of poor houses, misaligned with the one next to it. They resembled the upper and lower crooked teeth of a green yawning mouth. At the farthest point was a two-story house whose dark roof stood above fortresslike walls. It was grand in comparison to the other houses. But it was much smaller than I had imagined—much smaller than Lu Shing's home, which I realized now I had copied in my mind as my future home. I looked at Magic Gourd. Her eyes were rounded in astonishment.

"Am I seeing a dream of my past?" she said. "I hope the road goes far beyond this place and to another pond and house."

My mouth went dry. "I'm parched to death," I said to Magic Gourd. "As soon as we get there, tell the servants to bring us tea at once, and hot towels, as well."

"*Oyo!* I am your older sister, not your underling. You'll soon be serving *me* as penance for where you've taken me."

Magic Gourd's wind-whipped hair looked like an abandoned swallow's nest. Mine must have looked equally bad. We told Old Jump to stop and I found my traveling vanity kit. I lifted the lid and the mirror popped up. When I wiped away the grime, I gasped to see my dust-filled wrinkles. Two and a half months of sun and wind had transformed me into an old lady. I frantically pulled open the little drawers to find the jar of pearl cream. Some of those extra years were wiped away. We helped each other smooth and bundle our hair tightly at the back. Finally, we were ready. I told Old Jump to send one of his boys ahead to announce we were about to arrive. That way the family could quickly prepare a welcome for us.

We reached the outer walls of the Sheng family house. The

white plaster was cracked, and in some places, there were big patches of exposed clay bricks. Why had the house fallen into such disrepair? You did not need much money to smooth doors and repair hinges. Perhaps the servants had become lazy without the guidance of a wife.

The cart stopped at last, the wheels went silent. We were at the front gates. They were the height of two men. No one was there to greet us. For a while, I heard only the heaving breath and snorts of the tired donkeys and the thumping of my heart.

Old Jump called out, "Hey! We've arrived!"

The gates remained shut. A lazy gatekeeper must have fallen asleep. Old Jump ran his fingers over the bronze latches. Only a few sheaves of curled red lacquer remained on the two wooden doors. He looked up at the carved stone plaque at the top of the gate. They held some writing, but the plaque was too damaged to make out what it said. "Not bad," Old Jump said. "You can tell these were people of wealth and class at one time."

After the third shout, we heard a man shout back and then the scraping sound of the gate bolt as it slid to unleash the two thick doors. No firecrackers went off, no red banners flapped before us. It must not be the custom out here. Where was Perpetual?

Six women and six children stood stock-still and silent in the bare courtyard. Respectfully reserved, I figured, in an old-fashioned way. Their clothes were well made but of dull-colored cloth and in somber hues of blue, brown, and gray, and, as I had feared, in the style of widows and old women. Even the younger women were dressed like this. The clothes we had brought were not fashionable in Shanghai, but here they were unfortunate. We were peacocks among crows. Bedraggled peacocks. Perhaps they were waiting for me to speak first, as is the case with imperial visitors. Didn't Magic Gourd say their traditions harkened back thousands of years? Perpetual had said five generations lived under one roof. I quickly studied the faces of those who should receive my obsequious words. The oldest woman must be the great-grandmother. She had the driest face I had ever seen. Her eyes looked dull, as they do on those who are soon to depart this life. Another old woman had fewer wrinkles. The grandmother, I deduced, and the woman who was his mother was likely the woman with the stoniest face and upright posture, the mother-in-law I would have to win over or conquer. Sweet talk was necessary for now. There were two other women, one younger than me and another a little older. She wore a hairstyle that had been fashionable in Shanghai several years ago: parted at the middle, creating two curved locks that framed her face. I gave them no more than a glance, since they were less important. I searched for Perpetual's son. There were five boys and an older girl, and I soon recognized his four-year-old son by his ears, eyes, and eyebrows. He was studying my unbound feet.

My new mother-in-law finally spoke in a harsh voice. "So you have arrived. What do you think of your new home? Surprised? Pleased?"

I recited the stilted phrases I had rehearsed—extolling the reputation of their family, its ten generations of virtue, my honor in joining them as the First Wife of their eldest son, stopping short of saying I was undeserving of this position.

She turned to the woman with the curved lock hairstyle and said something, which caused the woman to tilt her chin up, and sneer at me, as if I had just insulted her. I noticed that she was actually quite striking.

Magic Gourd chattered in a simpering voice, "We were worried the entire journey that you were growing impatient. The roads, the weather, and there was a perilous mudslide that nearly swept us away—"

The mother-in-law cut her off. "We knew when to expect you. We even knew the color of your theatrical clothes."

Theatrical! Did she mean to insult us? Two men at the far end of the courtyard waved to us. The leering sons of the wine seller.

Old Jump yelled at his sons to unload our belongings. They smacked the ground and a halo of dust rose around them. A servant looked warily at the mother-in-law.

"Put her in the north wing," the mother-in-law said.

North! That was the worst corner of any house, the direction of wind and cold sun. Surely Perpetual would not have his rooms there. Or was it tradition to place a bride far from the main wing until the official marriage ceremony?

"And put her maid's things in the room next to hers."

Magic Gourd tilted her head and put on a fake small smile. "I apologize to even mention this. I am her elder sister, not her maid—"

"We know who you are," the mother-in-law cut in, "and what you both did in Shanghai." She sniffed. "This isn't the first time Perpetual has brought back a whore as a concubine." She looked at me. "But you're the first foreign mix."

I was too stunned to think or speak. Magic Gourd talked excitedly, "She was no common whore. She was—" She stopped herself just in time. She straightened up, gathered herself, and said in an authoritative voice, "She has come here as Wife, not concubine. That was the promise. Why else would we come all the way from Shanghai? You must talk to Perpetual to correct this misunderstanding."

"A maid is not allowed to say what I must do. I'll beat you senseless if you try that again."

My own senses returned, and I grabbed Magic Gourd's arm. "Never mind. When Perpetual returns, we'll put this in order." Finally I understood what this ill-treatment by a future mother-in-law was about. Did this rusticated bitch think I would be cowed? I had the skill to defeat the plots of courtesans and madams. She was no match for me. I would simply have to be patient and learn what was most important to her. There lay her weakness, which I would expose and wound.

"We're tired," I said. "Please show us to our rooms." The woman with the handsome face told the mother-in-law she would take us there. And the mother-in-law gave her an odd smile.

As we passed through the house, I noticed an odd combination of new furniture and old in ill repair. The altar table was large, of good quality, but the top was burned. The ancestor paintings had been torn in half and clumsily repaired. We went through the corridors of two courtyards, and finally we reached the farthermost courtyard, a neglected small place, more like an alleyway, and with only two bushes, a skinny scholar rock propped next to a dry pond, and two lichen-spotted benches. A spider's web lay across the door, as if to keep me from entering. I swept it aside and opened the door. It was worse than I had expected—furnished with a rickety-framed bed, without curtains on its sides, a wardrobe closet of cheap wood, a low stool, a bench, and, underneath the bed, a short wooden chamber pot. The room had been swept, but the corner pockets were dirty. If I stood in the center of the room, I could take only one step in any direction before I bumped into the furniture.

Magic Gourd peered into her room from the doorway. "*Oyo!* I am living in a chicken coop. Where are my eggs?" It held only a narrow bed, stool, and chamber pot. She cursed repeatedly. "What manners do people have here? We were not offered tea or food, only insults. They called me a maid!" She turned around and said to the handsome woman. "Why are you still here? To take glee in our misery?"

The woman called to a maid passing through the corridor. "Bring tea, peanuts, and fruits." Our bags arrived. I would not bother to open them. Perpetual would come any day now, and then my belongings would be placed in his room. I would have to see what I could do about Magic Gourd and her accommodations. I could not solve everything at once. We sat in the courtyard, and when the tea arrived, we drank greedily, dispensing with the dainty sips between idle chat. Why should I bother to impress this woman with my manners?

"Who are you?" I asked the woman.

"I'm Second Wife," she said simply.

I was astonished that she spoke Shanghainese. She must be the concubine of Perpetual's brother, or uncle, or cousin.

"That makes you Number Three," the woman said. "You can bow to me later."

Who was this Shanghainese woman? "You may be Second Wife or Sixteenth Wife to someone else in this house," I said. "But I am First Wife to Perpetual."

"Shall I do you the favor of telling you what kind of household you've come to? It will save you from as many beatings and heartache as I endured. Your shock and disbelief will only entertain others in this house."

"What nonsense," Magic Gourd muttered. She held herself stiffly, a sign she was nervous. "I'm sure you'll concoct all sorts of lies in hopes you can drive us away. If we leave, it will be because we choose to do so."

"I would not do that, Auntie," she said to Magic Gourd.

Magic Gourd shot back: "I'm not your auntie or anyone's maid, *Elder* Sister." It was a weak insult. The woman was at least ten years younger.

"Even if I wanted to chase you away, how could I? Where would you go instead? The man with the cart has left. You cannot hire another in this village. And why should I lie? I have nothing to hide. Anyone else in this house will tell you the same. You are Perpetual's Third Wife, just another Shanghainese courtesan who came here for a comfortable future."

My heart and head were pounding.

"Did Perpetual tell you about a first wife?" she said. "Azure. His true love before he met you. As smart as a scholar. Dead at age seventeen. Or was it twenty? Such a sad story, wasn't it?"

"He told me," I said. "There are no secrets between husband and wife."

"Then why didn't he tell you about me?"

What trap was she setting?

"Still don't believe me?" she said with mock disappointment. "Let me guess. Did he recite this poem: 'It was an endless time before we met, but longer still since she left.' Did he fail to say it was Li Shang-yin who wrote that?" I wanted to slap her to make her stop.

"You see!" Magic Gourd said. "I knew that man was a trickster."

"It's a poem that causes many a woman to lose her heart," she said. "Ah, I can see you are losing your doubt in me and growing doubt over him. The knife of knowledge is piercing your brain. It takes time to adjust, but once you learn your place, you and I will get along. But if you fight me, I will have to make your life miserable. Don't forget that we've all been courtesans and know the art of destroying each other. When we come to the end of our golden days in the flower house, we don't change our character. We still need to avoid being trampled."

Magic Gourd sneered. "What does a streetwalker know about golden days?"

"You don't remember the name Luscious Peach?"

There had been a celebrated courtesan by that name who came several times to my mother's house on party calls. It was always a big occasion when she did. But she could not possibly be the same. The Luscious Peach I knew had firm round cheeks and a gay manner, as if she were always amused by everything she noticed. This woman had dull skin. She had more of the no-nonsense harshness of a madam. She stood up and walked in front of us, and transformed into an age-less beauty, moving with the flowing water style, reminiscent of the old days. Her limbs were soft and loose, her hips gently swayed, her shoulders moved in turn, and her head tipped back and forth ever so slightly, all with a perfect rhythm of ease. It was the look of a seduc-tress, an adept yet pliant woman. Luscious Peach had been famous for it. No one could copy exactly how she walked and what she had done, though we had all tried.

She smiled, victorious. "I'm known as Pomelo now—a bit drier than a peach. I came for the same reason you did. A few poems, honorable wife in a scholar family, a fear for my future. When I arrived, I learned his wife was still alive. You heard right. She never died. He only hoped that she would. You've already met her. The woman who spoke to you when you arrived."

"I spoke only to the mother-in-law."

"That was Azure, First Wife. As you saw, she is quite healthy."

I felt the same as I had when my mother left me, not anguish, but anger rising as I realized all the ways I had been duped. What else would I learn?

"I think you've heard enough for now," Pomelo said. "It is too much to understand all at once. Just remember, we are not the only ones."

"There are others here?" I asked.

"Two others—at least two—but no longer. I knew one but not the other. Come to my courtyard tomorrow afternoon. The west side. We can have lunch and I will then tell you more about this house and how we happen to be here."

I couldn't speak. I expected Magic Gourd to recount all the warnings she had given me, all the reasons why she had not trusted Perpetual. She could have blamed me for a stupid decision that had brought her to this same madhouse. Instead, she looked at me with a sad mouth and pained eyes.

"Fuck his mother," she said, "fuck his uncle and fuck his wife's rotten cunt. What a pile of shit he fed you. He should lick his own anus where all it came from. And then a dog and a monkey should fuck his ass."

I went to my room. I took off the silk jacket and used it to wipe the dirt out of the corners of the room, cursing him the whole while. "Fuck his mother, fuck his uncle . . ." I opened the valise where I kept those things most precious to me. I pulled out his poems between stiff covers. I spit on them and tore them to pieces, then put them in the chamber pot and pissed on them. I took out Edward's and Little

Flora's photographs and I placed them on the bed. I said to them, "I've never loved anyone else," and I felt victorious because it was true.

The next day, Magic Gourd told me the wall between us was thin and she could hear that I forgot to say that a dog and a monkey should fuck Perpetual's ass. "You also didn't cry," she said.

"Didn't you hear me vomit?" Throughout the night, I had been gathering in my mind pieces of what had happened, what he had told me, what I had offered, what he had taken and what he refused until I offered it again. I compared those pieces against what we knew so far, and it was enough to make me sick. I didn't even know who he was.

"We have to leave this place," I said.

"How? We have no money, none of our jewelry. Don't you remember? He said to put it in a strongbox that he would carry for you. And then we went separate ways."

A maid came and announced the family was gathering for breakfast. I told her we were sick and pointed to the chamber pot. Magic Gourd claimed the same. We did not want to see the others until we knew more. At noon, we went to Pomelo's courtyard on the west wing. We sat outside under a plum tree. She did not invite us into her room, but by the number of windows, it looked much larger than ours.

The maid brought lunch, but I was not hungry. Although Pomelo had an honest face and open way of speaking, I didn't know how I could trust anyone in this house. As she spoke I listened with one ear attuned to lies.

Like me, when she arrived from Shanghai, Perpetual was not there. The coward did not want to be present when she learned the truth. When he finally arrived, he told her that he truly thought his wife would have been dead by then. She would not last much longer, he assured her, and soon, he said, Pomelo would be his rightful wife.

"Why did I believe him?" she said. "We courtesans are experts at spotting men's outward lies and half-truths. They leave out facts, the most important ones. We can still see through them. But with Perpetual, I was fooled. Why was that? When I came here, Azure really was ill. He took me to her room. There I saw a woman who looked like a skeleton. She lay motionless on the bed, and her eyes were open, staring upward like a dead fish. Her skin was pulled over her bones like a shroud. I was both horrified and happy that what Perpetual had said was true. Azure would soon die. Yet, I thought it odd that he did not go to her side and speak a few tender words. Hadn't he talked about their love as their reunion from past lives? What was it he had said about their fate? Their spirits were like twin constellations, fixed in the sky and eternal! That was it. He knew he was going to be devastated without her, so he had to prepare by pretending she was already gone. Imagine that! My heart was so wide open, I would have believed him if he had said he was the God of Literature and I the lowly Milking Maiden."

Pomelo learned over time that Perpetual had twisted the truth to its opposite in nearly everything about her. Bit by bit, the real facts came out. From the age of ten, he had been shackled to a marriage contract, unbreakable because of the large dowry paid. His family needed the money. What does a ten-year-old boy know about marriages, dowries, and who his bride behind the veil might be? Perpetual was sixteen when he first saw her, and he was aghast that she was a scrawny woman ten years older than he, with one squinty eye and a wide mouth whose upper row of teeth leaned out. The lower row was as crooked and discolored as the kernels in a bad ear of corn. He was angry—not at his family for taking the dowry—but at Azure for being ugly. He went to his wife's room only to perform his breeding duties. "Once she gave birth to our son," he told Pomelo, "I no longer had to seed the furrow." Thereafter, he traveled to other villages and satisfied himself with prostitutes.

"Furrow!" Magic Gourd said. "What kind of man uses an expression like that for the mother of his child? A donkey ought to seed his ass!"

"He told me he grieved as a chaste man for three years." Pomelo said.

"With Violet, it was five," Magic Gourd said, and snorted. I did not appreciate her letting Pomelo know I was even more of a fool.

"When I came I knew none of this. I could not tell how old Azure was or what she looked like. She was an apparition hanging on by a fingernail. But it was strange, very uncomfortable to see how little feeling Perpetual had for her. He never went to her room and I did not remind him of his years of being chaste. Like him, I was waiting for Azure to die, which I was sure would happen the next week, then the one after that."

Every few days, Pomelo had gone to the room to see how much more flesh had fallen off Azure's bones, whether her eyes were still moist or were dull and flat, signaling death had come.

"It was like staring at an old tortoise that never moved," she said. "I would have had sympathy for her if she weakened more each day until her face turned gray and she died. But she was the same every time I saw her. It made me so mad."

One day, Pomelo said, she decided to settle into her role as Wife sooner than later. She went to Azure's room and took a tally of Azure's furniture and other belongings. She wrote down what she wanted and what she did not, talking aloud as she criticized the jewelry or clothes. "Cheap stuff. This would make a beautiful woman look hideous. She sat before the mirror of the vanity table, and pinched her cheeks to make them rosy and healthy-looking. She practiced her facial expressions, which she then could pull out as needed—agreeable, trusting, willing, dutiful, pleased, and grateful. She put extra effort into looking enamored. She opened a drawer and took out a necklace that had been in the family for hundreds of years, a mosaic of pearls, rubies, and jade set into linked curved bars, with a large pendant of pink topaz. She draped it around her neck and looked in the mirror. It was crude in design and the stones were not the best quality. But it was the family heirloom that each generation of wives had worn.

Just as she reached to undo the clasp, she heard someone calling her. "Second Wife, Second Wife." It was a raspy whisper, like that of a ghost. She nearly jumped out of her skin, thinking that Azure was using her last breath to curse her for wearing the necklace before she died. But then Azure spoke again, and her lips actually moved. "He can be cruel," she said to Pomelo. "He cannot help it. He has a sickness in his brain. You should escape before you suffer from it."

Pomelo felt a chill run through her, because she half-believed that Azure was speaking truthfully. What reason did a dying woman have to lie? If he were indeed sick in the head, she would cure him of that after Azure died. But Azure did not die. Pomelo gave her reason to live. She was not a weak twig that could be easily snapped off. Her strength lay in her love for her son. She did not want her son to love a former courtesan as his mother. And she did not want him to become like Perpetual. He had his father's nature, but she would make sure he did not have his character. She wanted a son who would return the Sheng family to glory. And so Azure began to eat again. In a week's time, she could sit up and speak. In another week, she could stand in the courtyard and imitate bird songs. While ill, most of her teeth had further rotted and fallen out. She had them all removed and put in large and straight false teeth, which made her look quite fierce, especially when she smiled. She was strong, not just in body and teeth, but also in her will. She no longer bowed to other people's wishes, not even Perpetual's. Her mother-in-law was already dead, and Azure ruled the house unchallenged. One thing that Perpetual claimed about her was true. She was smart. She could discuss matters with the same reasoning as a man. And she had three other great advantages over everyone else in the house. The first was her family, who lived in a town fifty miles away. They were wealthy, and Perpetual depended on regular sums from them for the expenses of the house and his own spending money. The second was her son, the firstborn of the generation. Her son would inherit her family's wealth and she could use that fact to make Perpetual yield to her will. Her third advantage was her ability to think clearly, without becoming insane with jealousy or made stupid by beautiful lies. She did not weaken to his charms.

Pomelo had given us the gift of knowledge. And it was all bad. We shared an alliance based on the same betrayal. We had led sophisticated lives in Shanghai. We spoke the same language, and we had known our share of charming men. We had been enamored of some, and we each had one great and devastating love before we met Perpetual. With Perpetual, we had been caught in the same trap, chased by our own fear into what we thought was the safety of an ideal arrangement and lofty existence at a scholar's retreat. We had been equally foolish, and so we could be truthful with each other at times. But it was not with complete trust. We had both been tricked too often by too many people.

Without money, we were living in a prison. Magic Gourd and I went over Perpetual's lies matching them to what he had said to us in Shanghai. His so-called cousin Mansion had no doubt also been duped. I wondered who Perpetual really was. Who would I meet when he returned home?

Meanwhile, Azure was the one I had to be wary of. Azure was strong, the one who had spoken to me when I first stood in the courtyard wearing my fancy silk clothes, beaten and dried out after nearly three months of travel. She was the one who had called me a whore. She told Magic Gourd and me to eat our meals on our side of the house. We preferred that as much as she did. We had little to do with the rest of the family: the senile great-grandmother, the melancholy grandmother, the two wives of Perpetual's dead brothers, and the various brats of those women. Azure did not beat me. But she found ways to humiliate me, and the worst was where she had us live: the storage rooms of the dilapidated north wing, where it was the coldest during winter and the hottest during summer.

BEFORE PERPETUAL'S ARRIVAL, I prepared myself for more of his lies. I imagined every excuse he could make. I would cut loose the strings that held those excuses together. I would be businesslike and demand that he provide me with a separate house so that I could be the First Wife of that household.

He arrived a month late, by which time I was so miserable I could hardly leave my bed. I had become Third Wife of Nobody in this desolate part of the world. Where were the scholars, the respect, the peaceful gardens where I could wear my tailored clothes and feel the breeze blow through them? I cursed myself daily. How could I have let this happen to me? I once thought I could meet any adversity. But none of what I knew or thought or believed mattered out here. There was nothing to grab onto. No opportunity was going to pass by here. Magic Gourd tried to boost my spirits, but she, too, was listless in spirit and mind.

I cursed him when he came to my room. I refused to listen. But he knew me in a certain way—the weakest of me. And soon I was willing to take any scrap of an excuse from him as hope that his love for me had been genuine. That would be proof that I was someone important. All of my intelligence, common sense, and resolve were like sand through his fingers. He apologized, begged for forgiveness, and claimed he did not deserve me. I wanted to believe that, so I did. He confessed he had lied but only out of agonizing fear of losing me. He explained that his story about his wife was his way of showing me he could love me with excessive devotion. He claimed that the feelings he expressed were true, otherwise how could a woman experienced with so many men—hundreds—feel it was also genuine. He said I should hate him for the rest of his days and he would admire the fortitude of my character for doing so. He said he would make me First Wife if he could change the order of the universe decreed by the emperor. He said he would take me back to Shanghai, and buy me a house where I would be his wife—when the day came that he had the money to do so.

Until that time came, he said I would be the First Wife of the north wing. There he would be free to love me as the most desired of all. When he visited me, he fed me an elixir of words, and, for a while, I did not remember that this was where the wind blew through the cracks and the sun was cold. He had said all the things I needed to hear to recover from self-loathing and to restore my sense of importance, and with that in place, my other senses returned. He didn't love me, I didn't love him, and never had. But now I was like a bird, my wings once carried on a wind of lies. I would beat those wings to stay aloft, and when the wind suddenly died or buffeted me around, I would keep beating those strong wings and fly in my own slice of wind.

CHAPTER 11

HEAVEN MOUNTAIN

Moon Pond
September 1925
Violet

In Shanghai, Perpetual had declared his love for me with poems, and one of them guaranteed that Moon Pond's beauty would obliterate any lingering memories I might have of Shanghai. After seven weeks, I had still not suffered any bouts of forgetfulness. In fact, I could not stop thinking about Shanghai and all the possible ways I could escape Moon Pond and return. I should have read Perpetual's gloomier poems as hints of what awaited me.

I used to wonder why he glorified loneliness, a barren life, and the sentimentality of death. When I came to Moon Pond, I discovered he did not live alone; he had two other wives. He did not choose his poverty; he resented it. And all those high ideas? All along he had wanted wealth, glory, and lavish respect until it overflowed from his gullet. There seemed to be no end to the shocking surprises I was finding out about his character—not to mention what I discovered about the Ten Generations of Scholars. From the moment I arrived, I had a bad feeling I had been duped. Whenever the subject of ancestors or scholars came up, people around me fell silent.

Last week, I learned the truth while searching for my jewelry and money, which Perpetual had confiscated for safekeeping. In a document box at the back of a cupboard, I found Perpetual's personal account of his family's history.

When I was nine, my grandfather died of jaundice and was laid out in the reception hall. The corpse of his leathery yellow body frightened me and I feared dying of the same disease. My father took this as an opportunity to teach me a lesson. I paid careful attention. He was a great scholar, who held a high judicial position in the province. If I memorized the Five Classics, he told me, I would soon meet a hermit who would ask for a sip of wine, and upon my giving it, I would become immortal. Thereafter, I studied furiously. Within ten years, I had memorized all of the Classics of Poetry: 60 folk ballads, 105 ceremonial songs, and 40 hymns and tributes. I had also memorized many of the imperial speeches in the *Book of Documents,* a task so tedious it nearly drove me mad.

One day, the Number Six Wife decided to surprise my father with thoughtfulness beyond what had been provided by his other wives. She had found in a trunk the lucky gown worn by each generation of scholars during the imperial examination. She took it to the tailor to repair the frayed sleeve hems. When she told my father what she had done, it was too late. The tailor had discovered under the lining thin layers of silk on which the more difficult portions of the Five Classics had been copied. Unfortunately for my father, a recent rash of cheating on the examination had led to an imperial edict that all cheaters would be beheaded. A few days later, I watched two men lead my father to the middle of the square, which was already crowded by jeering people from many counties. He was known for issuing harsh penalties for minor transgressions, and his unpopularity went far and wide. One soldier kicked

my father behind his knees to make him kneel before a pile
of our family's most sacred possessions: scrolls of tribute to
the scholars of our family, thousands of our ancestors' poems,
hundreds of memorial tablets and ancestor paintings, and our
family altar and its implements for rites. My father was forced
to watch these treasures being smashed and set afire, which
exploded into flames as tall as trees. My father cried out, "I
didn't cheat. I swear it. I was a poor student and bought the
gown at a pawnshop." I was shocked that even to the end, my
father was dishonest. One man held my father's queue straight
up, and the other raised the sword. A moment later, I saw my
father's head roll to the ground and his body fall forward
onto the dirt. Our family's reputation was severed on earth
and in heaven. When we returned home, we saw the villagers
had set the house on fire, and thieving bastards were stealing
furniture and smashing whatever they did not take.

No matter how much I studied, I would be branded as a
son whose ancestors were charlatans. No hermit would come
asking me for a sip of wine. But I refuse to inherit shame. I
dare anyone to spit on the ground as I walk by. I will rebuild
our house and our reputation. I will rise on my own and create
a beginning for the next ten generations. I will receive what I
deserve.

This was the lofty reputation I had chased after. Like his father,
he gave out more lies to cover the first ones. He justified them. "If
I had told you the truth," he had said, "would you have come?" Of
course not. And now that I was here, I would not help him start the
next ten generations of liars. I wouldn't stay. Leaving, however, was
proving difficult. The compound was like a prison, and the village
was a larger one. Damn Perpetual. He knew we would be trapped.

From our first week in Moon Pond, Magic Gourd and I had been
scouting for escape routes. We walked the length and width of Moon

Pond in half an hour. The market square turned out to be nothing more than an open yard of beaten earth. By the time we arrived in mid-morning, the farmers had already packed up their goods for the day. There was only one lane of commerce—stalls whose trades-men provided the same service: the repair of pots, buckets, chisels, saws, and sickles, everything a farmer needed for ceaseless toil. The only other goods for sale were for funerals, the best of which was a paper mansion the size of ten men. Its faded colors and tattered edges made it evident that it had been on display for many years. The road we took to reach Moon Pond was half a day from the village at the other end of the valley. If we tried to take it, we would be spotted before we had gone a hundred yards. There were paths that led up into the mountains—to terraced rice paddies and the forests where old women chopped kindling and brought down a bushel on their bent backs. We saw the farmers trudging up early in the morning before the light of dawn and trudging back in the last light of dusk. Some footpaths became waterfalls with sudden rains. We noted them all and crossed off our list those that offered no escape. By the second week, we realized we needed clothes so we would not attract attention. I traded one of my fancy jackets and skirts for four pairs of plain blue tops, pants, and caps that the village women wore. Who knows where the woman who did the trade would wear her new fancy jacket? "She can put it on and enter a dream of being in a place where jackets like this are worn every day," Magic Gourd said. "That's where we're going as well. A dream." By the third week, it seemed like there were no other ways to leave without hiring a man with a cart. And we had no money to do that.

When Perpetual returned from a business trip, he offered to take me on an autumn walk to see a scenic spot that had inspired many of his poems. I was eager to go. It would enable me to look for other paths and roads. Before we went, Perpetual recited aloud one of the poems that the scenic spot had inspired, so I would fully appre-ciate the importance of where he was taking me.

"Where the hermit wears the shroud of night,

A half-full wineskin is his only friend.

No greater is he than the boulder on which he reclines,

Knowing that with the erosion of time,

Both he and the boulder will fall

The same distance, he to his death.

And the stars will still shine

Indifferently, as they do tonight."

The poem put me in a wary mood.

To get to the mountain path, Perpetual took me down the main road through the village. It was an odd choice. I could see from the road an elevated trail that cut into the foothills and went in the same direction. Surely it would have made a better choice to induce amnesia in me. But I soon figured out why he took this route. It was the best place to show me off—Perpetual's newest courtesan from Shanghai. He walked proudly with my arm through his. I observed how much he enjoyed the attention we received. The women gaped and made humorous remarks to each other. The men sucked on their teeth and leered. The villagers never did this when we walked alone.

Just past the bridge, we finally reached the path that went up Heaven Mountain. After climbing only ten minutes, Perpetual announced we had reached the spot. I surveyed the scenery below: the tiled roofs of houses, rice fields, and small sheds. I told Perpetual I was not tired and that we should walk farther up.

"The footpath is blocked by mudslides and crumbling cliffs," he said. "It's too dangerous."

"Why then did you promise to show me *'wondrous beauty as we walk in clouds up high'*?"

"We don't need to walk higher to reach the wondrous heights," he said. "We can make love right here and you can be as loud as you want. No one will hear you." He patted his groin. "See what you do to me? My sword is sharp. It's already risen out of its scabbard and wants to drive its mighty self all the way inside you, with your rump as its pommel."

I had to keep from laughing at his poetic attempts to arouse me.

"Only you give me this urgent need," he said. "I have never asked Pomelo to come up here."

"Pomelo has bound feet," I said. "She can't walk up this far."

"I had not thought of that. And the fact that I haven't is proof that I never had the desire to do so. Hurry and take off your dress. I'm in agony waiting."

I pointed to the sharp pebbles on the path and said it would make a miserable bed.

"You Shanghai girls are so spoiled. Turn around then and lean against that boulder with your bottom facing me. I'll enter you from behind. Are you damp yet?"

In Shanghai, his approach to sex had been circumspect to the point of bumbling. But the way he talked about sex now was vile. "I have my monthly flow," I lied. "I was too embarrassed to tell you."

"But you should tell me everything," he said gently, "always, no matter what it is. We agreed to share all of ourselves—mind, body, heart." Suddenly, his tone turned dark. "Don't keep secrets from me, Violet, nothing. Promise me right now." I nodded to keep him from growing angrier, and he became gentle again. He told me to go down on my knees to service him with my mouth. In moments, he was done.

As we walked back, he pointed out a few highlights I had failed to appreciate on the way up: a sour crab apple tree, the stump of a former giant tree, mounds of graves pimpling the hillside. I feigned interest while looking down for a certain road that Magic Gourd had just learned about from Azure's maid. All the maids shared gossip about their mistresses, and since they thought Magic Gourd was my maid, she was fed the same tattletale tidbits of the household. According to the maid, every three or four weeks, Perpetual told Azure he had to rent a cart and pony to go inspect his lumber mill, which, supposedly, was located about twenty miles away. Azure would tell him each time not to inspect another courtesan and bring her home. The maid said she had never seen the town. She had never even been outside Moon Pond. But a manservant, who we all knew was her not-so-secret lover, had offered to take her there one day. She reported that this offer must have been a marriage proposal. Her lover had heard it was easy to get to. "You take the main road through Moon Pond, go just a ways past the bridge, and keep on until you run into another road that's pretty wide. Head west into the blinding sun and keep at it for twenty miles or until the road stops and, soon, there you are: Wang Town." According to the manservant, it was a town, not a village, and it even had shops, brothels, and a port where small boats came and went. Whether that was true, he couldn't say. He had not yet been there. But once or twice a year, someone passed through Moon Pond, either on their way to Wang Town or coming back. They stopped in Moon Pond only long enough for the manservant to dredge as much information as he could about the world beyond the only one he had ever known.

I could picture those boats. I didn't care where they went. I would take one of them, any one, as far as it would go. It might be to another town, and in that town there might be other roads, and these might lead to other waterways, other boats. I would keep moving farther away from Moon Pond and closer to the sea, to Shanghai. But to do so, I needed money, which I would not have until I could find out where Perpetual had hidden our jewelry and money. I once told him that I wanted to wear my bracelet, and he said there was no need to put on airs in Moon Pond. It would make me look arrogant, and there was no one here to be arrogant to.

I would have no choice but to steal back what was mine. When I told Magic Gourd about my plan, she showed me its flaws. "How far would you get down the road past the bridge before someone spotted you? Any fool would recognize you. And even if you made it to the east road, Perpetual would come in a pony cart and yank you up by your mane and bring you home. We need to think of something else."

I imagined a dozen convoluted plans and went over practical matters. Which was worse: working at an opium flower house or living at the ends of the earth as Perpetual's concubine? The same answer came back: I would rather die in Shanghai.

Azure, meanwhile, was happy to live and die in Moon Pond. She had been making preparations for her lofty place in heaven, even though death was not as imminent as Perpetual hoped. As the mother of Perpetual's son, her spirit would receive daily offerings of smoky incense, fruit, and tea, as well as the forced obeisance of the rest of us. She had spirit tablets for Perpetual and her made out of the best camphor wood. There were none for Perpetual's ancestors, since they were disgraced and not worthy of being worshipped. So she brought over her own family's ancestors—scrolls, tablets, writings, and memorial portraits—so that her little son could lead the rituals.

I coyly asked Azure why there were no spirit tablets for Perpetual's ancestors. They burned in a fire, she told me. She did not say what the cause of the fire was. I then asked if the tablets would be replaced soon. "When there is money to buy the camphor wood," she answered. "If we did not have to feed your mouth, it would be sooner rather than much later." Even if I had not read Perpetual's account of "The Great Disgrace," I would have found out about it. It was a secret often told, different snatches relayed by the servants, Pomelo, and the half-truths Perpetual gave until I told him that I knew. I had a sour stomach for a week, angry at myself for having chased after a scholarly family's bad reputation all the way to this festering pond.

Twice a day, once in the morning and once in the evening, we had to make our way to the temple she was repairing, go to our knees on the stone floor, and murmur our respects to Azure's family. I had never had to do these rituals. My mother thought it was hocus-pocus. Edward knew nothing of ancestor worship. I had known a few of the courtesans who bowed and prayed in the privacy of their rooms. But most of the girls did not know whose family they had been stolen from. No ancestors would want a courtesan doomed for the underworld to buy them a better spot in hell using her ill-acquired hell bank notes.

Now that the rainy season was upon us, the temple roof leaked and drops fell on our heads and doused the incense. I thought Azure was stupid to spend money on fixing the interior of the temple without repairing its roof first. One day, as raindrops streamed down my face, I decided I should have a word with Perpetual and let him know my ideas were valuable, too.

That night, after Perpetual had satisfied himself in my bed, I praised Azure's devotion to the family ancestors. I cited my appreciation of every detail—the pillars, the table, the dais for the Buddha. How smart of her to make his spirit tablet of expensive camphor wood. I said, "Cheaper wood would attract insects and there's nothing worse than having your name chewed up by bugs. The oily camphor keeps them away."

I then told him what I had overheard that morning. "Some farmers were gossiping by my window about a neighbor's leaky roof. Everyone knew that the farmer's wife had been nagging her husband for years to fix the roof. This year, he joked that the spouts of rain were convenient for cooking and washing. So why was she complaining? As the story goes, a few days ago, the farmer's roof collapsed and smashed the stores of food kept just below the rafters. Rats devoured the meat, the dried corncobs were eaten by hens, the pigs got drunk on spilled rice wine and stampeded through town and fell into the river. Worst of all, the farmer suffered a broken arm and leg, making it impossible for him to tend his fields. His parents, wife, and children sought the kindness of neighbors, but the man had been feuding with everyone, and now the family was doomed to starve.

"The story left me trembling," I said. "In our house, all you have to do is look up and you'll see as many holes in the roof as there are stars in the Peacock Constellation. A few drops on your head are not a problem. But what if our roof comes crashing down and destroys what Azure has already worked so hard to restore? With all that oily camphor wood, everything could explode into flames and the entire house would burn, along with your poems."

The last part got his attention. I was about to add that Azure could be killed, but that might be what he hoped for. "In my opinion," I added, "the roof should be repaired as soon as possible."

He smiled broadly. "You've learned so much already for a city girl."

I felt as victorious as a courtesan winning a suitor whom another had desired.

"I want to be useful," I said, "even though I'm only Third Wife."

Whenever I mentioned my lowly position as "only Third Wife," he no longer apologized for deceiving me into coming as his First Wife, and I no longer complained—not aloud. Doing so had gained me nothing but his annoyance, which he showed in front of the other wives to shame me. I felt no shame. I did not care what he or the others thought. But if he was annoyed, he would then probably tell Azure to punish me by making my life more uncomfortable. Our food would be leftovers served cold. The laundry maid would return our clothes with spots.

"The roof has been a problem for many years," Perpetual continued. "Pomelo suggested last year that it be repaired. It seemed like a good idea until Azure pointed out that her ancestors are so happy that the temple is being repaired, they'll protect me from both disaster and a shortened life. So you see, the roof won't fall as long as Azure's fixing the temple."

He believed the reasoning of a madwoman, who lived with one foot in the afterworld. By telling me that Pomelo had made the same suggestion, I wondered if he was trying to pit us against each other. After all, she had been a courtesan as well and knew how to use humble subterfuge as her weapon. She had already told me that she could make me miserable if I didn't know my place, and that was at the bottom.

Thus far, I had not been able to detect any trouble she might be stirring up for me. From time to time, she came to our courtyard, always with the pretense of providing hot tea to warm me on a cold afternoon. I did not appreciate her visits but could not refuse her. It was awkward avoiding conversations that I felt could be used against me. I was polite but offered little beyond meaningless observations.

"When it rains," I said, "the ants make a grand procession across the floor."

"Have you sprinkled them with chilies?"

"I did," I said. "They enjoy eating Sichuan peppercorns the most."

I did not appreciate her visits for another reason. My courtyard and its rooms reflected my station, which I was sure gave everyone a good laugh. Magic Gourd and I had recently increased the size of our rooms by knocking down the walls of two storage sheds. But there was little else we could improve. Our courtyard was farthest from the main house, and to go from our quarters to the temple, we had to walk down a gloomy passageway that was green with slippery moss, which had sent me flying onto my rump twice already. From there, we had to walk along corridors whose roofs had burned in the great fire. In the late fall, the north courtyard remained cold and damp, even during the day, and I had to use a brazier—one just big enough to either heat a teakettle or warm my hands. Magic Gourd had a brazier even smaller than mine. We often set the two braziers side by side to cast off a bit more heat for the two of us. One day, as we fed the braziers' small mouths with coal, Magic Gourd recalled for me those days when I was the pampered daughter of an American madam. Right then, I decided I had had enough of cold misery and ill-treatment. I marched over to Azure's room. Her room was warm and dry. "We are about to die of cold," I said, "and the ground's too frozen to bury us. So we'll take a bigger brazier instead."

"There's none to give you," she replied, then pointed to her brazier on the floor. "Mine is no bigger than yours."

"That may be, but you also have heating flues under your *kang* floor, and the oven that warms it burns coal day and night." She could have sat naked and still be in comfort.

Her face showed mock concern. "*Ai-ya!* You don't have a *kang* floor? No oven? I didn't know. No wonder you're cold. I'll have bricks for an oven and flues delivered to your courtyard right away."

I was sure she was lying. But, the next morning, I found I was wrong. A pile of broken bricks blocked my doorway. I had to push out the ones at the top, one by one, to make a hole big enough to crawl out of that grave. Magic Gourd pointed out that even if I had a brick *kang,* there was no coal to feed the oven, certainly none that Azure would spare. "And don't expect me to chop kindling for you," she said. "I'm not going to turn myself into one of those hunchbacked women who carry a machete and eighty pounds on their back."

The windows in my room held no glass. They had been broken during the Great Disgrace. We had only shutters over the lattice screens, which had to be kept closed day and night because the window was a stone's throw from the compound wall next to the road. It was the main thoroughfare into town and a gathering place for gossip and conversation. I heard hearty greetings at dawn, and arguments at all hours, and the yips of excited dogs. Magic Gourd said the neighbors stood next to our compound's wall whenever Perpetual came to visit me. "They know exactly when he's spurting." She mimicked a donkey bray and a few pig snorts. "I have to chase away the boys who climb over the wall to look between the cracks of the shutters. Dirty rascals. I showed them a knife today and said I'd slice off their little stems!"

The shuttered windows made me feel as if I lived in a cowshed. Late at night, the watchman came by, calling, "Be careful of fire! Watch your fires!" He passed by my window so often I wondered if Pomelo or Azure paid him to do so to disturb my sleep. It made me nervous that he stood so close to our end of the house. To light his way, he carried two pans of burning coals suspended on a shoulder pole. One slip and those pans could swing out and send balls of fire flying. It had happened before. A month earlier a house across from my room had caught fire and part of a grain shed had burned. Perpetual said he wished all the houses around us would burn down.

I was nervous about the fire because Magic Gourd had heard a story from Azure's maid concerning a concubine who had died of smoke after her brazier tipped over. This had happened in my room, and it was only small comfort that the woman had died over a hundred years ago. Ghosts didn't get old.

"You used to feel the Poet Ghost come," I said to Magic Gourd. "Can you feel any ghost now?"

"I wouldn't be able to tell the difference between the cold breath of a ghost and the north wind blowing through this window."

When I went to bed each night, I imagined I was laying my body in the ghost form of the woman who died of smoke. I tried to use Western reasoning to convince myself there were no ghosts. Whoever that woman was, she may have died by accident. Or maybe the story was made up to scare me. But when I grew sleepy, my Western mind drifted away, and the ghost crept in with her ashy face. I dreamed that she sat on the side of the bed and said to me: "You and I are the same, aren't we? Like you, I was so miserable I thought I was losing my mind. The only way I could leave was on clouds of smoke. The other concubines—they were not as lucky." When I woke, I knew it had been a nightmare, but I could not stop thinking about what the dream ghost had said: "The other concubines—they were not as lucky." What did that mean? Magic Gourd poked around for clues, and Azure's maid told her in a whisper: There were two other concubines who died, and they both belonged to Perpetual. She could not say more. I had been in Perpetual's house for nearly three months and I was already nervous about everything. I had to stay strong and not give in to fear. What would my mind be like in another three months? In three years? If life became worse than this, would I be tempted to breathe in clouds of smoke?

I would not. I was determined not to weaken. Little Flora was my reason to live. She would keep me strong. I would do anything now to find her and I could endure anything to do so. Magic Gourd and I would use our clever brains and find our escape. We knew how to create opportunity, knew what to look for, knew the nature of risks and necessity. We had to be prepared to go through any sudden opening without question when it appeared. What clues did we have so far? A road to Wang Town. My money and jewelry, which were hidden somewhere. A concubine who died of smoke. Two other concubines who had belonged to Perpetual and were no longer here. What else? I felt as if I were picking up all the buttons that had popped off my blouses over the years, buttons that had rolled under the bed or a dresser, ones I had not bothered to pick up because I could hand my blouse to a maid to have repaired. I was now searching for any little thing that held a clue—and I found it, the button that had popped off my mother's glove just before we separated. She had not bothered to look to see where it went. She simply threw off the gloves. But I had seen it, lying next to my foot, a small pearl button that had somehow remained in my mind all these years. I decided right then: I would not throw away any of my chances just because I was angry at her. I did not yet know how to reach her. But I would, and when I did, I would tell her to find Little Flora for me.

ONE AFTERNOON, POMELO dropped by and insisted we come to her room to play mahjong and listen to music on her phonograph. "You have exhausted your excuses," she said with teasing sternness. "Perpetual is away for two weeks, and there are no call chits tonight to dinner parties in Shanghai. I'm longing for company. You and Magic Gourd have each other, while I am alone and have run out of interesting things to say to myself. After many years of solitude, a prisoner desires company of any kind, be it rat or scoundrel. You are neither, but I would still enjoy an afternoon together."

"Have you considered inviting Azure or Perpetual's sister," Magic Gourd said—rather unkindly, I thought.

Pomelo did not act offended. "Perpetual's sister talks about the accomplishments of her son, and without a breath in between. I was tempted so many times to tell her that the little brat was lazy, ill-mannered, and stupid beyond compare. That would have led to my demise. As for Azure, you know as well as I do that she keeps company only with statues of gods and the spirit tablets of her ancestors. I'm not inclined to bow down all day in that temple she's fixing. She's praying for another son."

Magic Gourd snorted. "That's nonsense. How can a baby come from her womb when Perpetual never visits her?"

"Oh, but he does, at least once a week. I'm surprised you didn't know. It should be obvious. Her family gives her money to run the household. Without that money, everyone would have starved long ago. Her parents live in a big town and are well-to-do."

I gave Magic Gourd a quick glance. We were both thinking the same thing: Wang Town.

"Her mother dotes on her," Pomelo said. "And since she's their only child, Perpetual's son will inherit everything. Another son would give Perpetual double assurance he'll inherit the family's wealth when Azure dies. And he expects that could happen at any time. Her health has never been strong. Come by this afternoon, and I'll tell you more." She gave us a sly smile and left.

I could not imagine Azure and Perpetual writing in bed. She never showed any affection or desire for him, nor he for her. Did he require her to act wild in bed? Or did they conjoin in a dutiful manner, like a name seal pushed into cinnabar paste before it's stamped onto a scroll?

In the late afternoon, Magic Gourd and I went to Pomelo's courtyard. "My flower sisters," she said. "I'm glad you decided to come." She sounded sincere. She gestured that we sit in the chairs by a table already set with mahjong racks and tiles.

"Let's be honest with each other," she said. "I know you're still wondering if you can trust me. I am probably as wary of you as you are of me. But I promise you this: I will not harm you, if you do not harm me. Did you ever hear a bad word said about me in Shanghai? In all the houses where I worked, I treated everyone honestly. I didn't steal their patrons. I didn't spread rumors. That's why the others did not steal mine. When you wound a sister, everyone feels free to wound you. This afternoon, we should let go of our suspicions and share a little amusement instead."

Like me, Pomelo had been able to take only a few of her belongings from Shanghai. Her luxuries were the mahjong tiles and a small Victrola. I foolishly took a portable vanity table, which survived the journey with a cracked mirror and a broken hinge. It mocked me daily. She wound the phonograph and an opera aria burst out. It reminded me of my days with Edward, so few and so long ago. The old grief returned and I pretended that the smoke of the brazier was stinging my eyes. I glanced around her room and was sick with envy. All the furniture was polished and free of gouges and burns—her chairs, stools, table, and wardrobe. Her floors were covered with thick rugs. Panels of yellow and red silk curtains floated in front of her bed. Four lamps hung from the ceiling and purged darkness from every corner.

"I worked hard to have these things," she said.

"I can imagine," Magic Gourd said.

"They are not gifts from Perpetual." She had found the furniture in the shed, she told us. They were the chairs and table that had been smashed and burned when the house was ransacked. She exchanged the broken leg of one chair with an unbroken leg from another, gluing it in with thick sap from a pine tree. She filled the gouges on the tables with sawdust, slivers of wood, and glue, then polished the wood with waxy leaves plucked from trees near the path to Heaven Mountain. To clean the rugs of stains and feces, she made a mud of fine dust and water and smashed it into the rugs and let it dry. She then beat the rugs for five days. To repair the scorched spots on the rug, she pulled out a strand of wool here and there from different areas, bunched them and glued them into place. The silk curtains for the bed, she said, came from two fancy dresses she had foolishly brought from Shanghai. The hanging lamps had been made by twisting together young twigs into the shape of a square then covering them with undergarments made of cotton gauze. Everything in the room, she claimed proudly, even the vases and mahjong tiles, had been repaired or fashioned out of useless belongings from either her trunks or the family's former glory days. I now saw the room with different eyes. The curtains had clumsy seams, the mended spots in the rugs were uneven, and the patches on the table were obvious. I was no longer envious of Pomelo. Instead, I admired her ingenuity.

She made a wry face. "If I live another hundred years, I'll be able to transform this room into the one I had in the flower house. I had a beautiful boudoir and was proud of it. I let pride get in the way of common sense. I waited to marry. I had patrons who asked me to marry, but I thought I could find a better man, a richer and more powerful one. One of my patrons turned out to be a gangster. He threatened to kill any man who looked at me. Word went around. The gangster soon took up with another courtesan a few months later. But all the old suitors avoided me out of lingering fear. All except Perpetual. And now you see, that's where ambition took me—here. It's dangerous to have pride and ambition together."

"There's no opportunity for that," Magic Gourd grumbled, "unless your ambition is for a grave on a higher hill."

"There are more chairs and rugs in the shed," Pomelo said to me. "I can help you repair them. Don't think I simply want to do you a favor. I'd rather be a carpenter than let my mind shrivel from boredom and lack of use."

Just as I thanked her, I felt a suffocating fear rise up. This room, with its shoddy comforts, had an air of sad resignation. This was as good as life would ever be. She had accepted that she would remain in this house forever. Her days would be spent making fake luxury out of debris, and in this wreckage, she would live out her days, breathe her last, looking at the faces of people she didn't like. Or did she still have enough warm feelings for Perpetual to suffer all else? I did not.

"I see hesitation in your face," Pomelo said. "Are you worried I'll extract a debt from you later? I won't. My offer stands if you change your mind."

Dusk came and she lit the lamps She brought out the mahjong set. As we washed the tiles, clacking sounds took me back to my Shanghai days: the hot afternoons as we waited for our parties to begin and our suitors to arrive. In familiar sounds, I could escape this place in memories.

Pomelo broke into my thoughts. "Did Perpetual ever take you up Heaven Mountain to a scenic spot? Ah, I can already see by your face that he did. Did he promise to take you to his poetic grottoes? No? He will. I endured pain to walk up that path. Perpetual did not offer to carry me. My foot bindings were bloody by the time I returned to this room."

"Did you reach the grottoes?" I asked.

"I'm not sure they exist. He told me the footpath had been cut off by mudslides the year before."

"Ah, yes, Violet was told that as well," Magic Gourd said.

"Even if the path were wide and clean," Pomelo said, "people in Moon Pond would not go up there. They think Heaven Mountain is cursed. If I were in Shanghai, I'd say it's just a made-up story to scare people. But I've lived here now for nearly five years. And I admit, just thinking about telling you the story sends a cold wave of fear down my back."

POMELO'S TALE OF BUDDHA'S HAND

At the top of the mountain, there is a white dome of rock shaped like a cupped hand. From the top, there are steep chutes that create four fingers and a thumb. The chutes stop where the dome flattens and fans out, making the palm. Three hundred years ago, a monk making a pilgrimage became lost and ascended the wrong mountain. When he reached the top, he saw a small valley and the dome shaped like a hand, but no temple. If he descended, he would face shame for his mistake. As soon as he thought this, the dome gleamed, and he knew that the Buddha's Hand was telling him to build a temple and thus change a mistake into a holy shrine. Infused with holy powers, he went into the forest and found large trees of golden-colored wood. With only a sharp stone, he chopped down five trees and rolled the logs to the center of the valley. He built the temple in seven days, and spent another day carving a statue of Buddha twice the size of a man. Its upraised palm looked exactly like the one on the dome. He chipped away at a slab of stone to create a dedication to Buddha's Hand. It included a description of his feats of carpentry. Anyone who made the pilgrimage here, it said, would have their prayers answers once they touched the Buddha's Hand. The monk then ascended to heaven without dying, then returned briefly to write this ending.

A short while later, a herder in search of his lost buffalo cow came upon the valley with the dome. The cow was by the golden temple, and when he went to fetch her, he saw the statue of Buddha through the open door. He wanted to make an offering, but in his entire life, he had never possessed even two coins to rub together. All he could offer was his corn cake, what would have been his meal for the next three days. He stuck the corn cake between the Buddha's thumb and forefinger. A moment later, he received his fondest wish: he could read, write, and talk like a scholar. He wept as he read the inscription on the stone plaque with ease. He even corrected a slight mistake in one of the characters. When he descended, he spoke elegantly of the temple and Buddha's Hand.

Soon, the temple became the holiest site in three counties, and many made the pilgrimage. The temple's holy reputation was bolstered by how difficult it was to reach. One could easily become lost. The path started at Moon Pond, and a half mile up, it split into two paths that went in opposite directions. A mile later, each of those two paths split into three and some went up and some went down. Two miles later, each of those six paths split into four, and those paths also went up and down and back and forth. All told, there were well over a thousand different paths winding through the mountain, although it was never clear who had counted them all. People called this tangle of paths the "Veins of an Old Woman's Hand That Take You to Buddha's Hand." All told, the distance was eight winding miles. It took a day of perilous devotion for a man to go from Moon Pond at the bottom to Buddha's Hand at the top. It took a strong woman two days. Many who went during the monsoon season were swept away. Sudden winds also claimed many. At the beginning of summer, venomous creatures emerged. In the late fall, there were tigers and bears hunting for food to last the winter. Those who did not become lost and who survived all the dangers would receive their fondest wish—that is, if they rid themselves of any thoughts of desire so that they could approach the Buddha with the right mind. If you desired a son, you had to tell yourself not to think about a son. If you wanted wealth, you had to stop picturing piles of gold. Unfortunately, by reminding yourself to not think about your desire, you were still thinking about it. That's why few had their desires granted.

There were two paths that took you to Buddha's Hand. One started on the south side of Heaven Mountain. That was the front of the mountain, as determined by the toelike shapes in the foothills. The other path started on the north side, which was the back of Heaven Mountain, as determined by the two heel-like shapes in the foothills. The back-of-the-heel path was the one in Moon Pond. No one knew how hard it was to get up one side and down the other. The only people who could have said never returned.

The temple's reputation lasted for over two hundred years, and then, a hundred years ago, a greedy man who did not receive his wish stole the Buddha's thumb. The temple immediately became cursed, the man turned to stone, and those pilgrims who made it to the temple met with a bad fate. Every family had stories: An old woman who wanted another grandson discovered when she returned home that her first grandson had died for no reason. A young woman who wanted her husband's paralyzed legs to be healed returned with her feet on backward. People told tales of falling boulders, flash floods, crumbling cliffs, and an assortment of bears and tigers, all of them passed along as family legend by those whose ancestors had suffered catastrophe.

One young man did not suffer from the curse of Buddha's Hand. He claimed that when he reached the temple, he saw ghosts moving in circles. He spoke to them, and they spoke back and told him a secret. And thereafter, only he could go to the temple without disaster befalling him or his family. That young man was Perpetual's great-grandfather. He passed along the ghosts' secret to Perpetual's grandfather and his grandfather told his father. His father died, however, before he could tell Perpetual. Perpetual says that without those words, he would not dare to climb the mountain to Buddha's Hand.

"That story is nonsense," Magic Gourd said. She said that so strongly I knew she thought it might be true.

"You can't convince people it's nonsense when it's family legend," Pomelo said. "Perpetual often reminds them that disaster awaits anyone foolish enough to seek Buddha's Hand. He describes the boulders that crashed down on those who did not heed the warning. Yet, I've asked myself, Why does he continue to write poems about drunken hermits in the mountain? Did he recite any for you? His father wrote many on the same theme. So did his grandfather and great-grandfather. There is something up there, and it's not a curse. Perpetual keeps his poems in a box near the altar. Did you find that box? No? How about the one with the story of his boyhood that describes how the family fell into disgrace?"

Pomelo must have gone snooping around for a reason as well. Was she looking for her jewelry?

"After I had been here about a year, I noticed that Perpetual was always busy writing a new poem the night before he left to inspect the lumber mills. I got up early one morning and spied on him. He was copying words from one sheaf of paper to another. He rolled up the sheaf of copied words and inserted it into a dagger sheath. A short while later, I overheard one of the menservants talking to my maid. He's the same fellow who told her about Wang Town, her lover. He said that Perpetual does not take the path just past the bridge. He goes a bit farther to a small trail hidden by bushes. And he always brings with him a full wineskin. I think I know what the true curse of Buddha's Hand is."

"What are you saying? Come out with it," Magic Gourd said.

"I've made a guess," Pomelo said. "Now you make one, too."

"He prefers the scenic path," I said, "and getting drunk on his way to the lumber mill."

"And the poems?" Pomelo said.

Magic Gourd frowned. "He's seducing some other naive courtesan with no taste for good poetry. Is she in Shanghai? If so, how does he get there and back in two weeks? Is there a train?"

"There's no mistress and no train," Pomelo said. "We can share our guesses tomorrow. That's my way of luring you to come back so we can play more rounds of mahjong."

THAT NIGHT I could hardly sleep due to Pomelo's riddle and its pieces: the lumber mill, the temple and the curse, the wineskin, the lies about mudslides and crumbling cliffs, the poems about a hermit. Given the lying nature of this family, I suspected that his great-grandfather had made up the story. The curse was a way to keep miracle-seeking people from climbing to the top of the mountain. There were no mudslides and there was no curse. There was something up there but it was not a dancing tribe of ghosts.

I puzzled over why Pomelo would tell me these things. She

should have worried that I might tell Perpetual what she had said. Yet, she knew I would not. She wanted me to know, and it was not out of sisterly love. She shared that secret because she had something to gain, and she must have considered I might not give it to her.

I now realized Pomelo may have lied about her feelings for Perpetual and his feelings for her. Perhaps she had loved him at one time—or convinced herself she did, as I had. I could not imagine she enjoyed his attentions in bed. In Shanghai, his lovemaking had been predictable and unexciting. Since arriving here, I had found he was no longer as considerate. He was demanding, crude, and rough on purpose. Then again, I was not as enthusiastic as I had once pretended to be.

Perpetual and I no longer engaged in lively debates. Out in the hinterlands, there was nothing to discuss. The only things that happened in Moon Pond were petty squabbles and outbreaks of illness. If Shanghai were in flames, we would not know it. Yet Perpetual had once said he admired my mind, the opinions I had gained from having lived in my mother's world of men and their businesses. That had been another of his lies. It occurred to me, however, that I should get him to talk to me more often. I could give him made-up confessions that would make him feel I shared everything. He would trust me more. He might talk about my confessions, give me advice, and I would act grateful and give him ecstasy beyond what the others could provide. And during those moments of disgusting intimacy, I would cry over his absence. I would ask when he would return and if he would bring me back sweets or a piece of cloth. He might unwittingly drop a few useful bits of information. There was nothing I would not do to make my escape.

When he returned from his next trip, I had tea and snacks ready for his visit to my room. As he ate hungrily, I made my first fake confession: I missed him terribly and worried he did not love me as much as he once told me he did. While he was gone, I had reread the poems he wrote for me to keep him inside me, so to speak. I found them erotic, even though he likely never intended them to be. When I read them, I remembered those times he recited them before taking me to bed and giving me other kinds of poetic delights. Masterly words and masterly lovemaking were inextricably linked. He was the mountain peak and I was the pond with his image inside me, rippling with excitement. When I read the poems alone, I said, I could not help but imagine his peak. He was happy to hear me say this. His love of himself was so great he believed that outlandish lie. He wiped away the crumbs from his mouth, and he fulfilled my fake fantasies by reciting a poem about a drunken hermit as he ground himself into me.

Afterward, as we lay facing each other, I told him another confession. I desired him so much that I worried that he had found another when he went away. I knew I should not question his fidelity. But those are the possessive thoughts of a woman inflamed with love and who already had to share him with two other wives. As expected, he tenderly assured me he saw no other women. I was his favorite, his empress of the north courtyard.

"Why must we be apart for those many days?" I said with an aching voice. "Please take me with you. If you did, we could make love anywhere along the road. Do you remember our time by the scenic spot?"

He told me tenderly he could not. He was busy with matters that required his full attention, and the temptations of my body would distract him.

I pretended to be coy and teasing: "What requires more attention than what I wish you would give me?"

He suddenly turned mean. "Don't ask me about my business. This does not concern you."

I knew it might have been a risk to push too quickly for information. I acted horrified that I had angered him and begged for forgiveness. I turned away and covered my face with my hands, as if to hide my tears. After a while, I said in a timid voice: "Is it too much to ask you to give me more poems to sustain me while you are gone? My favorites are about the hermit. You might be shocked to know that I imagine that you are the hermit and that I am your grotto."

He heartily agreed to give me more poems. He recited one, which was a variation on the same ones he had already written.

"Do you imagine a grotto when you write your poems? Is it one you'd want to visit more often than mine?" I slowly spread my legs.

"Yours is better." He rolled on top of me.

"Have you seen a real grotto like the one in your poems?"

He gave me a hard stare. "Why are you so full of questions today?" He rolled off and told me to pour more tea. I apologized and said I simply wanted us to be everything to each other, as he had once said we should be. I was not trying to be nosy. I threw on my robe and he told me to take it off. While working in the flower houses, I had long overcome shyness over nakedness. But now I felt vulnerable, as if he would be able to see whether I was lying or telling the truth. As a courtesan, I had learned what men were thinking and what they wanted by their movements and the tensions of their muscles. I made my limbs loose, my muscles relaxed. He sat on the bed and eyed me as I served. He bit into a bun and made a face.

He put the bun up to my lips. "Do you think it tastes stale?" he said. He stuffed it in my mouth before I could answer.

I turned away and covered my mouth as I chewed. I nodded. It was rubbery. When I swallowed the last of it, I tried to provide another confession, one concerning a desire to have his baby.

"Of course you do," he said, and shoved another bun in my mouth, this time more forcefully. "Is this one stale as well?"

I nodded. He was up to something. I needed to say flattering words to put him back in a better mood.

"Spit it out then," he said. I was grateful I would not have to finish eating it. He pushed down on my shoulders and told me to get on my knees, and the moment I did, he filled my mouth with his stem.

When his excitement mounted, he shouted, "Open wider, you whore!"

I struggled away. "How can you call me such a thing?" I cried, acting wounded.

He frowned. "Can I help what escapes my lips when I lose my senses?" He filled my mouth again, and again he called me names. "Faster, you slimy bitch cunt."

When he had finished, he lay on the bed, drowsy with satisfaction. He fell asleep. I sat at the other end of the room. What was going on? Clearly I had stumbled across important clues. There was a grotto and he wanted to keep me from knowing about it. It might take a while to secure more information. In the meantime, I would ask him to give me what he promised when I first arrived: to build me better rooms in another area of the compound, away from the noisy street and in a location that received a little sun. This was not to make my life here more comfortable. I hoped not to be here long enough for anything to be built. I had found with my customers that the more they paid for me the more they valued me. I was at the bottom now and he would treat me with less consideration until I raised my status in the household. I should be at least equal to Pomelo.

The next time he visited me, as I nestled in his arms following a successful bout of ecstasy, I cited the sunless cold, and the embarrassment of having quarters that were far less comfortable than what the rest of the family enjoyed. "The stone passageway carries our voices like a gramophone horn. Everyone can hear what we're doing."

"Don't exaggerate," he said with a laugh.

"It's true. Magic Gourd says the neighbors stand by the wall to listen to us, as if we're an opera troupe."

He laughed. "Let them listen. It's the most excitement they'll ever have in their lives. Why should we deprive them?"

I told him that I did not need an entire new wing. It would be sufficient to enlarge the courtyard wing so that my rooms were on the interior side, away from both the lane and from the echoing passageway. "It embarrasses me that Pomelo and Azure can hear us."

He was quiet for a few moments. "I haven't heard anyone complain about noise."

"The sounds carry in my direction as well." I made my voice tearful. "I can hear you making Pomelo deliriously happy. Your shouts let me know exactly what you're doing, whether she's on her back, her stomach, or flying through the air."

He laughed. "What an imagination you have."

"How can I sleep when I hear you telling her you belong to her, that she is your favorite?"

"I didn't say she was my favorite."

"You don't realize what escapes from your lips as you reach the clouds and rain!" I increased my tone of anguish. "How can I sleep when my heart is so wounded?"

He merely laughed. "My sleepless wife. I'll let everyone know you are my favorite. Turn over and cry out freely." He was rough from the start. His fingers were like the hard roots of dead trees. He grabbed my breasts and twisted them, causing me to yelp. He bit my neck, my ear, my lower lip, and each time I cried out in pain, he shouted, "Tell me I'm yours. Tell me you want me! Louder."

After this ordeal was over, I turned onto my side. I had used the wrong ploy. He stroked my hair, telling me that Pomelo now knew how much he cared for me. He reviewed what he had enjoyed the most and I blocked out listening to his repulsive words. I said nothing. He turned me toward him and I saw that his pupils were large and dark, animal-like. I looked down so I would not have to see them. He tipped my chin up.

"Look at me," he said. "Your eyes are so lovely. They are like openings into your mind." He kissed my eyelids. "Even when you're quiet, I can see into your eyes, all the way to where your true feelings hide. Shall I go in and see? What do you really feel about me?"

His pupils were two black moons. It truly felt as if he had entered me through my eyes. I felt an oppressive weight in my head. I could barely think. He was suffocating my thoughts, my will. I had to make my will stronger. He held on to my chin. I was determined to not show that I was nervous. I let my eyelids fall halfway closed to effect a dreamy look.

"Open them wide," he ordered. "I want to know all of you. I see it now. There it is, your precious thoughts. And here is mine: I will never let you go."

I startled, and he must have felt my body tense.

"What is it, my love?" he said. He turned my face back toward him. "Look at me. Tell me why you're frightened."

I could not speak at first. "I never thought I would hear you promise me that. I was surprised, and now I hope it will come true."

He continued to stare into my eyes and forced me to stare into his. "You belong to me. You always will. Do I belong to you?"

I felt again the oppressive sense of him in my thoughts. It took the remaining strength of my mind to fight off my fear.

"You belong to me," I said.

I felt what he was thinking. He was angry that I had lied. So I repeated it in a softer, tender voice, willing myself to look joyful and full of wonder that I was so lucky it was true.

MAGIC GOURD SAID her life was like that of a Buddhist nun. Subservience to idiots and fools increased her merit in the next world. Being with servants had its advantages, though, she said. It enabled her to learn what was being plotted—Azure was sick. Azure was pretending to be sick again. Azure was lying that Perpetual's son was sick. Pomelo was sick. Pomelo was pretending to be sick again. Pomelo complained about the food. Azure scolded her for complaining about anything. Pomelo gave Perpetual some kind of sex he liked and he gave Pomelo a bracelet. Azure said she could not find the bracelet intended for his son's future bride. Pomelo was angry when she had to return the bracelet. Perpetual was going away to check on the lumber mills and we would all have a week of peace.

Magic Gourd and I talked quietly, which for her was a feat of restraint. She was suspicious of Azure's maid, whom she had already caught snooping. To keep her from listening by our window, Magic Gourd spread a rumor that she had seen the ghost of a woman with a strangled look in her eyes walking around our rooms. Even with these precautions, we still whispered. Who knew if the other maids were listening—those who served the family on the other side of the house? I used to worry about Pomelo's maid until she got pregnant by an old man in Moon Pond and the old man paid Perpetual to give her to him. Azure would not use that money to buy Pomelo a replacement.

While Perpetual was gone, the heaviness of our daily lives was removed. Magic Gourd, Pomelo, and I spoke of old times, sometimes forlornly, sometimes with laughter. We told stories about our favorites. We did not relive humiliation. Nearly every suitor, patron, lover, courtesan, and madam was in our cupboard of stories. We could choose who to talk about at length: men who were louts, those who were generous, the good-tempered ones, the young men whose sex demands were endless. We agreed we had each had one customer who made our work effortless, whom we loved and wanted to marry, who later made us wary of ever feeling love. I told Pomelo about Loyalty.

I had once vowed not to think about him anymore. But it was impossible to keep the memories from seeping out. He had known me since I was seven and had seen me change from those days when I was a spoiled American girl. He knew what I had wanted from him, which I would have wanted from any man. He had suffered from my suspicions, my constant probing for more in him, for honesty. I recalled him telling me to take kindness when it was offered, to recognize love. Looking back, I could see how much he had loved me in his own way, but I had wanted more. The good memories of him now were gifts.

The best memories, of course, belonged to Edward and Flora.

The saddest ones did as well. The three of us kept our stories of great sorrow as the ones we most treasured. They were proof of love, and I told many stories that ached.

I had cried a great deal one afternoon over Little Flora. It was January 18, her seventh birthday. Magic Gourd and I talked about the day she was born. Remember the look on Edward's face as he held her? Remember the day she saw a little fly washing its hands? I hoped that she was happy. I feared she had no memory of me. All of a sudden, I heard a sneeze outside my window and quickly opened the shutters. Azure's maid was darting away. She had seen my tears.

In Shanghai, before I learned that Perpetual had been wooing me, I had freely talked about Edward. After all, he had poured out his grief for Azure. I had told him that the small moments with Edward were always large in my memory—a conversation we had had about the watchful nature of birds, the changing shades of both our eyes— little things like that. Perpetual had praised Edward's devotion to me—"your beloved husband"—and encouraged me to say more. We were compatriots in sorrow, he said, and I had agreed, not realizing how dangerous it was to proclaim to a future lover that I would never love any man more than the one who had died.

After Perpetual and I became lovers, he would gently ask if I still thought of Edward. I admitted that I did but would quickly add that I thought more often of him. Perpetual had cried to hear that. I gradually sensed he did not want me to remember anything about my past. So I would avoid talking about Edward. Over time, I had to pretend I had lost all memories of every happy moment I had ever shared with another. He wanted it to seem as if my life had begun with him and that he had released all my emotions. But Azure's maid had seen the truth: all those tears. She would tell Azure, who would give her a reward.

"Azure told me you've been weeping," Perpetual said that night as he entered the bed. "Are you sad, my love?" He looked concerned.

"Why would I be? Perhaps she heard me singing this afternoon. It was a sad song."

"Sing it to me."

My mind froze. "I'm too embarrassed. I can't sing nearly as well as I did in the courtesan house. I need to practice or I'll punish your ears with my squawking."

"Everything you do is charming. When it is imperfect, it is even more charming." He wrapped his arms around me. "Sing. I won't let you go until you do."

I racked my brain, and, luckily, I came up with a silly American song that I had hated. The flower sisters used to play it on the phonograph and dance a foxtrot, and the tune would remain stuck in my brain for days. I now sang those English words to Perpetual as sadly as I could.

> *"Lonesome little lovesick Chinaman,*
> *Packing up his grip, ready for a trip,*
> *on a great big ship.*
> *How he hates to leave his native land.*
> *After all these years,*
> *Time for sailing nears.*
> *He sings through his tears,*
> *'Good-bye, Shanghai.'"*

Perpetual clapped. "Your voice is still beautiful. But what do the English words mean? I understood only *Good-bye, Shanghai.*"

"It's about a sad girl who leaves her family in Shanghai."

"Were you singing it because you miss Shanghai?"

Where would this unfortunate song now take me? "I hardly miss it at all," I said.

"Hardly? Then you must miss something. What do you miss most? The parties, the beautiful clothes, the delicious food?"

I searched for something harmless. "I miss the fish from the sea, that's all."

He stroked my face, and when I looked at him, he said, "Do you miss the men?"

I sat up. "How can you ask such a question?"

"Are you embarrassed to admit it, my love?"

"I don't pine for my past," I said briskly. "I was simply surprised you would ask such a thing."

"Why did you look away just now?" He turned my face toward him. "I think you like to remember some of those men, certain ones."

"None. It was just business."

"You must have enjoyed a few of them, the handsome ones, the charming ones. Loyalty Fang. He was your first, wasn't he?"

I caught my breath. How had he known that? Did Loyalty boast to him? Did Azure's maid hear? "I have no special feelings for him," I said.

"A woman is always fond of her first," he said. "You must have welcomed him over the years without a businesslike feeling. He's far more successful than I am and must have given you beautiful gifts. Look at my face. Is he more handsome?" He pinned my arms and stared at me. I turned my face slightly. "Are you thinking of him now? Is that why you looked away? Would you like to pretend my cock is his? Turn over so you don't have to see my face."

He rolled me over before I could answer and rutted me like a lunatic monkey, grunting and shouting. He had gone mad.

The next night, he was calm, but I was on guard. We talked about his son, how tall he had grown. Perpetual's voice was gentle. He praised his son's diligence in doing his studies. He cited the clever things he had said. He was in a happy mood when he undressed me and pulled me into bed. But within moments, he changed. He wrapped himself around me and stared into my eyes. He said nothing, but I could feel him encircling my thoughts, removing them, replacing them with his.

"What are you thinking, my love?" he said. "Is it about Edward?"

I was prepared. "I am not answering questions about Edward." I tried to extricate myself, but he tightened his hold. "I don't understand why you're asking this. Edward is gone. You are here."

"Why do you lie? The lie is what keeps us apart. The lie means you are hiding him and he is still here. I know you miss him, and there is no shame in that."

It was true, I thought to myself, now more than ever. But I knew to say nothing.

"For me to love you completely," he said in a pleading voice, "you must let go of him, and see him for who he was. He was a foreigner who said he had married you so he could have a free cunt. Why are you trembling? Is it for him? Are you remembering what he did to you, how he fucked you like a whore. He's still here, isn't he? A corpse between us in this bed."

I resisted shouting at him. I spoke in a calm tone. "I don't want to talk about this anymore."

"Come on, my love, tell me the truth. What sensation did you have when he first touched you? Shivers? Did you want him in you immediately? You were an experienced woman. There is no holding back desire with women like you. I felt that when we met. You wanted me. But I held back. I made you wait before I took you." He embraced me roughly. His face was eerily expressionless. "How long did you wait for him? Did he take you from behind like a dog? Is that what foreigners do the best?" He turned me over and slammed himself into me. "Did he do this? Harder? Faster? Did you go to your knees for him? Why are you resisting? Show me what you did for him that you have never done with me. I want to have everything he had. I want what you gave to those men who were just business. I want what you've never given to any of those bastards."

As he pounded me, I had no breath to speak. He was pressing on me with all his weight. He was crushing me. I tried to push him back. He shouted encouragement to me, as if I were aroused. I realized I had to give him what he needed to hear. So I shouted that he was mine and I was his. I shouted for him to take more of me, all of me. He eased up.

When he was finished, he lay back pleased and exhausted. He became tender again.

"My love, you are so dear to me. What's this? Why do you look so unhappy?"

"I couldn't breathe. I thought I was going to suffocate."

"Did I hurt you? I lose control during lovemaking, you know that. I feel released and free, and I thought you were feeling the same. But I see that you weren't. Were you thinking of that lying American bastard?"

The old and uncontrollable grief opened up. I felt pure hatred for Perpetual. "Of course I think about him. You can't make my memory of him obscene."

He stood up and went to the table and stared at me. The lamp illumined his face from below and his eyes appeared to be deep holes. His face was contorted. "I can't believe you're saying this after what we've just experienced."

He shook me so hard my words came out in a warble as I yelled, "I'll always love him! He gave me respect and love. He gave me my daughter. And she's more precious to me than anyone else on earth."

Perpetual let go. He wrapped his arms around himself and his face crumpled in pain. "You love them both more than me?"

I was exhilarated that I had wounded him. I would wound him more until he hated me and would force me to leave. "I've never loved you," I said. "You should let me go."

He rose from the bed and came toward me. His face was as hard as gray rock. "I don't recognize who you are anymore," he said.

And then he punched me.

The side of my face went numb for a few moments before it throbbed, as if I were being punched again and again. I saw him through blurry eyes, a naked man wobbling back and forth, his mouth open in horror that he had hurt me. He reached for me and I told him to leave. I grabbed my robe, and as he apologized I continued to shout for him to leave. He grabbed my arm, and I shook him off, and walked away. I felt a nauseating kick to my back and I fell forward. Before I could catch my breath, he kicked me again, then grabbed my hair and pounded the side of my head with his knuckles. He was crying in a high-pitched voice. "Stop, stop, you must stop," as if he were the one being beaten. He was crazy and was going to kill me. I felt the dull kicks and punches, the shock shifting from my shoulder, to my thigh, to my stomach. I heard Magic Gourd shouting at him, and he left me for a moment, and I heard her yowl in pain. He returned to beating me with his fists. After each punch, I saw small white circles that grew and faded to reveal his lurid face. I felt an explosion at the back of my head and before me was only blackness. He had blinded me. He pushed me and I had the sensation of falling backward, waiting for my body to hit the ground. I kept falling and waiting, looking at blackness through my blind eyes.

I AWOKE TO see a stranger's hideous face swaying above me. I gasped. It was Magic Gourd. She had a black eye that had swollen shut. Half of her face was purple and red.

"I will slice off that little slug of his," she said. "Bastard scum! You think I'm joking? I'll find the sharpest knife in the kitchen when everyone has gone to sleep. If he's going to kill you, we might as well kill him first."

Her voice sounded soupy, as the words floated up and down. She had given me medicinal opium, she said. I was bobbing on cushions of air.

"I know his kind. Once he lets his cruelty out, he can't put it back inside. He saw how scared you were and it excited him. When you scream in agony, he becomes tender, full of love. And then—poom!—he changes and wants you to cower so he can be tender again. Cruel men are addicted to the other person's fear. Once they taste it, they have to feed it." She cursed Perpetual, but then I could no longer hear her and wondered if I had gone deaf.

When I opened my eyes, I saw Pomelo's blurry face moving in ripples. For a moment, I thought I had drowned and was viewing her from beneath water. I might be dead, but at least I wasn't blind. She looked stern one moment, then forgiving. Why did I need to be forgiven? I tried to ask her but could not hear my words.

The opium faded and I awoke in nauseating pain. My eyes darted about, looking for Perpetual. I could not run from him. My legs and arms were stiff, and when I tried to move, sharp hot pain shot through every part of me. Pomelo was putting herb poultices on the bruises, but the weight of them made me ache even more.

I don't know how many days had passed before Perpetual came with red-rimmed eyes, a remorseful face, and a gift. Despite my pain, I pushed away from him. If he killed me now, so be it.

"How could I have done this?" he cried. "I've made you afraid of me." He claimed he was drunk, and that love, despair, and wine had caused this to happen. He also feared that his father's ghost had possessed him. "All along, I did not feel I was myself. I was terrified by what was happening and yet I could not stop myself."

I recalled his whimpers. *"Stop. Stop. You must stop."*

He examined the welt on my jaw, the bruises on my shoulders, arms, and legs, kissing each, causing waves of nausea to wash over me. He described the bruises as the colors of fruits—plums, kumquats, and mangoes. "How could I have done this to your precious skin, my love?"

He laid a silk pouch on the bed next to me. I would not touch it. He opened it and pulled out a hairpin, a gold-filigreed phoenix of inset turquoise with a fantail of pearls. It had belonged to his great-grandmother, he said. "See how much you mean to me." He left it on the bed.

Every day he came and sat by the side of the bed for a few minutes. My fear had dulled to disgust. He brought fruit and candies. I did not eat them. He did not demand anything else. Two weeks after the beating, he asked if he could make love to me. He said he would be gentle. He wanted to do nothing ever again to hurt me. What could I do? Where could I go? What would he later do to me if I refused?

"I am you wife," I said. "It's your privilege." My body shuddered when he touched me. I had the urge to get up and run. When I could finally keep my body still, his hands felt like stone weights over my dead flesh. He was not happy with my lack of passion but understood that it would take time before we both loved each other again fully and completely. When he left, I vomited. Soon after, I heard him shouting with excitement in Pomelo's room. He bellowed to her and she shouted back that she belonged to him, every part of her. If she wanted him so much, she could have him every night. I would help her. I would insist.

About once a week, Perpetual would become livid and beat me. It was not like the first time when I thought he would kill me. He would roar and I would yell back, knowing what this would unleash. According to Magic Gourd, the neighbors would sit close to their windows, cracking peanuts while enjoying our opera. He was careful to not hit my face. He would slap the back of my head instead, circle me, and kick my rump and legs. He would shove me against the wall and force me to look at him, then yank my hair and shove me to the floor. When I was too nauseated to continue, I curled into a ball. Magic Gourd had been right about Perpetual's need to be cruel and later contrite. I loathed him and would not show him my fear.

When he was in my bed, I used memory to make him vanish. He could not see or hear my thoughts, and I brought back memory after memory until he left my bed. I went to the places I loved. The big salon where I chased Carlotta. She was batting a knotted ball of my mother's handkerchief. I went to a street where I took carriage rides. I waved to men. I walked along a lane with shops that sold books, lockets, and watches. I bought candy. I went to Edward. We were in the car and I was driving. I was screaming because I thought I was going to run over a duck and her ducklings. I returned to an afternoon when it was too hot to do anything but lie on the divans opposite each other in the library. He was reading . . . *The Golden Bowl*. Listen, he said. What was I reading? A passage out of his new journal. His journal. I read the passage aloud. I was driving. I returned to our bedroom and saw Edward standing with Little Flora in his arms. It was nearly dawn, and the room was warm with sepia light, and grew lighter and filled with color. I could see them both so clearly, the look on Edward's face as he murmured to Little Flora that she was miraculous. I felt the moment when he looked at me and said, "She's the perfection of love, pure and unharmed."

Why had he used that word *unharmed*? I had wanted to ask him later when Flora was asleep. There were so many things I meant to ask him, and now the only answers I would ever have were those I needed to believe. I knew what he was saying. I would protect her and all the harm that had been done to me would heal until I was pure again, no hate in my heart, only love.

MAGIC GOURD AND I went to Pomelo's courtyard two or three times a week to play mahjong. We had become old flower sisters, who had given up our suspicions and promised not to undermine each other. One day she mentioned a dish she had eaten in Shanghai. I said in a whisper that Azure's maid might hear and report to Perpetual that she was thinking of her old home.

"Azure's maid?" she said. "That little spy doesn't dare report anything about me. I have her by the neck. She and the young manservant are lovers, and I know for a fact he's been giving her food stolen from the pantry. But she still gets her reward from Azure for spying on you. I suggest you let her earn her reward. When you know she's spying, talk about your undying love for Perpetual and how much you admire Azure. Let the maid tell your lies."

Pomelo put a record on the Victrola. "The maid can't hear us talk with this music playing." During our latest visit with Pomelo, she began the conversation over mahjong with a complaint. "I've been meaning to tell you that you cannot outdo me in my affection for Perpetual."

I eyed her, wondering what she was up to.

"I can hear your business with Perpetual across the courtyard. You can hear mine. I sound more convincing than you. You've really become quite lackluster in your appreciation of his cock. I suggest you improve your actress skills. I was thinking we might compete with each other over who has fooled him the most with our fakery. We can be like the Shanghai flower sisters of our past, and vie for a man we don't want. Scream with pleasure. Declare you are his forever. Tell him you love him and only him. Do it for the pride we once had in our profession."

"I'd rather be beaten."

"That's what one of the other concubines said. She was strong like you."

I held my breath. I had been waiting for her to tell me this. Until now, she had refused to say more. "Did she live in my room?"

"She was in my room. I was in yours until I was promoted. Her name was Verdant," Pomelo said. "She once truly loved Perpetual, even after she came here and saw that he had lied. But when I arrived, she went crazy. She berated him for his dishonesty, mocked him for living in such a poor place. She no longer showed him any fondness or passion. And she would not cower. He beat her nearly brainless. He knocked out two teeth and damaged one eye so that she never could open that eyelid again. One night I heard her screaming even louder than usual. The next morning, she was gone. Naturally, I feared that Perpetual had killed her and already taken her body out of the house so that no one could see what he had done."

"*Ai-ya!*" Magic Gourd said.

I gasped and my stomach knotted. *Perpetual, a murderer.* This same end might await me.

"It turned out she had run away," Pomelo said.

I breathed again. Now I was eager to hear how she had done it.

"She took the path along the river. At the first bend, two women working in the field saw Perpetual and Verdant struggling. She broke free and quickly stepped into the river and wobbled forward over the smooth rocks below. The water was only knee deep by the banks and she must have thought she could easily cross to the other side. But the moss on the rocks was slippery, and the water was swift, and she fell a few times. Then it deepened, and toward the middle, the water was up to her thighs. Her clothes wrapped around her legs and she struggled to stay upright. Every time she fell, she moved a little bit farther downstream before she could stand again. But then the water deepened to her waist, and it carried her along like a leaf. She managed to steer herself to the bank and grabbed onto the roots of a tree. Perpetual found a sturdy branch and held it out to her, and she grabbed on. The women watching this were relieved. As Perpetual pulled her in, he shouted to her. She shouted back. The women didn't know exactly what they said because the water was running fast and loud. But one said Perpetual looked angry and he let go of the branch. Verdant was carried away with the branch still in her hand. Her head bobbed up twice before her body went tumbling over a small drop and was churned under. The woman said that Perpetual looked as pleased as a man who had caught a large fish."

I went numb seeing this in my mind.

"The other woman told a different version. She said that as they shouted at each other, Verdant got a crazy look in her eyes. She gave him one last shout and flung away the branch and let herself be carried away. The woman said Perpetual looked like a man who had caught a large fish only to have it escape and swim away.

"Verdant's body was found a mile downstream the next day, slapped against a boulder. The current was so strong her body could not be peeled off until summer when the water level went down. Whichever way it happened, people said, Perpetual could not be blamed for her death. After all, she ran away. She walked into the water. But if you ask me, I think it was she who let go of the branch. That was the kind of woman she was. She was like you."

My throat tightened. "You said there was another concubine. Did she die, too?"

"She is the one I have been waiting to tell you about. Charm arrived after me, and she left a year before you came. She used to be in your room."

I hoped Pomelo would not tell me that Charm had had a gruesome death.

"Charm and I became as close as sisters. We shared confidences about our hatred of Perpetual. We plotted ways to leave. She had two good feet and I had two bad ones. She suspected that whenever Perpetual said he was going to check on the lumber mills, he actually went up Heaven Mountain. Early one morning, she waited in hiding where the hidden trail starts. Sure enough, there he was, walking up briskly. When he returned home, she plied him with a lot of wine and a few drops of opium and exhausted him with enthusiastic sex. When he fell into snoring sleep, she went through the pockets of the trousers he had worn on the journey. She pulled out a small leather envelope and found inside a piece of paper that had been folded five times. It appeared to be a poem about the landscape of Heaven Mountain. It described a tree with a branch bent like a man's arm, a rock in the shape of a turtle—many different landmarks, including boulders on the trail that a person could climb over, but a horse could not. There were also words like *left, right, straight, up, down, the third one, the second one*. She realized she was holding the directions for going to the top of the mountain, to Buddha's Hand."

My heart soared. A means of escape. "Did you write down the answers as well?"

"Let me finish. When she left, she did not want Perpetual to know where she had gone. She tore a jacket and a pair of pants and showed them to me. 'Let him think that I followed Verdant into a watery grave.' She promised to send word when she reached a safe place. She left that night after she rendered Perpetual helpless again with her potion of drink and sex. She took with her the directions, the torn clothing, and a small satchel with food and water. Perpetual found the torn clothes in the river the next day. He was actually heartbroken. I cheered that Charm had escaped by going up Heaven Mountain. But after hearing nothing from her for two months, I thought she had died. I mourned her and hoped she did not die painfully."

So there had been a ghost in my bed after all. Charm.

Pomelo opened a drawer and removed a small folded sheet of paper. "Two days ago, I received proof that she is alive. A traveling shoe mender came by and said he had brought me shoes from my sister. The shoes looked familiar, and I accepted them. They had belonged to Charm. She had torn apart her shoes and refashioned them into a pair that would fit my bound feet. The seams were perfect and I searched for an opening in the lining—the one we courtesans make for hiding money or notes from our lovers. I carefully snipped open the back seam of the left shoe." She handed me the note:

> *Use the directions below to climb Heaven Mountain. At the top, you*
> *will see the valley and a dome of rock shaped like Buddha's Hand.*
> *Look down from the ridge and you will see the town of Mountain*
> *View. Go to the House of Charm and I will welcome you.*

I pictured a town that lay in the valley at the top of the mountain. Magic Gourd and I clutched each other with happiness "When should we leave?" I asked Pomelo.

"As soon as possible. I'll stay behind to tell them I heard you talking about running away toward the river. When you get to Mountain View, send a note in a pair of shoes to tell me how difficult it was to get there." She pointed to her bound feet. Although they were not particularly small, it was clear she would not be able to climb all that distance on her own. We spent a few minutes arguing, Magic Gourd and I insisting that we should go as three sisters.

Magic Gourd lifted her own feet up. "See? Mine were bound, too, and I'm willing to try."

Pomelo pushed them away. "Yours were unbound when you were a small child. They're as big as Violet's, maybe even bigger."

We continued to argue. We would find a way to help her. She insisted she would be a burden. We pointed out that she had given us the instructions and letter from Charm. In the end, she said, "You are both too good to me. I didn't even repair any furniture for your room."

I SAW LIFE differently after that night. I heard the farmers shout gruff greetings in the morning. And they seemed softer. I saw old men on the streets puffing on their pipes. A pack of dogs howled and barked and their ruckus dwindled as they ran away, and in my mind, I was running with them.

It was spring and the leaves were budding. At last, the rain was gone and the days were warming. Pomelo had already fashioned a pair of crutches from broken chair legs. She had glued layers of stiff leather on the bottom of her shoes and had a pouch of herbs for reducing swelling. She practiced by marching back and forth in her room every night that she was not with Perpetual and when the maids had gone to bed.

We brought other scraps of wood from the shed of broken furniture, which we used to make our effigies, which we hoped would fool people into thinking we had never left. The bottoms of small stools became our heads, half of a tea table top was used for a torso, and the table legs became our legs and arms. Magic Gourd insisted on fashioning faces for the effigies. She made a mixture of clay mud and sculpted mounds on the stool bottoms, then stuck different-size stones and pegs to create the eyes, nose, and lips. Our faces were quite frightening.

Magic Gourd and I had been hoarding food to last the three of us for three days. There was nothing I could not bear to part with. Everything would be a burden on either my heart or my back. I would bring only the clothes that would serve me best during warm days and cold nights. But then I remembered something I could not leave behind: Edward's journal and his and Little Flora's photos. I recalled the terrible day that Flora was snatched from me. I had looked at her photo and said to her, "Resist much, obey little." I had been following those words of advice. I slipped the photos out of their frames, and tucked them between the pages of the journal.

Magic Gourd set a Western blouse and long skirt on my bed.

"Why are you bringing me those?" I said.

She smiled slyly. "So you can turn yourself into the half of you that's Western. A Western woman traveling without a husband is not going to be questioned. People know foreigners are crazy and roam anywhere they please. It's worth a try."

"And if anyone asks why I'm traveling up a mountain, what do I say?"

"You will say in English, you are an artist. You travel to paint scenery. I will translate into Chinese."

I frowned. "Where are my paints? What is there to prove I'm an artist?"

She pulled from her bag two rolls of canvas. "You don't need to show me," I said. I knew what they were: Lu Shing's paintings, the portrait of my mother, the other of the valley. Every time I had thrown these paintings away, Magic Gourd had retrieved them.

"It's at least worth a try," she said. "I'll carry them. She unrolled one, the painting of the valley. "How could I give this up?" she said softly. "This looks like the place where my mother lives."

We waited until it was Azure's turn for a nocturnal visit from Perpetual. The moon was half full. In the afternoon, when Azure's maid was nearby, Pomelo made a show of inviting us to play mahjong, and we begged off at first and finally agreed after she insisted twice more. We had already brought our belongings piece by piece to her room over the last week. At seven, we went to Pomelo's for our game of mahjong. At ten o'clock, when all was quiet and Azure's maid was with her lover, we put on the simple clothes of farmers' wives. We laid out on the floor by the far wall our three effigies, donned in pretty dresses. We quietly placed the table and chairs on their sides, as if they had been overturned. We sprinkled the mahjong tiles and tea-cups on the floor, as if our game had been suddenly interrupted. An oil lamp stood in this heap, and we carefully doused oil on the bed quilts, the silk curtains, the gauze-covered lamps, and the rug. Alas, once the fire started, no one would be able to enter to save us—those ugly effigies with rocks for eyes. Pomelo and I left by the back gate just behind Pomelo's courtyard. Magic Gourd wound the Victrola, put on a sad aria, knocked over the brazier and oil lamp, then lit the curtains of the bed and darted to the gate where we were waiting.

We took the upper path along the foothills. After five minutes, we heard shouts along the main road below us. I imagined the horri-fied looks of those who saw our poor effigies lying just out of reach in the inferno, burned beyond recognition. Azure would be directing everyone to save the temple. And what would Perpetual do? What would he feel? How long would it be before someone entered the room and examined those bodies with skins of burnt bark?

The path turned up, and we looked over our shoulders fre-quently and saw how high the orange flames had grown. I wondered if the entire house was burning. Would the village burn down as well? I was stricken with guilt at the thought. We all talked bravely, but our voices gave us away. We were frightened. I had the sense that Per-petual would jump out of a bush in front of us. As the village receded, we could no longer see the smoke above the lower foothills, and we all felt relief.

We walked for three hours. Pomelo had to rest often because

her arms tired with the crutches. We were stopped when we arrived at a spot in the path that was covered with rocks. There was a way to get through, but it was dark and we did not want to risk anyone falling, so we found a place behind bushes and slept, two at a time.

With the new day, we were struck by the beauty of the open sky and the slopes and dips of the mountain. I had a sense of peace within me I had never felt. When we returned to the path, I saw that Perpetual had said one thing that was true. The mountain had slid down and covered the path with rubble. Magic Gourd and I could have jumped from boulder to boulder to cross. But we stayed next to Pomelo as she planted her crutch carefully with each step. She teetered over the larger boulders, and we had to be ready to catch her. When she reached the other side, she was exhausted, and so were we. We indulged ourselves in an hour of rest and a meal. Our progress was slow, and she thanked us often and profusely, apologizing as well.

"The world does not care for the woes of another when they have their own," she said.

Someone once told me: When you save a person, even unwillingly, you feel bound to each other for life. That's how we felt toward Pomelo. Magic Gourd often asked if she needed another rest. I asked if her feet were painful. And she asked if we had tired of carrying her little sack of belongings. We protested loudly that nothing was a burden, and, in fact, it was not.

By the afternoon, we had climbed high enough that the path had gone into the forest, where it was mercifully cool. We worried, however, that a tiger or bear might leap out from behind the trees. I confessed that I imagined worse: that Perpetual might appear.

"How could that be?" Magic Gourd said. "It would take him a while to learn we are not those fake corpses. He would also look first along the river. Why would he think to go into the mountains?"

We walked through the pine forest and began seeing patches of open sky, and soon, the whole sky. The oppressive fear immediately lifted from my chest. But soon it returned when the path narrowed into a foot trail that had been cut into the side of a cliff. I grew dizzy seeing how far down the bottom was. I remembered the story Edward told about the boy who flew over the edge of cliff trying to catch a doll.

"Look ahead and not down," Magic Gourd warned. "Where you look is where you'll go."

"According to this map, we are coming close to the grotto," Pomelo said. "It must be somewhere across there." She pointed to the other side of the abyss. "We should reach it in a few hours." Pomelo had a feeling our jewelry was hidden there. I imagined a hermit sitting in the grotto, just as the poems had described him. I always thought of the hermit as Perpetual. The idea that we might find him in the grotto made me shudder.

"Look!" Pomelo said. She pointed down the mountain. It was a small figure far below, and it was moving. We stared and agreed it was not a tiger or a deer. It was walking on two legs and could not be anyone else but Perpetual. He was the only one who knew there was no curse on Heaven Mountain.

We hurried up that dangerous narrow path, hoping to find a forest where we could hide. After half an hour, I could tell by Pomelo's grimace that she was in agony. Her arms and hands were blistered from using the crutches. And her feet were no less painful. She was wobbling over a narrow trail that was barely wider than her hips. If she stumbled, she would pitch over the cliff. Magic Gourd stood behind her and grabbed onto the back of her jacket to steady her as she swayed. I told myself not to look down. We had danger on one side and another danger coming up from behind. We finally reached a wider path away from the cliff. Magic Gourd and I quickly climbed up the path to get a better view and determine where Perpetual might be. We both gasped to see he was far closer than we had imagined he would be. What had taken us hours to traverse seemed to have taken him no time at all. He was clearly in a hurry. Was he chasing us? Or was he coming to the grotto for other reasons?

We took a zigzag course upward, making it seem as if we were going forward and backward, making no progress at all. I could hardly breathe out of fear.

Around yet another turn, I looked ahead and all hope drained. A rockslide covered a large swath of the path. It had taken us nearly an hour to pick our way through the last one, and until we climbed over this one, there was nowhere we could hide. My temples pounded. We looked at one another. One of us had to decide what to do. At his speed, Perpetual would reach us in less than an hour. I imagined he had a gun or a pickax, something to make it easier to capture—or kill—all three of us.

"You go on ahead," Pomelo said. She had numb, hollow eyes.

"Nonsense," Magic Gourd said. "What kind of people do you think we are?"

I agreed. But I also knew that if we stayed we would give up any chance of escape. I imagined the beating we all would receive, and once we were taken back, we would be locked in a burnt cage and suffer ten times worse the rest of our lives. We would do so together, and our unity would make it bearable.

"Keep going!" Pomelo said angrily. "After all our planning and effort, you would do me wrong to stay here. I'll pick my way through. Maybe there's a bush somewhere ahead. I can hide behind that."

That was unlikely, and we all knew that. A few months ago, I would have abandoned her without a second thought. But we had become old flower sisters and had worked hard together to save each other. How could we abandon her? Pomelo insisted again and said sharply, "I'll feel victorious if any one of us is free from that man. You can't waste the hopes I've had all these years to outsmart that bastard." She cried and pleaded for a few more minutes.

"We'll go ahead," Magic Gourd said, "but only to see if there is a place to hide. If there is, we'll come back down to get you. By then you'll be more rested." I wondered if Magic Gourd truly believed there was some hope to her plan. We did not say good-bye. We said we would come back to get her.

"Go, go," she said. She waved us away, as if we were nuisances. And we scampered over the rocks. I looked back every now and then and saw her on her knees, grabbing onto the next rock. My heart seized, and although she had ordered us to go, I felt I had betrayed her. After an hour, I could no longer bear it.

"We have to turn back," I said.

"I was thinking the same," Magic Gourd said. "He'll catch us later anyway. We cannot hide in the forest forever."

"We can try carrying her over the rocks," I said. "Together, it may be possible."

"It doesn't matter whether we can or can't. We will be together."

We hurried down with clouds of dust behind us. I was so scared I thought my heart would burst. At last we spotted Pomelo. She was seated on a boulder. We looked farther down the path. Perpetual was close enough now that we could make out his face, his thick eyebrows. He was swinging his arms forcefully, propelling himself forward. He must have already spotted Pomelo. He was shouting her name. She did nothing. She had given up, too tired to move forward even one more inch. I saw a bloody mark across her forehead. She must have fallen. She was shaking her head, as if dazed.

Perpetual was now two short turns beneath her. He stopped and raised his arm again. "I'll beat you bitches to death!"

Pomelo scooted backward by pushing her feet against a rock in front of her and loosened it. It slid and buried itself into the soft soil before hitting the path. She pushed against another rock, and we realized she was doing this on purpose. She pushed against a cluster of smaller rocks, and those tumbled and sailed in the air. A few hit boulders below and ricocheted in another direction, singing as they continued downward. They did not come close to hitting Perpetual, but he saw what she was doing, cursed, and pumped his legs even faster. She pushed at the rocks with her crutches, her feet, her hands. They flew at angles away from Perpetual. He had now turned onto the path right below her. She shoved rocks as fast as she could, and a dozen walnut-size ones hit the boulders below and soared in a new direction. One flew by twenty feet in front of Perpetual. He stopped and looked back, then forward and up at Pomelo. His face looked more determined and he rushed upward.

Pomelo's face was red from the effort. She leaned back on both arms and pushed hard. I held my breath and watched as dozens of rocks, thumb- to fist-size, tumbled down in clouds of dust, bouncing and knocking other rocks loose, whistling as they tore through the air between Pomelo and Perpetual. Perpetual dodged away from the tumbling rocks, and as he ran for cover toward a boulder in front, he glanced up, and a red explosion covered his face and twisted his head to the side then backward. His limbs looked boneless as he fell backward. Magic Gourd and I did not move at first, but Pomelo was stumbling to reach Perpetual, and we raced down to stop her. We all reached him at the same time and saw a red mash of flesh without eyes, nose, or mouth. His torso and limbs were turned the wrong way. Dust was still settling around him. Blood spread like a banner under him.

Magic Gourd nudged me and gestured to Pomelo. She was sitting on the ground. She appeared to be gleeful over what she had done. Each time she looked down at Perpetual's body, she leaned back with openmouthed gales of laughter. It was shocking. When we went to her, I realized she was wailing like a madwoman. She turned to look at us, and fixed on her face was an expression of helplessness and horror. She reached for us, and we sat beside her and cried without words. She continued to wail: "Bastard! Why did you make me do that?" She told us between sobs that she still hated him. She needed to kill him to save us and was too scared to do anything else but push and push. But at the very moment the rock smashed his face, she did not want it to happen. She had killed him and there was no wrongdoing. Yet to kill another—with a stone or by leading him over a cliff—taints your spirit and you set yourself apart from those who have never killed. Any one of us could have been the one to do it. I was grateful she had saved us from Perpetual and from being his executioner. I put my heart into her deep well of sadness as I imagined her agony in seeing what she had done over and over again, for the rest of her life. I now recalled that Edward had told me: "To kill another person is also violence done to yourself, and you bear the damage to the end of your days."

Pomelo wanted us to bury him. She said it was not decent to leave him to vultures and wolves. We convinced her otherwise. If anyone found him, they would think he had died because of a rockslide, and that fate had brought those rocks down, and not her two feet.

Beyond the forest, the path wound around the mountain, and when we emerged on the other side, we saw a shaded grove, a small pool of water, and a spring that fed it. We immediately set down our bundles and drank the sweet water, before splashing our faces. Farther ahead, another spring was set in a dark hollow. That must have been Perpetual's hideaway. I stopped when we were fifty feet away. I saw the back of a seated man: the hermit. For a moment, I thought the man would turn around, and we would see it was Perpetual. I picked up a rock, and so did Magic Gourd.

"Hey there!" Magic Gourd called out. The figure did not answer. She took a few steps forward and called again. He made no motion. Then she turned back toward us.

"It's what I thought. Our monk has meditated so long, he has become a boulder."

We hurried over and stepped around the boulder and found ourselves in the grotto. Against one side water streamed from a crack and onto a boulder worn down into the shape of a bowl. There was nothing else there. No treasure box. Not even a place to sit.

Magic Gourd became suspicious of a pile of rocks next to the grotto. She quickly knocked the rock pile apart, and we were suddenly looking into a small dark cave half our height. A rope lay at the entrance. She pulled, and the three of us joined in, dragging something heavy toward us. I hoped it was not a body. The first thing we saw were pale spiders scurrying over the top of a box. We jumped back. Magic Gourd broke off a branch and swept away the creatures.

The box contained books and dozens of small scrolls. We were disappointed. Where was our jewelry—the rings, bracelets, and necklaces that Perpetual had taken from us? Pomelo unrolled a scroll. It was a poem. She pulled out a book. It contained the edicts of Emperor Qianlong. I spotted something at the bottom of the box, and we quickly dug out the rest of the books and lifted out two slim cases.

One was made of hardened leather and was longer than a book. It had a gold-embossed illustration of a courtyard compound and its inhabitants. There was no lock on the latch. Pomelo lifted the lid. I held my breath—and there it was, our jewelry. I fingered my gold bangle, a pearl necklace, and the jade-and-diamond ring Loyalty had given me, which Magic Gourd had refused to sell, against my wishes. She had said the ring was like a bank account. All I had to do was wave it at Loyalty and money would flow.

Magic Gourd found her silver bangle and two gold hairpins. Pomelo had more: a diamond hairpin, two gold bangles, several rings, and jade and diamond earrings.

"Charm could have taken our jewelry," Pomelo said. "She could have reasoned we would never come this far. But she took only her valuables. She is a good person."

The other box was made of plain wood and had a brass latch. It was heavy. We lifted the lid and the three of us gasped at the same time. Inside were twelve little gold ingots and thirty-three Mexican silver dollars. When I reached the town at Buddha's Hand, I would have money to buy food, a place to stay, and respect.

We chose to rest that night in the grotto. I woke several times, startled by dreams that Perpetual was standing over me. Pomelo moaned: "He's come for me." I assured her she was having a bad dream. "I'm not asleep," she said. "I feel him standing nearby."

We left before sunrise. According to the map, we had only a few hours more before we would reach the top, unless the climb was steep or we found more rockslides. We were no longer being chased but being pulled by hopes that we would soon find a better life in the town.

"It's strange that no one from Mountain View has ever come down into Moon Pond," Magic Gourd said.

"Everyone across three counties knew about the curse and the ghosts dancing at the top," Pomelo said. "Why would anyone take the risk to come to an awful place like Moon Pond? Its reputation was widely known."

"Some people are stupid, they'll go anywhere," Magic Gourd said. "Or brave, like us."

I had never heard of a town at the very top of a mountain, except in fairy tales. But in her note, Charm had called it a town. Once we reached the ridge, we would be able to see it. In my mind, Mountain View would look exactly like the bustling city of Shanghai— with candy shops and restaurants, newspaper stands and bookstores, streets and streetlamps, a department store, a movie house, carriages, trams, and automobiles. The people would be educated and dressed in modern clothes. There would even be a river and a harbor busy with commerce—all on top of a mountain.

This Shanghai was not a place but a feeling of contentment. I was returning with myself whole and unbroken—limbs, mind, and spirit. I had discarded pride, that useless burden of self-importance I had carried around like my portable vanity with its broken mirror. Perpetual and I had pitted our pride against each other, and I would have died to prove I was superior. And if I had, would he have said, "Violet, you were better." I would rather live and do what was important—to find Little Flora, to let her know how much I loved her. I would do whatever was necessary.

When we were two turns away from the top of the mountain,

we slipped out of our farmer clothes and into our dresses. I was transformed into a modern Western woman. None of us spoke as we walked through the forest. We kept a steady pace because it would soon be dusk, then dark. I was sure that Pomelo's feet and arms were aching, but she did not mention it.

We came out of the forest and walked along a clearing and saw open sky. In front of us was a mound of rock. That was in Charm's note. And after that we would stand on the ridge. Magic Gourd and Pomelo wore the eager, innocent faces of young girls. We scrambled over the hump and there we were. Opposite was a white dome in the shape of a hand. Below was a small grassy valley. But where was the town? The valley was too small to hold a town. Even Moon Pond would not have fit in there.

"Charm said there's a town," Pomelo said, "so there is one."

The sun lowered and Buddha's Hand turned golden. I was walking in a place that was strange and familiar. I thought of the painting that had belonged to my mother, *The Valley of Amazement*. This place did not look like the painted one. But it held the same feeling, a riddle about myself. Was this place worse than what I had left behind? I was sure it was. But immediately, I wavered between doubt and certainty.

We quietly moved along the rim of the small green valley. Pomelo was panting, exhausted, and in pain. What a strong woman. We spotted a temple below in the valley. So it was not purely myth. From our distance, the temple looked gutted, nothing more than a skeletal perch for carrion birds. No ghosts danced around it. I knew Magic Gourd and Pomelo had looked for them, too.

The air was cooling, and soon the sun would be gone. The white fingers of the Buddha's Hand turned pink. We walked steadily along the ridge. The grass in the valley turned a deeper green, and the temple darkened to a burnt husk. "Ha! That temple's just a cowshed," Magic Gourd said. "Do you see any ghost cows circling around? The mind fools the eye. The eye makes us fools." She fell quiet again.

We were in that wedge of time that seemed peaceful one moment, and ominous the next. The sun kept sinking and the fingers of the Buddha's Hand turned a corpselike gray. Everything around us grew hazy and faded in color, and, in an instant, the sun was gone, and we were left with our thoughts. The town had to be close. We had come so far.

Pomelo asked for a rest. She allowed exhaustion to take over. The half moon replaced the sun. Faint stars appeared. By the time Pomelo was able to stand, the sky was a bowl of blackness and the stars that punctured it were sharp and bright. We lifted Pomelo, and she whimpered as she put her weight on her feet. We took small careful steps along the uneven ridge. It curved to the left, taking us closer to Buddha's Hand. How odd that the stars gleamed so far below, I thought. They seemed to be closer, not sharp and colored, but glowing. We could feel the warmth of them rising to us.

We shouted at the same time. "Mountain View!"

Charm was right. At Buddha's Hand, all we had to do was look down from the ridge.

It was too dark to see anything but the faraway lights of Mountain View. In our minds, we were nearly there. It might take us hours to reach it, or maybe a day, and even longer, if the path was covered with rocks and the trails became treacherous. None of that was a concern right now. We could not wait until morning. We had to start now.

We put Pomelo in the middle, and she threw her arms over our shoulders. I was surprised at how light she was, how light I felt. Together, we took our first steps and began our new life.

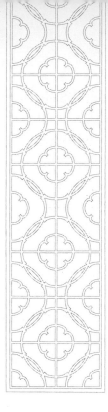

CHAPTER 12

THE VALLEY OF AMAZEMENT

San Francisco
1897
Lucia Minturn

I was sixteen when I saw what appeared to be a Chinese emperor standing in our doorway, looking as if he had just stepped off the page of a fairy-tale book. He wore a long gown of dark blue silk and a vest embroidered with symbols. His face was smooth and gently sloped, from chin to cheeks to the top of his head. He had a China-man's pigtail that ran from his crown to halfway down his spine.

"Good evening, Mrs. Minturn, Professor Minturn, Miss Minturn." He gave me only a glance. His English was unmarred and beautifully embellished with a British accent, his manners were formal, yet at ease. With my eyes closed, his voice sounded like an English gentleman's. When I opened them, the fairy-tale illustration reappeared.

Of course, I knew from the start that he wasn't an emperor, although I did hope for something illustrious like a Manchu Man-darin. Father introduced him as "Mr. Lu Shing, a Chinese student of American landscape painting, who comes to us by way of the Hudson Valley, New York, and originally from China."

"Shanghai," he said. "Those of us from Shanghai like the distinction." He wore a pleased look and radiated confidence, and I could tell he was proud that he was different from others. I was different, too, so right away we had that in common. I had been waiting for my spiritual twin to arrive, and while I hadn't imagined he would be Chinese, I was still eager to know everything about him. Before I could say to him one word more, he walked with my parents into the parlor to meet the other guests, and I was left standing in the foyer alone. They always took the best for themselves.

Right then, I wanted to possess him: his Chinese heart, mind, and soul, everything that was different, including what lay beneath that blue silk gown—a shocking thought, I know—but I had been promiscuous for nearly a year, so the leap was short between urge and frolic.

AT THE AGE of eight, I was determined to be true to My Self. Of course, that made it essential to know what My Self consisted of. My manifesto began the day I discovered that I had once possessed an extra finger on each hand, twins to my pinkies. My grandmother had recommended that the surplus be amputated before leaving the hospital, lest people think there was a familial tendency toward giving birth to octopuses. Mother and Father were Freethinkers, whose opinions were based on reason, logic, deduction, and their own opinions. Mother, who disagreed with any advice my grandmother had to give, said: "Should the extra fingers be removed simply to enable her to wear gloves from a dry goods store?" They took me home with all my fingers in place. But then an old family friend of my father's, Mr. Maubert, who was also my piano teacher, convinced them to turn my unusual hands into ordinary ones. He was a former concert pianist, who, early in his promising career, lost his right arm during the siege of Paris by the Prussians. "There are only a few piano compositions for one hand," he said to my parents, "and none for six fingers. If you intend for her to have musical training, it would be a pity if she had to take up the tambourine due to lack of suitable instruments." Mr. Maubert was the one who proudly informed me when I was eight that he had influenced the decision.

Few can understand the shock of a little girl learning that part of her was considered undesirable and thus needed to be violently removed. It made me fearful that people could change parts of me, without my knowledge and permission. And thus began my quest to know which of my many attributes I needed to protect, the whole of which I named scientifically "My Pure Self-Being."

In the beginning, the complete list comprised my preferences and dislikes, my strong feelings for animals, my animosity toward anyone who laughed at me, my aversion to stickiness, and several more things I have now forgotten. I also collected secrets about myself, mostly what had wounded my heart, and the very fact that they needed to be kept private was proof that they were part of My Pure Self-Being. I later added to the list my intelligence, opinions of others, fears and revulsions, and certain nagging discomforts, which I later knew as worries. A few years later, after I stained my undergarments, Mother explained to me "the biology that led to your existence"—the gist of which was my beginning as an egg slipping down a fallopian tube. She made it sound as if I had been a mindless blob and that upon entry into the world I took on a personality shaped through my parents' guidance.

In appearance, I could not avoid biology completely. I inherited a composite of them both, green eyes, dark wavy hair, small ears, and so forth. But the worst was my mother's flushed face when she was indignant, which on me showed as warm splotches that bloomed over my neck and breasts, and not a lovely pink blush either, but more like painful scorch marks. The splotches betrayed me at my most flustered, and at its worst, my entire face was enflamed, which caused me to flee to my room. My mother had learned to control her emotions so well she seldom showed anything beyond the sudden emergence of a healthy glow. I tried hard to control mine, but that proved as hard as holding my breath, especially when they humiliated me in front of people, saying things like "Lucia has peaks of emotion over stray cats." "Lucia has an unnatural aversion to flowers with thorns." "Lucia has whims. Wait an hour, and she'll forget what the latest was." They were hurtful and did not seem to know it. But that should not excuse them.

Mother and Father were eccentric, and that was not just my opinion. My father, John Minturn, had a respectable enough job as a professor of history and a scholar of art, renowned for his connoisseurship in figure painting. But the figures he liked best were those of nudes, "goddesses," he said, "whose diaphanous gowns had slipped to their classical ivory ankles." Father was also a collector of fetish objects from the Far East—and in his study he prominently displayed on one wall an erotic painting from Japan of a twisted couple with a look of insanity on their faces. In a glass case, you could view the thin ivory and horsehair whips that Chinese scholars used to chase away flies. And in that same case were the shoes of Manchu women who had lived in the imperial palaces of the Garden of Clear Ripples. The name itself made me long to be there until Father told me it had been burned and was ransacked. The shoes had been part of the loot. They sat on a tall blade of wood and resembled unmoored boats balanced on their fins. This impractical design, my father said, gave Manchu women the same mincing gait of Chinese women who bound their feet into hooves to give them greater sexual appeal.

My mother was the daughter of a botanical artist and amateur naturalist, Asa Grimke, who traveled for three years with the great botanist Joseph Dalton Hooker to Darjeeling, Gujarat, Sikkim, and Assam, where he made illustrations of newly discovered rare species of flowering plants. He had a minor reputation based on those illustrations, and that led to moving his wife, Mary, and daughter, Harriet—my mother—to San Francisco. He had received a large commission to illustrate the flora of the Pacific Coast. Unfortunately, he stepped in front of a spooked horse belonging to the very man who had come to fetch him, Herbert Minturn, a wealthy man who had made his fortune in the opium trade in China and the purchase of land in San Francisco. At the funeral, Mr. Minturn, who had recently lost his wife, said to my grandmother that he understood her grief. He invited our family to stay in his mansion until we found our bearings. My grandmother never found her bearings. She found herself in Mr. Minturn's bedroom due to numerous episodes of sleepwalking, a condition that she said could not be controlled, either by will or medicine. Since Mr. Minturn took full advantage of her malady, he married her. That was the story Mother gave in deriding her mother's disloyalty to the memory of her father.

As fate would have it, Mr. Minturn had a son, John, who was twelve years my mother's senior. Mother was six when they came to live in the house. He was away at college most of the time. But when Mother turned eighteen, the young man who had treated her as his baby sister made her his wife, and within a year, she gave birth to me. So that was the house I was born into.

Those were the people who raised me, and none of them were like-minded. We all lived separate lives under the same roof. Grandfather had once been an important man who seemed to lose more of his intelligence every year. He dispensed outdated business advice at dinner parties, but people were kind and said he was well meaning. My grandmother was not well meaning. She managed to insult people while acting as if she were nice. She was sneaky and started arguments with my mother, and once my mother had overheated like a boiler about to blow, and splotches had spread over her neck and face, my grandmother would say calmly that she saw no reason to argue and would walk away. We all called my grandmother Mrs. Minturn, even her husband did. Mother was often livid that Father was never as angry as she was. He said his mother-in-law didn't bother him because she was laughable, and that Mother should take the same attitude. Mother was further infuriated that their friends praised Father for his good nature, which my mother said was nothing more than ignoring problems as a way of solving them. In earlier years, I liked my father in some ways. He was social, chatty, witty; people enjoyed being with him and he paid special attention to me. He indulged me. He sometimes gave me rarities I longed for, or some version of them, like a garter snake, instead of a poisonous one. In later years, he seemed to be as aware of me as the stray cat that wandered in one day and never left.

Mother had two moods. She was either temperamental, meaning short-tempered and unhappy, or she was melancholy, meaning listless and unhappy. For the most part, she was a recluse. She spent warm days in the garden, planting flowers or cutting off their heads. She allowed me to choose only one flower, which I could plant in a sunny spot of bare ground near the cabbage roses. I chose violets, many species of them, purple and yellow, white and purple, pink and purple. The violets were unmanageable and invaded any bare spot under a tree or bush. My mother called them Johnny-jump-up weeds, and she would have pulled them out if I had not reminded her that she had allowed me to plant them, and so they were mine.

If it were not for that garden, I think Mother might have pushed harder for my father to leave the comforts of the family home and buy one of the row houses sprouting up on just about every hill, six or seven to a block. During melancholy times, she spent most of her days in her study, where she examined dead insects found in dollops of amber her father had given her—twenty-two pieces that he had found in an abandoned mine in Gujarat, which he had stuffed in his pockets like a thief. Her golden world contained flies, ants, gnats, termites, and other pests. She held a magnifying glass to them every day for hours. If I had allowed her to guide my interests, I would have wound up in an asylum.

She intended that I become an angry little suffragette from the day I was born. She named me Lucretia after Lucretia Mott, the orator. As I grew older, I disliked the name Lucretia more and more because the syllables reminded me of words with like sounds: *ludicrous, secretions,* and *cretin.* I went back and forth between the names Lucia and Lulu as alternatives. Mother said Lulu was ordinary, so that was the name I used more often around her, unless I wanted to be less ordinary, and that depended on whom I was speaking to.

As I already mentioned, my mother and father were Freethinkers. That extended to their freely talking about any subject in front of me. That lack of censorship might seem admirable, but I took it as neglect. They had no regard for my mental well-being, never stopping to think that perhaps they should not mention that Mr. Beekins had been found in the men's dormitory with his trousers around his ankles. He said this right before Mr. Beekins came to dinner. On numerous occasions, Father would tote out his collection of fetish objects to show other collectors, and I could tell by the glances that these people made toward me and their hushed tones that I should not have been there. When I was younger, I played with some of the objects in Father's study, not knowing what they were, one being a set of three-inch carved ivory manikins, whose details included penises and breasts, which I later discovered were manikins that women had used during masturbation. Despite all this frank talk about sexual matters, Mother and Father appeared to have no sexual urges for each other. They maintained separate bedrooms, and in all my years in the house I never heard the door of one opening and closing and then the door of the other opening and closing, sealing the sexual pact. Their relationship was more the former one they had as brother and sister.

I did not discover until I was fifteen that Father's urges were plentiful and he took them elsewhere. By then I was in the habit of stealing into Father's study to peruse his pornographic books, especially one with fifty-two photographs between blue cloth covers, showing muscular men and plump women engaged in a variety of coital contortions. *Classical Anatomy of Calisthenics* it said. I also found a large box made of burl wood with a top that slid off sideways. It contained love letters to him, many of them and in different handwriting, written by both men and women, which described lusty acts, memories of old or recent or soon-to-be consummated ones.

The more I read, the more upset I became. He gave many people his love, whereas it had been years since I had received any special attention from him. His lovers called him "the God of the Vortex of Love," "Thunderous Zeus," "Colossus of Cocks," "Grinding Goliath." They described themselves as his "Awakening Volupta," or "Voracious Vulva," or "Vibrating Vagina." They were factual about length, width, turgidity, timeliness, and durability. They talked about sex as if they were gluttons eating certain foods, which I would never be able to eat again: pudding, gravy, cream, and sausages. They praised my father for his effectiveness in causing geologic disaster and bad weather— fissures and earthquakes, floods and tornados, the upheaval of new islands out of ocean depths. And all I had wanted was simple affection. He had given it away, so freely to so many, and in an unfathomable variety of ways.

I was furious. I did not need his affection anymore. I had urges, too.

FOR MY FIRST sexual adventure, I selected the location before I did the boy. The grove was at the far corner of the grounds of the university where Father taught. The fall weather was warm, and the hydrangea bushes were softly lush with pendulous blooms. The grove reminded me of the settings of the paintings of nude gods and goddesses, an opportunity for divine fornication.

Only young men attended the university, and I gathered a lot of attention simply by sitting on a bench under an oak tree. The faculty knew me as Dr. Minturn's daughter, and thus, it was not unusual that I would be there, lolling on the lawn, studying up on calisthenics. The pictorial book lay in my lap, and to any young man walking by, I appeared to be both reading and waiting for someone. A number of boys who took the path near where I was seated paused to ask what I was reading. To the first six young men, I replied that it was a book on the principles of sewing. To the seventh, I said teasingly, "Wouldn't you like to know?" This young man was worthy of an audition. He had the requisite virile broad-shouldered torso and godlike features: thick dark hair and sky-blue eyes, beautiful strong hands, a sensuous pouty upper lip, and a deep furrowed philtrum, which, according to one letter to my father, was an erotic groove between lip and nosetip, which, like other grooves, should be thoroughly licked. I remember also that he had a confident attitude and was at ease flirting with me and let his language become quickly lurid—"I would very much like to see what's in your lap"—the sign of a man with coital expertise. He offered me his hand and pulled me up with such grace I felt like a ballerina.

Among the hydrangeas, he kissed me with earnestness, banging his lips against my teeth and covering me with saliva from nose to chin. I turned my face upward so that he could kiss my neck instead, and this sent ticklish chills of pleasure down my spine. He placed his beautiful hands, now rather shaky, around my adolescent breasts and kissed them through the cotton blouse. As my blouse grew damper with his kisses and with no sign that anything further would happen, I considered cutting short the audition. But then he unbuttoned my blouse and licked my nipples. I again felt chills of excitement. They soon died down as he fumbled with more of my buttons. I gave him a peek of just one page of the calisthenics book and told him to hurry. I waited as he struggled like a hare in a trap to unbutton his trousers with his beautiful but clumsy hands. At the very moment his penis sprang loose, we heard voices, and he pulled on his trousers and stuffed his cock back in with apparent pain. The image of his cock remained—how different it looked from the photographs, not smooth and still as white marble, but beefy, veined, and oddly helpless, like a blind hairless rodent seeking a milk-filled breast. I buttoned my blouse, smoothed my hair, and retied the bow. The voices passed. I stood up. I gave the young man my address and said to wait for me by the oak tree at ten o'clock that night.

He was precisely on time. I took him through the back door into the kitchen and we climbed the narrow stairs that the servants used. Halfway up, he asked if I was sure this was wise. "Wise?" I said. "How could this ever be wise?" We passed the landing to my bedroom and continued up the curling staircase to the turret. I had draped the room with Indian saris and covered the floor with a mishmash of small Persian carpets I had cut up, ones discarded because of cigar burns and spilled wax. A ladder of seven steps led to a sleeping loft adjacent to a bay window. A thick featherbed sat on the loft floor. This was my retreat, where I read and napped, where I sometimes hid when I wanted to kick and scream and did not know why. I had already lit the candles, sprinkled the quilt with rosewater, and set *Classical Anatomy of Calisthenics* in the bookshelf with its spine jutting out. We climbed up and I plopped on my back with a friendly smile, and we began. He provided kisses on my mouth and neck, these being gentler by my request. He undid the buttons on my blouse, but with more deftness than before, having practiced during the intervening hours, I suspected. I had already removed my undergarments, all of them, so we would not have to waste time with the rest. My Would-Be Vortex seemed hesitant about what we were about to do, because I had just told him I was Professor Minturn's daughter—and I admit, it was just to see his reaction. He was awestruck as he watched me take off my clothes, and he stared at my pubis, before surveying the rest of my illicit parts from breasts to buttocks with religious solemnity. After enough staring had gone on, I helped him remove his clothes. His penis swung out, and I ran a finger up one vein and down another. What a strange apparatus. He groaned and was about to fall on me when I told him to wait. I then pulled out the pictorial book from the low shelf and showed him the calisthenics exercise I thought we might try. My selection looked simple enough to do and required no standing, which would have been difficult because of the low height of the ceiling. The young Titan nodded, accepting the challenge. I swung my legs up and back, fully exposing all my privates, and he got into the correct position, one knee by my waist, the other by my rump, and his head squeezed halfway under the crook of my leg. But now his penis was out of alignment with my pudenda. So he checked the photograph, made an adjustment of his left knee, and that slight movement was enough for him to expend himself on my thigh. I was hugely disappointed—"You've ruined it!"—and was sorry I had not stopped myself from blurting that out. He was crushed. After half an hour, he recovered from embarrassment and we laughed about our overexcitement. But when we tried the same position, he achieved the same result. He begged me not to tell anyone and promised he would practice. The following night, he came fortified with whiskey. He chose an easier calisthenics position, and finally, after bearing down and pushing and making adjustments to see if he was in the right place, he penetrated me. I bore the pain well, I thought, and I was glad to be done with the opening of the portal. But all at once, he sat bolt upright, patted the sheets, and realized he had caused the spillage of virgin blood. He was deeply troubled. I said to him: "If you had known, what would you have done instead—packed up your pulsating penis and gone home?" We had another four encounters, which improved his stamina somewhat. But I did not think I was receiving full advantage, given I had not yet experienced anything I would have equated with geologic disasters.

Over the next year, I recruited half a dozen willing young men from my post on the university lawn. Most of them acted as if they had seduced me. They became solicitous once we were in bed. "Are you sure?" "Do you mind?" They were older than I by a few years, yet they were immature, exuding confidence one moment and then awkward boyish uncertainty the next. I disliked having to encourage the bashful ones without sounding critical or teacherlike. If my young man was nervous, I took this as a sign he felt that what we were doing was morally wrong. I would have none of that. One Adonis was quite effective. Bad weather appeared—a small whirlwind, high waves—but after two months of jouncing, I was bothered by his dull personality. I continued with him and took on another who was less adept but able to hold his end of a conversation after we were finished.

Mother and Father, meanwhile, were oblivious to my sexual adventures, just as they had been to nearly everything I did. I don't know why I expected more from them. If you have never had love, how would you know that you were missing it? Perhaps it had always been part of My Pure Self-Being to be born expecting a mother and a father's attention—their care, more important than a bug in resin or a fetish manikin. That place of higher importance would have made me believe I was loved.

I wanted Mother and Father to know about my promiscuity—to punish them and have them look at me with open disgust. I could then tell them in shouts of fury how selfish they were, how great my own disgust was, and I would name incidents I had written down. I would tell my father that I had enjoyed many volcanic eruptions, like those discharged by pen in letters to him.

ON THE NIGHT my Chinese emperor came to dinner, my parents invited eight other guests who were frequent visitors to our house: Dr. and Mrs. Beekins—an astronomer and his wife—an opera singer, Miss Huffard, and her lover, Charles Hatchett; my piano teacher, Mr. Maubert, and his maiden sister, Miss Maubert; the esteemed suffragette Mrs. Croswell; and a well-regarded landscape artist, Miss Pond, whose reputation included having had an illegitimate child she had had to give away. My father visited her often for well-described sex.

We gathered in the salon for sherry. Father introduced our Chinese guest as "Mr. Lu Shing. The first name, Lu, is actually his family name, and Shing is the given one."

"To Americans, our names are backward," Lu Shing said with an amused smile. "But in China, it's the natural order. Family comes first in name and duty. I go by both names, Lu Shing, always together, the son indivisible from the family."

Lu, I thought, like Lucia and Lulu. When it was my turn to be introduced, Father called me Lulu, and I corrected him and said: "Lucia."

"Ah, she is Lucia tonight," Father said, and winked. My face grew heated.

"Mr. Lu Shing," the astronomer said, "your English is better than mine. How can that be?"

"British tutors from the age of five. My father is in the Ministry of Foreign Relations and saw an advantage in speaking English."

He is privileged, I said to myself. He has social standing. He has a beautiful voice.

"Lu Shing is a student of Western art," Father said. "He has been under the tutelage of landscape painters of the Hudson River School for the last three years. And now he has the rare opportunity to apprentice with Albert Bierstadt, who is returning to California to capture the Farallon Islands and Yosemite once again."

Murmurs of congratulations followed.

"I am more of a butler and porter," Lu Shing said. "I arrange for accommodations and travel needs. But I am indeed privileged to help. I'll be able to watch Mr. Bierstadt at the earliest stages of his work."

Father started a lively conversation over the differences between American art and Chinese art, oil paints and black ink. Lu Shing talked easily, as if these people, many of them years older, had been friends through the ages. He was politely deferential at the right times, but anyone could see that he had outshone them in whatever he said. He showed appreciation when they expressed ideas he had not heard of before. He seemed secretly amused much of the time.

Father threw out more conversational topics, as if he were teaching a class: Chinese traditions and Western influence. The changing

society of Shanghai. Changing art forms. The influence of art on society and vice versa. Every time Father started another boring subject, I
wanted to shout, "Enough!"

"How do we capture a moment of emotion in art?" Miss Pond
said, and looked at Father.

Opinions made the rounds, and when it was Lu Shing's turn,
he said, "The moment is altered as soon as I try to capture it, so for
me, it's impossible."

How true, I thought. Moments are gone as soon as you think
about them.

Father was unstoppable, Mother was quiet, and Miss Pond
admired too often what Father said. And then Miss Maubert also
chimed in with much praise for Father, and with shining eyes, and
so did Mrs. Croswell, who had a coquettish tilt to her head. Even Dr.
Beekins, the astronomer, had a twinkle in his eye for Father. They
were enamored of him. Were they his coven of sex acolytes? Did Lu
Shing notice? Was I the only one who saw it? All around us, the conversation grew louder. They spoke as a chorus on Redemption. The
symbolism of gods. Christian salvation. Vice and virtue. Purgatorio.
Sins. Karma. Fate.

"Lu Shing," Father said, "what's your opinion on fate?"

"I am Chinese, Dr. Minturn," he said. "I cannot recommend it
highly enough."

I went to stand by him and tried to look calm and sophisticated.
"Mr. Lu Shing, I could not tell if you were joking. Do you truly believe
in Oriental fate?"

"I do indeed. We are all here by fate, Oriental or otherwise."

I was about to ask him more, but Father tapped his wineglass
and announced that we would now see what Lu Shing had achieved
while studying in the United States. He held up a small, framed painting. Even from a distance, I could tell it was a masterpiece. It had
lovely colors. And I saw by the faces on others that they had the same
opinion. The painting was passed around, and praise upon praise

were heaped on both the painting and the artist: "I did not expect to see such skill in a student." "The colors are rich yet subtle." "It captures a perfect moment."

Finally, the painting reached me. My first feeling was eeriness. I recognized the place in the painting. I had lived there. Yet I knew that was impossible. The light of the room behind me disappeared, the voices of the others faded away, and I was transported into the painting, to the long green valley. I felt its atmosphere as real and present, the touch of its cool air, and I had a complete understanding that this was my home, and the solitude was not loneliness but the clarity of who I was. I was that long green valley, unchanged from the beginning of time. The five mountains were part of me as well, my strength and courage to face whatever entered the valley. The sky held dark gray clouds, which cast shadows over part of the valley, and I understood that storms had once buffeted me and I had had to cling to the trees on the mountain. I had once feared that the dark clouds would evaporate and so would I. But look—the undersides of the clouds were pink, pendulous, and erotic. And most wondrous of all: a golden vale lay beyond the opening of the mountains. In that golden place was the painter of this utopia. I caught Lu Shing watching me with his pleased expression. It was as if he knew exactly what I was thinking.

"What do *you* say, Lucia?" my father said. "You are clearly taken with it."

I gave a more intellectual appraisal: "It captures many moments, many emotions," I began, looking at Lu Shing, "hope, love, and purity. I see in it immortality, neither beginning nor end. It seems to be saying all moments are immortal and will never disappear, nor will peace in the valley, or the strength of mountains, or the openness of the sky—"

I would have gone on but Father interrupted. "Lucia is given to peaks of emotion, and Lu Shing, your painting is the lucky recipient of that tonight." Everyone laughed warmly. I felt my neck flush.

Father and Mother always ridiculed me when they thought I was too emotional. I had peaks and peaks of emotion, a mountain range of them. They believed I had to control them. Mother did hers into a stupor. But did Father control his orgiastic peaks?

"I am lucky, indeed," Lu Shing said. "The truth is, I had the grandiose intention of capturing one moment of immortality and I believed I had failed. But Miss Minturn has lifted me with her compliment that I have captured all the moments of immortality. Truly, no artist can be more appreciative to hear that."

The room became shinier. The crystal drops of the chandelier sparkled and flashed, the halos of candles grew long. The faces of others had changed into strangers, and only Lu Shing was familiar. That was the moment I was knocked nearly senseless. I had never known this feeling before, yet I recognized it as being felled by love. I fought to remain calm in front of the others as I held on to my secret. I now noticed a small brass plaque on the bottom of the frame. I read it aloud. *"The Valley of Amazement."* Murmurs went around about the suitability of the name.

"I thought so, too," Lu Shing said, "when I came across its mention in a Chinese translation of a Sufi poem, "The Colloquy of the Birds." I took the title without knowing what it actually referred to and discovered later that the Valley of Amazement is not a pleasant way station. It's a place of doubt, and doubt is dangerous to a painter. So now I lack a title."

Everyone protested the Sufi's meaning. The Valley of Amazement aptly described the painting, someone said, and it bore no relation to the gloomier reference. "We are not Sufis," Miss Maubert said.

They were wrong to discount his feelings of doubt so casually. If he had doubts, he had to confront them, knock them down, and wrestle them to see that they were not real. Otherwise, they would remain in his mind. I could help him do this, simply by being with him, showing him how his own confidence could conquer doubt. I had done so myself countless times, I would tell him.

The conversation moved on to other topics, and then the maid arrived to announce our dinner was ready. Lu Shing was seated on my side of the table but at the far end, closest to where Father sat at the head of the table. Between us were the ample opera singer and Mr. Beekins. My view of him was eclipsed by the mezzo-soprano's breasts and voluminous hair. I was frustrated that I had been kept so far from him. Mr. Maubert was on my left side, and Miss Huffard was next to him. I looked around the table. The faces of the suffragette, Miss Maubert, and the astronomer were no longer engorged with adoration for Father. How strange this night was. The candles with their dense odor flickered as the cook set down a large leg of some animal swimming in larded gravy. When the opera singer sat back, I stole glances at Lu Shing's smooth face and the shaved bareness of his scalp, his naked splendor. He did not glance down the table at me.

Doubt came. Perhaps he felt none of what had taken over my mind and body. I had drunk an elixir, and he had not tasted a drop. He might find white women unappealing. He might have been intimate with a hundred beautiful women of his own kind. I had fooled myself in my craving for affection.

Through this gray cloud, I heard chatter and Lu Shing's voice rising above. The light in the room now had a greasy gleam. The conversation had moved to Mr. Bierstadt's stay at the Cliff House, where he would have a superior view of the distant Farallon Islands on clear days. Lu Shing had already portaged Mr. Bierstadt's trunks to the hotel and would prepare his traveling painter's studio.

"I've stayed at the Cliff House," Miss Pond said, "and each morning, when I looked out my window, I never ceased to be in wonder that the islands were twenty-seven miles away—except, of course, when I saw nothing but fog. Will you be staying there as well, Mr. Lu Shing?"

"An apprentice doesn't have the luxury," he said. "I found a small boardinghouse close to the Cliff House."

"You should stay with us," I said quickly. "We have plenty of room."

Mother looked surprised, and Father instantly agreed. "You must."

"We often have guests," I added. "Isn't that so, Mother?"

She nodded, and others agreed that he would be more comfortable. Lu Shing politely declined until Father said he would enjoy showing Lu Shing his entire collection of paintings while he was our guest.

Mother called the maid over and told her to freshen the blue room. That was the guest room on the south side of the second floor. Mine was on the north, and, of course, the turret was just above.

"Mother," I said, "I think Lu Shing would enjoy staying in the turret. It's small, but it has the best view of the Bay." Father hailed that as an excellent suggestion. Miss Pond volunteered to take Lu Shing in her carriage so he could fetch his things from the boardinghouse. I searched for signs that she wanted to seduce him. But then my father offered to accompany them.

Early the next morning, Lu Shing and my parents were already seated in the breakfast room when I arrived. How had they all known to rise early and why was I not told? I was excited to see his Chinese face. But then I noticed something was missing. He was wearing ordinary clothes: dark trousers, a white shirt and gray waistcoat. I wished he would change back into the Chinese garments. On the other hand, I enjoyed looking at his godlike physique. He was taller than father, who was of average height.

"Everyone who sails to the Farallons wants to see the sea lions, whales, and dolphins along the way," I heard Mother say. "That's the spectators' experience." She had her precious book of illustrated birds on the table. "I think that the variety of birds on the islands is far more interesting. Mr. Bierstadt evidently thinks so, too, since he painted many during his last visit. Among my favorites is the

Cassin's Auklet, which look quite ordinary from a distance, fat and molelike, until you know what to notice as you draw closer. The bluish feet, the white spot over the eye, and the rounded head and thin beak. That's the challenge with birds—to notice the details and their differences—those of murres, puffins, cormorants—" I had not seen my mother this animated in a long time.

Father broke in. "Harriet, you should accompany Mr. Bierstadt and our young friend on their voyage to the Farallons. They could use your sharp eye."

Mother was both surprised and flattered. She clearly liked the idea.

"I know Mr. Bierstadt would appreciate it very much," Lu Shing said. "But only if you can spare the time."

"I would enjoy a day of bird-watching as well!" I said.

Mother gave me a skeptical eye. "You suffer from seasickness."

"I would suffer to see the birds," I said. "You know I've always had an interest in birds." She gave me another doubtful look.

"There's time for me to study them ahead of time as well."

That night, I squirmed in bed, debating whether to sneak up the curling stairs to the turret. Lu Shing was sleeping right above me. I imagined him sprawled on the bed with moonlight washing over his naked body. What excuses could I use to enter the room: a desire to see a ship coming into the Bay, the moon, the stars, a book I had been reading and left behind? And then I remembered that there was, in fact, just such a book. *Classical Anatomy of Calisthenics.* A thrill ran through me and throbbed in my center. The next day, while Lu Shing was at the Cliff House setting up Mr. Bierstadt's painting studio, I darted up to the turret to find the pictorial book. I had tucked it under the feather bed. There it was. I pulled it out. I put it in the bookshelf, halfway pulled out. After fifty-two pages, he would be more than happy to welcome me.

The next morning, I greeted Lu Shing in the breakfast room.

He was friendly, but he did not give me fond looks or secret smiles, nothing like those Miss Pond gave my father. He must not have seen the calisthenics guide to love.

"I have a collection of favorite books in the turret," I said. "You're welcome to read any of them." I looked for telltale signs that he had already.

"Thank you. For the moment, I am reading as much as I can about the Farallon Islands and Yosemite."

"I think we have an excellent book on Yosemite. Look through the little bookcase in the loft."

We went directly from breakfast to Mother's study. She sat in one corner, scrutinizing her bugs, and we sat kitty-corner from her at a letter-writing table. The large illustrated book of birds lay between us. We dutifully noted coloration, shapes of beaks, wingspan, and tail length—a hundred details that provided opportunity for conversation consisting of: "That tail is longer than this one."

He turned pages to the right, and I turned pages to the left. I gave him my strongest flirtatious look: a glance over my shoulder with my eyes cast downward before they slowly rose and fixed on him. He returned a simple smile. Twice I made it seem that I had accidentally brushed my arm against his. He pulled away and apologized. When speaking to him about wingspan or migratory paths, I drew close to his face and whispered, purportedly so as not to disturb my mother's important work. I saw no signs of interest from him and grew more disheartened by the hour.

"Lucia," my mother called out, "don't rest your elbows on the pages."

I quickly leaned back and felt the flush of humiliation rise up my neck.

Lu Shing turned to me and said. "Lucia, Lu Shing. So similar. You Americans call it coincidence. We Chinese call it fate."

CHAPTER 13

FATA MORGANA

San Francisco
1897
Lucia Minturn

Three days before the scheduled voyage to the Farallon Islands, Mr. Bierstadt sent a hasty note of apology to our house, saying that he had to return to New York because his wife's illness had worsened.

"Consumption," Lu Shing said, "that is the rumor and concern."

My parents made murmurs of sympathy for the master painter. I silently cursed him. There would be no more bird studies, no romantic voyage.

"What are your plans?" Father asked Lu Shing.

"My family has been asking for the past year when I would return, and I can finally give them the answer they've longed to hear."

China. He was going to step back into the fairy-tale book, the covers would close, and that would be the end of the tale between Lucia and Lu Shing. Until now, it had not occurred to me that he would one day make the migratory return. If only he knew what was at stake for me, why I needed to escape to the green valley, wherever and whatever that was. I lived in a madhouse with soulless people. A mother who was in love with the bodies of insects. A grandmother who started the fires of argument. A grandfather who wandered use-less with sufficient wealth. A father who disbursed affection into the voracious vulvas of women outside this house. These were the lunatics who sat around the table, airing superiority at dinner, where Father presided like Sophocles chewing a pork chop, directing a debate about the meaningless parsing of art. I had to resist letting them change me, humiliate me, tamp down my emotions.

Our names, Lucia, Lu Shing. He said it was fate. But I was mis-taken. He did not mean we would cling together from those words forward. Fate blew us together, two grains in a cloud of pollen, and then it blew us apart. I had counted on too much because of my peaks of emotion. I was the fool, now overwrought.

I heard Lu Shing speaking about his disappointment in not being able to study with Mr. Bierstadt. He mentioned a mundane matter—settling the hotel bill and removing Mr. Bierstadt's belong-ings, booking passage on a boat to Shanghai, preferably via a fast route. He believed there was one leaving in a week. Mother asked if I was ill. I nodded, grateful for the excuse to leave before my face turned blotchy with shame. I went quickly to my room and sat at my desk to write down quickly what I was already losing.

The whole of me was contained in that painting. I cannot adequately explain it in words, except that knowledge of my Self-Being is already slipping away from view, and soon all that will remain are these words. I had felt my soul and now it is barely remembered—all of me at once that was truth, purity, strength, what was unchangeable and original, no matter how much was quashed and ridiculed by others. I wanted its creator, the mirage maker. I wanted him to show me his doubts, so I could show him mine, and together we could find the real valley and not just the one in the painting, but a real valley between two mountains, away from the mad world.

I know now it was not an ecstatic vision. There is no valley,

no vale. What I felt was not even my soul. I saw a painting and
I wanted to see and feel more than anyone else in the room.
I wanted the novelty of a Chinese man and to fool myself into
thinking he possessed Oriental Wisdom and could whisk
me away from unhappiness. He was from the fairy tale in my
childhood, someone would save me and love me. I became
infatuated with the painter, who could paint a place for me
to live. The feeling of all that has nearly disappeared, leaving
me, like life through the vale of death. Yet why do I still want
the painter? If he were here before me now, I would let myself
be deluded, fly off with infatuation to wherever lust would
take me.

The maid knocked on the door and startled me out of my reverie. She set down a tonic by my bedside. A few minutes later, Mother
entered my room—a surprise—she rarely visited me here. She asked
if I had caught an illness. Did I have a stomachache? Were there chills
and fever? How strange that she took an interest in my symptoms. I
think I have a fever, yes. She was concerned, she said, that I not pass
my illness onto Lu Shing. Last year, quarantine had been placed on
all Asiatics coming into San Francisco due to an epidemic in Shanghai of bubonic plague.

"If Lu Shing becomes ill, that might lead to the wrong conclu-
sion, and our house and we in it would be quarantined."

What a wonderful prospect. All of us remanded to this house,
Lu Shing and I imprisoned together, he right above my bed. My fever
was growing.

My mother went on. "Lu Shing would likely be sent back to
China and quarantined in the bowels of the boat. It would be an
uncomfortable journey home."

My fever was abating. "I don't think I am contagious. It was the
turnips," I said.

"Whatever it is," she said, "I hope it will improve in time so you can come on our trip to the Farallon Islands on Thursday. Your grandfather said there was no sense in our wasting the opportunity. He said he'll pay for everything, including a picnic of roast beef, just as he did twenty years ago . . ."

I made a miraculous recovery, thanks to this tonic of good news, which worked with such lightning speed I was able to join everyone for dinner and discuss further plans for the voyage. I caught Lu Shing looking at me with a smile, which I interpreted as meaningful—but not yet clear. I simply knew that between us lay fate and it had turned the boat around.

THE ECSTATIC MOMENTS would no longer be mine if I did not make haste. Sex would not bring us together in spirit, I now knew. Our union would be a carnal one, but more promising than what I had experienced with my other young men. I did not need excuses of ships with tall masts or the rise of the moon over an island. I put aside my fears of humiliation. I would lay myself before him and ask him to enjoy me. I had the confidence of a whore, knowing I would succeed in this one task.

At ten o'clock, I heard his footsteps and the creak of the ladder. I left my bed in my nightgown and I climbed the curling staircase and made two raps on the door. He called out, "Yes?" And I accepted this answer to enter the room. He was up in the loft, and the outline of his body was visible by the light of the oil lamp. But I could not see the expression on his face. I said nothing, and he did not ask why I had come. I went to the ladder and ascended. He wore no clothes above his waist and the rest of him was concealed by the sheet. He moved back to allow me room to slide in. I lay on my back and turned my head toward the bookshelf. I was not yet ready to see his expression, what he thought of my coming to him so boldly and unasked.

I saw the calisthenics book, just as I had left it, untouched. I did not reach for it. I did not want those muscled men and cheerful women in bed with us. I heard the foghorn followed by the barks of sea lions, their futile mating calls. If only he would simply begin and do what the other young men did, fastening their mouth on some part of my body.

"I'm not a virgin," I announced, "and my parents do not care what I do. I mention these things, if those are concerns." I turned my head and looked at him. His face was calm, or perhaps sympathetic or amused. I undid the top button of my nightgown to make my mission clear. But then he placed his hand firmly over mine to stop me. I had not counted on this. I felt the warm creep of blotches over my chest and neck.

"Let me," I then heard him say, and he slid his finger down the placket of the nightgown, and all the buttons popped out of their holes. He bent down close to my face, and I was taken aback by how Chinese he looked. I could finally touch him without the questions that lay between distances of what might happen or be allowed. I ran my hands over the smooth slopes of his cheeks, his forehead, the top of his head, his jaw to his chin. I looked into his dark eyes. "I leave in a week," he said. I denied it but nodded, and with that, I felt my gown slip off. The windows were open, the air was cool, and I was shivering. One warm hand glided along my body in a leisurely way, rounding over my shoulders, slipping along my side, his eyes following with the same calmness, and yet also curiosity, as if he were studying how I had been sculpted, how this curve had been made, how the length of my arm had been decided, how the curve of my ear had been shaped. I closed my eyes. His hand moved in light circles, slowly, more firmly, pressing along my inner thighs. I opened my eyes, and again I was surprised to see his Chinese face, and infatuation slowed my thoughts and blurred the light around him, so that all I could see in the clearest of newfound sight were all the details of his face. I closed my eyes and felt him move my hips into a new place. I opened my eyes, and his wonderful strangeness returned, yet now I knew him as I did in the valley of the painting, knowledge without words, and the joy of familiarity. He drew his queue down my belly—the forbidden sight, touch, feel of a Chinese man slipping his queue down and up my cleft, then slipping into me in a forbidden rhythm, watching his unfamiliar face, my mind floating into brief thoughts of the difference of our races and the indecency of joining the two, and then my mind falling back into the pleasure of violating taboo. I closed my eyes and asked him to speak to me, and he softly recited in his British speech.

> "Good little boat,
> good little boat,
> neither mast, nor an oar,
> in waves you float.
> You paddle toward shore."

I opened my eyes and saw a pained expression of pleasure on his Chinese face and I realized that to him I was also taboo, a wild white girl, exciting because I was forbidden and unfamiliar to him, different, rare, and unusual. I sighed, fulfilled in that valley where I was My Self. We stared at each other as he uttered the words that carried us along.

> "Trust me, trust me,
> I'll take you to dock.
> Go aboard, go aft
> Ride, ride on my cock."

My Chinese emperor closed his eyes and now he spoke his Chinese words, not a nursery rhythm but harsh sounds as he flayed against me, until our bodies were slapping, and he took me into the typhoon and geologic disaster.

I awoke when he lit the lamp.

"The sun will be up in an hour," he said simply.

Life outside of this room would soon return. "Let me lie awhile longer," I said, and hummed, settling against his body. "I've loved to read here since I was a little girl," I said drowsily, happily. "I was glad for solitude, although sometimes I was lonely. The room comforted me. Perhaps it had to do with its round walls. There were no sharp corners. The room was the same in any direction. Did you think about the roundness of this room?"

"I had disturbing thoughts—the impossibility of hanging a painting on round walls. I don't have the Oriental mysticism at my fingertips you might think I have. I am a very practical man."

"What were you saying in Chinese when we were having sex?"

He laughed softly. "The obscene words a man uses in the peak of excitement. *Chuh nee bee.*"

"What do the words mean exactly?"

"They're quite vulgar. How can I say this? . . . It has the meaning of pleasure as we connect, male to female."

"Those aren't the words. Pleasure as we connect! Male to female! That's not what you were groaning about."

He laughed. "All right. But don't take it as an insult. The words mean 'fuck your cunt.' Quite vulgar, as I said, but it indicates my passion is so great I've lost my mind and a more eloquent vocabulary."

"I like that you are uncontrollably vulgar," I said. I secretly thought about my young men. Most simply grunted, one was silent except for his panting. One called to God.

"Have you said those uncontrollable words to many women?" I stared at him directly so that he would think I asked only out of curiosity and not with a knife already pointed at my heart.

"I've never counted. It's customary to visit courtesan houses starting at the age of fifteen. But I didn't go often, not as much as I wanted. A man has to court them, give them gifts, woo in competition with other men and suffer heartbreak. I didn't have the money. My father wasn't indulgent."

He did not ask me about the young men I had been with. I was relieved, yet I wished he felt the need to ask, as I did to torment

myself, wanting to believe there were no others, or at least none who
had won him.

The next night, I again went to the turret, and this time we fell
more easily into the spell of intimacy. As we kissed I closed my eyes
to imagine him as the emperor. But I pictured only him, the face
beside mine. I did not feel surprised when I opened my eyes. I was
overwhelmed with joy to see him. The excitement of taboo remained,
a Chinese man having sex with an American girl. He whispered the
vulgar words as he entered me, and repeated them with each stroke.
In the mindlessness of swimming in each other's body, we were inti-
mates. He lifted my hips and my head soared and I lost all my senses
except for the one that bound us and could not be pulled apart. But
then we did pull apart and we lay on our sides facing each other,
growing quiet and with the distance of race spreading larger.

Despite my promise that I would not expect more than these
few days of pleasure, I could not avoid the creeping fear that I would
soon lose him. Had he thought of that inevitability as he caressed my
body? "Will you miss me?" I wanted to ask. On the third night, before
our trip to the Farallon Islands, I could not keep back the question.
I asked him in the dark when he could not see my face. I held my
breath, and when he said, "I shall miss you a great deal," tears fell
and I kissed him. And when I touched his face, I felt the dampness
of his own tears on his face. At least, I thought they were his, and not
the wetness from mine. Doubt was removed when he drew my hips
toward him, pulled my leg over his back, and plunged into me with
even greater need than before.

At that moment, I decided to go to China and knew instantly
this had been the answer all along to my spiritual malaise and loveless life. I was buoyed on crests of emotion, more exhilarated than I
thought possible. Bravery surged and conquered all fears. I could at
last feel deeply and unrestrained. How could I lock my soul away by
returning to the life I had before him? I knew it was mad and reckless to go to China, but this was the time to take risks and face dan-

ger rather than retreat into the living death of safety and stagnation. How could I stop myself? Our bodies were moving together, rowing to China, drawing nearer to the Valley of Amazement, where our emotions were free and we could wander together with our souls.

MY MOTHER SENT carriages around to bring the passengers to the dock. The opera singer, her lover, Mr. Maubert and his sister, Miss Pond, my father, my mother, Lu Shing, and I. We boarded with bundles of coats and baskets of food, sketchbooks, soft pencils, paints, and a guidebook to the islands.

During our sail to the islands, my mother gave lectures on the sea creatures we glimpsed from the boat. "Whales are not fish, but thinking mammals like us," she shouted into the brisk wind, making it either impossible or unpleasant to listen. The coats we brought were more fashionable than useful, all but Miss Huffard, who wore a thick fur coat, which, given her size, made her quite bearlike. The boat cut into the wind and the wind cut through my skin to the marrow of my bones. Mr. Maubert, his sister, and Mr. Hatchett wore greenish faces and periodically rushed to the railing. I was miraculously spared from seasickness, owing, no doubt, to the headiness of love. My mother went belowdecks and emerged with thick blankets, and we all stood about like Indians smoking peace pipes as we puffed clouds of breath into the cold air.

Lu Shing and I stood at the railing, supposedly keeping an eye out for whales, but surreptitiously glancing at each other. We spotted an occasional sea lion and let everyone know we had been attentive to our duty. At times, I pretended that the sway of the boat had caused me to lose my balance, and I fell against Lu Shing, who steadied me.

And then the boat did sway more forcefully. Its nose lifted and crashed, and everyone laughed, as if this had been arranged as a bit of fun. The small waves merged into rolling ones. I held my breath with each upheaval. There was no more laughter. Dark clouds blossomed above and tines of light fell onto the horizon ahead. The winds picked up and whipped our faces and turned our cheeks numb. The seagulls disappeared, and the choppy waters swallowed the flippers of sea lions. Lu Shing had wrapped his pigtail around his head and pulled his bowler down over his ears. He wore Western clothing, a thick wool jacket and trousers. I had plaited my hair at the back to match his. The wind had loosened it, and strands of hair latched themselves against my eyes.

The skipper shouted voiceless directions into the wind and nimble men jumped over to the boom and wrestled it around. A young dark-faced man handed out life preservers and assured us it was only a precaution. The boat pitched up and landed hard in the trough. He advised us to go below if we did not want to be splashed by waves. Miss Huffard and her lover were the first to take his advice and it required delicacy to ease the rotund singer into the small opening as she squealed when she missed a step on the ladder. Mr. Maubert and his sister descended next, then Miss Pond and Father. Mother followed reluctantly. Just before my father closed the hatch, he called to me, "Are you coming?"

"We'll brave it out. I think I glimpsed a whale just ahead."

Soon Lu Shing and I were the only passengers who remained on deck. We freely smiled at each other. It was the first time we had been alone that day. My chin was trembling and tears burned my eyes, and this was not due to love but the punishment of the wind. My teeth chattered like castanets. I imagined us standing on another boat in another week's time, that one going to Shanghai.

"It's so beautiful out here. I wish this boat would sail all the way to China," I said.

He said nothing. Perhaps he knew the reason I had said that. He was solemn, impenetrable, a stranger.

"I would like to go to China one day. Perhaps I could talk my mother into it if I make it an expedition to find rare birds." He laughed and said there were many. That encouraged me a great deal.

"I imagine it's difficult for Americans to live in Shanghai, given the differences in language and customs."

"Shanghai has a growing number of people from the United States—also England, Australia, France, many countries. I think they live quite comfortably—luxuriously even—and in a part of the city that is like a little country within the larger one."

I looked at him to judge the meaning of what he had just said. He might have taken me at my word—that I was thinking of coming to China with my mother. "Of course, if my mother didn't want to come, I could come alone."

He knew what I was thinking. He wore that same thoughtful look when I first went to the turret and lay down, unasked. "I'm already betrothed," he said. "I have a contract for a wife, and when I return I will marry her and live with my family."

I was shocked by his news and the bluntness in which he told me. "Why are you telling me this?" I said, feeling the heat rise to my face. I turned to the side so he would not see. "I wasn't suggesting I would marry you. I had hoped, however, you would have given me advice on how best to arrange a visit, just as you would have for Mr. Bierstadt."

I walked away before he could see how truly wounded I was and stood on the opposite side of the yacht, humiliated by my own actions. I hated myself for having revealed so much—and to virtually a stranger. How stupid to think a few bounces in bed would make him feel it would be unbearable to be without me. But if I now said I wouldn't go to China after what he had said, he would think that I was indeed seeking his love and not birds. A reckless thought came to me: I'll prove him wrong. I'll go to China and we'll see what he says to that! By the second, my anger and determination grew until I convinced myself that I truly did want to see China, regardless of whether he would marry another girl, instead of me. I could be independent and make a life of my own and be as different as all the people there.

The waters calmed. The wind died down. I heard a voice shout. I looked back, but it was not Lu Shing. It was the skipper. He seemed to be outlined in a cloud, floating in the salty air. He motioned with his spyglass to look ahead. Along the horizon were the peaks of the Farallon Islands. They were directly ahead. It was impossible that we had traveled this far so quickly. We had been at sea for only an hour. But then I saw that they were not peaks but the shadow outline of three enormous dragons. As I stared in awe, they became an elephant. I squinted my eyes. In another half minute, I saw a whale, which then shrank and became a yacht like ours. What was happening? Had I gone mad? I looked at the skipper. He had a maniacal look and was laughing. The crew was laughing as well, yelling the Italian words: Fata morgana. Fata morgana. A mirage.

My mother had told me she had once seen a fata morgana while looking toward the Farallon Islands. She said it looked like a ship and then a whale. At the time, I had thought she had imagined it. How strange that this had occurred right when I was thinking of going to China. This was a warning that I had seen an illusion of love. It was false and could change into many disguises. But I also considered it was a sign that I should go to China, that the life I wanted was closer than I thought. Just as I thought this, a sharp wall of wind pushed me, and a seagull directly above gave three sharp cries. The bow rose up on a jagged white crest and the boat pitched sharply to the side. We were being pushed to the mirage—or drawn to it, like Odysseus to the Sirens. This was a sign. Odysseus had to decide between vice and virtue. I had to decide between a puppet or being my true self-being. My hands were too numb to hang on to the railing, and when the bow pointed down again into the dark trough, my feet slipped, and I was shocked to find I was sliding on the deck. The blanket flew off my shoulders and my skirt ballooned out like a sail. I bumped hard into what looked like a spool of rope and tried to grab onto it, but from cold or fright I had no strength to grip it. I slid toward the railing on the other side and saw how easily I could glide smoothly under its opening and fall into the black waters. I screamed. A shout returned in a foreign language. I felt hands grab my ankles. A boy, no older than fourteen, with a Gypsy face and greasy hair, held on to me. He dragged me toward the hatch and I tried to stand, but my legs were wobbly, and he caught me as I collapsed. As he steadied me, I looked toward the horizon once more.

It was not until that moment that I looked to see where Lu Shing had gone. He was nowhere to be seen. Had he fallen overboard? I gestured frantically to the dark-faced boy. He assured me with his hands that the man with the long pigtail was fine, but he had lost his hat. He pantomimed the bowler sailing into the air. He gestured that Lu Shing was on the other side of the boat and was safe. I was furious. He was having a fine time, I was sure, unconcerned that I had nearly died. I would have gone over to him to curse him, but I was racked with cold.

As I stepped down the ladder on shaky legs, I felt the warmth rise over me, and my cheeks burned as sensation returned. The cabin was decorated like a parlor. There were divans and chairs, pots of ferns and Oriental rugs in colors of umber and ruby. Remarkably, nothing was in disarray. Mr. Hatchett said the furniture was nailed into place, all but the tea service. He pointed to a smashed teapot and teacups, and some scattered biscuits. A cabin boy was cleaning up the mess, pocketing the biscuits. My mother sat on a deep red ottoman, in earnest conversation with Miss Maubert, who lay against a fainting couch, looking green-faced, as if she might truly faint. Miss Huffard placed a mug of hot tea in my hands and told me to drink it and warm myself from the inside out. I heard Miss Pond telling Father how she had lost her sketchbook into the waves. Everything I heard now was meaningless. Miss Huffard rubbed my arms with her warm hands. She remarked at how little flesh I had on my bones. She turned me around and rubbed my back. She smelled of roses. "You nearly froze your little bum," she said. "What foolish things we endure for love."

I stiffened. What was she saying?

She patted my back. "I have done it many times, to my detriment, but never to my regret." She sang in full voice: "The heart has no memory, when love returns to me." Everyone clapped. She turned me around to face her again. "I have sung that many times, before a thousand admirers on the stage, and in my bedroom, terribly alone." Her kindness touched me. She led me through the companionway to a dark berth, laid me down, and pulled an enormous fur coat over me. It smelled of roses, too.

I was drifting off to sleep when I heard great shouts from above-deck. I jumped up and struggled in Miss Huffard's voluminous fur coat to reach the main cabin. Two boys were carefully lowering Lu Shing down through the hatch and two were below to receive him. His face was a grimace of pain. His leg was in a crude splint.

"He's broken his leg at the ankle," my father said. "The skipper said it was bent at a ninety-degree angle, as if it were boneless. It happened when we were lifted by that huge wave. They had to splint his leg before they dared move him below."

The green-faced Miss Maubert was asked to relinquish the fainting couch. All anger fled my heart. I wanted to ease his pain, give him courage through love. But many were crowded around him, assessing how to handle the new invalid. I finally pushed my way in. His face was white and he was biting his lip. I looked at his ankle as my mother unwrapped the cloth around the crude splint. The sharp end of the bone had punctured through his flesh. I saw pinpricks of light and then blackness. I fainted.

I woke to the smell of roses. I was still wrapped in the warmth of Miss Huffard's fur coat. She stood by. Everyone had disembarked. "You slept like a baby in a lullaby crib," she said.

"What's happened to Lu Shing?"

"Whiskey helped somewhat to ease his pain. The men just loaded him into a carriage. The doctor is already on his way to the house. There is another carriage waiting for you and me."

As I scrambled into my shoes, I heard Miss Huffard say in a

comedic voice, "Such a pity that he broke his leg. He won't be able to set sail for China for at least three months."

I threw my arms around her and cried.

"I would tell you to use the time to part from him gracefully rather than increase your misery. But I've never been good at following useless advice like that."

DURING LU SHING's three months of convalescence, I proceeded with my plan without telling him. I pawned my valuables. A gold watch. A ruby ring. A gold charm bracelet. I opened the box containing the silver dollars Mr. Minturn had given me over the years. I secured my passport and visa quite easily. I chatted pleasantly with the clerk, who had asked what means of support I had in China and I told him about a made-up uncle in Shanghai, who had invited me to teach English at his American school. "A teacher at age sixteen?" he said. I said I'd be seventeen in two weeks and had been precocious, which put my academic knowledge years ahead of students my own age. I continued to put my plans in place and was giddy as I decided what I should bring. After that task was done, I pondered over how I would reveal to Mother and Father—and Lu Shing—that I was leaving for China.

Lu Shing had been placed in my room to recover. I was given the blue room, but I stayed in the turret and came down regularly to tend to Lu Shing—bringing him books, his sketchbook, his meals, and a great deal of comfort as I neatened his bed, stroked his arm, and inquired about his degree of pain. In front of others, I sympathized that he had to delay his return to China. No one suspected that I might have other reasons for being his Florence Nightingale. Without watchful eyes, we enjoyed libidinous activities whenever we wished. Out of caution for his broken ankle, sex required geometric adjustments and careful positioning, easily supplemented by fellatio. I said no more about my plans to go to China. In fact, I created a subterfuge: I talked about going to a women's college back east and mentioned three I was considering. Thus, I allowed him to let down his guard. I talked about our friendship, which we would always keep, and I made lighthearted comments about certain coital activities that led to unanticipated surprises we might remember in the future with the old surge of desire. I told him about a fictitious young man who was courting me, and thus, Lu Shing should not worry that I would suffer once he left for China. I told him what the fictitious young man had said about my tantalizing attributes: my adventurous nature, my intelligence, the fact that I was not a virginal prude, and that I was unlike any girl he had ever met, different in a mysteriously intriguing way. Lu Shing agreed with my imaginary admirer and appeared to be relieved I had a lover waiting in the wings. He confided in me his dislike of certain Chinese customs, for example, the one that required him to marry a girl he did not love. He confessed he had doubts about himself as an artist. He feared that he lacked originality and the ability to express deeper ideas because he did not have any. He could only imitate technique. He appreciated my belief that he was wrong about his opinions about himself.

One afternoon, after tender sex and many sweet words, I lay in his arms and said that I would always remember him as my Chinese emperor. I felt him take a deep breath, and I knew he was stifling a sad sigh. How well I had come to know his body and mind. I asked that he think of me as his Wild American Girl. He replied he would remember much more than that. I added that I would not want thoughts of me to violate his vows of marriage.

"Marriage in China is arranged, in our family, and is not based on love. It is more akin to a business arrangement between old friends and meddlesome mothers. My future wife is a stranger to me. I don't even know if I will ever like her. She might be unattractive or have nothing interesting to say."

I pointed out that he could also visit courtesans, and he vaguely said he might. I went on: "My mother and father have a similar marriage. It does not stop my father from going elsewhere for his needs. They have an odd loyalty, based on their attachment to this house. They have been practical, yet their lives together grow hollow and they don't realize anymore how tragic that is. Who else could have loved my mother more dearly and pulled her out of misery?"

I was certain he was now thinking of the possibility of his own loveless marriage, a house barren of true companionship. "If you had been born American, I would have wanted someone like you for my husband." He fell directly in the logic of twin emotions:

"If you had been born Chinese, I would have wanted you as my wife." Before he left for China, I would try to change those words to simply these: "If you were in China, I would be happy to have you as my wife."

I had not intended to use pregnancy as the reason he should marry me. I would have preferred marriage by desire and not necessity. If he married me based on the advent of a baby, doubt would always exist over the reason we were together. Two weeks before he was scheduled to leave, I told him with hidden fear that I knew without a doubt that I was pregnant, and likely two months along. My fear was in anticipation over what he would feel and say.

He was shocked, of course. I saw him calculating in his eyes all that this meant, before he came and put his arms around me. He held me, and although there was no answer as to what we would do, I felt within his embrace protection and assuredness that we would find an answer.

"I cannot marry you and stay in the United States," he said.

I was angry that this was the first thing he said. I did not expect an expression of joy. But I had hoped for concern. "I will not risk my life with an abortion," I said. "And if I stay here and have the baby, I won't be able to keep it. It will be handed over to an orphanage. That's what happened to Miss Pond, and she's a Freethinker. She tried to keep her baby and she was shunned. Her work wasn't accepted. That baby was probably my father's, and he did nothing for that baby. He let it go to a warehouse. That's what would happen to our baby, and it would never be adopted because it would be tainted as half-Chinese with your blood. It would languish never feeling loved."

"The baby would not be accepted in China any more than here," Lu Shing said.

"Don't you have any suggestions other than what you cannot do?" I asked. "Am I alone in finding a solution?"

"I don't know what I could offer that would be acceptable to you. My family will not break the marriage contract, and because you're a foreigner, they would never permit you into the house, certainly not for the purpose of visiting me. At best, I could see you as my mistress, unacknowledged by my family. And I wouldn't be able to see you exclusively or live with you. I would be expected to have frequent sex with my wife for the purpose of producing a male heir—actually, as many sons as possible, and, if necessary, with several concubines if my wife proves incapable of having males right away. The expectations are more onerous in China than in America, and there are other complications you cannot begin to comprehend. I know that is not the answer you wanted to hear. I'm sorry."

He had merely recited the rules of his society. He had not considered breaking them. I defied my parents. Why couldn't he? He wasn't willing to consider other possibilities because he was not suffering as I was. He wasn't desperate to be rid of fear and confusion and wasn't on the brink of losing his mind. "Why can't you act on your own? Why can't you simply leave?"

"I can't explain the reason, except to say that what I think and do is lodged in my head, heart, character, and spirit. This is not a comparison to your importance to me. But no matter how much I love you, I can't extract that part of me and change into someone who would betray his family. I can't expect anyone could understand the enormity of my responsibility unless they were raised in China and in a family like ours."

"Tell me you don't love me so I won't ever hope you might. Tell me you would willingly let my soul curdle and die so you can bed a girl you don't even know. I will never trust love. I will feel only self-hatred because I let a weakling destroy my heart."

Finally, I saw anguish on his face. He looked as if he might cry. He embraced me. "I won't abandon you, Lucia," he said. "I have never loved anyone more. I simply don't know yet what we can do."

His words gave me great courage and expectations, and I inflated them. I took them with me when my family convened in the parlor after I told them I had urgent news. They sat stiffly, wearing expressions of worry. Lu Shing and I stood, he to the side and behind me.

"I'm pregnant," I said simply. Before I could say more about my plans, Mother leapt up and shouted at Lu Shing that he had violated "our hospitality, our trust, our honor, and goodwill . . ." Lu Shing said repeatedly that he was regretful and remorseful, deeply ashamed. Yet he seemed too calm for those feelings to be true.

"What good is your damn Chinese remorse?" Mother said in a sarcastic tone. "It's not sincere. You'll board a boat soon and leave this mess behind!"

Both Father and Mother turned on me and hurled words about my defects: that I was "ungrateful," "stupid," "prideful," "promiscuous." You said you wanted to choose your own interests, hobbies, and passions. So this is what you chose? Passionate sex with a man who is about to abandon you?

I felt the turmoil of a child who was ridiculed for who she was. But my face did not grow splotches of humiliation. I was angry.

"Passion and hobbies with a Chinese man," my mother said with a sneer. "A Chinese man with a pigtail. People will laugh at us for having taken him in as a guest! What fools we were to be generous." Those last remarks sent me into uncontrollable rage. She always thought only of herself. What about the harm she had done to me as a child?

I could not keep from crying, and I was angry at the same time that I was showing them the tears of a child.

"What do you care what happens to me?" I said. "I've always been nothing more than a shadow in this house. You never talked to me about what I wanted to do with my life, or what my feelings were. You never noticed when I was sad or happy. Have I ever heard you say that you love me? You made no effort. You simply neglected me. If love were nourishment, I would have been dead long ago. What kind of mother were you? Is it any wonder I went to someone who cared for me. Without love, I would have gone mad. I didn't want to become like you. But I had to remain here as a child and endure being humiliated for my ideas, ridiculed for having emotions. I was overwrought, you said. You wanted to quash any emotion I had so I would become like you. Loveless, selfish, angry, and alone."

My mother looked crestfallen, disappointed in me. I wanted her to feel so miserable, she would cry like me. The more I said, the more destructive I wanted to be. I could not stop. I was crazed and grabbed any weapon I could fling.

"What do you know about love?" I said. "You devoted more attention to bugs that have been dead for millions of years than you ever did to me. I was alive. Didn't you notice? Are you happy with your marriage? All you do is lock yourself in your room and wallow in misery. And when you come out, the greatest emotion you show is anger."

My voice became more mocking, more wounding: "No wonder everyone said Father was a saint for putting up with you. All your dear friends who you criticized laughed at your science experiments and said they could have saved you the time and told you the answer you sought: The bugs were dead. You were the mad scientist, deluded into thinking you would discover something useful. You wasted your life instead."

Mr. Minturn was too senile to understand what I was saying. "Why is she angry? Perhaps we should take her on another boat ride to cheer her up."

Mrs. Minturn gave my mother a superior look. "This is what comes of poor child-rearing practices. You should have locked her in a closet when she misbehaved. You wouldn't follow my advice. No wonder she has loose morals."

"Shut up! You're a stupid wicked woman, an evil presence who poisons this house. All your life, you've left rot behind you. Everyone hates you. Couldn't you feel it? And don't accuse me of loose morals. You used sleepwalking as your method for seducing Mr. Minturn into marriage. Why don't you suffer from sleepwalking now?"

"Calm yourself, Lucia," my father said. "You are saying things you don't mean and you may regret later. When you're less excited, we can talk rationally and you'll see that what you're saying is not true."

"You don't get to preside over this matter like you do at the dinner table with your boring conversations and pompous questions about art. You want me to hide my feelings just like you hide your lovers. Mother, do you know how many women Father has had sex with behind your back?"

He groaned. "No, no . . . stop."

"I read the letters from your lovers, praising your instrument of love and your skills, the positions you used, letters of gratitude from women and men alike. Men! Yes, Mother, he has had dalliances with men. Does any of this shock you? He's been servicing Miss Pond, too. Did you know she came to the house an hour before dinner the other night and asked to see his collection? His collection! Didn't you see her at the dining table, ogling him with postorgasmic affection? You call me promiscuous for having sex with Lu Shing. You're my model, Father. Lu Shing is not the first man I've had sex with. I've had students of yours. I used your books with the disgusting photographs of men and women inserting themselves in different positions. I used Professor Minturn's lesson book. It's a wonder I did not also become a sexual deviant like you, collecting nasty objects used for sex and masturbation. Am I wrong to want to keep this baby? Wasn't it your baby Miss Pond gave birth to? You gave up your own child! Whatever became of that baby? Don't you care if it's now languishing in a crib or if he one day works in a shoelace factory?"

I could not stop, and I did not know why I could not. I took all the secrets a family should keep from each other and made sure I had thoroughly destroyed them. All along I knew I was destroying myself as well.

Mother left, and I believe she may have been crying. Father had said nothing the entire time. But when he looked up, I saw in his eyes grief and terror. It was only then that I realized how cruel I had been. I had damaged the father I had once loved, and had severed him from me, as well as from my mother. I had become a monster.

I could not remain in the house another day. Lu Shing and I would stay in a boardinghouse. When I left the house, no one was downstairs to see me leave.

DURING THE LAST two weeks before we left for China, Lu Shing never questioned what I had said to my family. I told him that I had greatly exaggerated my experiences with other young men. I also admitted that I had lost control of my mind, and that while these were my feelings, and that everything I had said was true, I knew I had said too much. I wondered if I had scared him by showing him this turbulent side of my personality. I may have jarred him into thinking I would expect more than what he could give me. That was what I feared—that I would want more because my needs were bottomless.

Doubt crept in. I had made him feel contrite and forced him to say he loved me. He said he was thoughtless, that he did not deserve me and would never abandon me. A man being tortured would say anything. I did not remember how I had led him to say those words, but I knew he had not said them spontaneously or in a single confession of love. Yet I hoped that his piecemeal declarations were whole and strong.

At the last minute, I sent a note to Miss Huffard, the opera singer. She had passions, and only she would understand. I told her where I was going and that Lu Shing and I would marry once we overcame a few problems that could be expected between the races. I said I would write from Shanghai and asked her to wish me luck. I dropped my letter at the post office, and when they took it away, I felt that had been the final declaration that I was leaving my life behind and starting afresh. It gave me a boost of confidence.

When we reached the boat, I kissed him on the cheek. I did not care who saw. We were leaving each other for the next month. Lu Shing took one gangplank, and I another. His would lead him to a deck for Orientals. Mine would deliever to the decks reserved for whites. Earlier, when I had realized we would be separated by race, I had dismissed the rules as ridiculous. We could sneak into each other's room, just as we had in the house.

"If I'm caught in your cabin, or you in mine," Lu Shing said, "I would wind up in the jail at the bottom of this ship. They'll drop you off in Honolulu before you ever reach China."

He assured me he had a comfortable berth in a private cabin, and on a deck with other well-to-do Chinese. We would reunite when we disembarked. His family knew I was coming. He had written—at my insistence. He did not know what their reaction would be, but they sent a cable that they would be waiting.

On the second day out at sea, I unpacked the rest of my bags. At the bottom of one were two things I had not placed there. One was a red velvet bag. Inside was my father's spyglass. When I was a little girl, we used to look through the spyglass from the turret and watch the boats come in. I remember him naming the countries where the boats hailed from.

I then found a bag of purple chamois. It contained three pieces of amber with wasps. I wept all night, because I did not understand what the objects meant. I guessed that my father was rebuking me for spying on him. Maybe my mother was asserting that she did indeed love those insects more. I allowed a small chance that they were small tokens of love, which they must have shown me at one time. Otherwise how could I feel so palpably, so painfully that it might be love?

On top of the nausea from pregnancy, I was seasick the first three days. I used seasickness as my excuse for the sudden rise of a greenish complexion when I was with my dinner mates. I had been seated with five women traveling alone. The wives of diplomats and businessmen, they were rejoining their husbands in Shanghai. When they asked why I was going to China, I gave them the lie I had told the clerk at the passport office: I had an uncle who ran a school, and I would be a teacher of English.

"A school to teach the Chinese?" the eldest woman asked.

I nodded. "It is for the sons of diplomats." Lu Shing had been tutored among children of that standing.

"Then I know your uncle quite well!" she said. "Dr. Thomas Wolcott. We should arrange for all of us to have tea when you're settled."

I mumbled that it must be a different school, because my uncle was someone else, Dr. Claude Maubert. No one had heard of him. "It's a new school," I said. "He may not be taking students yet. My uncle has been in Shanghai for a short amount of time . . ."

"Here I thought I knew everyone," the woman said. "It's a very small circle of us foreigners in Shanghai. But everyone says that Shanghai is growing faster by the day." They encouraged me to join the societies there, a church, a ladies' circle to help orphans, another to rescue slave girls.

After we had been on board a week, I ventured to tell them an interesting tale I had heard.

"My uncle said he met a couple in Shanghai, an American woman and a Chinese man. They were married and living with his family. They even had a child. I thought that was a very modern arrangement."

The diplomat's wife scowled. "That cannot be true. There is no legal marriage between a Chinese man and an American woman."

I tried to hide my alarm. "Is that a Chinese law or an American one?" I asked. "I'm sure my uncle said they were married."

"Both. My husband works for the American Consulate, and he's told me about a few cases like this. Either a Chinese girl and an American man, or an American girl and a Chinese man. In either case, it never ends well for the woman."

I listened to their tales of terror. The American women were scorned. They had no legal status and were never accepted into Chinese families as wives because of the importance of lineage and the family's generations of ancestor worship. They recalled only two cases in which an American woman had lived in a Chinese family, but only briefly. In one case, the American girl was made a concubine—part of a harem, so to speak, treated like a scullery maid, and mistreated by the other concubines and the mother-in-law. Chinese mothers-in-law were generally a vicious bunch, they said in agreement, based on the tales. And that proved sadly true with this poor girl. She was beaten to death.

"The jurisdiction was in the Chinese section of the city," the diplomat's wife said, "and was handled by a Chinese court. There was no one to come forward on the girl's behalf. Who knows what the mother-in-law did or said, but the girl's death was deemed justifiable."

The other American woman ran away from her husband's family and became a prostitute. She had no money, and her family in the United States would not take her back. She went to work on one of the boats in the harbor, taking on sailors.

"If you are in touch with this young woman, you might suggest she go to the American Consulate and have them contact her family so they can send for her as soon as possible," the diplomat's wife said. I wondered if she knew that I was the woman in the lie I told. I was frightened by what they had said. I had argued against the warnings of my parents, against Lu Shing's as well.

I soon recovered from these waves of fear, just as I did from the nausea of pregnancy. I could win over Lu Shing's parents. I was clever and persistent. Lu Shing had written his father, as I had asked him to do. They had had time to absorb the news. And he had told them

I was soon to be the mother of his child, perhaps the firstborn son of the next generation. I reasoned that his father was educated, an important official in the Ministry of Foreign Relations. They must be modern in how they viewed Americans. All would eventually sort itself out.

A MONTH AFTER we left San Francisco, I stood on the dock and waited for Lu Shing to disembark from the Chinese gangplank. I was faint with nervousness, exhaustion, and the heat. I had not been able to eat since the night before. To my regret, I wore a dress suited to the foggy summers of San Francisco and not the Chinese bathhouse that was Shanghai. Coolies ran up to me to take my bags and I shooed them away. I was anxious for Lu Shing to arrive so that he could take care of these matters.

I finally caught sight of him. I was stunned. He was wearing Chinese clothes. He looked as he did when I first saw him in our doorway. There he had looked like an emperor from a fairy-tale book, the one I fell in love with. Here, amid a dock bustling with Chinese people, and passengers, he looked simply Chinese. A coolie in short pants stood behind him with bags clutched under his arms, dangling from his hands, and slung over his back. Lu Shing saw me, but he did not walk toward me. I waved. He still did not come. I walked quickly to him.

Instead of embracing me, he said, "Hello, Lucia." He sounded like a stranger. "I'm sorry I'm not able to embrace you, as I would like to." He wore his solemn look.

He had already warned me we had to be circumspect until his family had grown accustomed to the idea of our marriage.

"You look different," I said. "Your clothes."

He smiled. "Different only to you." His eyes looked at me kindly, like a stranger. "Lucia, have you thought carefully about this over the past month? Are you certain you want to stay in Shanghai? We may not succeed. You must be prepared."

He was supposed to soothe me, not frighten me. "Did you change your mind?" I said in a breaking voice. "Are you telling me to go back?" My voice must have been louder than I thought. Curious faces turned to watch.

Lu Shing remained implacable. "I simply want you to be certain. Our separation on the boat is just a hint of what lies ahead. It will be difficult."

"I've known that all along," I said. "I have not changed my mind." Secretly, I was frightened. But during that month, I had accumulated a different kind of courage—for the baby. The baby was no longer a problem but a part of me, and I would protect us both.

Lu Shing and the coolie conversed quickly. They sounded as if they were arguing. I was struck by the fact that Lu Shing was speaking fluently in Chinese. How odd he sounded. I had never heard him speak to another Chinese person. What happened to my English gentleman with a Chinese face? What happened to my handsome lover in his impeccably tailored clothes with his shaved pate and queue under a bowler? Where was his desire for me?

The coolie gave me a quizzical expression. He and Lu Shing exchanged more words and the coolie nodded. What had transpired? We walked toward the road, and when we reached the broad sidewalk, Lu Shing said: "My family is waiting across the road. All of them. My father, my brothers, my ailing grandfather, the girl I am contracted to marry, and her father and brothers."

"Why is that girl here?" I said. "Are you going from dock to chapel? Shall I be her bridesmaid?"

"I can't keep her from coming. This is not a welcome party, Lucia. It is the way things are done here to enforce family order. They have come here to shame me into adhering to my responsibility to family. They are my peers and elders."

His face was covered with perspiration, and I knew it was not simply the heat. He was nervous, and I had never seen him this way. He would soon have to stand up to his family, just as I had done with mine. I would be by his side to support his decision. The only question that remained: Would they allow us to live in their house?

"Where are they?" I looked around. Lu Shing indicated to an area about thirty feet away where two hansom cabs and ten covered rickshaws were waiting. It resembled a funeral procession. The coolie was placing Lu Shing's trunk in one of the rickshaws toward the back. Lu Shing walked toward his family. I followed.

He stopped. "I think you should remain here until I smooth the way," he said. "It would not do well to throw this in their face from the start."

Throw this in their face? Why had he said it that way? "I'm not going to be cowed," I said. "They can't ignore me."

"Please, Lucia, let me do it my way." He walked toward the first cab without me.

I motioned to the coolie to take my bags to a rickshaw. He looked at Lu Shing with a questioning face, and Lu Shing answered tersely. The man asked another question, and Lu Shing grunted. What was he saying? I understood nothing anymore. I was in a land of secrets.

Damn the bags! I marched without them toward the battalion of cabs and rickshaws. Lu Shing ran toward me and blocked my way. "Lucia, please wait. Let's not add to a difficult situation." I was exasperated that Lu Shing was more concerned with his family's feelings than with mine. I needed to let his family know from the start what kind of woman I was. I had brought with me my American free will and enterprising nature. I was accustomed to dealing with people from all walks of life, the pompous Mr. and Mrs. Minturn, the professors who thought they knew everything.

Lu Shing reached the first cab and began talking to a man seated in the back of the cab. I slowly walked a little way farther down the sidewalk, where I could see a stern-looking man seated in the cab. He was wearing a bowler like Lu Shing's. As the man spoke, Lu Shing kept his face turned down. I came closer until I was directly across and about twenty-five feet from the curb. I heard Chinese words flowing like water streaming over rocks. The man was Lu Shing's father. I could see that. He and Lu Shing looked alike, separated only by age. They were both handsome and intelligent-looking, and both wore the identical solemn expression, only the older man's was rigid.

Lu Shing spoke in a low apologetic voice, and his father's expression never changed. A pretty girl in the rickshaw just behind the second cab kept her eyes fixed on me. His bride, no doubt. I stared at her until she looked away.

All at once, Lu Shing's father stood up, shouted what must have been a curse word, and threw his hat in Lu Shing's face. Lu Shing cupped his eye. His father spit out more words, grating sounds torn from the back of the throat, sharp punctuated orders accompanied by chopping motion of hands. Lu Shing kept his face downward and said nothing. What did this mean? Why did Lu Shing remain motionless, wordless? Perhaps this was how it was done. Refusal through silence. It did not seem likely that the man would calm himself anytime soon. They would leave without us.

Just as I concluded that, Lu Shing turned toward me, walked over, and quickly stuffed money into my hand. He implored me to wait. A tragic expression contorted his face. "I'll be back as soon as I can. Wait for me here. Be patient, and forgive me for what is happening."

In the next instant, before I could overcome my shock enough to protest, he climbed into his father's cab. I watched this, as if in a dream. The driver jiggled the reins, and the cab with Lu Shing moved forward, away from me. The cab behind followed, and all the rickshaw pullers picked up their handles and ran. Lu Shing's relatives kept their faces turned forward, as if I did not exist. Only the girl stared at me with a scowl. And then they were gone.

I felt faint and sick. I could no longer stand. I spotted a tree far-ther up the road. How would I ever manage to carry my bags that far? Just as I thought this, I saw the coolie race by me with my bags under his arms. I chased after him, shouting, "Thief! Thief!" I would never catch him. I stopped and was about to fall into a heap when I saw him set my bags under the shade of the tree I had longed to reach. He arranged them to look like a settee then beckoned me to come sit. I walked over slowly, not sure what to make of this. He swept his hand out, as if he were a waiter seating me at a table in a fine establishment.

I noticed after a while that the coolie was still standing close by, staring at me. He wore a questioning look, then tapped his palm and made a motion of rubbing money bills. He wanted me to pay him. I looked at the Chinese money still clutched in my hand. I had no idea what any of it was worth. His fee could not be more than a few cents. But which of these bills was worth more? Which less? The coolie made gestures for eating and drinking, and rubbed his stom-ach, as if he were starving. Was this a ploy to have me give him more money? He said something incomprehensible and I answered in my own gibberish, "Damn this heat, damn this city! Damn Lu Shing!" I looked for a bill with the lowest number on it. Five. I handed it to him. He grinned. I must have given him a fortune. He raced away. Good riddance. I watched carriages and rickshaws come and go, each of them leaving me in deeper despair.

Ten minutes later, the coolie returned. He had brought a basket. Inside were two brown eggs with crackled shells, three small bananas, and a flask that contained hot tea. He also offered me what I thought was a cane. It turned out to be a parasol. He handed back some coins. This was surprising. Lu Shing must have hired him to take care of me. I examined the basket of food. I was dubious about the cleanliness of these offerings. He pantomimed that all was clean and I had nothing to worry about. I was famished and thirsty. The eggs were odd-tasting but delicious. The bananas were sweet, and the tea was soothing. As I ate, I kept my eyes trained on the road. It was a busy thoroughfare.

The servant motioned to me and pointed to the other side of the tree. He indicated I could shout if I needed him. I nodded. He lay on his side, and fell promptly asleep.

I was drawn to sleep as well. But I could not give in to it. Everyone would see my failure: a foolish American girl, alone and in trouble within the first hour of her arrival. I sat erect. I would show I was assured of my place in the world—which for now was under the tree on a thoroughfare, and in a city where I could not speak a word of its language, except the vulgar Chinese words *chuh nee bee*. I shouted them aloud, and the coolie startled.

I waited for hours on end, sitting on that ridiculous settee. Pride withered, my erect posture melted. My eyelids had a will of their own. I lay down and let sleep arrive and carry me away.

CHAPTER 14

SHANGHAILANDERS

Shanghai
September 1897
Lucia Minturn

In the quietest hour of the night, the coolie was the first to spot Lu Shing coming down the thoroughfare. He roused me and then ran back to the street and crossed his arms back and forth like a drowning man. It had been eighteen hours since Lu Shing had left me at the dock without my knowing whether he would ever return.

Before he could even step out of the rickshaw, my shouts cracked the air: "Damn you! Damn your family!"

He placed me quickly in the rickshaw, and the coolie jumped into another with my belongings. Seeing Lu Shing's grim expression, I knew we were not headed for his family home. I wept as I accused him of abandoning me like a beggar on the street—and in a strange city where I was unable to speak to anyone. Why didn't he stand up for me and go with me, instead of leaving me in the hot sun, where I could have roasted to death with a baby in my belly?

I was frightened near to losing my mind. At seventeen I had made a decision with inalterable consequences. I had devastated my mother and father by my hatred of them and their lack of love. I had revealed their vile secrets, the rottenness of their souls, and how ludicrous they were. Were there any sharp truths I had not flung at them? On the boat, I had already sensed the change in myself. I had taken on my parents' traits even as I condemned them, and I had further altered myself by my cruelty. Had I always had the capacity and desire to destroy another? I no longer had confidence and an independent mind. I was alone and without anyone I could show bluster to. I was dwindling the closer I came to Shanghai, to an uncertain future that depended on one person, who claimed he loved me, but who could not provide assurances of how he would be able to show it once I became the foreigner in his land. I went back and forth, like the pitch of the boat, clinging to the belief that I could conquer whatever obstacles I might encounter. After all, I had conquered the Chinese emperor's heart. But then I gave in to fear that American pluck would be transformed into Chinese Fate. Lu Shing was already different, no longer my Chinese emperor, but a cowed Chinese son.

When Lu Shing apologized, he said the words so quietly, so weakly, they sent me into a fury. How could he protect me? Each time he explained what had happened, I became even more frightened that he had no mind of his own. I did not know this man. In San Francisco, he should have told me he had no feelings for me whatsoever. He should have physically prevented me from getting on the boat. He had warned me, but he had also said he had never loved anyone more, which, I realized now, may have meant little if he had never loved anyone at all. Each meager hope conquered obvious danger. Those warnings belonged to the future, and I lived from one precious moment to another, harvesting love that would sustain me, no matter what arose. And now I was listening to weak apologies and useless explanations about why he had to choose his family over me. He did not understand my fright and what I endured for him. I wanted him to listen to the American women on the boat, saying that white girls had been beaten to death by Chinese mothers-in-law and no one had cared. I wanted him to starve and boil in the hot sun for love of me. I wanted him to destroy his family and his chances of ever going home, just as I had.

"Damn you! Damn your parents!" Out of exhaustion, I finally stopped shouting and simply cried. He lay my head on his shoulder, and I did not pull away from this small amount of comfort.

As we rode through the dark and humid streets, he explained he had spent all these past hours listening to his father shout at him about his responsibilities. His father had slapped him as he enumerated the names of all his ancestors over five hundred years, names that Lu Shing had memorized in his boyhood. His father cited his own position with the Ministry of Foreign Relations, to whom he owed duty and allegiance above family. People would wonder what moral defects he had passed along to an eldest son who would betray his family and destroy their reputation and future honor. His mother deserved a peaceful life in her old age, instead of his ushering her into a grave as fast as possible. She had taken to her bed, complaining of chest pains and a headache. His two younger brothers, the sons of his father's concubines, rebuked him, something they had never done. They said he would cause people to wonder if they, too, would take up with foreign women and debauchery in all the Western ways. What chance did they have in achieving a good future if he tainted them?

They are an educated family, Lu Shing said, but that did not mean they cast off tradition and filial duty. If he left the house to live with me, he would be disinherited and banished forever from his family, removed from their history, and never mentioned again—not as if he had died, but as if he had never existed. He would never be able to change his mind and return like the prodigal son in the Christian Bible.

"I would risk fortune and being banished into nonexistence for you," he said. "But I cannot destroy my family."

"I destroyed mine," I said. "I have nothing. And now you're willing to place your family's reputation over my life?"

"There was never a choice. You can't understand that unless you have been raised with the weight of five hundred years of your family's history. It was placed on my back the moment I was born as the eldest son. And I have to carry it forward."

"You're a coward. The moment you stepped off the boat you became a superstitious ghost-worshipper. If I had known that was who you were, I would never have come."

"I told you in San Francisco that my beliefs lay in how I was raised. I can't change that any more than I can my race or the family I was born to."

"How could you have expected me to understand what that truly meant? If I had said that I was raised to listen to my parents, to be guided by their advice, would that mean I would follow those expectations?"

"I can help you return home if you can't bear this."

"You coward! Is that your answer? I destroyed my mother, my father, and their marriage. I destroyed any chance of ever returning home. They didn't even come downstairs to say farewell. I'm already dead in their eyes. I have nothing to return to. I have nothing here, and you speak of reputation. You fail to understand how desperate I am. I have no bravery left. I'm falling and don't even know what abyss I'm falling into, but it's torment worse than death." I cried when I ran out of words to say.

The rickshaw took us along the waterfront and then turned onto a smaller street. We turned again and were on a wider street with gated stone mansions. We drove past a park, then more modest houses, English in style and set behind walls.

"Where are you taking me? A home for pregnant girls?"

"The guesthouse owned by a friend, an American. I've paid the rent in advance. It's not ideal, just the best I can do for now. And it's in the International Settlement, so you'll be among people who speak English. Rest there, and we can decide later what to do. But let me say now, Lucia, that if you stay, I will not abandon you. But I cannot abandon my family either. Although I don't know what answer lies in between, I promise to be truthful to you and to them."

I arrived at the guesthouse an hour before dawn. The gaslights were blazing. An enormous man named Philo Danner greeted us with much enthusiasm. He looked to be fifty. I thought he had sacrificed his sleep to welcome us. But he assured us that he slept during the vampire hours of rest between dawn and noon.

"You must call me Danner," he said as he led me to the sitting room, "and I will call you Lucia, unless you prefer something else. You can change your name quite easily in Shanghai."

Lucia was what Lu Shing called me, the name that fated us to be together. "I prefer to be called Lulu," I said in front of Lu Shing.

Danner was, in a word, flamboyant. He wore a light gold Chinese jacket over loose blue pajama pants. His hair was a dark mass of long angelic ringlets. His eyes were large and rimmed with long lashes. His nose was shapely, the patrician Roman nose of the English. Rolls of doughy flesh draped from his chin to the bottom of his neck. As he walked, his body rolled side to side, and he often ran out of breath and wheezed between words.

He owned this Yankee garden house, he said. It was a three-story building on East Floral Alley, in a good area of the International Settlement. It was built of thick stone walls that kept out the heat in summer and the cold in winter. Every inch of wall in his sitting room, dining room, and halls was covered with framed oil paintings of Western landscapes or scenes of Plains Indians. His tables and mantel held primitive masks, which gave the effect of other tenants staring at me, the interloper. Waist-high stacks of books stood in the middle of the sitting room, like a miniature Stonehenge. Danner maneuvered through the labyrinth with surprising gracefulness. I noticed tassels on the cushions of chairs, and then everywhere—purple, red, navy, and gold ones along the top of the sofa, on the tiebacks of curtains, on the door pulls, along the edges of sofas, at the corners of doorways, on top of the piano, on table scarves, at the corners of mirrors—an infestation.

Danner sat me on the sofa and murmured that he could see in my face that I had suffered a terrible shock. He looked at Lu Shing in an accusatory way. "What have you done to this poor girl?" I liked him immediately. A houseboy brought us tea and butter biscuits. When I quickly finished those, Danner told the houseboy to bring butter, ham, and bread. The food had a calming effect on me, and soon, Danner brought out a pipe.

"Let your troubles vanish into smoke," he said. "Opium."

Lu Shing murmured that I should not partake of any, and this caused me to enthusiastically accept Danner's offer. As Danner talked, the houseboy performed elaborate preparations with a dark brown paste. Danner handed me the pipe and said to inhale just a light puff. It was harsh at first and then my throat was instantly soothed. The taste was like pungent earth, then musk. It quickly changed into a sweet scent. The fragrance was at first like licorice and cloves, then chocolate and roses. Soon it was not simply a scent or a taste but a sensation, a silkiness, which enveloped me in its luscious sweetness. I was about to ask Danner a question but instantly forgot what it was because I was now conscious that Danner had the face of a genie. He was playing strange music on the piano. It sounded like heavenly voices.

I noticed Lu Shing sitting on the other side of the sofa, a sad gray figure in a colorful room. I was not angry anymore. He seemed lost. After another puff, I was ecstatic to find that the light from the lamps also made me feel weightless. The sweeping of my hand through the air made a thousand hands. The sound of Lu Shing's voice calling my name left sparkles before my eyes. His voice was beautiful, musical, so full of love. In looking at him again, he was in a halo of light, which emanated sexual desire. I yearned to have him touch me as he had the first night in the turret when everything surprised me. I had never known it was possible to feel peace and joy so deeply. I recalled memories of happy times as flat and thin, easily torn. In this marvelous smoky cloud of mind, I had no worries, only a glad sense that I would always feel as I did now. I had been awakened!

"Take me to bed," I said to Lu Shing, and the words floated out one at a time and reached him slowly. Lu Shing looked dazed as my words bounced on his face. Danner laughed and urged Lu Shing to do as I said.

We floated up the stairs. The lamp was lit and the light swirled around the bed like golden beads. Through a glowing doorway, I saw a bathtub that resembled a porcelain soup tureen painted with flowers inside and out. The water was shiny and still. The moment I dipped my hand in and paddled it like an oar, the painted flowers—tiny roses and violets—became real and swirled and scented the air. I quickly freed myself of my itchy clothes and slipped into the cool water, jubilant to feel its silkiness on my naked skin. Lu Shing kneeled behind the bathtub and kissed my neck.

"Lucia, I apologize—"

"Shhhh." I laughed. *Shhh* became the sound of rain drowning out his voice. "Shhhh." I was bobbing in waves of flowers and sprinkled by rain.

I felt his hands caressing me, stroking me. I sighed. He unbound my hair and kissed my neck. I murmured the vulgar Chinese words and asked him to say them. He repeated them in an oddly polite voice. I laughed and said to take me to bed and show me what those words meant. When he helped me stand, I felt the water stream down my skin like a waterfall. I lay on the bed and watched Lu Shing undress. His body shimmered. He lay next to me and caressed my back. I laughed and uttered the harsh vulgar words. He quickly entered me, and a few moments later, I saw with wonderment that I had become him. I was the face looking at me, and it appeared to be terribly sad, yet I was euphoric. "Good little boat," I said, and rowed against waves, and the ropes that had knotted his brow fell away. I watched myself in him as his eyes rolled back and he and I gave up fear. I repeated the vulgar words urgently, harshly, hearing those sounds also coming from him. Together our coarse words were scraping away his armor and mine, so we could reach more joy, more pleasure. I watched as the look on his face changed from desperate to ecstatic, and I felt victorious that I had conquered him and he was, at last, completely mine. I laughed that I had made this happen.

I AWOKE SO thickheaded I did not know who I was. Gradually, my mind returned. The room looked faded and flat without shadows and gold light. All my clothes had been removed and were not on the sofa where I had left them. I recalled that I had been exquisitely happy last night—but not a bit of it remained. The air was heavy and smelled of summer mildew. The old worries and anger had returned. Where was Lu Shing? Had he abandoned me again?

I left the bed and saw my dress hanging in an armoire, along with other clothes. Who had done that? Before I could step forward, a girl dashed into the room, and out of modesty, I gasped and tried to cover myself. She held up a blue silk robe and turned her face away as I slipped my arms into its sleeves. Slippers magically appeared at my feet and I stepped into them. She gestured to a small area behind the screen. The bathtub had been emptied. It was plain white and not a painted soup tureen. Nearby was a porcelain basin on a tall stand, and it was filled with water. She pantomimed washing my face. I splashed the water onto my face to remove the bleariness of my mind. I kept throwing cool water on me, until the bowl was empty and the floor was wet, but only part of me had returned. She took me to a cupboard with drawers. My clothes had been placed inside. She opened another drawer. Chinese pajamas lay neatly folded—light silky clothes. I understood why Danner wore them. The air was heavy and humid.

Downstairs, I found Danner talking in English to a gray cat, who was just as animatedly talking to him in its feline language.

"I know that it is six in the evening, Elmira, dearest, but we cannot begin supper without our guest. Ah—voilà!—Lulu is here."

How was it possible that I had slept for over twelve hours? I ate a supper of strange-tasting cold dishes: coin-size slices of beef and pigeon, eggs, salted raw cucumbers, and bright green vegetables. The cat stood at the other end of the table and ate from a china plate. Would all the meals be like this?

"I will not speak about your situation," Danner said, "unless you care to. I will, however, tell you what you need to know about the Chinese, and that is this: You cannot change thousands of years of Chinese custom about shame in the family. We create our own laws in the Settlement and govern what a Chinese person can do. But there is no law you can use to disallow their philosophical outlook. Shame, honor, and obligation cannot be cast off. You will not be happy with your young man, or with Shanghai, if you think you can change that."

I did not answer. I would not give up, and I would not return home.

"I can see your answer in your eyes, my dear. Hear my sigh. Every newcomer finds something disagreeable about the Chinese that they wish to change. I've heard all the complaints and have had some myself—their noisiness at odd hours, their standard of cleanliness, their selective understanding of punctuality, their inefficiency in doing something the way it has been done for a thousand years. They may alter it somewhat over much time, but they cannot change their fears, which govern much of what they do. And many a newcomer, like you, thinks she will succeed. It's that American pioneer spirit that scouted the rivers and mountains, opened new frontiers, and conquered the Indians. So why not the Chinese?"

I pretended to eat, but I had little appetite for strange food on a warm night.

"Some Americans give up and go home," Danner continued in a cheerful voice. "The sojourners who are required to stay for a few years grumble a lot to each other. The Shanghailanders, like me, who've made China their home, adopt a Chinese attitude about most things. We don't interfere. Live and let live. Most of the time, at least."

I discovered later that he was originally from Concord, Massachusetts, "a bastion of praying Puritans," he called it. While still young, he lived in Italy, where he began collecting paintings, which he sold at a good price when he returned to the States. He alternated between Europe and the East Coast and was known as a collector with a good eye for Eastern landscapes, traditional and, later, impressionistic. He moved to Shanghai nearly twenty years ago for undisclosed reasons. Many came to Shanghai with secrets, he said, or left them behind and developed new scandals. He brought trunks of paintings, kept the ones he liked, and sold the ones he did not in an art gallery, where homesick Westerners bought paintings that reminded them of familiar landscapes, where they had enjoyed quiet picnics in a land far removed from the cacophony of Shanghai.

Lu Shing had visited Danner's gallery from the age of twelve, when he first became fascinated with Western painting. His family expected him to achieve a high level of scholarship and pass the imperial examinations, but secretly he had hoped to become a painter. He spent hours copying the paintings in Danner's gallery—the popular landscapes with sheep and horses, the pretty cottages by the stream, the stormy seas with white boats. They were popular with Westerners.

"As you know," Danner said to me, "his work is quite good, even though they are imitations of the works of famous artists."

My head felt light. "He copied them? He wasn't at those places in his paintings?"

"He copied them well enough that it was hard to tell the originals from his."

I was afraid to ask about the painting that brought me to Shanghai. Would his answer make a difference? "Did you ever see one with thick rain clouds, a long valley, mountains in the background—"

"*The Valley of Amazement*. A favorite of his. I bought it in Berlin for pennies. *Das Tal der Verwunderung*, by an obscure artist who died young. Friedrich Leutemann. It hung in the gallery for years before I sold it. Lu Shing made many versions and added an element of his own. A golden vale in the distance. I have to say, I was not fond of the alteration. The original had a dark beauty, a quavering feeling of uncertainty. He took the uncertainty away. But he was a young artist then, searching for meaning."

I had wanted certainty and that painting had made me feel I was on the verge of finding it. I was glad he changed it. The golden vale he had added was original.

Lu Shing sold his imitations in the gallery until he had enough money to go to America—against his family's wishes. Danner sent a letter of introduction to one of his best clients: Bosson Ivory II, a collector of landscape paintings. The Bossons collected protégés as well, and he favored the idea of an Oriental one. For several years, Lu Shing lived in the Ivory house in Croton-on-Hudson, and in return, he presented Mr. Ivory with paintings. He wrote to Danner regularly and said that Mr. Ivory rolled up his unwanted paintings and put them away.

At the end of supper, Danner said that dinner would be served at midnight. Lu Shing would join us, along with the cat, Elmira, and, possibly, the guest on the third floor. She was a Chinese woman who tutored men to speak English, Danner explained. English lessons! That was the made-up story I had given those women on the boat. I told Danner about the coincidence.

"In a city with so many desperate women and so few opportunities, you will run across many coincidences. Her choice is a common one, and it is not really English lessons she provides, although her conversational skills are quite good. The truth is, she has an arrangement with two men, one during the day, one at night. She keeps them company on a regular basis, and they provide a stipend on a regular basis."

"How does she keep them company?"

"She is a lady of the night, my dear. *Prostitute* is too harsh a word. She is a professional mistress. Not mine." He chuckled. "You're shocked. I am not running a whorehouse, dear girl. The woman is an old friend, someone I've known since the days when she had a life that was quite respectable. But circumstances change quickly here, and a woman without a husband has few prospects. She could have become a rag collector, a washerwoman, a beggar. She could have gone to a cheap brothel or taken to the streets. She chose instead to take my offer to rent the rooms upstairs and take gentlemen callers. You will not be confronted with the comings and goings of her guests. They enter through the gate on the other side of the house, one alley over from ours. When you meet, you'll find her interesting and likable. Everyone does. Her name is Golden Dove."

Despite what Danner said, I was disturbed by the presence of the woman. I had a sickening feeling that my circumstances were already too similar to hers. I, too, had a gentleman caller and he paid my rent.

Lu Shing's coolie brought a note that Lu Shing would come that evening, and, as promised, he arrived just before midnight. Danner had many freshly cooked dishes laid out for dinner. I had no appetite. Lu Shing and I went immediately to my room and I searched his face to guess what had transpired. Failure and despair. I told him about the woman above me. If he abandoned me, her fate would be mine. He said I should not torment myself with terrible thoughts that would never come true.

"Did you try harder?" I cried. "Did you tell them about me?" Danner had said it was impossible to change a Chinese family. But I wanted Lu Shing to be as persistent as I was—and to be just as miserable. We lay on the bed facing each other.

"I am hesitant to give you too much hope," he said. "But I have thought of one possibility. It is to soften my mother's heart first, which will provide a path to my father's heart. If our baby is indeed a boy, he will be the first son of his generation. And because I am the eldest, his birth will have significance. I cannot guarantee they would accept him, since he would not be purely Chinese. But if he is the first, he cannot be ignored."

This possibility was my opium. The sweetness in the air returned. Gloom had vanished. So there was a way! The eldest son of the eldest son. I was so swept up with this answer that I did not consider that my baby would be anything other than a boy. I made plans for my new life within a Chinese family. Among the first things, I would learn to speak Chinese.

I introduced myself to the woman upstairs, Golden Dove, who was indeed likable. She was around twenty-five and pretty, although the two halves of her face were slightly askew, the cheek on one side being higher than the other. The right side of her upper lip appeared to curl under. I was happy to find she spoke English, not as perfectly as Lu Shing, but with enough ease that she and I could converse. She was open in talking about her life, guessing what I would want to know. She had been abandoned as a baby and raised in an American mission school. She fell in love with a handsome man and ran away from the school when she was sixteen, and after a year, he abandoned her, and she went to work in a courtesan house. It was not a terrible life. She had many admirers. She had freedom. She met Danner in a bookshop and they often had tea. But two years ago, she made the mistake of taking a lover, and this so enraged one of her suitors that he broke her jaw and nose. She healed in Danner's house and had remained ever since. "The life we receive is not always what we choose."

I did not ask about her gentlemen. In part, I was afraid I would find similarities to Lu Shing—a well-to-do family, a son who would not take her for his wife or concubine. Whatever similarities we had now would not remain. I was an American with more opportunities, although what those might be was not clear. In the meantime, I would improve my prospects. I asked if she could give me lessons in Chinese.

"You have elevated me to the status of a teacher!" she said. "At one time, I had hoped to be one."

Lu Shing came to visit me at unpredictable times. I waited every day for his coolie to come with a note telling me whether Lu Shing could come that day or the next. The coolie was the same man who had taken care of me the first day. I would hear him running through the gate shouting, in Chinese, "It's here!" and my heart would race. Lu Shing's message was written on cream-colored paper, enclosed in a matching envelope and placed in a silk bag so that dirty hands would not soil it.

"My dear Lucia . . ." they always began, and what followed was the same elegant handwriting, perfectly executed, whether he conveyed regrets or an announcement of his time of arrival, as if he had written it in a leisurely manner, unhurried, while enjoying his afternoon tea. His visit might be early in the morning or in the late afternoon or late at night. He never came during the hour for the midday meal or dinner. I tried to appear cheerful during his visits, aware that I had more recently fallen into moods like my mother's—angry and critical. But it was hard to stifle what I felt when Lu Shing seemed unbothered by the arrangement. I could not hide it when pink splotches spread over my chest and neck.

Rather than allowing me to sulk, Danner became my happy guide to Shanghai. Because of his enormous size, we had to take two rickshaws, and the pullers who saw him approach were always glad. Danner paid them extra. We ate at French restaurants, visited curio shops, attended a vaudeville show put on by Russian Jews, and took a boat ride on Soochow Creek. Shanghai provided endless diversions, and I strung them together to try to forget about my predicament and the absence of my lover. But as soon as our outing was over, I returned to fretting.

I asked Danner one evening if we could detour on our way home and go by Lu Shing's family house. Danner said he did not know where it was.

"I am not lying," he protested. "One day, I will indeed lie and you will see how poorly I do it. This city has many liars. You would think I would have learned to do it better. But I've never had a reason to be dishonest. I have no past as a criminal. I am not here to cheat people of money. But those who come to Shanghai always have a strong reason to do so. To make fortunes—that's a common one. You see in opium houses many who failed. In my case, I came with a dear friend whom I had known since our days at university. He was an artist and considered himself an Orientalist by aesthetic influence. We had a wonderful life together. He died of pneumonia nine years ago. So long ago, so recently."

"I'm sorry for your loss," I said.

He gave a slight laugh. "I've grown to the size of the two of us. We were as inseparable as twins, like Gemini, compatible in all ways— except for the tassels. They were his doing."

He was a homosexual. I thought of my father and his sorties with both men and women. I had been angry that he had given away his love to so many others but not to me. My father, however, had never spoken about any of them with any affection—none at all, not even Miss Pond. He never loved them any more than he loved me. I might have become incapable of being loved or loving anyone had I not met Lu Shing. Unlike Danner, I could not say we had a wonderful life together.

"What was your friend's name?" I asked.

"Teddy," he said.

Whenever we went to curio shops, I asked Danner what Teddy would have thought of this carving or that painting or those porcelain bowls.

"Teddy would have thought the gilded knickknacks were hideously pretentious. And these objets d'art are not art but vulgar imitations. He would have liked the coloration of these bowls." In time, I was able to guess what Teddy might have liked with uncanny accuracy, Danner said.

Whenever I was weepy or angry or frightened about the uncer-

tainties of my new life, Danner would comfort me. "I feel so alone,"
I said.

"Teddy once told me that it's natural that we feel alone, and
that's because our hearts are different from others and we don't even
know how. When we're in love, as if by magic, our different hearts
come together perfectly toward the same desire. Eventually, the differences return, and then comes heartache and mending, and, in
between, much loneliness and fear. If love remains despite the pain
of those differences, it must be guarded as rare. That's what Teddy
said and that's what we had."

Lu Shing brought his paints over. He wanted to do my portrait.
"How we see ourselves is never how others see us," he said. "So I
will show you what I see and what I feel. I'll paint you as Lucia, the
woman I love."

He seated me in an armchair and arranged the lamp so that it
illuminated my face. I wore nothing to cover my breasts, even though
the painting would depict me only from the shoulders up.

"I want the painting to emanate your sensuality, your free spirit,
your love for me. Without clothes you are freed to be yourself."

"With this belly, I am hardly myself." I was a bit cross, because he
had come late two nights in a row.

"I have always said it was impossible for me to capture an
immortal moment," he continued. "But you once said I had. So
I'm inspired to try." When I asked to see those immortal moments
emerge, he said I had to wait until it was finished. "A moment is not
the same as time."

On those nights when he was able to come to me, he painted
for an hour or two. I simply stared into his eyes when he looked up
from the canvas. His expression was somber, studied, and I felt at
times that he had no more emotion for me than he did for the chair

I was seated in. But then, he would put his brush down, finished for the night. His face would be flush with adoration and desire, and he would take me to bed.

I was impatient to see the portrait and know what he saw, who he thought I was. He had captured my immortal spirit in *The Valley of Amazement*. I remembered the surprise when I recognized myself in that long green valley and my soul in the golden vale. Who I was supposed to be had nothing to do with a neatly combed appearance, manners, or superior opinions of my parents. I didn't have to hide my faults. I had none, because I no longer had to compare myself to others. I held knowledge, the certainty of something important—but now I could not recall what it was. It had eluded me again. If I had it, I would not be tormented by doubt, whether I was loved, if I should stay or leave. I hoped the new painting would restore that sense of certainty.

Two weeks after he began, he presented the painting to me with an inscription on the back with both Chinese and English words: "For Lucia, on the occasion of her 17th birthday." My actual birthday had passed while I was on the ship. The painting was both beautiful and disturbing. I was set against a black background, in a formless empty space, as if I did not belong anywhere. My shoulders were milky white on one side and cast in shadow on the other. The painting extended to my waist, and over my breasts was a lustrous swath of satin, held up by one hand, conveying the erotic sense that I was both modest yet given to indecency. My green irises were thin rings, and my pupils were large and black, as black as the nameless place in which I sat. They reminded me of the first time I had looked close into Lu Shing's eyes and saw that his eyes were so dark I would never be able to see into them and know who he was. Anyone who saw the painting would confirm that I was the girl in the painting. While it was well executed, I did not want to be that girl with those blank eyes, unable to see anything but the painter, as if he would always be my entire world. This was not my spirit but what remained after losing it. Lu Shing did not know me. And what frightened me more: I did not know myself. He loved a girl who did not exist. He was not my intimate. Yet the thought of giving him up was inconceivable, because then I would have to destroy what was in the painting of the green valley: It was love for myself.

"You've made me beautiful," I said. I was glad we were in the dark, so that he could not see that my neck was flushed pink. I marveled over the painting, finding as many good things as I could to cover my disappointment. I then asked Lu Shing to paint over the name he had given me in English and Chinese. "It should read, 'Lucretia Minturn,'" I said. "If the painting is passed along to future generations of your family, they should know my true name." I watched for his reaction. He did not look at me.

"Of course," he said.

I asked for another painting. "The painting of the valley," I said. "Can you paint it from memory?"

He brought the painting to me three days later, leading me to suspect he had given me one of many copies he already had on hand, many depictions of where my true self could be found.

THREE MONTHS PASSED and I grew too large to wear the clothes I had brought. Danner and Golden Dove had a tailor make me new dresses and loose gowns. The ones I felt most comfortable in were like Danner's, loose-fitting pajamas and robes. The baby had become real to me, not simply a solution to gain acceptance into Lu Shing's family. My future lay with this baby, no matter what happened. I could not allow myself any expectations beyond that. Lu Shing might visit every night for a week. Rarely did he stay until morning. Just when I felt I could accept the arrangement, he would disappear for a week and I would feel cast into the nether world of the abandoned. When he returned, he always provided good reasons for his absence. He had been obligated to accompany his father as translator for an important meeting on treaty exemptions. His mother had fallen ill and called upon him for daily fortification of hope. I was suspicious of his truthfulness, but did not want to further question him and perhaps find that the queasy suspicions had been justified.

Over time, our lovemaking became distanced. I reasoned it had to do with my pregnancy, that he did not find a ballooning woman an attractive consort. But I also noticed that he seldom stayed longer than a few hours. He seemed hurried as he dressed. I could guess what he was hiding, and the truth knotted in my throat. I forced myself to be calm, to tamp down tears and cool my head and the blotches. When he stood at the door to say good-bye, he was awkward and wore a guilty face that belied his promises to be truthful.

"Are you married?" I asked with little emotion.

He paused and came to me. "I did not want to tell you until I was certain you were able to hear this news. But you were either in a sad mood or an extremely happy one. The time never seemed right."

The truth was upsetting but his reasoning was flaccid and insincere. "When would I have ever been able to hear it? When the baby was in my arms?"

"Lucia, you knew I had a contracted bride. The marriage changes nothing between us."

"Don't call me Lucia anymore. That girl doesn't belong to you anymore. My name is Lucretia."

"I was made to marry a girl I do not love. But you could still be my wife."

"A concubine."

"You would be known as Second Wife. It is not necessarily a weaker position if you provide the first male of the next generation. With our son, you could live in your own house, and the family would still recognize you as my wife. The arrangement will be far more comfortable than living in the house as First Wife. Ask Golden Dove if this is not true."

"And if the baby is not a male?"

"You cannot think that way."

Golden Dove confirmed the truth of what Lu Shing had said about my becoming Second Wife. "However," she added, "there is a difference between what is possible and what is realized, especially when it is the man who says what the possibilities are. I have learned from experience. Maybe your possibilities will not be like mine."

On the evening the baby was about to be born, what would have been the American observance of Lincoln's birthday, Danner sat downstairs, waiting for Lu Shing's coolie. Golden Dove had been with me all day, calling out in English: "Be brave. Be strong." After I had endured ten hours of pain, I could bear it no longer and I screamed and gasped. All her soothing English words were replaced with frantic Chinese ones I could not understand, which made me wonder if I was going to die. Finally, the coolie came back with the familiar cream-colored envelope and Lu Shing's neatly written message: He was obligated to attend a banquet and festivities for the sixtieth year of his aunt's birthday. "The sixtieth is one of the most important birthdays," he wrote.

A number was more important than being with me when our baby was born? The only acceptable reason he could have given was that he had died. Danner gave the coolie a note that I was moments from giving birth to our child.

An hour later, the Chinese midwife solemnly announced that my baby was a girl. She placed her in my arms. When the baby wailed, I wailed with her. I cried for the pain she would share with me. I cried that my hopes had evaporated. And then, while looking at me, she stopped crying, and I fell in love. I would protect her, care for her. I would not neglect her as my mother had me. I would not change her. She would know that I loved her for who she was. She would be like the violets I had planted in the garden when I was a child, the ones my mother deemed a weed that should be pulled out. I nurtured them to grow free, far and wide, and they spread, unhampered, until they were everywhere.

Danner was delighted to have a "miniature queen" among us. He would be her most loyal subject. When I told him that I had decided to name her "Violet" after my favorite flower, he said violets were among his favorites as well because they had beautiful and expressive little faces. He said he would send out a servant in the morning to find violets that we could plant throughout the garden.

Danner's nebulous note to Lu Shing had the desire effect. Within two hours, Lu Shing was running up the stairs. He came to me with eyes wide in expectation. A moment later, he knew the truth by my expression. When I unfolded the quilt around her, he did not move as he stared at her, and it was not with awe but with the slight hesitation that expressed his disappointment. He could not disguise it.

"She is beautiful," he murmured. "So small." He struggled to find other meaningless pronouncements on the features of an infant.

He glanced toward me with a questioning look. He was waiting for me to acknowledge what the birth of a girl signified for my future. I hated him at that moment. He thought I was disappointed that our baby had been born without a penis and that she was the reason I had lost my chance at being accepted by his family. And then it occurred to me that he saw Violet as the reason for his troubles. She was the reason I had come with him to Shanghai. I resolved I would not let Violet become anyone's disappointment. She would be welcomed for who she was. She was my child, my daughter, whom I now loved more than anyone in the world, more than Lu Shing.

"I named her Violet," I said, and without looking at him, I added, "I love her far more than you think."

He nodded. He did not ask why I had named her "Violet," nor did he comment on my declaration of love for her.

The following day, a woman arrived, who informed me that Lu Shing had sent her to be the baby's amah. I was heartened by the expression of love. Or was that love? An amah? I was bothered that I had to question everything that Lu Shing did. Each time Lu Shing visited, he brought her gifts, and I watched his face as he held her. He did not show delight. Later, when she learned to laugh, he delighted in her, but I still did not feel he loved her as I did. If he had, he would have fought to have her accepted by his father. When she cried with a red face and balled fists, he was concerned, but he did not feel her distress, as I did. He did nothing to soothe her.

"No father has those instincts," Danner said later.

"If he loved her, why would he not want to put his name on the birth certificate?"

"It would permanently cast her out as his offspring. Until you have an official position within the family, you should wait."

"Is it better for her to bear the stigma of being an illegitimate love child if I never have a position in his family? I can't let Violet go through life with others thinking less of her."

"I have a solution," Danner said. He left the house. Two hours later he returned with a wedding certificate that stated I had married Philo Danner. It was dated months before Violet's birth. He then held up a birth certificate for Violet Minturn Danner. "I've already had her registered at the American Consulate," he said. "She is an American citizen and will be required to sing 'My Country 'Tis of Thee.' "

I was crying. He had given Violet the gift of legitimacy.

"If you would rather be married to someone else," he said, "I can go to the same man who made the certificates. He is one of the best in Shanghai—all the proper-looking forms, red name seals, Chinese characters and English gibberish."

To celebrate his fatherhood, Danner bought Violet a bassinet and a silver rattle with a tassel. "My Puritan prayers have been answered. At last, I am a father."

Like me, Violet had brown hair and green eyes. Her skin was pale, but the shape of her eyes made her look more Chinese than white. Danner disagreed. He said she took after Teddy's Italian side of the family. As if by his decree, Violet changed over the next year. Strangers who saw and admired her guessed she was half-Italian or half-Spanish.

DANNER AND I had the life of a married couple in many ways. He would arrange for us to have our meals together. Golden Dove joined us as Violet's auntie, and we three took turns fussing over Violet. We noted everything new she had done, what she had shown interest in. When Violet was eleven months old, she called Danner "Daddy," and he cried and said that was one of the happiest moments in his entire life. When we took walks, we discussed her future—the schools she should attend, the boys she should avoid. We worried over her health together and disagreed over the best remedies to quell red-faced crying.

Danner carried her into toy shops and bought whichever object was the first thing she reached for. I finally told him that twelve jack-in-the-boxes were quite enough. She clearly loved him and laughed when he walked around, bouncing her on his enormous belly. But Danner, I noticed, tired easily with any amount of extra weight. He had to quickly sit down to catch his breath. I worried over his health and exercised the prerogative of his wife in demanding he lose weight.

By May, not even a year after I had arrived in Shanghai, Lu Shing had fallen into an unsatisfactory pattern of haphazard visits. He might be with me for three days and then I would not see him for a week. He had taught Violet to say "Baba," for father, but she did not lift her arms toward him when he arrived as she did to Danner. The disappointments I had with Lu Shing had been softened by Violet, who consumed most of my thoughts. She had given me the gift of fullness in my heart. When she fluttered her hands, she waved away anger. She crawled over the mounds of violets in the garden. Seeing her laugh in those pillows of flowers made my heart squeeze often with the surprise of happiness.

On a warm day in May, the Double Fifth, the alley was much quieter than on most afternoons. Most of the denizens—the Chinese and the foreigners—had gone to Soochow Creek to watch the

Dragon Boat races. In that serene garden, as Lu Shing stood with Violet in his arms, I told him my news: I was pregnant again.

LU SHING TOLD the amah to serve me foods that would strengthen the baby growing within me. He did not say the word *boy*. I knew we both should have had a cautious heart. But I was happy to let hope reemerge. It was not just for my chance to be accepted into the Lu family. I wanted Violet to be acknowledged as Lu Shing's daughter.

The baby came on November 29, 1900, Thanksgiving Day. Lu Shing had told me he would be away during that time to assist his father. Yet he came within three hours after my announcement had been sent. He held the baby and stared at his face, commenting on the great future that awaited him. He gloated that his son had been born on a special day, the day after his grandfather's birthday. Lu Shing would say that the closeness of the birthday marked one generation to the next. When he compared the resemblance the baby had to him, he described it as "the Lu family brow," "the Lu family nose." He caught me watching. "It's important that they see the resemblance," he explained, "so they know without a doubt that the baby is my son." He kissed my forehead and thanked me.

The next day, he returned laden with gifts. Chinese baby clothes, a silver locket, a rich silk blanket. He said that the baby should look Chinese when he presented him to his mother. He should look like he already belonged to a wealthy family.

He held the baby up to his face and talked to him: "Your grandmother has been waiting impatiently for you. She's made daily offerings. She was afraid she would have only granddaughters . . ." Lu Shing had spoken without caution, and suspicion immediately rose and made me ill.

"Did your wife give your mother a granddaughter?"

He was not apologetic. "Let us be happy today, Lucia. Let's forget everything else and believe that our fate has changed."

"You intend to make me your Second Wife?" I said.

"I am ready to try. We now have a better chance."

"What is your assessment of your family's acceptance of me? Warm embrace? Tolerance? Resentment? Be truthful. My happiness depends on it."

"It may take time." He spoke of his plans to approach his mother, to petition that I be recognized.

I was not listening. I had been thinking over the past hour of how my life might change once I moved out of Danner's house. I had freedom here and no one who governed what I did. Violet adored Danner, and he adored her. And Danner, Golden Dove, and I had become true friends who could count on one another without question.

"I prefer to keep the arrangement we have now," I told Lu Shing. "You can give me whatever position you want in your family, so long as both Violet and our son are accepted and also recognized as mine. I'll continue to live here in Danner's house and with our children."

Lu Shing looked relieved. He spoke again about his chances of winning his family's approval once he showed them our son.

"Until they are both accepted into the Lu family," I said, "they will be considered Danner's children. I will have an American birth certificate that says so. And even if they are accepted, the children will continue to live with me."

"Our son should spend time with his grandparents, especially on important occasions. That will secure his legitimate station in our family."

"What about Violet?"

"I will ensure she is accepted and treated well. But I cannot change how my parents view the first male of the next generation."

I never would have agreed to this arrangement two years ago. But I saw now that it had been folly and pride to foist myself on

Lu Shing's family and suffer from their rejection. My proposal was not a compromise, but my wish. I could let go of my resentments and Lu Shing his secrecy. That day, he lay on the bed with our son between us. He spoke tenderly with all the endearments I had not heard for a year. He would inform his family that he would divide his time between their home and the other we had on East Floral Alley. Despite our excited talk over the future, I was clear-eyed. His parents might not accept our son as the legitimate first male. And if that was the case, it would not matter. I would still have my two children. I might continue to be disappointed in Lu Shing, but I would not be dependent on him for my happiness. Danner was more a true husband than Lu Shing could ever be. He was more a father than my father ever was.

After Lu Shing left, I told Danner about my plans. "He declined to live here as Second Husband," I said. "So with you as First Husband and me as First Wife, our family will be just Violet, the new baby, and us. Lu Shing will come visit with us as before. Lu Shing can name the baby whatever he wants. But his American name will be Teddy Minturn Danner."

Danner was so overcome he sobbed to a state of breathlessness.

Lu Shing arrived early the next morning while Danner, Violet, and I were having breakfast. I could tell he was impatient to see his son. "The baby is sleeping," I said, "and can't be disturbed." Lu Shing asked to speak to me privately.

We went into the garden. I realized that my feelings toward Lu Shing had changed. I did not need him for happiness or a home or a future. I had been freed in mind to see him as he was: a man whom I had been infatuated with, whom I might still love, but that was not certain. I wondered if he sensed the difference in me.

"My mother has agreed to see our son," he said. "I told her that he has many of the Lu family features and that there is no question he is part of our lineage. From the moment I saw him, I said, he fastened his eyes on me and recognized me as his father."

I laughed at the lie.

"And I told her his name is Lu Shen. *Shen* means 'profound.' I would have chosen a name with you, but there was no time. I saw the opportunity to speak to my mother when no one else was around to hear what I had to say."

"I certainly can't criticize you for giving him a Chinese name. I've already given him an American one. Teddy Minturn Danner. Teddy not Theodore." Two names, given separately, a sign of how far apart we had grown. "I just now realized I never thought to ask you what your name *Shing* means."

" 'Fulfillment,' " he said, "a name that mocks me. I have fulfilled nothing—not to you nor to my family. I have failed as an artist. But our son will make up for my failures. He will one day be the head of a great family."

Those last words were opium to my soul. "When does your mother want to see him?"

"Tonight. She is already eager. It would be best that I take him to her by myself. If she wants him as her grandson, she would then present him to my father. And if he agrees, we can then tell them that you must be recognized as his mother."

"Tell me again what we would do if they do not recognize me?"

"You and I will raise him outside of the family. But he will not have legitimacy as a Chinese son, and so he would not be entitled to position or an inheritance, and I want those for our son."

I asked him to let me think and I would give him my decision tonight whether he could take our son without me. I posed the question to Golden Dove and Danner. They could reject him, I said. Or they could accept him but not accept me. We talked throughout the day. I posed the possibilities and they reflected with me. And if they gave me advice that differed from what I wanted, I did not hear it. I wanted my children—Violet and Teddy—to be recognized and given every opportunity for a good life of their own choosing.

I had Teddy bundled and ready when Lu Shing came that

evening. He had brought a nursemaid and silk baby pajamas. He held me in gratitude and professed love for me. Tomorrow afternoon, he would return Teddy to me and I would have had hardly enough time to miss him. I kissed Teddy's sleeping face. And then I let him go.

I could not sleep. I imagined what Lu Shing's mother would feel when she saw him. I imagined the worst, her look of disgust. Danner kept me company, trying to distract me with stories of Little Teddy's namesake. When I expressed worries that all would be for naught, I was grateful when he enumerated the reasons I could hope Lu Shing would succeed. He began with the desperate need of a grandmother seeing a grandson before she passed from this world. He said that she was likely indulgent with Lu Shing, since he was her firstborn son. He cited numerous families who were known to have mixed blood. He said that Teddy was too beautiful for any grandmother to refuse.

At 9:00 A.M., Lu Shing's coolie arrived with the familiar envelope in a silk pouch. "My dear Lucia, Our hopes are closer to coming true. She is very much taken with him." I gave out a shout of joy. I continued reading: "She is confident she can persuade my father to accept our son as his grandson. She will do so tomorrow when he returns to Shanghai. For now, she would like to spend more time with the baby. This, she said, will enable her to say just the right words to my father to overcome obstacles. We must be patient for another day."

I was not happy that Lu Shing's mother would keep Teddy. It had been difficult for even one night. I debated whether to send a letter asking that he return Teddy for the time being. If his mother was as pleased as he made her out to be, she would still be pleased when Lu Shing's father returned. I sent a note requesting that Lu Shing return the baby.

In the afternoon, when I expected him to return Teddy, I received his note in reply: "My dear Lucia, all continues with hopeful signs. My mother had a message delivered to my father, and he is returning early. He will arrive this evening."

I should have been happy that progress had been made. But I was not happy that Teddy was not in my arms. I should have insisted on being there. Were they jostling him too much? Did they allow him to sleep? And then another fear, the size of a grain of sand, crept in under my skin. Would she return him? The grain of sand went into my eye, and I became so anxious I walked up and down the alley. Danner could not follow me without becoming winded. He suggested I smoke opium to take my mind off what I could not change for the moment.

The next morning, Lu Shing sent more good news: "My brothers and their wives have seen the baby and were also very much taken with him. They, too, thought he has the features of the family. My father is already so fond of his grandson he talks to him of his future. All obstacles are being rolled out of the way."

I could not celebrate this victory until Lu Shing returned with Teddy. Danner and Golden Dove tried to distract me from worry. They talked about all the privileges my children would receive— education, respect, and power. My son could become a corrupt bureaucrat, if I did not instill good values in him. Danner bounced two-year-old Violet on his belly, singing a ditty and raising her above his head: "Ride a high horse, giddy-up up up . . ." Teddy would be home by the afternoon.

By evening, I was frantic. Lu Shing still had not arrived. If he had been delayed, he should have sent a note of explanation. I went through the different possibilities of what might have happened: Teddy had fallen ill and they did not want to tell me. Perhaps Lu Shing's father had a change of heart and his mother wanted to keep Teddy longer to encourage him to reconsider. Maybe Lu Shing's wife objected and more time was needed to smooth this out. But none of these fears was as great as the one that came true.

Late at night, the coolie handed me a note, this one hastily scrawled. "My dear Lucia, I am at a loss to tell you what has happened . . ." Lu Shing's father and mother had decided to keep Teddy. They would not recognize me as his mother. He would be the son of Lu Shing's wife. His mother had already taken Teddy away when she told him of her decision. He did not know where the baby was. "Lucia, if I knew where he was, I would have delivered him into your arms by now. I am sickened by what has happened, and I can only imagine your shock." He went on about a threat his family had made to never allow Lu Shing to ever see Teddy again if he attempted to see me.

I was shaking and could not make sense of the letter. I raced downstairs to find the coolie gone. I ran out into the alley and along Nanking Road. I cursed and wept. When I finally returned two hours later, Danner and Golden Dove were sitting at the table with grim expressions. They had read the letter several times to decipher what each sentence meant.

"This is kidnapping," Danner said. "We shall go to the American Consulate first thing tomorrow morning."

Moments later, horror washed over his face. During all the excitement of gaining the Lu family's approval, we had neglected to register Teddy as Danner's and my son at the American Consulate. How could we claim a child was missing when he never existed in their records? Lu Shing may have already made a legal claim.

I lay in bed for three days, neither sleeping nor eating. Golden Dove and Danner took care of Violet. I went through everything that had happened. I had felt the danger. I should have accompanied Lu Shing, at least in the carriage. I should have hired a carriage to follow the coolie. I wrestled with the idea that Lu Shing had been part of the plot all along. At last he was rid of me, his problem, the American girl who would never understand what it meant to be Chinese. He had no feelings for me or for little Violet.

Danner grieved nearly as much as I did. In little Teddy, he had resurrected his old companion and now had lost them both. Instead of eating insatiably, he stopped altogether. Golden Dove organized herself to find Teddy and assured me she would. She searched among her friends in courtesan houses for those who might know a man named Lu who worked for the Ministry of Foreign Relations. There are ten thousand Lu families, they said. What part of the foreign ministry? There are many foreigners requiring administration these days. What is your business? Why do you wish to find him?

When I revived myself and left my bed, I held Little Violet close to me, afraid that she, too, would disappear. She squirmed. I put her down and watched her toddle over to a pile of books and knock them down. She looked at me for approval and I forced myself to smile. For her, there was no such thing as hatred, betrayal, or false love.

A MONTH AFTER we lost Teddy, Danner stood up from the dining table with a groan and complained of indigestion. He went to bed at ten in the evening. He never woke up.

My heart was too worn to feel the sharpness of his death. I could not possibly feel more pain, and I refused to know what the loss of him meant. But over the days, a gnawing hollow of grief enlarged. Where was the man who had given me the fullness of his heart, his home, his compassion and love? He had felt my hopes and defeats, my fury and sorrow. He had given me decency and bestowed upon Violet a legitimate birth. He equipped me with armor to be brave and go forward. Danner had been the father I wished I had had. I should have told him. We were the little family he had wanted to have. We belonged to him and he to us. He knew that.

Upon reporting his death to the American Consulate, I discovered that Danner's possessions had passed to me—the house, the paintings, the furniture, and the tassels. I had been his wife and was now his widow. He had not forgotten Golden Dove. The rent he had collected from her had gone into a bank account in her name. She offered to pay me her usual rent so that she could stay and still serve her clients. I told her to live with me as a guest, and she said I was better than a sister. Although I had inherited the house, there was only a little bit of money for daily expenditures. We had already used much of that for Danner's burial. For income, Danner had sold a painting or two each month and always after great deliberation over which one he could bear to part with. I brought a few paintings to a gallery and was told they were worth next to nothing. I would not let Danner's paintings fall into the hands of cheats. I took the paintings home and told the servants that I could not pay them. Two left, but the amah and coolie stayed. They said it was enough to have a place to live and food to eat, and they even argued that they could haggle and buy provisions for prices far cheaper than a foreigner could get. I was grateful, yet we all knew we were delaying the inevitable. And then where would we go? I walked through the house, noting what I might sell—the sofa, the large armchair with its sagging cushion, the table and lamp—surveying all as I stepped between piles of books snaking through the house and piled on the mantel with swags of tassels. Books and tassels, the overflow of two spendthrifts, which now would sustain two frugal women.

At first, I was particular in selling only the books I would never read: the medical benefits of leeches, tide tables, the mechanics of musical instruments, the density of liquids. It turned out that they were the same books that no one else wanted to read. I then parted with the novels that would sell quickly among the American and British recent arrivals. Maritime history, historic accounts by British sea captains, and an atlas of maps were surprisingly popular. When the floors were cleared of books, I began with those on the shelves. I calculated how soon we would be broke: six months, less, if the remaining books proved unpopular reading. At bookshops, I always asked if a customer named Lu Shing had come by. I explained that I had found the book he was interested in. I always carried a pen with a sharp nib so if I found him, I would be ready to slash his face if he did not take me to Teddy. He should bear his shame publicly and forever.

Golden Dove and I made a list of all the possible routes for making money. She could teach English and Chinese. I could serve as a guide for Westerners wishing to explore "the mysteries of Shanghai." We left leaflets in the American shops, at the clubs, along the walls near the American Consulate. In between, I went to art galleries, looking for paintings of dark rain clouds, a long green valley, and mountains. Every day we walked through the streets of the International Settlement to look for places where we might promote our services and vowed not to give up, despite the ever-growing number of people crowding Shanghai—a million, Danner had told me, double what it had been not that long ago. Many of the men around the Bund, along Nanking Road, and other parts of the International Settlement were rich Chinese men dressed in tailored suits and wearing Homberg hats like Lu Shing's, and I would hurry to catch sight of their faces. I always returned home exhausted but never defeated.

After all that effort I had discovered one thing: No foreigners were interested in learning Chinese—all except the missionaries, and they had their own Chinese teachers. I found a few American men who were eager for a tour of Shanghai, but they also believed we were prostitutes who would provide a tour within the mysteries of female genitalia.

One warm day a man who watched me posting a notice of our sightseeing services asked if I knew where he could find a pub. I suggested the American Club. Too stuffy, he answered. I mentioned the bars along the Bund. Too boisterous and full of drunk sailors. He wanted a small-town pub that reminded him of the one back home. "Everyone claims Shanghai has everything," he said, "but I have yet to find a pub where a fellow can share a pint with friends, smoke a cigar, and sing old tunes around the piano."

"If it's homey you want, I know just the place. It will open its doors next week." I wrote down the name and address: "Danner's Pub. 18 East Floral Alley." When I returned home and told Golden

Dove the exciting news, she was elated. "At last!" she cried. Then she said: "What is a pub?"

"Whatever it is," I said, "we can do it."

Danner's Pub took shape over the next few months through the suggestions and dissatisfactions of our early customers. We started our first week with a pitiful stock: beer, cheap cigars, and gut-smoldering whiskey. Our greatest asset turned out to be sentimental songs. I thanked Mr. Maubert for having my extra pinkies chopped off, thereby enabling me to take piano lessons. In the piano bench, I found piles of sheet music—sweet ballads for the most part. I wrote down requests the customers gave for favorite tunes. I told them to return the following night with a promise they would be able to sing it. The next morning Golden Dove and I would scour the secondhand shops for music. Sometimes we were successful. Our customers also named their preferences for whiskey, beer, and cigars. Each day we took the profits from the night before and bought the better liquors and cigars, which we sold at ever-higher prices. I used my mother's technique of remembering the customers' names, so I could person-ally welcome them each night. I chatted with them briefly, enough to be able to ask them the kinds of questions that made them feel at home: "Have you received another letter from your sweetheart?" "Has your mother recovered from her illness?" I offered sympathy, congratulations, and wishes for good luck. Those small gestures, I found, brought our customers back again the next day, and the day after that. Within six months, business overflowed. We found a house in another alley with rooms to rent on the lower floor. Abandoned pianos were plentiful and so were out-of-work musicians. We called our second pub "Lulu's."

Golden Dove, I discovered, was insatiable for success. She sold increasingly better brandy, port, and special liquors, charging ever-higher prices. The pubs made plenty of money, but Golden Dove never felt it was enough. There were other opportunities, she said. Those who jumped quickly made fortunes. She knew this, because in the pubs, she often overheard Western men talking about new businesses. She had a talent for eavesdropping. Our customers did not suspect that a Chinese woman spoke English well enough to understand their plots. She had mastered the ever-smiling face of a woman who understood nothing and thus was invisible among them.

Through overhearing their conversations, she came up with the idea to start a small social club where businessmen could meet in an atmosphere that was fancier and quieter than a pub. It would also be more discreet than the American Club, and other places where your business was everyone's. We rented rooms in a statelier house—and there were many, made vacant by businessmen who came with schemes and had gone bust. We furnished the rooms with settees, small round tables with tablecloths, palm trees, gleaming brass, and marble floors. The best of Danner's paintings decorated the walls. The others were being sold by a dealer, a former friend of Danner's, an honest man who helped us sell them one at a time and at a fair price. We named our club The Golden Dove. In addition to fine liquor, we provided a tea service. Instead of favorite sing-along tunes on the piano, we hired a violinist and cellist who played Debussy. We offered small private rooms, where men could conduct business and make deals. As the hostess of a sophisticated club, I wore simple fashionable clothes. As I had done in the pubs, I greeted our "guests"—as we called them—by name. Golden Dove hired the waiters and trained them well. She monitored how much liquor was poured in a glass, one ounce and a splash more. And she watched and noted what each man's preferences were and what he had ordered, so that I could offer the returning guest the same table and ask if he would like what he had ordered the last time.

Golden Dove took her station standing at the ready in the private rooms. She whisked away empty cups and returned with clean ones that were filled. Among these well-to-do customers, the secrets were more lucrative. We heard which new businesses had immediately leapt onto waves of success, and which had quickly sunk, and we knew the reason why. We learned that certain banks had information ahead of time how to control the lion's share of the profits. We knew how they did it. We also gained knowledge of illegal plots, one involving men from four different companies who had inflated sales figures to a gullible investor. We knew how to recognize crooked deals.

"We know more about making money than most," Golden Dove said. "We just need to decide which business to start, so we can use it." It did not take long to find it.

In Shanghai, the same goods might be bought by both Chinese and Westerners, but not in the same shops. A well-known barbershop for Westerners soon had a counterpart for well-to-do Chinese men. A salon de coiffure for Western women was matched by a salon de coiffure for well-to-do Chinese women. In other words, whatever was popular and fashionable with Westerners could find a ready clientele among the wealthy Chinese. When we opened The Gold Club for Chinese clientele, we discovered that Golden Dove no longer held the same secret advantage: The Chinese guests knew she spoke Chinese and avoided talking about their secrets in front of her. And I did not know enough Chinese to gather the secrets—until I learned the art of *momo*—to be silent and write from memory. Golden Dove would greet the guests and I had to listen and later recite to her what I could recall. The first day I repeated the oft-used phrases: "When did you get back?" "When do you leave?" "That's bullshit." Within the year, I could understand the entirety of almost any conversation that concerned business, and I had a special vocabulary for animals, flowers, and toys, gleaned from Violet, who at age four spoke English and the Chinese learned from her amah, as if they were one language.

If a guest sought a foreign trade alliance with an American company, Golden Dove would mention to our Chinese clients a possible "new friend relationship." I would do the same for our Western clients. The twin clubs became purveyors of the jigsaw puzzle pieces needed in foreign trade. With small successes, we received a small gift. With larger ones, we drew handsome rewards. Eventually we charged fees and took a percentage of the profits. Golden Dove continued to be restless, and she passed her restlessness on to me. The richer the client, the more exciting the business, the more money we would make. "If we want to attract richer men," she said, "we should open a first-class courtesan house. And I know one with a very good reputation and whose madam is willing to sell."

Two years later, we opened a place that combined the two sides of our business: a social club for Westerners, a courtesan house for men. We named it The House of Lulu Mimi in Chinese and Hidden Jade Path in English. The path was where both sides met in the middle.

"In ten more years," I teased Golden Dove, "you will have bought ten countries, and in twenty years, it will be forty. You are insatiable. It's the sickness of success." She was pleased to hear it. "I have enough now," she said. "I needed to go back to my past and change it. Ten years ago, I had to leave a courtesan house with a smashed-up face. Now I own one of the finest in Shanghai, and to be truly successful, I must become a lady of leisure, never in a hurry, always calm, maybe even a little lazy."

I was neither calm nor leisurely. I had to take over her share of the work. After a week, when she saw my eyes were sunken hollows from lack of sleep, she said she would be a little less lazy. I think she wanted me to appreciate how hard she had been working, and I remarked on this often from then on.

Between the afternoons and parties at night, I played games with Violet, read stories, bathed her while singing songs in English and Chinese, and told her how much I loved her as I tucked her into bed and waited for her to fall asleep. Those were our habits of love. She could depend on me. Her amah took care of her in the morning while I was still sleeping. On occasion, I took a lover, and I was careful to choose one who was my inferior in money, or power, or intellect. I auditioned them, as I had my young men when I was sixteen, keeping those who were experienced, discarding those without wit. I used those men selfishly, greedily, without regard to their feelings. I allowed myself the exciting preambles of lust, the satisfaction of urges, but not the heady infatuation, nor any prelude that could be mistaken for love. My love belonged to Violet. By the time she was four, she had become a willful child. I was glad. She would not be confined in her thoughts.

Around this time, I discovered that the heart can also be like a willful child. It does behave according to expectation. If my heart quickened, I knew it was time to take out the hated paintings Lu Shing had left me. I would stare at the portrait he painted of me when I had already felt uncertainty but had still hung on to trust. Or had that merely been foolish hope? I would look closely and enter those large dark pupils, the portal to a mindless girl who loved the painter. Within those shiny black pupils, he had seen a mirror of his desires, my willingness to satisfy them, to be whoever he believed I was. I would then study the second painting, *The Valley of Amazement*, always with a sick feeling that I had once believed in the illusion of a Pure Self-Being, which required me to preserve my original qualities. I had not known what they were, but I had been determined that they not be altered or influenced. I let Lu Shing alter them. How easily I had discarded myself. I had let infatuation guide me and choose my direction in life—toward a golden vale that did not exist, toward a city at the other end of the sea. I went to that imaginary place and suffered the near demise of my mind, heart, and soul. I returned with the knowledge that I would be smarter than love. I was still determined to find Teddy. He was rightfully mine, but whenever I thought of him, I felt murderous rage, and not the heartache of having once cradled a baby who had recognized me and smiled. I tried to recall what he looked like. Instead I saw Lu Shing's face as he stared at his son, and I pushed his memory out of my mind.

The only being I would give myself freely to was Violet. I was her constant, the one who set the hours of dawn and dusk, who made the clouds by pointing to the sky, who warmed the day by removing her sweater, who turned it cold by donning her coat, who thawed her chilled fingers with the magic of my breath, who made violets sweet by twirling them under her nose, who clapped her hands as I declared her loved, at every hour, in every place, so that she would feel as I did: She was the reason I lived.

ONE OF OUR earliest guests at Hidden Jade Path was a charmer named Fairweather, a name, I told him, that was fair warning that I should avoid him. It was an affectionate nickname given to him by his many friends, he said. They invited him to dinners and parties and knew that had it not been for his finances he would have reciprocated their generosity and would yet one day do so twofold when his Shanghai ship came in. He confessed early on to me that he had been a brash young man who was disinherited from his wealthy family. He hoped to either make a fortune or win back the good graces of his father. Both would be ideal.

At first, I saw Fairweather as reminiscent of my first young man—the blue-eyed, dark-haired Greek god. But he was clearly more charming than men in my recent past. For one thing, he admitted from the start that he wanted to make me moan in the dark of night and laugh during the light of day. And from the start I did laugh—at his braggadocio.

"You avoid me, Miss Minturn," he said in a humorous fawning tone, "but I shall wait as Rousseau did for Madame Dupin." He often tossed off stuffy historical references like that, as well as obscure allusions and lengthy quotes to advertise that his background was refined. I devoured his wit as my opium. Within a week after meeting him, I let him into my bed, and unlucky for me, he proved to be a lover whose knowledge of a woman excelled the rest. It was his never-ceasing willingness to listen to a woman's complaints and the woes of her lonely heart, which he then followed by unlimited sympathy and consolation beneath the quilt.

And thus he listened to all my unexpected losses, the betrayals that killed my spirit, my guilt over damage done to others, those moments of self-imposed loneliness. He heard my weakness for intimacy, for the emperor of a fairy tale. He consoled me over the loss of Danner and Teddy and the death of my trust in all people. I told him more and more, because in trade, he gave me the words I needed to hear: *You have been wronged. You deserve to be loved.* For those counterfeit words, I was a spendthrift with my secrets, and he later stole all that was most precious to me.

San Francisco
March 1912
Lulu Minturn

Before Shanghai receded from view, I had already searched the boat from stern to bow, port to starboard. I burst through the door to our cabin ten times, expecting Violet to manifest like a magician's trick. I called her name wherever I went, and my voice cracked in the wind, and I was sick with the possibility that she was still in Shanghai. I had promised I would not leave without her. I could still see her face, her worried expression as I rushed about, packing the trunks, thinking about the needs for our new home. I had acted lighthearted, in part to allay her fear and doubt. But she could not be soothed—she was not as Fairweather led her away.

And now I tried to believe she and Fairweather had simply missed the boat. They did not get the required birth certificate and visa. Or they had not made it to the dock in time. But then I recalled the coolie who had come with a note from Fairweather saying they were already on board and that I should meet them at the back of the boat. He sent that note, I now realized, to make sure that I left. What could that possibly mean? I went over the details of his trickery. He told us we needed Violet's birth certificate with her. And it was not in my drawer. He might have stolen it the last time he was in my bed. There had been plenty of opportunities to watch me opening that drawer. Once I was gone, he must have taken Violet back to Hidden Jade Path. What else would he have done with her otherwise? Damn that bastard. I imagined Violet's angry face and Golden Dove calming her down. Golden Dove would explain how I had been tricked. She would let her know it would take a month to reach San Francisco and a month to return. And when I returned, I knew she would still be furious, because I had ignored her fears and put her in the hands of a man she had always disliked—despised. It would not matter to her whether I had left her by trickery or insanity. I had abandoned her.

The more I pictured her face, the more my fear grew. Something was terribly wrong. He must not have returned Violet to Hidden Jade Path. He would not have wanted Golden Dove to know what he had done. She would have contacted the authorities and had him jailed. Instead, Golden Dove would have believed Violet was on the ship with me. But why would he keep her? He thought she was a brat. And then it came to me: He might have sold her. How much would a pretty fourteen-year-old fetch in a courtesan house? Once this possibility entered my mind, I could not remove the terror that it might be true. I went up to a man in a white uniform. "I need to speak to the ship's captain immediately," I said. He told me he was a waiter. I ran into the dining room and asked the maître d' to tell me how to reach the captain. "I need to send an urgent message. My daughter is not on the boat."

By the minute, panic rose and I made demands of everyone I saw wearing a white jacket. The purser arrived. "This situation unfortunately is not uncommon. One person is on board, the other does not arrive in time. But eventually everything is sorted out."

"You don't understand," I said, "she is only a child and in the hands of a crook. I promised to wait. She trusted me. Please I need to send a message." He told me that messages were sent out only for purposes of navigation and emergencies.

"Damn your navigation! This is an emergency. How can you be so stupid? If I can't send a message, turn the boat around!" The ship's doctor was now by my side. He told me that as soon as we arrived in San Francisco, I would be able to return to Shanghai.

"Do you think my brain is porridge? It takes a month to get to San Francisco and a month to return to Shanghai. Where will she be in two months? I have to return now. Is there a lifeboat? Tell me now. Where are the life preservers? I'll swim back, if I have to." The ship's doctor said they would make arrangements for a lifeboat and a sailor to help me paddle. In the meantime, he said, I should calm down and have some tea and nourishment before the arduous journey back. "Drink," he said, "it will settle your nerves." And it did, because I did not awake for two days.

I AWOKE WITH violent seasickness and the realization that I had not dreamed this nightmare. For the rest of the month, I went over the details of what had happened, as if I were purling yarn, knitting it tightly, then ripping it apart to start purling again. I saw her in Hidden Jade Path, in my office, crying to Golden Dove, cursing me. I saw her in a courtesan house, in terror, about to be defiled. I saw her face as Fairweather led her away, full of fear and doubt. What had I done to her? What harm?

When we arrived in San Francisco, a man was waiting for me at the dock. He handed me a letter and left. I opened it and felt my legs grow empty and sank to the ground. The letter was from the American Consulate giving me the sad news that Violet Minturn Danner had been killed running across Nanking Road. Witnesses said she had pulled away from two men and shouted that she was being kidnapped. Unfortunately, the men ran off before they could be apprehended.

It was not true. It was another trick. Where was the messenger who handed me the note? I choked out a plea to everyone nearby to take me to the police station. Twenty minutes went by before I found a free carriage to take me. Once I was there, it took another thirty minutes before someone would speak to me. They spent another hour trying to quiet me. A woman finally directed me to a post office where I could have a telegram sent to Golden Dove. Because it was the middle of the night in Shanghai, I had to wait for her answer, and so I sat outside the post office until the telegram finally arrived.

> *My dearest Lulu,*
> *Deepest sorrow to tell you it is true. Violet died in an accident.*
> *Fairweather disappeared. Burial three weeks ago. Letter to follow.*
> *Yours,*
> *Golden Dove*

If I had lost only Violet, I would have grieved a lifetime. But I knew also that before she died I had shattered her belief that she had ever been loved by me. I knew those terrible truths because I had felt the same when love abandoned me. Those should not have been the wounds she bore as she left this life. I felt skinned raw as I imagined her suffering in her last hours. It did not matter how it happened—by accident or carelessness or deceit—she would have believed I had abandoned her. I could not stop seeing the fear in her eyes. It had grown to terror in my mind and the horror that I had traded her for a flimsy piece of paper—a false birth certificate that would have let me reach a baby I had held in my arms for less than two days.

She had always been such an observant girl, too much so, as I once had been. She knew what was false and what was evident. She could see with a clairvoyant's eye what selfishness could destroy. She saw that in me: selfish pride, selfish love, selfish grief. I had the strength to get whatever I wanted. I had ceased to see that she had been right in front of me.

She believed I loved a son more than I did her, so much that I would have traded her away. He was the baby I held briefly. She was the daughter who had tugged my skirts for fourteen years. I had wrongly believed she would always be there and that I could give her all that she needed the next day or the day after that. I knew her so well, loved her so dearly, and had shown her so little as she had grown older, and more independent, I thought, just as I was at her age. That was how I had justified devoting my time to my business. I had forgotten that at her age, I was not independent. I was lonely and I hurt every day thinking I was not as important as a dead bug or a pair of Manchu shoes from a burnt palace.

If she were here before me, I would tell her that I did not love that baby more. I was obsessed with a delusion that began when I was sixteen, which I could not let go. I was driven by anger to claim the life of all my foolish dreams. The baby was part of the delusion. And now, finally, I could also let him go.

I WENT HOME. The house had not been sold and occupied by strangers, as I thought it might be. It had survived the earthquake, just as Miss Huffard had said in one of her letters. My mother and father still lived there, and they were not shattered, as I believed they would be. Mother took my hand gently and wept. Father went to me and kissed my cheek. Mr. and Mrs. Minturn had died, Mother said, and in a tone of respect, I thought. We said nothing about what had happened.

For months, we lived a routine life, eating meals together but living apart. We were not falsely cheerful. We were polite and considerate, and in those little gestures, we acknowledged the damage we had done to each other. I saw Mother glance at me on occasion with tragic eyes. She still gardened, but I did not see her retreat to her study to look at her insects. The amber had been put away. My father's office had been swept clean of his collections. I locked away memories of Hidden Jade Path. Its importance to me was as meaningful as a pile of sand.

Our nights were quiet. There were no parties, where father presided. Mr. Maubert still came to dinner three times a week. His back was bent and he was shorter than I was. I played the piano for him and he said he was the happiest he had been in many years. How little he required.

Six months after I returned, I said to my mother and father: "I was married to a kind man named Danner and I had a daughter, and I lost them both." As I cried, they came to me and put their arms around me in a circle, and they cried, and we knew we were crying for all the sorrow we had caused and would always suffer.

March 1914

For two years Lu Shing sent letters postmarked from both San Francisco and Shanghai. In all his letters, he told me that he had waited for me at the hotel where we had agreed to meet. He repeated each time that he had been ready to take me to see my son. He added that his wife had agreed to my seeing him, and he would still take me, while adding that his son was emotionally tied to the Lu family. His son was the heir and he did not know that he was half-white. "We should spare him the shock," Lu Shing said, "of his complicated parentage." I went into a rage whenever I read that part of his letters. Did he believe I would deliberately hurt any child of mine?

His twentieth letter, which came two weeks ago, repeated much of what he had told me in Shanghai. But this time, he confessed something else:

I once said that our names were connected by fate: Lucia, Lu Shing. Our names were the sign we would recognize each other and a painting made us feel we belonged together. I still believe you are part of me. But, by the many ways I failed you, you showed me who I truly am. You did not remove my doubts. You forced me to see how I waver. You wanted a profundity of spirit; you did not realize there was nothing more of me to give. You live in deep ponds. I float in the shallows. I fear that this will always be as true of my art as it is of my character. Finally, at this point in my life, I can be rid of doubts by accepting that I am less than what I had hoped to be, far less than who you believed I was. I am mediocre, Lucia. I was not stinting with you. I was born with an impoverished heart. I regret that you were so wounded by my shortfalls.

I wrote back:

The baby I lost was two days old and his name was Teddy. I did not know him beyond those hours that I held him. After so many fruitless years searching for him, I finally recognize that the baby I was desperate to find does not exist. Lu Shen is not that baby. He is your son, completely yours, just as Violet is mine, completely mine. She is the only child I lost. She is the only one I grieve and will spend fruitless years searching for, even though she is dead.

CHAPTER 15

THE CITY AT THE END OF THE SEA

Between Buddha's Hand and Shanghai
June 1926
Violet

Charm had said that when we reached the top of Buddha's Hand, we would see the town below. We did not. I looked at Magic Gourd and Pomelo. They were biting their lips. We wound our way down, and continued along the small valley, and held tight on to stubborn hope, and saw nothing until we were at the very end of the green grass and stood on the ridge. Above, I saw through my tears the stars, ten thousand sparkles against black sky, and then I looked down and saw through those same tears ten thousand more sparkles. I pushed past doubt and told myself that it was not a bowl of stars in a pond, nor a cloud of fireflies, nor leaves flashing in silvery moonlight. I wiped away the tears and I saw what I wanted to believe. A town, and ten thousand lights glowing through windows.

We shouted to each other: "I knew it would be there!" "I could feel it!" "I saw it in my mind's eye and made it true."

The stars and moon lit our way along the winding path. In our excitement, Magic Gourd and I were at first unaware that Pomelo was stumbling behind on her swollen feet. We went back and each of us put an arm over our shoulders and joy so lifted our spirits we floated down, all weight removed.

As we drew closer to the town, I breathed deeply and filled my lungs with the fresh air, confident that whatever we found would be everything we did not have the day before. I once expected the worst and now I expected the best: a clean place to stay, a warm bath, hot tea, and a sweet pear. I pictured a river, the way back to Shanghai. None of those expectations was too much to wish for.

Pomelo insisted we find her friend Charm, who had escaped the year before. We wanted her to see she had saved us.

We summoned two rickshaws to take us to the House of Charm. Magic Gourd and I sat in one, and Pomelo had the second one to herself. She groaned and put her feet up, then sighed deeply. Within ten minutes, we reached the House of Charm, and saw that it was not extravagant, but it had a classic elegance, well suited to a modest town. When the manservant announced us, Charm must have jumped out of bed in two seconds. She rushed toward us in her nightgown, grabbed Pomelo, stared at her face, and shook her.

"You are not a ghost," she cried. "Wasn't I right? That bastard lied to us. There was a path."

"Perpetual is dead," Pomelo said simply.

Charm stepped back. "*Wah?* Are you sure?"

"As certain as can be. We saw his body and face. But now my feet hurt too much to tell you more."

Charm told the maid to take Pomelo to her own room and unwrap her bindings. She ordered warm water and herbs to clean her feet and draw out the swelling. We were shown to our rooms, beautiful boudoirs. A maid filled the bathtub with water hot enough to peel off rough layers of skin and make me soft again. As soon as I arose from my bath, another maid wrapped me in towels. I slipped into a loose jacket and trousers. Yet another maid set tea and snacks on a table. I ate greedily like the poor peasant I had become. And as soon as I drained the teacup, I lay down and did not wake up until late morning.

We sat around the breakfast table and Pomelo said we were so carefree she hardly recognized us. But whenever I cursed Perpetual, I flinched, expecting to be slapped or knocked to the ground. Fear had become a habit, and I knew it would take a while longer to be rid of it.

We spent much of the day resting our aching muscles. As two maids on each side of us massaged our legs, we took turns recounting once again all the ways we had helped each other. We had shared fear, and all three of us had lived to recall it. That was enough to make us sisters the rest of our lives. We let Pomelo reveal in her own way how Perpetual had died. In the telling, she must have seen it vividly in her mind. Her face became tight as she described climbing over rocks with feet that felt as if she were walking over coals. It nearly blinded her with agony. The sun would not stop pouring out oven-hot heat. The tigers had lain in wait in the dark forest, and she had jumped at every sound.

She now reached toward us and squeezed our arms. "They showed kindness more than a sister would have given. They could have chosen to save themselves instead of risking their lives to help me." We were humble and told her we were bored hearing about ourselves. Finally, she reached the moment when Perpetual was on the path just below her. She trembled and grabbed onto me, and looked down at the floor. We could see she was there again, on the rocky path. Her eyes bulged, her face contorted, and she gasped and huffed, unable to speak for a while. She pushed both hands out suddenly and set those imaginary rocks bouncing and flying, a dozen, she said, but only one was needed.

"I often wished he would die," she moaned. "I thought of killing him. But if I had known . . . what I would see, his eyes, his knowledge of what was coming, horror too great to imagine until I saw him lying twisted like tree roots, his face a red stump . . . asking myself: Did I do that? How could I have done that? Now I will forever see him without his face. Damn him." She angrily wiped away a tear. "I hate him for making me kill him. He made me inhuman."

Later in the day we spoke of those times when Perpetual tricked us. We all denied that we had loved him. We had been deluded into thinking so. We compared the poems, the promises, the gifts, and the stories of his family. *Wah!* He said that to you as well? We sifted through his fakery to find those pieces that might have been true. Had there been anything good?

"The bad poems were his," Magic Gourd said. "Why would he have stolen ones that were that awful?"

Charm spoke up: "Something was wrong with his mind, and it must have started when his father was disgraced."

"I refuse to feel sorry for him," Magic Gourd said. "His past does not excuse him. It is simply his past."

I did not forgive Perpetual. But I knew that feeling of being betrayed by lies you had believed in. It was like a crack in the wall behind you that widened without your knowing it until the entire house collapsed on top of you.

AT FIRST GLANCE, you might think the town of Mountain View was no prettier than Moon Pond in its setting by a mountain. But once you walked into town you saw lively people, clear water, and clean roads. Moon Pond had been a trick of the eye, beautiful from a distance, but once you were trapped inside, you discovered the pond was a swamp, the houses were crumbling, and the people were beaten down and had become suspicious and mean.

Pomelo decided to stay in Mountain View. With her share of the money, she would buy into Charm's business. The town was growing, and so was competition among the courtesan houses.

"Come visit," Pomelo said. And Magic Gourd said, "You come visit us in Shanghai when you are hungry for fresh fish from the sea."

Magic Gourd and I were given clean simple dresses, and Charm explained: "These are so that people in Shanghai won't think you came from where you just came from." We took a carriage to the next town ten miles away. It was called Eight Bridges, named for the number of bridges that crossed the river, which was wide and deep enough for passenger boats. On this side of Heaven Mountain, Charm said, there were roadways, riverways, and trains when you drew closer to Shanghai. On Moon Pond's side of Heaven Mountain, you were stuck in the worst parts of the past.

"To reach so much misery in Moon Pond," Magic Gourd said, "we had to suffer to get there as well." We reached another port, ate the local dishes of hot peppers and river fish, and stayed the night. We hired a car and drove to another river town and took another boat. The closer we drew to Shanghai, the larger the boats, the better the inns and food. No more mule carts, mud, and foul-mouthed carters. Two weeks from when we left Charm and Pomelo in Mountain View, we reached the train station in Hangzhou. We changed into our clean clothes, examined each other's faces, and groaned that there was no hiding the fact that one year had turned our skin ten years older.

On the way into Shanghai, Magic Gourd said we should open our own house. She gabbed about the style of furnishings and the distinguishing characteristics, which would quickly build the reputation of the House of Magic Gourd.

I had my own plans, and it would begin with a visit to Loyalty Fang—this time to ask, not for a favor, but for a job.

October 1926

I did not go to his home. I walked into his office at the company building. He was seated at his desk and was stunned. "Are you a ghost?" We had not seen each other in a year and I viewed him through different eyes. He was now in his middle years, still handsome, and, in fact, more attractive because his face had the lines of maturity and character. Or so I thought.

He grinned. "I've missed you." He stood and was about to come around his desk to greet me in the usual way—a kiss, a pat on the rump, and a deep inhalation of my scent, as if he and I were dogs.

"Don't be polite," I said, and sat down. "We're old friends."

He nodded. "I forgot. You're married. So how is marriage to that yokel from the countryside. Have you tired yet of mountain clouds and waterfalls?"

"Perpetual is dead."

His smirk vanished. "I apologize."

I would not show Loyalty my true emotions. "The marriage was over before he died. And now I'm back, starting over."

He called for tea. It was served in the porcelain teacups and saucers his company made. "You look fetching. The countryside and fresh air agreed with you, I see."

"Liar. I aged ten years in that miserable place." We had often bantered with each other. But his teasing was more wounding than humorous. I knew I was not attractive in the way he was accustomed to seeing me—certainly not stylish—and intentionally so. I had chosen a dull blue Chinese dress and a gray sweater. My hair was pulled into a plain bun. I wanted no misunderstanding over what I was asking. I was not dressed for seduction.

"I need a job," I said.

"Of course I'll help. This evening, I'll make a list of the houses that are doing well, and tell you more about each one. Then you can choose which ones might suit you, and I'll put in a good word for you."

"At the House of Aged Courtesans? I'm twenty-eight, not some naive child with future heartbreak ahead of me. I'm not seeking to go back to an unprofitable life. I want a job here, with your company."

His eyebrows rose. "What's this?" He laughed slightly.

I remained calm. "You know I have valuable skills other than my talent for wheedling gifts from your pocket. I understand the world of business. I grew up in it. I listened to businessmen having dinner together at the courtesan house. In fact, I gave my opinions at a dinner party you hosted, when we first met. And, as you know, I speak English, Shanghainese, and Mandarin, one as well as the other."

Loyalty looked as if he was amused. "What do you propose? Do you want to become vice president?"

"I want a position in the company as a translator with your foreign trade business. I don't merely translate words, unlike those translators who went to English language school. I've heard my share of them at Hidden Jade Path. They make mistakes so often you could find yourself buying a donkey instead of a company. I do not translate like a bad dictionary. I can express subtlety in negotiations. That's one thing I learned from my mother. If I do well and am qualified for other jobs, you can promote me. If I do not meet those expectations, you can demote me to some dull position. Or you can fire me. Or I can quit."

He grew serious. "Years ago, I said you were surprising, and this was what fascinated me about you. Now you are even more surprising. I am indeed intrigued with the possibility of your working for my company. However, I can't give you a job simply because I know you from quite a different business. You're a woman, and none of my customers would trust what you are translating."

"Put me in a room without windows and have me translate letters and documents, your advertisements and signs, which, by the way, are full of mistakes that you would find embarrassing if you knew what they were. If you had been a better pupil of English, you would know how qualified I am."

"You're asking me to be your boss—and you're already nagging me before you even get the job? All right, but you'll have to prove yourself. You can't rely on my fondness for you."

"When have I ever relied on that? I'll prove on my own that I'm more than worthy of the job and I'm counting on proving this in an office, seated on chairs, and not in your bed. I have put that part of my life away forever."

TWO WEEKS LATER, Loyalty pronounced me accurate and indispensable. Besides my work with his correspondence and documents, I had suggested he give his company an English name and not just one written in Chinese and rendered into Western script as Jing Huang Mao. "No American can pronounce that, so how could they remember it?" I suggested its English translation: Golden Phoenix Trading. I had a sign and business cards made. He gave me a full-time position.

Now that I was sure of having a job, it was time to fulfill the promise I had made to myself, my reason to live, which had enabled me to endure being trapped in Moon Pond. I wanted to find Flora and to know that she was well. And I also needed to reach my mother. After Flora had been taken, I finally read the letter Lu Shing had written me about her—about her grief that she had been tricked and that I had died as a result. He promised that he would not tell my mother that I was alive, nothing about me, unless I gave him permission to do so. If he had kept his word, then she would still believe I was dead. I had always viewed her leaving me from only the perspective of an aggrieved child. She never should have left. She never should have believed I was dead. But my grief over losing Flora had gradually changed me. I saw Flora through a mother's eyes. I now saw my mother with the same. We feared that our daughters would believe they were unloved and deliberately abandoned. Flora might not remember anything about me, except that I had let go of her arms. I wanted Flora to know and feel that she had always been loved. I was ready to tell my mother that I knew she had loved me. I did not hate her as I had before.

Yet I could not forgive her for what had happened. She had been tricked, yes, but it started with her desires. I bore the consequences, and it was not just suffering of the heart. What was forgiveness anyway? Cleansing her of guilt? Giving myself the reward of heaven? What godlike power would enable me to gladly make her whole, while knowing I would never be? I wished I could forgive her and release the pain in me. But part of my heart was missing—where forgiveness and trust had once been. It was empty and there was nothing left to give.

"I want your help in reaching Lu Shing," I told Loyalty. "He'll know the address of both the Ivory family in New York and the address of my mother in San Francisco."

"I can probably get the address from the Ivory Shipping Company," Loyalty said.

"I don't want to raise suspicions. They would tell the Ivorys you went seeking their address, and they would send their spies to learn why. In any case, I want Lu Shing to understand Flora's importance to me. He is her grandfather. He has to take responsibility. Once you have the Ivory family address, we will send them a letter from you, which I will write, of course. This letter will explain you were a good friend of Edward's from the days when you did business with the Ivory Shipping Company. We'll say that you spent much time together during his first year in Shanghai—that was before he knew me. We'll tell them you have something that belonged to Edward, which you had borrowed—some cuff links, which I will buy. You will then say you kept them when you heard that he had died and, at the time, you did not know who you could return them to. That will make them think you did not know me. It wasn't until recently that you heard he had a child living in New York, and so you want to send Edward's daughter the cuff links to cherish as a keepsake. The package will arrive before Christmas, and it will include a gift from you—a charm bracelet perhaps—a Christmas gift from Uncle Loyalty. Yes, you'll be an uncle! You'll say you're following the Chinese custom of being an uncle to any child of good friends. A family like the Ivorys would show good manners and have Flora write you a thank-you letter. And then, every year, Uncle Loyalty has an excuse to send her a Christmas card and a little gift. When Flora sends you those thank-you notes, I will have this little part of her as my own keepsake."

"This is a very good plan," he said. "I like being an uncle. I know why you want to reach your daughter, but why also your mother? You once told me you hated her."

"I once hated you."

"You did?" He looked wounded.

"Only a little, for a short time—until you got rid of that little tart, the virgin courtesan who tried to give me trouble later. My feelings toward my mother, however, have been more difficult. I'm finally ready to tell her I'm alive." I did not turn away soon enough to keep him from seeing my tears.

He came to me and put his arms around me. "I will find a way," he said.

LOYALTY CONTACTED HIS friends who might have known Lu Shing. One of them heard he was in San Francisco and asked a friend there to find him. "All Chinese people in San Francisco know each other," he told Loyalty. We sent his friend my letter, so that he could pass it along until it reached Lu Shing. Within a month, we had a letter from Lu Shing.

"My Dear Violet," it began.

> *I am grateful you have written. I know it was not easy to do so. The addresses for your mother and the Ivory family are on a separate sheet of paper at the back of this letter.*
>
> *I think of you often. You may find that hard to believe, but it is true. Since I did not receive your reply to my last letter, I honored your request to say nothing to your mother. In any case, I have*

*not seen her since our meeting in Shanghai in 1912. She did not
contact me. After numerous efforts to reach her, I finally received
a letter from her in 1914. She told me she no longer wanted to see
me—nor her son. As I told you in my last letter, she grieves for you
constantly. She lives with her mother and father in the house where
she grew up. Since she refuses to see me, I cannot tell you more
than that.*

   If I can assist in anything else, please let me know.
   As always,
   Lu Shing

I had already composed my letter to my mother weeks ago,
changing parts of it many times. When I received the address from
Lu Shing, I read my letter to her again, and with a pounding heart,
I sent it:

Dear Mother,

   *I know you must be shocked to learn I am alive. Fourteen years
have passed and many of them were difficult ones for me. I will not
go into the details in this letter. I would not know how to relate all
that has happened. Suffice it to say, I am well.*

   *I received a letter from Lu Shing, in which he informed me you
had not known that the news of my death was false. He said you
had blamed yourself and had never stopped grieving. When he told
me that, I was not able to write to you and I made him promise to
say nothing. I still had a child's heart and I refused any explanation
as to why you had left Shanghai at all. I believed I would never let
go of my hate.*

   *But now I have the heart of a mother. I lost my child when
she was three and a half years old. Her father died during the
pandemic and his family took her from me by force in 1922. I
have grieved for a living daughter for nearly four years. I have
had no word about her since and have grown increasingly*

*desperate for her to know I did not let her go willingly. I am
haunted that she might believe that I did not love her. I fear she
will become like me: a girl who felt betrayed by love, who later
refused love, and could not recognize it or trust it. She must know
I have loved her continuously since she was born, and more dearly
than anyone. She is now seven. I would like your help in finding
her. I need to know she is happy.*

*I once believed with a child's heart that you left me deliberately.
I hated you. I know you were tormented that I might believe that.
I feel the same torment, deeply and constantly. While I cannot
forgive you completely, I don't wish for you to be tormented any
longer.*

Your daughter,

Violet

Mother's return letter was hastily written and covered with
splotches, which I guessed were tears.

My dearest Violet,

*I had to reread the first line of your letter a dozen times to make
sure it was true. And then I was lifted from the hell of my own heart
in knowing you were alive. I sank into another when I realized you
believed what I had feared—that I had not loved you enough to save
you. There are no excuses for a mother's failure and I will bear a
black mark on my soul forever.*

*Would it ease your heart even a little to know I nearly went
mad on the ship when I suspected what had happened—that I
ordered the captain to turn the ship around, that I was sedated
so that I would not try to swim back? When I received the letter
from the consulate, and then another from Golden Dove, both
confirming that you had died, I imagined your last thoughts—
that I had not loved you as much as I did a phantom baby. For
fourteen years, I woke up every day seeing your frightened face*

looking at me as I was promising I would not leave without you.
I have gone over every false step I took that led to your demise. I
have condemned myself for weaknesses. And it all returns to seeing
your frightened face looking at me.

I can never earn your forgiveness. But I take it as an enormous
kindness that you have written to me. And I am grateful that you
have asked me to help you find your daughter and with shared
understanding of a mother's loss of a child. I undertake this
mission, not as penance, but with the fullness of love.

I want to say so much to you, my dearest Violet, and yet, I
know I should not let my own emotions spill over more than they
already have. So I will simply say for now that I hope you'll one
day believe, without doubt, that there has been no one in my heart
more precious than you.

   Mother

Mother and I began a tentative relationship through an exchange of letters. She understood so well my need to reach Flora—my young and helpless child, who was more gullible, more easily contaminated by the thoughts and feelings of others. And Mother was right to hope I would be comforted to know she had suffered losing me, although her description of my fright and wavering trust brought back my own sharp wounds.

In her next letter, she pulled out the strength of optimism she applied to build Hidden Jade Path. "Nothing is impossible," she wrote. "We simply have to have persistence and ingenuity. I will deliver her back to you." I was grateful and more hopeful than ever by her determination. With anyone else, I would have thought that what she said were empty words. I knew that Mother would never give up. She would do what no one would have thought of to do.

The letters went back and forth more quickly. I gave her accounts of Flora, and then Edward, information that was factual at first, and eventually included the emotions around the facts. She in turn told me about a memorial she had made in her garden, where violets ran wild. She had already removed the tombstone and put a birdbath in its place. She wrote at length about a man named Danner—not Tanner, as I had mistakenly heard the name when I was a child. He had given me my legitimacy as an American citizen. We were certain the Ivorys knew that my birth certificate existed and had bribed someone to destroy it. Mother said she would secure it for me, if I wished. We reminisced about Golden Dove, both what I believed about her and who my mother revealed her to be—her guide and mentor, who conquered obstacles and stacked them like building blocks. "Without her," Mother wrote, "I likely would have remained a helpless American girl railing against my stupidity and his spinelessness."

In those early letters, she was far more forthcoming than I was. Her mother and father were odd, she wrote in one. I did not write back that I now understood where my own mother's eccentricity had come from. She recalled more about her mother and father with each letter.

I had confused my parents' oddities as being my enemies, their neglect as lack of love entirely. Neglect is a surreptitious slayer of the heart. It has as its accomplice carelessness. My parents' oddities faded with age and were replaced with the frailties that await us all. The mother and father I had rebelled against no longer existed. They were new people—gentler and more endearing, flawed and puzzled to be so. They needed me. When they died—my father first, then my mother—I truly mourned them, especially the part of them I had refused as a child to see.

My mother, the one I had grown up with in Shanghai, no longer existed either. She had been replaced with a new person, both a stranger and a familiar. I could start afresh in deciding whether I could trust her. She allowed me to see who she was through what made her vulnerable to losing her heart, losing her soul, losing her way in the world, and losing me. She was honest, and at times shockingly so, when she gave me confessions no mother and daughter would freely share.

> *I shudder in remembering the murderous words I flung at my mother and father. I told my mother that everyone talked behind her back and she was cracked for spending years in her room looking at insects that had been dead for millions of years. I told my father I had his lovers' letters, and I recited the vulgar and laughable nicknames they had given him to describe his sexual prowess. The Vortex of Sex! I think he nearly died of embarrassment. Looking back, I'm aghast that I condemned them so violently to justify my love for a mediocre painter. Happily, my poor taste in art resulted in you. I'm glad you can't see me blushing as I recall again what I found so compelling about that Chinese painter and why I believed those paintings were stunning masterpieces. My God! I'll only say this, Violet. You're lucky you have your father's looks.*

Our letters were frequent, at times almost daily. I shared the moments of my life one at a time. In the beginning, they did not include those days in the courtesan house. They were about the day Flora was born and the day Edward died. I described Perpetual as my last resort for respectability. I admitted that I met Loyalty in the courtesan house, but I did not tell her about his purchase of my defloration. In matters of sex, I remained discreet because those subjects made me acutely aware that she was, after all, my mother. It did not matter that we had been in the same business.

And yet, in many ways, I could speak about my hopes and despairs and moments of happiness far more freely than I could with anyone else. I finally understood them. Often I was not writing to her, but to myself, to my spiritual double, to the lonely child I once was, to the woman who once wished she was someone else. She had said something similar about the act of writing those letters. She likened it to passageways in a house that began at opposite ends, which we entered with trepidation, which became wonderment, when we found ourselves together in a room that had always existed.

In one very important way, she was the same mother I knew in Shanghai, and that was the persistence and resourcefulness she had applied in making Hidden Jade Path a success. She applied the same qualities to finding Flora. When her scheme was in place, she told me what she had done. "I have rented a bungalow in Croton-on-Hudson, a half mile from where Flora lives. The town is lovely and boring enough to provide forced serenity and ample time to go spying."

She quickly learned where Flora went to school (Chalmer's School for Girls), which church she attended (Methodist), and where she took her equestrian lessons (Gentry Farm Stables). Mother even attended a school play (*Whispering Pines*), posing as a talent scout for an anonymous but famous Hollywood movie producer. That fictitious affiliation made her a most welcome guest. "A front-row seat," she bragged. She revealed to the principal the next day that, unhappy to say, she had not found the child actor the famous director sought—a girl with dark Mediterranean looks and a fiery temper. The principal affirmed that none of their girls qualified in any way. My mother tactfully praised the play and inquired if they would want to use her services as a volunteer in the drama department. "I was an actress," she said, "mostly silent films, but also a few talkies. You wouldn't recognize my name. Lucretia Danner. I was never the lead, always the former girlfriend of the leading man, and, more recently, the mother of the misbehaving bride." She named the films: *Hidden Jade Path, The Lady from Shanghai, The Young Barons* . . . The principal claimed to vaguely recognize one of the made-up films. Mother explained to the principal that she and her husband had lived in Manhattan but enjoyed weekends in Croton-on-Hudson. "He adored this town. Having nothing to do is one of life's greatest luxuries, don't you agree? Nonetheless, I do believe one can occasionally be useful." She became a volunteer for two school plays a year. She helped in designing sets, making costumes, and teaching diction suitable for each character, and she bragged that she had excelled in volunteerism. However, there was nothing she could do when the idiotic director assigned Flora a meager role as a scarecrow in one play and the screeching chorus of three milkmaids and their mooing cows in another.

My heart beat in my throat every time I received a letter postmarked from Croton-on-Hudson. Mother had promised me she would not hold back in her reports. If Flora was happy, she would tell me. If she was not, she would tell me that as well.

> *Flora has the same independence of mind you showed at her age, but she also doesn't seem to care for anyone in particular. As you may recall, in the school play, Flora had a very small role as one of three scarecrows in a field invaded by birds. After the play was over, the odious family—Minerva, Mrs. Lamp, and Mrs. Ivory— descended like vultures on Flora. I have seen no sign or heard mention of Mr. Ivory. He is either an invalid or dead. The three women lavished praise on Flora's performance, and Flora showed no happiness or shared pride. Her apathy concerned me. But later I remembered that when you were a child, you went through periods when you pretended you cared for no one. Furthermore, it was a dreadful play, and it's ridiculous that anyone would praise a child for standing with arms spread out on a wooden cross, as if she were Jesus's dead sister wearing a checkerboard tablecloth.*
>
> *I must say, however, I have never observed Flora showing any affection for Minerva. She never seeks her out. That was unlike you. You were a skirt puller for attention, at that same age.*

I was glad at first to hear Flora was not close to Minerva. But later I worried. If Flora felt no happiness or pride, this would be terrible. If she did not feel love for anyone, this would be tragic. I hoped her lack of feeling had more to do with the loathsome people she lived with. A few days later, another letter came from Mother:

> She is cordial with her teachers and cooperative with the other students, but none are special to her. She does not seek them out. They do not seek her out. She prefers her solitude on the school grounds. She has a favorite tree and a squirrel that eats from her hand. From that spot, she observes the others. She appears to be quite fond of her tan-colored horse at the stables where she takes her riding lessons. And her favorite companion is a little perky-eared dog, the color of a dirty mop. I learned this after I accidentally tore out a small hole in an ivy hedge that surrounds the Ivory family's estate. The dog runs around her in circles, does tricks, and barks in a piercing shrill voice. I went to the library, and after a search in the encyclopedia with all things that start with the letter C and D, I determined the dog is a cairn terrier, whose talents are limited to digging and stealing food. I will obtain one soon.

"Uncle Loyalty" received a well-written letter of thanks from Flora for her father's cuff links. "She has very good handwriting for a seven-year-old child!" he exclaimed. He slowly read aloud the English words: "Dear Mr. Fang . . . Mr. Fang? Why not Uncle Loyalty?" He looked puzzled, as if his own child had disavowed him. He had developed avuncular feelings toward Flora simply by helping me scheme how to reach her. I told him this should not discourage him from sending another gift next year from Uncle Loyalty.

MY VALUE TO Loyalty's business grew. He had me attend meetings with his foreign-trade customers. I was his so-called secretary who took notes of what was said. As his translator did his usual work, I took on the role of being *momo*. With his English-speaking customers, I transformed myself into the secretary who spoke only Chinese. With the Chinese ones, I became the foreigner. By plan, Loyalty and his translator were called away at least twice during those meetings, which gave his customers a chance to speak confidentially among themselves, assuming I understood nothing. If they glanced toward me, I gave them a friendly smile. Later, I would give Loyalty my report, the customer concerns about quality, or speed of manufacturing, or cheaper competitors, or honesty.

I gave him yet another observation. Many of his new customers talked about going to the latest nightclubs. They discussed ways to get out of going to the party Loyalty wanted to host at a courtesan house. I told Loyalty that courtesan houses were less in fashion and some were known for fleecing customers. For a while, Loyalty resisted my suggestion that he set up an account at one of the more popular clubs. He had once been looked upon as the epitome of a successful and sophisticated businessman, but he had not changed with the times. He wore the same fashions, which I said suggested he was not that successful anymore. Eventually he let go of his stubbornness and bought new suits, which he wore to the Blue Moon Club, where, with my help, he became a member and, soon, a favorite customer who was always seated at his preferred table.

"Violet, you are always surprisingly clever," he said one day after I suggested he give his American customers souvenirs of Shanghai.

Since our early days together in the courtesan house, he had often said I was "surprisingly" this and "surprisingly" that. I should have seen it as a compliment, but, given our history, I felt he was implying that he had expected little of me. I used to worry that one day he would cease to say he was surprised, and I would feel I had met only his low expectations. I finally told him that the word annoyed me.

"Why is it bad that I say this? My other translators do nothing surprising. You will always be surprising to me, because you are better than most, and that is true not just in your work, but also in who you are to me. This is your nature, which I appreciate and is the reason I've always loved you."

"You haven't always loved me."

"Of course I have. Even when you married—both times—I kept my loving feelings. All these years, I have never loved anyone more than I have you."

"You mean not anyone else besides your wife."

"Why do you persist with that? You know that was a marriage in name only. We're divorced now. We stayed together only for our son. Why don't you believe me? Shall I have you talk to her on the phone? Let me call her right now."

"Why are we talking about these old matters? From now on, you can say I'm surprising, but don't tell me you love me, because I know where on my body you want to put that love."

"After all these years, you still don't know how to accept kindness and love when it's offered."

Loyalty and I succumbed to our old intimacy within four months of my starting my position at his company. I had to admit to myself that he made me laugh more than he wounded me. He appreciated me. And I enjoyed his attentions in bed. He knew me well in so many ways. But our relationship had become different as well. I did not tie his affections to the number of gifts he gave me, nor did I have the same fears and uncertainty in waiting for him to decide whether he would see me. He did not decide any of it. He was not my customer and I was not his courtesan. I lived in my own apartment and saw him daily at the office, and at other times two or three times a week. I called him "my friend" and not "lover," as he suggested.

"A friend is someone who is not as special as a lover," he complained.

"Magic Gourd is a friend, and we are very close. A lover could be a man who is close to your body." I told him that I wanted a lover who was dependable and faithful, and not someone who made me wonder what he was up to when he was away from my side for even thirty minutes, which was all it took for him to flirt with a woman and suggest further flirtation elsewhere. He had done that. And he continued to go to courtesan houses.

"What man does not look at a pretty woman without imagining more? That's not being unfaithful, just curious. If you found a man like the one you describe, I would say there is something unnatural about him. Would you really go off with someone like that?"

"Don't you want honesty and trust in business? If you suspected a partner or employee had cheated you, wouldn't you be reluctant to do further business? Maybe you think I should expect less from you because I was a courtesan, and customers could never be expected to be faithful, not even with a contract. Even when I worked in that world, I still wanted love so strong that the man would have no interest in another woman. Maybe you will always be incapable of giving that kind of love. You tell me I want too much. And maybe I do, but like you and your imagination, I can't help but be that way."

I ended our relationship many times, shouting he was an unfaithful bastard who gave me fake love—and sometimes with accusations that particularly tender moments had been false, which wounded him.

"You're the one who wants to quit," he would say to my reason for ending our affair. "So who is trustworthy and steadfast?" His logic was maddening. He said my feelings were illogical.

He continued to philander behind my back, visiting courtesan houses at least once or twice a week. One day I spotted a gift in a red silk bag sticking out of his pocket. He admitted he was going to a courtesan house, but the gift was not for anyone in particular. He was carrying it in case someone sang or told a good story. My feelings for him vanished all at once. It was strange how quickly it happened. Instead of being infuriated by his lies, I felt free. That's when I knew I could end our relationship for good. I was calm when I told him. I explained that we were two different people who were not compatible in what we wanted. He started to argue about the gift—that it didn't even cost that much. He pulled out a hairpin. I told him it wouldn't have mattered if he didn't go to courtesan houses at all. I simply didn't love him anymore.

He was shocked and gradually his face fell into sadness. "I see it in your eyes. It's finally happened. I've lost you. How stupid that I didn't treat you better. I'm sorry." He fell quiet. His eyes looked lost. "All my weaknesses didn't mean my love for you was weak. I treated you badly and felt I could count on you to forgive me. After all, you didn't forgive your mother, yet you forgave me many times. It's too late to take back the suffering I caused you. But I can't bear the thought that I may have caused you to distrust love even more. You have to believe I've always loved you. From the beginning, I felt you knew me. When we were apart, I felt something was missing. No matter how many friends were with me, I felt alone. I felt dissatisfied no matter how much success I had. I never wanted to admit this, Violet, but with you, I could be a child again, innocent and good. Imagine that! Loyalty, who is so successful—just a naughty little boy, who would wake in the middle of the night, so scared by how much he loves you, he needed to touch your face to make sure you were there. It was as if you protected a hidden part of me. And when you were not there, I felt I was going to die alone. I wish I told you many years ago." He had tears in his eyes.

I took back the little boy and I stopped breaking up with him. I moved into his house, and we still fought, not as much, and we always conceded that we loved each other. We did not declare we loved each other. We did not profess it with the giddiness of a secret finally revealed. We admitted it.

One afternoon, after we returned from a cousin's funeral, he said, "Promise me, Violet, you won't die before I do. I couldn't stand it. I'd lose my mind without you."

"How can I promise that? And how can you be so selfish in hoping you'll die first when that would leave me to be the one who suffers?"

"You're right. You should die first."

We settled into the routine of a married couple, knowledge-able about our habits, likes, and dislikes. We noted how our bodies had softened with age, and how the atmosphere of Shanghai had gone crazy with decadence competing with decadence, which we did not find attractive. How odd that we had become the old-fashioned ones. We agreed on more things than we disagreed and could let go of most annoyances, and only a few of his faults reignited the same arguments that had once torn us apart.

We had been together around three years when Loyalty told me that he had been finding it harder and harder to empty his bladder. It had been going on for a while, but he did not want to tell me, lest I think he was worried, which he was. He downplayed his fear by saying it was probably something like constipation of the penis. A few days later, he saw blood in his urine, and he came to me white-faced. I made an appointment to see a doctor.

We sat holding hands when the doctor told us he had can-cer of the prostate. He would need radiation. The doctor said this would give him the best chance, and if it did not have the desired result, they would try another treatment. Loyalty feared the radia-tion would shrink his penis and testicles, and that the second treat-ment would involve cutting off both, leaving him a eunuch. He had always acted like a strong man, and would never show any kind of weakness. It made me ache to see the unmasked despair and fear in his eyes.

"I refuse to let you go," I said. "We've been fighting so much over unimportant matters. Now I'll fight to keep you. You know how strong I am."

"My dear Violet girl, if a strong temper can cure, I will soon be well."

While he underwent the Western treatment, I went to the Chi-nese doctors for medicines. I bought large amounts of the immortal-ity mushrooms, once taken by emperors.

Loyalty laughed weakly when I told him that. "Immortality? Where are those emperors now?"

"They were murdered by their wives."

The Chinese doctor came with his acupuncture needles every day. I made Loyalty do *chi gong*. I fed him the freshest foods that were balanced for yin and yang. I hired a feng shui master to rid the house of disturbed spirits. It did not matter whether I believed that spirits existed. It was my declaration that I loved him and would do everything possible.

"Even though I've treated you so badly," he murmured, "you still love me. You are still here. You are always surprising, Violet. Everything I thought was important is not. The business, the flower houses, none of it is lasting. Only you are important. My sweet girl. I want only you with me to the end of my days, whether they are few or many."

"Ah, but if I cure you, my boy, will you claim the disease affected your brain and you do not remember the part about no longer visiting flower houses?"

All at once, pain and fear left his face. He seemed healthy again. He took my hand. "Please marry me, Violet. I'm not asking you now because I may be dying. I've wanted to ask you many times in the past. But you were always mad at me. There was never the right moment to declare we should be together for the rest of our lives when you were yelling at me that you would never sleep in the same bed with me again."

We married in 1929. His family objected. He was marrying a woman who did not appear to be entirely Chinese, and who had no family history except a murky one. I shed a flood of tears that he had stood up to them. When I was fourteen, I had dreamed of marrying him. When I was twenty-five, I lost Flora because I was not married. I had married Perpetual out of desperation and fear for my future. And now I had married Loyalty for love. Eighteen months after we married, the doctors told us Loyalty no longer had the cancer. Both

the Western doctors and Chinese doctors took the credit. Loyalty said
he was alive because of me.

"All those foul-tasting soups you made and your constant nagging to drink them," Loyalty said, "even the cancer could not stand
it and left." Over breakfast each day, Loyalty kissed my forehead and
thanked me for letting him see the new morning. He served me tea.
That one act was an astonishing show of appreciation and love. Loyalty was used to others taking care of all the comforts of his daily life.
He had never had to think of mine or anyone else's.

We still fought on occasion, always over petty things. I found
it maddening when he gave women the long gaze. Most of the time,
it did not lead to any interest on the woman's part. But when they
smiled, he smiled back. If it happened at a party, he would find some
reason to move in the woman's direction and let his eyes linger even
longer. When I accused him of lusting after other women, he denied
doing anything of the kind. The way he looked at people was the
way his eyes worked, he claimed. I asked him why they didn't work
that way with men. Whatever his eyes were doing, he said, at least he
wasn't going off with other women. So why wouldn't I be happy with
him for that? We would then break into the same argument about his
dishonesty and my illogic, which ended with my sleeping in my own
bedroom, and him knocking on the locked door, sometimes in the
middle of the night, and sometimes two nights in a row.

Our best times were the mundane evenings when we ate our
dinner together at home and he kissed me for cooking a dish he particularly liked. We listened to the radio and talked about the news
or about Flora or my mother. Sometimes I reminisced about Hidden Jade Path. I took him back to those times when I overheard the
courtesans talking about their misfortunes, what I noticed about nervous men at the parties, and what I saw and heard when I hid behind
the French doors between Boulevard and my mother's office. And
we recalled at least a hundred times the evening we first met, both
of us adding made-up details to exaggerate how big Carlotta was or

how scared Loyalty was, until I was reduced to gasps of laughter when Loyalty said he pissed in his pants when he heard me say I would have to amputate his arm right there and then.

He often ended by saying: "You told me to wait for you to grow up, and that one day we would join our fates together. I was too stupid to do it sooner, but now, you see, here we are." And then, he took me to bed, as he always did when we talked about our intertwined fate.

There were many moments when he would see me cry silently and he would drop whatever he was doing and come to me and wrap his arms around me, without asking me why I was sad. He knew it was about Flora, or about Edward, or about how I felt the day my mother left. He simply rocked me, as if I were a little girl. Those were the reasons we both knew how deep love was, the shared pain that would outlast any pain we caused each other.

MAGIC GOURD LIVED a few blocks away. Her big plans to open a courtesan house were quickly forgotten when she ran into an old client, Harmony Chen, who had once been rich and now owned a modest business selling typewriters and "modern office supplies for modern businesses." Harmony had been her patron and remembered her well. He said the wiggle in her hips was still memorable, and he didn't mind her personality. So he married her, she said, so he could see that wiggle every day. Harmony told me she made him laugh all the time.

"He's a good man," she said. "Considerate. The best life you can have as you get into old age is good food, good teeth to eat it with, and few worries when you go to bed at night. A good husband is extra and can vary whether the number of worries you have is more or less. Mine are less."

Whenever she came over to visit, she liked to recall the difficulties she endured on my behalf. Her eyes would light up when she recalled something new. "Hey, remember that man who drove the cart—what was that scoundrel's name? Old Fart? Did I ever tell you he hinted that I should have sex with him? The bastard said we should go into the field and see how big the corn was."

"That's terrible."

She huffed. "I told him we didn't need to go in the field. I knew the corn was only this big." She held up her pinkie. "He was snorting mad the whole day."

She often brought up Perpetual. "Hey, remember when that bastard was beating the life out of you? I didn't tell you that I tried to pull him off. That's why he punched me in the eye. I almost went blind." I thanked her. She waved her hand dismissively. "No, no. There's no need to thank me." She waited until I thanked her once more before starting up again. "Hey, remember that night when we thought the whole village might burn down? I just got a letter from Pomelo and she said it was just her room and a shed. She got the news from tradesmen who go back and forth between Mountain View and Moon Pond. The path that went past Buddha's Hand is like a highway now. Someone was smart enough to turn that white rock into a shrine and now the place is crawling with pilgrims who buy sugared corn cakes and walking sticks. One of the pilgrims found Perpetual's body a year after he died, just some of his bones and scraps of clothes, also a leather pouch holding a poem. And listen to this! Nine months after Perpetual died, Azure had another son. She claimed it was Perpetual's, but one rumor has it that the father was her maid's lover, the manservant. There was another rumor: the mother of the baby was the maid and the father was Perpetual. In any case, Azure claimed it was hers."

WHEN MOTHER AND I started discussions about her coming to Shanghai to see me, Magic Gourd pretended to be enthusiastic. "You'll be so happy to have your real mother back." I had to reassure her many times that she had been more a mother to me than my real mother. She had risked her life. She had suffered for me.

"You worried about me," I said. "Constantly."

"That's true. More times than you know."

"I worried over you as well."

She gave me a doubtful look.

"When you got influenza. I thought you might die, and I sat by your bedside and held your hand. I begged you to open your eyes and come back to us."

"I don't remember that."

"That's because you were dying. I think my words might have made a difference."

Whether they had or not, Magic Gourd was deeply touched. "You worried?" she said over and over again. "No one in my life ever worried over me. Not before you."

She worried whenever I threatened to divorce Loyalty. I didn't mean I really wanted a divorce. I was just saying how angry I was. It was always the same reason: He had been flirting with a woman. She came over and listened to me, agreeing with everything I said. He was so bad, so thoughtless, so stupid. "But you don't need to divorce," she said. "There's an herb you can put in his tea. I heard it shrivels desire and other things. You just don't want to do it too often, otherwise it's permanent, and that would be too bad for you as well." Then she gently cajoled me into seeing that Loyalty was not that bad compared to some husbands. "Loyalty may be naughty but he is never mean. He's handsome, too, and a good lover. And he often makes you laugh. Four things. Most women don't even get one."

Shanghai
1929

Mother and I finally agreed that she should come to Shanghai. We did not write the exact words *before it's too late,* but that was what we were both saying in various ways. I told her that I did not think we should attempt to undo the past by talking about what might have changed the course of our histories. We had forged a relationship of confidantes between two adults, which was more than friendship but not that of a mother and daughter. We had intimate written conversations, yet they were faceless exchanges, separated by distance. Our confessions and remembrances required trust, and while our words flowed freely most of the time, we knew we could retreat behind the safety of a sheet of paper, and we did not need to explain why. We did not worry about offending each other when we were more measured and doled out sparingly the selected words that stood for an unresolved mix of feelings. A face-to-face meeting in Shanghai might expose us to the damaging past and undo what we had forged and was important to us. We both decided it was worth the risk. I warned her that I might not want to embrace her any more than I would a piece of paper. I didn't know what I would feel seeing her in the flesh. It might raise emotions I had forgotten I had, and thus she would have to be prepared, and not wounded, if I did not throw myself into her arms as a mother and daughter might when happily reunited. She agreed it would likely be awkward and unpredictable, and that she was prepared for distance between us. I thought about that reunion the entire month before she arrived, feeling the gamut of emotions, from being the child who had felt betrayed, to the woman who knew that I had been more important to her than Lu Shing and her son. I would see her, knowing she had been tormented and had grieved for me, as I did for Flora.

As we waited for the boat to arrive, I warned Loyalty to not give her one of his long flirtatious looks.

"How can you even think I would do that?" he said with mock offense.

"You would give an old woman in a coffin that look."

He laughed and kissed me. "I will be right here with you. Squeeze my hand if it is unbearable and I will find excuses to take you away."

Even though we had exchanged photos by mail, I had pictured her in one of her high-fashion party dresses, and not in a plain brown suit. Her features were striking, but outside of her world of business, she did not have the mesmerizing qualities that drew men to her side. She did not move gracefully but with jerky nervous movements as she searched for her luggage. She went to me, stopped ten feet away and stared, as if she were seeing a ghost. She was biting her lips as she looked me fully in the face. "I know we agreed to hold off speaking about our emotions. But I have kept seventeen years of your absence inside me, and I cannot hold back the words I had wanted you to hear. I love you so very much."

For the second time in my life, I saw her cry. I nodded and let her put her arms around me and I wept freely, too.

After a few minutes, she let go, and wiped her eyes. "There! Now that's out of the way. We can go back to being nervous about what we say."

Loyalty treated my mother with much respect. "It was in your house where I first met your lovely daughter as a seven-year-old brat. She has not changed much, except in age." My mother liked him immediately. She talked to him in her rusty Chinese. It was a relief to have him there to change the conversation to safer topics whenever either of us became uncomfortable. They recalled people they both knew, the scions of wealthy families, and he gave her an update on what had happened to some of them—whether they were doing the same, worse, or better. Most were doing worse.

Magic Gourd was waiting for us at our house. Many of my letters had mentioned her, and the first time I did, I reminded Mother that about twenty-five years ago she had asked the courtesan Magic Cloud, as she was known then, to leave Hidden Jade Path because of a matter having to do with a ghost and a patron. Magic Gourd, I went on to say, had been with me when I met Edward, when Flora was born, when Edward died, when Perpetual nearly killed me, when we escaped from Moon Pond—during all the moments of my life since my mother had left. I did not say anything about Magic Gourd's role in training me to be a courtesan. But I had made it clear that Magic Gourd had been like a mother to me. Over the distance of letters, I could not see my mother's face when she read those words, *like a mother.* The handwriting in her return letter, however, was more neatly written than usual. She expressed sadness that she had treated Magic Gourd so poorly, especially considering how she had taken care of me and how she embodied the attributes a true mother should have, one who was protective, who sought the best for her daughter over all other matters, who was selfless and would sacrifice her own life before any harm befell her child. In those words, she had spoken of the ways she had failed me. In each of her following letters, she asked how Magic Gourd was doing. Magic Gourd also politely asked the same about Mother.

Before coming to Shanghai, Mother already knew that Magic Gourd was now called Mrs. Harmony Chen and that Happy was her given name—Happy Chen in English. She was proud of her status and did not appreciate anyone using her former name. I was the only exception.

In the car on the way to the house, Mother and I talked about how she might introduce herself to Magic Gourd. We were nervous. She could hardly pretend that they had never met. And Magic Gourd was not one to hide her feelings. I had also forewarned Mother that she would not recognize Magic Gourd. She was past fifty and stout. Her jowls and the corners of her mouth hung down when she was nervous or disapproving. But when she smiled or was excited, they lifted up and added to her ample cheeks. She still had large beautiful eyes, and they were more often kind than critical.

When we walked in the door, Magic Gourd and Harmony were having a leisurely cup of tea. She acted surprised to see us. "Is it that late?" she said. "I thought you wouldn't be here for another hour."

Mother went to her and began by saying that she had read about her in so many letters, and it was good to finally thank her. She got no further than that.

"You remember me," Magic Gourd said. "You kicked me out. The reason had to do with the ghost of the house and a rumor that a greedy courtesan spread. It nearly ruined the business of the entire house. I wished the girl who spread the gossip a bad life, and then I heard she wound up in a Hong Kong gutter next to a fish market and without her teeth, and after that, I told myself, 'You don't need to think about that anymore.'" She smiled. "None of us do."

Mother was free to continue with her expressions of gratitude, using the words *like a true mother* and mentioned the attributes of one. This unleashed the first of endless stories Magic Gourd had at the ready about the harrowing times we had shared. Beginning with the Hall of Tranquility, she informed Mother about how she had trained me so that I would not fall into the dirty hands of cheap customers. Mother did not appear shocked. She said, "She could have wound up in the streets without your guidance." An hour later, Magic Gourd described the lavish feast Loyalty threw for me when I was fourteen. Eventually it came out that Loyalty had bought my defloration. She turned to Loyalty. "Don't be embarrassed. It was going to happen with someone, and Violet was lucky it was you."

Magic Gourd said to her, "You know what I think? It wasn't just luck. It was fate that you were on that boat. If you had stayed, Violet wouldn't have met Edward. She wouldn't have had Little Flora. She would not be here with Loyalty. What happened to Violet was terrible, and I'm not saying fate happens without blame. But when fate turns out well, everyone should forget the bad road that got us here. We should now concentrate on having Little Flora meet her true mother. With everyone's help, there's no way we can't succeed."

We took Mother to the old neighborhoods. She saw that Hidden Jade Path was now the private residence of someone powerful enough to have guards with rifles standing by the gate. "Gangsters," I said. "Or politicians who are friends of gangsters. Fairweather fell in with them, did you know? He met with a very bad end, I'm not sorry to say." She asked for details, and when I told her, she winced. She spent the second week in Soochow with Golden Dove, who, by her own description, had become fat and lazy. She was plump, but hardly lazy. Two years after she moved from Shanghai she married a man who had a furniture store. She turned it into an emporium of dry goods. In her late thirties, she told us, she gave birth to a son, who was making her life less peaceful. So she was happy.

Mother returned home after three weeks. Our letters resumed, and we critiqued our reunion. We admitted that we had secretly wanted to re-create that day she left Shanghai. We wanted to stand in her office, listen to the scoundrel's lies, and for her to see the danger, so she would know to protect me. But we could not re-create a different past. It was more like going to a movie and already knowing the ending, and also seeing that the movie stars did not look as we had expected.

Although my mother and I were glad to embrace each other at the beginning and end of the visit, we agreed that we preferred the intimacy we had in our many letters. In person, we had been careful about what we said. We had looked at each other's expressions, gestures, and the direction in which we turned our eyes to judge what we could talk about. There were others who tried to defray tension when there was none, or who added discomfort we could have easily avoided. Overall, however, the visit was a success. We wrote with greater openness and understanding. Magic Gourd had said we should forget the in-between years. But we did not want to. The wound had made it necessary to reveal to each other as much as we could.

MOTHER RETURNED YEARLY to Croton-on-Hudson to be near Flora a few months out of the school year. She took on the role of nosy neighbor. She ran into Flora at the fair, at church, in the park, or along the sidewalk walking the dog.

> *I once saw her dog take off to investigate another one across the road. A car nearly hit the beast and Flora screamed, "Cupid!" I felt the peril in my granddaughter's heart and the relief when the dog returned with head, tail, and legs attached in the right places.*

That was the first time she had called Flora her "granddaughter." I knew she had undertaken the task of finding Flora out of love for me. She had acquired additional reasons, and I was glad.

> *I bought a perky-eared cairn terrier like Flora's, thinking the two dogs would be eager to play with each other. I named her Salomé. Sure enough, Cupid saw her and bolted down the sidewalk to see her, and their leashes wound around us as the maypole. In the struggle to free herself, Salomé tried to kill Cupid. Fortunately, once the two dogs were untangled, they became quite chummy, in fact, rather lewdly so, which required further extrication.*

With Salomé's help, she ran into Flora often at the park. She carried dog biscuits to ensure Cupid would always seek out Salomé and her. She asked Flora if cairn terriers were the best choice of dogs as far as intelligence went. Flora shrugged and said, "I dunno." I believed Mother would have taken equestrian lessons to be with Flora had she not been terrified of horses. She did brave her distaste for religion and joined the Methodist Church. Through her reports and photos, I saw Flora from that distance. I learned that she kept her hair short, wore a plaid dress, and liked to sketch. When Mother posed questions to her—about the weather or the fair coming to town—the answer was always the same: a shrug and "I dunno."

When Flora was sixteen, my mother reported concerns that Flora's friends were "not the best kind." A particular boy came by often, and she would run to the car, and the boy would be slouched against the door and hand her a lit cigarette. That was his greeting. Mother saw her storm off one day after church, shouting to Minerva, "That's not for you to know." She hopped into the waiting car of the boyfriend. The boyfriend leaned across and gave Flora a long kiss. Minerva was left standing amid the churchgoers, distressed and embarrassed. Mother observed in Flora the signs of rebellion, which she believed were normal for a sixteen-year-old girl. But she also saw trouble. Flora was reckless.

The following year, Flora had settled down, my mother reported. She seemed quieter. She had bobbed her hair even shorter in a rather unattractive style. She took long walks through the park and drew in a sketchbook. Mother once asked to take a look. Flora answered: "Suit yourself." She had seen Minerva praise everything Flora did, which Flora almost seemed to resent. She would sigh and walk away. Mother knew to be more measured, one of her old skills from the days of Hidden Jade Path. "I find the perspective is quite interesting. It creates a trick of the eye. That's how I see it. But everyone sees something different in any work of art." Flora said, "That's what I wanted, many perspectives, but I don't have it right yet." It was the first time Flora had responded in any real way to what Mother had said. When Mother introduced herself as Mrs. Danner, Flora said: "I know who you are. You tried to make movie stars out of us."

IN 1937, AFTER high school, Flora went to college, and my mother did not know where. She continued to rent the place in Croton-on-Hudson so she could return in the summer, in case Flora did, too. But she did not see Flora and was bereft.

I was about to respond to her letter, but the war with Japan had started in full force. There had been incidents here and there. But in August, bombs fell on the South Railway Station and killed nearly everyone there. And then bombs from the Chinese air force accidentally fell on the Bund, and on another day, one fell on Sincere Department Store. Each time that happened, we were uncertain whether we truly were safe, even though the International Settlement was not in the war zone. The Japanese surrounded the Settlement, ready to pluck any Chinese with anti-Japanese sentiments who was foolhardy enough to sneak out. That included many. Within a few days of each bombing, the nightclubs started up again, life went on eerily as before. Loyalty warned me every other day to not go near Nanking Road or anywhere near the border of the Settlement. He was afraid I would think I was American enough to go anywhere I pleased. "For my peace of mind," he said, "I want you to think of yourself as Chinese. No half safe, half not."

IN JANUARY 1938, Loyalty put a letter in my hand. It was from Flora and it was addressed to "Uncle Loyalty." It was the first time Loyalty had been acknowledged as Uncle, and he shed a few tears as he pointed a shaky finger at the word *Uncle*.

December 26, 1938
Dear Uncle Loyalty,

If you got any letters of thanks over the last nine years, they weren't from me. I never saw your letters until today. Minerva Ivory, erstwhile mother, intercepted them, as well as the gifts. First let me say, I'm impressed that you kept my father's cuff links, fountain pen, and book of poems. You two must have been really good pals for you to go to the trouble of shipping the stuff all the way from China. So thanks for sending me his things. It really does mean a lot to me.

Thanks also for the Christmas gifts, especially the little carved jade horse. I never knew that was my sign in the Chinese zodiac. I'm guessing the eyes are not real rubies. The charm bracelet would have fit me when I was ten, and it's a shame I didn't get to wear it then

*because I adored charm bracelets when I was that age. You have
no idea how much. Actually, I'm kind of surprised that you would
have guessed that a girl would like something like that.*

*By the way, while looking for your letters, I found some written
by my father. They made it clear beyond a shadow of a doubt that
Minerva Ivory was not my real mother. (She's the liar who wrote the
letters to you.) I had always suspected that was the case, and I'm
glad to know it's the truth for all kinds of reasons I won't get into.
The fact that she's not my mother naturally makes me wonder who
my real mother is. In the last letter my father wrote, he told Minerva
he was married to a woman in Shanghai and she was going to give
birth to their baby (me). The problem is, he did not give her name.
This is a shot in the dark, but do you happen to know the name
of my real mother? I know it was ages ago, and for all I know, she
died in the pandemic, along with my father. Anyway, it's not that
important. I'm just curious. But if you do know her and run into
her, give her my regards from New York.*

Sincerely,

Flora Ivory

*P.S. I never really liked poetry, but maybe I'll give it another try,
now that I know how much my father liked the book you sent. You
never know.*

Loyalty was angry. "She never got my letters! That dog-bitch
mother wrote the letters. Dear Mr. Fang. All these years, I could have
been called Uncle."

"Flora knows." That was all I said.

I debated what to write. Should I say she was ripped from my
arms, with the two of us screaming for each other? Should I say that
Minerva and Mrs. Lamp made it impossible for me to keep her? In the
end, I expressed to Flora my great joy at having found her and that my
fondest wish had always been to be reunited.

I have much to tell you about your father and how much he and
I loved you. In the meantime, if you wish to meet your grandmother,
she is right there, in Croton-on-Hudson, where she has watched over
you for all these years.

We received Flora's answer by telegram. She wanted to meet her grandmother.

MOTHER SAID THAT she arranged for Flora to meet her in the park, and as soon as Flora saw her standing at the little bridge, she snapped: "I knew you were up to something. I was always running into you. I thought you were spying on me for my parents. Later I thought you were just some crazy lady."

She did not show immediate affection for her grandmother. It was mostly curiosity, and with caution. Mother understood this and told Flora that she had only wanted to assure her real mother that she was all right.

"You can tell her what you want," she said. "But how would you know the difference between what is all right for me and not? I don't even know if I'm all right."

She told Mother that she had learned the truth about me when she was home during the Christmas holidays. Her mother had gone to Florida on a two-week honeymoon with her new husband, "the professional leech," she called him. In the mailbox, Flora found Loyalty's letter in a Christmas-wrapped gift containing a scarf. She found it puzzling that he mentioned "another Christmas greeting" and that he thanked her for her last thank-you note. She then ransacked her mother's desk, shelves, and closets. Minerva was a pack rat, and Flora knew it had to be somewhere. In the attic, she found several shoe boxes bound with string. Inside were letters—not just from Uncle Loyalty, but also from her father. She read them all, feeling sick to her stomach as she gradually realized what had happened. Most of the letters were dated before she was born. They were pleas from her father for Minerva to grant the divorce, and they came with declarations that he would never return to her, that he didn't love her and never had. The earlier letters mentioned Minerva and Mrs. Lamp's trickery that had roped him into a sham marriage. There were later letters disparaging her for using lies about his father's health to lure him home. And then Flora read the letter that said he loved another woman and he had made her his wife in Shanghai. "A baby will soon be born," he had written, "a real one, and not the kind you made up to trick me into marrying you. Isn't that enough proof that I will never return?" That letter was dated November 15, 1918, and it was his last.

Flora told Mother she wanted the truth—who was her real mother, why was she in Shanghai, and how she met her father. "Please don't give me pretty lies. I've been fed them all my life. I don't want to find I've been fooled again in other ways. If the facts are bad, I can take them. I don't care what they are, as long as they're the truth."

I began by telling her that her mother was half-Chinese. Flora was stunned at first, but then she laughed and said, "Well, isn't that ironic?" It turns out that when she was thirteen or fourteen, she had begged Minerva to take her to a Chinese restaurant in Albany. Minerva insisted she wouldn't like it. Flora asked her how she knew that. She was furious when Minerva said nothing else and kept driving. When she was sixteen, she and her boyfriend— the bad one I told you about—drove to the city and ate Chinese food. She said she did it to spite Minerva, but she discovered she also liked it. I told Flora she probably ate more Chinese food than Western when she was little. And she said, "Of course I liked it. I'm part Chinese."

I then told her the more difficult truths. I said, "I gave birth to your mother out of wedlock, and your mother gave birth to you

without being legally married. That was the reason the Ivorys were
able to take you away from your mother." Flora didn't say anything.
She showed nothing on her face. Finally she said to me, "I want to
meet her. If I don't like her, I won't have to see her again. But I'm
guessing that if she's like you, she can't be that bad."

March 1939

Mother and Flora went to San Francisco first, where they would
board the boat to Shanghai a week later. During the time they stayed
in San Francisco, Flora slept in the bedroom that my mother once
said would be mine. I could still picture it: the sunny yellow walls,
the window with the large branches of an oak so close you could
climb onto them. That bedroom had been a symbol of happiness. I
imagined Flora climbing onto the branches of that tree.

Mother said the house had become a ramshackle place in need
of much work. It was too big for one person and held more sad memories than good. When she told Flora she would probably sell it, Flora
said, "Don't. Maybe I'll fix it up and come live here. I want to move as
far away from Minerva as I can, and I'll need a place to stay." She did
not say that Mother could live with her as well. Then again, where else
would Mother live?

The moment came that Mother had been dreading. Flora wanted
to meet "the Chinese part of her," meaning Lu Shing, whom Mother
had not seen since 1912. She had ignored Lu Shing's entreaties to get
together so he could apologize and had hoped he would vanish from
her existence and memory. But she said she could not blame him
for luring her back to San Francisco with promises she could finally
see Teddy. She had let herself be lured and now did not want to be
reminded of the many bad decisions she had made in the name of
love. I suspected she also might have been afraid that love would be
rekindled.

I received a letter when Mother and Flora were already on the boat. It was dated the previous week, when they were still in San Francisco.

I've been a jumble of nerves just thinking about this meeting. It's been twenty-seven years since I last saw him. And I can still remember what a charmer he was. I fear that he'll charm Flora, and she will want to keep this delightful Chinese grandfather in her life. She said she wanted to know the truth about everything, but I had to be careful to present the facts and not my emotional opinion of him. So I told her about his dual relationship to Mr. Ivory; her grandfather, the art collector; and my father, John Minturn, her great-grandfather, the art scholar. I was in the midst of telling her that Lu Shing had been Mr. Ivory's protégé and had lived in his house for several years. Flora then said, "Wait a minute. I heard about him—I mean, I overheard what my grandfather said about a Chinese man who had lived in the house years ago. He called him 'that double-crossing two-bit slit-eyed bogus bastard Chinese painter—seduced John's daughter right under his nose!' I thought that what my grandfather had called the painter was hilarious. It was like a tongue twister. And I said it all the time, faster and faster. 'Double-crossing two-bit slit-eyed bogus bastard Chinese painter—seduced John's daughter right under his nose.' Now I get why he said it. The daughter was you, and you gave birth to my mother, who my father then fell in love with, and she made a mess of the family tree by giving birth to me. I can't wait to meet this double-crossing two-bit slit-eyed Chinese bastard painter, who seduced you." I then told her more about Lu Shing, just the facts, like his taking my baby and disappearing for the next twelve years.

I received another letter the next day.

Flora has an unnerving way of saying things. Yesterday we were all set to see Lu Shing. I was agitated, as you can imagine, after not laying eyes on him for twenty-seven years. Back then, that man could peel my clothes off just looking at me. Before we stepped out the door, Flora told me I had on a very nice dress that went well with my green eyes. I thanked her. Then she said, "It's new, isn't it?" Before I could recover from being flustered, she said, "The beauty parlor did a good job on your hair. Frankly, the way it was before, it made you look kind of dotty. I bet the two-bit painter is going to regret the day he left you!" She gave me a wink. Can you believe it? To be honest, I did want to look my best when I told Lu Shing to beat it. "Beat it," by the way, is a useful phrase Flora taught me. It's a polite way to say, "Fuck off."

We arrived at 10:00 A.M. at the art gallery in Nob Hill where Lu Shing sells his paintings. It's no bigger than a bread box, but he apparently owns the place. Who else would sell those paintings? Flora was polite and wore her usual quiet blank expression. She looked carefully at Lu Shing's face as she shook his hand. I wondered what she saw. To me, he looked so worn out, so lacking in spirit, although I confess, he was still handsome, and his voice—so melodious and British. He's always had an imperial Chinese quality to him that makes you think there's more to him than there actually is. At one point, I caught him smiling at me, and I wondered if he was thinking, "Poor Lulu, she's turned into a dotty old hag. At least her hair looks nice." He came over and thanked me for coming. His eyes were sad. "It shouldn't have been this way," he said. "I'm sorry." All my resolve to curse him vanished. I felt wistful.

"How's your wife?" I said in a cheery voice. He said in a respectful tone, "She died." A bit of hope came back—not real hope but a memory of it—that he would one day be free to marry me. You'll be glad to know that my senses came back two seconds

later. *"I'm sorry to hear that," I said. "And I'm sorry to say none of my husbands died. I had to divorce them. I'm on my fourth." I'm sure he knew I wasn't telling the truth, but what could he say?*

Flora was walking around the little gallery and seemed to be studying the art—or rather, the products. There were scenes of boats on the bay, some with calm waves, some thrashing dark ones worthy of Mutiny on the Bounty. *He had painted cable cars going up the hill and into the stars. He had many of the new Golden Gate Bridge, which he painted gold, even though it's red. There were a few sea lions on rocky islands. My eyes caught one painting in particular. You know it.* The Valley of Amazement. *There were a dozen of them, some depicting a sunset, another a sunrise, one before a storm, another after a storm. One had a carpet of purple flowers covering the valley floor. Another had them in blue. A few showed miniature cities of gold lying beyond the opening between the mountains, illuminated by the beams of heaven.*

You'll be pleased to know your daughter is an astute art critic. She remarked to Lu Shing that he seemed to specialize in happy scenes. She pointed to one of the Valley of Amazement *paintings and asked if he could paint a larger one and add birds in the sky. He said he could do that quite easily and often customized paintings to what his customers wanted. Our sly girl said, "I thought so." He asked if she would like one, and she declined, telling him, "I was just curious to know how you make a living." I could tell that he knew what she was saying, and I felt sorry for him because I was remembering that he once admitted to me in a letter that he was a mediocre painter with no depth of spirit, and he knew enough about himself to be disappointed with his life. At that moment, I could not be angry with him anymore. I pitied him.*

After we left the gallery, Flora told me that Lu Shing was a phony artist. Everything he did was a copy of what someone else had done, she said, and it was not even well done. "It felt like all the truth got whitewashed with fake happiness," she said, "only it was not happy and it was worse than fake. It was dangerous."

LOYALTY, MAGIC GOURD, and I were at the dock to greet Flora and Mother. I was light-headed, hardly able to breathe. I told Loyalty and Magic Gourd once again to be careful about what they said. I wanted no mention of Perpetual, Fairweather, or courtesan houses.

"You've told us ten times," Loyalty said, and squeezed my hand. "I'm nervous, too."

"She'll know who you are the minute she sees you," Magic Gourd said to me, which made me even more nervous. "In the photos, she looks like you."

I saw Mother first, and a moment later, Flora came into sight. They were standing on the dock amid the hustle-bustle of hundreds of passengers and coolies sorting through baggage. I could not see the details of Flora's face, just the green cloche she wore. She was tall compared to Mother and those around her. She had Edward's height. I watched her move toward me, gliding through chaos. As she drew closer, I saw more of Edward's face, his serious expression. She had his complexion, his hair color. She stopped before she reached me and pointed to a trunk and nodded to a coolie, spotted another and pointed. I had seen photos of her when she was seven, ten, thirteen, seventeen, and the most recent one, taken six months ago, in which she looked more sophisticated. But in my heart and mind I still kept two strong memories of her: the laughing gurgling baby and the screaming little girl being taken from me. I had lived with those two memories, and they had equally torn my heart. I had imagined feeling the weight of her as she slept in my arms. Little Flora was not this tall stylish woman with red lipstick and bobbed hair.

Mother was suddenly before me and gave me a quick embrace. She had aged over the last ten years. Her hair had gone completely gray and she was now shorter than I was. Her hair looked freshly done, and she wore a dress that complemented her eyes. Lu Shing must have seen her looking like this when they met at the gallery. She was still vivacious, still in charge. She waved back at Flora and pointed to me, and Flora looked my way and nodded. Her expression did not change. She showed no surprise or happiness.

Magic Gourd put her hand on my shoulder. "Eh, see? She has that same expression you have when you're trying to pretend you don't want what you want. See her mouth? That's what you look like right now." She rubbed my chin. "It's pinched tight."

I forced myself to smile, and my mind flooded as I went through a repertoire of introductions I might use. "I'm glad to meet you." "I'm Violet Fang." "I'm so glad finally to see you again, Flora. I'm your mother." "I'm your mother, Flora." "I'm Violet Fang, your mother." "Do you remember me, Flora?"

But all those practiced phrases flew out of my head, and when I reached her, I said, "How was your voyage? You must be tired. Are you hungry?"

She said the trip was all right. And she was neither tired nor hungry. I searched for her baby face and found it in her eyes. When tears welled up, I turned away. I felt a hand on my shoulder and heard her say, "Here you go." She handed me a handkerchief. After daubing my eyes, I looked up at her to thank her, expecting she, too, would be teary-eyed. Her eyes were dry. I was scared. She felt nothing for me.

Mother was speaking in Chinese to a coolie and told him to be careful. Her Chinese was even rustier than the last time she was here. I instructed the coolie to take the trunks to the other side of the road, where our car was waiting.

"It's kind of strange hearing you talk in Chinese," Flora said. "I know you're half, but you don't look it until you speak. I'll get used to it, I suppose."

"You spoke Chinese when you were a little girl," I said. "Your

Auntie Chen and you spoke nothing else." I pointed to Magic Gourd, who nodded excitedly.

"I spoke Chinese? That's a hoot."

I brought Magic Gourd to Flora and said: "This is Mrs. Chen. She's my dearest friend who took care of me for many years. She's like a sister to me."

Magic Gourd nodded and said in practiced English. "You call me Auntie Happy-Happy."

Mother sidled up to me and gave me a quick hug. "I told you she looks like you. You wait and see what else she does that's like you."

Loyalty was waiting patiently to be introduced. Flora went up to him and shook his hand. "You must be Uncle Loyalty."

He beamed. "Yes, yes, that is true. And you are my—I forgotten the word—my English is so bad—my daughter."

Flora smiled. "I suppose."

Grandmother, mother, and daughter sat in the backseat of the car. Mother had placed me in the middle, on purpose, I knew, so that Flora was next to me, on my left. It was a torment that I could not stare openly at Flora's face, so I kept my eyes trained ahead and told the driver to take us along a route without Japanese check-points on the border of the International Settlement. I did not want to scare Flora. The car was silent. Distress welled in my stomach. I felt I was going to burst into tears. This was not how it was supposed to be. It did not feel right. All those years of waiting, and I could not release any of the pain or joy. Flora did not know me. To her, I was a stranger who looked white and spoke Chinese. The baby who had clung to me was now indifferent to the mother who sat next to her. Minerva had made her incapable of feeling. I tightened my throat. Mother had already warned me that Flora would come across as cool. "After days, she's lukewarm," she wrote.

After a month, I would say she is warmer. But she has never called me "Grandmother." I am Mrs. Danner to her. Don't be too

hurt, Violet, if you find she's not the cuddly child you've held in your
memory all these years. Remember how odd we felt seeing each other
after our long separation.

I was about to ask Flora if she wanted to see anything special in Shanghai when I saw the heart-shaped gold locket around her neck. She had kept it. Minerva had not taken it away. Had she ever pulled it apart to see what was inside? "You're wearing the locket I gave you," I said. "Do you remember it from when you were little?"

She fingered it. "I remember playing with it in a room with yellow walls. I also remember a woman trying to take it away. I think it was my mother. I mean, Minerva. I can't ever call that woman my mother again. Anyway, Minerva kept trying to take it, and I bit her and she yelled and that made me think I should bite her again. I wore it all the time. But I didn't know you had given it to me. Minerva claimed it was from her side of the family. Everything about her was a big lie."

"Did you open it?" I asked.

"I never tried until I read the letters from my father. And then I got this feeling there might be something in that locket. I had to work hard to pry it open, and then I finally got it apart. I saw the photos, you and my father, the two of you together. If you hadn't soldered the damn thing shut, I might have known the truth a lot sooner."

"I didn't want the photos to accidentally fall out. You chewed on the locket all the time. Did you see those teeth marks?"

"So that's what those dents are." She put her palm over the necklace. "It's always been special to me, even before I knew where it came from. It was like a little magic heart, and I could touch it and it could make me strong or invisible or able to read people's minds. I sort of believed that when I was younger. I wasn't crazy, though. It was just something I needed to believe."

My eyes welled up yet again and I turned away, toward my mother.

"Did you lose the handkerchief I gave you?" I heard Flora say. I nodded. She put her hand on my arm. "It's okay. You can cry if you want."

In between my daughter and my mother, I sobbed.

On the way to our house, Loyalty pointed out a few sights. When he indicated we should look to the left, I took that opportunity to study Flora's face. She glanced my way every now and then and smiled slightly.

"I can't get over the fact that you speak Chinese," she said, "and that I look like you."

"Actually, you resemble your father more," I said. She looked at me straight on, puzzled. "The shape of your eyes, the color of your irises, your eyebrows, your nose, and ears . . ."

Flora leaned over and looked at Mother. "Is she blind?"

Mother said to her: "I told you, Flora. You look like your mother."

FOR THE FIRST two days, I said nothing about the past. The four of us took Flora on a tour of Shanghai—as much as we could see within the International Settlement. She was interested in the architecture, especially in the roofs with their curved eaves. "There's something about a roof that's like a head and a face tilted at the sky." She practiced speaking simple Chinese words with Magic Gourd: "tree," "flower," "house," "man," "woman." She could recall them an hour later.

On the third day, she said over breakfast: "I'm ready to hear about you and my father. Just tell me and don't try to make it proper and all that. Don't leave out the good stuff."

"I met your father," I said, "because Uncle Loyalty introduced him to me as someone he could have conversations with in English. Your father also thought I was a common prostitute in a cheap brothel. We did not get along at first." She enjoyed hearing about the misunderstanding, and Loyalty's role in that. When I described

Edward, she listened, sitting perfectly still. I found it difficult to put into words all who Edward had been to me and who he was to her. I told her how beautiful his voice was, and I sang the morning song he made up. I told her he was serious, sometimes sad, gentle, and funny. I told her briefly about his despair over the death of a boy named Tom who fell because of a prank he committed. She was interested in knowing what her grandfather and grandmother thought about it. When I said they said he was not to blame, she sniffed and said, "I knew it." As I related what more I remembered, I found Edward coming back in more detail, released from the photograph, the immobile memory, and back to life.

I went to a table where I had laid Edward's journal. I put it in her hands, and she ran her fingers over the soft brown cover. She opened it and read aloud the title that Edward had declared grandiose.

To the Farthest of the Far East
By B. Edward Ivory III
A Happy Wanderer in China

I showed her the passage Edward had written when we went to the countryside and he taught me to drive. As she read to herself, I was with him again. He urged me to go faster, to feel the speed of life, as we raced away from death spreading over the land, when he wanted to feel only happiness because he was with me, the woman he loved. I turned to him, and he saw that I loved him, too.

"That was the love we had and gave you. He made me pure. I was no longer the courtesan I had been forced to become. I was loved, and that was knowledge I would always have. When Mrs. Lamp called me a prostitute, she could not take his love away. Instead, they took my baby. They took you and made you forget who I was."

Flora was somber. "In a way, I didn't forget. That's why I wouldn't let anyone touch the locket. As long as I had it, I knew someone like you would come back. I waited for you. And every day, those awful people told me that you didn't exist, that it was a bad dream. Every day they said this until you became a dream." She looked at me with a desperate face. Her eyes were like Edward's just before he confessed that terrible story of the boy who fell off the cliff.

"They took me away from you and tried to make me someone else. I'm not them. I hate them. And I'm not you either. I don't know you anymore. I don't know who I am. People see me and they think I look so sure of myself. Hey, lucky girl, you're rich and have no worries. But I'm not who they think. I'm wearing an expensive dress. I'm walking with my shoulders back like a confident girl who knows where she's going. But I don't know what I want to do in my life. I'm not talking about the future after I finish college—if I finish. I don't know what I want to do day after day. There's nothing that strings the days together. They're all separate days, and each day, I have to decide what I want to do and who I will be.

"Minerva tried to make up who I was. Her daughter. But she knew I didn't love her, and she didn't love me. I used to try to believe she did. But somehow I knew love was not what I felt from her. I thought there was something wrong with me. I was a girl who was unlovable, who could not love. I saw the girls at school with their mothers. They decorated Easter baskets and they'd say, 'Blue is my mother's favorite color.' I had to pretend that I was as excited as those other girls. And then I grew tired of pretending. Who was I pretending for? Who was I if I didn't pretend?

"Like father, like daughter, I was raised in the good ol' Ivory family tradition. You can do no wrong. You're always right. You can lie through your teeth and make people do what you want because you have enough money to buy your way clean. You can buy admiration, buy appreciation, buy respect—all of it fake, of course. To them, flimsy cardboard facades were good enough. And I did my best to prove they weren't.

"I stopped studying when I was a kid and flunked my tests. If I knew the right answer, I wrote down the wrong one. My family accused the teachers of treating me unfairly and they bullied them into letting me take the tests again at home. They hired someone to fill in the answers. I became a stellar pupil!

"I started shoplifting when I was eleven. It was exciting because it was dangerous and I could get caught. I had never had such strong emotions—not that I could remember—and I felt I needed to do it. I stole a little tin soldier from a toy store. It wasn't anything I really wanted. But when I took it home, I suddenly felt it belonged to me and I had a right to take it. My right. I stole things that were valuable and other things that were not: a silver baby cup, an apple, shiny buttons, a thimble, a silver dog that fit in the thimble, a pencil. The more I stole, the more I felt I had to steal. It was like having a huge Santa Claus bag inside me that I had to fill and I didn't know why. I figured I wouldn't know why until I filled it. Finally, I got caught, and my erstwhile fake mother sat me down and asked if I lacked for anything. I said nothing because I couldn't tell her I had the empty Santa bag inside me. She said I only needed to tell her what I wished for and she would provide it. She gave me ten dollars. I threw the money away when I went outside. It made me mad that she thought she could pay to make the bad part of me go away. I went back to stealing. I wanted to be caught again right away. But no one noticed. So I stole bigger things and in plain sight—a doll, a piggy bank, a wooden puzzle. I knew the shopkeepers saw me, but they said nothing. My erstwhile mother, I later found out, had set up an account with the shopkeepers, and they would mark down the cost of what I had stolen. The amount of money would be paid from the account. It was like a joke to them.

"I didn't want to be bad. That wasn't who I was. It just felt closer to who I might be, because I wasn't like them. Being like them meant I had to feel nothing was wrong with them, with the world, with those who rubbed their hands and pretended to respect them, when it was really their money. Being them was believing love was a kiss on the cheek. Love was supposed to make you feel happy and that you weren't alone. You could feel something you didn't feel with anyone else. And your heart would squeeze when there was love. That's what I had with my dog. People say true love is constant. Well, no love is constant, too.

"When I was older, I took up with the kind of friends the Ivorys thought were the scum of the earth, and especially a boy named Pen. I know Mrs. Danner saw him when she was spying on me. He and I smoked cigarettes. We drank booze. I did all the things I shouldn't do, and then I got pregnant. When I realized I was going to have a baby, I felt like I had finally done it. I had changed myself. I was now different. My body was different. The way people would see me was different. Girls who got pregnant were immoral and stupid. But now I didn't like the change. I wasn't immoral and stupid. I got into a *situation* and with a boy I didn't love. I used to think he was different, because he didn't care what people thought. He was fun and dangerous. But I knew I didn't love him. I wanted to, but he was not that smart. The cream didn't rise to the top, if you know what I mean. And now he wanted to make me an honest woman, he said. He said he loved me and asked if his love was reciprocated. Reciprocated! That was the biggest word he had ever used. He had a chance to marry Little Miss Moneybags and he had gone to the dictionary to figure out how he could do it. Even he had become fake. The baby was the only one who wasn't.

"So what was I going to do? I had not plotted it out yet, but I would. I knew I would soon have to leave home. I would not let my baby grow up to be like the erstwhile family. And they would be glad that I left. They could not pile on enough lies to cover up a belly that was going to grow bigger and bigger. It took Minerva two months to notice something was wrong with me. I was vomiting every morning in my room. One day, I got sick at dinner. She was about to call the doctor, thinking I had a stomach ailment. I told her, 'Don't bother. I'm pregnant.' She closed the dining room doors, so it was just the two of us. I told her I didn't know who the father was, just to further upset her. It could be any of a half dozen boys, I said. She said the strangest thing: 'I knew this would happen. You were born without morals, and for all I tried I couldn't change that.' I didn't know she was referring to you. She told me I had ruined the family reputation, the Ivory family's social standing, and that I would be the source of a lot of gossip. It was thrilling to hear her say this. 'Young lady,' she said in a shrill voice, 'you've crossed the threshold into the devil's playground.'

"I burst into laughter. She shouted for me to stop. Her command made me laugh even harder. I was laughing hysterically. And then I realized I couldn't stop, and it was frightening. How could laughing be frightening? She kept shouting and I kept laughing. She said that if I went off with this dirty boy, I would be living in a slum with the baby. I laughed and laughed, until all I could do was wheeze because I could hardly catch my breath. I was suffocating on my own laughter. And then she shouted that if I ran off and had this baby, I would receive no money from her ever again. And suddenly, I was able to stop laughing. I said, 'I'm the one who is going to inherit the money, not you. You're the one who will get *no* money.' She got quiet.

"I told her that, like it or not, I would live in the house and have the baby, and if we were the pariahs of the town, I would at least be honest about it. She immediately changed her tune and said in a fake soothing voice that I should put my mind at rest about the baby and my future. Everything would be fine, she said in her phony voice of concern. 'Don't worry, my dear,' she said. 'I'll call the doctor now to prescribe something to help with your nausea.' She called me 'my dear.' My inheritance had bought those words and made her choke them out. I was grateful when the doctor came. I was sitting on the side of the bed, doubled over. He set down a bottle of medicine on the nightstand and told Minerva to give me a pill three times a day. And then he said he would give me a shot to help me feel better right away. The needle went in, I said, 'Ow,' and I remembered nothing else until I woke and was in terrible pain. Minerva said that this was normal with nausea and gave me a pill. I fell asleep. I awoke again, and she gave me another pill.

"Three days went by before I knocked away Minerva's hand as she brought the pill toward my mouth. I knew the dull ache in my womb was not nausea. They had gutted me. They had taken out what they felt was wrong, what had embarrassed her and would have ruined her social standing. Minerva wore her phony kind face and said through lying teeth that I had had a miscarriage. She said it so sincerely. She said I didn't remember it, because I had been in such pain it knocked me out cold. I cursed her with every name I could think of. I was screaming, and Minerva said I would be just fine and it was natural to suffer melancholy after what I had been through. And then I was quiet. Why was I screaming? What would change? I couldn't win against her, because there was nothing to win. I was an orphan. I belonged to no one. I had nothing and nobody to hang on to. The only person I could trust and rely on was me. But I was helpless and wanted to give up, because I didn't want to be strong anymore. What was the point?

"I felt like I was dying and I would never know the difference between who I was and who I did not want to be. I ran away as soon as I was able to get out of bed. The police found me and brought me back. I ran away again. I was caught again. Every time they caught me, something else died in me. I slashed off my hair. I cut my wrists and ran through the house letting the blood spurt everywhere. I guess you would say I had a nervous breakdown. The doctor was called again. Instead of taking me to an asylum, Minerva hired nurses to watch me until I felt better. They slipped medicines into my food or drink to make me docile. I stopped eating and flushed the food down the toilet. I grew weaker and weaker. And then I thought it was stupid that I would let myself die just because I hated them. I knew what I had to do to escape. I would be the good girl who lived a false life. I would smile at the table and say what a nice day it was. How lucky we were not to be starving like some people. How lucky we weren't Jews in Poland. How lucky we were not like other people who lived on the other side of the river. I studied, passed my exams without any help from paid tutors, and I was accepted by a school in New Hampshire that took hours to get to and on winding roads, which I knew made Minerva throw up.

"I didn't return home, except twice. The first time was when my grandmother, Mrs. Ivory, died. The lawyers gave the official word that I had just inherited the Ivory family estate. It had passed to me and not to Minerva. But she, as my purported mother, would have the power to determine how to spend that fortune on herself, until I was twenty-five. Practically the first thing she did was marry a man who claimed to own an oil well. If he owned a well, it was a well in someone's backyard into which he had thrown a bottle of Crisco. The second time I came home was last Christmas, when I knew Minerva was away with her new husband in Florida. I had gone there to remove more of my belongings. I didn't want any part of myself to remain there. That was when I found Uncle Loyalty's letter and gift in the mailbox.

"When I learned Minerva wasn't really my mother, I could feel myself being turned upside down. I felt like all my emotions had been in a saltshaker, tapped out a little at a time. And now everything had poured out all at once. Finally, I understood so many things. Minerva resented me. She hated my face because it was the face of the woman my father loved. She couldn't love me. I couldn't love her. There was nothing wrong with me, except that I was someone else's child. I was elated. I could be me! But then I immediately became scared. I didn't know who I was. I was like that big empty Santa bag.

"So here I am, the smart-alecky girl who doesn't really know who she is yet. I'm lost. But I feel better here in China because everything is so different and anybody coming here would be lost. I don't mean lost on the streets. I mean it's confusing and jarring and strange and new. The language is different, and you don't know the rules. And all this confusion here is pushing aside the other confusion I've had. I can start over. I can be three and a half again. I can learn a few words: 'milk,' 'spoon,' 'baby,' 'pick me up.' And I do remember those words. I feel part of me is in those words and part of me is coming back. A memory of me. A memory of you. I remember saying, 'I'm scared.' I don't remember if it was in Chinese or English. I also remember being a little girl in my mother's arms, your arms. I know it was you, because when I first got to Shanghai and we were seated in the car, I was looking at your chin. I remembered seeing that same chin when you held me and it was at eye level. I used to poke your chin, and when you smiled, it changed, like a little face. It was different when you were talking or laughing. It was different when you were sad or angry. In the car, I saw your chin was bunched up and I knew you were afraid, because I remembered being in your arms when I was little, bouncing as you ran. I was holding on to your neck. I said, 'I'm scared.' You told me in our language, 'Don't be afraid! Don't be afraid.' And then I felt someone pulling me away from you. I was reaching for your face and I saw your chin was bunched up hard. You were calling my name and you were afraid. So I was, too."

FLORA AND I took walks in the early morning and we watched everyday life pour out of doorways and onto the widest boulevards and narrowest alleys. She wanted to understand my life in Shanghai and what her father had experienced. What was it like to be Chinese? What was it like for a Westerner? Whose morals were more severe? Who did I think I would have become if my mother had not left?

I used to ask that last question all the time. Who would I have become? If I had lived in San Francisco, would my mind have been different? Would I have had different thoughts? Would I have been happier? "I wanted to live somewhere else," I told Flora. "But I didn't want to become anyone different. I wanted to be who I had always been. And I was and still am."

We went to the house on Bubbling Well Road, where Edward

and I had lived. It was now a middle school for the children of foreigners.

"Foreigners," Flora said. "I'm a foreigner."

The big tree was still in the courtyard garden. We stood in its shade, as we had just before she was taken away. The stone bench was there, and it bore a plaque with Edward's name. Beneath were violets. Mother and I had placed the plaque there a week ago and replanted the flowers. She had given the school a nice contribution and also paid for a gardener to tend it.

"Is he really buried here?" Flora asked.

I nodded. I remembered watching the dirt falling on the cabinet that had served as Edward's coffin. The old sorrow came back: Edward, how could you be leaving me?

Flora brushed her fingers over the violets and closed her eyes. "I want to feel he's holding me in his arms."

I pictured Edward rocking Little Flora, looking at her with a wondrous face, soothing her, telling her she was pure and unharmed.

FLORA AND MY mother stayed for a month. A few days before they would leave, I felt she was again being pulled from me.

"You should come to visit us in San Francisco," Mother said. "You have a birth certificate under the name of Danner that says you're an American citizen. I can help you get it. Although maybe you'd be too wary to let me try that again."

"We wouldn't be able to get a visa for Loyalty. Thousands of Chinese citizens want to leave, and the consulate knows they wouldn't return. I can't leave Loyalty by himself," I said. "He wouldn't know how to take care of himself." I did not tell her that Loyalty had already made me promise that I would not leave without him. He was afraid I would be pulled to America, now that I had found both my mother and my daughter. When people go to America, he had said, they don't come back for a long time. "After the war, Loyalty and I will both come," I told Mother. "Or you come back here and bring Flora. We can go to the mountain that Edward and I climbed, or to Hong Kong and Canton, places I've never been. We can see them together."

Mother gave me a sympathetic look. She knew I wanted to see Flora again. "I'll see what I can do." She squeezed my hand.

Three days later, Loyalty, Magic Gourd, and I stood on the dock with Flora and Mother. How long would it be before we could see each other again? How long would the war last? What other terrible things could happen between now and when I would next see them? What if I did not see Flora again for ten or fifteen years? What if Mother died in the middle of writing a letter to me? They were leaving me again. It was too soon.

Magic Gourd shoved a large sack of candied walnuts into Flora's arms. She had been cooking them for the past two days. "She looks like you when you were that age," Magic Gourd said. She had said that nearly every day since Flora arrived. "I used to wonder what would happen if someone saved you and you left and I was all alone. I wanted you to be saved, but then . . ." She put her fist against her mouth to keep from crying. "Watching her leave is like watching you go." Flora embraced her and thanked her in Chinese for her good care when she was little.

"She has a good heart," Loyalty said to me in Chinese. "She got that from you. Three and a half years was enough time to give that to her. She's the daughter we might have had. I'll miss our daughter." He made Flora promise to send a cable as soon as she arrived so that we would know she was safe.

And then it was time. Flora came to me and said in an oddly stiff voice, "I know we'll see each other soon. And we'll write often."

I thought she had warmed to me and was stricken to realize it wasn't true. She couldn't leave now. I needed more time with her. I was panicking, shaking.

She took my hands. "It's not as hard this time, is it? I'm leaving, but I'll be back." She threw her arms around my neck, hugged me close, and whispered, "What did I call you when I was little and they were taking me away? Was it Mama? It was, wasn't it? I found you, Mama. I'll never lose you again. My mama came back from a memory, and Little Flora came back, too."

I whispered back that I loved her. And then that was all I could say.

"No more heartbreak," she said. She kissed my cheek and pulled away. "There's that face on your chin." She poked my chin and rubbed it until I laughed. "We don't need to be scared anymore," she said. She kissed my cheek again. "I love you, Mama."

She and Mother walked toward the gangplank. She turned back three times to wave, and we waved as well. I watched them ascend, and at the top of the gangplank, she and Mother waved again. We waved furiously until Flora put her arm down. She stood still and looked at me. And then she and Mother went inside and were gone.

I remembered the day when I was supposed to leave Shanghai for San Francisco. My mother should have waited for me. She did not. She should have returned. She did not. The American life that should have been mine sailed away without me, and that day I no longer knew who I was.

On sleepless nights, when I could not bear my life, I thought of that ship and imagined I was aboard. I had been saved! I was its only passenger, standing at the back of the ship, watching Shanghai recede—an American girl in my sailor dress, a virgin courtesan in a high-necked silk jacket, an American widow with streaming tears, a Chinese wife with a black eye. A hundred of me over the years were crowded on the deck, looking back at Shanghai. But the ship never left, and I would have to disembark, and begin my life again each morning.

Once again, I imagined myself as that girl in the sailor dress. I was on the ship, standing at the back of the boat. I was going to America, where I would be raised by a mother who took me to San Francisco. I would grow up in a beautiful house and sleep in a bedroom with sunny yellow walls and a window next to an oak tree, and another that looked out upon the sea. From that window, I would be able to see all the way across to a city at the end of the sea, to a dock by the Huangpu River, where I was standing with Magic Gourd, Edward, Loyalty, Mother, and Little Flora, waving to the girl in the sailor dress as the ship receded, waving until it disappeared.

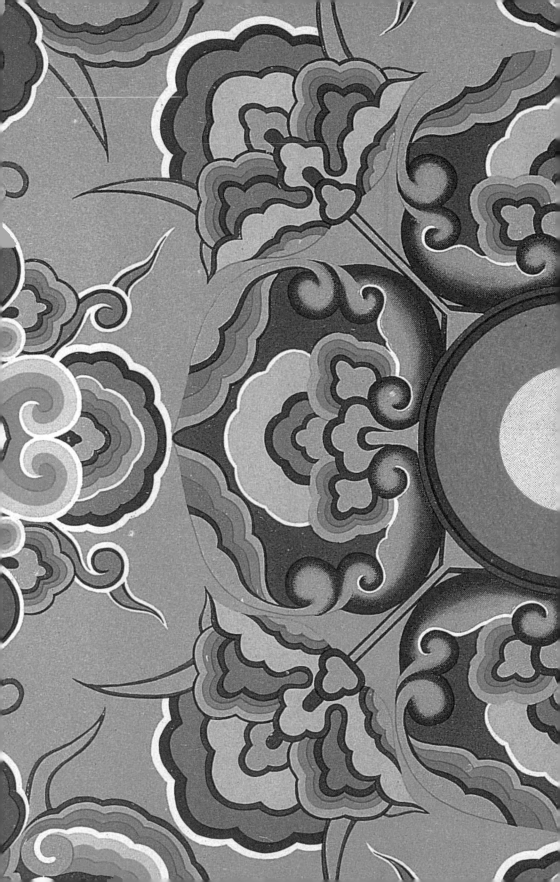